"Carol Berg is an absolutely gorgeous writer. . . . She does incredible, intricate world building that moves along like a deep, powerful river: It looks, on the surface, as though it's carrying along at a reasonable rate, with occasional dips and swirls into eddies, but beneath that is an absolutely tremendous current pulling you along toward inexorable rapids, and you barely know it's happened until you're already over your head. And then, just in case that's not enough, she does exactly the same thing with the character development, resulting in works of stunning scope that are also enormously internal journeys of discovery for not just the characters, but the reader."
—C. E. Murphy, author of the Walker Papers series

"Among my favorite fantasies EVER! Carol Berg develops her characters, story, and world with a well-rounded brilliance seldom seen in fantasy, and a beauty that leaves a reader breathless."
—Janny Wurts, author of *Wars of Light and Shadow*
(on *Flesh and Spirit* and *Breath and Bone*)

"Carol Berg's writing is some of the most lyrical and flowing I have run across. Her books all have some innate grace that serves as a marker against which I measure almost every other book I read. Berg's books aren't just books; they are art, and she's a master of the wordsmithing craft. Her writing style gives all of her books a dreamlike quality that I love. Her stories are more real than real, and her characters are so vibrant, you live those mor---------you read, and you learn so much about yourself as you do it."

Dust and Light

"[A] captivating and satisfying fantasy epic. . . . With an impressive command of language, sure-handed plotting, and perceptive characterizations, Berg traces the arc of Lucian's arduous quest to solve the murders of several illegitimate royals."
—*Publishers Weekly*

continued . . .

"Carol Berg has spun a tale of magic and politics, of intrigue and betrayal. Set in a rich world, told through the eyes of a compelling and sympathetic hero, her story twists and turns, building to a conclusion that satisfies while hinting at more adventures to come. I eagerly await the next Sanctuary novel."

—D. B. Jackson, author of the Thieftaker Chronicles

Breath and Bone

"The narrative crackles with intensity against a vivid backdrop of real depth and conviction, with characters to match. Altogether superior."

—*Kirkus Reviews* (starred review)

"Berg's lush, evocative storytelling and fully developed characters add up to a first-rate purchase for most fantasy collections." —*Library Journal*

"Replete with magic-powered machinations, secret societies, and doomsday divinations, the emotionally intense second volume of Berg's intrigue-laden Lighthouse Duet concludes the story of Valen. . . . Fans of Marion Zimmer Bradley's Avalon sequence and Sharon Shinn will be rewarded."

—*Publishers Weekly*

"Berg combines druid and Christian influences against a backdrop of sorcerers, priestesses, priests, deep evil, and a dying land to create an engrossing tale to get lost in . . . enjoyable." —Monsters and Critics

"An excellent read . . . a satisfying sequel." —Fresh Fiction

Flesh and Spirit

"In Carol Berg's engrossing *Flesh and Spirit*, an engaging rogue stumbles upon the dangerous crossroads of religion, politics, war, and destiny. Berg perfectly portrays the people who shape his increasingly more chaotic journey: cheerful monks, cruel siblings, ambitious warlords, and a whole cast of fanatics. But it's the vividly rendered details that give this book such power. Berg brings to life every stone in a peaceful monastery and every nuance in a stratified society, describing the difficult dirty work of ordinary life as beautifully as she conveys the heart-stopping mysticism of holiness just beyond human perception."

—Sharon Shinn, national bestselling author of *Royal Airs*

"Carol Berg has done a masterful job of creating characters, places, religions, and political trials that grab and hold your attention. . . . Don't miss one of 2007's best fantasy books!" —Romance Reviews Today

"It's challenging to create a main character who's not exactly a good guy and yet still elicits reader sympathy. Carol Berg's newest novel, *Flesh and Spirit*, features a man who has committed quite a few misdeeds and yet remains likable. . . . Berg also excels at creating worlds. . . . It's like we're exploring this world alongside its characters, and this technique works remarkably well. . . . I'm eagerly awaiting the duology's concluding volume, *Breath and Bone*. This first installment is an engrossing and lively tale with enough action to keep you hungry for more." —*The Davis Enterprise*

The Daemon Prism

"[Berg's] insight into the nature of human good and evil, the constantly ebbing and flowing relationships among lovers and friends . . . consistently raises this novel above sword-and-sorcery routine." —*Publishers Weekly*

"An amazingly complex and rewarding story. *The Daemon Prism* is certain to reward the devoted students of the Collegia Magica trilogy." —*Booklist*

"One of the best fantasies I have encountered in years. . . . Berg takes chances with her characters . . . that leave them imprinted indelibly in your memory and heart . . . wonderful." —Science Fiction and Other ODDysseys

"Enthralling and not to be missed." —*Kirkus Reviews*

"Filled with action and feeling as if it occurs in a Berg version of the Age of Reason; fans will appreciate this stupendous story." —Alternative Worlds

BOOKS BY CAROL BERG

THE SANCTUARY SERIES
Dust and Light

Ash and Silver

THE COLLEGIA MAGICA SERIES
The Spirt Lens

The Soul Mirror

The Daemon Prism

THE LIGHTHOUSE SERIES
Flesh and Spirit

Breath and Bone

THE BRIDGE OF D'ARNATH SERIES
Son of Avonar

Guardians of the Keep

The Soul Weaver

Daughter of Ancients

Song of the Beast

THE RAI-KIRAH SERIES
Transformation

Revelation

Restoration

ASH
— AND —
SILVER

A SANCTUARY NOVEL

CAROL BERG

A ROC BOOK

Published by New American Library,
an imprint of Penguin Random House LLC
375 Hudson Street, New York, New York 10014

This book is an original publication of New American Library.

First Printing, December 2015

LIBRARY OF CONGRESS CATALOGING-IN-PUBLICATION DATA:

Berg, Carol.
Ash and silver: a sanctuary novel / Carol Berg.
pages cm.
ISBN 978-0-451-41726-8
I. Title.
PS3602.E7523A9 2015
813'.6—dc23   2015019866

Printed in the United States of America
10 9 8 7 6 5 4 3 2 1

Penguin
Random
House

FOR PETE, THE EXCEPTIONAL SPOUSE,
MY TRUE HEART AND MY BEST FRIEND, EVER AND ALWAYS

ACKNOWLEDGMENTS

Thanks to my extra eyes—Susan, Curt, Courtney, Brian, and Saytchyn. And to Brenda, ever-inspiring and ever-generous with home and heart. To the Writers of the Hand for companionship on the journey and for energy, fun, food, wine, and focus, focus, focus. To Mike, Stella, Richard, Twila, and all the crew at the Hand for providing a refuge when life got too hectic at low altitude. To Marcus the Fighter Guy for combat advice. To my editor, Anne Sowards, for her gifts of commentary, trust, and understanding of life's knotty seasons. To my faithful readers for support and unending encouragement. And most especially to Linda the Muse for twenty-seven years of friendship, mentoring, incisive questioning, plot-twisting, and lunch. Looking forward to many, many more.

The teeth of spring bite sea and stone. Storm and mist shadow the cove. The glade starves. Where is the fire? Where is the heart? Where is the gladness of the season, when danger lurks amid trees yet barren, and in the sea yet cold and dark? Dance, my brother. Spin, my sister. For root and sap, for wave and worm. Call glory to banish grief too long lingered.

—Canticle of the Spring

ASH

— AND —

SILVER

PART I
SEA AND STONE

CHAPTER 1

YEAR 1293 OF THE ARDRAN PRINCIPALITY

YEAR 216 FROM THE UNIFICATION OF ARDRA, MORIAN,
AND EVANORE AS THE KINGDOM OF NAVRONNE

YEAR 3 INTERREGNUM,
MOURNING THE DEATH OF GOOD KING EODWARD

LATE SPRING

You are not a murderer. The curious fact had been served to me that morning like cold fish on a platter, to be digested as I took my daily run.

My bare feet slapped on the mudflats, instinct bound with magic leading me inerrant between pools and mud and the sucking sands left behind by the tides. Cold damp slicked my bare arms. Fine soft particles of sand and clay coated my feet.

That I had ever taken life unsanctioned by law or duty would never have occurred to me. It was true, the story of my years before coming to Fortress Evanide remained a gaping void inside my skin. And some of my comrades here had almost certainly escaped from rough entanglements with Crown law. But my habits and inclinations, so carefully examined and strictly groomed in my training, suggested nothing like in my own nature. Yet if I had not been similarly entangled, why would my guide choose that fragment of my past to return to me—infused by way of enchantment so that I recognized its indisputable truth?

My destination had not yet emerged from the thick fog, though its chill stone bulk loomed scarce half a quellé ahead of me. Formidable. Hidden. *Fortress Evanide*—its name derived from the Aurellian word for *disappeared*, like those who worked, studied, and trained here. Supposedly the few hardy travelers who ventured this tide-scoured coast believed the place a stronghold of the gods . . . or demon gatzi . . . or even more elemental creatures of air and sea who sent the rampaging waters to drown any who ventured close.

My arm blotted the salt sweat stinging my eyes.

Every day at Evanide I raced this course. Some days it stormed. Some days the sea never entirely relinquished the flats. Still I ran—or swam if it was impossible to stay afoot. At first, two hovering guards had watched amused as I floundered in sinkholes and tide pools and retched from unfocused terror and unaccustomed exertion. Later I ran with a companion of my cadre, a paratus, a man lacking only his final months of training before taking on the arms of the *Equites Cineré*, the Order of the Knights of the Ashes. Now that I was myself a paratus, I was required to run alone, just as I now slept alone for the first time in all my days here—two years, more or less, by my reckoning of the seasons.

Commander Inek, my guide, had told me that the solitude prevented more men from taking the last step from paratus to knight than any other aspect of our training. I'd been skeptical until I, too, experienced these solitary hours when questions and fears, so long suppressed, rattled around in the emptiness inside my skull. *Where is my home? Who are my people? How have I come to be here?*

No one came to Evanide unwilling. Magic powerful enough to remove memory could not be effected without some measure of consent on the part of the subject. *Why would I have agreed to such a thing? What had I been?*

Not a murderer. That, I supposed, was a comfort. I was a sorcerer of more than average skill, although my deepest talent—the inborn bent that was the keystone of every sorcerer's work—had been deliberately hidden in the same moment my past was ripped away. Instead, my masters at Evanide had taken the retching, wretched tyro, who'd had to crawl the last quellé across the mud those first days, and made a warrior of him.

Screeching gulls mocked my passing.

Warrior. That was an ill-fitting skin as yet. My initial weakness, physical ineptitude, and ignorance of defensive and strategic magical practices testified that my life had been a comfortable one, focused on more sedentary pursuits. But once convinced I was not going to be purposely drowned or driven entirely mad, I had grown to relish Evanide's rigor, living and breathing the lessons of magical warfare, preparing to combat the evils of a world I could recall only in the abstract. Every day I reveled in the satisfaction of growing strength and agility. And the magic seared my soul with wonder and glory— defenses and attacks, *obscurés* and veils, encryption, exposures, strategies of wit and illusion to support an ally or confuse an opponent, weapons crafted from light, heat, and cold as well as steel and wood. The Order's training stretched body and talent in ways I could never have imagined, no matter what my previous life.

Our masters had made us empty so we could learn without boundaries, Commander Inek had told me in the days when the ache in my head and the vacancy inside kept me constantly breathless and nauseated. Only now that I was left alone to consider it all had the questions returned a thousandfold, less fraught with emotion, but plaguing nonetheless. *Who* was *I? Who am I?*

A deep and resonant horn call split the muffled silence of the fog—the tide call, its rising note sounding as much in my gut as in my ears. A second blast followed. The sea was ever our first enemy. A single long blast meant the turn—the ebb was done. The double warned of the deluge.

My feet sped up on their own. The tidal onrush in Evanide's bay bore the strength of an avalanche, spawning deadly whirlpools and vicious currents as it raced across the mudflats and up the rivers and swamps of the level coast. Though an hour yet remained until the onslaught, my body had learned its lessons well.

Every tyro of Evanide was dragged from sleep at least once during his months of initiation and sent onto the mudflats at low tide, forbidden to return to the fortress until the rising water had reached the octaré mark on the tide pillar—the height of eight men standing on one another's shoulders. Two of my cadre's five had drowned in their test, unable to muster wit, strength, and magic enough to survive the maelstrom. For the rest of us, the experience lived on in our nightmares, ground into our bones and sinews, as our commanders knew it would be. We never began a day unaware of the tide charts. And when the hour warning sounded, our feet ran.

"Get a move on, Greenshank!" Dunlin, the scarred, cocky second paratus of my cadre, was perched on the rocks beside the water gate like his namesake bird. He didn't unlatch the gate for me. The spells for all entries and defense works changed randomly throughout the day and night, and it was each man's responsibility to unravel them for himself. Agility was not just for feet and hands. "Inek has a change of work detail for you this morning."

"Gods be thanked," I said, as my fingers investigated the tendrils of spell-work that entwined the bronze latch and my inner senses responded with the counters. "Totting up bundles of reeds and quivres of salt and calculating factors' commissions have me ready to leap from the seaward wall."

All were required to train in the business of the Order as well as its martial purposes.

"You must have been well behaved of late." Dusky-skinned Dunlin picked his sound teeth with a sliver of reed, a show of nonchalance. "Fix is readying a boat for you."

"A boat . . . I'm sent *out?*"

Once raised from tyro to squire, I'd been off the island numerous times. To fields and forests for training in open combat and riding practice. To remote villages to practice enchantments of stealth and illusion. To isolated crossroads to stash casks of reeds, salt, inks, or dyes for retrieval by our trusted factors. But always I had been in company of a knight or a commander and other trainees. To be sent on a mission away from the fortress alone was a measure of trust, a recognition of honor. A test, too, of course. Every activity in Evanide was a test.

A moment's focus to release magic through my waiting fingers, and the gate swung open.

"You'll find Inek in Fix's chart room."

My smirking comrade chortled as I smacked him on the shoulder and dashed up the steep, narrow steps. I splashed through the cold footbath and left a trail of wet footprints through the stone halls as I hurried to my sleeping cell in the South Tower. A quick blot with a towel and I donned wool shirt and hose from the wooden chest, leather jaque from the peg on the wall, along with my knife belt and gray mask. Our full-face, clinging masks were the pervasive symbol of our life. The *Equites Cineré* lived by secrecy, stealth, and anonymity.

Left behind in my chest was a fragment of a small rectangular stone called a relict—given me on the day I joined the Order and broken in half on the night I arrived at Evanide. The relict's design was intaglio, a thin layer of black over white, so that the engraving showed white against an ebon field. When whole, it portrayed the emblem of the Order, a quiver with five disparate objects poking out of it—a staff, a sword, a whip, a hammer, and a pen. The relict's matching half was hidden away in a safe place, or so I'd been assured. I prayed to every god that was true, for the missing fragment of stone held the sum of my lost memories.

I could leave Evanide this day, running as far and fast as I wished. But unsanctioned departure meant relinquishing those memories, that life, for all time. No past. No future. No identity.

The sea tide was but a gentle urgency so far upriver. I shipped my oars and stretched my shoulders as it carried the skiff onto the muddy embankment. Plovers and quacking teals arrowed skyward from the vast stand of man-high reeds.

When the prow nudged the bank, I sloshed through the chilly water, dragging the little vessel into the reed forest, away from the sea's grasping fingers.

The man I was assigned to meet was nowhere within range of my senses, even honed as they were with practice and magic. Just as well to have a moment to clear my head. To reach the river's mouth across the vast bay had been a two-hour wrestling match, and the trip up the estuary another hour's row through the tumultuous dance of inflowing tide and outflowing river current.

Sitting on the prow, I removed my mask to let the misty air cool my cheeks. The mask was sewn of fine gray linen woven with a faint thread of green, like the bird who supplied my name. Once invested as a knight, I would receive a meaningful name and, consulting the wisdom of my superiors, choose how best to help right the wrongs of the world—chasing down bandits, unseating cruel landlords, protecting travelers, the noble work the Order had done for centuries. The work of justice.

Assuming I passed my testing, of course. Assuming I was willing to give up my past forever. Not my bent; at some time along the way I would reclaim my inborn magic to use in service to the Order. Nor would I forfeit my knowledge of the world; it mostly remained with me already. But I would relinquish all knowledge of my personal past—people I'd known, those I loved, family, home, enemies, pastimes I had enjoyed, childhood dreams and fears, youthful ambitions. How could one decide when all you had were fragments?

My age was eight-and-twenty or thereabouts.

I had been born in the kingdom of Navronne, three years embroiled in a war of royal succession.

I had once been contracted to a necropolis.

I had once been wealthy but had fallen on hard times—which likely explained the necropolis.

I was not a murderer.

Those were the scraps that had been tossed me. None of them struck the fire of memory. None hinted at value worth forsaking the Order. Perhaps that was the point.

A piping trill drew me to my feet, perhaps only another bird alarmed at my intrusion. But a second and third trill in rapid succession announced my visitor. I slipped on my mask, letting its enchantments settle it smoothly around my features.

Most sorcerers in Navronne wore half masks. Only those of the *Equites Cineré* covered our entire faces. All that we were was kept hidden from the world.

"Dastardly, damnable place to meet." The wheezing complaint accompanied the hollow rattle of the head-high reeds. "Endless muck. Grim, gloom, cold as Magrog's ass, with nary an awning to block the rain. Villains who hide their faces and leave a man's notions in a muddle— Oh."

The man might have been a mud creature, thick-boned, brown-skinned, and bundled head to boot in dirt-colored wool. His beard was weedy, plaited in numerous short braids that stuck out from his chin like spikes of spreading saltwort.

He grinned—his teeth brown, too—when he caught sight of me. "A locale of opportune meetings, however."

"Identify yourself," I said, fingering the silver-inlaid wooden token Inek had given me.

"Kitaro," he said. "Ganache de Kitaro, scholar, adventurer, sometime scoundrel—though never when dealing with your kind—and occasional purveyor of rare materials. Tell me your requirements and I can provide." With a flourish he whisked a small wooden disk from his pocket.

An invisible thread of magic bridged the air between his disk and the one in my hand. His token matched mine, its magic, as well as its face, identical. My preparation for the mission had informed me of his appearance and manner, but it was the token witnessed his authenticity.

"And your name, sirrah?" he said.

"My kind do not deal in names, Scholar Kitaro, as you well know." Inek had warned me of the fellow's glib tongue. Information was as valuable as his rare materials. "I believe you've brought one of your rarities for my superiors. I have the agreed payment."

I produced a small bag and hefted it for him.

His brown smile widened at the heavy chink. "Then let us fetch my prize before this mud swallows me entire."

He pivoted smartly and plunged back through the reed thicket. I stayed close, senses alert, probing the stillness beyond his rustling passage. Rain, little more than gossamer fog as yet, whispered over the landscape. A beast that was neither bird nor fish created a pocket of warmth and stink beyond the reeds, but no other human creature lurked anywhere close.

Eventually Kitaro's path of broken stems yielded to a broad expanse of marshland, a low, gray-green vista stretching as far as eyes could make out through veils of rain and fog. A stout donkey waited patiently at the verge of the reeds.

Clumps of spreading, fat-stemmed glasswort provided more solid footing than did the sodden muck. Kitaro stepped awkwardly from one to another to retrieve a bundle from a nest of plants. He stripped burlap wrappings from a small green jar and proffered it gingerly.

"Have a care, masked one. The substance you require is immersed in water and must remain so, else Deunor Lightbringer's wrath will consume your hand and body in flame that can reduce city and forest, bone and mountain to ash. Break the jar and you unleash the holocaust."

Inek had told me much the same. But he'd also cautioned me against trickery.

I pulled long, slim pincers from my knife sheath. "Open it. You understand I must verify the contents."

Holding the jar as far as possible from his body, Kitaro did as I asked.

Magelight revealed a yellowish, thumb-sized lump suspended in the water. I probed the waxy glob with the sharp-tipped pincers and picked off a nub the size and color of a maggot.

"Think of it as a gatzé's cod," gibbered Kitaro, blanching as I drew the pale nub from the jar. "Pop it and we'll have burning holes in our skin."

Holding the pincers well away, I sent a touch of warmth along the handle— only enough to take off the day's chill. Then I dropped the bit on a mound of sodden weeds and stepped back.

The tiny lump pulsed with a yellow-white gleam, softened a bit, and sent out tendrils of vapor. A sudden burst of white light, more brilliant than magelight, almost made me drop the tool.

"Told you. *Cereus iniga*, also known as bonefire. Now I'm off before this rain rots my weary bones." The brown-toothed grin spoke glee. The outstretched hand spoke naught but business.

Shaking off amazement, I tossed him the heavy bag. He peeked into it and sighed with pleasure. "May Deunor's light illumine your soul, masked one."

My fist touched my breast to acknowledge the blessing—one I heartily welcomed.

Yet good manners could not make me forget duty. Kitaro mounted the donkey, and as he turned the beast inland, I called out, "One more matter, Ganache de Kitaro! Return my master's token."

He looked back, grinning, and held out the wood disk. Magic ripped through my fingers into the splinter of silver embedded in my own token's center. A silver arc streaked toward Kitaro's hand. Though less showy, the power manifested far surpassed that of the green jar's contents.

Kitaro's token fell to ash. His expression fell slack, his gaze gliding through me as if I were but another reed brushed by the rain. Wide brow creased ever so slightly, he dusted his tingling fingers, clucked at his donkey, and rode away.

He would recall nothing of our transaction save for its initiation with the carved token, his comfortable familiarity with the masked strangers, and the gold coins he'd reaped. Those few things he would remember only if he was presented with another one of our tokens. All else, even this location and the particular material he'd brought here, would vanish from his mind over the next hours and days, as if a maidservant with a dust broom swept up his footsteps as he passed.

For two centuries the *Equites Cineré* had held the keys to manipulating human memory—astonishing, intricate, awful magic that only those of extraordinary power and proven honor could or should wield. I'd been taught the ways of it already, and in the coming months before my investiture as a knight, I would learn the practice. Once I'd understood that gift to come, no personal doubts and no challenge my commanders threw in my path had been sufficiently difficult to deter me. For out of all my lessons at Evanide, one thing had come clear: The skill to master such magic was in me. If I developed the strength needed to use it, I could help untangle the horrors of the world. Who could ask for a richer life?

Carefully I bundled the jar in its burlap wrapping and hurried back through the path of broken reeds, hoping to catch tide's ebb to ease the passage back to Fortress Evanide. My eyes stayed fixed to the green jar, so wary was I of its contents. Only when the rippling of the drowned river intruded on my consciousness did I pause and extend my senses to check for danger.

Amid the odors of fish, cold brine, and sea wrack floated an entirely untoward scent—a mix of meadowsweet and sun-warmed grass. Summer came to mind, and places far from Evanide.

It seemed impossible that such slight variance in the air—likely some marsh flower bloomed early—should rouse sensations so entirely alien to the life I led. My knees softened like warmed dough; my chest grew tight as shutters swollen in the damp. And a heat roused my nether parts, a sensation I'd assumed had been excised along with memories of friends and lovers.

I crept forward slowly. Paused at first glimpse of the flooded river.

A woman was singing, her eerie melody heating my skin. Perhaps it was so affecting because I'd not heard a woman's voice in so very long. But how had I not detected her coming?

Not entirely bereft of reason, I summoned power. I'd no permission to show myself to strangers, even masked. Touching eyes, lips, ears, tongue, and brow, I drew an enchanted veil around me and slipped out of the reeds.

She sat in my skiff, legs crossed, a pile of marsh grass in her apron. Thick, unruly curls the hue of chestnuts fell over her face and shoulders. As long, deft fingers wove the yellow-green stems, her song fell into humming.

I dared not breathe as I tried to decide how best to oust her from my boat. She must have heard my step, for her head popped up. And to my horror, my veil enchantment was flawed, for when she shook the lush curls from her face, her eyes, fiery green and slightly angled, locked with my own. The corners of her lips quirked, emptying my lungs of breath and my mind of thought. Then she smiled, breaking the gloom as if the sun had burnt away the fog.

"Fully masked, now? Oh, take it off, please, that I might look upon thy comely face once more. My shy, dear, gentle Lucian, how I've missed thee!"

CHAPTER 2

I should retreat. But the woman occupied my boat, and though the tide had begun its ebb, it would be hours before I could cross the bay afoot. And her greeting . . .

"You mistake me for someone else, mistress," I said, trying not to sound like a pithless boy.

Though I might wish it otherwise, she could not possibly know me. Wherever the knights had recruited me, they would have ensured we were not followed, bringing the full power of the Order's memory magic to bear on anyone who tried. Anonymity was our lifeblood. Our safety. Our first and strongest weapon.

"Get out of my boat." No magic sparked anywhere about the woman. My veil enchantment felt solid. How was I to explain such failure? Inek would have me a squire again!

The woman laid aside her weaving and her smile, concern clouding jade-hued eyes. "Sure I've not changed so much. Whereas thou . . ."

She jumped lightly from the boat, graceful as a leaping deer. Slender as the reeds, taller than I'd thought, near matching my own height, she swept around me like a summer eddy. Long fingers plucked at my knuckle-length hair, then brushed my shoulder and upper arm, near sapping what composure I had left.

"'Tis true thy bearing is something different, and hair sheared so close hides the ebon sheen I so adored. And thou'rt grown in strength, most surely. But this"—she leaned her face to mine and inhaled deeply—"I could never mistake. Thy sweat is ever clean, unlike so many of thy brothers. Thy appetite yet favors grain and fish and green things more than blood meats. And though 'tis fainter than before, I catch the scent of thy beloved inks and pages."

She pressed the tip of her finger to her lips, hesitant, and then reached toward my face. "This custom I do sincerely regret, as I did in those sweet hours we spent together. To hide thy face entire—"

I jumped back when she touched my mask, shaking off the mesmer of her beauty as two years' training snapped into place . . . with no small sting of panic. Was I so weak as to be taken in by brilliant eyes? This mission must be Inek's test.

"Who are you? What business have you on a desolate shore where no one comes save those summoned? Perhaps you followed the trader. You'll come with me and we'll find out."

Sadness wafted over me like incense. "Oh, Lucian, I cannot. I do not fear, as I know 'tis thee behind the mask. We are ever bound by what we did together, closer than thine own heart could imagine. Yet thine eyes tell me—"

She stepped back, her manner grown sharp and wary. "Is this some game or some dread penance since I beheld thee last? Humankind is ever fickle. Cruel . . ."

"You're a stranger to me, lady, as is anyone named *Lucian*. I wish you no harm, but I'll not allow you to carry tales." Spinning a net spell to keep her close, I reached for her arm.

She slipped my grasp as deftly as an eel and . . . vanished.

I spun in place, blinking raindrops from my eyes. How could anyone move so quickly?

"Come to this place again one day," she said, from every direction at once, "and thou'lt find proof of our friendship. My people sorely need thy counsel."

And then she was gone. Neither trained senses nor magic could detect a breath, a heart's pulse, or a spot of warmth in the failing light. And though I inhaled half the wind, no meadowsweet freshened the stink of the marsh.

Lucian. The name itself held no meaning for me, yet when I spoke it aloud, I fancied other names waited just beyond hearing. Glimmers of light trailed in the wake of her presence, fading just at the point other images lurked.

I possessed no personal memory of any woman. Even so I knew she was extraordinary. Not just in beauty or grace. Her passions blazed from deep inside, shining through her skin and her words, through every expression and movement. Was it possible I'd known her in my former life, despite being bound up with rules and protocols as all purebloods were?

She was correct about many things. The change in my physical bulk, certainly. My preference for fish, bread, and lettuces over heavy meat. My hair that was, indeed, black as a magpie's head. Anyone at Evanide would know those things. But *beloved inks and pages*? No comrade of the Order, not even Inek, could possibly have guessed the aching pleasure the scent of ink and parchment roused in me. Yes, I was bound to explore every passing thought and feeling with my guide, but that one had always seemed too trivial to mention, in the same wise as my mask having a coarse thread that itched my left ear. Did she know that, too?

I dragged the skiff into the water and hopped in. As I unshipped the oars, I forced aside all thought of the woman's mystery. I had a long row ahead in dangerous waters and failing daylight. Distraction would see me dead.

Knight Commander Inek had served as father, mother, counselor, tor-mentor, employer, tutor, and priest for two years, since the night two of his knights-in-training had dragged me gibbering across the bay at mid-tide and dropped me on Evanide's great stair at his feet. Wreathed in fog, tall, stern, serene, and ageless, he had seemed a silver-haired god whose favored rites I had never learned. Shivering and dripping, the world yet swirling like the black waters of the bay, I had groveled at his feet, offering eternal service if he would but return my life to me. "I accept," he'd said. "But it will be a life forever changed. And it begins now. On your feet, tyro . . ."

He had guided me through every step, and I respected, honored, and loathed him. I craved the hour I could be shed of his cold presence for the last time. Yet that event must surely be a small death I would carry with me always.

As I moored the boat, Fix the boatmaster told me Inek was likely in the armory, as it was time to advance the enchantments on his current tyros' blades. I dared not delay reporting. Fix had witnessed my return. Inek would know of it before I reached him.

Thus I hurried smartly past the boathouse and up a short stair and winding ramp into the sleeping citadel, through the cavernous undervaults where we competed in games of strength or agility, and then upward into the Common Hall, where all at the fortress ate and where tyros, squires, and retainers slept on the floor like household dogs. Outdoors again and across the Inner Court. Shivering in my wet garments, I ascended the steep and exposed stair up the north face of Idolon Mount, Fortress Evanide's foundation.

In the vestibule at the top of the stair, I lowered my eyes, touching forehead and heart in respect for the two standing watch. "I am in-mission, sir knights, as yet unreported. I was told Commander Inek worked in the armory."

"Blessed return, Greenshank," said a soft-spoken knight masked in gray and red. "The commander is where you say. Enter."

A maze of passages burrowed deep into the rock. They led to our three most secure rooms: the armory, the fortress treasury, and most precious of all, the dark, ever-misty cave of the spring—the source of fresh water that allowed any but birds to live on this rocky islet.

A beam of magelight led me deep into the armory. Darkness obscured most of the vast cavern's stores of spelled swords, knives, shields, and armor, the bundled staves, bows, arrows, and caskets of medallions, tokens, and jewels. A basket held tiny squares of silver called untraceables, used to ferret out those who might be alerted to enchantment without revealing the magic's nature or origin. A lacquered box held silver splinters, which could be linked to transfer enchantments as did those embedded in memory-wipe tokens.

A magelight globe hung over a long worktable illuminating a well-used sword. From his coarse tunic and slops, the lean man hunched over the sword might have been a smith's assistant or the squire who catalogued the armory. Until he glanced up, that is, and the ice-blue eyes scraped one's skin raw, and the sculpted lines of his face registered his judgment. His knuckle-length hair was entirely silver, but he could have been any age from thirty to seventy. And, in truth, if one heard him command the sun to rise in the west, one would believe entirely that the orb would reverse its habit.

I bowed and touched my brow. "Knight Commander Inek, I report my mission complete."

"Blessed return, Greenshank. Unmask and speak."

I stripped off the mask and set my bundle on the end of the table. "The purveyor of rarities carried the proper token," I said, pulling away the wrapping. "Once sure of that, I tested the substance as ordered. I judged it *cereus iniga*, yielded the payment, and excised Kitaro's memory."

As I spoke, the commander's attention returned to his work modifying the protections on his tyros' swords. Enchanting weapons to minimize sepsis or loss of limbs, while maintaining the feel and proper risks of sword- or knife-work, was a delicate business. Inek altered the protective spells frequently as his students advanced, sometimes tightening them if the moves to be practiced were particularly dangerous, sometimes loosening them to keep us wary. Sometimes it seemed he did exactly the reverse. It kept his students on edge, alert and focused, as we were always required to fight to our personal limits. We were never quite sure if we might die or wound a comrade on any particular day, but reading an opponent's weapon was the first step to preventing either disaster.

At Evanide, one either learned the necessary lessons or broke or died. Rumor told that only one in fifty tyros became a knight. No gossip ever tallied how many of those nine-and-forty failed, their memories of the Order and Evanide erased. Or how many withdrew from the journey with honor, the most trustworthy allowed to retain knowledge of their time here. Or how many died.

I began again. "I practiced a veil as I was waiting."

He glanced up sharply. "You were masked?"

"Yes. I arrived early. I donned my mask as soon as I heard Kitaro's footsteps. But the veil enchantment failed, though I detected nothing wrong with it."

I could not have said when I had decided to withhold the tale of the woman. If this was a test and Inek already knew of her, punishment was certain; at Evanide, omission and dissembling were equivalent to deliberate untruth. But if she was what she claimed—a friend from the past—and I reported her, Inek would certainly strip away my memory of the incident, while our Knight Marshal decided if her presence compromised the purposes of the Order. I had to know more before I could allow that.

"I thought to work another veil tomorrow and ask one of the senior parati to inspect it."

"Ask Cormorant. He's expert at veils." Inek's forefinger drew a scarlet flame along the sword's cutting edge. Very, very carefully. "What of your navigation? Night fell on your return. . . ." As he had known it would when he set me the mission in the last hour of a rising tide and said it must be done that day.

"I made good speed, though I depended too heavily on the Seal Rock beacon. If it had been submerged, I might yet be trying to extricate myself from the Spinner or Hercal's Downspout. I'll need to practice the same route when the full moon grows the tide." Deception grew like a fungus. But I needed to get back to the estuary.

"Full moon's six days hence. Highest tide seven." He lifted his finger from the blade and pinched off the light at the sword's point. "I'll note a practice crossing in your training schedule."

"As you say, *rectoré*."

Scarlet, vermillion, blood . . . the sword pulsed every hue of red for a few moments. Inek watched it intently, and I took the anxious moment to order my thoughts.

When the color faded, Inek set the blade aside and laid a second one on the table. His fingers flexed, ready to work. "Is there anything more?"

A thousand things more, threatening to burst my chest. "Questions plague me, *rectoré*, as you warned. Not doubts. I am entirely committed. I cannot believe the past holds anything to compare to the gifts of power and good service offered me here. But surely to *know* myself would make the final relinquishing all the more significant."

As ever, his glance of assessment scraped my spirit raw. "You've a great deal more to learn before we speak of commitment or the final relinquishing. You've held paratus rank for what . . . forty days? You've not even begun to feel the plague of questioning you'll suffer. And inevitably, doubts will follow. Don't tell me of your resolve, Greenshank; prove it."

"Yes, *rectoré*."

"You did well today. Three of our brother knights will use the *cereus iniga* to save a great city from a terrible foe. Think of the price *they* will pay, once it's done—the price you will pay to do such service if and when your time comes. Then see how long you can stave off doubts."

As always, he was right. "They'll not remember what they've done," I said.

To preserve our ability to serve those who needed our skills, and to ensure that those who joined us did so for the right reasons, knights sacrificed not only their past, but also their glory.

"Nor will those whose future they save remember who it was defended them," he said.

A knight retained everything of his training and experiences inside Evanide. But once he submitted a mission report to the Archivist so that all could study it, the knowledge of his own part in that venture was stripped from him. His body's understanding of the lessons learned would remain, but if he happened to review that mission in the archives, he wouldn't recognize it as his own. A harsh, rigorous life, but one that made sense to me. It felt honorable and clean, unlike my wavering conscience.

"*Rectoré*, I need—"

"Enough, Greenshank. You've an early call tomorrow, as do I. And if I'm to prevent our lackwit tyros from slaughtering one another, I need to finish this. Go to bed."

I touched my forehead. "*Dalle cineré*, Knight Commander."

"*Dalle cineré.*"

From the ashes. The emblem of the *Equites Cineré* ought to be a phoenix, as we were each of us built anew from the ashes of the past.

Sleep eluded me. For seven nights I flinched at every sound, afraid Inek had come to throw me in the bay or sentence me to the Disciplinarian's lash for my lies. Days were filled with training in magic and combat, with running, with practicing veils that even Cormorant, the parati-exter—the next to be knighted—could find no fault with. But through the long nights, my mind revisited the woman's words, analyzing, questioning until they felt graven in my skin.

The full moon brought the highest tides to the bay. No matter my frenzy to be gone, I spent a pre-dawn hour in the chart room studying, and presented myself to old Fix at the docks as if this were no more than the navigation practice Inek had scheduled.

Fix was one of those servitors who must have been at Evanide since its founding. His weather-scored face was not masked, so he was no knight. And no one addressed him as adjutant—one of the skilled trainees who had failed to reach knighthood, but chose to stay on and serve the Order. He was just Fix, who knew everyone who resided at Evanide and everything that went on. I tried always to take a moment to exchange a word with the old man. His knowledge of the sea and boats dwarfed even Inek's. This day it required patience to heed the boatmaster's gloomy predictions that storms inevitably accompanied the demon tide.

As I crossed the bay to the estuary where I'd met Kitaro and the woman, I could afford thought only for rampaging sea, spell-wrought beacons, and faint lines of magic that stretched between submerged rocks. But as I entered the river Gouvron's mouth, dismay slapped me in the face like a dead fish. The demon tide had spread its waters deep and wide. There were no more muddy banks. The half-drowned reeds were arm-high, not man-high, and all looked the same.

Cursing, I trolled up and down the lower estuary but the sea had washed away all remnants of Kitaro, donkey, *cereus iniga*, and magic. No one lurked but birds, insects, and sea creatures. How could I imagine the woman would be waiting? This was surely Inek's test. So simple a mission. And so abject a failure.

Mind numb, stomach in knots, I tied the skiff to a random clump of reeds. My shoulders were afire, and surely a giant had battered my back and legs with the trunk of an oak. Like a raw tyro, I'd eaten nothing that morning and drained my water flask early on. To find any water fresh enough to drink on the day of the demon tide would mean rowing upriver past the salt boundary, another five quellae at least. But I'd need every scrap of my strength to get back to Evanide alive. How many names were there for fool?

I would rest for a quarter of an hour, then head back. . . .

. . .

A hard edge rapped my skull. I jerked instantly awake, sprawled in the bottom of the skiff. The restless river had tumbled me from my seat, cracking my forehead on the sternsheet. Great gods, how long had I slept?

The painter angled sharply upward. Either the reeds had grown dramatically or the ebb was well begun. At least Fix had called the weather wrong. Blue sky teased behind thin, high mist, and the reed shadows had begun to stretch across a golden world of water and marshland. Past time to go. Time to survive the passage, confess my sin, and take my punishment. Inek would likely be waiting at the dock, coolly disappointed that his test had snared me.

As I stretched out cramps and reclaimed my seat, a black cylinder rolled along the bottom of the bobbing skiff. A spare water flask, I thought at first, as pleased as one could be when facing such an ordeal. But the shape was wrong; it was straight sided and tied at both ends. The leather covering was not stiffened and hardened, but wrapped about something else and sealed with resin. *Proof of our friendship* . . .

Cold fingers fumbled with the damp leather ties and pulled a rolled parchment from the casing. Magic assured me there were no enchantments to harm or trick, no poisons or pricking needles. But certainly a deeper enchantment suffused the fine parchment, heating a knot just behind my breastbone. My body named the spellwork benign, though reason could not explain why. I spread the page.

The world paused. Surely the squalling gulls were halted mid-flight, their rapid hearts stilled . . . as mine was. An ink drawing depicted a naked woman reclining on a grassy hillock bathed in afternoon light. The lines of her hip and thigh were long and elegant, her legs firm and powerful, her thick hair a cascade of curls over her shoulder. The drawing itself was masterful, assured and balanced and so real . . . so true . . . that I could smell the meadowsweet and sun-warmed grass her body crushed. The very woman I had met here.

But unlike the previous day, her bare skin was marked with fine and elegant drawings. Luminous images of honeysuckle vines entwined her arms and legs. Simple threads wrapped her fingers. A butterfly graced one hip. A lynx curled amid a stand of aspens on her back, and a nightingale on her cheek spread its wings across her brow and down her neck. Danae . . .

Gods' witness, the image was truth, and tales of the world's creation— knowledge the Order had not taken from me—spoke of only one sort of creature whose body gleamed with nature's own artworks. Danae—the earth's mythical guardians. Tales said the exquisite lines would gleam every shade of blue—lapis and azure, cerulean, sapphire, and indigo. Legend explained how she could be here and then not, for Danae could travel at will through the world and dissolve into earth or sea. Gods and myth held no sway at Evanide, but this . . .

Yet it was neither divine revelation nor sheerest wonder that made my hands tremble. As my fingers traced the curves of her shoulder, her neck, and the perfect wing scribed on her brow, I knew what ink had been used, the width of the pen, the technique used to shadow the cheek to reveal the slender bone beneath or to reveal the brilliance in her eyes. Magic swelled in my breast, where the fiery knot burned. With a touch I should be able to quirk her lips as I'd seen them the previous day, for that, too, would be truth, or extend her finger as she had done to touch my mask . . .

My bellow could have roused every bird that nested in the Gouvron Estuary or the coastal marshes. This drawing was a fragment of my soul as much as that chip of stone hidden in Fortress Evanide. And yet I could not remember her name, nor what we had done together, nor how I could possibly know a being of myth. If this was a test, then it demonstrated a measure of cruelty that could change my every perception of the *Equites Cineré*.

The discipline that embodied my present life quickly tamed inner chaos. Yet as I rolled the page to store it away, one more detail of the drawing leapt out at me. In the lower right corner, the artist had scrawled his name. I touched that, too, and it felt as familiar as the ink and parchment.

Lucian de Remeni-Masson. His name. My name.

Evidently I drew portraits and my magic instilled them with truth. Yet I could not remember doing so, nor when or where I'd learned the skills. Save for the burning in my chest, all of it was gone.

CHAPTER 3

According to Fix the boatmaster, Knight Commander Inek could be found in the sparring arena with Dunlin and Heron, the third paratus of my cadre. But when I reached the arena, Inek was nowhere in sight. Dunlin knelt beside our grimacing third, tightening a bandage about his bleeding thigh. Patchy enchantment mottled the air about the two, so I didn't interrupt. Healing enchantments were a critical portion of a knight's training, though mostly futile for anyone who wasn't born with the bent for it.

Like Lucian de Remeni, who instead carried a bent for portraiture. I crushed that thought. No more thinking until I spoke to Inek.

"A rugged session?" I said when Dunlin sat back on his heels and tossed the roll of linen into the wooden box.

Dunlin crooked his head in distinct mockery of our swordmaster. "Is it possible we forgot our nether limbs again, Paratus Heron?"

Heron, a scrappy, spindle-limbed fellow with sinews like drawn steel, hopped up from the blood-spattered stone muttering a curse upon Dunlin's unknown heritage. He wiped down his sword and sheathed it, and waved off my outstretched hand as he hobbled away. "I'll be in the infirmary. This hamfist's bandaging will likely have this cursed leg rotted by morning."

"Now you, Greenshank, a bit of extra work?" asked Dunlin, making a great show of wiping the blood from his blade. "You seem a bit soggy."

I shook my head. "I'm yet in-mission, hunting Inek."

His face sobered immediately. "Blessed return. Inek was summoned to the Marshal not a half hour since."

"I'll be ready for a match later," I said on my way out. "*Any* weapon." My swordwork was ever in need of extra practice, but it was the fight I needed more. The hard row back had kept inner turmoil at bay, but since I'd left the boat, guilt, desire, and confusion raged inside me in a whirlpool worthy of Evanide's storm tides. I had to tell Inek the truth. Perhaps having the unsanctioned knowledge ripped out would keep my skull from crack-ing. Yet I wasn't sure I could allow him to do that. *Danae*. Holy Deunor . . .

The Knight Marshal of Evanide had no name. At the Rite of Breaking, when the knight-in-waiting smashed the fragment of stone that held his past, he announced the name he would carry for the rest of his life. *Unless* he was eventually named Knight Marshal. When the knights chose a replace-ment for a deceased or retired Marshal, only the Knight Archivist, the care-taker of our memories and the Order's history, knew the identity of the one selected. If the man chosen accepted the office, his former name was marked as *knight-deceased* throughout the archives and excised from the memory of every member of the Order—including his own. Anonymity meant freedom to make hard decisions for a man who must send his knights into the most dangerous places in a dangerous world.

Early in my residence at Evanide, our Knight Marshal had died of a fever. This new Marshal had appeared at his vesting wearing a full mask and robes of pure white. He even wore white silk gloves so that no one could identify him by scars or marks or any trace he left that might be detectable by magic. Every quat of his flesh was hidden, save eyes and mouth. Eerie to imagine I might have met him, trained under him, or studied his deeds as I viewed the missions stored in the Order's archives, yet neither of us would know.

Some said the Marshal walked the fortress unmasked from time to time to observe its workings. I doubted that, but certainly straightened up when-ever I encountered anyone halfway familiar whose name eluded me.

Hurrying through the Hall and up the South Tower stair, I prayed Inek's business with the Marshal would be short, lest I lose my nerve to confess my deceit. The sheathed portrait, tucked into an oil-dressed sack, weighed on my shoulder like an iron plate.

The Marshal kept his eye on the world from a series of chambers on the southern flank of the fortress. It seemed strange that a man who rarely left the citadel could gather sufficient information to choose our tasks wisely, but as Inek had often reminded me, the Order was hardly isolated from the world. Knights brought back detailed reports of their missions before their memories were erased; we were trained to be observant. Parati-exter who chose not to be invested as knights left Evanide with honor and served as good sources of information. And the Order maintained a wide network of well-paid informants who knew nothing of who we were, just as we main-tained a network of factors for our business interests. Squires' gossip whispered that a few Order knights served as spies, too, but no one knew for certain.

Thyme and rosemary scented my path across a courtyard garden to the far colonnade where a guard paced. The knight pivoted smartly at my approach. I halted, touching fingertips to forehead, then fist to heart, eyes lowered.

"Ah, Greenshank, I do so appreciate your fine discipline. I assured Commander Inek that no search parties were required, as you would dutifully seek him out no matter the lateness of your return." The Marshal's doorward, a jovial knight-retired named Horatio, knew the name and status of every trainee who'd been at Evanide more than a month. "They wish you to go right in."

"Go in?"

Naught could measure my dismay. I'd been planning to snare Inek as he left, not intrude upon his meeting with the Marshal. And *search parties*? Deunor's fire, were they ready to dismiss me even before my confession?

Horatio rapped twice on the thick oak and pushed the door open. "Retain your mask."

I hooked my cloak at the shoulders, straightened my mask, shirtsleeves, and leather jaque, and cinched the ties of the leather sack. Best not have the portrait fall out in front of the Marshal. Goddess Mother . . .

I had met Evanide's Knight Marshal exactly twice. Once at the rite that advanced me from squire to paratus, and once shortly before that occasion when I had sat with him for a personal interview to judge my readiness. With a voice as mellow and mysterious as a night breeze in softer climes, he had probed my perceptions of the Order and our mission, my experiences during my training, and the seriousness of my intention to pursue investiture as a knight. I had come away stripped bare, and yet strangely exhilarated, the way before me clear. And now, so short a time later, all was murk and confusion—the true penance for lies and dissembling. Never again.

That interview had been held in the Marshal's outer chamber, so the hard benches and lack of a fire to chase away the damp did not surprise me. The beautifully rendered map labeled *The Middle Kingdoms and the Known East* yet held the place of honor at one end, while at the opposite end was a shimmering mosaic of our three ruling Knights in full armor: the Knight Marshal in white and silver, the Knight Archivist in deep red-gold, and the Knight Defender, his mail and helm gleaming black, his tabard, cloak, and mask of midnight blue.

These three knights were the bones of the Order. The Knight Marshal focused his eyes outward, presiding over our missions and training. The Knight Archivist gazed ever inward, ensuring the integrity of the Order's history and our memories. And the mysterious Knight Defender had eyes everywhere, for he saw to our security and integrity, and no one had any idea who he was. Though it was assumed the three consulted one another, their demesnes were separate and inviolate.

The door leading into the Marshal's inner chamber stood open. I swallowed hard, told myself that despite this one transgression, I remained a worthy warrior, and entered.

I had never visited the inner chamber. Though it was no less plainly furnished than the outer chamber, its prospect must steal the breath of any person with eyes. Across the far wall stretched an expanse of windows measuring five times my armspan. Its center span, paned with remarkably clear glass, gave view to the crescent spit that cupped Evanide's bay to the south and the lighthouse that marked its tip, already afire on this murky eve. Beyond all lay the gray, heaving expanse of the Western Sea and its seamless joining with the sky.

But at either end of the clear window was an equal wonder—glass panes stained the colors of emerald, sapphire, ruby, and citrine, cut and joined to shape images. On the right they depicted the fortress, stark against a field of pale blue sky, surrounded by the swirling waters of the bay. Centered at the bottom was the small white-on-black emblem of the Order—the quiver and its five implements.

On the left, the panes shaped a woman—a goddess, by her haloed face. Her finger pointed to a twin-peaked mountain, though her eyes were turned away, weeping. Sprawled across the slopes was a city of graceful towers, bridges, and flowered boulevards. Atop one of the mountain's peaks stood a modest keep and its three towers. Its twin was crowned with a ring of standing stones. People crowded the ring of stones and others streamed up the lanes and boulevards toward it.

Centering the lower glass was a cruder version of the Order's emblem, the five implements no more than sticks. About the mountain city was laid an array of slivered panes of ruby and citrine. One might think the slivers benign—the artist's suggestion of enchantments or the divine—and the goddess's tears a mystery. But it struck me that when the sun made one of its rare appearances and shot its beams through that window, it would set that glorious city afire.

Such a horror rose in me, I could not drag my eyes from the image, even when a man cleared his throat behind me. I didn't understand it.

"Greenshank, attend!"

My gaze snapped away to two men seated beside a small hearth and a third, a glaring Inek, who stood to one side of them. I dropped to one knee, touched my forehead and heart, and lowered my eyes. "Knight Marshal, Knight Commander." I nodded to the seated man in the white hood and mask and to Inek in turn. "I report my mission complete."

"Blessed return, Greenshank." The two said it as one, though the voices were entirely distinguishable—the Marshal's deep and mellow quiet and Inek's that might have been hammered in the armory. Neither of them said *speak*, the command to continue my report.

I stood. My stomach—which had lodged itself in my throat—settled a bit.

"Have you met our guest, Greenshank?" The Marshal opened his hand to the man seated beside him. "Attis de Lares-Damon, respected linguist and a curator of the Pureblood Registry—a leader among the pureblood sorcerers of Navronne."

No wonder I'd been told to retain my mask. Ordinarily one bared one's face before the Knight Marshal, but not with an outsider present.

"I've not been formally introduced, Knight Marshal, but the curator has queried me on several occasions."

This Damon was a frequent visitor to Evanide, one of the few outsiders permitted here and the only one I knew of allowed to speak directly with those in training. He observed our work with sharp interest, yet his questions were mundane. *Are swords or polearms easier to enhance with spellwork? Is your combat training more involved with pureblood opponents or ordinaries? Do you focus primarily on individual combat?* Inek could have answered more completely than I.

"Damon has requested an interview with those new raised to the paratus rank," said the Marshal. "Answer without reservation."

Without reservation . . . meaning without protecting what I knew of Order secrets. Who was this Damon? A glance at Inek's lean face illuminated nothing, though as one who had spent two years with my life hanging on his whim, I detected an unusual fury smoldering behind his chilly shell.

Damon rose and bowed to the Marshal. A small man, he affected a particular neatness about his hair, close-trimmed beard, and plain garments. His complexion was the hue of olives—visible because his mask covered only the left half of his face. That named him pureblood.

All men and women born with magical talents were descendents of long-ago invaders from the Aurellian Empire. Purebloods were those whose magical lineage had not been diluted or obliterated by familial interbreeding with common Navrons. Surely most of us at Evanide were of pureblood descent and would have been raised among people like this Damon—in a society almost as restrictive as the Order. I could list the rules and disciplines of that life, but to think about it too closely made my head ache in the way it had when I'd first been brought to Evanide. I had learned to hold such matters at a distance.

"I regret the unfortunate timing of our meeting, paratus," said Damon. "You've just returned from a rigorous exercise, and I understand your desire to deliver your report and be off to rest and replenishment. My questions may seem frivolous, but I assure you they bear upon the future of our beloved kingdom and thus upon the future of us all."

I inclined my back, deferring to the Marshal's obvious respect for the man. For the moment, curiosity shoved aside my personal concerns.

"Know, first," he said, "that I am aware of what is done to the minds of those who train at Evanide. So tell me, what do you recall of the war that rages in Navronne?"

His manner invited answers as sober as his questioning. My recollection of history was extensive, but I began with a summary.

"The noble king Eodward died some three years since without a writ designating which of his three sons should inherit his throne. The eldest, Bayard, Duc of Morian, is accomplished in arms, but considered brutish and poorly educated, ill-suited to rule. Osriel, Duc of Evanore, son of Eodward by a pureblood mistress, is a reclusive halfblood, reputed variously to be a weakling cripple or a dangerous madman who practices demonic magic in his mountain strongholds. Perryn, Duc of Ardra, seems nearest his father's son, and yet demonstrates signs of weakness . . . cowardice, dishonesty, guile. The bitter contention of Perryn and Bayard gave rise to this war that ebbs and flows across the kingdom to its sorrow. It grants opportunity to Sila Diaglou and her murderous Harrowers, who seek to raze our cities and send us back to living in caves. She preaches that such groveling misery will appease some nameless gods who have sent us these years of plague and relentless winter. I could give more detail. . . ."

Damon waved it off, even as he stepped closer. His unblinking stare pricked uncomfortably. "Which faction holds your allegiance? Prince . . . priestess . . . ?"

How could he be so familiar with the Order and ask such a question?

"I am incapable of answering that at the moment. As a paratus of Evanide, I defer to the Marshal and his commanders."

The Marshal leaned forward slightly, intent. His fingers brushed a silver pendant, the only adornment to his stark white.

Still Damon probed. "And yet your account hints at personal feelings about Perryn and about the Harrowers."

"Who could not despise savagery that raises ignorance to the state of a god?" His probing crept under my skin, lending inappropriate sharpness to my words. "As for Prince Perryn . . . perhaps I misspoke to mention rumor less founded than those regarding Bayard." Indeed I could not raise particular incidents about the Ardran prince to match Bayard's firing of a Hansker plague ship with all aboard or his stripping of already depleted village storehouses in famine-ridden northern Ardra. "I was attempting to provide some equity between the three. My apologies if I overstepped, *Domé* Lares-Damon."

His observant posture grew only more intense. "Is it your broken memory that makes you incapable of opinion?"

"I don't—" And here I stumbled. It was not as if I'd no mind to consider what I heard. And yet, who knew what specific understanding had vanished along with the person I had been—this Lucian?

Damon did not relent. "And if so, how will you judge rightly when you are a knight and have sacrificed the personal beliefs shaped by a past you've just hammered into dust?"

"On that day I will be a new man," I said, reaching for the surety of purpose the Marshal's interview had left in me. "My foundations will be renewed in this Order which I deem worthy, which I *choose* to be the compass that will guide my course." Yet my answer sounded over-simple and left me entirely unsettled.

Damon strolled toward the center of the chamber and faced the grand windows, where the pearl gray of sea and sky had darkened to the hue of slate. "Magnificent," he said. "It struck you as you came in, Greenshank, did it not? This window?"

"Aye, *domé*. The prospect makes a man seem quite small."

"But it was not the center panel that arrested your attention so much as the left, I think. Why?"

Two years in the Order had accustomed me to such intimate probing from Inek, my guide, the one charged to take the dust and splinters they'd left me and reshape them into something worthy. And the Marshal was the commander of us all. But this stranger . . .

I glanced at Inek. The fire beneath his skin had flecked his eyes with sparks. Yet nothing in his soldierly posture gave me permission to withhold such privacies. Nor did the Marshal, whose expression remained unfathomable behind his white mask.

"The depiction filled me with horror and . . . grief." To speak it felt as if I peeled my skin away. "To burn a place entire must surely make a goddess weep."

Damon spun round as if I'd kicked him. "How could you know it burned?"

I could not judge whether this was dismay or eagerness or merely surprise. It was tempting to say something outrageous to see what he might do. Did he think I *remembered* something?

A chill left me acutely aware of my damp clothes, of my illicit venture to the estuary and the damning portrait in the sack on my shoulder. More than ever I did not want the portrait exposed here.

"The arrangement of the slivered glass . . . the color of it, citrine and red . . . and imagining sunlight passing through . . . suggested burning. The female figure's tears seemed to affirm it. Perhaps that's an incorrect interpretation. The work, so large and detailed, is stunning no matter its subject."

Damon gestured dismissal, as if the ripple in his composure had never happened. "Clearly you've a good eye for detail. I never noticed those slivers of glass. Perhaps we could summon the next paratus, Knight Marshal. I'm finished with this one."

As Damon returned to his seat, the Marshal opened his hand to me. "Thank you for your clarity, Greenshank. Commander Inek, you and your charge are dismissed."

"Knight Marshal." Inek touched his forehead and heart.

I echoed his farewell, but on one knee. I had earned no true rank at Evanide. Not yet.

I followed Inek through the fortress like a lamb behind its dam—or its butcher. I would be shed of this matter, even if he bucked me back to tyro and threw me in the bay.

To my surprise he did not take me to one of the private cells where a guide met his charges for individual tutelage, counseling, or whatever personal scouring they needed. He led me to the armory.

"Bare your face. Then light the warning lamp and barricade the door." The molten fury I'd seen in Inek was ready to spew. Of all days . . .

I hastened to do his bidding. No need to make things worse. The red globe outside the wide doors warned all who had business here that someone was working dangerous enchantment inside. I fired the globe with mage-light, then threw the bolts, touched the release pins for the defense bars, and let magic flow through my fingers. Fingers are the conduit of magic.

Steel beams shot out from the sides of the doors. As they slammed into their holding brackets with a resounding boom, Inek launched a shield across the armory and bellowed as I'd never seen him. Then he whirled on me, his eyes like the fire of the *cereus iniga*. "Do you know this Damon? Lie to me and you will sleep tonight in the bottom of Hercal's Downspout with chains about your ankles."

"No, *rectoré*, how could I possibly—?"

"Because for certain the devious wretch knows you, and for seven days you've lived a lie."

CHAPTER 4

"I've no knowledge of the man, *rectoré*. I swear it," I said. "Indeed, I had an eerie sense when he asked me about the window glass, as if—"

"As if you had remembered something you should not. He believed your memory excision flawed or broken. Is it?"

"No! Truly, I can tell you naught of Damon but what you heard and saw, and I was strictly honest throughout his questioning. But the other—"

"The lies?" Inek had regained control of himself. His glare fixed on me and his words bled disbelief, but at least he didn't look ready to throw anything else.

"I omitted an incident in my report seven days ago. This is not excuse, *rectoré*!" I cut him off before he could say what I already knew. "I fully understand the depths of my fault, and in no way do I expect this confession to offset the penalties you assess. I returned tonight with full intent to tell you all, because I believe in the Order's way. The life you and your brothers live has a purity and purpose well worthy of what an aspirant must sacrifice. But events have clouded my resolve, and in order to find my way again, I must step back. . . ."

I laid the leather sack on the floor between us. "Knight Commander, I report my mission of seven days ago complete."

"Blessed return, Greenshank. Speak." His every ritual word was a hammer and a warning.

"My earlier report on Kitaro, the purveyor of rarities, was exact. He rode away, his memory correctly clouded and his Order token left in ashes. But as I returned to the skiff with the *cereus iniga*, I heard a woman singing. . . ." I told him all.

He did not interrupt. Not to call me the names I'd called myself. Not even to remind me that a paratus who puts his life at risk through Evanide's fiercest tides to serve a lie is betraying his brother knights, both those who have nurtured him and those in the future who could suffer for lack of his strong arm and trained magic. Instead, he paced in ever narrowing circles, arms tightly folded. By the time I unrolled the portrait, he was crouched beside me.

"Goddess Mother of earth," he whispered.

Anyone who looked on the portrait would recognize its authenticity, whether they had met the woman or not. But for a person who lived with magic as we did, its truth was indisputable. And truth spoke that this woman was not of humankind, but a legend made flesh. Even stony Inek could not contain his awe.

"*You* did this."

"I must have done. The name holds no meaning, but my fingers recognize the signature as my own. When they touch the page, magic courses through me and I know I could alter the image, if I wished, and it would remain true. I understand that my bent is but hidden and will be returned if I succeed at my endeavors here, and that the name Lucian will not matter when I choose another on the day of my investiture. But this woman . . . the very same who sang and vanished and professed she was bound to me in ways a *human* could not understand . . . *Rectoré*, my every bone, every sense, every perception insists she is Danae. She says her people—Deunor's holy fire, her people whom tales name guardians of the earth—need *my* counsel. What does that mean? Who, in the Sky Lord's mercy, *am* I?"

Inek stared at the portrait. Shook his head. "Is there more?"

"No. I came here straight from the estuary. I do sincerely desire this life, but if you say you must strip these things away— How can I turn my back on a mystery that any man or woman in this kingdom would give a limb to pursue? My soul is ripped asunder with the argument."

Inek blew a long exhale and sat back on his heels. "Were these things brought me by anyone else I'd have him whipped for brazen lies. But you . . . I've long held suspicions about you."

The air shifted as Inek resumed his pacing, tapping the rolled portrait on his open palm. What could he possibly *suspect*? Commanders had access to our memory relicts, and for two years I had poured out every scrap of thought and feeling to him. He knew far more of me than I did.

Bracing my shoulder on the stone wall, I pressed the heels of my hands into my eye sockets. My head pounded as if the ceiling of the armory were caving in on it, one stone at a time. Not since that initial journey to Evanide, when every moment was a frenzy to squeeze out some scrap of memory, had I experienced the like.

As I grasped a tenuous hold on my wits, Inek halted his pacing in front of me. Resolute.

"I do not know who you are. And I've never understood how you came to be here—or why. Though physically inept and inclined to sentimentality, you were naturally well disciplined, intelligent, your innate power for magic clear. Why was your place in the outside world untenable? Why would you consent to this life? Even yet those answers elude me, for from your first day I've been forbidden to examine your archived memories to plan your training as I do for the others. The old Marshal told me that condition was set by those who recommended you to the Order."

A single flaying glare, then he shrugged and continued. "That happens from time to time. Family contention is the usual cause. He gave me sparse information about your talents and weaknesses, which has proved accurate for the most part.

"But about the time you were made squire, that Marshal—a hale and vigorous man—collapsed and died. Inexplicably. And not a month after this new Marshal—a strict disciplinarian—takes his office, a former senior paratus who *failed* his final testing is allowed to speak to selected squires . . . and of all Evanide's trainees you are the only one selected for his notice on every single occasion."

"The Marshal. And Damon." The implication was like a kick to the knees. "You believe—"

"I believe *nothing*. I state only fact and a coincidence of time and events."

"But this Damon . . . a *failed* paratus! How is it possible he even knows of the Order?"

Any trainee who failed, no matter what his rank, was stripped of all memory of the Order before leaving Evanide. Only a paratus-exter, a man at the brink of knighthood, who decided he could not in conscience take the final step, was allowed to leave with both his own memories of life before Evanide and his awareness of the Order intact. And even then he carried no memory of the Order's particular magics.

"Damon's status was not an easy thing to learn," said Inek, "and I'll not deny it seeded me with doubts. Yet, his questioning seemed benign. Thus, I've held discipline all these months, even as I wondered about him—and you. Now you bring me undeniable evidence of the magnitude of your talent, and this extraordinary mystery of your past on the same night I learn that this same Damon, and *not* the Marshal, chooses which fragments of memory are returned to you. And now, it seems, Damon will also assign your off-island missions."

"My missions!"

"These things are not righteous." The air trembled with Inek's indignation. "They compromise the independence of the Marshal, which compromises the integrity of the Order."

"What kind of *missions*?" His outrage fed my own. I had submitted as was necessary to survive in this place. I had seen worth enough early on to yield my trust as well as my obedience, mostly because of this demanding mentor and what he'd taught me of resolution and endurance, of the knights and their selfless service. And then, the Marshal's passion had captured my soul's aspiration. But if outsiders—a failed trainee—held sway over the Marshal and his decisions so far that *Inek* would doubt, my faith was upended entire.

"I'm to be told at *the proper time*. Until then we are to continue your training as before."

"So you'll erase my memory of all this. Leave me naked before the wolves." Anger, and no little fear, depleted what manners I had left. My life . . . my mind . . . were in the Order's hands.

Inek glanced up, blue eyes cold, fully my guide again. "Your training will certainly continue as we are charged. You are a strong and disciplined man, displaying *possibilities* of becoming a true knight. But you are unfinished, and you will need to be stronger yet—and far more wary."

"No. I can't accept—"

"Do not interrupt! The Marshal apparently supports Damon's purposes and though I deem this violation of the Order's founding principles serious enough to bend my god-sworn oaths, their ultimate goal may be as holy as Mother Samele's breast."

"You don't believe that!"

"Silence your insolent tongue and listen." He scrabbled through a wooden box, and then swung around holding two wide silver bracelets. "I'll not strip any of this from you—not the mystery of the woman nor your true name nor awareness of Damon's interest in you. But for your every hour in this fortress, you will bury that knowledge so deep Kemen Sky Lord himself could not discover it. *Off*-island, however, whether dispatched on exercises I choose or Damon chooses, you may draw upon that knowledge as you do all else that bobs to the surface in the slurry pit of a paratus's mind. Upon your return, you will give me complete reports of everything you discover. We shall speak of these things only here in the armory."

I gaped at him. Missions off-island . . . allowed to remember . . . to pursue answers. Even as my spirit leapt, my blood pulse quickened. His plan was enormously risky.

Inek ran his fingers over the bracelets' embossed surfaces, seemingly bemused . . . until a stiletto of magic pierced the air.

"I'll not excise your understanding of my own violation, either." Inek continued as if he had not just made the world thrum with power. His magic always sang. "I've spoken slander, given you unsanctioned information about your background, and allowed you to retain memories you should not have. One hint of this conversation could result in my ruin. Even so, I will not relent in your preparation. I trust you to keep me safe—to keep us *both* safe—as we do what is necessary to preserve the honor of our brother knights' service. If we learn, as I must hope, that I am mistaken in my suspicions, we shall confess our violations to the Marshal, allowing him to determine our future as we have committed ourselves to do. Elsewise . . . we shall see."

His courage left me speechless. He was trusting me with his mind . . . with his life . . . for a violation of his knightly oath could surely see him stripped of one or the other. He would allow me opportunities to learn what we needed, yet, by maintaining the integrity of his teaching, the path to knighthood remained open to me. Fear shook me to the boots. If this man, the most righteous of knights, was driven to compromise his honor, then his suspicions of conspiracy must run very deep.

For Inek, if naught else, I had to make this work. "Will I be able to distinguish tasks of your devising from the others?"

"When I send a paratus on exercises away from the fortress, I often provide spellwork he is not yet privy to. Often linked to something like these." He dangled the silver bracelets from his thumbs.

Silver was an extraordinary medium for spellwork. Even the most complex spells could be linked to an artifact of silver and they would retain their cohesion for years. And somehow silver's brilliance, its malleability, its delicate variability—so easily blackened, so easily restored—masked the enchantments it carried, leaving them undetectable to even the most skilled sorcerers.

"These will serve as an armory for your own favored—and perfected—enchantments. And from now on, as you prepare for an off-island task, you will leave them with me for a few hours. Fix will have them waiting for you with your boat. Pay attention, and you'll easily discern whose mission you undertake."

He tossed me the bracelets. Eyes closed, I traced the intricate designs. My fingers saw the shapes they traveled, here an embossed star, there a flower or a ring, an engraved spiral or triangle. With practice I would be able to locate each inerrantly, no matter distraction. My exploration continued until I came upon the residue of a small magic humming on a raised circle. *Inek.* The name popped into mind, quite distinctly.

I slipped a silver band over each hand, and snugged it about my wrist with its double latch. "The raised circle will tell me the author of the mission."

A tilt of his head affirmed it. His hand motioned dismissal.

"One more question." I could not ignore the most unusual part of the interview with Damon. "What is the image in the window? Damon *cared* what I knew about it. It was my description of fire that shocked him, made him think I knew more than I should—which I did not. I spoke only what I saw."

Inek's arms were folded again, his face inexpressive. "I'll not answer beyond this: The image is the foundation story of the Order, the reason for our existence and our way. The story will be revealed to you on the day you are vested as a knight, if you should live so long and prove worthy."

That wasn't enough. "Is it possible the meeting was set for the Marshal's inner chamber so that I would see the glass and Damon could gauge my reaction?"

"Possible." I was glad Inek was unmasked, as his brow creased just enough before his answer to reveal he'd not considered that.

"As you leave, douse the warning light." He retrieved three swords from the rack and laid them on the worktable.

One more curiosity. "*Rectoré*, why the armory?"

His snort made his opinion of my question clear. He never liked the question *why* from his subordinates. "Tonight, I deemed you a participant in this corruption of our way. I believed Damon put you here for a purpose, and whether or not you recognized him, I believed you to be working toward that purpose. That may yet be so. The sheer number of enchantments in the armory makes it impossible to be overheard. Thus, no one would hear as I beat you until you told me the truth."

"That's not as easy as it was when I arrived," I blurted. Foolishly.

"Try me, paratus. And as you bleed, you will still have to walk the seaward wall for the first quarter tonight and the next thirty nights you reside in the fortress, as punishment for your lies."

Fortress Evanide's seaward wall. Had anyone ever devised so miserable a place to stand watch? As if one could actually *watch* anything while facing the Western Sea in the pitchy dark after midnight. As if any boat would dare approach the sheer cliffs of Evanide's western face at any hour, come to that. The sea would smash it to splinters in an eyeblink.

The seaward watch was one of Inek's favored reminders of failure, this time exacerbated by his hatred of lies. He had assigned me a quarter's watch each night. Six hours. The normal duration of the seaward watch was two, because a moment's lapse of attention could send the unwary guard plummeting into the boiling black water below. The walk itself was forever slick from spray, fog, or rain, and narrow enough two men could not pass. That those who built the damnable shelf had seen no virtue in a parapet more than calf-high did nothing for a man's anxiety. And, of course, full mail was required. The weight of chausses, thigh-length habergeon, pauldron of plate, and all the sodden padding underneath added to one's weapons ensured death from a fall would be quick, though perhaps preferable to six continuous hours of aching back, neck, and legs, and unceasing wet, cold, and salt spray.

On top of normal training—sparring, running, unending study and practice with ever more complex magic—and four hours of dead sleep if I was lucky, my punishment ensured I had no time to ponder Curator Damon's purposes or fret over how I might investigate the Danae mystery. Indeed, those hours taught me to shove all distracting questions deep, as Inek commanded.

Raimo, the second armorer, helped me choose what spellwork was the most useful to affix to my silver bracelets. He insisted I do the work, of course, which was quite fine with me as long as I could keep awake. It wouldn't do if I got in a pinch and forgot that I'd linked a veil to the spiral sigil on the *left* bracelet and instead produced a gout of fire from the spiral sigil on the right.

On the morning after my third night on the seaward wall, I returned to my cell to shed the cursed mail—and wipe it down with oil, of course—find something dry to wear, and stumble to the Hall to see if anything was left from breakfast. I had made it as far as the wiping down when the curtain in my doorway flew aside. A dark-haired paratus in a mail shirt leaned easily against the doorframe. His grin flashed through his gray mask, warming even my cold skin.

"Ah, Greenshank, I thought I counseled you never to get on Inek's wrong side. Thirty nights on the seaward wall . . . Did you curse his forgotten mother?"

There was only one possible response to Cormorant, Evanide's paratus-exter, the next to be knighted. I grinned back.

"An omission is the equivalent of a lie," I said, quoting Inek's first and most serious lesson to any tyro. "Perhaps when you beat that into me with such exquisite care, you managed to beat it right back out again."

Honorable, generous, supremely gifted, Cormorant had been my paratus-mentor when I was a tyro, soothing the constant pain and terror while teaching me innumerable skills.

"Of all things, you idiot!" he groaned. "Perhaps another beating is in order."

"The wind has done a sufficient job of that," I said, resuming my blotting and oiling. "Please don't tell me I'm to spar with you this morning. Or just go ahead and skewer me now."

"Though I'd relish the occasion, alas, not. I was just up to the armory and Inek dispatched me here. I'm to fetch your bracelets to him, and announce that your training schedule is canceled for the rest of the day. He wishes to see you in his chamber at midday and recommends you sleep until then."

Slug-witted and cold, I stared at the heap of dripping chausses and the towel in my hand. "Bracelets?"

"Paratus, would it be those on your wrists, do you think?"

"Yes." Blood surged into my head. "Yes, of course." Bracelets meant Inek's spellwork for a mission . . . a mission off-island.

I unlatched the metal clasps, slipped the wide bands over my cold hands, and passed them over.

"*Dalle cineré*, Greenshank."

"*Dalle cineré*, Cormorant. How many days left?"

"With the Sky Lord's grace, five-and-twenty." Five-and-twenty days until he crushed his relict—destroyed his past—and was invested as an *eques cineré*. A resolution spoken with joy and without doubt. How I envied that.

Once the curtain fell still behind him, I redoubled my efforts at the cleaning. The salt water could set rust in mere hours . . . and who knew how long I might be gone? Would the task be Damon's or Inek's? I doubted I could sleep for the questions roused by the coming venture, but somewhere between habergeon and mitons, I crawled over to my pallet and collapsed.

"Your task will be simple information gathering," said Inek, shoving a small map across the table. Evanide's bay and the Gouvron Estuary made it easily recognizable as our own coastline.

"We've reports that one of Navronne's warring princes will visit the town of Ynnes in the next two days. Prince Bayard's ship docked at Tavarre three days since, and he rides down the coast road with a small party. No one has been able to ferret out what business he may have in a place so out of the way as Ynnes, but I doubt it's sampling their fish. As Navronne's war will shape the future of the Middle Kingdoms for generations to come, it behooves us to know as much as we can about the man. Our usual sources might be noticed in such a small place."

"We're well placed for such a mission," I said, studying the map. Ynnes lay perhaps thirty quellae north of Evanide and five or so inland, on the north banks of the river Aluelle.

"This is not practice. The dangers will be real and serious. Bayard is an experienced warrior, and is on alert for his brothers' assassins. He has pure-bloods in his service, thus enchantments will not pass unnoticed. Move fast, learn what you can that may be of use, and get out safely. Stay masked, and carry no weapon but a knife. You're given no permission to shed blood, and there is nothing here worth dying for—that we know of." No suppressed humor broke my guide's grim demeanor.

We spent most of an hour going over matters such as transport and what the Order knew of Prince Bayard's recent movements. Inek provided a pair of wood tokens set with silver splinters that would allow me to erase an informant's memory of a masked man asking questions and had me fix an *obscuré* spell on my mask so that an observer's eyes would slide away from my face without remarking it—a common technique when we walked among ordinaries. I hadn't thought of either. What else hadn't I considered?

"The tide surges in an hour," said Inek, standing. "Fix will provide your map, provisions, and purse." And my silver bracelets, I assumed. "Have you any questions?"

"None, *rectoré*."

Inek stood. "Go in safety, Greenshank, and return in honor."

"In honor, Knight Commander." The ritual words carried a deeper significance this time. Our lives and fortunes rested in each other's hands.

An hour later, Fix untied my bowline and tossed it into the skiff. Map and provisions were stowed. The silver bands gleamed from my wrists.

"*Dalle cineré,* paratus," called Fix, lifting a hand as I caught the tide.

"*Dalle cineré.*" *From the ashes* . . . Perhaps so. The bracelets told me this was Damon's play.

CHAPTER 5

Ynnes was a most ordinary river town. Flat, cold, wet. Everything smelled of fish. The docks where the fishing boats set a course down the river Aluelle to the sea. The bloody gutting sheds hanging over the river. The smoke from the drying house. The streets that were little more than rivulets of mud overhung by top-heavy houses of gray timbers that had never seen paint. The hairy men clad in dun canvas, and the pinch-faced women bundled in cloaks the color of mud.

It ought to be a cheerful place. The lord who owned the land thereabouts had granted Ynnes's fishermen their catch decades ago, and though Navronne was well into its fourth year of famine, I'd watched a drudge ferry three cartloads of fish from docks to drying house in two hours. Yet children sat dull-eyed and listless while their gaunt-faced mams ground fish bones into a gray paste—a nasty ration I'd had the misfortune to taste on training missions. I wondered if the hard-eyed men guarding the drying house were protecting the town stores, not from outsiders but from their own townspeople.

I had arrived at Ynnes's rotting palisade at dawn, after spending a rainy night on a hilltop overlooking the road. No royal party had ridden past.

The pole gates stood open, but two townsmen perched on barrels in the center of the opening. With no other travelers to mask my entry, I was entirely too noticeable. I tried a muffled call from out of the morning fog, made other strange noises, and even loosed a will-o'-the-wisp to lure the men away, but only one of the guards succumbed. Unwilling to waste the memory tokens so soon, I resorted to a veil and crossed the town's threshold unseen—only risky if a skilled sorcerer nosed about. A quick exploration yielded a good sense of the town's layout and a fine observation post atop the ruin of a glassworks.

Half the morning I perched on a strip of broken slate roof joining a pair of brick chimneys—one of them easily climbable. Though I had to share my aerie with pigeons and fifty years' legacy of their tenancy, it provided good cover and an excellent view of docks, street, and gate. I dropped my veil early. Veils sapped one's magic too quickly to be held long. The mask would keep me anonymous; its *obscuré* would prevent anyone noticing it.

The only travelers to arrive since I'd taken up my watch were a party of three men and two women, mounted on sturdy, well-fed horses. Not war-horses. None of the men fit Bayard's description. The women's plain but well-made capes, one blue, one gray, named them a merchant family, perhaps, but not royalty. None wore pureblood cloaks or masks.

The traveling party left their mounts at the town stable, and I noted the house they entered, above a potter's stall. It was far from the best house in the miserable town. I doubted Prince Bayard would give it a glance, much less visit. If he came.

Another hour passed. A steady rain poured from the inexhaustible clouds. At its making, my hooded cloak had been infused with spells to repel the wet. But spellwork that challenged the fundamental processes of the world so directly had little endurance. The bay crossing and most of two days out had soaked the thick wool through. Even so, it was not mail and I was not walking the seaward wall. Grateful, I ate the dried apples I'd stuffed in my jaque that morning. The provision bag remained with my horse in a stand of beeches south of the river.

At mid-morning, sharp hails drew me onto my knees between the chimneys. A party of six at the gate, this time all men, four of them heavily armed. The gate guards touched their brows as the six rode in, recognizing the travelers as men of rank. None of the party pressed the guards to proper reverence for a prince who aspired to be king, and yet . . .

The two who were not so obviously men-at-arms were both big men, and the larger of the two could surely be Prince Bayard, called the Smith for his build and his brutish hand. Tall and broad in back and chest, he wore a thick beard and a wide hat with the brim curled rakishly on one side. Though his garb was common leather and russet, he sat his mount with the ease of a knight and the assurance that the world was his to command.

The man who rode beside and slightly behind the bearded man dismounted with equal swagger. He was broad in chest and back as well, but he'd scarce reach the other man's shoulder. More significantly, his fur-lined pelisse was the color of good wine, and no hat or hood adorned his head, just a mask that covered the left side of his face. A pureblood sorcerer.

As the others waited, the pureblood knelt in the center of the gateway and laid his hands on the earth. My fists clenched on their own, and my senses reached deep, as if I might feel his magic flow. Did he lay down a trip thread to warn if anyone followed or a trap to prevent their crossing? Or did he seek evidence of magic? The Order trained us to minimize the leavings from our spellwork, but if the man was exceptionally skilled at detection, he might notice a slight residue from my veil. Information worth the knowing. I'd best get an estimate of his skills before I left.

The pureblood rose and wiped his hands on his braies, then touched his forehead and bowed before speaking to the man in the hat—his contract master, then. A pureblood, seeing himself divinely gifted with magic, deferred to no ordinary, even royalty, save the one who had paid handsomely for his services.

Contracts were the foundation of pureblood life in Navronne, providing the sorcerers' families wealth and security in exchange for their magic. Before relinquishing my past to the Order, so Inek told me, I had been contracted to a necropolis. I had assumed that my bent, the unique talent inherited from the bloodline of one of my parents, must be weak. But if I could create such artwork as that portrait, why could my family find no better contract for me than a city of the dead—a burial ground?

My head pounded its usual warning to stop reaching for memories that weren't there. The task of the moment must come first. The big man in the hat was most assuredly a wealthy man to own a pureblood contract. But why would a prince of Navronne visit this dismal town while embroiled in a war that engulfed the entirety of the kingdom?

As the leader and his men-at-arms dismounted, the pureblood eyed the town, scanning slowly, carefully, from the river to the palisade, across the mud streets, the unpainted houses and sheds, and upward . . .

I lay still as the broken bricks, though my heart raced like that of a raw tyro.

Ridiculous. He couldn't know I was up here.

I peered around the chimney again. One of the four men-at-arms led the horses into the farrier's yard, while another took a post just inside the gate. The pureblood, his master, and the remaining two soldiers had been joined by a plump townsman with spindle shanks and a great beak of a nose. Likely a town official, as a red badge adorned his tabard. He bowed deeply and waved a hand toward the fish-drying house.

As the party moved toward the long, low shed, the awkward fellow bowed every other step. After he tripped over his own boots, near knocking the imposing visitor into the muck, a soldier grabbed the bumbler's collar and quick-marched him the rest of the way into the shed. The door swung shut behind the five of them and the hard-eyed town guards resumed their watch.

Dried fish. Was that the story of this venture?

Determined to know more, I shinnied down the chimney. Two women emerged from the wellhouse down the lane and sent me scrambling into the tangled weeds of the ruined glassworks. Would Damon think a visit to the drying house confirmation enough of Bayard's mission in Ynnes? The pureblood had me uneasy; a quick departure would be welcome. Yet if the big man was indeed a prince of Navronne, why would he be buying his own fish?

Once the women had trudged past with their heavy buckets, I slipped around and across a muddy wagon yard to come up on the drying house from behind. The place lacked windows, but it did have back doors—ill-fitting doors, one wide enough for wagons, the other human-sized. By squeezing between a broken-down wagon and the wall, I could peer through a sizeable gap beside the smaller.

Dim . . . smoky . . . stinking . . . It was difficult to make out anything through the racks of fish. A thin gray-lit outline marked the entry door on the far side of the interior. Several shadowy figures stood beside it. A bit more focus and I sorted out the tall man in the wide-brimmed hat and the spindle-legged official.

As resolving vision built people from the shifting shadows, hearing picked out intermittent words from the smoky interior.

". . . as soon as possible . . . my men sufficient to guard . . . Max, give . . . payment." The commanding voice could only be the noble's. ". . . a dry place to wait . . ."

"Honored, honored, excellency . . . fire in the hall . . ." The dithering official. "Willem! Three wagons ready within the hour! You, Herc, and Voilo."

The shouted orders birthed two scrawny figures in the shadowed interior. They headed straight toward me. Or rather toward the wider door and the wagons in the yard behind me. I twisted around, squeezing past the broken wagon, only to have my cloak snag on a splintered slat.

A rattle behind the wall was a beam being lifted. Hinges scraped and the wagon doors yawned. Impossible for me to get loose and all the way across the yard without being detected.

I touched the spiral on my left bracelet and held still. The veil enchantment slipped over me like a silken glove, just as two slovenly youths emerged from the opening maw, yelling for Herc. Wrenching my cloak free, I sped across the yard, hoping no one noticed footprints and cursing my stupidity. Inek would roll his eyes in strained patience while reminding me of the necessity of escape routes and other useful tactics to remain unseen, especially in the vicinity of purebloods.

Once back to the crumbled glassworks, I tried to convince myself I'd sufficient information. If I left now and traveled through the night, I could return the horse to our hostler and take the morning ebb back to Evanide.

But I couldn't. Inek might have assigned me a simple spying exercise to nose out such weaknesses as I'd just demonstrated. But Damon had chosen this mission. What purpose did this venture serve for *him*? He was expecting more than dried fish.

At the least, I should see the party off. If they departed within the hour with three wagonloads of fish, I'd go.

Once ensconced in my aerie again, I dissolved the veil. If the pureblood had sensed its invocation, he'd be watching for it. Unlike wisp lights or sparking powder one could buy from an itinerant Ciceron, veils were nothing anyone in the town might use.

The obsequious official escorted the visitors past the potter's house and a breadseller's stall to the grandest structure in the town—a rickety building that proclaimed its importance with four carved wood pillars and evidence of paint. My morning's exploration had identified it as the town's common hall. One of the men-at-arms accompanied the master and the pureblood inside, while the other made a circuit of the building before taking his post outside the door. The official hurried back to the drying house.

I watched and waited. The rain intensified. Nine small boats returned to the docks empty. The fishermen trudged away, several into houses along the lane, others continuing on toward a taphouse farther down the lane.

Then my every sense flared to life. The pureblood emerged from the commons house. He looked up and down the street, then crouched and touched the churned-up muck of the lane. What was he looking for? Me?

After a moment, he wiped his hands on a kerchief, stared at the ground in brief contemplation, then rose and trotted up the lane . . . but only as far as the potter's house. He knelt yet again and touched the stoop before going inside.

I held my breath, fascinated.

Moments later, the pureblood emerged in company with one of the women travelers. She was tall and slender, draped in a long blue cape. She raised her hood, but not before I glimpsed pale hair and smooth flesh. She was no crone.

The two dashed through the rain to the commons hall.

Instinct . . . training . . . everything in me screamed that this was not some royal fancy to while away the time by bedding a random traveler. Perhaps it was my vantage, observing so much from this height. This was the next move in a single game and it was not a game about dried fish.

My descent from the chimneys took only moments. Perhaps the pureblood's moves were naught but usual caution, but I had to assume he'd sensed the veil I'd worked at the drying house. That left my choice of tactics slim.

Veils were powerful magic. A veil confused the observer's eyes so they failed to see an object. An *obscuré* was quieter. It made the eyes slide away with little or no impression of the object. A suspicious sorcerer could detect either one. Neither prevented ordinaries from bumping into the hidden person's limbs, hearing his steps, or sticking sharp objects in the approximate area of his gut. The sorcerer could tell a swordsman exactly where to find that gut.

Inek had said this wasn't worth dying for. So, how was I to get inside undetected?

Without a good answer that avoided bloodshed, I had one alternative. Force them out. I wanted a better view of the woman and an idea of who she was. If I did it right, no one would notice the magic until I was well away.

I swung by the deserted docks and set a fire spell smoldering atop a broken cask. With some damp scraps of wood and rope arranged beside to feed it, and an infusion of extra magic to ensure the rain didn't douse my sparks, it should make a pretty blaze by the time I finished my other preparations.

Shouldering a hoop of rope and tugging my hood low, I trudged down the lane past the commons house, as if on my way to the taphouse. Instead, I turned into the alley between the bread stall and the commons house. Circling around as the prince's careful guard had done, I traced a line along the wall, my touch scribing a conduit for enchantment.

Now, a little work with my bracelets. I bound a spell of heat, one of smoke, and one of penetration into a single construct and linked that back to the bracelet. Like the other bracelet spells, it would be available for my use, just waiting for an infusion of magic to bring it to life. My plan would have to unfold fast, before the pureblood could react. He would be expecting something, so I'd let him have it. But first, some bread from the stall.

"Five loaves for the noble guest," I said, as the hollow-cheeked woman's gaze fell away from my *obscuré*-spelled mask to the coins in my hand. "Your freshest—in a basket."

I left her puzzled, not sure who had bought her loaves. The basket of bread I linked to a fire spell just large enough to hint at a bigger conflagration to come.

"For the prince, sir knight," I said, tugging my hood to the soldier guarding the commons door. "Spindle-shanks done sent this, as he says it might be longer than an hour 'til the wagons are readied. I can take it in. . . ."

"I'll take it." As the man snatched the basket from my hand, I infused the fire spell with magic. He disappeared inside. I sped to the corner of the hall where my trace began and linked the new spell from the bracelet to it. My fingers poured magic into the path around the building. Heat and smoke would penetrate the wood walls from three sides. The bread basket would explode into flame. And those inside would, I hoped, feel an urgency to come out.

Noting a satisfying orange glow from the docks, I burst into the house directly across the lane. "Fire at the boats!" I shouted at the three grizzled fishermen I'd seen entering.

I dodged out again. As the three ran off, shouting the alarm, I ducked into their doorway and waited. Smoke billowed from the commons house, along with curses and bodies. A clanging bell emptied every house in the town.

A man-at-arms appeared first, his sword incising a path in the river of men and women now rushing from the taphouse to the docks. Pureblood and master emerged next, shielded by powerful enchantments and the second guard's sword. Close on their heels was the woman in blue.

I shoved two fishermen aside to reach her before any of her own people arrived from the potter's house.

Raising my cloak as if to shield her, I touched her arm. "Lady, may I assist you?"

"Remove your hand or I'll cut it off." Indeed she carried a short sword drawn from a sheath at her waist. Her glance traveled from my hand on her arm to my face and did not drop at the sight of my mask. An incredibly strong-willed ordinary to see past the *obscuré*.

Her pale skin was stretched over fine bones like sculpted marble, flawless save for a diagonal scar that etched each cheek from cheekbone to chin. Her eyes were the color of spring sky in fairer climes, but as frigid in their disdain as ice shards at the winter solstice. "Who are you?"

"Only a . . . p-poor fisherman . . . lady." Shock, not fear, loosed my grip and backed my feet away from her. No artifice contrived my stammering. "I would not have harm come to you."

The precise, glaring scars on the slender woman's cheeks would have told me enough, but the scarf around her slender neck confirmed it—a trailing scarf of bright orange, the colors of the ravagers who believed that cities and sorcerers and nobles should be slaughtered in repentance and the rest of humankind hide themselves in caves. The colors of the Harrowers. She could be none but Sila Diaglou, the priestess turned prophet who had slashed her own face in a public marketplace to amend the kingdom's sins and now commanded legions rampaging across Navronne's fields and cities.

She drew up her hood and bullied her way toward the potter's house, where her four companions engulfed her. The man in the hat and his protectors were nowhere in sight. Townspeople thronged the lane in front of the commons hall, shouting about smoke with no fire in the commons, and flame with no spark at the docks. Ynnes likely hadn't seen such doings in decades.

The city gates stood open and deserted, tempting me to run. But I needed to see if prince and priestess met again or left together, and I'd no wish for either party to overtake me on the road. Sila Diaglou slaughtered sorcerers.

I slipped back around the palisade and up the glassworks chimney. The risks of such a perch were not lost on me. But no house seemed safe with everyone awake. In a different season I might have hidden in the river, but the only way I could survive the frigid water for any length of time was with magic, which would draw the pureblood like a bonfire.

The two parties rode out within the hour—Sila Diaglou and her four companions first, the prince, his pureblood, and four soldiers a short time after, along with three wagons heaped with fish. The town gate was closed and locked behind them.

Ynnes was soon as dark as Sila Diaglou's soul. Sad piping came from the direction of the taphouse. Somewhere in the night a man and woman argued. I slithered down from my aerie and slipped across the yard to the docks. I'd no time to hike upriver to the ferry crossing and no inclination to swim.

A youth sat on a barrel, bundled in a blanket, his mouth sagged open as he dozed. The star on my left bracelet provided a spell to deepen his sleep— not so much that any would think it unnatural. Infusing the spell with magic, I touched his cheek. His head lolled.

Magic frayed the mooring line of the most decrepit boat of their lot. Once across the river, I wedged the dinghy in a snag. Perhaps the boy would notice when he woke.

Avoiding the road, I ghosted over the countryside. Shivering in the rain and deepening cold, I sought some worthy reason a son of Eodward would parlay with a priestess who slaughtered purebloods, nobles, and priests with equal savagery. Her Harrowers were not weakened by the brother princes' war, but proclaimed it more evidence that every god but theirs was a lie. Would Bayard, unable to defeat his brothers honestly, truly ally himself with Harrowers to make himself king? Even a paratus with half a mind recognized that as a foul and dangerous bargain.

Half an hour took me to the swale where beeches grew. The bay mare waited patiently where I'd left her. To my weary disappointment, she was not alone.

CHAPTER 6

Touching the magical perimeter I'd left around the mare gave a measure of the power used to breach it. Considerable, expert, though more kin to a smith's sledge than an etcher's needle. The mage who'd done it hid warm and breathing in the deeper shadows, eating the rest of my apples.

I could walk away with a clear conscience. Inek had given me no permission to engage Bayard or his men in any fashion, and a sorcerer who traveled with battle-hardened soldiers posed no small danger. Yet a confirmation of the noble's identity, and a hint of his dealings with the Harrower priestess would be invaluable.

My senses probed the air around and the earth below as I trudged into the beech grove. No magics hung in the air—no snares, no paralyzing bolts. No tremulous loops waited to open a void or buckle the ground beneath my feet.

"Are you as wet as I am, Betony? I think it's time for home." I scratched the mare's nose, ran my fingers down her legs, and tightened the saddle girth.

"So where would a faceless apparition have a home?" A soft gleam of magelight spread across the wet grass, as the short, bull-necked man I'd seen from the chimney perch stepped into the open. His wine-colored cloak was fine and thick, his black beard heavy and trimmed close to his square jaw. Naught else was visible in the faint glow.

"That's a more complicated question than you could imagine, pureblood," I said, keeping the horse between us. "Do you intend a fight? I've far to go and would prefer not."

He edged around the clearing where he could see me better. "I doubt a fight would be useful."

"Then I'd thank you to leave a bit of provision for my journey. Your noble master likely pays you well enough to feed yourself."

He snorted a laugh. "Tell me what family permits such unseemly garb and what master commands you create disturbances in fish towns, and perhaps I'll leave you these"—he peered into the leather sack—"haycakes?"

I shook my head decisively. "No bargain there. Only a goat would actually eat those cakes—they're mostly salt and seagrass. I've heard naught to entice me to break privacy. But I'm still listening."

"I really must know who you are. You smoked us into the open—a most unusual and powerful spell combination that has left me in bad grace with my master. He ordered me to discover your purpose or not come back."

The pureblood leaned his back against a tree, folded his arms, and crossed an ankle, the very image of relaxed power. Yet spellwork soon threaded the air about him like a haze drawing over the sun—binding magic, pain inducements. Dangerous magic.

My thumb touched a small cross on my right bracelet. The spell waiting there had taken me months to learn. Called an impenetrable wall, it could provide an instant's protection from any magical assault. Though extremely short-lived and extremely costly, it could save a man's life when he'd no leisure to judge a threat. I sincerely hoped not to need it.

"It's always satisfying to hear one's mission is accomplished," I said, feeding the mare the last sliver of apple from my pocket.

"Accomplished?" His sneer would have been obvious to a blind man. "I doubt that. You created a clever and perfect opportunity for assassination, yet you're satisfied with a bit of confusion?"

"You assume my mission was your master's harm," I said. "Well, perhaps that *was* the task assigned, but then a thousand things can go wrong with assigned murders. Consider, I attracted your attention. I did *not* take the perfect opportunity to damage your lord. I displayed a fine sample of my skills. And you're here, are you not?"

Tension rippled through his easy posture. "You *wanted* to draw me here?"

"I am in search of a new master. My current one is . . . um . . . eccentric. His requirements put me at odds with my own kind—"

I gestured at my plain leather and russet, the full mask, the black cloak, all of them egregious violations of the protocols mandated by the Pureblood Registry—Damon and his cohorts whose iron hands governed pureblood life.

"—and his activities put both life and soul at constant risk. I would prefer less . . . spiritually grotesque . . . service. Yet, being a practical man, I could only accept a master of the same rank and prestige as my own, and there are only two such to be found in Navronne. So I examine what Serena Fortuna puts in front of me and, lo, today I glimpse one of these verisame two! Not only is he a lordly figure, but he has at least one formidable sorcerer at his command already. Thus I decide to investigate what opportunities might exist for a sorcerer who could bring exceptionally useful information, as well as exceptional skills, to that lord's service."

I could almost hear his mind open at my wild story. "One of my lord's peers . . . an eccentric . . . Sky Lord's balls! You serve Osriel the Bastard!"

So satisfying when a play bears fruit. The man in the hat, so clearly *not* Prince Perryn the fair-haired popinjay, was indeed Bayard, Duc of Morian.

"Discipline forbids me affirm your guess, *eqastré*," I said, addressing him as an equal, "and my current discipline is *extraordinarily* cruel." I waved my silver bracelets, and let him imagine what he would. "But I'll say my master heard unsettling rumor of an alliance to be sworn in Ynnes this day and dispatched me to make an end to such a possibility. Indeed the meeting I witnessed makes me hesitate in my resolve. I already serve a demon. Why would I risk proximity to a witch who lusts for the death of all sorcerers?"

The pureblood's hand waved in dismissal. "My master pursues what's needful for Navronne's future. He sees a great deal of litter that can be advantageously swept up before he takes his rightful place and returns the kingdom to good order. His servants do not question him. Yet, as all of our kind learn sooner or later, it is possible to . . . guide . . . ordinaries once we've proved ourselves loyal and clever."

Litter? What sordid arrogance to use rampaging lunatics to broom away inconvenient opposition. And what extravagant idiocy to expect such allies to be dismissed easily in their turn. History demonstrated that fanatics were as dangerous and tenacious as hounds with the frothing sickness.

His magelight brightened. Eager, coal-dark eyes gleamed from his face, the masked side as well as the exposed. "As to your contract, my master would not wish to offend his brother. Yet he would welcome your information. So little is known of the Bastard. How could we trust you to be forthcoming and not take what you learn of our stratagems straight back to the demon prince?"

I spread my arms wide. "I've risked a great deal to speak with you," I said. "You've no measure of my master's wrath should he find out. But my contract is up for renewal, and if we manage the new one through the Registry, my lord could do nothing about it. And be sure, once free of his household, I'd bleed myself dry before going back."

He crossed his arms and took my measure. "The Registry would need your name. And of course, His Grace would have to approve the negotiation first. But I'll say . . . he'll surely bite."

Well he should say so! To bring Bayard an intimate of the reclusive third prince who lurked atop the riches of Navronne's southern mountains would surely reap substantial reward.

"Come with me now," he said, taking a few purposeful steps. A thread of insistent magic twined about my limbs.

Clearly I'd milked all that was useful from this encounter. I inclined my back, touched my forehead, and extended my hand. "I would be forever in your debt, *eqastré*. This is my family crest. It will reveal enough to forward our business, and I can swear truthfully to my master that I spoke my name to no one."

He took the wooden disk and shone his light on it, wrinkling his brow. "But what—?"

Magic arced from the token in my hand to the one in his. He jumped a little and wiped his ashy fingers on his braies. They stung, I knew, as if they thawed after frostbite.

The pureblood's twining magic dissolved, and I slipped into the shadow of the beeches. He passed me by as if I were one of the sodden trees and spoke only to the horse. "So who are you, lady beast, and what are you doing in the midst of nowhere? I'd some notion . . ." He frowned and shook his head. "Well, come along. No use letting you stand out here and take a chill, while I walk halfway to Tavarre. The soon-to-be king of Navronne will make good use of you."

He swung expertly into the saddle.

"Damn all arrogant purebloods!" I mumbled as he rode away.

Inek was not going to be at all happy at my losing a horse and tack. And I'd have to hurry or lose hours to the demon tides. Yet I dared not use magic to reclaim my mount; to be seen would undo the memory wipe.

Fortunately, nothing on or about the beast could lead anyone back to the Order nor to the hostler that tended our mounts. And the urgency of my news would trump all else. Bayard's alliance with the Harrowers would change the course of the war . . . of Navronne's future and that of all the Middle Kingdoms. Rampant savagery condoned. Pillage and ruin of towns and trade routes not avoided but encouraged. Prince Perryn's weakling legions could never stem such a foul tide. Something had to be done.

Bayard's sorcerer would head north, toward his master's ship. My course lay south. I sped across the barren hills to the coast road, then settled into a smooth gait along its grassy verge.

. . .

My path through the dark hours became a tunnel that seemed endless. The world blurred as I focused solely on controlling breath and muscle. I paused at stream crossings just long enough to slurp water. To stop was to invite the chill into tiring muscles. I encountered no other travelers.

At some time, the fog vanished, as if swallowed by a monster of the night. Multitudes of stars pricked the ebon sky—a rare beauty in these climes. I couldn't enjoy it. Though the summer solstice lay but days hence, clearing brought the kind of out-of-season frost that had blighted Navronne's weather for the past seven years.

A marker I'd left at the roadside sent me scrambling down rocky steeps toward the thrashing sea. Though my knees ached as I jogged along the rough shingle, the need to return to Evanide was implanted deep in all who trained there. The fresh water in the boat's cask, a bite of Malcolm's cheese, and an hour's rest would allow me to catch the ebb and make the crossing without foundering.

So I continued. But somehow when my arm swept the stinging blur from my eyes for the five-hundredth time in an hour, the crash of waves had yielded to the shifting of reeds and the burble of streamlets and mudholes. My feet no longer traversed a rocky shore, but the marshlands that protruded into the western sea like the Goddess Mother's apron.

The change shook me. Had I fallen asleep? How could I not have noticed entering such treacherous terrain?

A fan of magelight guided my steps toward the cove where I'd moored the skiff. Safely across a soggy mead, I pushed through chest-high reeds, testing each step. The low-pitched slop of surging water—the river Gouvron itself—welcomed me . . .

A spongy hummock gave way and I plunged, backside first, into frigid swirling water. Down and down. Cold, thick, the fingers of the tide reached through a submerged tangle of reeds drawing me deeper into the blackness.

Training took over. *Slow the heart; steady the nerves; let the body's reserves give time for magic.*

But exhaustion slowed my response, and the grip of sea and river tightened and dragged me down faster and deeper. My chest burned. . . .

A burst of musical laughter rippled from the depths, bathing me in summer. Was the Last Ferryman a *woman?*

A warm, powerful current shoved me sideways and my feet found solid purchase. I arrowed upward. Hands and head broke the surface, greeted by blustering wind. Gods' fire, as if I weren't already freezing!

Gasping, coughing, and spitting, I ripped slime and sea wrack from my head. Salt and mud had me blind. I scrabbled for a handhold to drag myself out of the sink.

"Wait, my poor Lucian! Let me help."

Splashing and laughter accompanied hands of warm flesh that enclosed my wrists, and with a shallow chuff of effort, she hauled me onto the cold mud. No Order comrade could have done it so smoothly.

"Though I relish this intimacy," she said in my ear, "our dance is entirely graceless."

Astonishment and a mouth full of muck left my appreciation garbled. I scrubbed at my eyes with sodden sleeves, desperate to look on her.

"Stay—" Crouched close, she halted my frantic flailing. "Let me guide thee till we can wash them safely."

One wrist in hand, her other arm slid around my back. Her presence heated me like flooding sunlight, as she guided me blind over squishing ground. Only on the inside was I shivering. She knew me. She was Danae.

Wary of tricks and illusion, I tried to resist such a mad certainty. "How did you find me, lady?"

"Did I not say we are bound by our deeds? Ever and anywhere can I find thee. Since I left the scroll, I've yearned for yon fortress to spit thee out again, so I've taken . . . residence . . . close by. 'Tis only thy urgency and direction these few days made me wait till now. Thou didst ever remark my persistence!"

As I fought for some hint of memory, my skull throbbed its usual refusal.

"I recall nothing of you before I found you in my boat," I said. Though it violated all caution to reveal weakness, she had me at her mercy in uncountable ways. "Until I saw the portrait, I'd no idea I could do such work, or that you are . . . what it claims you are . . . or how I could possibly have come to know you. Lucian de Remeni's life is an empty canvas to me."

"Empty!" She halted, but kept her hold on me. "By the Everlasting, Lucian, did we break thee? We had devised the torment as a penalty for thy trespass—twisting the boundaries of the world with thy magic. Naari said he touched thee with it in a fit of anger and quickly stopped when you suffered such distress. Naari does not lie, but if he misjudged . . ."

Tales called the Danae tricksters, who delighted in tormenting humans, but *this* trick, at the least, could not be laid at their feet.

"It was those I live and work with now who broke my memory. They needed to teach me things I couldn't learn, living as I was. I agreed to it." Somehow. For some reason. "What trespass—?"

"*Thine own companions* broke mind and memory?" Her outrage aborted my questions. "They stole away thy beloved artwork and the studies of history thou didst value so deeply? What folly can match that of humans?"

Her grip tightened, as scorn dripped like acid from her tongue. "Mere movements and sequence do not define my dancing, no matter how perfectly I execute them. If I have no spirit, no exuberance drawn from my living to infuse my steps, the dance will remain dry and meaningless. How canst thou do any work of value lacking thy own true spirit? From the first moment I heard thee speak of Navronne's history, I recognized how extraordinary was thy spirit, and I witnessed its fullness on that sweet afternoon you worked magic for me, lay with me, and used thy pens and inks to show me what I am to become."

Even with her support, I near stumbled over my own feet. Her words rattled my ignorance like hailstones on tin—names, places, studies of history, magic that twisted the boundaries of the world. That my art had shown her what she was to *become*; I dared not imagine what that meant.

Yet something worse shadowed all. Always I had believed that the most important pieces of my life must be engraved on my spirit, and that no matter my experience with the Order, the right spark must eventually bring those things back—in recognition or understanding, if not exact detail. To hear that I had known this fleshly, passionate woman, that I had *lain* with her, and that the experience was entirely lost staggered me. "Lady . . ."

"Come," she said, pushing my hand from my eyes yet again. A few steps more and she drew me to my knees near the source of a quiet burbling.

Her hand cupped my forehead. "Lean forward just a little. And take off that dreadful mask. Trust me, my friend. I've seen thy comely body entire in all of its joyful parts."

The cold was certainly no problem. Her touch, her smell, and the merry jibe scorched my every part. Half embarrassed, half roused, and entirely confused, I seemed incapable of words. Then, with a sure hand supporting my head, she sluiced my face with fresh, frigid water. Once, and then again, and again.

"Ow!" I spluttered and spat.

Scolding, she swatted my hands aside as I tried to rub away the sting. "Clean thy hands before touching the eye!"

I dipped hands and gritty mask at one, then pressed the water from my eyes. With a careful breath—terrified I might see no one and know myself mad—I blinked them open.

The woman from the boat knelt beside a small pool that glittered with starlight. Her cheeks and brow were flawless, unmarked as I had seen her at our previous meeting, but . . . ah, sweet Goddess . . . water dribbled from her tangled curls onto shoulder, arm, and breast clad in naught but exquisite images of vines and trees, butterfly and lynx, inked in blue fire. Danae fire.

"Envisia seru." The words rose from my marrow, though I'd no idea what they meant.

Her sober expression bloomed as if an early sunrise had intruded on the fading stars. "Ah, dear Lucian, thou'rt a delight to my eyes, as well. Somewhere along this strange path hast thou learned a proper greeting for one of the long-lived."

Emotions poured from her body like scents from an herb garden—pleasure, eagerness, regret.

"It was not I who taught thee, secret as I was in those sweet days." She brushed drips from my brow in such intimate fashion my cheeks burned like summer sunrise. "Was it the other—the sentinel marked in silver you told Naari of? If her lessons remain in thee, then surely the answers to our questions can be found, as well."

Enthralled by her every breath, every lineament, every word, I could only stumble onward.

"I know naught of these things—penalties, twisting boundaries, silver marks . . . you. I don't even know your name." Nor what she liked to do, nor where she lived, nor how we'd become friends. Purebloods were discouraged from forming friendships. How had a pureblood artist come to know a dancer—a Dané masquerading as a dancer?

"Then our dilemma is indeed dire." She pressed her folded hands to her mouth and frowned. "When the severity of thy trespass became apparent, Tuari Archon, he who speaks for the long-lived, sent me to the city called Montesard to learn of thee. I was only a youngling, but skilled in ways that passed me easily for one of humankind. *Not* easy was it to tease past the rules that surrounded thee like an oyster's shell . . . and then past thy own shy nature."

Her fleeting smile was quickly enveloped by a worry that tightened my gut.

"When I saw the drawing wrought on that wondrous afternoon, I could no longer deny that I had learned what was needed—and so very much more.

The archon was anxious for my report, and thy grandsire was so very angry with thee that I left. Upon my return to the true lands, I told Tuari all I had learned. He commanded we stay close and watch thee, Naari and I. We tried to warn thee of the trespass thy magic wrought. The last time Naari gave warning, you spoke to him of another of the long-lived, one who named herself a sentinel—one who watches the boundaries of the true lands."

She stretched out her arm and its glimmering cerulean, indigo, and sapphire marks.

"Thou didst say her gards were not colored with the hues of sky as ours are, but with bright silver. Thou didst claim she spoke of *Sanctuary* . . ."

Her pause invited me to speak, but I shook my head. None of this held any significance.

"Now Tuari's patience grows thin. He has commanded me to fetch thee to him, as the tale of silver gards and Sanctuary is of great concern to us. But without thy remembrance . . . if he sees no worth in thee . . . Lucian, his wrath is terrible. He does not value humankind."

Joint and sinew softened with her fear.

"The trespass thy magic wreaks opens our boundaries to dangers unimaginable. I am bound to take thee to the archon, but how wilt thou answer what he asks?"

A meadowlark riffled its melodious call from the hills beyond the marsh, startling me out of my beguilement. The stars had faded. Morning and the tide's ebb were upon us. Curiosity, no matter how maddening, and wonder, no matter how deep, could not define my duty. Not today.

"Two years have I fought to remember my life, lady," I said. "It is impossible. And I can't go anywhere with you just now. Duty demands I report to my commanders with all haste. But I need an hour's rest before I go, and if you could just teach me of these matters—the true lands, trespassing boundaries— I would be ever grateful. And perhaps something of this grandsire you named. Gods, you know more of my own family than I do!"

But she leapt to her feet, her countenance riven with worry. "If thou canst not come with me, then go. Others are on their way to meet us. Please, Lucian, be safe . . . but hurry. 'Tis much more difficult to argue thy necessity when there are five of my kin surrounding thee, even if they mean you no harm."

No harm. But she had already told me that this Tuari had no use for humankind and her worry was indisputable. I could likely hold together a few more hours and row.

"I'll go. But tell this Tuari I'll gladly speak with him as soon as I can. Let him test me and see that I've no will to do injury to your kind and no knowledge or magic that would permit it—even if I did before." Certainly she would have to explain more before I could even know what to deny. "How will I find you?"

"Return to the estuary at any time. Touch its waters and I'll find thee. Until then, travel land and water with the greatest care."

Rolling fog swallowed the new-birthed sun as I bowed to her. "Gracious lady."

"Ah, Lucian, my name is Morgan."

"Morgan." The name was tart and sweet on my tongue, but not at all familiar.

She smiled as she vanished, as if her pleasure captured the last beams of the morning's sunlight.

Her tale sparked naught of memory, only a seething confusion. What, in the name of every god, could have compelled me to give up such gifts—an exceptional and unusual bent, studies that she said I relished even more, as well as the mystery, wonder, and affection embodied in this glorious woman? Was it greed or folly or a falling-out with this angry grandsire? Had I been a coward, unwilling to face the consequences of my choices in life? What had I done?

A future with the Order had seemed so clear a path, so honorable, so right. But Morgan's assertion that a future made no sense without a past struck me hard. What if she was right? New doubts companioned those grown from Damon and the Marshal's collusion, threatening to sear my resolution to ash.

CHAPTER 7

"The Marshal commends your getting us the news so timely." A plaudit could hardly be delivered with less appreciation than Inek's. "He says tell you that word of Prince Bayard's unholy alliance now spreads throughout the kingdom to every knight, to every informant, to every ear that heeds rumors of treason. He dispatched messengers as you wallowed in your bed."

It was mid-afternoon on the day of my return from Ynnes, and Inek sat on his armory worktable. He didn't approve of what he saw. My clothes were still damp, stiffened with salt and mud. I had wakened late after a blessed six hours of sleep and decided it wise to report immediately. I could scarce recall what all I'd told him when I staggered into the armory that morning.

"And the Order itself will take action?"

"The Order, yes, after due consideration. *You* will resume your training this afternoon—and your seaward watch tonight. Twenty-two nights remain of your punishment. Be glad I've added none for losing a good horse or coming here stinking, ungroomed, and unprepared for work."

"But I hoped—"

"You hoped I would free you from your duties and send you back to the estuary. I will not. You hoped I would answer the questions this woman—the purported Dané—has posed. I cannot. I applied to the Marshal for permission to review your archived memories. I told him it was critical now you are eligible for solitary missions, but he refused yet again. Unless the Archivist should permit it on his own—an unheard-of interference—I'll not have access to them. And I've certainly no relevant personal knowledge. Silver-marked beings? Magic—magical portraits—that assault some mythical boundaries? What are these *true lands* the woman speaks of? Divine Idrium? The Karish heaven? Hansk, or Pyrrha, or Aurellia itself?"

"I should study the lore of the Danae," I said, trying to moderate the urgency that felt like to burst my skin. "And references to places of sanctuary. Temples are traditional sanctuaries, as are Karish churches, now they're widespread. But I've an idea she speaks of something other. I could search the archives for historical references. Legends. Stories."

The plan had seemed brilliant in the fogs of waking from half a day and a full night of sleep. But I didn't need Inek's you-are-an-utter-imbecile glance to hear how feeble it sounded now I was walking. He'd warned me that he would not relent in training.

He abruptly left his perch on the bench and wandered over to the sword rack.

"No. A paratus has no reason to dally in the archives. The Archivist has no true loyalty but to the Order, and on any day he would be equally likely to laud you for studying beyond your narrow concerns or report you for neglecting your proper work. And he and the Marshal . . . it often seems they speak with the same voice." He fingered the sword hilts, but pulled none from the rack. "Neither spit nor bone of these matters makes sense. Truly, had I not seen that portrait, I'd follow you onto the seaward wall tonight and shove you over as a liar and a lunatic whose madness will be our ruin. As it is"—he blew an exasperated breath and pivoted to face me—"I can likely come up with a reason to read up on legends. And I'll devise a new mission to get you back to the estuary in the next few days. That won't be easy. You'll have to talk your way out of any consequences from this woman's master. That their grievance with you is related to Damon's interest seems unlikely, and yet both seem to concern your magic. I was told at the beginning that your bent was strong and would be useful to the Order. But what she said . . . You're sure she said you portrayed her as she was to *become*? Were those her exact words?"

So I'd told him that, too. I'd babbled until he'd summoned his tyros to drag me to bed.

"Yes. But I'm not sure what she meant. Maybe the light-drawings. Those on her body are exactly like to the portrait, but in person she has none on her face. Yet the portrait depicts unquestionable truth. If I'm able to draw something that's not occurred as yet . . ."

"That would certainly explain Damon's interest. But how could a sniveling portrait painter's magic, extraordinary though it be, worry these so-called Danae?"

His testy skepticism rankled. "You believe the portrait truth, as well, Knight Commander. What else could she be? She can vanish and appear from nowhere. She spoke of humans as *other* and said my magic interfered with the work of *her kind*—the kind she calls *the long-lived*."

"What work? To nurture the earth as our grannies tell?" he snapped. "I think they fail. Shed this sentimental drivel. Reasoned thought would be useful."

Something deep was disturbing Inek. Anger, irritation, disappointment had never before spilled over into petty insult. He glared at me as though I were some plague-ridden sailor, drawing pestilence from foreign airs to taint Evanide and the Order. "The next time you are off-island, find out how your magic works to bother them, either from her or by putting pen to page and exploring the sensations it arouses."

"As you say, *rectoré*." Gods, if only I could go now!

"Now off with you. I've work to do and so do you. And Greenshank—"

"Knight Commander?"

"Control yourself. Your actions. Your responses. Your frustration. Changes are expected when a squire becomes a paratus. But every variance will be noticed."

I inclined my back. "And you, *rectoré*, perhaps the same?"

His eyebrows shot upward. "Your tongue flaps too freely of late"—his bite yielded to a long pause—"but indeed, you are likely correct."

It was the nearest to an admission of fault I'd ever heard from Inek. I headed to the sparring arena in a better humor than I'd expected. I yelled at my cadre and set parati, squires, quivering tyros—and myself—to work.

F ive days of normal work—with unusually virulent magics and exceptionally sharp swords, it seemed—and six miserable nights on the seaward watch left little opportunity to think beyond the moment. Only one thing came certain. Leaving the Order was not a viable choice. Running away without sanction meant forgoing my past, and my hope that time and events could restore its most significant pieces was fading. If seeing a gloriously beautiful Danae woman could not rouse the memory of lying with her, then I could look on my own father, mother, or brother and not know them, or I could stand before a mortal enemy and see no danger.

A *sanctioned* withdrawal meant the Order would give me back my past, but a recovered past surely brought its own complications. My initial journey to Evanide had been a blur of constant panic, constant nausea, the restraint and punishment when I tried to run, the inevitable conviction and terror that I was mad, and the unending, murderous pain in my head. I'd no idea where the journey had begun, what dangers had lurked there, or how long or how far we had traveled. And I would be stripped of all knowledge of the

Order. Even if I were willing to abandon Inek to investigate the possible corruption of the Order on his own, would my memories tell me why a curator of the Pureblood Registry had such an interest in me? Curators were powerful sorcerers with wide influence. For all I knew, *Damon* could be my angry kinsman.

Inek was correct in his strictures. Such uncertainty could drive a man to madness sooner than true danger. The best I could do as I awaited my next assignment was keep ready and bury all thought of our treacherous pact.

On the sixth morning after my return from Ynnes, I raced into the Archive Tower Seeing Chamber for a mission study session. Though I'd done naught but throw on a dry shirt after completing my hours on the wall, I was late. The fire in the Hearth of Memory already blazed a searing yellow and white. Dunlin and Heron, two knights, two parati of other cadres, and three of Inek's squires were already seated on the half-circle bench that fronted the cavernous hearth. The Archivist stood rigid with impatience, his whipsnake fingers tapping the tall table where only one vial of his amber potion remained beside six empty ones and the bottles of acid-green eyeglim and its antidote.

"My apologies, Knight Archivist." Excuses were irrelevant at Evanide.

"Drink and take your place." The Archivist could have stepped off the massive basalt chimney before us. His tall, lean frame and his rust-colored mantle and mask made him a brother of the two knights—one defiant, one fallen—carved in relief on the ruddy stone.

I downed the bitter draught and took my place without delay, gripping the wooden arms that separated the seats on the bench as the world began to spin. The initial dizziness as the potion refocused eye and mind could topple even a seasoned knight.

Every mission the Order ventured was committed to a relict—a thumb-sized rectangular block of black-and-white stone—in the same way as every trainee's past life. Trainees and knights alike studied these missions to learn strategies, tactics, and history.

Squires did not receive the amber potion or the eyeglim. They would watch the unfolding events of the mission in the flames—the images wavering like reflections in a rippling pond. They would have studied the written transcript of the mission earlier and discussed the points of relevance with their guide. The viewing was to provide visual examples to reinforce the particular strategies or tactics they studied.

For knights and parati, the study was entirely different. The potion, the eyeglim, and the rest of the Archivist's magic allowed us not just to see, but to experience the unfolding events as if we were the participants, training mind, muscle, and reflexes quite like practice sessions in the arena. The accumulation of these experiences, along with those of his own training at Evanide, were the foundation of a man's knighthood, remaining with him until he died.

My eyes, already bleary with salt spray and lack of sleep, blinked rapidly. The Archivist tried three times to dispense the eyeglim droplets that would allow me to experience the history our commanders had chosen. His growling annoyance hinted at a temptation to send me away—which would be a boon after six hours on the seaward wall. Alas, he got the drops in.

A blurred movement and a chink meant he'd tossed the relict into the flames. All I truly saw was the brilliant flash of yellow, white, and blue that transported me into another man's body existing somewhere in the past. . . .

A bitter-cold evening, touched with smoke. No matter that the grapes were barely in—what grapes the corrupted seasons had left in the world. Winter's onset was no longer a gradual melding of golden fields and fragrant grapes with windblown leaves and frost-touched mornings, but the first blow of a brutal hammer that crushed us for nigh on three quarters of the year. We ran, my brother knight and I, pelting through the vineyard rows, uphill and down as fast as we could while holding complete silence.

I, the paratus known as Greenshank, settled quickly into the knight's mind and body. At least thrice in a tenday we were sent into these missions from months or years past, living as a knight who had given up this personal memory of one of his missions. It was so strange, near impossible, to think this might be one of Inek's missions or that of the knight sitting beside me, neither of them able to recognize it as his own. Rumor had it that some knights matched the wounds suffered in a session with their own scars, but they could never be entirely sure; that was part of their sacrifice.

The sessions had been horribly uncomfortable at first, as if two minds wrestled inside my one skull, but I had learned to yield to the magic and open myself to the narrative the knight had provided, as well as his actions and sensory experience.

The pair of us had been diverted from another mission a half day since and set on the trail of a Harrower raiding party bound for a slaughter. The news of an imminent attack had reached the Order late and we were closest. Why this raid of some rich man's house held more importance than protecting a caravan bringing grain to the smut-blighted villages near Raspor, we weren't told. I didn't like it. But a knight trusts his orders, even when they make no sense.

Any opportunity to shed Harrower blood was welcome, of course. I'd seen the carnage they left behind, sometimes, I believed, with my own eyes and not the Archivist's contrivances.

We'd found the abandoned Harrower encampment near the Earwine ford as we'd been advised. Seven riders. As long as their number didn't grow too much along the way, we two should be able to take them easily. Harrowers were not combat trained for the most part, and all of them believed magic to be corruption, anathema to their gods. First we had to catch them, though. The camp was two days old at the least.

Counting on our instruction as to the raiders' destination, we'd not followed their track, but cut through roadless hills. A day and a night we'd pushed our mounts, shorting them on rest in trade for speed. They'd got us most of the way before they'd blown. We turned them loose and ran.

We picked up the raiders' trail near Pontia. Two new companions on far better horses had joined them. The tracks skirted the walled town and led us into these hills crosshatched with vines.

My legs ached. My back seized in the biting cold. But the smoky air lured me on, as if I might find home fires lit to welcome. Even after so many years vowed, certain scents pull me. Smoke on a cold night is one. The stink of Harrowers another. This night I had both.

As we neared the summit of the hill, we detected living beings near. Flattening ourselves to the ground, we crept upward and took a quick scan over the top. Beyond a scattering of dark outbuildings—stables, from the smell of them—a great, sprawling house blazed with light. Faint music twined with the smoke. In between were . . . horses. Sky Lord's balls, *hundreds* of horses. Amongst them lanterns flickered and voices murmured or broke into quiet laughter. Had a Harrower legion joined the nine? Did no one in the house see the host poised to come down on them? What fools to be so careless in these days.

My second slid down from the summit on his back and lay beside me for a moment, staring at the stars. Appalled, no doubt, as I was. No matter our skills and magics, we could not stop such an onslaught. Training said we should leave immediately. A warning would only precipitate what was to happen and cost our lives for naught. And yet . . .

Harrowers did not laugh or show lights as they waited to swarm their prey. I lifted my head and tugged my second forward again. We lay there, chins on the dry grass, watching long enough for the truth to reveal itself. To smell the hay and oats. To hear the quiet slosh of water poured in troughs. To recognize the click of dice near a lantern. Callow laughter mixed with grunts as two bodies wrestled. These were guests' horses pastured in groups or hobbled. A few grooms and servants worked and loitered among them.

Strong threads of magic wove a confusion about the landscape, impossible to sort out. Defenses? Weapons? More likely spells of fertility, water cleansing, or such usuals found about a grand demesne. Perhaps this wealthy man employed a pureblood or was one himself. Harrowers loathed purebloods. So where were the nine we hunted?

My partner guided my seeing as if I were a tyro. A snuffed lantern. A grunt. A heavy fall. Another light doused farther on. The shadowy figure left a trail of voiceless black through the field. Another thud. A restless horse whinnied and shifted, disturbing a few more. Four threads of death led toward the rear of the great house.

Three mounted men carrying torches patrolled the peripheries of the residence. I readied a blazing arrow and a sirening call to warn them, but before I could launch, flames shot skyward on every side of the house. We had delayed too long.

Never had I seen such a conflagration grown so quickly, save in the Order's own battles. Harrowers disdained magic . . . or so we believed. Perhaps not this night.

Shouts rose from the burning house, just as flaming arrows arced from the three riders toward the interior courtyards. So many people there must be inside . . . hundreds of souls. God's mercy, why did they not come out?

"You for the sneakers; me for the cursed horsemen," I yelled. Without another word, the two of us raced down the hill, bellowing cries of war and vengeance. Stealth would be wasted.

We dodged packs of panicked horses charging toward the fences and others bucking wildly trying to rip out their pickets. All the grooms were dead. I tripped on a headless youth, but gritted my teeth and lurched onward, staying on my feet. A crackling as of lightning from my left marked a firebolt streaking from my second's hand. A dark-clad figure glowed like sunrise for an instant, then collapsed with a grunt. My knife made sure of him.

"Down, First!" My partner's call.

I ducked and rolled as a second firebolt struck a man not three paces from me. The Harrower's sword flew, glittering orange in the firelight, like the scarf round his neck. I bounced to my feet and finished the devil with a thrust, but not before his knife carved its image in my ankle.

When near enough to cast, I spun a net of paralyzing filaments toward the three horsemen. It should have taken all three easily, but half the net flared bright green and shattered into quickly fading sparks. I'd no idea what I'd done wrong.

The remainder of the net snared only the rider farthest from the house. Lacking his firm hand, his mount bucked him off and bolted. I didn't see if he was trampled, for a wild man ran at me sword in one hand, axe in the other. More practiced than I expected, death lust glowing Harrower-orange in his eyes, he pressed me hard, closer and closer to the burning house.

The roar of flames could not drown the rising chorus of screams from the house. Were they locked in? Sky Lord's mercy, we needed these lunatics dead so we could open a way inside.

I cast a tangle spell to snare the madman's feet. This easiest of combat spells shattered in green sparks. Stunned, I scarce countered his thrust, and it caught me in one shoulder.

He laughed and bore down on me again. But he was a fool. I let him dodge and weave and think his tickling touches worried me. Inevitably, he overreached, and I feinted low—my lucky move. When he matched my move, I slashed open his middle, spinning just in time to parry a cut from a second horseman charging past. He immediately dragged his mount into a turn. The bones of his face were knobby and long, his eyes alight with Harrower madness.

"Come on, demon-spawn!" I yelled, doubting if anyone could hear over the hellish din. "I can take you without magic." But I backed away from the inferno and dodged behind a fountain that splattered over a corpse, forcing my pursuer to turn after me.

The horseman charged and I triggered another net spell. Half of it flared green and shattered; half snared his sword arm and wrenched it out of position. Surely a magical void line was confounding us! The fractured net showed me. Spellwork nearer the fire than a hundred paces more or less failed.

The bony-faced rider galloped past, harmless for the moment, but pulled round again, shifting his angle of approach. His tactic was clear: drive me toward the house. Toward the void line, the boundary where magic failed.

How had Harrower rabble put up such a barrier? And why? They could not be expecting knights of the Order to come rescuing. Which likely meant the barrier was aimed at those inside. The confusing variety of magic around the demesne had suggested this was a pureblood house. And so many horses . . . two hundred sorcerers or more could be trapped where their magic could not work. Where they would burn.

As the horseman raised his sword and charged again, I scrambled uphill and through a gate narrow enough he could not pass. Stumbling between trees, hedges, and stone benches of a walled garden, I sought another gate. In the end, I scrambled over the wall, back to the field of death, for I was desperate to locate my second. He needed to know about the void line. And, great Deunor forgive, even if we failed to save the poor wretches inside, we had to learn how it was done.

Too late. The third horseman herded my partner deliberately toward the blaze. Weaponless, my brave brother laughed and raised his hand. His fingers, outlined against the flame, spread in his favorite pattern. A lightning crackle—

My own firebolt shattered in useless green sparks, as I feared it would—just after his did the same. Just after the rider cleaved his skull.

The rider swung around to find where my bolt had come from. I drew up a veil for long enough to scutter into the night across the paddocks and up the slope. I needed a wider view. There had to be some way to get the people out.

Five dead—the four sneakers and one horseman. The same two horsemen—Magrog stew them in their own blood—yet patrolled the front and stable side of the burning house, as if to ensure no one escaped. That accounted for seven. Where were the other two? Blocking some other entrance? Behind me?

The horses were mostly gone, over the fences, into the fields. Those left were dead or injured or huddled together at the farthest corner of their paddock. Halfway up the hill, a fallen beast grunted his agony at his splintered leg. I relieved him of his distress and wedged myself beside his carcass. My head spun and shivers racked me. My wound had bled buckets down my arm. If I didn't bind it soon, I'd be wholly useless. And the Order had to hear of this attack.

My hands shook as I pulled a rolled linen from my belt. With teeth and fingers, I bound it tight about my upper arm. Blood doused the pale bandage before I tied it off. Now to salvage what I could.

The fire was demonic in its nature. In an explosive burst, the walls caved in upon themselves, silencing the last agonized wails. When only pulsing embers and bitter stars lit the dreadful ruin, the two Harrower horsemen whooped and rode away.

Only then, as I tried to comprehend the magnitude of such horror, did I glimpse the remaining two riders. A dark-cloaked pair appeared abruptly on the road not a hundred paces from me. Shadows masked their identities. One stood average in height and slender, one shorter and a bit stooped. I named them male from the timbre of murmurs I could not quite decipher—and a pleased laugh.

A lust for vengeance and retribution for all who had died this night pushed me to my feet, sword and knife in hand, and magic at the ready. We were well outside the void line. But I'd swear on my mother's womb that magelight sprang from their fingers, lighting their way, as they strolled up the road away from the destruction. And in that moment they turned, half of each face remained shadow, half pale. They wore half masks. Purebloods.

"Gods' mercy . . . gods' mercy . . . gods' mercy."

"Stop dawdling and get out of here, Greenshank." The Archivist's rusty voice seemed like a pinpoint of light at the end of a very long, very dark tunnel. "I've other things to do than tend you like a nursery maid."

I could not tell him what was wrong. Numb, shaking, dizzy, angry, outraged, appalled . . . I could not possibly speak it all. Even separating mind and body from those of the unknown knight wouldn't help.

Determined hands pressed a square of linen into one hand and a small glass cup into the other. An astringent smell swept away the remnants of the seeing . . . the memory of life I had just experienced. Of its own choice, my hand brought the cup to one eye. I blinked enough that the infusion of euphrasy could dissolve the eyeglim, repeated the wash on the other eye, and used the linen to blot the dregs. The impatient Archivist snatched the cup away.

"My apologies, Knight Archivist," I said. Again no excuses. Impossible to come up with one, anyway, save that I'd begun the study overtired and anxious.

The hearth fire was dead. I shuddered and was glad of that. More surprising, the bench was empty. The two knights were walking out together, murmuring softly. Their masks hid their expressions, of course. I hoped mine did, too. Inek had told me to control my responses.

One of my hands, the one that held the linen square, stung fiercely. I stared at it stupidly. The arm of my bench seat was cracked and a great splinter protruded from the heel of my hand. Clutching the damp linen, I touched my forehead in deference and hurried toward the door.

"First!"

The call struck me in the back like a lance tip, and I spun so sharply I almost knocked over the table holding the empty vials and bottles. But it was only Dunlin, my own second, waiting.

"Inek came by to scoop up his clutch of squires. He said tell you we'll discuss this session later, as he'll be busy for the rest of the day. You're to keep to your schedule. No sooner was he out of sight than a summons arrived for you. As soon as you have 'recovered from this study and had a chance to refresh yourself from your'—ah-hem—'stalwart service on the seaward wall,' you're to report to the Marshal. I'm thinking you have a quarter of an hour until he sends a troop of tyros after you."

"Yes," I said. "Thank you."

Body and spirit might have been an arrow point made from a sliver of glass. Did I say more, did I allow myself to feel more, the archer would send me flying, and when I came to a stop, I would shatter. So I didn't do either.

Dunlin cocked his head. "Are you all right? Did you know your hand is bleeding?"

"It's nothing."

I left the Seeing Chamber and hurried down the tower stair, across courtyards and down causeways. My feet moved faster and faster through tunnels and undercrofts, until I was running up the narrow steps to the seaward wall—the only place in the fortress where one was almost assuredly alone. As thunderous waves battered the wall and fog masked the rest of the world, I fell to my knees and vomited over the side, vicious spasms that purged every remnant of bile my body could produce. Every time I thought I was done, it came on me again.

I had no name for the sickness that raged in me. No reason beyond horror that one human, gifted with magic, could do such things to another. But I knew it was more and that it was important and that like the Danae portrait, the scene I had just witnessed had touched a piece of my soul. That piece just wasn't there anymore.

CHAPTER 8

Though my belly remained empty, I managed to be clean-shaven and wearing dry clothes when I applied for admission to the Knight Marshal's chambers.

"Proceed directly to the inner chamber, Greenshank," said Doorward Horatio. "Unmasked, as usual, please."

Once the thick door closed behind me, I removed my mask and hooked it over my belt. Its absence left me feeling naked nowadays. Especially after Inek's warning.

I breathed deep and composed my features.

"Come, Greenshank, no need to muster extra courage before joining me."

My eyes blinked open. The Marshal, enveloped in white, stood in the inner doorway. Polished to brilliance, his silver pendant hung from his neck on a simple black cord. The pendant was inlaid with gold. Its reverse, which I'd glimpsed at my first interview with him, was also gold or brass—perhaps the seal of his office.

"Tell me I'm not so fearsome as all that, especially to a paratus who has served us so well."

A month previous I would have told him that I no longer feared him. Not anymore.

I dropped to one knee, touched my forehead and heart, and lowered my eyes. "Serving justice is my desire, Knight Marshal."

"I believe that. Come in."

Lagging behind him, I seized the opportunity to examine the great window again. I was grateful for the fog and gloom. To see the sun firing the slivered glass would be near unbearable after what I had just witnessed.

"Take a close look," said the Marshal, gesturing toward the left panel before he'd even turned back to face me. As if he had read my thoughts. "It's why I brought you here."

So close on the heels of the morning's viewing . . . Was the Marshal responsible for the morning's subject—another fire? Was Damon? A quick glance around confirmed that the curator was not present. Yet I could not shake the sensation of his cunning eyes watching.

"Commander Inek said that the story depicted on the glass would be revealed to me on the day I was vested as a knight, if I should prove worthy." And live so long.

"That's the usual way."

The Marshal joined me at the window. Surprising to note we were exactly the same height. He seemed so imposing.

"You and Inek work well together," he said. "My predecessor believed that would be so. He had great hopes for you, as do I."

"Your encouragement has helped me through difficult times, Knight Marshal."

The window displayed a city centered on two peaks, not a house in a verdant vale like that I'd seen destroyed an hour past. Even standing so close, I found no evidence of connection between the two scenes besides the murderous ring of fire—and, perhaps, a goddess weeping.

"This is the Order's story," said the Marshal softly, "this and the other pane. I thought to tell you some of it today that it might ease some of the doubts that plague you of late. Do not mistake. It's not my goal to coddle you by making this questioning time easy. Introspection is but a finer grit in your shaping. But you've difficulties enough to deal with, and I'd rue the hour the lack of a simple answer would drive you to unfortunate choices."

Had Inek mentioned my anxieties about my past when he'd applied to review my memories? Surely he'd not mentioned Danae or our suspicions of Damon. Or was this interview simply another step in Damon's mysterious plan? Why were they so cursedly interested in me?

"Please understand, sir, that what doubts I have are naught to do with my desire to pursue this life, but only with my fitness."

"Naturally." He shifted his gaze from me to the window. "When our Aurellian ancestors discovered that their sorcery took on such exceptional vitality in the lands we now call Navronne, they settled where their particular gifts seemed strongest. The majority of our people pushed south toward the benevolent climes of Ardra. But one small group of families made their home in Morian, near the northern sea. Because of the great distance between their settlement and the others, they went their own way about many things, producing a harmonious society that nurtured great art, philosophy, and a richness in the land itself that was exceptional, even in beauteous Navronne. They prospered from the sea trade and the overland routes to the old kingdoms of the east, built themselves a magnificent city, and made their own rules. The rules included those regarding magic and how it was to be nurtured and protected. Tales call their magic unparalleled."

What was this power the Marshal had to touch the spirit with his storytelling? Knowing of his violation of the Order's traditions, I'd not expected he could enspell me as he had in our private interview those months ago. But as a master musician with his lute, his story immersed me in nuances of wonder and grandeur, mystery and sadness.

"Even as the Empire of our ancestors challenged great Caedmon for sovereignty of Navronne, the future promised decades of instability. The northerners reached accommodations with the local peoples and continued on their path, while those of the south believed it necessary to solidify—unify— our presence in the kingdom. So began a long struggle between the two factions. Decades later, as Aurellia itself began to shrivel, and our ancestors were left to defend our presence without fresh warriors from our homeland, unity took on a terrible importance. But those in the north relished the life they had made and refused to yield. And so, a cadre of three hundred pureblood sorcerers—one from each great family who had settled the south— their skills honed in war, were sent to *insist* our kin of the north join with them to ensure their mutual safety."

"To swear allegiance or die," I said. A pernicious dread crept through my veins. History unfolded in certain ways, ever and again. "And they died."

"They died. Every one of them. It wasn't meant to be that way—not the children, not the artists or scholars or the musicians, the elders, or the ordinaries. Only the recalcitrant leaders, those men and women who refused to accede to the wisdom of their southern kin, were to be chastised. But the cadre's plan went terribly wrong. They had set a ring of fire around the great city to flush the northerners out, and as the people fled through the gantlet of sorcerers, the traitors would be arrested. But the northern folk did not leave. Instead they fled to sacred ground—this ring of standing stones atop the second peak. The flames consumed city and people alike. Some tales say the gods took pity and the earth swallowed the city, or it sank into the sea before it could burn. Some say—"

"Xancheira!" I blurted.

The symbol at the bottom of the window should have told me. The white on black emblem was not a degenerate version of the Order's mark. It was a five-branched white tree on a black field, the blazon of the duchy of Xancheiros—the greatest historical mystery of Navronne. *That* was a story I knew.

I could not hold quiet. "Historians have always written that it was Aurellian soldiers—loyalists to the Empire—who razed Xancheira and massacred its people as King Eodward drove them from Navronne. But that would have been over a century later than the time you speak of, and no one ever found evidence of it. None have suggested it might have been the Aurellians who *stayed* who did the murders."

Three hundred families had sworn allegiance to Caedmon's line and the kingdom he founded, because they wanted to remain in the land where their magic was strong. They held to his Writ that balanced political power in Navronne between the Crown, those who served the gods, and those who held the gift of the gods' magic—themselves. Sorcerers.

"Knight Marshal, you're saying the Pureblood Registry burned Xancheira and massacred thousands of innocent people."

"One could conclude that," the Marshal acknowledged with quiet reason, "but without blame or accusation. It was long ago. Many worthy societies are built on faulty ground. And today I'm telling the story of another such society. Built by those who witnessed a horror they had no mind to cause." He waited.

"The cadre of sorcerer-warriors," I said, as the links snapped into place.

"Though some had wives or children or parents, they could not go home to them, not after slaughtering wives and children and parents. To a man, they vowed to pay for what they had done—to cover their faces in shame and use their strong arms and their magic in service to those who needed justice . . ."

"To forgo glory, pride, and even thanks for their deeds," I said. "The *Equites Cineré*—the Knights of the Ashes." The Order.

So much explained. And, as everything of late, the knowledge brought with it a fear that shook me. Was that how they chose who joined them—men guilty of sins that required a lifetime's expiation? Was that why a portrait artist called Lucian de Remeni-Masson had abandoned his gift, his life, and a friendship that few mortals had ever known to stand the seaward watch at this dismal fortress? What had *I* done?

You are not a murderer. The fragment given me took on a wholly new significance. If I was here because of a crime, at least it was not murder.

"How did they end up here?" I said, pointing to the rightmost window and its depiction of Evanide. "This fortress is centuries older than the Aurellian migration."

The Marshal dipped his head and laughed, not in his usual easy humor but in amusement tinged with vinegar and rue. "Many reprobates have found safety in Evanide. Warlords. Thief lords. Sea lords. Exiled royalty. In the time of the Order's founding, this was a hospice, a place of refuge for those mighty, god-gifted purebloods who were unable to control the power of their magic here in Navronne. Of necessity, those who cared for them had learned a great deal about mind and memory."

"And shared those skills with the knights."

"Indeed, their great work became our greatest tool. This story is not yours to speak to anyone save Commander Inek. He, of course, is privileged to know everything of you."

A warning sounded in my soul as brazen and clear as the tide horns. The Marshal had just lied with the same quiet clarity that he questioned and probed and reassured nervous trainees. Inek's request to know more of me had been refused.

I lowered my eyes that he might not guess what I'd heard. His lie betrayed the very honor he claimed for the Order. "Thank you for this, Knight Marshal. I'll speak the story to none who lack the right to know."

Yet why was I privy to it? And why now? Nothing Inek might have reported about my doubts or questions had to do with the Order's origins.

"*Dalle cineré*, Greenshank. May you surmount all difficulties and find your proper destiny."

And so was I dismissed.

"*Dalle cineré*, Knight Marshal."

In a swirl of white robes, he retreated to his chair. Interesting to note—his feet were bare. They were not the callused, dry feet of an elder, but those of a man near my own age.

The afternoon's duties were tedious. An hour sorting lists of needed supplies to be parceled out to various merchants. Two hours practicing basic combat spells without full use of one, two, or all four limbs. An hour squeezed in to clean my armor from the night's watch. At some time I ate and drank.

Though I found occasion to visit the armory twice and Inek's guide

chamber several times, he was not to be found. I even exerted my prerogatives as first of our cadre and engaged Dunlin in extra wrestling practice,
just to have an excuse to visit the arenas.

"You've not seen Inek this afternoon?" I said as Dunlin and I sat panting
on a butt of hay and canvas used for target practice.

"No. He left *me* to spar with his squires after they finished reviewing the
mission study. Hand of Magrog, that was a rough viewing." He glanced
sidewise at me and passed me his water flask. "Was that what spurred this
fight? I'll not be able to take a full breath for a tenday."

"You're getting lazy. I'm your first, and it's my responsibility." It was the
truth. I'd been neglecting my second and third, trying to balance discipline
and comradeship. But we were knights-aspiring, not gossiping friends. I
needed to do better.

Dunlin was right, though. Fighting when outrage seethed so near the surface risked loss of control. Pain, fear, and anger must be used to feed strength
and skill—Evanide's unending lesson.

Yet the screams from that burning house would not be silenced. Purebloods murdering purebloods. *Exterminating* them. No more fitting word
could describe what I'd seen. And the story of Xancheira declared that
extermination was a part of the Registry's very foundation. It could not be
coincidence that the Marshal had summoned me right after the study session. Had Damon arranged it?

It was scarce believable Damon could be privy to mission studies. But he
was choosing my missions. The more I considered it, the angrier I grew.
Damon was a curator of the Registry, a direct successor of those who'd sent
executioners to Xancheira. If magic was the gods' gift, then the Registry were
the worst kind of apostates.

Inek did not reappear that night. We were told he had taken his tyros
and squires off-island. As always, our cadre's training schedules would be
posted each morning in his guide chamber. Without his word to the contrary, my punishment schedule remained unchanged.

Inek's absence chafed. I needed to know if he'd been able to learn anything of the Danae or references to a place called Sanctuary. I needed to speak
to him of the Marshal's tale that fit so horrifically with the study session, to
ask how the story of pureblood infamy might fit with Damon's presence here,
and to explore why, in the name of all gods, the incident had shaken me so. I
had promised Inek to bury all knowledge of Damon and the Marshal and my

role in their conspiracy while in the fortress, but that was impossible. If my guide didn't return timely, I'd soon be manic as a twistmind.

Fortunately or unfortunately, the swordmaster and the combat spellmaster announced that the quarterly combat tourney required for all parati would begin the next morning. After the first hour of serious bouts, as a healer stitched the laceration that spanned the length of my forearm, I determined to bend every thought to avoiding further bodily damage. As when wrestling the demon tides, distraction would see me dead—or at least a patchwork of stitches.

By the fifth night of the tourney—the sixth of Inek's absence—body and mind were pounded to paste. As midnight struck, I stood at the bottom of the steep, narrow, exposed stair to my watchpost atop the seaward wall. The ascent appeared as unassailable as a mountain must to an ant.

Are you tired, Greenshank? Do we push too hard? Will you always manage to be fresh and rested on your knightly missions? Can only those born in armor serve the world's needs? I didn't need Inek's cold assessment to judge how weak I was. An ink dabbler aspiring to be a knight. Perhaps that was the problem.

I cursed and set my boot on the first step. Whenever he returned, Inek would not find me lame and would not find me shirking.

Relief at nearing the top vanished as I emerged from the shelter of the wall and the sea wind blasted me full in the face. I tried to plant the heel of my lance, but the step was too narrow and I wobbled sideways, dizzy, toppling. . . .

I lunged for the wall, scrabbling and heaving myself upward for my life. Stone had never felt so welcome as that narrow walk atop the seaward wall. Until I thought about getting up.

I lay straddling the walk, one foot dangling over the deeps, the other over the courtyard far below—a lesser drop than the plunge to the sea, but more than enough to leave me a heap of broken armor and bloody meat. My right hand yet gripped the lance, but the shaft was trapped somewhere between my torso and the wall.

Worse yet, the low parapet did not begin for a body's length from the stair on either side. Encased in heavy armor, buffeted by a constant gale that could fell trees, my limbs displaying all the strength of butter in summer, I could imagine no possible way to get to my feet without falling.

What a damnable predicament. I pressed my forehead to the stone, trying to slow my thudding heart and pumping lungs. If I could just clear my head . . . so foggy . . . so drowsy . . .

A gust of wind slapped me in the face like a cold, wet hand. My extremities were grown frighteningly numb. I had to move, and I needed leverage and more width than the wall walk provided. The stair was somewhere behind me.

Gripping the wall with my knees, I wriggled backward and stretched my right leg along the wall to locate the stair. Nothing.

Again.

When my boot at last scraped the edge of the blessed stair, I almost wept. I wriggled and stretched again, but just as I found a solid purchase, a shadow flapped over my head. Not a bird, for a firm weight pressed on my back.

Fear had me reaching for my knife, only to realize that it was the very lump grinding divots in my hip bone and entirely impossible to extract. Which made no difference whatsoever when someone grabbed my waist and dragged me, armor, lance, and all, backward along the damnable wall and onto my hind end right beside the stair.

"Choose, paratus. Get your own feet under you or dive off. Anyone so infernally stubborn is like to die young anyway."

My chin rested on my chest, not from the humiliation, but from sheer difficulty in lifting it. Indeed, I was helpless to suppress the laughter that bubbled through my aching chest. "How long have you been watching me, Commander Inek?"

"A very long two years and sixty-eight days. But for tonight, near an hour. Your snoring belied any notion you were dead, so all I had to do was make sure you didn't fall. I wished to judge what I must add to your schedule of punishment for sleeping on watch, and I wasn't about to help if you didn't make a move to help yourself."

Asleep? A chill rippled my skin as though a wave had strayed up the wall. I pushed up to standing. My knees buckled, but I planted the lance and willed myself into a proper stance.

"My life is yours, Knight Commander." This was the correct acknowledgement to a comrade who had saved one's life. Once my spirit settled, I might argue that I was very close to saving myself, but the night had a while to run as yet.

"I don't want your life. I want your attention. The stair verge is hardly the best position to stand watch. You should consider a station more useful. Perhaps near the north bend?"

"As you suggest, *rectoré*." But he was already vanished into the dark. Northward.

It took me a while to follow him, planting the lance and each foot with perfect caution, making sure my gelatinous limbs would hold me up. I even cast a light. My night-seeing was acute and most times I could walk the wall by feel, but I dared not rely on it this night.

By the time I reached the bend in the wall where the Archive Tower blocked observation from any other point in the fortress, Inek sat draining a flask of . . . ale, by the smell of it. His legs dangled over the precipitous drop as if he perched on a fence in a homely meadow.

I doused my magelight, took my stance facing the sea, and held proper silence. No more reprimands this night.

"No one but the Marshal knows I've returned from Lillebras," he said from the sheltered corner. "It will remain that way until you encounter me inside the fortress."

I dipped my head. The gibbous moon sailed out from behind gnarled clouds—a welcome brilliance. He must have known the sky would clear—thus the move to this hidden spot to prevent his being seen. I shifted a few steps over to where I *could* be seen, if anyone had a mind to check on my whereabouts.

"Heed me closely, Greenshank. A battle is shaping northeast of Lillebras. Perryn's legions began a move northward four days ago—shortly after he received word of his brother's infamous alliance. And we've reports that Bayard's second legion has joined him at Tavarre, and they march east from the coast, on a line to meet his brother in the valley of the Brasé. It remains to be seen if Sila Diaglou's rabble will join Bayard before he engages his brother or hold back as a surprise mid-battle."

He stoppered his flask and shoved it into a bag under his cloak. My parched throat resented that enormously.

"The most interesting report claims that Prince Osriel has been sighted not twenty quellae from Lillebras. The man in question travels with a small party and little state. But our informant has seen Osriel before, and we've heard the Bastard can sniff out a battle before it happens, as if the fester of hostilities draws him."

Stories told worse than that about Osriel and battlegrounds. The bastard Duc of Evanore commanded only his province's mountain warlords. Those were fierce, but few, and no match for his elder brothers' armies. Yet soldiers feared him far more than Bayard or Perryn. They spoke of mutilations and demonic rites, or gatzi summoned to couple with the injured to birth demon warriors to fill the prince's legions. Wounded soldiers begged comrades to kill them rather than leave them lie where Osriel might find them.

"You're not asleep again?"

"No, *rectoré*."

"And so we come to your part. The Marshal wishes you to determine whether Prince Osriel has dealings with the Harrower priestess or either of his brothers. I suggested that we proceed as before—that our more experienced spies locate our quarry, and we bring in Greenshank only when we have an idea of the Bastard's activities. If you were to bide close to Lillebras, a triggered beacon could draw you into play quickly. I've recommended that the journey between here and Lillebras—rugged country threaded by streams and rivers that might slow your progress—should begin immediately, giving a raw paratus ample opportunity to find his way. Is this very clear?"

Ferocious pleasure infused my bones with a bit of vigor. Inek had contrived an opportunity for me to speak with Morgan. "Aye, *rectoré*. All seems clear."

"Leave your silver bracelets in the armory when you go off watch. They'll be fitted with the summoning beacon. Fix will provide the bracelets when you depart for Lillebras. Heed me. No matter delays along the way, you *must* be ready and in place when the spy's signal comes."

"I will."

"Go in safety, Greenshank, and return in honor."

"In honor, Knight Commander."

He rose, lithe and easy as a juggler. The wind flapped his black cloak. "I've had no opportunity to work in the archives of late. And we need to explore your reactions to the mission study. But I doubt your stone skull could comprehend a discussion of history or tactics at present."

"Aye, Commander." My desperation to speak of the incident had to yield to necessity. I had four more hours to stay awake and alive, and it would take everything I could muster.

"But I do wish to hear how you've performed in the spring tourney. Clearly you've thrown yourself into it with your usual extravagant diligence."

Why in the Sky Lord's midnight did he care for such trivialities?

"I stand first in archery, third overall," I said. "Out of eleven remaining."

"Better than my estimate."

Yes, it was a decent result; I'd worked hard on my blade skills since the last quarterly. Inek, of course, demanded that I finish first before the end of my training.

He moved as if ready to go. The walk was too narrow for him to pass, so I had to move past the stair to let him down. My knees whined at the prospect.

"One more matter, Greenshank."

I paused.

"Answer me this: If your brother knight was ill or injured, unfit to venture his next assignment to the danger of his life, what would you do?"

Inek, ever the schoolmaster. "I would offer to take his place, *rectoré.*"

"And what if he was most honorably set upon doing his duty—a noncritical duty, as it happened—and refused your offer? Would you let him die for his pride?"

"Of course not. I would speak to his commander—" My glib answers hung on the blustering wind like branches snapped from a tree . . . about to pummel me on the head, I feared.

"It is a guide's duty to push. It is your duty as a knight-aspiring to strive; strength, skill, and duty are your pillars. But, as you've said, it is also your duty to push back when it is clear a brother's life is in danger. And why would it be important to save your brother's life and not your own? Perfection is ephemeral, Greenshank, and true wisdom is the knowledge of when to bend. Now, have you anything more to say to me tonight?"

Even my dull wit could not miss his meaning. True wisdom it might be, but the speaking was bitter. "Knight Commander, I am unfit for duty. But I can—"

"You are dismissed—to resume this watch at the usual time only after you have accumulated no less than ten hours of sleep. All other duties remain as scheduled."

Clouds had swallowed the moon again. I cast light enough to guide my feet back to the stair, but moved past and waited, allowing Inek to descend first. A small way to demonstrate relief and shame . . . and respect.

But he remained a short distance away, facing the sea. "I'll go down later."

"As you say. *Dalle cineré, rectoré.*" The Order's motto held immediate significance, when body and spirit were so weary. The prospect of sleep approached rapture. Perhaps tonight I wouldn't dream of screams drowned in ash, of purebloods watching, of Damon's cunning eyes peering through the Marshal's white mask. . . .

The embers of outrage flared hot and bright.

"Rectoré?" I had descended but a few steps, and leaned into the upper stair as I shifted round to speak. Inek was scarce visible atop the wall, his black cloak billowing like a raven's spread wings against the midnight clouds. "Who were they, the two at that burning house?"

"How could I know? Have you forgotten their identities are purged? Go to bed and wake up with your wits about you."

"Not the Order knights, but the purebloods—the two who watched, laughing, as the walls collapsed. The knight saw them on the road as soon as the remaining Harrowers rode away. He thought it looked as if they dropped veils, and he assumed they were the last two of the nine riders. Did someone identify them, call them to account for such a crime?"

For a moment I thought he'd vanished.

"Commander, you've seen this study. Your squires saw it. You must know."

Inek abruptly drew his cloak tight and joined me. He sat on the wall, feet on the top step, his face on a level with mine. "I never imagined you were yet spellbound when I took the squires away. You were engaged, yes, but that mission is a terrible scene, and I knew it would hit you hard, prey to sentiment as you are. But my squires did *not* view that piece at the end, nor did your fellow parati. No trainees are allowed to experience it; it deals with complexities most are not ready to deal with. What else were you shown?"

Sitting on the steep, narrow steps was impossible. Rather I perched like a steel bird.

"Nothing beyond that," I said. "It sickened me, as you expected. Worse. I believed I could never witness anything more vile than people, especially those so gifted by the gods, amused at such savagery. And then, within the hour, the Marshal told me the story of the Order's founding. About Xancheira and the Registry. Something I wasn't supposed to know as yet. Why would he? And why the two together?"

"He said naught of Damon or his interest in these matters, I suspect."

"No."

Another pause. "The two purebloods remain unidentified. Rumor spoke that one pureblood and one ordinary were executed for involvement in the crime, but neither matched the descriptions of those two. It is a strange case—"

He fell so abruptly, so utterly silent, and the night was so black, I almost believed he'd gone. Or toppled from the wall.

"Commander?"

"Enough. You'll be crashing down the steps, and I'll not leap down to catch you. Be about our plan. Prepare as I've taught you. Nothing of this mission should require more of you than you can handle." I fancied I glimpsed his blue eyes glittering. "But watch your back at every moment and speak to *no one* of seeing the purebloods at the end of the study. There are friends and there are enemies, and some that are neither one nor the other. I cannot yet sort out who is which. But be sure of this, while you're off, I'm going to find out what in all Magrog's hells you are."

PART II
THE TEETH
OF SPRING

CHAPTER 9

The sandy inlet up the Gouvron provided no easy mooring. I had to haul the boat up a steep bank so neither demon tide nor spring flood would wash it away, and tuck it into a tangle of tufted sedge and round-headed rushes so some wandering thief would not think it his for the taking.

All morning as I rowed upriver, I'd watched for Morgan. Listened for her singing. Called myself mad to imagine she was what I believed or that she could find me anywhere as she claimed. Once the boat was secure, I perched on a rock, ate, drank, and hoped.

The sun, thin and silver, slid past the zenith. With deflated spirits, I hefted my pack and cast a bit of magic to plump the crushed grass where I'd dragged the boat. Shorting a loop in the river left me a day's walk to the hostler. Three days' hard riding northeasterly would take me to the forest outside the town of Lillebras, where I'd wait for the signal. It was but a short ride from there to a hidden lake above the prospective battleground, where I'd meet the Marshal's spy. I'd best move.

"Lucian!"

The woman came running along the grassy bank, chestnut hair and brown cape flying. My eyes were so expectant of naked flesh and blue fire that I almost didn't recognize her. But with her every step closer, the day grew brighter.

"Morgan!"

Names were rich with association. Inek's name evoked his commanding integrity, the pillar centering two years' chaos of fear and striving. Dunlin's name evoked easy humor and brotherhood—not friendship, but shared purpose, experience, and trust. Morgan's presence struck sparks, no doubt—awe, excitement, urgencies of spirit and flesh. But her name—like the one I believed to be my own—fell upon my soul like a pellet made of lead. Though I hungered for it, it woke nothing deeper.

"I'd almost given up on you," I said. "Is something wrong?"

"There's no giving up." Her brow was drawn tight, and her eyes darted everywhere but my face. "Tuari's anger is grown to fury. I'm sworn to bring thee to him as soon as possible. But I've a thought how we might enliven thy memory before we face him. 'Tis a distance to travel. Please tell me thou hast no urgency to prevent our going!"

"I've four days' travel to my destination and a deadline of seven. Thus, assuming weather or ill chance doesn't delay me, I've three to spend. But not an hour longer. I cannot fail my commander." Inek pursued a dangerous course to unravel this mystery of the Order and me. The best I could do to repay him was to execute my duties with precision.

Morgan squeezed her eyes shut, considering, then nodded sharply.

"'Tis fortunate I've lived among humankind. The long-lived do not measure or tally the sun's travels as humans do. And in truth, our tallies would not come to the same, as days spend differently in the true lands. But all should be well if we keep a good pace. Once Tuari is satisfied, I can hasten thee to thy destination."

"And he *will* be satisfied?"

"He must."

Not exactly the answer I wanted to hear.

"So where are we going? I've a map." Perhaps she could point out what she named the *true lands*, and explain what in Deunor's holy fire Danae thought my magic did to its boundaries.

But the rolled skin wasn't even out of my pack when she stilled my hand. "My kind need no pages. But I do need my gards. I cannot find the way while clothed in human garb."

She unlaced her bodice and threw off her skirts and tunic. Her feet were already bare.

Body and mind became hopelessly tangled. My eyes flicked away and back again. And again.

She laughed and thrust the bundled clothing into my arms. "You can carry these."

Before I could get my mouth closed and the garments stuffed in my pack, she struck out south and east, away from the river, at a pace that precluded easy conversation. Just as well. Eye and mind were wholly occupied with the grace and power of her form. As the sun teased through high clouds, the marks on her skin—the gards, she called them—came to life, not in shades of sapphire and lapis, but cerulean and sky, blues so pale as to seem silver.

"You said your archon was disturbed when I spoke of others of your kind who were marked in silver," I said, when she stopped to scoop water from a rain pool nested in a lonely slab of rock. "But yours . . ." I pointed to her arm, though I dared look at it only sidewise.

"'Tis the sunlight fades my gards. And wearing human garb too long causes them to vanish almost entire. But these are not what you described to Naari. The sentinel's gards were *bright* silver, you told him, drawings inked in starlight. We've lore that speaks of such, but few have seen the like. Come"— she hurried me away from her clear discomfort with the subject—"we've no time to dally."

The rock-strewn barrens yielded quickly to softer country laced with willow-banked streams. No matter the summer solstice just past, spring had scarce touched the land. The silver birches and spreading chestnuts dotting the grasslands still sported new green.

As I marveled at Morgan's sure navigation through drenching rain, I noticed oddities in our course. When we climbed out of a wet green vale onto a heath, startling a flock of dithering crakes from the oat grass, I would have sworn the cone-shaped hills on the horizon were not those I'd seen when we descended into the vale. And the grass was bone-dry.

I blamed the stormy light. But over the next hours, I carefully studied the sky and the distant uplands. In late afternoon, we emerged from a woodland of deep-green yew and beech into a sunlit landscape of hillsides that were similar, but certainly not the same as the ones carved on my memory. If magic was responsible, it was wholly undetectable—which was entirely worrisome.

"Hold, lady."

She turned around, the sun paling the glistening gards that had deepened in color in the wood. As before, her eyes darted behind me and to either side. "We must keep moving."

"I need explanation." At the least, if she could so confuse me on the journey, how in the Sky Lord's mercy would I ever find my way back? We'd not come near so much as a farmstead, much less a village or a road. "How is it that what I see ahead when we leave the wood is not what I saw when we entered? I'm not mistaken."

"We cannot dally, Lucian. Tuari is surely hunting us by now. He'll know I've met thee, and his displeasure will grow hugely—worse than that, if he thinks I've spoken of matters humans are not meant to know."

My patience was worn thin with all the things I was not *meant to know.* "I've trusted you for all these hours," I said. "But you've told me neither where we're bound nor what I've done that so offends your lord. My first duty lies behind us, and I daren't go farther without understanding."

"Oh, friend Lucian, canst thou not touch the ground here and call up thy magic to understand the paths we walk?"

"I touch ground to detect traces of magic. I've tried it along the way and found nothing."

"But thou didst once read *history* from the land."

History! That made no sense at all. "You mentioned that I studied history, but— Why would I touch the earth?"

"To see images of the past, you told me, to hear music or scraps of words, to follow threads of meaning. It was the magic thou didst value more than art, more than me."

"That's not possible." She had described the signs of a magical bent for history, yet the portrait witnessed that Lucian de Remeni's bent was portraiture. Dual magical bents were exceedingly rare, and *no one* carried both to maturity. The Registry required one to be excised in childhood, for two mature bents led inevitably to madness . . .

Lead settled in my belly. Was that it? Had incipient madness prompted my family to consign me to Evanide?

"Perhaps I only wished for such a skill."

Morgan spun sharply and sniffed the damp breeze from behind us. "We must go, Lucian."

I smelled naught but the mingling of damp earth and the land's late greening. No trace of the sea. Despite our speed, that seemed impossible.

"Even if reading history with magic was my talent, it is dead or muted. Please, lady, just tell me what's going on."

"I dare speak only this," she said. "Those of my kind spend our lives learning the land, its shapes, smells, and sounds, the life that abounds in every field or pond, stream or hillside. We can use this familiarity to find our way . . . quickly . . . from one place to another that is very like. This—"

"No. You speak of magic. You couldn't hide such enchantments from me."

A smile softened her worry lines, a rich, sweet sadness flowing from her like a spiced tisane. "'Tis not magic, but what we are. What I am. It's why I could not stay with thee in Montesard. It's why I could never stay with thee, no matter the delight we shared in those days or our childish whimsies of abandoning families and traditions and making a life together. It's why I must answer to Tuari and not thy commanders or kings. Though we share the same form, gentle Lucian, I am not human."

Not human. Wordless, breathless, I nodded.

My intellect had spoken it from the moment I saw the portrait. Spirit had disagreed; she was so vibrant, so womanly, her emotions and expressions so recognizably . . . human. Now, surrounded by woodland and meadow, her gards taking fire again as daylight failed, my spirit, too, believed. She was no human's sister or daughter or lover. She was lightning.

"Trust me. I mean only thy good, and I'll do all I can to protect thee from Tuari's wrath. But we *must* pry open thy memory, else matters will become very difficult for us both."

Robbed of answer, I motioned her onward. But as her long limbs devoured the steep slope ahead of us, I stayed close and kept my eyes open.

"So then, at least tell me where you're taking me to get my memory pried open and how you think to accomplish it," I said. Perhaps her kind had their own sorcerers.

"We're to join my partner, Naari. He suggested a way to crack this mud clot. His plan seems well reasoned, if a bit . . . risky. 'Tis more likely a stick will break the clot than a feather, yes?"

My blood rushed hot as if the tide horns had sounded. "What *stick*? I'm trusting you—"

She pointed to the horizon. "Atop those twinned hills lies a spring in a mossy crevice. When we ascend the next slope, we shall look down on the great city men name Palinur."

"Palinur! The royal city? That's not possible!"

Of course she had just told me how it was possible. But it would take an inordinate amount of faith to accept that we had walked from the Western Sea in the far northwest of Navronne to Palinur in the kingdom's heart in half a day. "You're saying we've walked more than seven hundred quellae! And without glimpsing so much as a plowed field."

She shrugged. "We have walked the true lands, where measuring has no meaning. And my kind do not plow any more than they build. As I told thee, time spends differently here, which means we must hurry on if we're to get thee back to do thy duty."

And so we continued. It was unnerving, at best, to contemplate what *stick* awaited me from beings who could drag me across Navronne in a day's walking.

The city that sprawled across the grassy hills was indeed great Caedmon's city—the royal city of Navronne. Neither its massive size, the thousand flickering lights, nor the clashing bronze of so many bells sounding the quarters had convinced me. The grand gates and thick walls might have belonged to any number of northern cities, and I told myself the dead vineyards might once have harbored some hardy northern grape and not the exquisite vintages of the Ardran hills. But as we crossed the great roads that funneled mobs of travelers into the city, threading a path through hostlers, food vendors, bawling tavern-ers, scurrying pickthieves, and smirking procurers who thrust half-dressed girls and youths into our paths, I knew it must be Palinur. Only Navronne's greatest city would be so alive and so wicked, so late.

I had refreshed the *obscuré* spell on my mask, and Morgan—her Danae light hidden under bodice and skirts—had pulled up the hood of her cape, so none paid us mind as we hurried along the ring road outside the city walls. Though she'd indicated that our destination lay on the "sunrise side" of the city, we passed up the calmer easterly gates just as we had the chaotic southern portal.

Morgan adamantly refused to say how they thought to make me remember.

Neither of us said much. The long day wore on me, and once past the gates, a profound stillness fell on the road. We encountered no travelers, no vendors, nor even the beggars' village one might expect outside any city's walls. No stock pens accounted for the foul wind coming down from the north.

Watchfires atop the city wall illuminated scorch marks, stains, pits, and gouges in its smooth face. The ground itself was broken and pitted, too. Here and there the cart road squeezed through heaps of rubble or circumnavigated some gaping pit or a pile of tar-splattered beams and metal—telltales of Bayard's fruitless siege two years' past. This destruction would be but a dusty corner of history compared to what might come now Bayard had allied with Sila Diaglou.

My legs expressed their gratitude when a steep portion of the looping track at last reached more level ground. My lungs would have, as well, save that the foul stench I'd noticed earlier was ten times worse on the windy flat.

Morgan didn't slow. She left the road and headed toward the gray strip of the city wall that had climbed the same hill, only in a straighter path. Watch-fires marked the wall's bend around this high plateau before straightening again on its northward course.

"Come on," she said over her shoulder. "We're looking for a gap in this wall."

But I stayed behind, squinting into the patchy night.

The cart road had split, the main branch servicing the once impressive gate-house to a walled compound—a temple perhaps. The siege had crumbled the top half of one gate tower and knocked holes here and there in the compound's wall. But stone cauldrons flanking the gatehouse blazed with wind-wild flames, illuminating the undamaged statues of two gods grappling—Deunor, Lord of Light and Magic, and Magrog the Tormentor, Lord of the Underworld.

"What is this place?" I said softly, though Morgan was well out of hearing by now. Familiarity teased at me, like a strand of hair flapping against my cheek. I had been here since my change. As I'd never traveled so far from Evanide, I must have been here on that first confused journey to the fortress. Yet even to consider what place it might be set off warning thunder in my head. Which meant that this was a part of my past, as well. Was that how Morgan thought to make me remember? To shatter my skull?

The lesser branch of the cart road extended into the blackness east of the compound—the side away from the city—most likely to service a side gate or postern. The worst of the stench came from that direction. Horribly fascinated, I continued straight on toward the source of the stink, using my body to shield a soft magelight from any watchers inside the compound.

Quiet clicks and rustling, and soft whapping sounds slowed my steps as I reached the rim of the plateau and looked down. Tatters and scraps of rotted leather and linen fluttered in the wind amid piles of . . . bones. *Goddess Mother preserve!* At my feet lay a hillside of skulls and bones, heaps and piles of them, most picked clean by crows or the scuttering creatures whose eyes gleamed in my light. Here and there someone had thrown dirt on more solid remains, for some were not so old as the others. Had I not seen people at the city gates, I would have thought the entire population of Palinur lay dead on that hillside.

Scritching feet or wind set a skull rocking—a skull half-cleaved through by axe or blade.

Hair rose on my neck. The brutality of combat was near surety in an *eques cineré*'s future and such a sight could not but feed the doubts grown so large these past days. How could I aspire to such a life?

Yet this display was Prince Bayard's doing and Sila Diaglou's and surely that of the weak-livered Perryn, as well. The weapons the Order provided to the cause of right were extraordinary, and despite my novice faults, I knew I was good at what my masters taught me—both magic and war. And if I was suited to such skills, how could I refuse the call to use them? Someone had to stand in the way of tyrants and fools.

Had I not known better, I would have said Inek had brought me here instead of Morgan. Morgan . . . First things first.

I doused my light and retraced my steps.

"Over here," she called softly.

I joined her at the verge of the road.

"I thought I'd lost thee," she said, as we hiked across a lumpy field.

"I need to know why you've brought me to this cursed place."

"Soon enough."

We squeezed through a narrow opening in the thick city wall. Massive bars of iron and wood were set into the mortar—enchanted in place—making it impossible for beast or armored soldier to squeeze through. Beyond the narrow gate a twisting footpath plunged steeply into a dark tangle of scrub that stank of sewage and sodden ashes. The foul wind rustled new-leafed trees.

Before I could demand better answers, Morgan lifted her head and cupped her mouth. "Yai! Yai! Yai!"

The rapid biting cry mimed that of a white-tailed eagle.

An answering cry came from the trees below—along with the shimmering of blue fire. Danae.

Fingers ready on my bracelets, I backed away from her. "What have you done?"

She raised her hand to stay my flight. "No, no. This is Naari, my partner, come to help. We shared the watch on thee after we left Montesard. He more than I. We'll not approach Tuari till thou'rt ready."

The Dané who climbed up from the tangled darkness was tall and well-made, his sinews taut, his long hair caught in a braid. Every quat of his flesh, even his privy parts, were scribed with drawings of light. A white-tailed eagle wrapped his pale brow, sculpted cheek, and long neck, as if drawn in ink compounded from sapphires. He smelled of rosemary.

Chilly eyes took stock of me as he left the steep path. "I didn't think he'd come. Our last meeting was not so friendly."

Unlike the structures beyond the wall, naught of this Dané felt familiar.

"He has agreed to answer to Tuari, as I told thee he would." Morgan touched the Dané's arm. "*Envisia seru*, Naari."

"'Tis delight to see thee, as well, sweet Morgan." His expression warmed.

My magelight caught Morgan's smile. Brilliant, intimate. Foolish that it should cause such a tightness in my chest. I didn't know her. They were not human.

Naari jerked his head my way. "Is it shame makes them hide their faces?"

"Custom, not shame," she said. The last of her smile vanished. "Hast thou word from Tuari?"

"Not yet, though the night suggests he is on his way. Our source is in place. Shall I trick the man to come out or show thee where he plies his watch?"

"What man? Source of what?" All I could think of were the thousands rotting on the hillside. Surely no one *lived* in this cursed place.

"Show us," said Morgan, eager. "Thou'rt certain he's the one?"

"Certain." Naari pointed through the gate back toward the temple or whatever it was. "Every nightfall he comes out and prowls round the outside. Then he retreats, fixes a lock on his gate, and kindles a fire just within. He fancies himself the night lord of this dead ruin."

"If we're to learn secrets, we need Tuari delayed," said Morgan. "Wilt thou venture it, Naari?"

"He'll not hold long, but for thee I'll try." Naari touched Morgan's cheek, then gestured the two of us toward the gate and dissolved into the night.

As I yet gaped in wonder, Morgan took my hand. "Come, Lucian. We're off to find thy remembrance."

We moved swiftly back across the muddy field toward the gatehouse. An orange speck glimmered behind the spiked iron bars of the gate.

"Who's in there? A priest? A diviner? A sorcerer?"

I reached to catch her arm, but she swept onward with all the force of Evanide's tides. So I matched her stride for stride, trying to slow her with words. "You must understand, lady, no common magic can change what was done to me."

"We've no idea what kind of person waits behind that gate. Nor if he knows aught of magic. But he knows *thee*. In the winter before thou didst make a home in the sea fortress, 'twas thy habit to frequent this place of death. After only a few days, thou didst vanish, and for a long while, we thought thee dead, too. I was near lost in grieving. But then thy magic manifested stronger and more intrusive than ever, and Tuari sent Naari back to find thee. Naari watched *this* man fetch thee back here from the city, bound, muted, and ill. And ever after, he—the one who waits yonder—kept thee in rags and chained. He is thy enemy."

"Chained?" I had been a prisoner? *Here?* That fit no pattern I understood. Pureblood sorcerers were not kept prisoner save in the Registry Tower, and I could not even state an explicit reason *that* might be so. The most terrible crimes—treason, kin-murder, using magic for murder, torture, or rape— reaped swift execution.

You are not a murderer. The fragment the Order had given me sounded a fragile reassurance.

Lesser crimes were settled by swift punishments—whipping or public humiliation—and unrestricted contracts. . . .

My feet kept moving over the rough ground, while I worked to create order from throbbing chaos. If I reached too deep, the pain in my head would put me beyond reason, but Inek had revealed something of my last contract.

A *place of death,* Morgan had called this compound. What if it was no execution ground, but rather a *necropolis,* a city of the dead? Its size, the crowded roofs and pinnacles outlined above the compound wall, would make it the principal burial ground of Palinur. I had been a man of wealth, the Order had told me, a pureblood fallen on hard times and contracted to a necropolis. They'd *not* told me I'd been kept in chains. Madmen might be kept chained. *Great Deunor preserve!*

"We thought confronting thy enemy might jolt thy reason," said Morgan with soft urgency. "He's not like to recognize thee, fully masked and changed as thou art. And even if the memories we need remain hidden to thee, *he* might know these things."

"Yes. Questioning could be useful."

Nothing in me could confirm that I had once lived here. And I had no naive imagining that laying eyes on a person—even a hated jailer—would undo the magic that blocked my memory, but I could surely squeeze out some information.

"We can restrain him, if need be. But a story might get us past his gate. Travelers lost?"

"No," I said, shaking my head. "I'll do this. Just follow my lead."

After two years with the *Equites Cineré,* I was not the same man who'd been kept prisoner here, but I knew a great deal about his world. Indeed from the moment we'd sighted Palinur's walls, the truths, habits, and understanding of pureblood life, which for two years had seemed as remote as information read only in a book, had infused me like new bones.

Few men were bold enough, skilled enough, or vicious enough to chain and mute a pureblood. Either this man waiting was pureblood himself—which these vile surroundings made ludicrous—or he was a bold, devilishly wicked, and dangerous kind of ordinary. A contract for a madman's services would be quite inexpensive if one had stone walls to confine him and some use for his particular magic.

We halted a dozen paces from the gate. The fire from the stone bowls lit a brass plate above the arch. It read NECROPOLIS CATON.

"Who's out there?" The challenge from inside the gatehouse rang so loud it could have waked the bones on his hillside. "If ye think to rob the dead, be assured 'tis already done."

"We're no grave robbers," I said, masking everything but pureblood hauteur. "I am a traveler passing through this city with my maidservant. We've had an unfortunate incident on the road. I wish to know if this place can provide proper grave rites for a pureblood."

"*Pureblood* rites? In the middle of the night? And so I must let you inside—in *these* times?" The bellowing laughter threatened to bring down the rest of the broken gate tower. "That's the damnedest ruse I've heard since a lackwit constable demanded to inspect the tombs, claiming Harrowers had taken up residence inside them. 'Tis almost enough to let you in just to see what kind of lackwit *you* are."

A touch of my left bracelet snapped the lock on his gate. A second in quick succession exploded a bouquet of five cold torches waiting in an iron cask into flame. My boot's harsh impact swung the iron gates open.

"Bring a torch, Fanula," I said, giving Morgan a gentle nudge. "The good man will show us in or find his gatehouse crumbled on top of him."

CHAPTER 10

Morgan played her part to perfection, dipping her knee and fetching a torch.

A thickset fellow waited just inside the necropolis gates, behind a flaming brazier. Steady, thick-fingered hands held a well-maintained sword at the ready. He'd once been a soldier, I guessed; his stance was expert. Though his height did not top my own, the breadth of his solid chest, shoulders, and arms would lend significant weight to his blows. I would not count him out in a test of arms alone. As for his nature . . . a tangle of wiry, sand-colored hair and beard, threaded with gray, left his features unreadable, save for a pair of eyes that burned with the same heat and color as his fire.

For certain, he was no pureblood. Not only was his hair entirely un-Aurellian and his garb laughably unfit for Registry standards, but the only magics anywhere close were my own. A brittle emptiness where I would expect threads of magic suggested the compound had been stripped clean of enchantment at some time not so long past.

"I am no lackwit, ordinary, but neither am I overzealous." I opened my arms in largesse. "The times are unsettled and the hour late. Sheath your weapon, and I shall overlook this impudent violation." To draw on a pureblood was to beg a hangman's attentions.

He lowered the sword, but did not sheath it and did not relax his posture. Morgan remained near the gate as I encroached farther on his demesne.

"You've violations of your own that might draw interest, pureblood," he said. The hot eyes flicked from me to Morgan and back again. "No proper cloak . . . and a most unusual mask. No brocade, no pearl buttons, no jewels, no escort save a fair young woman who wears no mask. Sneaking about in the night. A man might almost think you were . . . ordinary. Or hiding. Or *renegade*."

Which was exactly what I wanted. Let him believe I had dangerous secrets.

I'd rather tease information out of him than use force. As expected, neither sight nor sound of him caused a miraculous resurrection of memory.

"So you're familiar with pureblood customs," I said. "I was told that might be the case."

Had I not been watching for it, I'd never have noticed the slight lift of his head and hardening of his shoulders. "Who told you that?"

"Being a stranger in the city and tangled in a . . . family difficulty . . . I made discreet inquiries. I was told Necropolis Caton had a pureblood under contract."

"And so I do." His inspection slid quickly from my mask to my hands and Morgan. "Family difficulties can be a bother. My pureblood taught me that right enough. Why are you here?"

I held to the story that had popped into mind as Morgan and I crossed the field. His belief was not so important. I needed to learn.

"A traveling companion was taken ill on the road and died. He must be buried according to his station, so that his family may offer prayers and libations when they learn of his end. But I cannot afford delay." I peered into the murk beyond the brick tunnel. "Is there a priestess here? Or do you take care of everything from anointing to digging? Surely this pureblood doesn't dig. . . ."

He glanced behind me, in his turn, and then rested the tip of his blade in the dirt and folded his hands on the hilt. "Oh, I can see to a pureblood burial with proper rites. Where might we find this unfortunate friend? I take it he's not in company with you right now, unless your *maidservant* carries him in her pocket."

I fidgeted with my rucksack. With my knife sheath. I bit my lip. If he thought he could learn something profitable, he might reveal enough that I could formulate useful questions. "Prove to me you know enough of our customs. If I'm satisfied, I'll send my servant to have him brought. Naturally, I'll pay well for proper attention and . . . discretion."

"Naturally. I've a decent room to lay him out, a few stone vaults that have space proper for elevated folk. I've a box of ysomar that looters haven't found, so we can anoint his fingers that carried his magic, and a resourceful sexton who can likely find silk to wrap them. And if his own clothes happen to be fouled, she can find some to make do once he's washed. It's not likely she can find quality to suit you, but being travelers, you surely have extra. Mayhap his own. What else do you wish to know?"

"Good. Those things are good." Certainly he was no fool. I fidgeted a bit more. "But this pureblood . . . I wish to consult him before we fetch my poor friend. That would tell me more. Yes, I insist on seeing him."

A grin blossomed in the thatch of his beard. "That won't be possible."

"But you said—"

"I said naught of any pureblood *being* here. You see, I am a loyal servant of the king—whomever that might be at the moment—and his law. And I've been especially well trained not to run afoul of the Pureblood Registry. Just think: You might be an ordinary yourself, a felon teasing me with illicit magics you've bought in an alley."

"I'm certainly not. How dare you—?"

"Or you could be yet another bothersome Registry inquisitor come to discover if I've by chance encountered my *recondeur*"—his right hand flew up as for an oath—"and as I've sworn up my granny's sagging ass to the full count of her three-and-ninety years, I've neither seen a nose nor heard a spit of the snake-tongued blackguard. So you may take that back to your masters and leave me in peace with the dead."

"Your pureblood is named *renegade*?" Shock and dismay near choked me.

"He vanished two years ago during the Great Siege. The Registry brought me notice that the cursed spelltwister had gone rogue after murdering one of their own, and that if he ever showed his nose in Palinur, anyone who listened to a word he said would be dead in the next hour. I told them I'd kill him myself if I ever ran across him."

Named murderer *and* a *recondeur*, though beside the second, the first was nothing. To run away from the responsibilities that came with the gift of magic was the most abject betrayal a pureblood could commit. *Recondeurs* condemned their kin to everlasting disgrace, and brought a death sentence to any ordinary who might possibly have aided, condoned, or merely failed to notice the escape. For themselves they reaped the most severe Registry punishments short of death, forbidden to marry, to sire children or bear them, to negotiate their own contracts, to walk free, to speak with other purebloods, to teach or study . . . everything a person might desire from life. They were forever subject to unrestricted contracts. Masters could confine them, work them to death without consequence.

"I think he's more likely dead," said the man. "Three thousand citizens of Palinur died that first month of the siege, most in the first three days. More than half the people who labored in my yard here. But I never saw his body, and you can be damned sure I looked for it. Still, a Registry inquisitor comes nosing around here on and off, and I have to dispatch another complaint to the Tower, lest they forget I'm an aggrieved customer, owed for the unfulfilled contract."

He squinted into Morgan's torchlight as if to see me better.

"But you're not one of *them*, are you? And I'm thinking you'd not wish me to file a complaint this time." His gaze slid away yet again.

"No . . . I'm no inquisitor."

If the Registry had declared me renegade, rather than dead or traveling or held out of contract by my family—whatever story my family and the Order had arranged—then every moment I took a breath outside Fortress Evanide was a dreadful danger. The Registry never stopped hunting *recondeurs*.

Though my every muscle twitched, I had to stuff myself back inside my playacting—which at the moment was uncomfortably near truth. "And no, don't contact anyone. Just . . . don't."

Had I run before? Was that why he'd been allowed to chain me? Or had I run from his cruelty? And how could the Order think to make a knight of one so despicable as to abandon his every kinsman and acquaintance to disgrace or death? Unless the man's aberrant magic—two bents grown to maturity—had driven him mad. The Order likely had ancient knowledge of how such an affliction might be amended.

Learning about my history was rapidly losing its allure.

"I am not a trusting soul." His fingers flexed about the hilt of the sword. "Unless you're a murdering devil like a number of your kind, willing to magic me to death right in front of this lady, who does not in the least fit my notion of a maidservant, much less the escort of a pureblood man who is strictly celibate until his family tells him whom he must marry"—he bowed mockingly in Morgan's direction—"you'd best explain a bit more."

Morgan laid a hand on my arm. No words were needed to tell me of her growing anxiety. I was near drowning in it.

This man was not at all what I expected. Dangerous and wily, I had no doubt. But perceptive. I welcomed the dancing shadows and the way the *obscuré* shoved his eyes away from my face. But I needed more information before we ran.

"You're correct that this lady is neither pureblood nor servant. Rather, I am her protector. I hoped that a sorcerer contracted to a necropolis might be willing to help me with certain matters. Private matters."

"Because he must be a sorcerer of poor talents or poor judgment to be contracted to this kind of place?" Scorn and bitterness tainted his tongue. "You believed he must be lax in your pureblood discipline, a ne'er-do-well who could be hoodwinked into doing some magic you need done without questioning. Or mayhap, a man of no honor, who could be paid to violate his contract."

"I didn't say that."

" 'Twould not be so foolish an assumption." He glanced around, as if assessing what a stranger might make of his strange haunt. "You just could not be more wrong."

And there it was—a contradiction that set my blood racing and my head pounding its warning.

"Then why would anyone believe he turned *recondeur*?"

"That is a very long story."

All calculation fled, I seized the opportunity. "I'd be interested to hear."

The sword returned to its sheath, the man squatted beside his fire and pushed a battered pot closer to the pulsing coals. "Aye, you would. No doubt of it. But even the troublesome spelltwister himself would say it's not your business, save perhaps as a warning not to get crossways with the Registry. Though you likely know that already, what with a dead pureblood out there waiting."

Fragments of history—gleaned from the Order, from this man, from Morgan—glittered in the dark like shards of the Marshal's colored glass. Only no matter how I rearranged them, these made no sensible picture. Even if this fellow knew so much more than he was telling about his pureblood—about me—was it possible I would have told him about some encounter with *Danae*? Who knew what a madman might babble?

I had to know.

"Without the benefit of your pureblood's magic . . ." I shrugged. "Truthfully, the man is not dead. Not yet. Only devilishly persistent."

Making a show of reluctance, I retrieved Morgan's torch and took her arm. "We'd best be off before he finds where we've gone. Unless . . . Might my lady rest by your fire a few moments before we go? We've had a long journey already, and must make it to our refuge before dawn."

Surprise drove his wiry eyebrows upward, yielding quickly to calculation. "If you think to squeeze out a bit of my pureblood's story, then be sure I'll want to hear more of what use you thought to make of him. Tit for tat. Untimely death, whether actual or contemplated, holds a particular fascination for me."

"If my lady agrees."

I drew Morgan close. "I doubt he can help with Tuari. But he can tell me things. . . ."

"I understand thy need," she said softly into my shoulder. "But I fear to stay. Naari cannot long delay the archon." The anxiety pouring from her body chilled my blood. But information given willing was always better.

"Until the bells ring the next hour and then we go," I said, shifting round to our host. "My name is Viridian." He would take the giving as a measure of trust.

"As you say." He grinned and shrugged, as he filled a mug from his pot. "I am Bastien de Caton, Coroner of the Twelve Districts of Palinur, paid by the Crown to investigate suspicious death. Sit, *Domé* Viridian and his lady. If you've a cup, you can share my posset. Alas, it's but a bread posset and the bread was acorn bread, but 'tis made from sack, which makes up in potency what it lacks in spice."

A coroner . . . not just a gravedigger, but a Crown official of the same ilk as local magistrates. That likely explained his cleverness and his ambition to own a pureblood contract, though it said naught about what work a pureblood kept in chains might have done for him.

I gave Morgan a hand to sit on the filthy cobbles next the fire, then retrieved the cup hanging from my belt. As I held it out to be filled, Coroner Bastien's eyes remained fixed on the spot from where I'd taken it—the slight bulge where my cloak had fallen back over my knife sheath.

"Might I see that dagger?" The half-strangled words were his first that lacked perfect composure. Though his mouth and chin were tight as a tabor, his extended hand shook a little.

I passed it over, curious as to what had caught his interest.

The knife's only distinguishing mark was the white-on-black symbol of the Order on its hilt—the quiver and its five implements symbolizing magic, arms, discipline, memory, and justice. We did not expose the emblem gratuitously, but like the mask we wore to prevent recognition, we felt the value of its use outweighed the risks. Even in the frenzied confusion of combat, one could recognize a brother knight who carried the blazon on his weapon or his tabard. For any person not privy to Order secrets, the image would be quickly forgotten. It carried its own kind of *obscuré*.

He examined the dagger carefully, holding it near the fire, then he looked up at me standing over him. The dagger slipped to the ground, and this time his gaze did not slide away.

"It's you! By all gods of grace and mercy, Lucian, what the devil is this playacting? Yet you're so . . . changed . . . and this girl isn't your—" His gaze dropped to Morgan, even as he took a great breath. "Holy Mother, this is the one you described to me, the girl who started this all back in Montesard. Is that where you've been—chasing a woman? I thought you dead, you bastard, or run off with the damnable Cicerons! You swore you'd be here to help on that dread morning"—his litany of astonishment and indignation drove him to his feet—"and when I found the mask Constance made you left on the slot gate, I knew you'd been close. Be sure, I cursed your name to the ends of the earth, for the Smith's legions ran us over that morning like we were straw men, left half of us dead or dragged off to fight, and then Perryn's devils swarmed through and took the rest. I prayed they took you, too, for thanks to your perfidy, it's only Constance and me left, even my Garen taken for Perryn's legion. . . ."

Though every syllable crashed a battering ram between my eyes, I tried to piece together meaning. He knew of Montesard and Morgan, likely more than I did. How could I ever have told my contract master—one who kept me bound and in rags—of such indiscretion? Had he beaten it out of me?

Yet if I was mad, then how could he be angry that I'd broken an oath to him? What oath would I possibly have offered an ordinary beyond the requirements of a contract? Yet clearly he had taken it as sworn. A madman's ruse would never have fooled so perceptive a villain. And Cicerons . . . what would I have to do with a clan of roving pickthieves and sleight-of-hand artists?

Keys to a lifetime were laid in front of me and no matter how deep I reached and twisted, not a door did any of them open. Great gods, he called me Lucian. What ordinary called a pureblood by his personal name?

". . . been two years, and it's taken all I can do to keep the Registry at bay. That Pluvius has near driven me to murder with his threats and wheedling, as he's so sure you're alive and claims he can help you . . ."

"Slow down," I blurted. "Stop!"

He stopped, hands on his hips, seething. Wary.

"I know naught of any of these things—these people . . . oaths . . . dealings with Cicerons," I said, pressing my hand to my forehead, near panting with the thunderous pain that increased with every attempt to understand. "Answer me one question: Why did you keep your pureblood in chains?"

"What?" He stepped closer.

Without conscious consent, my feet moved backward, as if his simple proximity might land the final blow to shatter my skull.

"It *is* you," he said. "Yes, your voice is something different—deeper, maybe. And you carry yourself . . . stronger. Like you finally know where your balls are kept. You may have your face covered, and I'll wager my own balls you've put that *lookaway* magic that I can't recall the name of on that mask. But I'd recognize that pureblood nose and the bearing of that stiff neck anywhere this side of divine Idrium. So what's wrong with you?"

Morgan shook my arm, and I pushed her hand away. Her fear and anxiety only worsened the growing agony of brain and bone.

"Just answer the question," I said, through gritted teeth. "I have to know. Before we speak another word. Why?"

"Phhht." Shaking his head, he blew a note of disgust. "Because you told me to, you stubborn prick. So's you could abide by your damnable pureblood rules. So you could survive to use your magic. So you could keep the rest of us—those who stood between you and the Registry—safe."

Now it was my turn to stare, though my eyes were bleary and watering. Even so grotesque a masquerade as he described stirred no memory. But it spoke of truths I recognized about myself, and a few shards slid into place, presenting the last image I could possibly have expected.

"We were *friends*?"

The furrows in his wide brow deepened as he forced his gaze to stay fixed to mine. "Wouldn't say friends. You didn't know much about friends. But partners. Aye, that."

"Lucian, this cannot wait." Morgan near ground the muscle of my arm into the bone. "My kinsmen come. If this man cannot answer for thee, we must run, else the pain in thy head will soon be far worse than this. Tuari Archon can afflict the mind. His companions can break thee."

Worse and worse. Squeezing my eyes shut, lest the blaze of light and incomprehensible answers do the job beforetime, I nodded. "One more question, then, Bastien de Caton. Did I ever tell you anything about Danae with silver drawings on their skin or speak the word *sanctuary* alongside?"

"What's wrong with you? Has someone thrown you in a pit again?"

Of course he thought me lunatic with such a question. "Please, I just need—"

"Yeah. You told me some."

"Mighty Deunor's grace!" Relief made porridge of my knees. "Would you be willing to bear witness to that—tell someone else whatever I told you? Just that. If so, I can promise you a sight to astonish your children's children. And then after, we can sort out some of this mess."

"Well, that would be amazing on many counts." He picked up my dagger he'd dropped by the fire and passed it back to me. "You found the Path, didn't you? You've *been* there and it's changed you. Is that what's happened? And now— Is this the Registry come to question you? They'll have you prisoner again before you can spit, and me dead besides."

I needed to understand all he spoke of, but Morgan's urgency was squeezing the air from my lungs. "Not the Registry. This lady's kin. They don't care for people like you and me so much. But all will be well for you, if you but tell them the truth." I glanced at Morgan.

"Offer no violence, and my kin will not harm thee, good Bastien."

"So will you do it?"

"But you said not to speak of those things to anyone."

I had to focus on the present situation, ignoring his doubts and resentment and what might have caused them. "Imagine that I— Please, explain your meaning as you would to a stranger."

He inhaled sharply. "Gods' bones, you truly don't remember. Not me nor the lily-child nor the Registry portraits nor how you ended up in the fix you did."

"No, I don't. I've no time to explain. But as we said, it's just this one matter that's of immediate concern. Her kin are on their way."

His eyes flicked from me to Morgan. "Are you a prisoner? Have her people done this to you?"

The snappish questions heartened me. "She's trying to help. Perhaps . . . Morgan, can you tell him the questions they'll ask?"

"I can guess them," she said, her voice tight. "In the days when Lucian lived in this city, he worked some very powerful magic that caused a disturbance in the world. Dost thou know what I speak of . . . what kinds of things he did and why?"

"Aye," he said, folding his arms across his broad chest. "A bit. But I'll not say it just yet. Pose me more questions, and then I'll decide." He jerked his head at me. "If he's fuddled, maybe he doesn't know what he's getting into by speaking of it."

Fuddled was not half. Was anything stranger than having two people discuss such intimate matters as my magic and the woman I'd lain with, while I had less knowledge of those matters than either of them?

Morgan laughed a little. "I do think we've found thee no enemy, but a worthy ally, Lucian. Good Bastien, my kinsman will ask when it was that Lucian saw a sentinel of the long-lived—one of those humans call Danae—

with silver markings on her skin. He will ask what were their dealings. He will ask what she said of a place called Sanctuary."

"I can speak to those things, though there's little enough to tell. What else?"

"He will want Lucian to take us there—where the sentinel is."

"Humph." He glanced at me. "Don't know if that's possible."

"Only if you can tell me how," I said. And if he could rebuild all the memory that went with my bent.

The yip of a white-tailed eagle ripped the night. Another cry echoed the first, so close I knew we'd see them did we step outside the gatehouse.

With a look of concern that set my chest burning, Morgan brushed her hand across my brow. "I'll go out to meet them," she said. "Come when I call. I beg thee both, mind thy best manners. My kinsman has no patience with those unlike himself."

I smiled in what I hoped was a reassuring fashion, while focusing on matters that would not threaten to explode my head: Inek back at Evanide, pleased that I would be able to bring back some answers; my hope that this business would be dealt with in plenty of time for Morgan to get me back to Lillebras to do my spying. Wondering whether she would disrobe to face her kin. No matter that I could not recall our time together or feel the intimacy she hinted at, she must surely be the most beautiful woman any man ever looked on and I had been at least two years celibate. . . .

"Manners?" The coroner took Morgan's place at my side, staring at her back as she ran through the gate. "Who's coming? Are you sure we should be doing this?"

"Partner Bastien, I don't think we have a choice."

CHAPTER 11

"Sky Lord . . . Goddess Mother . . . Blessed Lord of Vines, preserve me. I didn't dare imagine they would be—"

"Just be respectful," I said. "Their grievances—whatever they are—are with me, not you."

Only the need to keep my witness steady held my own voice calm as we walked out of the gatehouse into legend. Five Danae awaited us. Their gleaming gards made the darkness around us tremulous, altered, as if the ugly dregs of winter and war were brushed away and replaced with starshine, summer, and scents of pond lilies and seagrass. Alas, save for Morgan's faint smile, they lacked a shred of welcome amongst them.

Morgan stood apart from the others, arrayed only in her gards, hands clasped at her back and head held high. Bastien nearly choked when he recognized her. "Gods' bones, I've no manners taught for this," he whispered. "Do we kneel? Can we look?"

"We don't kneel," I said. "You are an official of the Crown. I am . . . what I am . . . and a pureblood. Looking seems to be expected."

There was no question as to which of the five was Tuari Archon, the one whose commands ruled Morgan as the Marshal's ruled me. Big, well-muscled, hair twined with leaves and bound into a tail that fell over his shoulder and reached his waist. Though his face and body seemed ageless, his presence rivaled that of the oldest trees or the sea beyond Evanide. Every lineament expressed pride and disdain for us grimy humans.

A female stood at his side, a wisp beside his imposing height and sculpted sinews. She did not cling, though. Her own lean body spoke of impressive strength. A delicate swan drawn in sapphire graced her small face, and her hair curled about her head like a cap. Spidersilk draped one shoulder, was caught at her waist with a thread, and drifted around her legs in the breeze.

Naari, Morgan's partner in watching, stood at Tuari's left, a hoop of braided rope over one shoulder. Another sturdy male, lacking any markings on his face, stood on the woman's right. His grim demeanor and the sizeable club in his hand suggested a role as bodyguard, and his arms and shoulders testified of his fitness for the role. *Breaking*, Morgan had mentioned. I had foolishly imagined the weight of supernatural argument, not wood.

"Come, Lucian, show thyself to Tuari Archon and Nysse, his consort. Honored *sagai*"—Morgan bowed to Tuari, arms crossed over her breast, and then to the woman—"*elegai*, this is Lucian de Remeni-Masson, a sorcerer of exceptional gifts and a man of honor who reverences beauty and truth."

I halted well out of arm's reach and touched my fingertips to forehead in the way of purebloods greeting contract masters or purebloods of similar rank.

"*Envisia seru*, Tuari Archon." The greeting seemed presumptuous. "And you, as well, Nysse of the long-lived. Forgive any rudeness. I am unschooled in proper greetings for your kind." Danae likely held additional grudges for those addressing them incorrectly. Purebloods did.

The woman dipped her head in acknowledgement. Cool. Not at all friendly.

"Why is a second human brought to intrude upon our senses, *sengai*?" said Tuari. His voice carried the throaty power of a seaward gale. "Is the masked one not the person who spoke the mystery to Naari? The same who dared touch thee in mating frenzy?"

Resentment . . . and danger . . . shaped his every word.

Morgan deferred to me. "Please explain, Lucian. Thou has naught to fear from my father, who is the just and honorable lord of our kind."

Father. The revelation so neatly dropped in my lap left me near speechless, and instilled such a fervent desire to turn tail and run, I almost missed Naari and the bodyguard's quiet movement toward our flanks. Almost.

"Hold!" I spread my arms, pointed at the two, and stepped back.

Bastien's hand flew to his sword. I gestured him to hold it there, as I closed the gap between us so we could press our backs together if matters came to a fight. The two Danae halted, glancing back at their master.

"Purebloods, who carry the gods' magic, do not answer summonses, save from their own masters," I snapped. "Yet with the greatest respect, I have chosen to attend you, Tuari Archon. I demand respect in turn and will not be outflanked by servants with ropes and clubs as if I were a frolicsome hind. Though my memory of my dealings with the long-lived is damaged, as your daughter has explained, I have brought a witness willing to repeat what I told him of the matters that interest you. Your daughter has assured me that my efforts to answer your concerns will reap honorable treatment in return."

"My daughter presumes much to make such assurances." Tuari snarled. "Tell me why I must respect a trespasser, a destroyer who uses his very nature to endanger our lands and our work."

"I cannot conceive of any circumstance where I would willingly endanger your kind. Our lore and teaching speak of Danae as guardians of earth and sea, beings who bring fruitfulness and health to the land. My own magic surely derives from the same immortal power that gives you that responsibility, whether one names it a god, as humans do, or something else."

"The Everlasting and its Law," said Morgan. "That is the name we give to the true lands and the great ordering that both encompasses and lies beyond them."

"Then I swear that I reverence the Everlasting and heed its Law with the same serious mind as you do." I did not mention lore that named Danae treacherous enemies of humankind.

"Humans have no knowledge of reverence," said Tuari, with chilly conviction. "They destroy all they touch. The true lands are blighted and the human realms suffer. Thou art the principal violator, more than any of thy kin."

His accusation near robbed me of speech. What in the gods' heaven did they imagine I had done?

The woman, Nysse, touched the archon's arm. "Yet he speaks mannerly, my love. Let us hear his witness before we judge his fault."

Tuari grunted sourly, but covered his consort's graceful hand with his own. "Let him answer."

I did not mistake their concession for indulgence. "Will you speak for me?" I said to Bastien. "It seems a bit more serious than I first thought."

He didn't answer me directly, but squared himself and inclined his back respectfully to Tuari. "I speak for Lucian de Remeni-Masson," he stated with the gravity of a hearing before a king. "My name is Bastien de Caton, Coroner of the Twelve Districts of Palinur, and I am accustomed to hearing witnesses in cases of untimely death. I do swear on the Law of Navronne and your Law of the Everlasting that what I speak is true."

"Proceed," said Tuari, grudgingly.

"I understand that you seek to know of Remeni's magic, of his encounters with the sentinel—the Danae woman whose skin was marked in silver—and of his mention of the word *sanctuary* in regard to these matters."

He waited until Tuari nodded. Hearing witnesses—I didn't know coroners did that. But watching him induce Tuari—a force of nature—to bend his neck, I dared imagine this Bastien might be very good at his job.

"Remeni was contracted to me for just over half a year for the purpose of drawing portraits of the dead. Several times over the course of those months, as he told me, he encountered beings he came to believe were Danae. On the first occasion, two of them, marked in blue, as you are, showed themselves to him in the streets of Palinur. Attacked him, as it were. They knew his name and warned him that his magic trespassed the boundaries of the world. They said he needed to learn about the *true lands*, and threatened him with punishment. He had no notion what they meant. I am an experienced judge of liars and thieves, and I believed him."

Half a year . . . portraits of the dead. I almost missed his continuation for astonishment. If only I could consider my missing past without axes cleaving my skull.

Bastien folded his hands at his back, as if he testified to impossible events before mythical beings every day of his life.

"For much of the time he was under contract to me, his own people wrongfully kept him prisoner in their stronghold. But it was while he was a prisoner, desperate to learn why he was being held, that he invoked his inborn magic and first saw the Danae woman marked in silver. Though it seemed he truly existed in another place altogether, he believed the experience to be a dream or that his mind was clouded from being kept in the dark so long. The woman marked in silver reacted with pleasure at his coming and spoke of a beacon that had drawn him there. As if he were expected. She said that his *makings* twisted the boundaries of the world, the same charge as the two in Palinur's streets. But the silver one expressed no venom, only that her people were divided as to what to do about him: lead astray or grant *sanctuary*."

Tuari's eyes had widened just enough to tell me he had heard something of interest at last.

"This vision was interrupted, as it happened, by Remeni being set free. Again, he swore he'd no idea what she meant. Again, I believed him. Once back here, he tried to force such a vision to manifest, bringing every scrap of his native bents to bear. On several occasions—not every attempt—he glimpsed this other place. He described it as five promontories ribbed with white rocks, so that it appeared as a white hand protruding into the sea.

"But it was no dream. I watched him. Each time, he vanished from the room where he worked. He tried again and vanished for near a quarter of an hour. And on that occasion, he met the silver-marked sentinel a second time."

How had my magic taken such a turn? Nothing I knew of Aurellian magic, whether inborn bent or other practice, could transport a person to another place.

"And what did the sentinel tell him?" Tuari could not mask his eagerness. If he hadn't asked, I would have blurted the question myself.

"She called those like you her *kin marked in blue* and said her people were waiting for one like Remeni—with his particular talent for magic and the strength to use it."

"She *desired* him to use this perverse power?" Tuari's face purpled. "To what end?"

"She gave no hint of her purposes, saying only that Lucian must prove his *quality* before she would tell him more. To our frustration, she failed to tell him how to accomplish this proof, but seemed to think he would understand and wish to do so. She spoke no more of sanctuary. After that day, turmoil in the city caught us up and Remeni vanished. These words are true upon my swearing."

I teetered on the brink of a chasm. *His native bents.* I had not mistaken; the coroner believed I had more than one. Art. History. And *transported* to another place. Who would ever have heard of such a thing? Trying to resolve these new pieces set my stomach into rebellion. I had to listen, absorb the words, but dared not think about them. Knowing bits of the missing past only worsened the pain of reaching for more.

"Where is she?" Tuari demanded. "Why would she give such direction, yet fail to say how to fulfill it or where to find her?"

"She explained herself no more than you do," said Bastien. "You all seem to expect that he knows. He did not. And, apparently, he still does not."

"Then show us," said Nysse. "Prove thyself, Remeni-son. Show us this magic that caused the sentinel to greet thee."

"You're sure it's my *bents* that made it happen?" I said to Bastien, forcing detachment. "Not some other kind of spellworking?"

"Certain." He dropped his voice. "One or the other of them. You were drawing portraits when I saw you vanish. You were examining the history of the Registry Tower when you encountered the sentinel the first time."

Which was not going to help this argument at all. I took a breath to settle my gut.

"I would gladly do as you say," I said to the archon and his consort. "But it's impossible. The same affliction that prevents me remembering these encounters has hidden my inborn magic. Hearing Coroner Bastien's testimony is like hearing a fireside tale of another man's life, and I can no more work that particular magic than I could a stranger's."

"A convenient flaw." Tuari blew a note of anger and disdain. "But I've heard enough. Thou shalt have no chance to trespass again or use thy skills in service of any marked in silver."

Something flew through the air and dropped around me, ensnaring my ankles.

A flash from my side was Bastien's sword slashing Naari's rope that threatened to yank me off my feet. Another loop flew and another, but I burnt them through before they could ensnare Bastien or me.

"No more, Archon!" I bellowed. I raised a shield of fire between the two of us and the Danae. "Hear me. I swear I bear you no ill will. If you'll but tell me what you think I've done . . ."

But he ignored me, and though the two younger Danae paused, they did not retreat.

"Thus is a human's true nature revealed!" Tuari's fury rumbled beneath my feet and set the very air quivering. "What now, daughter, who promised the violator meant no harm and would answer peacefully? Never should I have sent a softhearted youngling to mingle with humankind. Thou art tainted by his touch and nimble tongue. How am I to punish thy foolishness? Perhaps the span of a gyre in beast form?"

"Sagai!" Morgan's horror—and Naari's and Nysse's—told me more about the punishment than the words.

"I do not lie, Tuari Archon," I said. "My memory is broken, and without it, I've no way to access my deepest magic. Morgan can testify that I did not know her when she found me in the estuary. But I swear on anything you choose that I *will* give you answers as soon as I have them for myself. If that means drawing a portrait or whatever I did to make this transport happen, I'll do so."

"And lead me to this aberrant sentinel?"

"If it is possible, certainly."

"Then on my daughter's future, thou art sworn," he snapped, glaring at Morgan and then me. "And wilt thou swear the same, daughter? What if I say that if he fails in this oath, thou shalt live as a beast until the end of thy days?"

"No, wait . . ."

"Yes." Morgan garbed herself in pride and fury. "Lucian swears he will answer to you when his memory and magic are restored. I believe him. I know him. I pledge my life on his word."

"A *human's* word?" The Dané shook with rage.

"Yes."

My horror cried out, "Morgan, you mustn't!" Who knew how Tuari would interpret *help* or *answers*, *truth* or *possibility*?

Tuari shook off the shocked Nysse's touch as if she were a gnat. "So be it sworn." With a jerk of his head, the four of them vanished into the night.

Morgan stared after them, as if she could see them leaving long after human eyes failed. As the city bells tolled the hour, she folded her arms across her breast and begin to shake.

"Lady, what have you done?" I said. "I meant what I swore, but what if my memory is never restored completely or if I can't make the connection happen again? Bastien says it didn't always."

"I told thee, Tuari has no use for humans. Nor for daughters who care for humans, it seems. Even daughters who share his rash temper. I hope— Gentle Lucian, thou must find thy memory."

Her wan smile sent arrows up my spine. Could Tuari truly change Morgan into a beast? A fox or a hind . . . prey to hunters, to larger beasts. Surely not. But her fear enveloped me, more real even than my own.

"I'd best find my human clothes. We must go." She stalked back toward the gatehouse.

Steel sliding on leather spun me around. Bastien had sheathed his weapon. Shaking his shaggy head, he squatted and fingered the Danae's braided rope. "I'm not thinking that went as planned."

"No. I'm grateful for your clear witness. I've a thousand questions, as you can imagine. But I have to go. I've duties . . . and I must see this breakage remedied."

His head popped up. "You've a way to do that?"

"It's not simple . . ." Deunor's holy fire, what if the Marshal—or Damon— refused to sanction me leaving the Order with memory restored? "I may be back, begging for answers and your posset to soothe the discomfort of hearing them."

"Aye, I can see it's rough. But lest you can't fix things, there's more you ought to know."

"I'm sure of that, but too much at once will have me gibbering." And

Inek's position and mine at Evanide depended on my being back to receive the Order spy's signal.

Bastien jerked his head at Morgan, who was lost in thought as she pulled on skirts and cloak, masking her glory for our trek around the city. "There's more has to do with this matter."

"*What? You withheld?*" Did he want me to strangle him? "But you swore!"

"Now just hold on to your boots. Everything I spoke was the truth. I just left out a bit. The sentinel told you her blue-marked kin were *excitable* and that their *view of human usefulness* differed from that of her own people. She also said that you were the answer to a long waiting by some of her kind—and some of *our* kind, as well. So I'd say she was more friendly to human folk, yes? Lest you didn't notice, this Tuari is itching to hurt somebody—you for certain, but not necessarily just humans. He near burst his heart when you said the silver one was waiting for someone with the strength to *use* talents like yours. And I'm thinking, as the world is a dreadful mess right now, one wouldn't want to go starting another war—between folks like these."

"Yes. Truly."

"So I thought you'd likely want to learn a bit more for yourself before spilling it to them. The sentinel told you what you had to do to prove your *quality* was to follow something called the Path of the *White Hand*. She said they would welcome you at the end of it."

"White hand . . . the path . . ." I whipped out my dagger. "This blazon made you think I'd already gone to her." Easy to see the confusion. From a distance the Order's emblem would be very like.

He dipped his head toward Morgan. "Do you trust her fully in this matter?"

"I must," I said. "As you said, if not for her, I might be dead right now—or broken. And my resources to explore what all this means are quite limited at present. Besides, she's honestly terrified at what he threatens."

Morgan joined us, looking almost ordinary in her maiden's skirts. Quick and sharp, Bastien's gaze swept her, seeking evidence of the marvels—and perhaps the loyalties—behind the drab fabrics. I knew so, because my own gaze did the same. I yet felt the luminous wonder our eyes could not see, as when the sun's warmth heats a wall at one's back. But I didn't know her.

The coroner averted his eyes. "I've someplace to show the two of you. 'Tisn't far."

Morgan touched his chin, deep buried in his beard. "Know this, worthy

Bastien, before we go farther: I am my father's loyal daughter, but I do not share his despair. I have lived amid humankind, and learned of the great variety of human souls—those of cruelty and careless greed that he despises, yes, but also those of generosity, of wisdom, and even some who match my own people in grace and art." Her alter hand brushed mine, shooting lightning bolts through my spine. "And lest the two of you plan to speak more secrets, know that my hearing is exceptional."

Bastien opened his mouth to speak, but thought better of it. Instead, he bowed. Grinning. "*Envisia seru,* gracious lady. Even in human garb."

Her laughter rang sweeter than chiming silver, though it faded quickly. Beneath her generous sentiments lay profound hurt and a fear seated too deep to let it pass.

"What is all this about?" I said. "Your father has just condemned you to this dreadful fate, and if the risk was merely my trespassing on something sacred to your kind, a knife to my throat would end it. Why do silver gards and sanctuary concern him so? Please, tell me."

She withdrew her hand from mine, and turned away. "The song of sanctuary is long and must wait for another time. But the silver gards . . . Indeed, my father has laid my future in thy hands, Lucian. And reason says I must trust thee with things we do not share outside our own. But the questions silver gards raise touch on privacies no human can ever know and I've promised my father to honor our tradition. Trust me; his fears are justified. Be wary if you speak to the sentinel again. Listen and observe her carefully."

"Morgan, how can I—?"

"Our time is short." The air crackled. "If there is more to see, do it quickly."

I shrugged helplessly at Bastien. "Show me what you would."

"Come this way." Bastien struck out across the field toward the city wall, for the same gate where Morgan and I had met Naari. "I'm going to show you where my knowledge of this mystery ended. I believe the place to be important, but my damnably stubborn pureblood never deigned to tell me what he learned there. And as we go, I'd best tell you a few more unhappy truths."

CHAPTER 12

"First off, Lucian, if you show so much as a hair in Palinur, the Registry will bury you so deep Magrog himself couldn't find you. This Curator Pluvius, who visits as regular as the gatzi's itch, claims he can help you, but you could never decide whether to trust him or not. I'd not trust a Registry curator with a crumb of dirt."

"Pluvius." I rubbed my aching brow and packed the name away with the rest.

We kept a brisk pace as we crossed the muddy field toward the wall, Bastien on one side of me, Morgan on the other.

"They've put about that not only are you a madman and a renegade, but that you killed one pureblood and mutilated another with your magic. I gather you yet understand what that means."

"Yes." I swallowed hard. Perhaps if I judged his words as the story of someone other than me, my eyes wouldn't dissolve as they were currently threatening. "Did I?"

"Don't know. You might have had good reason. Certain nobles of Prince Perryn's court will also have your head off your shoulders if they catch a glimpse of you. And don't imagine you can shelter in a temple. There's been recent upheaval in Arrosa's temples—some of our better work, I think. But I doubt you need to hear more about these things right now."

"Probably so," I said, wholly confused. How could a portrait artist make so many enemies?

"It's all to do with your two bents"—he might have read my thoughts—"the artwork that you practiced and the gift for history that you thought had been burnt out, but was not or grew back or whatever. The work you did here made you reach deeper for your magic, so you told me, and you believed the two talents somehow meshed with each other. You were convinced that this joined talent enabled you to shift to this other place. And the silver one said they were looking for someone with your *particular talents*."

He peered around me. "Lady Dané, does it make sense that the magic that transported Lucian to this other place would be the same that stings your sire so fiercely?"

"Indeed," she said. The power of her worry slowed our steps and drew us close enough that my shoulder brushed hers and Bastien's mine. "I'll tell thee a portion of the great mystery of the world. But 'tis a violation. . . ."

Her posture, usually so fluidly graceful, was rigid as an oaken beam until we each swore to protect her secret.

"My people walk lands that take the same shape as these that humans walk. But they are also set apart. Consider the reflection in a pond which is very like what it shows, but of a different quality, defining a different realm. The long-lived pass between the true lands and the human realm without a ripple. Lucian witnessed this on our journey here."

"A different realm. That's why I saw no evidence of human habitation."

"Aye." Morgan's eyes closed as if to avoid witnessing her own sin. "Few humans have ever been able to cross into the true lands, and always by pathways we know. Sentinels guard those ways, for humans bring danger and disorder wherever they travel. Thy magic, Lucian, thins the boundaries between our lands and thine, and my father, who is responsible for the ways our kind heed the call of the Everlasting, fears thy workings forge new paths we do *not* know."

"How could I possibly have known that?" I said. "And why would I damage these barriers apurpose?"

"We don't know. But it does not escape notice that we first felt the wrenching of thy magic in the very seasons this diseased and unyielding winter took hold of the world."

"The *winter*?"

"The health of thy fields and rivers, forests and sea derives from the health of the true lands. When the disease took hold, we searched for damage afflicting the boundaries. We found thee. Thus, against all custom, was I sent to learn of thee."

"You think *I* am responsible for the *weather*?" For dying sheep, frozen vineyards, famine, plagues . . . not just a single death, but thousands. Certainly true magics altered the natural world, but . . . "Bastien, did you see me do any such thing? Did I speak of it, hint at it? Holy Deunor, was I such a monster?"

"Pssh. Never a whisper." His skeptical spewing reassured me. "The worst you learned was that your drawings exposed sins people didn't want known.

Besides, the magics you did for me drained you dry, and it never changed the season a whit!"

"Surely I believe thy saying, Lucian," said Morgan. "But is not my sire's fear understandable? What are the consequences if thy magic destroys the barriers that keep our two realms separate? Such a shift in the Everlasting must carry terrible risks. Humans moved across the boundary on that very day Naari last spoke to thee in warning, yet we've never found them."

Muddle-headed as I was, I knew this was wrong. Even such magic as I worked at Evanide filled me with wonder and purpose, a beauty, a rightness that soothed the wounds of lost years. It could not be so unnatural as to create this plague of winter.

"I'll not believe this until I see evidence," I said. "You told me you kept your true nature hidden from me when we met. Yet your portrait showed truth, a truth I could not possibly guess."

"Indeed, it showed truth and more." She touched her smooth, unmarked cheek.

"If *truth* is the work of my magic, it cannot be this unholy thing your father fears. Tell me, lady, has the winter eased these two years past? Have flocks and vineyards grown healthier? For it's been at least that long since I used my bent."

She shook her head. "The world has grown more ill since thy move to the sea fortress. But it could be that thy hand in the sickness is hidden, as are the seasons of thine own history." The pearly light from my hand revealed tears glistening in her green eyes. "The Law of the Everlasting requires us to eliminate such a threat as you are. But if we knew more of the sentinel with silver gards, it might help soften that harsh judgment."

Only stubborn faith could refute her logic. I had pledged my loyalty to the Order, they who *could* mask my bent—magic that was a part of me as much as my spine or my rattling heart—they who could erase all recognition of the two extraordinary people at my side. But despite my faltering trust in the Marshal, the Order was not just one man. It was Inek and Cormorant, and the knights and trainees who sacrificed lives and glory for just purpose. And truly, I could account for every moment of my stay at Evanide and every scrap of magic I had expended there.

As one, the three of us resumed our hike to the wall. I felt like a ghost risen from the boneyard of Caton, floating in a world I had no senses to comprehend.

"Hmmph." Bastien's grunt broke the silence. "If Lucian's magic is so fearsome, why does this sentinel say her kind would welcome him? She even mentioned the boundary twisting, but she wasn't anywise afraid or angry."

Morgan shook her head. "The sentinel with silver gards is a great puzzle."

When we reached the wall, Bastien didn't slow, but led us through the slot gate and down the steep track into the deeper dark. The city's outer wall and an inner, older one, built atop rocky ramparts, formed a deep ravine. It was a dismal place, swampy, musty, overgrown with willows.

"Best keep voices down and light spare," said Bastien. "The Guard Royale patrols Caedmon's Wall, though fewer and fewer are left to do it. Prince Perryn's snatched up all but dotards and weanlings for the summer's campaign."

The ravine widened a little. The night was pitch in the bottomland, and despite Bastien's warning, I widened my magelight, lest we founder in mud or break our heads. Swathes of ground were treeless and sterile, littered with blackened stones and broken carts. Wagon ruts cut deep through the mud.

"Two years ago this was Hirudo Palinur," said Bastien, his voice muted in the heavy quiet. "Some two hundred people lived here, mostly Cicerons, and a few who didn't mind living amongst them. The barber-surgeon that did jobs for me at Caton had a hole down here. No other place would have him, as most of his fees went for nivat paste or corpses he could cut apart to school himself. Never knew a twistmind could keep his mind sharp before I knew Bek."

Every city spawned such a district, rife with disease and perversion, where one could hire a thief, a whore, or an assassin, or lay wagers of coin or blood.

Bastien kicked a charred timber out of our way. "All this burnt on the morning Bayard laid the siege."

We crossed a muddy flat, pitted with old fire rings, rusted wheels, and rotting barrels. But my interest snapped to the city-side wall, the older of the two confining boundaries of the ravine where a strong *obscuré* tried to divert my attention. Concentration revealed a squat stone hut butted up against the rubble underpinnings of the ancient wall.

"I've come down here on and off over the years, so the magic doesn't make me look away anymore," said Bastien, nodding at the hut's dull red door—a door unscratched and uncharred.

"The Cicerons called this their commons house, as if they were a righteous village here at the city's bung hole. Their headman was named Demetreo, an honorable sort for a knife-wielding thief. You and he had dealings, Lucian, some of which you told me, some of which you didn't."

"Dealings with a *Ciceron*? Why?" He might have told me I'd had dealings with badgers.

"Not long before the siege came down, you and a friend of mine had been out doing some work for me—"

"What work?" I said, the need to know overwhelming good sense.

"We solved murders," he said, his teeth gleaming white. "You ran your fingers over a dead face as you drew, reached deep into your magic, so you told me, and your portraits showed things you couldn't possibly know . . . useful things. Folk pay well to know how their kinsmen die, who did the deed, and where they're laid. Folk pay to know their enemies are dead, or their neighbors' farm has no man to work it anymore. Nobles pay decent. Merchants pay better. It was good work. Decent work, even for a pureblood."

"The work of justice."

"Aye. Exactly that. You liked it better than sitting in the Registry Tower drawing identity portraits for purebloods. Though you came to believe that some of *those* portraits told the secrets that left you in chains."

I ignored the warning throb in my head while enjoying the sweet irony, then let it go. "Go on."

"My friend and you were wounded, and Demetreo brought you here. That was the first time you'd been inside. Touch the door."

Just before my finger encountered the painted wood, the door swung open.

"You see? Those invited in get to come back. Door won't open to anyone other."

Magelight revealed a single chamber, centered by a circular stone firepit. Plastered walls were hung with lamps. An armchair with a high back, the old wood splattered and stained, sat near the back wall. Far more interesting was the variety of small enchantments that filled the room, around the door for certain, but also about the hearth, the lamps, and even the dice abandoned on a three-legged table. Common spells, precisely executed by a variety of hands. Not at all what one might expect in such a place. A *Ciceron* place. Yes, Cicerons claimed to have magic, but their spells were always proven to be fools' fakery.

"This house is not what it seems." Morgan remained in the doorway, her brow wrinkled in puzzlement that reflected my own.

Bastien's eyes, intent and curious, fixed on me. He pointed to the back wall. "Shine your light up near the rafters."

"Deunor's fire!"

Just beneath the timber rafters, at the time the plaster was wet, an artist had painted a black lozenge. On the field of black he had depicted a white hand, thumb and fingers spread.

"The Path of the White Hand," I said. "What could a Ciceron commons house have to do with Danae or a way for a sorcerer to prove his quality to them?"

"Such was your question that night, too," said Bastien. "Demetreo said he'd tell of the symbol, but only to you. He'd done us a service, summoning Bek to stitch up my Garen and keeping you both safe here. So we worked a bargain. In exchange for telling you about that bit of paint, he wanted an hour of your assistance. He didn't allow me to stay."

Bastien's meaty arms wrapped his broad chest, and he strolled over to the armchair. "These stains are blood, you know."

He swiveled around, his sharp glance puncturing me. Judging . . . what? Guilt? Confusion? But he continued the story. "When you got back to Caton, you refused to say what you'd learned. You said you'd done a portrait, but wouldn't say whose."

But Bastien had been angry. He had spewed resentments when he recognized me. His grimy leather jaque was straining to hold them in even now.

"Three days after Bayard laid his siege and you failed to show up at Caton, I came down here in search of Bek. We had wounded who needed his skills. I found a few of Demetreo's fighters lying dead out there, left in a heap for rats and vultures. But every other Ciceron was gone, as was my surgeon. Soldiers told me they'd never seen any but those few. But then"—he pointed a thick finger at the floor—"I came inside here. And right where you stand was Demetreo with his skull caved in, laid out as if he were a hero prince, wrapped in a cloak I'd last seen on you, exactly the kind of nicety you'd do. And beside him lay his granny Oldmeg—a crone who could have been the Goddess Mother's own granny—with her wrists sliced open, a stab wound through her heart, and a bloody knife laid careful on her breast. Guess you don't recall what that could be about, neither?"

I shook my head. Why Cicerons?

"I had plenty of reason to fear the Registry had taken you. Killed you. Buried you. Whatever. But that morning I came to suspect you'd run off with the Cicerons."

"Nothing inside me supports such a story," I said. Cicerons were the dregs of every kingdom.

"Gods' bones, what's happened to you?" Bastien's frustration spewed like boiling water. "Did someone drop you on your head?"

"I can't—"

"Our answers are there." Morgan pointed to the back wall beneath the fresco. Her voice was tight. Her hand kneaded her stomach fretfully.

"What is it, lady?"

She waved me forward. "I dislike all walls. But that one is more than a wall. Learn, Lucian. I would not spend my life a beast."

I shoved the bloodstained chair aside. Though touch deemed the rough plaster solid, the stone quivered with illusion. None of my working, though my hand named it familiar, the sensation very like seeing my own ghost.

With a touch of my left bracelet and an infusion of power, I ripped the illusion away.

Perhaps a third of the plaster vanished, exposing a stony bulwark—not the even courses of pale blocks found in the city's outer wall, but age-blackened, undressed stones, laid and mortared as they were dug from the ground. Set into the wall was a low, round arch, worked of bronze hammered into flowers, vines, and a variety of beasts and birds.

It was the interior of the arch stunned me, however. Shifting patterns of light in thready colors I could not name filled the man-high space. Shapes of landscapes, cities, temples, and faces formed and vanished so quickly I wasn't sure if they were actually there or only imagined, as one might glimpse wolves or cats in cloud shapes. The harmony of the enchantment's design and the perfection of its creation settled into my spirit like good wine. The magic used . . . its substance and texture . . .

"Extraordinary," I breathed. "Though I've no idea what it is." Again, my fingers twitched, it felt so like my own work.

"What's so damned remarkable about a bit of metal set in a rock wall?" grumbled Bastien. He ran his hand across the brilliant display. Tapped it with a hairy knuckle. "Looks like a door was bricked up when the wall was built. But why would anyone hide it behind magic? Or did you just pull down the plaster and vanish the leavings?"

"You don't see colors or patterns inside the arch?" I sensed no *obscuré* or veil. My finger touched the wall of light. . . .

I staggered backward, only my eyes testifying hand and arm remained uncharred. Two more attempts gave the same result. Bastien looked at me as if I'd fallen in a fit.

"You didn't *feel* that?" I said. "Morgan, surely you— Are you ill?"

Halfway across the chamber, she sat on her haunches, pale and stricken, hands knotted at her breast as her gaze fixed on the wall. "'Tis a crack in the world. The abyss. The unending dark whence beasts come to devour the Everlasting. Long have we spoken of such, but never have eyes beheld it."

"I see light and color that scald my hand," I said, exasperated. "No brick. No beasts. No abyss. Why would we three perceive it so differently?"

Morgan shook her head, her fear and horror choking me.

"There is something *here*," said Bastien. His fingers rubbed a cluster of grapes halfway up the left side of the bronze arch, and then a spot exactly opposite on the right. After a careful examination, he tapped a third spot at the apex of the arch. Each place was darkened with paint or dirt or—

"Old blood," he said.

"Blood-sealed spellwork! That would explain the old woman with cut wrists and a wound in her heart."

I touched the stains on the sides of the arch. "Blood of the left spirit—the side of the soul, where anger and outrage lie, the part of us that is passion and ferocity. Blood of the right spirit—the side of peace, of reason, learning, and skill. And the blood of the heart"—the stain at the top of the arch—"which binds the two into a whole and makes us human. A blood seal is extremely rare—used only to protect objects of the most profound consequence. . . ."

"So did Oldmeg's blood close up this mystery or open it?" Bastien's question drew me out of the tangle of implications.

"From the age of the arch and the rocks, I'd say she unsealed it, until her blood dried and the enchantment reverted."

"A portal locked and unlocked with death blood?" Tears dribbled down Morgan's cheeks. "That's what sickens me. Lucian, this blood magic was perfectly devised to bar my kind from what lies beyond this wall."

"Perhaps your 'crack in the world' is devised for the same purpose," I said, "while what I see is supposed to intrigue me enough to pursue answers. Certainly I didn't create the seal."

Because the blood seal was Order magic, like the memory spells inherited from our beginning. From Xancheira. Xancheira, whose blazon of the white tree and five branches was so like the Order's white quiver with five implements, which was so like the white hand glaring above the arch in all its mystery . . .

The clues fell upon me like raindrops. A silver-marked woman who told me to follow the Path of the White Hand. A rivalry between those marked in blue and those marked in silver. A doorway marked with the white hand

and locked in a way that would keep Morgan's people out. It would keep ordinaries like Bastien away, as well; he could not even see possibility. But a clan of Cicerons had vanished on the day of Bayard's siege, and fighters stayed behind, perhaps to ensure that the others got away safely. . . .

I wandered over to the little table and fingered the dice left lying there, working to maintain detachment. "Bastien, did this Demetreo or his granny mention leaving the city?"

He cocked his head. "Not exactly. But you told me the crone warned of dangers to come on that morning of the siege. It's why you vowed to come to Caton to help."

"But I couldn't, because I was waylaid. First by Naari, I think"—who believed humans had crossed into the true lands by virtue of my boundary-thinning magic—"and then by . . . others." For I myself had been in the process of vanishing into the embrace of the Order. It would explain the hint of familiarity with the necropolis. Perhaps I had met the knights while on my way to keep my promise. But knowing of the white hand, if I'd seen the knights' blazon . . .

Puzzle pieces shifted and aligned. Cicerons, the Order, Xancheira. White hand, white quiver, white tree. And Danae. Only one answer came, however unlikely. "What if these Cicerons passed through that arch seeking *sanctuary*? Somehow I helped them . . . or showed them . . . or interpreted the magic by way of the portrait I did for them, using my joined bents, thinning the boundaries."

"Then they're dead." Morgan's voice broke. "The world is broken. There is no sanctuary."

"But I don't see the abyss," I said. "Perhaps that is but one possibility, while the light and images I see are another. The evidence says the magic was unsealed by an old woman's sacrifice, so perhaps her headman and his fighters died for *hope*. That's not a matter for grieving."

"Why Cicerons?" Bastien's resentments were bound with grief. "They may not be the blight everyone thinks, but why not other ordinaries? Thousands died that day. Thousands disappeared. Some of them . . . We might never know when they died or where."

"That makes no sense to me, either. You said the silver-marked Dané spoke of her kind and *my own kind* waiting for me to prove myself. Maybe my *test of quality* is to solve this puzzle. Sanctuary. The sentinel said no more of it?"

"Only the one mention—that her kind could grant it."

"Morgan, you say there is no sanctuary, yet your father wants to break me if I don't tell him more of it. And there is a song. . . ."

Morgan stood at the open doorway, drawing in great breaths of chilly darkness. Unfortunately, I could give no comfort. "Lady, I need your help."

"What I see is no illusion," she said without looking back. "The land you visited is real. Perhaps it is even safe . . . for now. But the abyss yawns beneath it. Thou canst not imagine the danger."

She stepped outside. "We must go, Lucian. Thy duties wait."

Duties, yes. The Order. The war. I'd promised Inek to be ready when the spy gave the signal. He was risking all to help me.

Yet I felt so near to solving this great puzzle—all these pieces at my fingertips. Why they had come together in me seemed the greatest mystery of all. Throughout this journey I had tried to understand how I had ended up in the Order, why I would have given consent. And I'd learned it was naught so simple as madness or murder or a rebellious nature, but this verisame mystery.

I pulled out my dagger. I had followed the White Hand.

"I don't suppose I ever spoke of a city called Xancheira?"

"So I'm to hear more of *that* mystery, as well!" Bastien's acid could have etched steel. "Let's just say I was never nearer bashing your hard head against a wall as when you told me to bury the little *sample of Xancheiran needlework* we'd gone to so much trouble to retrieve. You were never a good liar. The thing terrified you."

That seemed ludicrous—though no more so than Cicerons seeking refuge behind a blood-sealed doorway. "Can I see it? How did we come by it?"

"It's a deal of trouble to fetch, as I did exactly as you said. It's buried deep, and all my diggers are dead or conscripted. As to how: You believed the mystery of Xancheira was somehow connected with that"—he pointed to the fresco above the gleaming arch—"and you found it in a chest full of artifacts from your grandsire's investigation of Xancheira."

"My grandsire . . ."

My throat constricted. All other considerations fled. Never could I have imagined Bastien would know anything of my family. Contract masters were never privy to such personal information, save that Bastien and I had evidently been more than master and pureblood.

". . . a historian, is he?"

A great wave of understanding blunted the sturdy coroner's brittle edges. "You don't remember them, either? Your *family*?"

"Lucian, we must go." Blistering with urgency, Morgan reached for my arm.

My hand stayed her. "*All* of my past is locked away. Not destroyed, but hidden, so I can focus on my work. I've accepted that. It's likely wise, save when one has problems with the Danae. But I would ask"—grace of the Goddess Mother, did I truly want to hear this?—"does my family, too, believe me a murderer? A *recondeur*?"

"Stars and stones, Lucian, how do I answer that?" His distress was near as palpable as Morgan's.

"You know so much of me," I said. "You've this skill . . . to perceive. If I told you about my family, then I've a notion you can guess what they know, what they believe happened— Please, tell me the truth."

He glanced frantically from me to Morgan and back again, and then puffed his cheeks and blew a note of resignation. "You once told me that your family was more precious to you than the crown of Navronne to its princes. From what I know, they thought of you the same. But they're all dead these three years, every one of your blood kin save one young sister. And she— She's a spark of a girl who gave you fits, but you loved her dearly—your only kin left in the world. When all the trouble came down on you, you sent her away to the safest place you could think of, a place where she could still practice her magic. I've neither seen nor heard mention of her since then. But you left some valuables to take care of her should she ever come to Caton in search of you. I've kept them safe."

"All but one dead." Body and soul had become unmovable weight as if I'd been melded into the ponderous wall in front of us. How could one grieve properly when the faces and voices were no longer a part of the soul? "How? The war? Plague? What?"

"Murdered in a Harrower raid is what you were told. But you came to believe— Damn, damn, damn. I oughtn't—"

"Say it!" Of a sudden my entire body was shaking.

His mouth opened but either he didn't speak or I couldn't hear. Surely the bones of my skull fractured, as fear, anger, and certainty boiled out to devour patience, setting a storm raging in the great void of my soul. "They burned, didn't they? My family." *Hundreds of sorcerers . . . couldn't get out . . . trapped inside . . . purebloods laughing . . .*

"You thought some Registry curators had a hand in it. The night before the siege was laid, you sneaked into the Registry Tower to look at the curators' portraits you'd done the previous year. You believed your joined bents had shown things you couldn't know—crimes they'd done that caused them to do murder. Some had tried to kill you and your sister. Some wanted you buried in that prison. That Curator Damon wanted you to run . . ."

"Damon!"

I would have crushed the words from Bastien had he not continued. "He came to the necropolis one day near the end. He was the first of the curators seemed willing to listen. But he was shifty. You didn't trust him. He told you to run, that he knew of a house of healing and reflection where you could hide."

"Healing!" The laugh that scraped my chest was more a donkey's bray than a human sound. The months of terror and nausea, drowning, bleeding, fighting. And it was Damon's Registry who had broken me to begin with. Damon had sent me to the Order . . . and because of the white hand mystery, I had consented.

"I never saw you again after the night you went to examine the portraits. That's why I believed they had you. I do know you accomplished at least one task of value that night—in a matter of justice, though it was a small thing compared to the troubles of the world. So, if you weren't dead or captive of the Registry or bolted with the Cicerons, I suppose you ran?"

"I suppose I did," I said, hauling in the torn threads of my composure. "But you can be sure it has not been healing or reflecting and certainly not chasing women. I thank you for your help, Coroner Bastien. I would be ever grateful if you would retrieve the Xancheiran artifact. I'll be back to fetch it as soon as I can."

"I will," he said, peering at me curiously. "I'm ready to help however you need. You need not do this alone, Lucian. Whether you remember it or not, we partner well."

I jerked my head in acknowledgement, though I doubted anyone could help me understand save the spider at the center of this web. Damon.

CHAPTER 13

I crouched on a rocky outcrop above the restless lake, my senses extended to detect the approach of the Order spy. Midnight was long past; dawn, yet hours away. The waning moon was setting over the hills.

If I needed any proof of Morgan's contention that seven days had passed since leaving the Gouvron Estuary, it was that slouching moon. When I cast off from Evanide, a mere three days past, so mind and body insisted, the moon was pregnant, approaching full. Morgan said time's river meandered differently in the true lands. Confusing, impossible. Like so much about that journey, it didn't bear thinking about. My family slaughtered, save for a sister. And not one, but two bents. My spirit ached from holding it all at bay. But it was necessary. I was in-mission.

Wind-shifted trees, ruffled lake, and weak moonlight provided good cover for a practiced spy. I awaited the signal.

Muffled harness chinked softly at the spot where the track from the village emerged from the wooded ridge. A pearl of light winked not far from the source of the noise. A slow second and rapid third wink followed.

I responded with a slightly different pattern. When a green flick answered, I breathed again.

A dark figure scrambled quick and quiet as a gray spider across the spread of boulders tumbled from the ridge into the lake. Had I not known to watch, I doubt I could have spotted him. By the time he found my perch, I was standing with knife drawn.

"Well met, Paratus Greenshank."

"Blessed respite, sir knight."

"You may call me Grey."

We sheathed our weapons. Though he wore his mask for our meeting, Grey's dagger did not bear the Order's mark. He lived outside our bounds.

We retreated behind the rocks. He was slender built for a knight. His hair, a shaggy tangle of mud-brown, spoke little of his age. But behind the alert intelligence I expected, the eyes examining me through the mask carried a weary burden. No matter that their personal memories were erased, knights felt the weight of the battles they'd fought and the sights they'd seen.

"I've a skin of Malcolm's cider," I said. "And bread, a bit aged, and olive paste." Losing four days along my path had preserved my supplies.

"A swallow of cider would be fine," he said, lowering himself gingerly to the ground, back to the rock. "No time to linger, as I must be back before dawn with my horse not blown. I daren't be late. Prince Osriel's bodyguard, Mardane Voushanti, has no patience for tardy guides. And he is surely marked by the Tormentor. Look him in the eye and your soul shrivels."

I passed Grey the aleskin. "Do you travel everywhere with Prince Osriel?"

"Sky Lord's benevolent mercy, no. It sounds perverse, but we were fortunate this battle's come together near Lillebras. My cadre did advanced training hereabouts, so I've every rock, tree, and crevice charted in my bones. When the Order learned Osriel required a local guide, they made sure I was hired. I volunteered for the mission, but I'll never be so grateful as when I pass it over, for if the servant is Magrog's right hand, the master is surely the Tormentor himself."

"I've heard it so," I said, interested to hear rumor confirmed.

"You'll never see even so much of Osriel's face as you see of mine, but until the end of your days, you'll never mistake his presence. 'Tis like cold oil that slowly sheathes your skin, fills your ears, slides over your tongue and into your nostrils until it drips into belly and lungs and you cannot breathe nor hear nor feel anything but him. . . ."

Grey shuddered, then took a great swallow from the skin, closed his eyes, and sighed in gratitude. Evanide's brewmaster pressed a fine cider.

I left him the moment. Soon enough he opened his eyes and scratched at his half-grown beard. "Here's what you need to know. The battle was joined three days ago—sooner than we expected. The fight has gone ill for the Ardran legion. Perryn's lost two of his best generals, one dead, one captured, and his lines are in increasing disarray. This coming morning's assault is surely going to break them. Sila Diaglou and her madmen have infused Prince Bayard's legion with new vigor. They'll chase Perryn all the way to Palinur by summer's end."

"And what of Osriel? Does he spy on them? Plot against them?"

The knight leaned forward, arms around his knees. "I've been with them three days now, and certain he's been in no hurry to do anything. We arrived in the vicinity of Lillebras yestermorn. All day and into this night the Bastard has bided his time in a hovel with a squire, two soldiers, the bodyguard Voushanti, and a formidable Evanori warlord called Stearc. If he's got more men in the vicinity, they're well hid. I've neither seen nor heard aught of them."

"Are the servants pureblood? I'd expect one, if not two." Osriel was the richest of the three princes, thanks to the gold beneath his mountain stronghold.

"I attempted to discover that very thing." Grey shoved his shaggy hair behind his ears. "I dropped an untraceable at a crossroad. The only man it brought to the alert was the Bastard himself. Fire-god's holy heart, I'd heard he was halfblood, yet I didn't believe— Well, I'd thought him asleep in his saddle. Three hours he had us scouring the surrounding wood for spies. When none was found, he concluded it was the *power of the crossroad* had intruded on his *meditations.* But ever since, he's displayed an uncanny sense of where I am. He tells his men when I'll get back from a scout, or when I'll arrive in the morning. Hold rein on your magic unless you're desperate."

Another swallow of the cider and he passed the skin to me. "Weren't you supposed to be mounted?"

Heat flushed my cheeks, though my answer was strictly true. "I never found the hostler's. I thought it better to be here in plenty of time."

"You may regret that," he said, dry as ash.

I returned to the more important subject. "So the battle's almost over, and Osriel's not shown a pennon. What could he be up to?" Rumored horrors rose to mind.

"No idea. 'Tis unlikely he's to meet with anyone. He's sent no messages along the journey. Before I raised your signal, the whole party was asleep save for the warlord taking the midwatch, and he's not moved ten steps from the prince these three days."

"Then why did you fetch me here?" I wasn't to go in until he had some sense of Osriel's plan. Then I could observe whom he met or what he did from a reasonably safe distance.

"Because they've told me I'm to guide them to a particular spot tomorrow—one I'll be told only at dawn—and then I'll be free to leave with my pay, as they've a *map* to take them the rest of the way. If I argue, they'll get suspicious, and if I follow, he'll know. And once I'm dismissed, they could head out anywhere—to the battlefield, the village, the river . . .

caves . . . springs . . . the region is pocked with places. So drink up your cider, paratus, and take up your pack. You must stay close on our trail tomorrow. When Osriel's coin touches my palm, the mission is yours."

We made it to the hovel where Prince Osriel lay by first light. It sat atop a greening hill creased deep with rock gullies like an old man's warty face. The site provided excellent views of the rolling landscape on every side and escape routes in any direction. From the size of the steel-capped man circling the hut—the formidable warlord, Grey said—the prince could sleep nowhere safer or better guarded.

As Grey rode up the hill, I remained flat on the ground in a beech copse. He'd promised I'd see which way they went. I'd told him to have a care.

Sentimental, Inek called me, to speak such things aloud. It was a knight's duty to take his best care—for the success of his mission and his brothers of the Order. But then, some of us had to be reminded of that.

Was it my own stubborn ignorance that had half the kingdom wanting to kill me and my family? Goddess Mother, I had a sister. Why hadn't I asked her name? A spark, Bastien called her, a girl that I loved. Even beyond magic, how could I not feel her existence? Unless I'd failed at keeping her safe and they'd killed her, too . . .

No. After the mission I would think. For now, I had to watch and be ready.

Damp seeped through my braies and crept slowly up toward my shirt. I dug fingers into the stony earth and dragged myself forward. History and art together would be useful for a knight. To discover truth . . . to solve murders . . . to show people how to unlock complex spells and save themselves . . . The work of justice.

A wrenching jolt in my head warned me to stop. But I could not let it go. Since my first days at Evanide I had hungered for greater magic, devouring and relishing each day's advancement. Knowing some mysterious talent dwelt inside me, inaccessible, had been difficult enough. But to touch this soil under my fingers and know that in other times I could unlock its past was an exquisite torment.

Inek said a paratus's bent could be unmuted at any time the Marshal judged appropriate. Its use could be woven into the last months of his preparation. But what of *dual* bents? Would the Marshal risk giving both of them back? He could not afford a knight to go mad.

The real question was what did *Damon* intend? Damon, who had sent me to the Order and who chose my missions. This one, too. What game was he playing and what gamepiece was named Lucian de Remeni?

A good thing Morgan had laid some kind of sleep over me when we arrived at the lake. A gift of the long-lived, she'd said, as she kept watch at my side. When I'd waked, she was gone, and two smoked fish and a pile of raspberries awaited me. Thus, unlike poor Grey, who'd not slept in over a day, I was rested and fed. Just more than half crazed.

A distant call brought me alert. Grey's horse grazed on the hilltop, but he was nowhere to be seen. And where was the warlord? *Idiot!*

Just before panic sent me running up the hill to search for tracks, a soldier rounded the corner of the hut. Then Grey came up from behind, leading three horses. A youth followed close with three more. Four men emerged from the house and joined the guard and the youth. Easy to pick out the prince. Five wore leather and steel. One wore robes and hood of spruce green.

Stories named Osriel the Bastard a horned monster, deformed by his evils, or crippled from bribing his mentor Magrog with limbs or heart or balls, depending on who was telling the story.

In truth he was no giant, but average among his servants. Most other details, including horns or deformities, were hidden by his shapeless garb. But though history named him a man near my own age, his back was slightly bent, and he walked with a noticeable limp.

Before mounting, he stepped away from the others and turned slowly, as if surveying the terrain through the drooping folds of his hood.

I did not think of myself as prone to frights or megrims, but I did trust a brother knight's instincts. I did not twitch an eyelash until he turned away to his mount.

The party wound slowly down the cragged hill on its western flank, Grey in the lead, the prince behind with a stocky warrior close at his shoulder—the bodyguard. The warlord in the steel cap brought up the rear behind youth and two soldiers.

They'd need no map to find the battleground. Thin pillars of black smoke scarred the deep blue of the western horizon. The death stench was likely my imagination, as the day was still and windless, with a gathering haze that dirtied the light. But when they reached the bottom of the hill, their route twined northward through the mounded hills.

Afoot, I scuttered between hillock and rock; paused to make sure they'd rounded another bend; ducked behind a stand of hazel or leafless larch until they were out of sight again. Tracking a riding party of seven was simple.

Staying close enough that they could not leave me behind would be the challenge in country variously open, rocky, and wooded.

The luck of the landscape took us quickly into a dense woodland of oak, beech, and pine. The track was rough and little traveled and wandered through thick underbrush of tor-grass and fragrant juniper. Boulders of every shape—twisted, bulbous, conjoined, heaped, some shoulder high, some taller than three men—protruded from the fragrant earth. The air was heavy under the trees.

An hour or more along the increasingly wild path, the party halted and dismounted. Their discussion was of an even temper, though it was impossible to make out words from behind a tree. When the solid thud of hooves came my way, I slipped to the ground and shrank into a knot.

A single rider approached, retracing the route we'd taken. Not in a hurry. Humming, and . . . jingling coins. I grinned as Grey rode slowly past, tossing two coins in the air one more time before stuffing them in his waist pocket, even as the weight of responsibility settled on my shoulders. *Dallé cineré, brother,* I bade him in fervent silence.

Stretched out on my belly, I slithered forward through a patch of mushrooms.

The prince perched on a fallen tree, his back to me. The bristle-haired bodyguard and the warlord crouched before their master, the three heads together over a sheet of parchment. Their discussion remained damnably quiet. I'd have to be sitting on their boots to hear.

The two other warriors stood well away, faces alert and scanning the wood. The unarmed squire minded the horses, examining hooves, legs, and girth straps. When done, he led the beasts one by one to a leaf-choked pool overhung with willow and birch. Its murky water leaked into a shallow rivulet that vanished quickly into the woodland.

What was here to interest a dark-minded prince in the midst of a war for his father's throne? Carefully, without invoking any spellcraft, I closed my eyes to the visible world and opened myself to magic.

A lovely enchantment, intricate as spiderweb and strong as silk thread, hung amid the prince and his men. I recognized it immediately, as it was so like that of the map hanging in the Marshal's outer chamber—a Cartamandua map, one of the finest made. It was said that Cartamandua maps could lead one to places you wouldn't find otherwise. Was that what Osriel was about—hunting some secret place, a place of magic or omen, treasure or revelation?

Yet another enchantment lurked in close proximity to the map, this one a simmering evil that robbed me of breath, an enchantment crafted of pain and fire, blood and despair. In all my training at Evanide, in countless mission studies, I'd never encountered such a thing. Without using magic of my own, I could not even guess at its nature. I was glad. The thought of probing deeper sickened me, in the way of sticking my hand in a dead man's rotting belly to retrieve his heart.

Rising emotion raddled one man's unintelligible words. Anger? Frustration? The warlord sat back on his haunches and bellowed, "Mount up!"

The warlord's command might have been a dog biting the squire's backside or the guards' boots. Packs and waterskins were quickly stowed. The squire brought the horses.

An Evanori warlord was dedicated and trained from birth to defend his lord, his mountain fastness, and his hoard of gold. Mumbling under his breath, this one fussed about his warhorse, doing everything the squire had already done before swinging himself easily into the saddle.

The prince's bodyguard gave Osriel a hand up to a bay gelding. Still no sight of Osriel's face. But the bodyguard's . . . Goddess preserve. Half his face was a crumpled, leathery ruin. Burnt, I'd guess, but more than that. Bones crushed, leaving jaw and cheek sunken and the eye but a dark slit. A bristle of gray-brown hair left this horror fully exposed. *He* should be wearing the hood.

The prince led the way toward the willow grove and the shady pool. Bodyguard and squire followed close. The warlord held an urgent conversation with the two soldiers, and to my dismay, the pair wheeled their mounts and took the path Grey had ridden an hour previous.

"Your heads roll if you're not back before sundown!" called the warlord after them. "Camp here."

Ride with the wind, brother! Concern for Grey beckoned me after the pair. But I knew what Inek would say. Grey, too. The mission lay ahead of me, not behind. The Order needed to know what wickedness this prince planned. If that single dread enchantment I'd detected was the prince's work, it justified their concern.

When the prince's party disappeared behind the shaggy willows, I skulked after them. Had I not watched them squeeze between a protruding boulder and the pond, I'd never have found the path.

The pond was far bigger than I'd thought, being the bottom end of a long lake. The upper end was sealed by a jumble of earth, wood, and stone, as if a divine sculptor had dropped all the waste from the earth's making there. The far shore was a scrubby bank of earth and loose rock.

But the four horsemen traveled the nearer shore. A massive scarp hemmed the lake along this side. The vertical stone was taller than five men, seamed with dirt and roots from the forested swell above. Between the foot of the scarp and the lake, a shelf of stone scarce wide enough for a single horse served as a path.

The path's direct course was not at all friendly to spies. Did I step out to follow the four, a single backward glance would note me. So I held still until they were but tiny figures at the far end of the lake. They dismounted.

I waited. And waited. Squinting into the watery sunlight, I picked out horses . . . but no men. *Towers of Idrium!* Where had they gone?

I pelted along the shelf path, sparing naught to prevent all this from being a waste. Yet even a hundred paces from the towering blockade that bounded the lake, I saw no place they could have gone. I'd felt no surge of magic. My gaze scoured the path-side cliff and the massive debris pile that ended the lake, though I could not imagine a limping man in robes climbing either one. Nothing moved but songbirds, squalling at circling crows, and trickles of water that seeped through the debris to feed the lake.

Had I gone blind?

The horses waited patiently, tethered to branches protruding from the scarp. Soothing the beasts with whispers and pats, I squeezed past them along the verge of the lake, and discovered a natural illusion that rivaled anything of magic.

What I had believed to be the leftmost portion of the lake's terminal blockage was, in fact, a flat wall that protruded from the scarp to the water's edge. Color and texture blended it into the actual background, neatly blocking an observer's view of the last section of the waterside path—a hundred paces at most. A ledge just below the surface of the lake—one boot long— would allow one person at a time to get around the end of the protruding wall. Carefully.

Time to choose. Go forward, or retreat to the mushroom patch to wait for the four—and the other two soldiers—to return. Instinct said that if I retreated, I might as well abandon the mission.

Not a breath or shuffle could I hear from beyond the wall. Setting my inner foot gingerly onto the underwater ledge, I gripped the largest knob I could find and swung my outer foot around until it found a horizontal surface. Shifting my weight forward and inward, I pushed myself to standing on level ground beyond the wall.

Impressions pelted me like hailstones of lead.

A glimmer of torchlight inside the gaping maw of a cave.

An astonishingly familiar splash of white above the cave mouth.

And the certainty that I, the fool of a paratus, was not alone.

In the eyeblink's gap before the battering ram slammed into my head, I had already turned halfway round to note the man-sized niche in the protruding wall and the monstrous face and thick body that occupied it. My bracelets and a burst of magic generated a rope of light, mitigating the blow that laid me out. Thus I could see straight into the bodyguard's red-centered eye glaring down at me and recognize it as a well of pain and fire, blood and despair.

CHAPTER 14

The half-faced bodyguard tried to drag me into the cave by one arm wrapped around my neck. I elbowed him in the knee. Dizzy and confused, I was unsure what that might accomplish, but after so many hours in Evanide's training room, it was wretched to be hauled about like a piglet.

I shouldn't have done it. Nor should I have bothered with any other move I attempted in our brief grapple. Never in my fiercest bouts at Evanide had I suffered such overmatching skill. His fists were very hard and very experienced, and he knew how to inflict the maximum discomfort while ensuring I remained conscious to appreciate his technique. Eventually he left me flat, convinced my bones were dust and wishing the rest of me was, as well.

One advantage of surrender was that I got a good look at the splash of white above the cave mouth. The image of a splayed hand had been carefully cut from white stone and embedded in the gray rock.

Then the bodyguard threw me over his shoulder with shameful ease and carried me into the cave. My senses reported naught but a blur of rock and torchlight and shadows blacker than seemed righteous. Every particle of my being hurt. Yet once deposited on my knees on a hard floor, with my head shoved downward in submission, I concluded that naught was actually broken save a tooth. I did not presume that my condition would improve. Anyone who could create the enchantment that bound this powerful man must own a roster of torments so vile I could not imagine them.

"So this is our shadow, the wisp of cloud who drifted in our wake for most of a day." Cold, clear, heavy with dread portents, the voice came from everywhere at once. Whimsy, painted in poison. "So odd he is, don't you think, Voushanti? But with skills, you say?"

Were it my heart's deepest desire, I could not have lifted my head. My hands drooped limp and useless beside my knees.

"Some, lord. Not so much as he presumes."

Inky shadows darted across the stone floor. Whirled in tornadic frenzy. Brushed slowly across the scrapes on my hands, stinging like brine.

Gatzi's teeth, I could feel them—the shadows. Invisible fingers traced the contours of my face and slid down my arms to my fingertips. Had I been able to move I would have tried to scrape them off. As it was they left a sticky taint like pine sap, though the odor reminded me more of the boneyard outside Necropolis Caton.

"The full mask is most curious," said the lord. "Not at all what pureblood masters prescribe, yet these hands have talents. And these silver bands"—a light tapping on my bracelets by no instrument that I could see set my skin creeping—"I do believe wonders lurk inside them."

Only the most perceptive sorcerer could detect magic lurking behind silver's brilliance. Yet Osriel was halfblood, anathema to our kind, one who represented a pureblood parent's careless extinction of the divine gift. In Osriel's case, it was his mother, a pureblood who'd become the mistress of a beloved king and died a few years after giving birth to . . . what? A charlatan? A coward? Or a monster who dabbled in evil to enhance his degenerate magic? The Order needed to know. *I* needed to know why he sought a cave marked with a white hand.

"Who is this man of clever illusion?" I said as haughtily as one could from his knees with bowed head. "A shadow twister with a brutish, devil-marked servant?"

A leash whipped round my neck, dragging my head forward and down until my nose touched the floor. Stinging neck and scraped chin testified the instrument was no illusion, yet neither was it made of leather or fiber. The Order's ropes of scorching light tangled limbs, but vanished as quickly as they touched their marks. The frigid tail of Osriel's leash did not let go.

"Insults are a fool's tactic," he said. "Think of something better." The choke strap tightened.

Don't panic. For all he knows you could be his brother's man. He'll get nothing from your corpse. But the world spun dangerously, and I wobbled. The constriction eased half an instant before ending my life.

I gulped breath, blinking until my head cleared.

The strap tightened again ever so slightly, nudging me toward the verge of death. Most people didn't understand how brief a pressure to the neck would kill. This man did.

Dizzy again. No matter resolution, panic nibbled at my belly, at my groin, at my lungs and spirit, even when the pressure relented long enough for my eyes to refocus.

I willed myself calm. Using magic to take a life could drain a sorcerer past his own capacity, warping his talents or obliterating them. One so skilled would know that. But there were things to be learned here. I had to live.

"Dead men answer no questions," I croaked, twisting my head slightly to ease the pressure, perfectly designed to keep one dizzy with terror.

Cold, wicked, mirthless laughter cascaded through the cavern. "What say you, Voushanti? He thinks death would free him from answering."

"I say he is an ignorant spy, lord." The bodyguard grabbed my hair and wrenched my head back, as the invisible leash slid away, its edge keen as a razor knife. Warm blood dribbled down my shirt.

The man in spruce-green robes sat not ten paces from me, perched atop a slab of rock broken from the cave's low ceiling. The height of the slab would put his head on a level with mine were I allowed to stand. From my angle a pale, square, clean-shaven jaw was just visible below the drooping hood. Elsewise one might question whether he was a man at all. His limbs—whatever he had of them—were swallowed by voluminous sleeves and flowing gown.

Voushanti let go of my hair and moved to his master's side. A taint of red gleamed from his ruined eye. His shadow rippled, and his master's garments shifted as if moved by the breath of a great beast. No matter the need to observe, I averted my eyes, my spirit sick.

"I would know what you are, masssked one." The viperous hiss issued from the hood.

The lord's power left no path to avoid danger. His demand left no time to devise elaborate plays. And deception bore its own risks. Yet neither was this his own fastness in Evanore. He had no great numbers of servants and messengers at his beck. Might a bit of truth lure him into revelation?

"I am a historian of pureblood birth, exiled from the society of my kind."

"I doubt that." My heart near leapt out of my skin. The cold, deep whisper sounded just at my ear, as if he knelt at my left shoulder, though he remained motionless on his rock seat. "A *recondeur* walks willing into a gatzé's den? Next you'll say you've no idea who I am."

The pressure bending my back eased. But I didn't wish to invite more choking, so I stayed still.

"I am no *recondeur*, Lord Osriel, Duc of Evanore and Prince of Navronne. Rather I am condemned by family and Registry to walk the world without name, face, or home until my exile is reversed. I use the time to learn. Being a historian, I seek out secrets of the past. Powerful as you are, you can surely test my truth in this."

"Oh, indeed I shall." This time in my other ear. I hated that I jumped, even when expecting it. "What leads you to believe I hold secrets of the past?"

"You may hold secrets or not, Your Grace, but this cavern surely does." Using a magical map to come here, he must know something about the white hand. If I was to learn what he knew, I had to offer something plausible of my own.

"Kneel up."

It was no easy matter to raise up when every muscle and bone felt like a pounded meat custard. And more difficult yet to lift my eyes and face him as if I were an honest man. But he'd bitten my hook.

"The vanished city of Xancheira has ever intrigued me," I said. "A great city founded by Aurellian sorcerers in the days we came to this land. A city renowned for beauty, art, just governance, and most especially, its magic. Then, in the matter of a day, so imperfect history claims, every Xancheiran soul dies and their great city vanishes from the earth, a mystery spawning a thousand hypotheses, but no evidence to prove one or the other as true. I've wandered throughout Navronne listening to tales from mighty hall to Ciceron fireside, while hunting the symbol of Xancheira. Son of a king, you may be familiar with it, a white tree with five branches. . . ."

"I am familiar."

I inclined my back to acknowledge and smiled inside. The shadows had quieted. Though not a comfortable quiet, to be sure.

"Amongst these bits and pieces that make no sense, I've run across mention of another symbol that is very like—"

"A white hand."

"Indeed, lord. Sometimes throughout the span of history, words, symbols, or stories become intertwined, shifting form until one cannot judge whether they are the same or different. My search for the mark of the white hand led me to Lillebras, but there it stalled. I have scoured the countryside with no result. And what should I hear on the eve of a great battle? The Duc of Evanore and a small party—no warlike legion—required a guide intimately familiar with the district. And I think perhaps this lordly prince, reputed a powerful mage in his own right, might have an interest in legends of Xancheira's magic. And so I set myself to find him, and . . ."

I lifted my hands as if to say *here we are.*

"Bring him here."

Voushanti grasped my upper arm with a grip like a bear's jaw. Forthwith, I stood an arm's length from the prince. A hand emerged from the folds of green velvet, a hand that might once have been slender and fine-boned, but was now mottled purple, gray, and red, misshapen at knuckle and joint, the fingers curled in upon themselves.

"Give me your hand, masked one, and say again that you speak truth."

I dared not delay, lest I think too much and shade my declarations with untruth. I laid my grimy fingers in his slightly opened claw. It required every shred of discipline I possessed to keep my hand steady. Surely the fires of Magrog the Tormenter's furnace raged beneath his skin.

As a gale on the seaward wall, power rushed into me, sweeping away thought and caution. I clung desperately to the bones of my story and walled off all else. My hope to dissect Osriel's magic vanished along with the world and time and reasons, until I stood naked in a freezing dark while those scorching fingers examined every part and portion of flesh and spirit.

No, no, no! My spirit recoiled from that touch as it crept closer to the raw and gaping cavity in my breast. And then the bitter touch . . .

My screams set the cavern's fire and shadows dancing with wild abandon. I knew so, because I writhed and fought to escape that darkness, to hold back his touch, to appease the agony in my brow . . . in my breast . . . and in a fiery bridge between the two. Only Voushanti's bear-jaw grip kept my head from slamming into the prince's rock.

"Bring him ale." The hollow command sounded a thousand quellae distant.

The monster shoved me to the floor, where I huddled in a knot, rocking, one fist to my head, one to my breast. *Mask your weakness, madman.* Danger lurked on every side like wolves gathered about a hunter's dying fire. What had he learned? I needed to attack, to obscure, to avert his gaze.

I swallowed the next scream that rose like lava from the pits. But to breathe was a mighty effort, and I could not think of a way to begin. . . .

A tin mug appeared in my shaking hands. I downed the lukewarm ale and grasped reality: the world of gray, shifting light, my mission, the Order. What childish hubris to invite such an assault. Had I exposed my brothers or yielded my name or my will? Goddess Mother, for a mirror glass to look on my own eyes, to ensure they had no red center of pain and despair to mark enslavement.

"My question remains, masked one: What are you?"

"My question for you, prince," I croaked, "is what have you made of me?" I riffled through two years of memory . . . of the meeting with the Danae, with Bastien . . . through the bits and pieces I had learned in the past days, through will and desire and hopes. All seemed my own—Greenshank's. Nothing of Lucian de Remeni.

"Shaping you to my service would pleasure me beyond description." His raw lust oiled my throat and churned my bowels. "But what sculptor can choose proper tools when he cannot describe his medium? Clay? Steel? Diamond? Silver? Yes, perhaps silver. So much lies hidden beneath your tarnished surface as would provide a long winter's study in my mountain fastness. I have never encountered a soul so fragmented as yours."

Pain subsided, leaving body and spirit a raw wound. My mind's fingers grasped at reason and gave me hope that I'd held firm. So, test it . . .

"I am condemned to exile, lord, as I told you."

"So you are. Indeed all you spoke was truth . . . which does not imply that I believe your story. But enough that I shall invite you to examine what I came here to find."

On my feet again, I bowed with what dignity I could muster, chilled to the marrow. Osriel's was no degenerate halfblood magic, but complex beyond my experience and dangerous beyond knowing.

"I offer my knowledge to the task, and an apology for this pitiful show. Your power, lord, humbles me. Alas, disconnection from the practices of my own kind has broken me in many ways."

"Perhaps so." The tenor of this pronouncement leached all ambiguity from the phrase. What did he see in me that confirmed my breakage so firmly?

Heaving a great breath, trying to ignore the whirling particles of night visible from the corner of my eye, I extended my open palm. "Show me, if you will."

Perhaps the prince gestured. Perhaps he spoke. I neither saw nor heard his command. But the half-faced Voushanti shoved me toward the back of the cavern. Firelight danced on a high wall, the mottled gray rock carved into grotesqueries by seeps from above and undercut into swirled alcoves by ancient floods. Our boots crunched on a dirt floor pocked with rubble and milky puddles.

The steel-capped warlord squatted beside a few saddle packs and a small fire built on a stretch of sand. Though I glimpsed no way forward beyond the cavern's back wall, there had to be one. The party's fourth, the squire, was nowhere to be seen.

The warlord stood as we approached, a small leather case in hand. His hawkish face and solid bulk might have been hewn from the granite of his home mountains. An icy glance slashed me as he hurried back toward the prince on his rock throne.

A torch mounted in a rusty bracket marked one of the shadowed alcoves. At closer distance, it came clear that this overhang, scarce a handspan higher than my head, housed a deeper cove than the rest, and an opening at its back.

Voushanti waved me through the alcove into a wide passage. The wavering light of the cavern quickly faded behind us, and the bodyguard carried no lamp. Perhaps the red light in his eyes sufficed for his vision, but I cast a pale magelight. We had to climb over a few rockfalls and duck under low-hanging rock, but in the main, the way was easy enough until my senses detected a tangled shimmer in the air akin to a wall of spiderwebs.

No matter how forcefully I stepped through the enchanted barrier, I got nowhere. Even when I spied a palm-sized rock and with utmost concentration stepped past it, the motion left me where I started. The rock remained in front of me. To one who could not sense the magic, the passage would seem endless.

I doubted the enchantment was the prince's doing. It reminded me of naught so much as the Ciceron commons house and its strange portal. The logic, the colors, the nuances might have been worked by my own hand. A close examination suggested this one was not so impenetrable as that one. But should I break it? Giving aid to Osriel must give any man pause.

I turned to Voushanti, making sure my eyes did not shy from his monstrous face. A further show of weakness would do me no favors. "Has the prince moved beyond this enchantment?"

"The proper question is: Can *you* move beyond it?" His words crackled like flame.

Of course they were testing me. But answers lay ahead. The squire, too, I'd guess.

My blood heated as I examined the spellwork more thoroughly, appreciating Evanide's never-ending practice in locks and barriers. The spell's release was buried deep, but not difficult. I infused a bit of magic. The barrier vanished like smoke.

The passage opened into a small chamber, where expectations were quickly unsettled. No squire waited. Indeed, no one had visited this place for a very long time.

Dust lay thick on the stone floor, unmarred by footsteps. A pile of rubble collapsed from the ceiling filled half the chamber. Ancient artists had painted horses, deer, and ox-like beasts in red and blue over the walls, punctuated here and there with unfamiliar god-signs. Yet it was not dead men's art that set my heart racing, but the round arch of hammered bronze set into the far wall.

No weaving of threaded light filled the bronze frame. Only rock, scarred, cracked, and pocked as any cave wall, half grown over with hardened seeps. It had narrowly escaped being blocked by the rockfall.

Shadows flitted across the wall and the arch, graying the light. I whipped my head around. The hooded prince stood in the tunnel doorway, Voushanti at his side. "So our journey is not wasted, after all."

"He opened the way without blinking," said Voushanti.

"I suspected he could. I deem him a man of many useful talents."

The portal in the hirudo had been hidden behind a simple illusion of plaster and barred with a blood seal, but this one . . . I touched the stone inside the arch. Prepared this time, I did not flinch when fire shot up my arm, as it had when I touched the tapestry of light. Yet, even knowing what to look for, I could detect no magical seal, only the fire. Perhaps the portal was dead.

The prince joined me beside the arch. I did not step away, which was as difficult as anything I'd done on this journey.

"What kind of portal is filled with stone?" he said. "There should be light. Motion. A spell to unravel to open the way." One of his misshapen fingers traced the line of a curling bronze stem, making my own hair curl with a frisson of enchantment. Or terror. Osriel knew exactly what he was looking for. Where had he learned it?

"A *portal*, you say, lord?" I tried to sound surprised. "A blocked doorway, it seems, or unfinished."

He touched the stone, but just like Bastien in the hirudo, he did not recoil. Why did I experience the fiery rejection, when neither Osriel or Bastien did?

"I wish you to use all your skills to tell me what you find here." His will was as palpable a presence as his bodyguard. How would I know if he was forcing me when the command was exactly what I wanted to do?

"This is real stone," I said, rapping my knuckle on it, "solid, no illusion to hide a portal."

That was true. Perhaps in my old life I could have drawn the right person's portrait to reveal the mysteries of this portal, as I'd done for the Cicerons in Palinur. But even if I remembered how to invoke my bent, I wouldn't do it for Osriel.

"What did you hope to find beyond this wall, lord prince?"

"You said it. Magic."

The word was shaped with the craving of a twistmind for his nivat. It whispered of torments like those I'd seen in his bodyguard's eyes—of pain, despair, and hopeless ruin, of a man who well might seek unholy spoils on a battlefield. If the place called Sanctuary was a part of what the Danae called the true lands, and these true lands were somehow bound to the health of the world as Morgan's father believed, what would it mean if a skilled sorcerer without scruple could walk free there?

I could not hold back my shudder. Did that please the one whose gaze burned through his green hood?

Osriel wandered away toward the wall paintings and the rune-like god-signs. "And you, masked one?" he said over his shoulder. "What do you seek here?"

"A story," I said, in all honesty. "What more could a historian desire?"

Damon had not chosen my missions and the Archivist's revelations at random. What great purpose linked an ancient massacre and a recent one with the warring sons of a great king, and a man with two bents? With Xancheira and Cicerons and Danae? I'd never seen any hint that Damon knew aught of my dealings with Danae—or anything called the true lands or the Everlasting or the boundaries between them. Surely the tale was bigger than Damon.

Gods, what I would give to know. Damon's purpose—that piece of the mystery—had torn my life apart. But my head felt like an anvil. Somewhere deep between my brows the pain of Osriel's ravaging yet lingered. Please gods, let that be all he'd left there.

My fingers strayed to the bronze frame. The flowers and beasts wrought in its gleaming surface were exquisite, so real I could smell the sweetness of the blooming lavender and hear the mawk of the crow and the rustle of the vines. Veins and sinews heated as I touched a pair of dancers twined in an eternal arabesque.

Without consideration, I reached deep, letting magic flow through my fingers . . .

. . . and I near drowned in light and sound and sensation. *Men in velvet gowns, women in embroidered caps or long scarves, and children decked out in ribbons of every hue danced through cobbled streets to rippling lutes and sawing vielles. Solstice fires blazed in healthy fields. Boisterous gaiety erupted in answer to sprays of brilliant fireworks against the night sky . . . shifting into whispered reverence. As the fireworks ceased and bonfires burned low, ears heeded fainter music, while lights of blue and sapphire flickered through veils of mist. . . .*

I strained to see. *No, wait!*

The image vanished as if whipped by a sea gale, and still the deluge came. *A quiet invasion from the distant east, impoverished Wanderers from the ancient homeland, their small magics used for thieving crops and horses, cattle and sheep, careless burning and rapine. Annoyances became years of violence. Vengeance that scarred the land. Riders in black tabards charged across the plains, whooping as they chased down the ragtag Wanderers. Lances of fire and ropes of light ensnared the wild ones—fierce men and women with curved blades and dangling earrings—and they were marched back to the city where pennons blazoned with the white tree flew. Shouts rang out: City of glory! All Hail, City of the Everlasting!*

In a blink, all vanished. But when I closed my eyes again, images and sounds and words raced across my mind's canvas, blurred before I could grasp their story. Reason insisted I could control the chaos, but it could not tell me how. Yet only one thing could be its source—the furnace between my eyes pouring molten streams of magic down neck, shoulders, arms, and through my fingers. The magic of my blood. My bent.

Exultant, I watched the sun blaze and listened to storms of years roll across mountains and plains. Only sensible to consider the mysteries that dogged me. Xancheira, Cicerons, Danae . . .

A wintry gale howled through a ring of standing stones . . . curved blade and fire lance lay crossed on the center stone in the eternal sign of truce . . . blessings of peace rung in by cascades of joyous bells. Boughs of fir and yew on every lintel as the crowd gathered. Hosannas faded to awe as tall figures, male and female, skin scribed in sapphire light, laid their own solstice wreath atop the weapons. Meanings fluttered on the wind like prayer flags in mountain temples, like the return of birds in spring, like the first green of field and forest: a pledge . . . a promise of hope . . . a profound holiness shaped of generosity and mutual sacrifice. For the truest danger came from the south . . . from purebloods . . . from the Registry . . .

Too soon that image faded, leaving eyes pricking and heart full, though I could explain none of it. Only time and peace might fit the pieces together. Meanwhile the flow continued. *Towers rose above the town, markets bustled, and everywhere grew flowers of red and yellow . . . which too quickly yielded to hisses of anxiety and the roaring, blistering heat of a furnace, the acrid odor of molten bronze and a splash of bright enchantment.*

"Must have these ready tonight," said a fading voice, as its owner tapped on a

bronze frame just like the one my hand touched. "The archon will open the ways only a short time . . . the Wanderers must pass . . . until the time is right and they return with our salvation . . ."

Before I could grasp the meaning of these things, my stomach lurched, and the world dropped out from under me. And when I opened my eyes, I was in a wholly different place.

CHAPTER 15

"Seasons have I waited to meet thee again, Lucian. I feared thee lost or broken, our hope failed."

The Dané sat on a narrow hilltop of emerald grass, pocked with white stones and buttercups. Her bare feet scarce bent a blade as she rose. The weighty gray-blue evening sky promised storm. Yet did it portend whirlwinds of epic magnitude, it could not rattle heart and bone like the sharp-edged silver of her gards.

With all the grace I could muster after Voushanti's beating, I bowed. "*Envisia seru*, Sentinel. Mortal danger stalks me every moment I am here, so before all I must ask: Where are they, those humans who traversed the portal two winters past? Are they safe?"

A sea breeze teased my neck, ruffled the Dané's drapery of spidersilk, and tangled her red-brown hair. Her green eyes, very like Morgan's, glinted with silver lights as she examined me.

"Protected, else what is Sanctuary?" But she did not smile. "Thy deed was worthy, knowing thine own passage was not yet possible. Indeed, the travelers have testified to thy quality."

"They took all the risk," I said. "Such courage to step through. I doubt I helped with that."

"Thou didst send thy heart with them. Braver than sending thine own self." Her fingers brushed my brow, shooting sparks into every part of me. "But if thou'rt in mortal danger, I deem it best not to tell where the travelers bide or aught that might betray us."

That, of course, made damnably good sense, though I'd no idea what she meant about my heart.

"What is it you want of me?"

"To set us free, of course. All of us—your kind and my own. Thou'rt the only one can do it. Come back when 'tis safe, and I'll tell thee all."

"This place," I said, pulling away so as to see our surroundings. "It's real. . . ."

For certain I no longer occupied a Navron cave with Osriel the Bastard. To the north the hillside descended into a folded landscape of grassy knolls, white-boned knees, and soft hollows that cupped ponds or lakes. At its foot, five white-ridged spits of land protruded into the heaving sea. Exactly as Bastien had described the landscape of my transports. The white hand.

The view to the south revealed this hill to be isolate in a crescent bay. A short bar of land—the wrist of the hand—connected the hill and its spits to a rolling coast forested with new-leafed birches. The wrist was of a width that perhaps two horses could traverse it abreast. No horses were in sight anywhere, nor were towns or villages or any sign of human habitation.

I'd no time to question. Every moment vanished from the chamber risked Osriel's interest.

"A great deal has happened since last we last spoke. I can't remember how to go back or how I might visit you again. My magic doesn't always bring me."

"It is my choice as sentinel whether to give thee entry, even when thy magic opens the boundaries. 'Tis often too great a risk, for the danger here grows mighty and terrible. Thou needs must find the surer way to come—the Path of the White Hand. Till then, I cannot let thee tread this land too long nor expend thy magic here nor draw upon the land to replenish it. Trapped wouldst thou be, unable to return to thine own lands until the Everlasting births another human of thy power and . . . quality."

"Trapped! Unable—"

"I'll send thee back." Her fingers swept my eyelids closed.

"Wait!" I said. "Before I go, lady . . . tell me your name and what you are."

"My name is Safia. I am summer evening light upon sweet grass. Sun and shadow." Her sadness touched my heart, though I had no reason.

Then her hand brushed my brow.

The dusty closeness of the cave cut off the sea wind. My eyes refused to open, for surely they'd see the bastard prince awaiting explanation. Bastien said I vanished for mere moments at a time. No one with Osriel's skills could have missed the power of my bent, but had he noted my absence?

"Now, historian, tell me your story." The hooded man rested his back against the painted wall, faced in my direction, though *direction* and *seeing* seemed to have no connection where Osriel's observation was concerned. "Complete this time."

"I should have warned you," I said, as lies and half-truths, spells and diversions battled for primacy. What could I possibly say to blunt the malevolence filling the chamber like black smoke? Would the choke leash come next?

"Warned?" Neither Osriel's quiet intensity nor his manic shadows eased my jiddering gut. "Need I prove to you how sorely I take offense at deception?"

"You need prove nothing, lord. Your deeds have witnessed both to your puissance and your strict requirements. My breath comes short already, even before I feel the noose."

I scrambled for ideas and words to express them. All I wanted was to get away from this devilish prince and consider every word and image of the last hour. That wasn't going to happen easily, with Osriel ten steps away. Voushanti blocked the only way out, and if my vision had not failed me, the steel-capped warlord waited just behind him. And what use a blast of fire or even my last resort—the *impenetrable wall* enchantment—in this rat-trap of a chamber?

"These years of exile have taught me much of my weaknesses, poor discipline, and self-indulgence. Did I babble obscenities, lord? Or curse at you, or gods' save me, did I threaten you with violence or unseemly . . . intimacies?"

"No."

Curse it, villain! Tell me what you saw. "Terrible aberrations that should have been trained out of me when I was a child seem to expose themselves when I probe deep-layered history. Please take this as no insult, Your Grace, but do you know how a historian's bent presents?"

"Sensory manifestations, so I understand, a rushing river of impressions derived from the object of study. And the historian's skills must bind and constrain that river and its tributaries into—as you said—a story. *Tell* me the story."

I held up my hands as if they might diffuse his dangerous impatience. "There, you see, you've hit upon the *other* thing I failed to warn you of—my skills. You see, my superiors prisoned me for a matter of months. I was very close to madness. And whether from that or other circumstances, I lost my skills of interpretation. Imagine me standing in that river, as you so perfectly described it, and feeling it flow over, around, and through me without the ability to constrain it. Over these years of my exile—easy to understand the shame I brought upon my family—I've not improved them. Perhaps if we were to speak of what I experienced just now, a wise and knowledgeable prince might make sense of it. I've seen the city of Xancheira, I believe, and battles and peacemaking and even—I hesitate to say, lest you think I'm mad again—two Danae standing—"

"Faugh!" bellowed the monstrous bodyguard. "Have you not heard enough of this babble, lord? He tells you only what you want to hear. Let me twist his neck twice around and perhaps he can find a word of explanation that is not a lie!"

The prince stretched a grotesque finger Voushanti's way, and with a single burst of scouring enchantment, dropped the big man to his knees. "I did not ask your advice, dead man. And do not speak of my desires again, lest I starve you."

When the finger swung round to me, I kept my palms spread and open. Did I touch my silver bracelets at that moment, I'd not have given a dried pea for my chances of taking another breath.

"You saw two of the long-lived beyond this portal?"

"Not beyond the doorway, lord, for as I said, it is blocked. I glimpsed them in an image drawn by my bent." This was not the time for embellishment. Nor to ask him how he knew the term *long-lived*. I'd never heard it, save from Morgan and her kin. What would I dare risk to hear what he knew of the Danae and their true lands?

The prince's arms wrapped round his chest, squeezing as if to crush his human heart. His silence grated on my spirit worse than his threats. Nor did I know whether the pressure squeezing my own chest was his wrath or simple terror. But I dared not speak before he did.

"Get him out of here." Osriel waved that dreadful hand at the kneeling bodyguard. His voice, so smooth and cool, had taken on a heated roughness. "Ensure he takes no notion to leave us, for I would talk of vanished cities and mythical beings with this smooth-tongued historian. But my own dread master demands an accounting just now."

The stone beneath my boots trembled, and the dead cold chamber took on a furnace heat and a morbid shimmer that raised every hair on my body. I'd scarce choked back the invocation of my last resort, when Voushanti gripped my arm tighter than ever. The hawk-faced warlord stepped aside to let us pass, revealing the missing squire hiding his face in his hands. Had any adder brought to a market faire ever inspired such a careful dance as Osriel of Evanore?

The iron-fisted Voushanti and I had not gotten so far as the thready remnants of the web enchantment when the prince called after us. "And then, *historian*, we shall strip you of your mask and your lies, and hear how it was you vanished as you stood in your river of magic."

It was well the prince called the warning. My greedy soul had already been contriving how I might learn what he knew before taking flight. But out on the seaward wall, Inek had warned me how it was hubris to taunt Serena Fortuna when she provided us a way out of an impossible situation. My life had value. I had answers the Order needed. And being in the grip of a devil, with an Evanori warlord and an angry Osriel the Bastard close behind, was as near impossible as I wished to visit.

For a handful of moments when we emerged from the passage and the shadowed alcove, Voushanti and I were alone. As I knew he would, the furious bodyguard shoved me to the pitted floor. Controlling the fall, I rolled to my belly. With a touch of a bracelet and a short burst of magic, a hand of flame shoved the bodyguard toward the rear wall. Another touch, another burst, and a whirlwind picked up dust and gravel and released it in the direction my finger told it—straight into the passage we'd just left.

I leapt to my feet and ran, grinning as Voushanti roared. I'd shaped the fire spell to feed on a victim's anger. The more furious Voushanti got, the hotter he would get and the more ferocious the pressure backing him to the wall. But an agonized scream from deep in the portal chamber quickly erased all childish pleasure. What unseen *master* tormented Osriel the Bastard?

I bolted for the cavern mouth, eyes over my shoulder, cursing when my feet got tangled in a leather pannier left near the fire. My stumble knocked over a stack of fist-sized caskets of tarnished silver, tumbling their contents in the sand.

Everlasting mercy!

Eyes. The silver caskets had spilled out eyes cut from a human body, washed clean and wrapped in dread enchantment. Eyes that had once given light to a man's knowing. That had looked on his lover or his children or the sun.

Sky Lord's wrath, what could make a man who had felt the pulse of divine magic in his veins resort to such profane cruelty? Many people believed the soul resided in the eyes. I hardly knew what I believed of gods and souls, but even with half a mind I knew the world's glory shone through our eyes, as did its pain and despair, and every aspect that made us different from beasts.

A rain-soaked evening waited beyond the cave mouth. I'd hoped for darkness, but charcoal sky and steady rain would serve for decent cover. I swung quickly round the masking wall onto the lakeside path. The horses were gone.

My curses could have scythed a hay meadow. Without a mount to speed my escape, the path was now as dangerous a trap as the portal chamber. The two soldiers had been ordered to return to the lower end of the lake by sundown or forfeit their heads. I'd no reason to doubt they were there. Voushanti and the warlord could arrive at any moment. Osriel, too, if his *accounting* left anything of him. I needed to get off the path. Up or down; cliff or water.

The cliff was not so high, but every moment climbing I'd be exposed. Any man who'd trained at Evanide could survive in the water, as long as he had magic to aid him when the body's reserves ran out. But I'd no idea how much power I had left. Only experience enabled a sorcerer to judge his reserves, and I owned no memory of using my bent. For certain, once the signs of depletion set in, it would already be too late. Submerged in the middle of this lake, with the cold sapping my strength like a tyro downs ale, would be no time to discover the price of my historical venture.

So it had to be up. And fast. And quiet.

Again I blessed Inek and the hateful hours he had forced us up the cliffs on the coast south of the lighthouse, no matter fog, rain, or sleet. Though dauntingly vertical, this scarp was not a tenth the height, and was seamed and cracked like an old sailor's face. I scrambled up.

But beyond the blocks and cracks, easy hand- and toeholds vanished. Rain slicked the rock, erasing every bulge where my boots might hold the face for a push upward. Water sluiced over my head and spattered into my eyes. Twice I had to retreat and seek an alternate route, when encroaching night and rain left me blind to a next hold. But fear of the exposed and vulnerable position drove me upward as fast as I could haul my battered carcass. At least the pummeling rain should cover my noise.

Perhaps halfway up the wall, a tenuous handhold gave way in a splatter of grit and pebbles. My heart rattled like a sculptor's hammer when a toehold did the same. Only a meager protrusion and my left hand jammed in a crack held me on the wall. My wrist bone near snapped before I could find more reliable support.

Too fast, idiot. Too fast. I clung to the wall like a spider. A cold, terrified, miserable spider, unable to see top or bottom, unable to see anything but myself in a bone-shattered heap on the lakeside path, with Osriel of Evanore and his red-eyed monster standing over me, flensing knives in hand ready to expose my bones—and harvest my eyes. Yet immobility wasn't going to keep me unbroken either, for the longer I held still, the less feeling I had in fingers and toes.

With infinite care, I stretched and reached. My fingers clawed at the little pocket hidden above me, ensuring a firm hold remained once the debris was clear. Then I found a solid foothold. Shift weight. Push upward. Reach . . . Again . . .

Where were they? Terror had erased all sense of time, but surely Osriel and his party should be below me with torches . . . magelight . . . paralyzing magic. The enchantments I'd thrown at them were well made and persistent, but anyone with the prince's skill should be able to counter them. I wasn't mistaken about his power. Of all things I had been taught, it was how to judge my enemy. And this prince was my enemy. He sought power in the realms of the Danae. Where else had he sought it using human eyes to pay his tally? I'd no reason to believe he would not survive to use what he'd bought.

I'd heard both knights and trainees at Evanide dismiss Eodward's third son. I had to survive this and tell them we dismissed the Bastard at our peril. At the world's peril.

So I climbed. And when I hauled myself over the rim of the scarp, scraping my face on the gnarled roots and rocks that kept the forest lands from washing into the lake below, doubting I could crawl another body length, I grabbed a sturdy sapling, stood up, and staggered forward.

Once away from the rim of the cliff, I dared a faint magelight to help me find the track down to the clearing at the lower end of the lake. Two narrow trails petered out quickly. But a third seemed more promising, definitely wider, and it penetrated a more open woodland. More interesting, a most definite aroma of horse rose from my boots. Fresh in the last few days. Multiple horses heading *up* the hill.

How likely was it a party of horsemen had come up this way so late in the day with no destination closer than Lillebras, probably a day's ride?

Had the squire taken the horses up to graze while I was being interrogated by his master? Facing a long slog afoot with a mounted chase, I'd best find out. I reversed course.

Doubts crept in as I trudged up the ever-steeper hill through the rain, getting ever closer to a man I feared, albeit separated by thick layers of earth and rock. To leave their mounts so far out of reach seemed careless. Twice a rustling in the brush sent me to ground, dousing my magelight.

About the time the rain stopped, the trees thinned and vanished. The track leveled, curving around the slope. My footsteps and weary breaths, so pronounced under the trees, vanished into open air.

Squatting low, I extended my senses as far as I could without magic . . . and then a little farther yet. Ahead were a muddy hillside with nothing growing higher than my knees, a rocky outcrop the size of a house, and horses. Four of them. Right in the middle of the rock. Or rather, as I discovered when I crept closer, left to graze in the lee of the giant rock pile. No human was anywhere close.

The lack of pursuit puzzled me. Perhaps Osriel assumed I could not get far on foot in the night and the rain. He knew I was alone. I didn't like to think what else he knew of me, after his ravaging. Yet how could I complain, when the knife he'd used to pry out my truth had somehow cut the bonds of my bent?

Summoning whatever calm an escapee altogether too close to a devilish pursuer could muster, I strolled past the horses, giving them wide berth. I brushed the bushes and hummed to let them know I was near. They were clearly well trained and experienced, as they'd been left with naught but ground ties, but a bit of caution ensured they'd not run until I was safely mounted.

I chose the warlord's bay. He was likely strong enough to get me back to Evanide and unlikely to be spooked by gouts of magic being flung about along the way.

"Hey, young sir," I said, softly, standing to one side. "Might a tired para-tus request your aid? He'd be a lighter burden than your master."

He turned his head in my direction, and I held out my hand. "I'm not so fearsome as those you travel with. Sadly I don't have anything for you, either. You've likely eaten better than I today."

He watched, unbothered, as I sidled close, and I was soon stroking his muzzle and his neck. A beautiful beast. And Goddess Mother, so warm.

"Come, good fellow," I said, stroking the bay's neck, soothing as best I could with my own spirit in tumult. "We've a way to go and none must stop us. It will be mostly up to you, but I'll provide a little direction."

Laying a hand on his muzzle and the other on his lead, I whispered "home-ward" and let magic flow through both hands at once. No need to visualize what home I meant. Evanide was all I knew. Once I'd threaded his lead under and around one cheek band and through his mouth, I grabbed hold of mane and withers, and threw myself onto his back.

He wasn't sure of me at first, but I got him headed for his companions. We needed to scatter them. The squire's sturdy mare grazed nearest the rocks and as I slapped her on her rump, I noticed a dark, gaping hole in the granite . . . a cave . . . and a shadowy movement just inside.

Instinct screamed warning; realization slapped me. This hill surely housed the portal cavern that opened onto the lake. The cursed hole must connect to it . . . its postern gate. My enemies had only to stroll through tunnels to meet me.

"What a bold rogue you are, masked one, prying where you have no business. We shall surely have a game for the ages once you are in chains!" The cold challenge and the massive blast of power arrived at the same time, scarce a heartbeat after I touched the raised arrow on my left bracelet that triggered my *impenetrable wall*, draining every particle of magic in me to feed it.

The collision of Osriel's magic and my own set off a concussion that rumbled the earth. The rock behind the shadowed prince cracked with jagged orange fire, and the horses I planned to scatter galloped wildly into the night. The bay tried to do the same, and I held on with every shred of strength I could muster and let him run.

If I could but stay on his back, and he could avoid breaking a leg or careening off the cliff into the lake, my spellwork would guide us home to Evanide. Once there I'd serve the works of justice, as well as a cold fury that would not be appeased until I saw Osriel of Evanore, Prince of Navronne, in his grave.

CHAPTER 16

Somewhere in the moorlands west of Lillebras, I slid off the horse. That's what must have happened. The bay cropped the thick grass ten paces away from me, unspooked. I lay flat, and though my body complained of aches and bruises aplenty, a tender cheekbone, and a swollen lip courtesy of Osriel's monstrous bodyguard, it displayed no additional signs of blood or breakage. Wringing out my wet clothes would have made them more comfortable, but with plump clouds hung so low over the distant hills like ripe grapes, there was no use in it.

So I lay there on my back too cold to shiver, too empty to hunger, too weary to think beyond the green, wet wilderness. After using the impenetrable wall, it would be days until I could summon magic. Maybe forever. I needed to get back on the horse.

"Stay with me, beast," I mumbled. "We need to move."

When the rain came, I opened my mouth and drank until my belly bulged. Refreshed enough to recall the dread prince who must surely be in pursuit, I stepped on a long-fallen beech and dragged myself onto the horse's back. We rode on until I found myself on the ground again.

What are the proper boundaries between sleep and dream, thought and vision? Though the wan daylight and soggy moorland were banished outside my eyelids, the inside was populated with the events and revelations of the past days. Necropolis. Hirudo. Portal cavern. Scraps of information twined about each other like snakes in a basket.

I made it as far as sitting up, head on knees, as rain drizzled on scalp and shoulders. If I could not ride, I must at least think. The story I sought was inside me. I just had to find it.

The Danae did not make the bronze portals. Foolish that I'd ever thought so, now I'd seen Morgan in the wild where she belonged. Humans—the skillful, stubbornly independent Xancheirans—made them. The Xancheirans, known for their magic, their art, and—what had the Marshal told me?—*a richness in their land itself that was exceptional, even in beauteous Navronne.* Which led me to the Danae, who tended the earth's health.

My bent had shown me the Xancheirans observing some Danae rite on the solstice. Surely that demonstrated a closeness—friendship grown from generous deeds or the land itself. Mayhap from their mutual reverence for it. And when invaders with curved swords and dangling earrings—Cicerons, I thought, still Wanderers in our own day—damaged the land with their own kind of magics and their war, the Xancheirans stopped them. Yet they didn't slaughter the newcomers. Instead they made peace, a holy peace, blessed by the Danae at the standing stones I had seen in the Marshal's window glass. A city of glory, they called their home, the City of the Everlasting . . . to honor the Danae?

Hoping to enliven my sluggish mind, I massaged my forehead, the origin of the magic that had blazed from me into the sculpted bronze.

What of that bronzework? *The archon will open the* ways *only for a short time*, the anxious sculptor had said. Morgan had spoken of *pathways*, passages that led between human lands and the true lands, as she had guided me to Palinur. If the Xancheirans were bound in peace to both Danae and Cicerons, perhaps the Danae had opened similar pathways for Cicerons to carry the bronze portals, cast and infused with magic by the Xancheirans, to hidden caves or a ravine in the shadow of Caedmon's Wall.

The bronze sculptor had also said the Cicerons would return with the Xancheirans' salvation when the time was right. How could *Cicerons* be the salvation of Xancheira? And why would they have been sent away from the city, while the other Xancheirans were left to face the danger from the south—the Registry? I had assumed the Palinur Cicerons had gone through the portal to find sanctuary, but this history suggested they were supposed to return to *Xancheira* . . .

I blew a long, slow breath and let the drizzle cool my head.

When the Registry fire surrounded them, the Xancheirans retreated to the standing stones. And died. Or vanished.

The sentinel had implied that Palinur's Cicerons had indeed found sanctuary. She didn't want to tell me where, lest I reveal it to the wrong people. And if I stayed with her too long, or used my magic in the place where we met, I would be trapped—and would have to wait for another to be born with power like mine. Trapped until one was born with the ability to thin the boundaries between Danae lands and human . . . and set them free.

Like gnats, revelations circled just in front of my eyes. I stilled, lest another movement knock them away again.

I had assumed she meant I was to set the Cicerons from Palinur free. Somehow bring them back to the human world. But she'd said "set *us* free." What had Bastien told me of her first words to me? *You could be the answer to a long waiting. . . . My kind and your own.* And that had been spoken *before* the Palinur Cicerons had passed the portal, which had been on my last day as Lucian de Remeni. My own kind . . . impossible! Two centuries had passed. But my mind would not stop. . . .

My journeying with Morgan from the estuary to Palinur and back to the lake where I'd met Grey had seemed to encompass but a single day, but more like seven had passed in the world of humans. Two centuries . . . seven to one . . . less than thirty years.

Goddess Mother preserve! Were they *all* still there, hidden in the place Morgan's Danae couldn't find, the place called Sanctuary? The Palinur Cicerons. The Xancheirans. And the silver-marked Danae, prisoned by a sacrifice of friendship to save the lives of their human friends.

"Morgan!" I bellowed to the earth and sky.

The bay looked up sharply.

"No . . . no . . . don't worry." Burying shock and agitation, I shifted around where the horse could see me. "Naught to do with you. You, fine horse, are going to save my life. I likely saved yours when that cursed prince threw his magic at us. . . ."

If Morgan was watching, she gave no sign, and if not, how could she hear me? She spoke of a bond between us, but I couldn't feel it. And she had left me so abruptly at the lake, never mentioning when we would meet again or how I might find her. But her future depended on my finding answers. Surely she would come.

I led the horse for a while, until I found a rock tall enough to use to mount him. My legs hadn't spring enough to get me up again. If I could just find a spot out of the rain, find something to put in my belly, sleep a bit, maybe I could muster magic enough to build a fire, lure a rabbit. . . . For now, I just hoped to stay on the horse.

"Is it not possible to serve duty without leaving thyself a husk, gentle Lucian?"

"Unff," I said, shrugging. My mouth was fully occupied with smoky fish and its tender green wrappings. The concentration required to avoid choking on bones sapped my reply of any meaning other than thanksgiving. Strength and purpose came flooding back with every mouthful. Questions and answers could wait the brief time until Morgan's holy gift was demolished.

She had found me the third—or perhaps fourth—time I fell off the horse, about the time the scent of the sea had lured me into lustful dreams of her floating in Malcolm's cider. She had helped me regain my seat and led us to this place where no chase could follow. I slept until she woke me with fish.

Now I sat cross-legged on a windswept height, feasting, while Morgan squatted between me and a rivulet of clear water that dribbled from a pile of boulders. The sea was but an imagining on the purple-gray horizon.

I tossed bone and head aside with one hand and snatched up the last fish with the other. "Did you hear me calling?"

"Hear? No. Felt thy need, certainly." Her thumb rolled a pair of dark berries about her palm. They seemed to require all her attention. "But I've other duties, too. And when one is at odds with Tuari Archon, it is well to attend them."

She glanced up, her smile flashing pale like distant lightning. "Dost thou understand that?"

"Very well, else I'd never have left Palinur without prying more answers from the coroner. And doing my duty has benefited me as much as the alternative this time, I think. But certainly you must teach me how to avoid leaving myself a husk. Honestly, I don't enjoy it."

Her laughter brightened the hazy sun. Her hair, more red than brown in the afternoon light, was threaded with white campion, and the clean, sweet lines of her body could not but make me ashamed of my mud-soaked garb and unshaven filth. She had begged me to remove my mask; now it was tempting to hide behind it. Instead, I averted my eyes. If I *appreciated* Morgan any more, I would forget the questions that so desperately needed answering. "Tell me of Sanctuary."

I needed to understand.

"That's more difficult than it seems," she said, ruefully. "The long-lived carry knowledge of mighty things—the land and seasons, woodlands, rivers, and the sea—and also of small things. I know a tree whose roots touch the river above the estuary; a family of otters makes its home there. I know how patient is the shellcracker bird whose chicks take half a year to learn how to feed themselves. I know a rocky snag that houses a thousand little creatures who thrive through salt tide or river flow. It is the nature of the long-lived to keep such things in our minds, but when I was a wanderkin, I thought it burdensome. When we two bided in Montesard, 'twas thou who taught me what *duty* meant—not needful tasks commanded or required of thee unwilling, but joyful purpose, no matter difficulty or hardship."

I wished I could warn that naive young man. He didn't know his family would be burnt alive or that the very men and women who taught him duty were executioners on par with Harrowers.

She twined a stem of campion around her fingers. "Remembering is our duty. Thus it troubles us when we realize something is missing from our memory, especially when it touches great emotion."

"Like something mentioned in a song."

She dipped her head, then tossed the wilted campion aside.

"On winter nights we oft sing of a wanderkin, a young one of our own who spends her days exploring and learning of the world as preparation for her duties. Against her elders' warning, she sneaks into a human city, fascinated at the vigor of life there, undaunted by the crowds or filth."

"Was it you?" I blurted.

Her cheeks . . . indeed her neck and breasts, too, took on a rosy hue. "Nay. But certainly this song made me curious to learn what beauty she found in a city. Rhiain made a friend as could ease the longing for her own life. As did I."

Now it was my cheeks heated.

"The song can take us from moonrise to moonset, so I'll tell, not sing." She shifted her position abruptly as if to shake off sentiment. "A cruel woman recognizes Rhiain as one of the long-lived, lures her with nivé, and enthralls her. Books of lore have told the woman how to nourish a wanderkin's spirit just enough to keep her living, and the wicked dame shows off Rhiain in the market for coin, like some do birds or bears. One morn while sitting outside her mistress's house, filling a stone basin with her tears, Rhiain meets a human youth. When he asks what causes such grievous sorrow, she shows him what she is and begs him take a message to her father and mother that she is fading. Instead, the kind youth tries to steal Rhiain away. But he is himself enslaved—beaten, starved, and forced to harsh labors."

She glanced up from her tale, a spark of mischief in her eyes. "Not *all* of our songs tell dreadful stories of humankind. This one . . ." Her shoulders rose in helpless good humor.

Though my skin was near bursting to hear of the tale's significance, I returned her smile—happy to see it on a day she seemed so somber. But as the earth's face changes when clouds cross the moon, so did Morgan's revert to melancholy. Her gaze grew distant. . . .

"Rhiain steals her mistress's books of lore and brings them to the youth where he lies chained in terrible suffering. 'My people know a place of safety for those who've no escape,' she says. 'I never listened when told of it, as I am but a foolish wanderkin who believed the world's ills could not touch her. Help me discover the way to Sanctuary, and I'll take thee with me, for thou art brave as our heroes of old, and dearer to me than my own kin, who in all these seasons have not ventured the city to find me.'"

Again, Morgan emerged from her tale, face and spirit retaining Rhiain's grief so that I could not shed it either. "As thou hast seen, there is truth in the tales of the long-lived just as in thy magical drawings. It is that truth we hear when we sing Rhiain's Song."

I touched her hand as if that might ease her sorrow. "And how does her tale end, gentle lady? What do we learn of Sanctuary?"

She shoved my hand away. "Nothing at all. For season upon season we strive to remember. The song says Rhiain and her youth found refuge there and stayed until they were healed of their afflictions. Rhiain renounced her kin, but devoted herself to our work, celebrated amongst us until her passing. The youth, healed from his travails, lived for many years in harmony with our kind, before choosing to return to the human world. Even the books of lore eluded us, as Rhiain and her friend burnt them before finding their refuge."

I was very confused. "And before her passing, Rhiain didn't tell anyone what Sanctuary was like, where it was, or how she got there?"

"She may well have. But don't you see? We've forgotten everything of Sanctuary, save the mention in this song. And we don't know why."

I pressed the heel of my hand to gritty eyes, trying to follow the threads. "Rhiain and her friend *left* Sanctuary. They weren't . . . trapped . . . there?"

"Certainly not. It would be no sanctuary were it just another prison."

Exactly. So, something had changed. I had been so anxious to tell Morgan my mad notion about the Xancheirans, but now I wondered. Was she bound to tell her father everything I learned? Before revealing all to an angry Tuari, I needed to understand the consequences of what I'd promised him. I had to speak to the sentinel again.

"It grieves me beyond saying that my magic has put you at odds with your kin—" And even as I spoke the words, a terrible realization struck me about Morgan's danger—and perhaps her unusual melancholy. Gods save me, I'd violated my oath.

"—and I must tell you something astonishing that happened yesterday!"

I told her of following the prince into the cavern of the white hand, of his rapacious interrogation, and of finding a second portal so like the first. ". . . and when I touched the frame, seeking to understand its meaning, images and sounds and emotions, sensations of all kinds, flowed through me like a rampaging river. Somehow in the prince's ravaging, my bent for history had been unmasked, and I used it—"

"Oh, Lucian!"

She lunged forward and pressed her hands to the sides of my face, bringing her rosy lips and fathomless eyes within a finger's breadth—which near made me forget what I'd just said.

"I was so afraid! I felt it, the twisting of the boundaries, and thou didst not tell me. For certain my father felt it, too, and I would have to tell him you withheld . . ."

". . . which would endanger you."

"And thou, as well. But Tuari knows of this dread prince and sorely mistrusts him. He will certainly believe this saying and rejoice that you can now take us to the silver one."

It was as if her own full-faced mask had fallen away to reveal a different person altogether. How lovely, how ripe and alive she was. Her soft cheek brushed mine. Her arms slipped around me, enveloping me in relief, fears, and desire. Her breasts, gleaming with blue fire, pressed against my damp shirt. . . .

No, no, no. With screaming reluctance I retrieved her wrists, pressed her curled fingers to my forehead in apology, and placed them back in her lap. My actions had already left her life at risk; I dared not even think how Tuari Archon would react if I turned my attentions to her as my younger, foolish self had done. Especially when I refused to take him to Safia.

"Sweet Lucian, let me—"

"I cannot, must not, make your danger worse," I said, hoarsely.

Tangled desires did not mesh well with indignation. And no matter her words, her generosity, she was a stranger to me. If I could just *remember* those days I knew her—what we had talked about, how we had felt, what had made us each risk so much to be together. My violation of pureblood discipline regarding the body's urges could have drawn lifelong punishments, as could her dalliance with me, it seemed.

"What kind of villain threatens his own daughter with such a fate?"

Morgan's face blazed scarlet, stricken as if I'd slapped her. "My father is no villain. His concern is the *world's* fate!"

"That's but an excuse for lack of faith," I snapped. "Not just faith in humankind, but in his own kind, in you and himself. Prisoning you determines nothing of the world's fate, save to diminish its glory."

She did not respond. She wanted honesty. But honesty could wound, and anything I might add would only make things worse. I munched on the purple berries I had dropped when she embraced me. They were hard, bitter, and gritty with mud, like so much of truth.

I could not but contrast Tuari's rancor with the image of Danae and Xancheirans amid the standing stones and the surety it had raised in me of a profound holiness, shaped of generosity and mutual sacrifice. I wanted to believe *that* image was truth in the same way the portrait of Morgan was truth—the harmony with her surroundings, the brilliance and beauty of her nature.

She drew up her long legs, wrapped her arms around them, and rested her chin on her knees. "Thou didst speak with her again . . . the silvered one."

"Only for a moment, lest Osriel notice me vanished. She claimed she was the one who allowed me to cross the portal or turned me back." That scalding fire that only I could feel.

"That is the proper task of a sentinel. Did she say more?"

"She said I mustn't use my magic when I was there—which would be impossible, anyway, as I can't do other magic while using my bent. But she didn't explain why."

Only that I would be trapped.

Morgan puzzled at it. "Her saying makes no sense. Thy magic is of the Everlasting and thus draws on the land—the true lands and the human lands that are forever bound one to the other. 'Tis why thy ancestors came to Navronne, yes? What would forbid its use in Sanctuary?"

"It makes no sense. But for now, we need to go," I said. "Your feast has restored me. My horse should know the way, but I'm not sure he can take me to my boat . . . not from here."

"Set the beast free. I'll have thee to the estuary before moonrise," she said, unfolding herself. "And whenever thou hast need of me, dip your hand in the water of the estuary and call my name. I'll come as soon as I can."

We strolled down the hill side by side, my cramps and bruises easing. I tried to notice when she made the subtle leaps that would shorten the distance like gathering a loop in a rope or carrying a boat across the meander of a river, but it was near impossible in the rainy gloom. Her cool silence grieved me.

"My oath stands," I said. "And I *will* tell you all, but I am so ignorant about all this. I need to understand what I've experienced before I can describe it. And I'm often hasty, so anxious to do my duty, I get myself and others in trouble. I'm trying to do better. Like not leaving myself a husk."

"Dost thou regret thy oath to my sire?"

"To respect and honor your kind and do them no harm? No. To do what's needed to keep you safe and free? No. I'm only afraid that I've not the knowledge or power"—or the right?—"to do as he wants. As I told him, the gift I bear is not unrighteous. But I've got to find out why it seems so. Now I have at least a part of it back, maybe I can learn."

Morgan had said we were bound by what we'd done, that she could sense my needs. Perhaps that's why I felt her emotions so clearly. It was my own were a mystery to me.

The breeze gusted stronger as we descended a rocky hillside, certainly not the one where I'd eaten fish, onto the flats of the upper coast. The air was thicker. A heavy scent of briny deadness twined with old woodsmoke sent Morgan back easterly out of our way.

"It's naught but the salterns," I said, tugging on her arm. "Someone's worked them in the past month. But I doubt anyone's working so late, unless they've a boil going in the hut."

The flats and the tides made collecting the salt water and trapping it between the earthen dams to settle easy. But even the constant wind on the flats was too damp to dry the salt completely. Thus Evanide's servitors poured the brine into lead pans in the shed and boiled the water away. But not this afternoon.

"I'll not walk there," she said, shaking me loose. "I cannot. Find thy own way through. I'm not needed." She forged on to the east.

"No, wait. Please." I caught up with her. "I need to hear one more story. You have to tell me about the silver gards."

"Only if we go another way. I'll not be forced."

"But why? None will see you." Understanding escaped me.

"'Tis the salé," she said, exasperated. "It . . . sickens me. Does that please thee to know?"

"The *salt*? But you walk by the sea, live near the estuary. You eat fish. I didn't know."

"'Tis just . . . so much at once. The dry crystals. Come, I'll tell thee willing of silver gards. 'Tis long past time."

Only as she drew me away on a path to avoid the saltern did I recall tales of greedy landlords and villeins who wished to trap Danae in their fields to ensure a rich harvest. They put out feast bread made with nivat—or even the seeds themselves if their purse was heavy enough—to draw the Danae near. But under the loaf or the pile of seeds they'd hide a fistful of salt, because the salt crystals would bind a Dané to the land like an iron chain. If that were true . . .

"I didn't think," I said. "I'd never trick you, never force you to do anything against your will."

"Ah, sweet Lucian, I know that. But this matter of the gards . . ."

Anger ebbed, she stretched out one hand, inspecting it, as if she'd never considered the wonder of it. The sapphire and lapis vines glowed brighter, their colors richer in the cloudy light.

"We are sworn not to reveal such things to humans. Yet thy need demands it. Perhaps I can explain it in the manner of our tutors in Montesard—telling while not telling."

She took my hand and strolled across the barrens. "What if thy king's eyes were the hue of ripe plums and the color of his eyes determined what crops would grow in his land, the course of his rivers, what stories are told, how many younglings are birthed there, and the talents of the subjects who serve him? The sign of this kingdom's right ordering is that all these good subjects have the same color eyes as their king, despite a variance in hue. When they see through their purple eyes, they experience the world in a similar way and go about their work. When the king and his people join together to give an accounting of their lands and grapes and children, their harmony binds the kingdom in safety and health until the next time.

"And then, one day, the king hears rumor of one with green eyes. How does that one see or experience the world? It cannot be the same as he does, yet the very vitality of his people depends on their experience of the world."

"It's natural your father would be anxious if the silver gards have never been seen before. When my ancestors came to Navronne, the people here had never seen magic. They were afraid of us, and yes there were struggles. . . ."

"Wars," she said. "Thousands of deaths. Recall, I studied human history alongside thee. But the long-lived have no historical writings as humans do. We've no stories of those with silver gards nor do we recall seeing them. And yet my elders fear them, not as strangers, but as if the warning is writ in their bones or carved in the trees that *do* live in their memories. It is not just my sire. When I saw the abyss through the portal in the human city, the fear that afflicted me was the same in kind as when I hear of the silver gards. What lies beyond that portal is terrible and dangerous, though I cannot explain why."

"Is it only silver that worries you?"

"My sire insists that any difference would afflict him the same. But others of more generous mind tell me that if they heard tales of green gards or gold, it would concern, but not frighten, them. We know that the Everlasting expresses itself in glorious ways, and when we find a flower, tree, or fish that none have seen before, we rejoice. As you've seen, our gards pale in sunlight, which is natural. But I've thought that silver might be so fearful because when we fade, as Rhiain did, from a life that is not whole, and our gards pale to silver in night as well as day, sometimes we do things that make no sense . . . turn our work to harm. . . ."

Her voice shook so terribly, I stopped and drew her around where I could see her face. Shame and horror were writ on her. "What is it? I don't understand."

"Madness," she whispered. "Just like humans, we can go mad. And if this sentinel you've seen is mad . . . if there are more like her . . . who knows what is the truth of Sanctuary?"

CHAPTER 17

"**B**lessed return, Greenshank!" Fix the boatmaster snatched the line I tossed up to him and secured the bucking skiff. "Brought a storm, I see, as well as my best boat and mercy to my ears."

I glanced up. It was difficult to comprehend the old man's banter. Now I was free of oars, rocks, and deadly whirlpools, foreboding choked the stormy afternoon, shrouding the fortress until my spirit could scarce breathe. Mad Danae . . . Goddess Mother!

It was necessary to heed Fix. He was the first judge of anyone returned from a mission. Perhaps the best. Though the lowest of servants, he saved lives—knights and trainees both—by detecting wounds of body or spirit that pride sought to mask.

"Have the squires stoppled your hearing, Fix, hoping to raid the kitchens undetected?"

None had ever figured out how the boatmaster stayed abreast of every person inside Evanide.

"Nay. Seems like every hour of late, some's pestering as to whether *Greenshank's* come back. Knight Commander Inek's worst at it; he feels shorted, no doubt, as ye've yet to complete your nights on the seaward wall. No guide likes his punishments interrupted with missions."

"Would Inek be in the armory, do you think?"

"More like the archives. He's studious of late." His ruddy brow crinkled. "But then, he's not there neither. He's likely on his way to the Marshal, as the Marshal's laid first claim on your carcass. And 'tis a mealy carcass at that. You look like summat Malcolm scrapes from the bay at low tide."

"I've no complaint," I said. "Not drowned. No holes in me."

It was tempting to intercept Inek on his way to the Marshal. But we'd not have time enough to cover all I needed to tell. Best get the mission report out of the way first.

"Who besides Inek's been pestering?" A crash of thunder and the rising gale had me shouting.

"More than's usual for a shag-tail paratus. Oughtn't say more. Wouldn't want to put you above yourself."

"Just want to know who I've got to see before I can sleep." I stowed oars and bailers, and passed Fix the skiff's small water cask.

Fix twisted his craggy face, speculating. "Well, Paratus-exter Cormorant for one, about his investiture. And a knight, name of Bearn."

"Cormorant's investiture!" I'd completely lost track of the days. "It's not happened already?"

"Nah, you've come in time."

"Excellent!" Cormorant, the first of Evanide's senior parati, was a brother I respected and valued. Now he was to take his final step to knighthood, the first of the trainees I knew well to do so. That he cared I should be here for his night of glory pleased me greatly.

As for the knight, I didn't know him. To have a stranger *pestering* about me seemed odd. "Did this Bearn mention what he wanted or where I could find him?"

"He's an odd one. Said he'd find you, as he was in and out on mission. Didn't say what he wanted. But the Marshal's got first claim anyways. The others'll wait."

"The Marshal knows I'm here already, eh, Fix?" The rapid communication of arrivals was another of Fix's mysteries.

"Mayhap." The old man grinned, as the wind tangled his gray hair and forced his gleaming eyes into a squint.

The truer question was whether Damon the Spider was waiting as well. I'd lay odds he was.

Fix shuffled up the quay, the water cask on his shoulder. Thanking him for his good service, I hurried past him to the first stair, then up and inward toward the southern flank of the fortress.

Patchy torchlight showed the way through the afternoon's storm-wrought gloom. Trainees, knights, adjutants, and servants strode past about their business. As usual.

Astonishing I'd been away near a half month; mind and body insisted it had been but four or five days. Holy Deunor, so much to sort out. The sentinel, Safia, had been sad and secretive, yes . . . and afraid of some increasing danger. But mad? Surely not.

Knight-retired Horatio barreled past me through the kitchen passage, clattering down the stair toward the training rooms. That was not so usual. The Marshal's doorward couldn't stand watch every hour of every day, but his absence at mid-afternoon, and his urgency, could not but leave me curious and wary. Indeed, as I crossed the upper courtyard herb garden through a deluge and charcoal light, no guard stood outside the Marshal's chambers. Or was there . . . ?

"Speak your name." The dark-cloaked man stepped out from the shadowed colonnade, his pale complexion entirely bare. An outsider. Unmasked.

My knife and spellwork were at ready in the space of an eyeblink. "Who commands it?"

"Speak your name. Once assured of your identity, I shall reciprocate. If you're expected inside, I'll allow you to pass."

His steel-timbred voice scraped my nerves.

"You've no authority here," I said, cool, but loud enough I hoped someone else might hear.

"Does it ease your concerns if I say my own master is inside with yours," he said, "and that the two of them commanded me stand watch while Doorward Horatio is away on other business?"

He moved farther into the lamplight, a tight-bodied man something near my own age. His richly black clothing and fair complexion, the black hair, slicked straight back, and the pale hands that held a very fine sword put me in mind of our relicts—so starkly black and white. His capable stance and a scar that creased a granite-hewn brow and cheek belied any impression of softness.

"Curator Damon is your master, then," I guessed.

He inclined his back in the way of acknowledgement rather than deference. "I was given a list of those permitted to enter. If your name does not appear on that list, you're to return tomorrow."

So he was an unmasked pureblood or an ordinary with iron balls. Having seen Horatio barreling through the halls gave weight to the man's explanation, but it signaled further Registry intrusion into the Order's business. I didn't like it.

"I'm Paratus Greenshank," I said. "In-mission and reporting to the Marshal as required."

"Well met, Paratus Greenshank. Your name is on the list. I am *Fallon*, Curator Damon's military aide." He put a slight emphasis on his name, as if I might know some other military aide. "As is customary, your weapon must be sheathed before you can proceed. You are commanded to retain your mask."

Inek would be livid that we had outsiders on guard in the fortress, outsiders familiar with our customs. And since when did Registry administrators have military aides?

Since the beginnings perhaps, when they dispatched sorcerer-soldiers to fire Xancheira or Harrowers to exterminate entire bloodlines . . .

As Fallon stepped aside to let me enter, I returned my dagger to its sheath. His quick, firm hand atop mine prevented me yanking it out again when his body pressed my back and his breath teased my ear.

"If you would hear a private warning from one deeply in your debt, *Domé* Remeni, pause at yonder font on your way out." Then he backed away and vanished, as if he'd never been there.

He *knew* me—Lucian.

My hand did not release the knife or the spell invocation hovering at mind's edge until I stood in the Marshal's outer chamber with the thick door between me and Damon's man. The outer chamber's protective enchantments remained in place. Before stepping fully into the inner chamber, I verified that the two men beside the hearth were the only ones present. The white-robed Marshal was seated; Damon stood at his shoulder. No Inek as yet. Hearth fire and torchlight glimmered on the great windows, but it was lightning from the storm beyond that set the panes of citron and red ablaze, curdling my gut.

"Come, come, Greenshank! All is secure." The Marshal's many-layered voice embodied welcome and reassurance.

"The presence of an unmasked outsider at your door trumped a warning, Knight Marshal," I said. That I offered an excuse was a measure of my unsettled state. What debt could Damon's military aide owe me?

As ever, ritual provided clarity and focus. I sank to one knee, touched forehead and heart, and lowered my eyes. "Knight Marshal, I report my mission complete."

"Blessed return, Greenshank." He gestured me up, his eager posture bearing assurance of his sincerity and interest. "You find us met in haste. We've anxiously awaited the results of this mission, and without a word, you've already astonished us by your quick return."

I swallowed all reply lest I stumble into places I didn't want to go. Of course they would know when Grey signaled me. With the foreshortened traveling distance through Morgan's true lands, only four days had expired since I'd left Grey, not the six or seven they might have expected.

"Perhaps the paratus ran away from the nasty halfblood," said Damon, brisk as the sea wind.

"Speak, Greenshank," said the Marshal, ignoring the jibe. "As Commander Inek is delayed, you may summarize for now. Where was Prince Osriel going? What was his objective?"

Inek's absence disappointed. For once, Fix's infallible instincts had failed him.

Hands at my back, I told of the mission as clearly and concisely as I could. "Prince Osriel's objective was magical power—searching out sources of it. Some from story or legend. Some from grotesque and unnatural rites. I assumed the mission in a woodland glade east of Lillebras . . ."

Once Morgan had left me at the estuary, I'd given careful thought to this report. The map, the lake, and the cavern were fair game, but the portal must remain my secret—and Inek's whenever I was able to tell him about it. I told how the prince had used a Cartamandua map to find the cavern. I described Voushanti and the warlord, and my decision to risk capture in order to discover Osriel's purpose.

". . . convinced we needed to know more of anyone who uses such dreadful magic as what I saw in the bodyguard. On reflection, it was likely prideful and foolish to assume *I* had to be the one to discover this, but I know how rare it is for Osriel to leave his strongholds. So I devised a ruse . . ."

This part would be risky. I wasn't supposed to know of my bents.

"Why a historian?" snapped Damon when I paused for a breath.

"Flimsy, I know," I said, "but it was the first thing that came to mind as a reason to be following princes and exploring caves. It allowed me to keep close to the truth. Indeed, the prince cast some spell to assess my truth—a complex and most intense enchantment. Though he judged my words accurate, he doubted my story as a whole. Yet he was curious enough—or greedy enough—that he sent me to examine the inner chamber that had drawn his interest. There were paintings of beasts and god symbols on the walls, as are often found in Navron caves. But the only magic was of the subtle kind one finds in any holy place. . . ."

All while I spoke, the little curator paced in circles. Every moment he was behind me, my back clenched in anticipation of a knife. Which was foolish, of course, as he clearly had some use for me. Yet his man had offered me a *private* warning.

I brought the report to a rapid conclusion, speaking of Osriel's unnerving power and of my escape. The Marshal was appalled at what I'd seen in the silver caskets. Damon was not.

"Have I not told you?" Damon burst out. "So much work . . . so much hope when Eodward took Lirene as mistress and produced a son. The spawn should have died at birth."

Damon locked up his fury and snapped his attention back to me.

"What is your opinion of this prince compared to his eldest brother, paratus?" he said.

"My *opinion*, curator?"

"Which is worthy to sit Eodward's throne? How do you assess their prospects?"

His interest in my opinions of the warring factions still seemed ridiculous, but the horror of Osriel was too vivid to silence.

"What is to choose between a bully without conscience and a demon gatzé? Allied with Sila Diaglou's savages, Bayard's might in warfare is perhaps more formidable. But Osriel is personally more dangerous. He demonstrates subtle, intricate magic and explosive power. Every rumor of his depravity should be given credence. I believe he seeks access to power beyond that available to mortal men."

That was as near Osriel's determination to cross into Danae lands as I dared go.

"A valuable assessment of a dark situation," said the Marshal, unruffled by Damon's odd outburst. "Well done, especially for a paratus whose training is incomplete." Was that a jab at Damon? "You should review your tactical decisions with Commander Inek as always, whenever he makes an appearance. Likely his tyros have been trying to drown themselves this morning."

No. Not Inek. Tyros would not keep him away.

"Now, Greenshank, your next assignment." Damon's icy armor bore spikes. "At sixth hour of the morning watch, you will report to the Archives Seeing Chamber for a review of a relict I've selected. You will speak to no one about the appointment or anything else concerning me. I will not be a topic of speculation among parati and squires."

As the sun fired the image of burning Xancheira, a Registry curator spoke as my commander. Why did the Marshal allow it?

Discipline shattered. "My service is not pledged to you or your Registry, curator," I said, pivoting sharply to the man in white. "Knight Marshal, what is *your* command?"

"Paratus Greenshank, you will not question any order given in this chamber." The Marshal's ferocity near drew blood.

It was astonishing my mask did not blaze from the fire in my flesh. I knew it was not yet time to challenge them. And Inek's own teaching commanded me: Think *before speaking words you can't take back.* Yet submission to Damon rankled.

It was clear what was expected. So I shackled pride and silkbound indignation and bowed to the Marshal. "Accept my apologies, Knight Marshal."

The spider had moved to the window and stared out at the lightning-riven blackness. Though it was near physical pain, I bowed curtly to his back. "My apologies, curator. I shall meet you in the archives at sixth hour tomorrow, as you command."

I offered no excuse.

"The storm is on us, paratus," said Damon. "Men and women of intelligence, courage, and conviction must face it together, else all we value will be swept away."

"Indeed," I said, wondering if we valued the same things at all. Yet I—Lucian de Remeni—had chosen to pursue the mystery of the white hand to Evanide, knowing Damon intended it.

"Your mission is discharged, Greenshank," said the Marshal, rising as if to preclude any further exchange. "You have returned at a most fortuitous time. In a few hours our brothers gather to celebrate Paratus Cormorant's investiture. He requested you to stand his vigil with him. Commander Inek stood in until duty called him away. Dunlin took up the watch yesterday afternoon. But as you've returned, you may vest yourself, serve out the last hours, and escort him to the Common Hall. Cormorant will be pleased."

"I'll be honored to serve him." And I was. No matter the taint of Damon's presence and the Marshal's cooperation with him, I believed in the Order's way because of men like Inek and Cormorant. No worries or anger could overshadow such an occasion.

"*Dalle cineré*, Knight Marshal. Curator."

"And one more thing, Greenshank . . ."

"Sir?" I said, halfway through the door already.

"As you are unwounded and shall be well fed at Cormorant's investiture feast, Inek, wherever he is, would insist you take up your punishment duty as required at midnight. The sooner your nights on the wall are done, the better. I give you leave to shorten your watch by time enough to be prompt to your morning appointment with Curator Damon."

Great Deunor's fiery balls! I wanted to slam the two heads together—the white and the dark. No chance to visit the archives on my own. No chance to hunt for Inek. At least he'd know where to find me. Where was he?

"As you command, Knight Marshal," I said. "*Dalle cineré.*" I would honor his office, even if unsure about the man who sat in it. What hold did Damon have on him?

The font stood in a corner of the herb garden outside the Marshal's quarters. I cupped my hand and took a welcome drink, while every sense stretched out to locate the dark-clad Fallon. A cough from the colonnade that led to the infirmary cued his position, and I strolled in his direction, head bowed and arms folded as if meditating on the unsatisfactory interview. My dagger sat firmly in hand, tucked under my arms.

"My master swore you'd not recognize me," Fallon said softly, making his empty hands visible. For one who moved as quickly and smoothly as he did, that was only moderately reassuring. "Is that true?"

"Yes."

"Nor even your own true name nor what you were before"—he waved his empty hands—"all this?"

"You spoke of debts and warnings."

He inclined his back. "We've a history, you and me. My father was Prince Perryn's *consiliar prime*—his right hand—and you got him hanged."

His hand dipped into his jaque, screaming danger, *debt*, and vengeance.

"Hold right there!" My body pivoted sideways, braced and balanced, knife at the ready. Fingers of my left hand lay on my silver bracelet.

But it was only a folded scrap of parchment he offered me. "Perhaps this will raise a memory."

"*You* open it."

My pale magelight illuminated an ink drawing. A girl child of ten or twelve, a beggar child, I assumed, her hair cropped short and ugly, her white shift stained dark, her large light eyes sad. Knowing. Resigned to things no child should understand. Yet her cheeks were plump and smooth, her hands clean, and the shift intricately, beautifully embroidered. The depiction was not some allegorical work pulling together the contradictions of prosperity and poverty, but a portrait. Magic had infused the image with truth.

Pulse hammering, I noted the scribbled lettering in the lower right corner:

LdR-M.

"Who is she?" I said, wary of Fallon's every heartbeat.

He folded the page and slipped it back where he'd got it. "My eleven-year-old half sister. My father debauched and strangled her, and you—

perhaps on a night you cannot remember—gave her justice at the peril of your own life."

"I've no knowledge of any such occasion," I said. The necessary words. This man served Damon. They were also the truth, though horror and wonder had me hungering to know more.

My dagger lowered, Fallon stepped closer. "My master believes I blame you for my father's fall from power, caring nothing for the circumstances of the crime. Lest you've not noticed, political gaming is my master's lifeblood. But this shame was my devil sire's own doing. *Then* and *now* I rejoice in justice done for an innocent. Though I serve the curator and share in many of his purposes, I've sworn to repay your service."

"So you believe I had a hand in your father's fall."

His white teeth shone in the dark. "I watched the man who drew this portrait force Perryn of Ardra to execute his own *consiliar prime* as they were trying to steal the throne of Navronne. That man held the prince at bay until he had evidence the deed was done. His courage shamed me, because I'd not had the balls to call out the vile prince or my despicable sire."

Great gods, no wonder I'd had to run!

Fallon's urgency drew me on. "You cannot be unaware of my master's interest in you, Remeni . . . or whatever you're named here. Unfortunately, he's not shared his plan for you in my hearing. But you need to know that he has summoned the Three Hundred to a Sitting. Do you understand what that means?"

"An earthquake!" Shock choked me. "A hurricane."

Sittings of the Three Hundred—assemblages of the heads of family for the three hundred senior Registry bloodlines—were held perhaps once in fifty years, and only for events of dramatic significance. Strengthening the breeding laws with the requirement of Registry approval before any pureblood child could be conceived. Or tightening the restrictions on pureblood interaction with ordinaries or adding draconian penalties for ordinaries who aided *recondeurs*. The very first such assembly had ratified Caedmon's Writ—the foundational truce between Crown, Temple, and Registry. Many purebloods still named the Writ anathema for its accommodation of any civil regulation of purebloods and their divine gift. What was in Damon's mind?

"Go on."

"This Sitting," said Fallon, "is set for the first day of autumn at Cavillor Castle, the seat of the family Canis-Ferenc. Kasen de Canis-Ferenc is not only one of the wealthiest purebloods in Navronne, but he is well-known among

Navronne's *ordinary* legions as a master of strategic warfare. He has refused to serve any of King Eodward's sons. Cavillor and the town bearing its name lie twenty quellae north of Lillebras—approximately five days' ride from the Gouvron Estuary. The Three Hundred shall address the matter of corruption in the Pureblood Registry."

"Corruption!"

"For two years, as he's planned this event, my master has traveled to the seats of more than half of the Three Hundred families, carrying with him a folio of portraits, each bearing this same signature." Fallon patted his jaque where he'd returned the girl child's portrait. And waited.

The scenario he painted bespoke a man building support for a plan to be proposed at the Sitting. But why with a folio of my portraits?

"Have you an idea what he thinks to present at the Sitting?"

"No," said Fallon. "With each Head of Family he reiterates the Sitting's stated purpose of addressing corruption. All other discussion is family matters or news of the day. I stand only as his aide and bodyguard, beneath notice of your kind, but I've good eyes and ears. The folio of portraits is always with him. And when he leaves, the Head of Family is always afraid."

Portraits that could reveal hidden truths. Blackmail.

"Damon intends for you to be present for this Sitting, Remeni. In what capacity, I've no idea. But I'd say this is a move of power as we've not seen in Navronne since the Writ, and when serious, determined men make moves of power; it behooves their servants . . . and their instruments . . . to have a care. I certainly shall."

I had to make some answer. If he spoke truth, this man had just put his head on the block for me. "I've no memory of these matters . . . the girl child . . . the folio . . . But I'll stay vigilant. And if ever there were dealings between us that laid this geas on you, let their burden be lifted now. Go in safety and with my thanks."

A shake of his head denied my grant. "This debt is for my lifetime. Ysabel was small in the world compared to duty and ambition. She died in torment because I did not pay attention, and it was not her brother the warrior who fought for her, but strangers. A portrait artist and a coroner. Do either of you ever need my service, I will answer."

Fallon melted into the shadows, leaving me awash in fear, curiosity, and an undeniable satisfaction that intellect insisted belonged to someone else, yet I hoped might belong in small part to me. Very like a Knight of the Ashes might feel when hearing of a righteous deed well done.

. . .

Aspeedy visit to the lavatorium and its ever-flowing, ever-frigid water, and the layered shirt, habergeon, and black wool tabard didn't itch as they might have otherwise. My lighter cloak and spare mask completed my toilet, and I raced through the citadel and up the exposed stair on the north face of Evanide's granite heart.

No one I met had seen Inek that day. His absence nagged. The commander was not one to prattle about his duties, but he was serious about his students. He would never miss an investiture.

My skull was like to burst with all I'd learned—and now this news. A Sitting of the Three Hundred less than two months hence, to be held in a pureblood house far from Palinur. Secret, then. And very near Evanide.

Bypassing the armory and treasury, I plunged deep into the mount, arriving at a stair that had likely been in place centuries before the fortress itself was built. The steps were little more than a suggestion. Follow the stair downward into the bowels of Idolon Mount and one reached the misty Cave of the Spring, the source of our fresh water. Ascend and one emerged at a rocky nest called, appropriately, the Aerie—the highest point on Evanide's islet. There, exposed to wind, weather, and whatever view of the wide world Erit the cloud goddess provided, did a paratus-exter spend two days and two nights considering the decision that would alter him forever.

An iron gate stood at the top of the stair. My fingers worked out the spell, and I ducked through the low arch. Lightning flickered at the end of the short, steep passage beyond the gate, silhouetting a man standing guard. The thunder growled and rumbled, almost without break.

"Who goes there?" Dunlin's challenge was firm, but voiced quietly, though indeed Cormorant was unlikely to hear us over the storm.

"'Tis your First, Paratus Dunlin. You are relieved."

Dunlin came to attention as I joined him at the verge of the grotto. Rain blurred my view of the gray-cloaked man nestled in a crotch of the craggy rocks behind him.

"I am relieved. You have the watch." Dunlin's enthusiasm was clear. "Well met, Greenshank!"

As my second passed me his lance, his entire posture changed. He yawned, scrubbed at his head, and stretched out his shoulders. "He hoped you'd arrive before the ceremony. The idea pleased me, as well."

"A near thing," I murmured. "But the storm held off its worst till I got back."

"Unless I fell asleep and missed the last bell, we're nigh on three hours from seventh when his vigil ends. There's the standard you're to carry before him." Dunlin waved his hand at a long pole wrapped in silk and a small carved chest sitting far enough inside the passage to keep them mostly dry. "His robe and hood are in the chest, as are the two tunics." Black for acceptance; white for rejection.

"From the bell he'll have half an hour to robe and get to the Hall. He's to stay silent and not show you his choice until he's dressed. But honestly after two days in the weather with only his future to chew on, he'll likely need help to distinguish white from black. He's not twitched since I got here yestereve."

"I'll see to him," I said.

Dunlin stared past me and cocked his head. "Can you guess his choice?"

"No guessing needed," I said. "Cormorant was born for knighthood."

"Agreed. He'll be the next Marshal, wait and see. Though he's not got this Marshal's ferocious rigor that will have his knights cursing his ancestors to the tenth generation while they die for him. Cormorant is simply everlasting fine at whatever he does."

I'd never understood Dunlin's estimate of the Marshal. I saw no rigor. Nor did I perceive Heron's Marshal—the priest of a mysterious warrior cult only initiates understood. It was the Marshal's passion for right and his vision of a just world that spoke to my soul. Except today.

"Of course, we'd never know it was Cormorant," said Dunlin, screwing up his face until his mask look like a dune shore. "We're all mad, you know."

"Aye." Some of us more than others. "Would you give Inek a message for me?"

"Certain."

"Tell him it's urgent I see him, and the Marshal's sent me back to the wall tonight."

"Your never-ending punishment tour. Do you imagine Inek will relieve you?"

"I doubt it. Maybe distract me, though."

Dunlin waved and vanished down the stair. I took my formal stance, back straight, legs spread, lance extended. The bluster whipped my cloak and pelted my back with rain.

Three hours left. I should ask the gods to guide Cormorant in his decision. If he chose to stay, the rest of us would witness his Rite of Breaking, as he hammered his past life to dust. We'd see him presented with new sword, armor, and knight's tabard, and share a feast unmatched on any other occasion at Evanide.

If he chose to leave the Order, he would announce whether or not he had decided to retain the memory of his life here. No matter which, he would leave the fortress in the same hour. The rest of us would still feast, raising our cups to his good service and his free choice, wishing him well on his life's journey.

Thunder crashed and cold wind gusted behind me. "Greenshank! At last . . ."

I whirled around. Cormorant stood just behind me, dark hair dripping, his normally lean face pinched.

"Sorry if we disturbed you." I said. "Are you—?"

"You've got to find Inek."

The worry lurking in my gut took fire. "The Marshal said duty interrupted his vigil yesterday."

"I doubt that. Listen"—he drew me away from the arch and across the Aerie into a cove of giant slabs. The cove offered a bit of shelter from the rain and wind, and no one lurking on the stair or in the passage would be able to see us, much less eavesdrop on our conversation.

He leaned his back on the slabs, drawing his sodden cloak around him. "A few days ago, Inek asked me to name you as my vigil companion. As you were in-mission and not expected back, he intended to take your place."

"Whyever?"

"He admitted it was a strange request and unseemly to trespass on the rite, but he asked me to trust him that he'd no alternative. If you're like me, you'd trust him with your mother's life. . . ."

I nodded, though yet confused. "Go on."

"He told me only that he had business regarding *the most important mission he'd ever undertaken*, and that I was to speak of it to no one but you." He threw up his hands. "I didn't know a Knight Commander took on missions beyond training! I even suspected it might be some part of my final testing. They throw some hard things at you in these last days. . . ."

Like the lightning, Cormorant's brilliant grin—the kind that could lift a man's spirits in the most desperate hour—flashed and faded quickly.

"Naturally, I agreed," he said. "We paraded through the Hall, spent a few difficult hours in the archives, and then came up here as the rite dictates. The Marshal roused me with his usual *call to excellence*, as I was a bit of a wreck, and then left, taking everyone but Inek. That was at seventh hour of the evening watch, two days ago. A few hours later, near midnight I think, when the fortress was quiet, Inek left, saying he'd return by midday at the latest. They bring me water at midday." He glanced up as if to ask if I understood.

"He intended to be back before anyone knew he was gone."

"That was my thought. He swore me to secrecy yet again, and gave me his most solemn oath that his business was honorable and necessary. And he said that if he didn't come back, something had gone very wrong, and I was to send you after him, as soon as you joined me here."

"And he didn't come back," I said, "and the water carrier noted it. So Dunlin was sent."

"Aye. So the Marshal must know what's going on. That's good, but I promised . . ."

But the Marshal had failed to tell me that Inek was missing—which could have perfectly honorable reasons.

I didn't believe that. "Where were you to send me?"

"To the Knights' Relictory. You're to go undetected and look for anything out of order. If you cannot find him—and only then—speak to the Archivist. And he added the strangest thing. 'Tell Greenshank that if the occasion arises, he should draw me.' Which made no sense at all, as he didn't say what you were supposed to draw him into or out of."

I ducked my head, so he could not note my astonishment . . . or my understanding of the danger Inek feared. My guide didn't want me to draw him into anything, but to *draw* him. To seek the truth with my bent. Desperation . . . and so much faith in me. Inek knew of my bent, but not that Osriel's ravaging had opened the possibility of its use. He thought he was going to die.

"Certainly, I'll go. I hope you're wrong to worry. And I'll do my best to be back to escort you to your night of glory—whatever you decide."

"Find him, Greenshank. He was afraid."

CHAPTER 18

Hood and cloak drawn close, I took a circuitous way through the fortress. The paratus supposed to be standing vigil watch with Cormorant must not be seen flitting about the halls. Inek had installed himself and then me in one of the few duties at Evanide unlikely to be interrupted.

Inek . . . who had allowed Cormorant to see his fear. *Draw me.* It was all I could do not to run.

Unusual for afternoon, only a few were abroad. A servant swabbed a wet floor. A paratus limped toward the barracks wing, sweating and bloody. A knight commander—not Inek—herded a trio of soggy, exhausted tyros just come in from a dunking in the bay. I slumped to disguise my height and strode purposefully into the Archive Tower.

No guards or locked gates barred entry. A variety of spellwork webbed the precincts—spells of preservation, illumination, magnification, the occasional piercing bent of a knight or adjutant who was scribe, cartographer, or historian. A few warded rooms required the Archivist's permission to enter, but I knew those, and none were my objective. Unfortunately, I had no idea where to find my objective.

The Knight's Relictory held the Order's most precious trust—the memories of those who trained here. None below the rank of commander were allowed to know its location. Not even rumor made a guess, save the occasional speculation that it was up the testy Archivist's backside. Though entering without permission could get him dismissed from the Order, I suspected why Inek had gone there. He'd sworn that night on the seaward wall that he would discover what I was.

So where was the place? The second, third, and fourth levels were warrens of small chambers furnished with writing desks, book chests, scroll cases, and presses stuffed with documents. The fifth was a single large room, containing the map repository and long tables for spreading them out. A quick inspection confirmed that there were no masked doorways and all space was accounted for.

The Seeing Chamber occupied most of the ground level. Two centuries of archived missions sat in their own relictory behind a heavily warded door.

A scattering of squires and parati worked here and there throughout the Tower. None had looked up as I whisked by in search of the hidden relictory and *something out of order.* Curiously, neither the Knight Archivist, easily identifiable in his rust-colored mantle, hood, and mask, nor his second, similarly garbed in dusky blue, was anywhere to be seen. *That* was definitely out of order.

The two men lived in this tower and rarely left it. That served the balance of the Order, the same that kept the Marshal in his windowed chambers and the Knight Defender wherever he lurked. So where were the Archivist's personal quarters? The only place I'd not searched was a slate-roofed structure that joined the square tower to the seaward wall.

A door in the wall next to a coal store, easily overlooked, opened into the auxiliary passage. Lamps illuminated several doorways hung with woven rugs. Two led into cells scarce larger than the one where I slept. A rust-colored cloak and mask hung on pegs in the first, ones of dusky blue in the second. The Archivist's cell held the luxury of a padded armchair, a footstool, and a small writing desk. The second's pallet was covered with a thick quilt of sewn-together scraps. A basket of scraps and a spool of cotton suggested the man was making another. Neither cell was occupied.

A kettle sat on the cold hob in a third chamber. A cheese rind, half-empty cups, and unwashed soup bowls littered a table of scrubbed pine. A fourth chamber was a storeroom, its presses filled with neatly ordered ink horns, cups, pens, and the like.

Draw me. I snatched up a pen, a stoppered ink cup, and a tied roll of clean parchment and stuffed them into my pockets. But when I returned to the passage, I felt a fool. There were no more doorways.

Rain drizzled from an overhead grate at the end of the passage. Neither the lightning flashes nor magelight penetrated the heavy blackness, and yet boring hours on the seaward wall insisted a full third of the passage remained beyond that grate.

I squeezed past the dripping water and found the hidden stair mostly by feel, as every common light spell failed. The stair twisted downward in a tight, steep spiral, three times blocked with subtle wards that needed untangling. So carefully hidden, this had to be the relictory.

The last twist in the stair brought me to a vestibule so small as to hold a single man. Surprisingly, unnervingly, a thick iron door snarled with stinging enchantments stood wide-open.

I stretched my senses through the blackness beyond the opening. . . .

White daggers speared my eyes with such blazing ferocity, it was all I could do to stay upright. My sword flew from its sheath, clattering against stone and iron.

Staggering sideways, I fumbled for my bracelets, but mitons of ice sheathed my hands.

"Greenshank! I'd given up on you." Too rough a voice, and too . . . old . . . for Inek. Demanding. Impatient. Rusty.

"Knight Archivist?" I shielded my eyes with my club of an arm.

"First Inek, now you, blundering into forbidden places like scoundrel boys stealing apricots. I might have expected such indiscipline from a paratus, but by the Sky Lord's lance, not Inek."

"What in damnation is going on here? Where is Commander Inek?"

I wasn't feeling very respectful. He'd muted his beam, but I could see naught but molten steel against a yellow haze. I'd swear two holes had been burnt into my face.

"*What is going on here* is an excellent question—which your *rectoré* asked just before I sent him into a sleep from which he may never waken. And which Second asked, just before I put him into a state from which I may or may not revive him. Here"—clamping cold hands about my arm, he shoved me into a chair—"stop rubbing them or you'll go blind. I'll get the salve."

Glassware rattled somewhere I couldn't see. My hands regained feeling as I sat on them, the only way I could avoid touching my scalded eyes.

A rustle of slippers and the Archivist bent over me. "This will sting, but you'll be seeing quicker. All to the good, yes? Better than Silverdrake fared."

"Silverdrake?" I thought I knew all the parati and squires.

"Inek. Even as a tyro his hair was silver."

Inek as a tyro. My mind stretched . . . and brought me to my senses before a man I didn't know and couldn't see put more enchantments in my eyes.

I freed a hand and shoved the Archivist's arm aside before he could dispense his salve. "First, if you would, Knight Archivist, tell me where is Commander Inek."

"Inek is resting comfortably out of his mind not fifty paces from here. *Out of his mind* because there was some alteration in the infernal trap and I don't know how to repair the damage it's done. Cursed pattern's entirely crosswise, like to finding thorns on ivy."

"Out of his mind!"

"I've put him in stasis, hoping the damage is arrested as well, but I've no way to tell. He says you might. Were it anyone else . . . I ought to have you drowned for harboring such skills without me knowing of them."

Inek had told Cormorant that if I couldn't find Inek himself, I should consult the Archivist. Which meant he had some measure of trust in the man. "So *you* didn't harm him?"

"Deunor's fire, he told me you were intelligent! I am the Knight Archivist of Evanide. I could have fractured his memory in a hundred different ways at any time I wished over the last thirty years—a bit longer if you count the last year of our training together, the year we studied Evanide's greatest magic together, and I discovered it was my calling and certainly not his."

Which answer, I noted, was neither yes nor no.

"Late last night," he continued with wounded patience, "a concussive magic drew me to this chamber. It wasn't the door wards. Inek let himself in very easily, because he recognized the spellwork on the door—maybe years ago, maybe sometime in between, maybe in the same hour he came creeping in here to steal your relict. We developed the ward together. I should have created something different when I was named Archivist, but I had far too many other things to learn, and Inek is imminently trustworthy. . . ."

Steal your relict! "Please, Knight Archivist. Dispense your salve and start at the beginning, if you would. I'll be missed when seventh hour rings."

I'd no sense to follow his meanderings with my eyes smoldering like a dragon's gut.

"Head back." Just as he always commanded in the Seeing Chamber.

I tilted my head back obediently. The gooey globs of salve he dropped into my eye sockets spiked needles of ice into my skull, and when he wiped it off, the pressure drove them deep. I pressed the heels of my hands to my forehead. "You were speaking of my memory relict. . . ."

"Inek sneaked in here night before last, evidently to steal it, though I don't at all understand why. He's been bothering me about it for two years, which makes no sense at all, as he knew it was interdicted. But then who ever tells the Archivist anything of importance?"

He paused his rattling narrative. I felt more than saw his accusing glare, as if my very existence offended him.

"In his search he encountered a trap," he continued. "A nasty, dreadful bit of spellwork that began snarling his memory. *Like snakes*, he told me when I found him. His cries were terrible. It was the convulsive energy of the trap spell that drew me here, you see. I tried to reverse the damage, but concluded quickly that I'd no idea how to do so. It was a cleanly worked trap spell, but damaged somehow . . . perverse . . . difficult to read— Well, it had no business being where he encountered it. The Order's discipline is falling to ruin."

Distress was tearing at the old man, whether due to the Order's lacks or Inek's condition or his own incapacity was unclear. But it had shaken loose more words than I'd ever heard from him.

"Before I put him in stasis, Inek had enough sense remaining to tell me that his mewling paratus Greenshank might have the magic to help sort him out, and that he'd left orders for you to find him. I questioned Second, of course, as he can access the relictory at any time. He denied altering the trap, but he had a memory hole where your name should have been. I put him down for the time being, until I could probe deeper. Then I waited. Either you would show up or . . . someone else . . ."

Perhaps the person who set the damnable thing? Did he suspect someone? Feathers stroked my spine.

"Is it common for a trainee's name to be excised from someone's mind?"

"Not common at all. But then nothing's been usual since—" He stuffed a linen square in my hand. "Such matters are beyond a paratus's concern."

Blotting sticky tears, I rose. The leather straps dangling from the chair I'd just vacated choked off argument, especially when I noted similar straps binding the limp Second Archivist to another chair.

"Please take me to Commander Inek. I'll try my best to help him."

"I should hope so. You're an oath-sworn paratus of the *Equites Cineré*."

He led me past an alchemist's bench to a desk burdened with a hundredweight of books and papers. He retrieved the seven silver medallions that were the symbol of his office from a glass box, pulled their silver chains over his head, and flicked a hand at the ceiling. Lamps flared into life, one and then the next, into the depths of the chamber.

The blooming light revealed a sight that staggered me. The rear half of the chamber was filled with bronze racks, row upon row of them, one stacked atop another. Arrayed on the racks, each in a frame of its own, were identical cubes of thick glass, each edge the length of my finger.

Only as I looked on them—thousands of them, stacked ten racks high— did the subtle majesty of their massed enchantments settle on me. Each cube was bound in layers of spells, designed to protect the intricate, powerful enchantment that held a man's memory—the black-and-white relicts just visible through the cloudy glass. Some cubes were empty, though, save for wisps of flame that spread a golden glow through the glass walls like stray sunlight.

"Memories," I whispered, as if these scraps of souls might hear me. "There must be one of these for every tyro to train at Evanide. How in the name of the gods do you keep them straight?"

"They are as individual as every man. And we key them with magic, of course, bound to the tyro's soul."

The touch of his finger caused silver tracings and sigils to appear along the bronze rails. Some I recognized from my studies here; others were strange.

"Some say we should toss out the relicts of those who fail or die. But I agree with my predecessors. They are holy, in the way a man's or woman's bones are holy, no matter the person's worthiness in life. So they remain."

"What are the cubes with a flame?"

"Those of the knights, of course. In our early years, the residue of a knight's destroyed relict was returned to its vessel. But terrible spells can be worked with fragments of a soul."

"That's why the knight throws the dust of his relict into the sea."

To move between the stacks was like swimming through liquid glass. At the far end of the chamber Inek lay on a pallet of blankets and cloaks. His eyes were closed, skin flushed, hands clenched. But he did not breathe.

My own breath halted, as if one of the massive pillars supporting the fortress had collapsed. "Dead . . ."

"No. In stasis, as I told you. Unchanging until I wake him and the snakes devour him from the inside out, or he remains in this state for more than a month and his body hardens and crumbles. So what is it you do? How can you possibly help?"

Something . . . gods, please . . .

"At one time my magic could reveal secrets. I'm not sure I can—"

"Your *bent* has been returned to you?"

"By chance. I don't— It just happened."

"Hmph. A bent often breaks through on its own, especially if it was used intensively before it was masked. Masking bents is one of the most difficult things I do." Lecturing seemed to soothe his frenzy. "Bents are nature's imperative, as much a part of physical memory as of intellect. If some external spellwork cracked your mask, which from the way you prevaricate sounds likely, I'd be very interested in hearing about it. But I think you can have some confidence your talent will serve you—and confidence is a great part of our skill, yes?" He sounded almost friendly.

"Yes, certainly." From Fallon's testimony and Bastien's, I had used my bent for portraiture very deeply indeed. "I've no idea how long it might take to produce something useful, but if you would . . . I must return to Cormorant by seventh hour."

"I'll be needed for tonight's rites as well. But if you can give me some idea of what's been done to him, I'll work the rest of the night if need be. Reach deep for him, Greenshank."

Whether for guilt or friendship, he cared deeply.

As did I. "I will."

I settled on the floor beside Inek, unrolled the parchment, and sharpened the pen. Opening the ink cup released the oaky smell of tannin and the sour stink of green vitriol. In these two years the smell of ink and paint had roused longings I could not name. Now I could.

Bastien said I ran my fingers over the faces of the dead as I drew them. Easy to understand. I'd learned a great deal about magic at Evanide—about the huge role our senses play in designing the structure of our spellwork, allowing precision I hadn't known was possible. It was why we worked so vigorously to stretch our sensory perceptions. I would have to trust that my instincts knew how to link those perceptions with my two bents, and that my right hand recalled how to create a likeness, for I needed to reveal not just Inek's nature but what had happened to him.

Thus, as Inek hovered between death and life, uncomfortably exposed without his mask, my left hand traced the lines of his prominent cheekbones, his high, straight brow, his stern jaw. Then I dipped my pen, reached deep for the magic burning in chest and brow, and began to draw. . . .

"Greenshank!" My wrist seemed to be caught in a foot trap. Fruitlessly, I tried to retrieve it. "Let go!"

"The last quarter's rung and you must run for the Aerie. But Deunor's fire, look what you've done. I've studied it as you worked."

The heat of my bent had cooled a goodly while earlier. But I was trying to push deeper, to find more. I'd surely failed.

No more noble figure could ever have worn the silver mail of the *Equites Cineré* than the man looking out from the page. His right hand wielded the warrior's sword; his left gripped the staff of magic. But the eyes peering through Inek's mask were solid black. Black blood streamed from a terrible, ragged gash across his brow and pooled near his feet. Images crowded the pool—a palatial home, an old man's scarred hand, a woman's face, a drowning tyro . . . But none of it gave a hint of Inek's assailant or any key to his healing. The background remained blank—solid white.

"There must be more," I said, "if I just knew how to reach for it."

But the flame in my breast had died. I felt a surety of completion. The image inside me was exactly this, and as well as I knew anything, it was true.

"But this is extraordinary!" said the Archivist, tapping the page in a woodpecker's rhythm. "Don't you see? This wound is devouring Inek's memory, certainly. But notice that all of the images are in the pool—perhaps the past that he has already given."

"But the drowning tyro is his present life. Surely . . ."

"That *could* be a tyro, but I see no other sign of the Order. Silverdrake is lost in all this whiteness, but he holds on. Look at his fists—bloodless and pale—clenched about his weapons. And this neck chain"—he tapped on the thick-worked loop about Inek's neck—"is no simple decoration. Memory work is all about symbols, and this chain surely details the spellwork that binds him. Each link is a glyph. The symbology that memorists work with is a language to itself—because the concepts we deal in require thousands of words. And those words could be in any dialect of any language, though truly I've never seen glyphs representing any but a variant of Aurellian—which comprises only about three hundred dialects . . ."

Time pressed. "Knight Archivist, will Inek—?"

But he wouldn't stop. "If I could determine what alteration has been made to the original trap spell, Inek might have a chance. There are thirteen links in the neck chain, thirteen glyphs, which are not half enough for such a working, but all of them are familiar pieces of a memory trap. Perhaps—" He held the page just under his nose. "Yes, see this one!"

Manic, he snatched the pen from my hand and pointed the tip to a link in Inek's habergeon, a link right over Inek's heart. It was brighter than others, as if a layer of tarnish had been polished away from that particular curl of steel.

"This is the same as the first in the neck chain. There's more of the pattern hidden in his mail. Just pray it is the key to unwind the spellwork, and that I can find and decipher it in time to help him."

He dipped the pen and scribbled some of the patterns in the white space of the drawing, aligning them in various arrangements. "Get out of here! I've work to do. Say nothing of these matters to anyone."

"Aye, sir knight."

"I'll be in the Hall when Cormorant— Oh, wait!"

I was halfway to the door when his biting call stopped me. He fingered one of his silver medallions, then beckoned me down an aisle of the glass cubes. He touched one at just about head height.

Dissipating magic buffeted my face like a gale, as the cube's front face melted away. The Archivist pulled out a half-relict—a broken fragment that held a man's life—and laid it in my hand with gentle reverence.

World and time stood still. I glanced up, unable to speak, choked with words, thoughts, imaginings . . .

"No, no, Greenshank," he said, impatiently. "This is Cormorant's, not yours. You must carry it to his rite. Second was supposed to do it, but—" He shrugged.

"Of course." The flood drained away. "So mine remains in its glass. Inek didn't find it."

No matter his mask, I could read the Archivist's discomfort clearly. The tale it told left me as still and empty as Inek. He led me down an aisle and pointed at the fifth cube from the end on the third row from the bottom— the glass that held my memory. I sank to my knees in front of it.

"Inek begged me to tell you he did not do this," said the Archivist, his rust-colored robe brushing my shoulder. "The corruption in the glass tells me it has been this way for more than a year—perhaps from the day you arrived. Saints and stones, if Inek had only known that the man occupying these robes was his partner from the day we were tyros. . . . He could have come to me, explained why learning more of a nothing paratus like you was so important. I could have shown him where it was, and I'd have seen that perverted . . . corrupt . . . wicked enchantment waiting. But he didn't know whether he could trust the *Archivist*, so he sneaked in, broke the seal, and touched what was inside."

The cube's glass front was dissolved. What lay inside was no thumb-sized fragment of stone, but black dust and white splinters and a purulent enchantment that could set snakes devouring a mind.

CHAPTER 19

"Paratus Cormorant, it has been an honor to serve with you. The hour has come for your choice."

The man in sodden gray gave all the appearance of sleep, tucked into the rocks as he was. But my hand on his arm roused his grin before he even opened his eyes. "Call me Terryn for now. Terryn de Pescatori-Salvados. Let me hear it."

"Gods' bones! Terryn de Pescatori-Salvados . . . they gave you your—"

"A secret not to be shared," he whispered. His face was animated, filled with life and experience and . . . *knowing.* "They give you back everything. So you can choose fully to hold or yield it. It's terrible and wonderful and painful, and you've only the two days. But to see your life beginning to end, to make sense of the world and reasons and where you belong . . . It gives a man confidence."

Unless there was nothing to give back. The shock was only beginning to settle in. My past . . . and the man shaped from those years and experiences . . . was dust. Unrecoverable.

"Gods!" Cormorant slapped his head. "How could I—? Greenshank, did you find Inek?"

"He lives, but a spell trap has damaged his mind. The Knight Archivist is looking into it. For now, you've other things to think about. You know Inek would wish this night to go forward."

Cormorant examined me carefully. "You're injured as well."

"To see a fine man laid low by someone in this fortress"—outrage elbowed its way past self-pity—"we are all injured."

His hand clapped my shoulder. "Whatever I can do to forward justice, I will do. Until then, I'll hold Inek in my thoughts. And you as well, brother. It's been clear for some time that Inek believes greatness awaits you."

Laughter emerged as a mirthless bleat. "I'll hold to that as I walk the seaward wall tonight. Come, you must dress. I wonder if they left you a towel . . ."

He needed no help, so I didn't see which tunic he chose, though I believed Dunlin correct that it would be black. *Cormorant* . . . Terryn de Pescatori-Salvados . . . whatever name he chose to carry forward . . . was destined for greatness.

A trudge down the Aerie stair and through the deep passage led us to the armory. As we passed the armory door, I unfurled the Order's ensign—the white quiver blazon on a field of black—and led my brother into the lingering daylight on the side of Idolon Mount. Angled sunlight bathed the fortress in gold, the storm but a few bloated clouds in the east. To the cheers of three hundred knights, and a hundred parati, squires, tyros, and adjutants, we descended the outer stair and joined the Marshal and nineteen knights-commander in procession to the Common Hall of Evanide.

The anthem of the Order, sung with such strength and belief by the assembled brothers, raised the hair on my neck. But it did not send my soul soaring as every other time I'd heard it.

Inek should be here. To make a knight from ash and splinters was a work worthy of celebration. To harm one, as Inek had been harmed, was a work worthy of mortal judgment. I had to assume that the person who destroyed my relict was the same who had laid the spell trap, even if the deeds were two years apart. But it was the latter crime for which he would pay.

How could I waste six hours on such a useless exercise? Every moment of my first hour on the seaward wall that night, I seethed, tempted to climb back down and tell the fortress watch commander—or the Marshal himself—I was unfit for duty. But that would be a lie.

Appetite had deserted me during the celebration of Cormorant's investiture. Sir Conall of the *Equites Cineré* he was now and would ever be. But the day with Morgan—the food she'd given me, the sleep she'd guarded, the very air I'd breathed—had refreshed and renewed me beyond measure, so that even the bay crossing and the invocation of my bent had not drained me. I had no excuse but frustration.

Inek had reasons for me to be on this wall. I'd hold faith in that if naught else. I wanted to have faith in the Archivist, too. At the end of the feast, it was announced that the Second Archivist had found Commander Inek in the armory, severely injured from an enchantment's backlash. Who would dare contradict the story? I'd wager the Second Archivist himself sincerely believed it.

Yet the Archivist had so much as said he knew of the trap spell and that it was *alterations* had devoured Inek's mind. Who would destroy my relict and leave a poisonous enchantment for anyone who tried to learn about my past?

Damon, surely. He had sent me to Evanide. He had a use for me beyond a folio of portraits that frightened the senior pureblood families. And Damon was a linguist, who had been trained in Order magic. Who better to create a dialect of symbols to alter a spell? But why?

In the second hour of the watch, fog blanketed the fortress so thickly I could not see my feet. The only proof the fortress yet existed were the tide horns and the bell that struck the hours. Please gods no brother had been caught out on the sea this night.

Though necessarily focused on balance and calm, I could not banish thought entire, not with so much learned and experienced in the past month. Yet I could not afford the distraction of wrestling with puzzles, thus thoughts and questions flowed as they would.

My past might be gone, but my bents yet lived. What a marvel that a despicable prince's scouring had freed them. Yet drawing Inek's portrait had not returned me to the five-fingered land. What if Safia never allowed me through again? The Duchy of Xancheiros had been home to thousands. Was it possible they were yet trapped there? And Morgan was beyond my help if I could not satisfy her father.

Bastien said I'd had him bury evidence of my grandsire's investigation of Xancheira . . . a spindle . . . needlework of some kind. Evidence of the massacre, perhaps, or some hint of the city's fate. And surely if there was a route to Sanctuary in this world, it would lie wherever that city had once stood. I needed to get that spindle.

My grip was near bending the lance. My fingers had gone numb. I wriggled them inside the mail mitons to ensure I didn't drop it.

This Bastien knew more of my past than I ever would. Did Damon know of our unusual relationship—not just master and pureblood, but partners? Friends? What if the curator decided to eliminate anyone who knew me? Somewhere I had a sister. I needed to warn them both, keep them safe, Bastien and—

Why hadn't I asked Bastien my sister's name or where I might have thought safe enough to send her when the Registry proclaimed me a murdering madman?

The answer sailed past like flotsam on the flood. Because she wasn't real to me. The horror I felt at my family's murder I would have felt at any other family's massacre. Yes, the sight of the fire had hit me very hard that day, but I'd felt no personal loss even after Bastien's telling. The outrage was the deed itself and that it had been committed by people like me. I'd never imagined so much of feeling and attachment was lost with the specific memories.

No matter what else I did, I would make that young girl real again. Get to know her in *this* life. Make sure she was safe and well cared for and not alone. She was likely safer at distance from me and Damon. *A spark of a girl*, Bastien had called her. *You loved her dearly . . . your only kin left in the world . . . sent her away . . .*

Under layers of padding and mail, my sweat chilled. What had the silver-marked Dané said? *Thou didst send thy heart with them. . . .*

A cry of anguish rose in me. Was it possible I had sent my only living family—my young sister who trusted me—through a magical portal with a ragtag band of Cicerons to a mythical place called Sanctuary, where she was trapped until *I* could get her out? Where those who waited to greet her might or might not be mad?

Balance! Focus! Eyes forward into the murk. Curl your toes and feel your feet . . . your ankles . . . knees. . . . The wall is solid beneath your boots only as long as you feel it.

The remaining hours on the wall crawled by. Damon had set something huge in motion. Something involving the Order, the Registry, and a Sitting of the Three Hundred. I had to learn what he planned, as well as what part he expected me to play in it. But my life's work, inside or outside the Order, would be to ensure that he could not do to my sister, my friend the coroner, or anyone else, the horror he had done to Inek.

D amon, muffled in a wine-colored pelisse, warmed his hands at the Hearth of Memory as I hurried into the Seeing Chamber. No one else was present.

"I worried I'd be late," I said. Sixth hour had rung as I threw on a dry shirt, splashed the salt from my eyes, and forced aside every concern but Damon the Spider. "Perhaps the Knight Archivist is delayed by the fog, as I was." Or perhaps he was busy working to save Inek's life.

Damon didn't bother to turn around. Clearly he didn't realize how close I was to throttling him. "The Knight Archivist will not be present. I shall administer the eyeglim and potions myself."

"And work the Archivist's magic?"

He pivoted and examined me sharply, as if he thought I might not be the Greenshank he expected. "Are the skills of a Registry curator so far beneath those of an Order pedant that you fear to engage in this session?"

"I'd no intent to offend, curator. And I'm certainly willing to observe whatever you wish to show me. It's only that the enchantments required are quite specialized to the Order. I must confess, I cannot grasp your position here or your interest in my training or opinions. Sometimes it seems as if your purpose and that of the Order must be the same, but recently . . . I'm no longer sure of that."

The unmasked half of his face expressed only detached observation. But the quirking mouth and gleaming eye beneath the purple silk evidenced enjoyment of feint and counter. I hated that.

"Be assured, Greenshank, the Knight Marshal and I are of a single mind. My position and purpose have not been your concern to this point. But the time of secrecy is rapidly coming to a close. Now tell me: After last night's celebration and your ridiculous tour of the seaward wall, are you quite capable of engaging your mind? You will experience a series of complex scenes from a single perspective, and you must link their threads to make a story— as a *historian* does."

"Quite capable, *domé*. The seaward watch teaches a man his limits. It's taken me a while to understand that. The time can also provide a certain clarity of thought. It is my duty to learn what every aspect of my training can teach."

With Inek's fall, Damon and the Marshal had cracked open the door of their plotting. Now Damon seemed to have dropped all pretense. *So push him. Give him what he seems to relish.*

"Why am I the only one privileged to observe this seeing? Is it some particular flaw in me that draws the Registry's concern?"

"The Order has you well practiced in dealing with uncertainty. You will be told what's needed when the time is right."

"What makes you believe that I will listen to your needs at any time?"

Even such insolence did not ruffle him. "Because I know you better than you know yourself." He poured the amber potion and passed me the cup. "Experience what I have to show you. Then we shall discuss your future."

As ever, I used magic and all my senses to examine the amber potion and the eyeglim. Occasionally, the standard formulas and enchantments were purposely altered to sting our eyes or empty our bowels—lessons not easily forgotten.

Both potions were as they should be. I would have to trust Damon's skills to do the rest. Curiosity trumped caution.

The amber potion quickly had me dizzy. Settled on the wooden bench, I allowed Damon to administer the eyeglim. And I did not fight when the blurred hearth fire flashed a brilliant yellow and I fell into another man's skin. . . .

I hurried down the iron stair, nauseated as always at its tight twisting as much as at its destination—the dank pit where our cruelty festered and our hope was nurtured in darkness and filth like a tender mushroom. Why my colleagues picked the middle of the night for their games was unfathomable. It was just as black down here at midday as at midnight. Did they think the hour would hide their corruption?

I knew better. Light was coming to reveal their sins. *Our* sins. No deeds of worth allow the doer to remain unsullied.

It was inevitable the fools had fixed their minds on the portraits. Were I one of my single-minded peers, I would have burnt the damnable things the moment I saw them and buried the artist right then. But Pluvius-the-not-so-much-a-fool-as-he-pretended swore that all of pureblood society would notice the paintings' disappearance. Over the months of their creation, he'd made a great fuss about Remeni's brilliance and how we would hang the portraits whenever the new king took his throne, celebrating the Remeni—and thus the Registry—connection to the Crown. Exactly the kind of attention we could not afford. And then there was the matter of the massacre so close in time, making Lucian's fate more noticeable. We'd had to wait. I'd approved of Pons's solution to keep Lucian out of sight. Unfortunately, it just hadn't worked.

"Damon!" Pons waited at the bottom of the stair, torchlight turning her thick skin yellow. My protégé was a singularly unattractive woman. "Do you know what these idiots think to do here?"

"Hide their crimes," I said, "as you did, my friend."

Pons's maturity had produced a formidable intellect, and she had performed admirably as our newest curator, as I knew she would. Her connection to Remeni and his cowardly grandsire had been invaluable; her fitness for the duties of her future unquestionable. Never had I known any person at once so diabolically ruthless and so morally conflicted as Elaia Pons-Laterus. I planned a grand future for her. And she was perfect.

My heart hammered so violently, it yanked me out of the magic for a moment. I drew a great breath, willed my body to slow down, and dived back into Damon's memory. Into Lucian de Remeni's past. My past.

The remaining four of our six—Gramphier the Blood-handed, Pluvius the Idiot, Scrutari the Holy Hypocrite, and Albin the Devil's Insufferable Cock—waited in the cell they'd set up as an artist's studio. The blindingly white plaster that masked the iron walls had taken a month to install. The worktable bowed with the weight of inkhorns, pens, and artist's paraphernalia, the fodder for their schemes. The chair where they'd bound sleeping ordinaries in hopes of seeing Remeni vanish as he drew them had been pushed to the side. Did they not listen to Pons's tales of the man's stubborn righteousness and extraordinary discipline?

Through session after session, slobbering from the potions and magics they used to force him to speak after months insisting he mustn't, Remeni claimed that his magic could draw out a man's soul. He refused to draw anyone who was alive. We could kill him or not, he'd said, but the gods would never forgive him such a crime.

His confusion and weakness had been subterfuge. None of the others recognized it. And none of them had the grit to haul in a corpse for him to draw—which gave him the victory, albeit a small one, as my magic ensured he would not remember it. After six increasingly brutal attempts, Albin and Scrutari, at the least, had come to believe the *vanishing* was a lie. Their illogic never ceased to astonish me.

Let them believe it. The tides of history would sweep them aside.

A clattering in the passage announced his coming. My colleagues, shy of being seen by the jailers, veiled themselves.

The knaves hauled Remeni in naked and chained, his hands silkbound, his eyes blindfolded. No matter how often I'd told them it made no difference, they always insisted he be bound "lest he remember being without."

The imbeciles could not comprehend magic that could so precisely expunge a man's experience. They shoved him to the floor.

"Unbind him," I said. "How can he possibly do what's needed while trussed like a goose?"

Remeni, head bowed and eyes squeezed shut, twitched as nervously as a twistmind craving his nivat. As the jailers removed his bonds, he buried his eyes in the crook of his elbow. It was hard on him coming into the brightness from the pitch-dark cell.

Unfortunately, that darkness, too, was necessary. Lucian de Remeni-Masson was a stubborn, disciplined man. Breaking him was never going to be easy, and these games in the cellar hadn't helped in the least. I didn't have forever to grind him down and rebuild.

Crouching beside him, I laid a hand on his cold flesh. He jumped, and I sent a bit of soothing magic into him. Not too much. We needed him lucid. "I heard you've been dreadfully sick, Lucian. Is that so?"

Lucian wouldn't speak without magical coercion. He knew the rules of his confinement, and discipline comprised his very bones.

He squinted over his arm, trying to blink away the tears flooding his eyes so he could get a good look at me. The flash of hope that followed was always the most painful part to witness. He couldn't remember how often we had done this.

Today, though, he just stared dully, buried his eyes again, and nodded. Good . . . we were getting close to the end of this business.

"I'm truly sorry for that. We've tried to keep you clean and healthy. If I find your minders have been careless or have maliciously dosed you to make you ill, they'll be soundly thrashed."

I glared and dismissed the brutes.

"We've a different task for you today. A bit of painting. Some of my colleagues are uncomfortable about their portraits. Small alterations can ease their concerns. No souls involved. No betrayal of your bent. No magic at all, save that mundane sort which lives in any fine portrait artist's hands. And just think, you'll learn your masters' intimate secrets!"

His breath visibly slowed. He was considering it. I wondered if he could manage the work. His hands trembled like terrified rabbits.

"I swear on my hope of a nobler world, Lucian, that once this task is done to our satisfaction, we'll have no choice but to consider your madness much improved and perhaps relent in the strictness of your confinement. Come, stand up. . . ."

His body had not deteriorated as much as five months' imprisonment would lead one to expect. I made sure he was fed adequately and kept free of vermin. Silence and darkness would make him stronger. Physical inaction would leave him all the more ready for the Order's molding. A mad starveling would do the world no good at all.

Still blinking, he let me lead him to the stepstool and the great easel where the man-high painting stood waiting under its sheet. As I unshrouded Pluvius's portrait, the Master of Registry Archives unveiled himself. I wasn't sure Remeni even noticed the man. He stared at the painting.

"Do you have all the materials you need to make a few small changes to this work?" I said. "Lucian! Tell me."

The prisoner jerked his eyes from the canvas, glanced at Pluvius and then at the worktable. His hand, steadier, poked through the materials—dishes of ground pigments, flasks of oils, resins, and sharp-smelling chemicals, rags, brushes, scraping knives and tweezers of all sizes. His fellow portraitist Gilles had made the selection. Poor Gilles, to be sacrificed as so many others had been . . . and would be.

Lucian dipped his head and held out a hand, palm up, as if to ask what he was supposed to do.

"Tell him what you want repaired, Pluvius. . . ."

It was a very long time until I slipped back into my own body, imagining I could yet smell the paint and ethers I'd used to alter four paintings of my own making. But I did not open my eyes or move or give an indication to whoever might be watching that I was yet returned. How could I ever comprehend what I had just witnessed?

Only Morgan's testimony and Bastien's convinced me that the half-mad prisoner was me. How unnerving, how extremely odd, to observe oneself in such a state. Odder yet to believe to my depths that the scene was true, and to have absolutely no recollection of it. Over four sessions in that white room, my art had hidden truth to mask a multitude of sins. I felt dirty. To alter the truth of one's divine bent was a corruption of the soul.

Curator Pluvius, who had been my contract master at the Registry, had told me to erase a symbol of Xancheira's white tree that hinted at forbidden Registry secrets in his possession, and to replace a missing hand, an unwelcome reference to a second bent, excised when he was a child. The genial old

man had also called me *son* and *lad* and talked of persuading the other curators that he should have custody of me until my madness was deemed cured.
His kind talk might have had some meaning had I not been naked, mute,
and half mad, doing his bidding in a prison cell.

I had originally depicted Curator Scrutari-Consil, a small, ugly man, at his
desk writing. The official seals of the king of Navronne and the two highest
clergymen in the kingdom, already pressed into red wax, lay beside the document. The seals were not *attached*, however, and none of the three men were
present—the makings of a royal forgery. Damon had goaded Scrutari to confirm that the document was a false will that named Perryn of Ardra as Eodward's heir. At the behest of his contract master and Prince Perryn himself,
Scrutari had executed a forgery that would give a cheating coward the throne
of the mightiest kingdom in the world at a time of its gravest crisis. I had obliterated the evidence.

Bastien had told me I'd eventually gone back to the Tower to see the
altered portraits, and that a small matter of justice had come out of that visit.
Was it the matter of Fallon's dead sister?

Curator Gramphier, the gaunt, aristocratic First of the Curators' Council,
had me remove a bloody dagger with Xancheira's white tree on its hilt and
blood on his hand. Together they exposed his complicity in the murder of
anyone other than purebloods who attempted true magic—and anyone who
came too close to revealing Registry secrets. Gramphier laughed as he told
me these things, sneering as he spoke of murdering purebloods, entire bloodlines, and any Ciceron who crossed his path. He knew I'd not remember
anything he told me.

None of them mentioned the particular *Registry secrets* the white tree
represented. Damon, whose body I occupied, who so freely exposed my
identity, my unusual bent for portraiture, and the other curators' crimes,
never considered those secrets either. Yet the symbol itself gave me a clue.
Xancheira. Were any of these villains aware there might be witnesses to the
Registry's guilt yet living?

Lastly, Curator Albin, a ferocious toad-like man, insisted I alter a background landscape that exposed the subtle truth of his portrait—evidence of
his connection to the Harrowers hired to slaughter a pureblood family.
Again and again I refused, for I had recognized it as my own family's murder. In his fury, he came near slicing off my hand. Perhaps it was the threat
of mutilation that made me comply—or simply that I was too worn down
to fight. Damon believed I'd reached the nadir of my confinement at that

confrontation and expressed readiness to set his plan for me in motion. His thoughts did not reveal what that plan might be.

According to Inek, a prominent pureblood had died for my family's murder. Goddess Mother, let it be the loathsome Albin, who never in all those scenes bothered to tell *why* my family had to die.

At the end of each session, Damon had handed me a wooden token that contained a splinter of silver, and using the identical one in his hand had erased my memory of the men, the room, the work, and the secrets. Each time the jailers chained me and dragged me, uncomprehending, back into the dark. Order memory magic. *Sky Lord's wrath!*

"I know you're back, *Lucian*. Is the truth not what you wanted?"

For a moment it seemed the emotionless voice was inside me instead of out, for it was so exactly the voice of the body I had occupied for these untold hours. Damon was exactly what he seemed.

Flesh touched mine, pressing a soft square of linen into my palm. Then the cool glass of the eyewash cup. The smell of the eyeglim's antidote seared my nostrils. The world I knew existed outside of me, while I yet dwelt in that other with a most unsettling conviction. I did not know everything yet.

Damon could not possibly imagine I would judge him innocent just because he desired no alteration to his own portrait. By his own admission, he had approved my abasement. All because he wanted to grind me down, so he and the Order could rebuild me. And he no longer cared whether or not I knew it. What had changed?

Inek's loss, surely. And my obvious mistrust of the Marshal. Damon believed I had no one left to confide in, no one to trust. He wanted me angry and he wanted me alone. He had shown me Lucian, but he wanted only Greenshank. Why? Had the Archivist told him that I'd seen what had happened to my relict? Did he enjoy watching me live his past, knowing it was the closest thing to remembering I would ever have?

The roar erupted from my chest like scalding tar from a siege wall. Yet it did not empty me. Anger and hatred boiled inside, so virulent it must surely leak through my pores and eat holes in the stone beneath my feet, all the way through Evanide's rock to the Tormentor's mighty forges.

"Do you need a while to consider what you've witnessed?" he said, as if asking me which jerkin I might wish to purchase at a leather-worker's stall.

My hand launched the eyewash cup, which bounced off the hearthstone and clattered across the floor. "The other session. The burning house. That was my *family*!"

And, of course, the truest horror here was not that single event, as awful, dreadful, and savage as it was.

"You *allowed* it," I snapped. "All of you. You knew what that *animal* had done. You let him force me to hide the flames of my own family's burning lest he be exposed as a traitor to all purebloods, to Navronne, to the gods. The rest of you watched and chatted about nothing until he threatened to leave me useless for magic-working. But worried about your own sins, you dared not leave me incapable. And when I gave in, you scoured my memory of it and sent me back into the dark. All of you—the six most powerful purebloods in the world—are tainted with conspiracy and murder and false imprisonment, with decades of slaughter. And . . . great and holy gods . . . you masked a conspiracy to steal the throne of Navronne! What measure is there for such corruption?"

"The Marshal reminded you that many worthy societies are built on faulty ground."

"The Pureblood Registry is *not* worthy!" His equanimity but threw more tinder on the fire scorching my gut.

"So, what are you willing to do about that?"

Something woke in me at this quiet goad. Something deep and huge, snarling, as dark and cold and unrelenting as this dreadful winter. The molten anger did not dissipate, but hardened into rock. This was the answer. This was about Damon's purpose, the reason he wanted me at the Sitting of the Three Hundred.

"What do you *wish* me to do about that, curator?"

"For now, I want you to lend your mind to the first problem. Tell me how we reform the Registry."

"Magic is the gods' divine gift to the world," I said. "It must be nurtured and shared. It must remain independent of the politics of ordinaries. But the Pureblood Registry, formed to ensure exactly those things, was founded on slaughter, and it yet wallows in murder and political corruption. It must be purged. Cleansed. Reduced to ash and bone, as are we of the Order, and refitted into something worthy." Even as this spewed from me, I knew it was no contrivance for Damon's ear. I believed it heart and soul, in bone and sinew.

Damon preened like a proud parent. "Exactly so. To make ready for this day, I have been forced to lie low, to cooperate as I plumbed the depths to which we have sunk. That has tainted me irretrievably, as you have suspected. And as I've shown you today, I've played a role in your own life's dissolution, as well as its resurrection here at Evanide. I vow to you here that I seek no position of authority for myself. I have dedicated my life to guide this cleansing and then yield to those worthier than I to lead this new Registry forward. But to do what's needed, I must have a right arm strong in magic and resolute in purpose, ready to do terrible deeds. I need a voice that carries the weight of righteous anger to persuade three hundred families and their thousand offshoots that this work must be done. I have consulted with your Marshal, with his predecessor, and with your most excellent Commander Inek to bring you to this day. You will be that arm and that voice."

Surely this was madness. "Why me? What is it you want me to do? Burn cities? Empty pureblood houses the way the Registry rousts Ciceron slums? To be your *Harrower*?"

"You've seen the gift your art provides—to depict the sins all men and women wish to hide. In the coming months, I'll ask the Archivist to unmute your bent. You are already disciplined and well trained, and soon you'll own skills that only the Order can provide. Alongside others dedicated to returning Navronne to a righteous path, we shall devise our campaign."

Only that campaign was two years under way. He hadn't needed my arm or my voice to leave purebloods in fear. Only the folio of my portraits. And he spoke of my investiture and skills I had yet to learn, but those could take a year or more, and the Sitting was two months hence. There was more to his plan.

It took no time to decide how to answer. Even if I killed Damon now, nothing would change. These other demon gatzi would keep doing as they did, and I wouldn't know who else was involved at the Registry or in the Order. Fallon had judged Damon's purpose a *move of power* as we had not seen since Caedmon's Writ—a truce that had defined Navronne for almost two centuries. I believed him.

Thus, begging forgiveness from the ghosts I would never know, and asking the gods to strike me down were I to become an arrogant monstrosity like this man before me, I straightened my back and faced the author of my dissolution. "I will not kneel to you, curator. The taint you bear I cannot forgive, and one day we shall meet in reckoning. But for now, your purpose is my own."

A terrifying truth.

Then, knowing he would accept nothing less, I laid a fist on my breast in the Order's binding submission, and lowered my eyes. "Command me."

— PART III —
SHATTERED
STARS

CHAPTER 20

Damon's first command was to continue my training in all areas, with special attention to archery and memory magic. Though his insistence on archery was curious, not only was I better at it than swordwork, I preferred it. And I could not get enough of the memory work. Still, I chafed at this first tug of his leash. Not a magical leash, but certainly the will of a very powerful man.

The choice to take up my old life was gone. So I must build my new life from the elements Damon had left me. Magic. Mystery. Deception. War. Justice. But I'd not let him define or shape those elements.

My new commander informed me that the Marshal wished to see me. No surprise.

Wreathed in concern, the Marshal greeted me beside his great window—the center span that looked out on a misty midday. "I was told Commander Inek was attempting to attach a powerful memory enchantment to a silver bracelet when the spellwork rebounded so terribly. But no one can tell me to what purpose. Have you any idea what he might have been about?"

"None, Knight Marshal. Will he recover?"

"The damage from backlash is variable, but the Archivist is not sanguine. Ah, Greenshank, Inek's loss would be immeasurable."

"Immeasurable," I said.

I hated the Marshal in that moment. How could he speak with such conviction, such sympathy, so believably, when he knew the truth? The water carrier who discovered Inek missing from Cormorant's vigil would have reported to the Marshal. He would have spoken to the Archivist.

"I am going to ask a great deal of you going forward, Greenshank, and of Knight Conall. Conall has his own changes to deal with, but he is mature beyond his rank and already familiar with Inek's tyros. He will continue to drive the tyros toward their testing. Inek's current squires will move into another knight commander's cadre. Inek had no senior paratus save Cormorant, which leaves you, Dunlin, and Heron."

He faced me straight on, hands clasped at his back.

"A mentor unfamiliar with a paratus's training history makes an ineffective guide. Thus I shall take on the duty of personal reviews and counsel. But I've no time for close supervision. As First of your cadre, you will direct the other two in their day-to-day training, relying on the combat masters, the Archivist, and other tutors for skills beyond your knowledge. You will drive them hard, as Inek would wish and report to me daily at sixth hour of the evening watch beginning tomorrow. Is that clear?"

I felt bad for Dunlin and Heron. It was laughable to think I could substitute for Inek in any way. "Of course, Knight Marshal. If this is what you think best."

"I *do* think it best, Greenshank, and yes, Curator Damon will be intimately involved in your development, as he has been these past months. I recognize your resentment of him. He sees it. Inek saw it, and shared it to a certain extent, I believe. Damon is an outsider, a Registry pureblood who is not subject to the disciplines of the Order."

The Marshal wandered from the window as he spoke, and spoke to his meaning as if he were arguing with someone else in the room. "I have committed my life to the Order, and I believe firmly and entirely in its goals and practices. But I also believe in what the curator said yesterday. A storm rages in Navronne. This war . . . these unworthy princes . . . this savage priestess and her followers. We cannot focus solely on small injustices. At some point, we must address the larger ones. I believe that time is upon us."

I could not argue. Though I hated agreeing with the two of them about anything, the smaller injustices were certainly symptoms of a disease that needed to be healed. I just believed that Damon himself—and likely this Marshal, too—were a part of that disease.

"Is that all, Knight Marshal?"

He pivoted sharply, and his eyes—an unusual gray-green, and hard and sharp as polished malachite—locked onto mine from his fine white mask.

"Despite what I've said here, you must have a care, Greenshank." His voice had dropped. "Curator Damon is quite single-minded. I think it is unfair to drive you forward blind when small things might illumine your choices. Remember: You *do* have choices, as does every member of the Order. I would tell you something in confidence."

Careful, Greenshank. This could so easily be a trap.

"Curator Damon is not my Order commander," I said. "I may share his purpose and his vision, but he is not privy to my soul. My dealings with Evanide's Knight Marshal are not his business."

"As is proper." If a masked face could beam, his certainly would. "Before accepting the recommendations of my predecessor to heed an outsider, I studied Damon's history. Attis de Lares-Damon was a trainee here. As you can imagine, he was intelligent, skilled, and driven to excellence in all his endeavors. He reached the rank of paratus-exter, awaiting his final test and the same rites we celebrated yestereve. But the Marshal of those days refused to set a day for Damon's investiture. He wrote in his journal that he could point to no flaw in Damon's record, yet could not, in conscience, bring the man into our brotherhood. He believed Damon to be wanting in some indefinable way.

"Damon, understandably, demanded a resolution. Even a Marshal's doubts cannot deny a paratus-exter his final choice. But the Marshal *can* alter the terms of that choice, even to making it the paratus's final test.

"'Ordinarily you would have to choose either to reclaim the memories of your past and leave Evanide or to abandon your past and embrace a future of service in the Order with use of all the skills you've learned here,' he told Damon. 'But for your final testing, I've changed those terms. Heed me carefully. I will invest you in our Order, allowing you to embrace our discipline of service. But I will also require you to accept your past, giving you a perspective no other knight possesses. The price of this enlarged perspective will be half the knowledge you have gained here. That will necessarily limit your service, but benefit our ultimate objectives, I think.'

"Damon asked what was his other option. The Marshal said, 'To fail. I will destroy your relict and send you back into the world without your past. But in respect for your accomplishments at reaching the rank of paratus-exter, I will allow you to retain your memory of the Order and your time here, though, as before, recalling only portions of the knowledge you've gained. Which do you choose?'"

"Tell me, Greenshank. Which do you think Damon chose?"

It took me a moment. I was so fervently hunting misdirection in this Marshal's story I hadn't comprehended the actual events and the strange, skewed choice. Reclaim his past life and join the Order, or relinquish both the past and his place here. But in either case, he would retain only a part of his Order skills.

The answer that glared at me explained a great deal. About the oddity of a *failed paratus* who held knowledge of Order secrets. About a man who could unapologetically expose his partnership in savagery, while pursuing a righteous cleansing that would sweep him and those like him away. It explained a sorcerer who had seemingly mastered Order magic—some of the most complex known—and yet needed an Order knight shaped to his specifications to be his *right arm*. Fallon might be more experienced in war, but I had the magic.

"He chose the second path," I said. "He wanted neither his former life nor the disciplines of our brotherhood. And the Marshal gave him his wish."

The white hood dipped in confirmation. Damon had left the Order with heart and soul free of entanglement—no connection from his true life and unbound by the selfless discipline of Evanide's brotherhood. But only a part of his Order training was intact. Which part?

Perhaps more important, this Marshal had just given me an insight into his partner's weakness. The Marshal had his own purposes, not entirely bound to Damon. As did Fallon. As did I.

"*Dalle cineré*, Greenshank." The Marshal's abrupt dismissal caught me formulating questions. But there would be time enough for those. I would be speaking with him every day.

"*Dalle cineré*, Knight Marshal." *From the ashes*. In the past day, our benediction had taken on an entirely new meaning.

My proper destination upon leaving the Marshal's chamber was to search out Dunlin and Heron and review their training schedule. But I was driven to a far more urgent errand.

I'd once spent three nights in the fortress infirmary, out of my head with fever from an untended wound turned septic. As was drummed into me from all sides, I was fortunate to survive with the leg intact. The incident had resulted in my sole visit to the Disciplinarian and his whipping post. Never again had pride ruled sense in the matter of wounds or illness. Overwork and excessive risk were a more difficult balance, as both Inek and Morgan had pointed out so recently. I was determined to block out six hours of sleep before I stood my midnight watch. But first, the infirmary.

Evanide's infirmarian was an adjutant—one who had completed a part of his training and withdrawn with honor, but had petitioned to stay on and serve the Order with his bent. His oaths were strict and his past naught but dust.

"Are you bleeding or fevered?" Adjutant Tomas gave me a sour glance as he hurried past the door where I stood. He didn't like people wandering in and out of his demesne. His capable hands were the color of good earth, a rich contrast with the five large rolls of linen bandage he held.

"Neither," I said to his back. "I've come to visit Commander Inek."

Tomas set a bandage roll and towels beside each of five vacant sling beds, where bowls, potion flasks, and leather packets that looked uncomfortably like surgeon's tools already waited. The sixth bed at the far end of the long room was hidden by a folding screen.

"There's naught to gawk at," he said. "The commander maintains. The Archivist has finished three hours of trials and says he needs to 'work out more glyphs,' whatever that means. So be off. I've work to do. The Tyros' Tourney begins today."

The infirmary would indeed have a bloody afternoon.

"I'm not here to gawk. Can Inek hear?"

"Hear?" Tomas was already on another visit to his linen cupboard. Laden with sponges and extra sheets, he made another distribution pass. Each bed was set by an embrasure. Whatever sunlight it captured shone on the sick man, even while the narrow opening helped keep out the cold. "Can a memory-strangled man in stasis hear? However would you tell?"

"Perhaps one tries and then asks him when he's healed." I grabbed a load of blankets and ten more towels from the cupboard and dropped a share at the end of each bed. Tomas stared, then deigned a jerk of his head. I stepped behind the screen.

I wanted to avert my eyes. They had stripped Inek naked and laid him on a clean sheet, but despite a raw morning, they'd not bothered to cover him. The infirmarian believed excessive heat was unhealthy and promoted malingering.

Ensuring Tomas's back was turned, I fetched a blanket I'd just dropped at a vacant bed and spread it over Inek. If one supposed a memory-strangled man in stasis could hear, then it was easy to conclude he might feel the cold.

"Knight Commander," I said, quiet enough none could overhear, "this is Greenshank . . . Lucian de Remeni. I need to speak to you about several matters."

This seemed foolish now I was at it. He didn't move, of course. Not even a hint of breath. But his pallor was more ivory than gray. He wasn't dead.

"First, I hope you don't suffer.

"Second, I pray for your recovery, though as you well know, doubts about the gods plague me. Perhaps I pray to the universe or the forces of nature, though that would include Danae and they are not at all benevolent. Indeed if there are gods, I believe they've sent us the Archivist, yet praying to the Archivist would be most uncomfortable. Did you know he is your cadre brother from your days as a tyro? He called you Silverdrake. Though my mind screams doubts and mistrust about everything nowadays, I believe he deems you friend and brother and works diligently to help you recover. If something in you fears what he attempts, thinking he means you harm, and if you're willing to accept my whim on a matter of trust, do not resist him."

Gods, this was babbling idiocy. Yet, I couldn't abandon it, now I was here.

"Third, I sincerely believe what you told the Archivist, that you didn't destroy my memory relict. I would swear to Kemen Sky Lord, seated on his chair of judgment, that Damon did so. He sent me here . . . drove me here like a stupid sheep. He has a plan for me, and it does not include any weakness derived from family or personal connection. He forbids himself the same. On another day I'll tell you how it is a failed paratus knows Order secrets.

"And last, by strange and unlikely chance, I've recovered my bents. I used them to draw your portrait, which the Archivist thinks might be of use in deciphering your malady. Thank you for your faith in me. I beg you hold that faith, no matter what you hear of me while lying here or after your recovery. Believe me, that in everything I do and every choice I make, your voice reminds me of strength and honor and how to make hard choices. This is the foundation of my new life, as I attempt to carry out the mission we took upon ourselves."

They had wrapped Inek's hands in linen and barrier enchantments, likely to ensure there was no residue from the terrible trap spell to pass along. So I touched his shoulder and bade him peace.

"Did he hear you?" asked Tomas, escorting a limping, blood-streaked tyro to bed one.

"We'll see," I said. "I have faith in him."

After a brief visit to the chart room, I sought out Dunlin and Heron in the sparring arena. They were finishing a bout with polearms in a masterful, vicious, bruising draw. I brought them water and let them recover their breath, then relayed the Marshal's command.

"I swear to give you my best," I said, "to drive you hard and myself no less, to judge in equity, and to refer all questions of technique to an appropriate master. If you've a difficulty with my appointment, go to the Marshal now. I'll not interfere and will bear no grudge. But once you accept the state of things, that will change. That is, I'll consider any complaint offered to the Marshal and not to me as deception, and it will reap appropriate punishment."

"I hope you'll take better care with our lives than you do with yours," grumbled Dunlin, nudging Heron. When they broke into laughter, I laughed with them. It would likely be the last time.

"Inek gave me a hard lesson about that," I said. "If you're stupid, I'll pass it on to you. So?"

Heron, naturally more sober, straightened his back and sank to one knee, fist to his breast. "I accept the Marshal's wisdom and your vow, First. Command me."

Dunlin followed. My hand gestured them up as if it already knew what it was supposed to do. The weight of the moment settled on my shoulders right beside Inek's fate, my sister's, Bastien's, Morgan's, and perhaps a bit of the world's.

"Your orders, First?" They spoke in unison.

"Proceed today as you would any day Inek is away. I'll review our schedules, speak to the Archivist about our additional memory work, and post any changes before tomorrow morning. At sixth hour I'm going to bed, as I've had no sleep in more than two days and I've the seaward watch at midnight. Inek's unable to rescind the order, so I'll finish out the remaining nights."

"But that's daft. The Marshal could—"

One twitch of my finger silenced Dunlin's natural outburst. We were no longer equals.

I would miss that. Did knight commanders ever join together in comradeship? I'd never witnessed it. Every time I'd sought out Inek, he'd been at work with his students or alone.

M y application to see the Archivist before supper was refused, so said his edgy assistant. The slender Second Archivist's hands reached for things that weren't there, and the eyes looking out from the dusky blue mask darted hither and yon, as if he were missing something.

"He'll see you tomorrow at midday in the place he saw you last." His off-kilter face twisted into even more confusion. "I s'pose you know where that would be?" Clearly *he* didn't.

"Yes. Thank you." Who could forget the dust of one's past? Which reminded me I needed to dispose of that dust safely.

With no memory work instruction scheduled, I saw no need for Dunlin,

Heron, and me to deviate from Inek's plan for the next day. So I stopped into the barren little cell where Inek had shredded tyros' fears, squires' foolish pride, and parati's doubts and prepared to scrape the wax tablet he kept for schedule changes. Two entries remained on it in Inek's slashing script.

KC. 1M Aerie—Corm
KC. 11E SW—Bearn

This would have been changes for that last day. *KC* meant Knight Commander. Cormorant's vigil in the Aerie began at first hour of the morning watch. When Inek abandoned Cormorant in the Aerie, he had gone to *SW*—the southwest tower? the seaward wall?—and met with this same Knight Bearn who had been pestering Fix about me. Curious that Inek had given him some of the precious time he'd arranged for his venture into the archives.

The Archivist was the person most likely to know about this Bearn, and I couldn't query him until the next day. As I scraped the tablet and wrote my own brief status message, weariness took hold. Even scribing the cold wax was an effort.

Unfit for service? Close to it. I planned a long, hard night and could not afford to be dull. So I skipped afternoon sparring and the regular run on the mudflats. Rather a visit to the kitchen garnered a massive wad of bread and butter and a bowl of whatever was in the pot on the hob. It might have been washing water, but vanished too quickly to judge. I took extra bread for later, then went to bed.

The tide horn woke me, as I'd planned. The single short blast—high tide. Eleventh hour of the evening watch.

I ate the extra provision I'd brought from the kitchen and prepared what was needed for my night's venture. Armor for the seaward wall and my spare cloak, three flasks of water, two of ale, and some dried fish I kept handy for missed meals went into a leather bag. Then the bells were ringing the second quarter before midnight, and I had to don the damnable armor.

By my reckoning this was my twenty-second night on the seaward wall. I believed I was the only one counting. We would see about that.

If anyone was interested, they could have watched me charge through the Hall cursing Inek's nasty punishments and clattering helm and mitons against the plate pauldron because I'd not put them on as yet. I wanted to be noticed heading for my useless duty.

As I ticked away the endless first hour, focusing on darkness and balance and staying alert, I brought Inek to mind. Ever straightforward and supremely skilled. Exceptionally private. Though he spoke of how a knight's bent could shape his service to the Order, none of us even knew what Inek's bent was. What had brought him to his state?

He'd planned the venture to the archives for days—to take my relict or borrow it to review—for he'd told Cormorant to choose me to stand his vigil. The meeting with Bearn had not precipitated the act, for he'd told Cormorant of his destination well before he'd met with the mysterious knight. And he'd left the message for me, *knowing* something was going to happen to him. *Then why did you touch the dust, Knight Commander? Of all people, you would have noticed its virulence.*

Gods' grace . . . had he done it apurpose? He'd wanted me to draw him. Not just to find the way to save his life or reveal that someone wanted my mind wrecked. I was certainly the logical person to examine my own relict, yet I would have listened to any warning he spoke. No, he wanted to *demonstrate* something. About the Archivist—whose loyalties were so oddly tangled? Or did he think his portrait might reveal more than just how to cure him? I needed to examine it again.

But that had to come later. Some matters could not wait for another opportunity. I needed to warn Bastien that Damon was destroying all links to my past. And if I could get a look at the Xancheiran artifact he'd buried, perhaps we'd know why. I knew only one way to get a message—not to mention a coroner—halfway across Navronne in time to help.

When first hour struck, I shucked my armor and left it tucked in the slightly wider spot on the wall. A dollop of magic doused the weak torch in the courtyard below. Wrapped in my spare cloak, I shouldered my provisions bag and crept carefully down the wall stair, through the quiet fortress, and down to the docks to steal a boat.

CHAPTER 21

Fix was nowhere to be seen when I slipped away with the ancient flat-bottomed squinch he kept in the back of the boathouse. It was the only boat that might not be missed should sea or circumstance make me return later than I planned. The squinch was watertight, but could tip easily if not well laden. But that was only one of my problems, rowing from Evanide to the Gouvron mouth in the nightwatches.

What little light the crescent moon provided was unreliable thanks to the patchy fog hanging low over the water. The crossing stretched my navigational skills beyond comfort. I had to depend on magic, locating the beacons affixed to rocks drowned by the high water, drawing theoretical lines between them, and using the familiar patterns to navigate between the bay's multitudinous hazards. Sea and storm could displace the beacons at any time or distort their lines of magic. Magic is of nature, too.

At least twice while fighting the drag of downspouts, I lost hold of the patterns and had to rebuild them quickly before my sense of where to look escaped me. Errors likely wouldn't drive me out to sea, but grace of the Mother, I'd rather not be plowing up and down the coast until dawn, searching for the estuary.

After the long, nervous row, it was good to feel the deep undercurrent of the Gouvron joined with the growing ebb in its battle with the sea. The whisper of reeds and dank, ripe odors of fish and sea wrack welcomed me to the estuary. Morgan had said I'd find her there.

Steady rowing and an occasional push off intrusive reeds kept me moving up the deeper channel. No need to go far, just enough to prevent getting lost in the reed forest and find a semblance of solid ground. Time pressed hard. The trip back was always longer than the outcrossing.

A little way upriver, I found a placid shallows and planted an oar in the mud. Holding tight with one hand, I dipped the other in the water. "Morgan!"

A hurricane of squealing birds erupted right over my head, startling me in turn, so that I lost my grip on the oar. My anxious grab tipped the boat.

Righting the cursed squinch before it took on too much water, I grabbed the planted oar before the lazy current could swirl me out of reach. Boots and cloak slurped up more water than I could bail. Between sweat, spray, and flooding, I was drenched. The night was dark as pitch and the scent overtaking the sweet rot of boglands warned of rain in the offing. Heart thumping, I rowed farther up, until I could tie off to a clump of reeds.

The scheme had seemed so simple. Slip across the bay in the middle of the night, stick my hand in the estuary water, and a naked woman of surpassing beauty whom I dared not touch though she made my body hunger so fiercely I could scarce breathe, would instantly appear and agree to take my urgent warning halfway across Navronne, convincing a man to bring a mysterious bit of my past all the way back here. Next time I visited Inek, I would tell him of my plan. Surely the shock of my idiocy would force his disciplined mind to function, just so he could wake and assign me a lifetime on the seaward wall.

The imagining roused a hoarse chuckle. I could be a fixture on the damnable wall, like old Fix at the boathouse. Navronne might go up in flames, but no marauder would dare attempt Evanide's western flank, for Greenshank's armor has rusted and holds him there for all time.

What would Damon think of his *righteous voice* and *strong right arm* foundering in the Gouvron Estuary, his great plot to reform the Registry undone by a flock of birds?

But then again, on the afternoon I'd come here to find Morgan's portrait, I'd hit my head on the gunwale. Perhaps *I* was the one lying naked in the infirmary and everything that had transpired since was a concussive nightmare!

I reached over the stern, both hands this time, and splashed as hard as I could, soaking the last few bits of me that were dry. "Morgan! Come find me! If I'm in a dream I need to know it now!"

"Tsk! Art thou a husk again, Lucian de Remeni? Come, sweet friend, let me tend thee. . . ."

No need for magelight. She sat crosslegged on a sandy islet in the middle of the river, the blue flame of her gards painting streams of sapphire and lapis in the flowing river. Her invitation arced across the water to my boat like the token magic and erased every thought in my head.

Never had oars dug so deep into a river. Never had boat moved so straight across a current. Never had wet clothing been shed so swiftly or bone-deep hunger been so gloriously satisfied.

"I shall convince the worthy coroner that his safety is precious to thee," she said, kissing my fingers and bundling my hand in hers. "And I shall bring him to speak with thee and ensure he carries thy grandsire's artifact of the lost city."

I unwrapped her fingers and gently extracted my hand, so that I could continue pulling up my soaked woolen braies. But in a lissome glide, she curled around behind me and traced a finger up my spine. Such heat spread across my back that the thought of dragging the cold, sodden wool shirt over my skin was near unbearable. "Lady . . ."

"Recall, my name is Morgan, not *Lady*. And it grieves me sorely to see these ugly, stinking garments cover thee. Do I not protect thee from the cold?"

Her arms twined round me, crushing her breasts to my back, nearly losing me in frenzy yet again. But the islet had not changed in size. Every moment I stayed made my return to Evanide riskier. The tide charts testified this ebb would not leave the mudflats barren. But rocks one could ignore in the flood became your enemy when exposed. Did I dally too long, I would face the rise.

"Would that I could offer you half what you've done for me," I said, pressing her glowing hands to my brow before disentangling her. "You've warmed me in uncountable ways. Gifted me a new memory that is not terrifying, but kind and generous, and most assuredly warm—everything of beauty. You've no idea what that means. . . ." Words were insufficient to explain how low I had been. "You remind me of why I must make these terrible things right. But to do that, I have to go. I just— If I've made matters worse between you and your father—"

Her finger silenced me. "This was no simple lusting, Lucian. Never think that. The long-lived nurture and heal the living world, and we are free to choose the recipient of our gift, whether it be a field, a grove, or an estuary. Why should I not choose a human man? Tuari cannot blame me for doing what I have been birthed to do. Go with my blessings. Come back after the moon is reborn, and if thy worthy ally Bastien is not too stubborn, he shall be here. I know a sea cave where I can house him if he chooses not to bide in the estuary."

Her eyes sparked like new stars. "Didst thou not think Bastien very like an otter with all that hair? He might well be content to burrow in drowned roots!"

Laughing as I'd never laughed at Evanide, I pulled on clammy tunic and shirt and fastened my cloak, then pulled her into an embrace I wished might never end. "Very like. But I think the cave might do better . . . if his offer of help yet stands. Tell him I could dearly use a friend. *Another* friend."

"I shall ever be thy friend, gentle Lucian, delighted to ease thy sorrows. Someday, perhaps, we can talk again of history and why humans do the terrible things they do, or argue how matters might be different if everyone had magic or no one, or if artists could actually paint what magic looks like. Our discussions in Montesard were always lively."

"That would please me, as well," I said. "Bastien said I didn't know much about friends. But perhaps that was only because I'd already found one who could never be matched."

Morgan had warned me we could never be together, different as we were. And I scarce knew myself. But if I satisfied her father . . . made him understand my good intentions . . . friendship could grow.

As I loosed the bowline from a clump of gnarled roots, she bent over the gunwale and pulled me to her again. Her lips brushed my ear.

"Not at all a husk," she whispered. "Not this night." Then she gave the stern a shove and sent me on my way downriver laughing.

There was nowhere on Evanide's perimeter to land the boat other than Fix's little bay. Which meant I'd no way to avoid the hunched figure silhouetted by the graying light. What could I possibly tell him?

"Blessed return, Greenshank," said the boatmaster. "How has old Dorye performed this night?" His question lacked the gentle jabbing of other returns.

"I tried to sink her, but managed not," I said, knowing the jest would fall flat. "Fix—"

"You've duties elsewhere just now. But before another night passes, you *will* sit with me and explain."

"Please, Fix, the Marshal must not—"

"I am not bound to the Marshal. This is between you and me. Now be off. Sixth hour's gone."

Astonished, disbelieving, grateful, I raced through the fortress like any other trainee returning from a hard night's work. I narrowly avoided crashing into Dunlin and Heron. Their voices flattened me to a pillar outside the Hall, heart pounding.

". . . so where's his ass?" grumbled Dunlin. "If we're still to run or swim before eating, how is it he's not out?"

"Maybe he fell off the seaward wall."

"He'd never. Wouldn't be righteous. He'll be made Disciplinarian before he's knighted."

"Or Knight Defender, securing Evanide by keeping us all fit and pure, every knight taking his turn on the seaward wall!"

Choking back a laugh, I ran on as soon as they'd passed headed for the eastern wall to swim. No mudflats today. We needed fast hard work, not just slogging through chest-deep water.

Only as I balanced on the wall, struggling to buckle on chausses just so I could be seen before taking them off again, did Heron's mention of the Knight Defender wake a mad notion. Evanide's cliffs and seawalls made it near invulnerable save through the sheltered inlet, the only bit of the islet that was ever connected to the mainland by land. So the Knight Defender . . . Fix?

I dismissed the idea in the next breath. It was true Fix said he was *not bound to the Marshal*. He could carry a filled water cask with ease and drag even the larger skiffs about like toy boats. And there were his pointed insights, his awareness of everyone in the fortress, his convenient skill at notifying what-ever commander was awaiting you. I certainly needed to talk with Fix. What might he know about the old Marshal and the current Marshal, or the Archi-vist and Inek?

But truly my whim was ridiculous. The boatmaster was not a day younger than seventy years. No matter what his other skills, a Knight Defender was the last defense of Evanide. He chose his own successor from the elite warriors of the Order—those who could best any opponent with or without magic. Not even an exceptional man of seventy could do that.

The seventh strike of the bells jolted me. I dumped the rainwater from my helm, abandoned mitons to retrieve later, tossed the lance into the court-yard below, and hurried—carefully—to the stair. Within the hour I was swimming in the bay, racing with Heron and Dunlin. Heron reached the lonely rock called Doom's Knob first, but I beat the two of them on the return, even in the face of the incoming tide.

"I'm speaking with the Archivist at midday about our lessons," I said, still breathing hard. "Instead of sparring later, let's do this again. One of you had better beat me. I've been awake since midnight."

"Standing still on—" Heron's kick made Dunlin bite off his jab. "As you say, Paratus Commander."

"Now!" Grinning, I dived from the seawall into the swirling water. Energy and resolve pounded through me. For the family I'd once loved and this family at Evanide, I was going to make things right.

T he fortress bells struck midday as I crossed the unoccupied Seeing Chamber heading for the Archivist's quarters. Even after the night's bay crossing and two hard swims to Doom's Knob, my steps were brisk.

Only when I reached the cellar relictory's iron door—closed tight—did my rosy outlook fade. All the bits of information I needed from the Archivist thronged into my head like hungry tyros: Inek's progress, tales of Sanctuary, of Xancheira, Knight Bearn's identity and purpose. Allowing my near useless magelight to die, I yanked the bellpull.

Latches and bars clanked on the inside, and the hinges ground noisily as the door opened a crack. And then a little wider. I shut my eyes. Magelight flared bright as clear sunlight through my eyelids.

"Reporting as ordered," I said.

"Come, come." He left me to close and bar the door. The enchantments crashed together behind me like steel gates, as I caught up to the angular figure in rusty red.

"A terrible crime was done you, Greenshank, leaving you bound to silence about the event and lacking a guide. I should have had you back to speak of it, lest you do something stupid."

The frosty assessment chilled my remaining good humor, holding no more concern for my well-being than a hail from a watchman at a city gate. "I believe I've come to terms with it, though I would dearly like to know who did it and why."

He blew an impatient note. "I can't help you with that. I still don't understand what makes you of such interest."

Nor did I. "For today, I'm more concerned with Commander Inek. How does he fare?"

"The puzzle is most complex. No approach has made improvement as yet."

Inek's portrait lay on his desk amid a clutter of parchment sheets. The pages were entirely covered with little diagrams paired with lists of words, some of which I recognized as Aurellian—the language of all pureblood ancestors—and some not. He had circled some twenty-five or thirty links on Inek's habergeon, each of an unusual shape and a slightly brighter shading than the rest.

"Is it possible the person who created the spell was a linguist?"

He glanced up at me sharply. "You speak of this outsider the Marshal favors. Do you have evidence to make such an accusation?"

"Not unless you've detected—"

"Then how dare you besmirch his honor—or, by implication, the Marshal's which is the honor of the Order itself?" His anger set his magelight quivering. "Any further such nattering will earn you more severe consequences than the seaward watch. I can leave your mind like seaweed. I can seed dreams that will stain your every waking hour. I can have you looking over your shoulder, forever convinced you're being followed."

His blistering fury left no doubt of his will or his capability to do as he said. His jaw iron-like beneath his rust-hued mask, he carefully rolled the papers and portrait together. "I will continue seeking the solution. You and your two orphaned parati will meet me in the study chamber on the second level every day at ninth hour of the morning for memory work."

"We'll be there. Is there anything else, Archivist?"

He tapped the rolled portrait on his palm. "This is useful. I don't see why you're here and not contracted to some devilish ordinary."

"It mystifies me, as well, Archivist," I said. "I've been thinking of trying another portrait of Inek. To spark my bent I'd like to examine historical information about this kind of spellwork." Surely that would lead me to mentions of Xancheira, the source of our memory magic. "If you could direct me—"

"Ridiculous!" he snapped. "You will pursue the proper business of your training, and that does not include lending your superior intellect to matters you imagine I've overlooked!"

"I meant no offense, Knight Archivist. And I've one more inquiry." I yielded no time for him to refuse. "Inek's log mentioned a meeting with a knight called Bearn on the same night as he was stricken. Perhaps Inek told him of his venture to the relictory, of his plans or suspicions."

The Archivist's anger vanished in an eyeblink. "Bearn? The name's not familiar."

He pondered, his brow creased, while idly fondling the silver medallions on his breast. Perhaps *not* so idly. As his thumb rubbed one of them, a spark of magic stung my skin. Were the pendants some extension of his archives?

"We've no knight named Bearn—never have. Is this *another* outsider?"

Surprise nearly choked me.

"He must be," I said, though doubting it. "Boatmaster Fix would never

have named him a knight if he weren't. Perhaps Bearn isn't his real name.
Perhaps he's one of the Marshal's spies."

"Spies?" The door he'd slammed on his anger burst open again. "The
Order is the last bulwark against chaos. Now we've outsiders sneaking around
the halls. The Marshal's honor questioned. Relicts destroyed. Insolent parati
strutting their talents. Great Deunor raise our Knight Defender!"

"Thank you, Knight Archivist."

I left him fondling his medallions. Perhaps it had been foolish to ask him
about Bearn, for his eyes burnt holes in my back all the way to his door.

An altogether unsatisfactory meeting. I trusted the Archivist to care for
Inek, and he seemed to accept my story about my returned bent. But his testy
defense of the Marshal left me wary of telling him anything more of my other
business. Neither Damon nor the Marshal had demonstrated any awareness of
my involvement with the Danae, and I had few enough secrets.

So where was Xancheira? I headed up to the map room. The Marshal's
story of the Order's founding and Bastien's and Morgan's mentions of Montesard placed the city near the coast of the northern sea, which agreed with
my observation of the five-fingered land. . . .

Another wasted hour. The archive map room had no detailed coastal
maps. Fix's chart room held the portolans detailing Evanide's own bay and
Navronne's western coast that we studied every morning. Perhaps he kept
all of them.

I'd promised to return and explain my borrowing the squinch. I could
ask him then. But I'd go after nightfall. Better to spend the daylight hours
demonstrating my devotion to rigorous training. Damon would be watching.

The day was full to bursting. My three-man cadre viewed a short mission study Inek had scheduled to demonstrate the virtues and pitfalls of
lightning shocks embedded in a blade. We followed it with two hours' work
with a spellmaster and three with the master Armorer to create such a blade.
My meeting with the Marshal to report my cadre's activities was brief and
allowed no opportunity for further confidences or questions. Damon was
there. He did not speak.

After a hurried meal and a few hours' sleep, I sped through the quiet fortress and down to the docks. The north-side dock lamp burned red, so someone was out on the sea this night; Fix would be awake, waiting. Lantern light
gleamed inside his stone cottage at the south end of the quay.

But I didn't make it so far.

"Thinking to take old Dorye out again, paratus?"

The dark shape that stepped from behind the boathouse was almost invisible in the gloom. But the voice was unmistakable.

"Nay, boatmaster. I've come to speak with you, as you said. My new responsibilities complicate my days."

"Aye, they would," he said. "Come along. With Inek downed by this mysterious *rebounding enchantment*, curious eyes are everywhere. Many of them on you, which I doubt you want."

My skin prickled as Fix led me down the quay. I'd come ready to ask his help, but if he believed I was involved with Inek's wounding, I daren't reveal anything. If only I could see the old man's expression.

"No one could possibly believe I was responsible for Inek's injury," I said. Though I feared I was.

"Maybe, maybe not," he said. "But most believe Inek is the least likely sorcerer in the Order to stumble into a magical rebound. What do you think?"

Fix pulled the door open and light flooded onto the quay, illuminating his face—masked! The perfectly fitting slip of linen was deep blue—as were the shirt and breeches that outlined a body entirely unlike the hunched boatmaster. His hair was not mottled with gray but black and thick, yet if I closed my eyes I knew it was Fix. The smell of him was brine and ale, tar and rope. The voice grated with the raw edge of a man constantly exposed to cold, salt air, and rough weather. Alertness wreathed him like a lamp's glow—an alertness I'd always thought admirable for a man of his age. But either I had sorely misjudged that age or this mask and garments bore some illusion. . . .

His *garments*. Their blue was the particular midnight hue I'd seen in the mosaic in the Marshal's outer chamber—the depiction of the Order's three ruling Knights. Of a sudden my whimsy took on an astonishing logic.

"It might be more important to know what *you* think . . . Knight Defender."

"I detest believing one of our own might have done such a crime, but . . ." He lifted his shoulders and motioned me inside.

No clear answer save a hard gleam in his dark eyes. Fix's eyes.

"Now what did you wish to talk with me about, Greenshank? Or were you really hoping to speak with someone else?"

A glib response stuck in my throat when I saw the dirty white-haired man bound and seated on Fix's floor. He wore an Order cloak and mail shirt, and a full-faced mask lay scorched and shredded on the stone beside him.

The prisoner's first glimpse of me had him grunting and straining at his bonds. He was certainly a sorcerer. Cords of silk bundled his fingers, ensuring he could not feed a spell; a rag binding his mouth ensured he could shape no words of magic. Shackled feet and sturdy ropes ensured he was going nowhere.

"Greenshank, meet Knight Bearn—or, as you might know him, Curator Pluvius of the Pureblood Registry."

CHAPTER 22

"Pluvius!" I said, once I found my tongue again and suppressed an urge to kick him in the balls. "I heard that name in a relict-seeing . . ."

In which the old man had expressed sympathy and regret while forcing a naked, half-mad Lucian de Remeni to hide his particular secrets.

"Why would he be here disguised as one of us?" demanded Fix. "He came asking for you, Greenshank—in particular. Perhaps you summoned him. You've been alone off-island. Could have sent messages. Could have betrayed us, betrayed your oath, your commander . . ."

The keen-edged words slid over my cheeks, burning like the kiss of a sharpened blade. Fix was the true danger here. I met his hard gaze.

"Everything I've done has been with Commander Inek's approval and with the Order's integrity in mind. I've no idea why *anyone's* interested in me. Likely you know far more of Curator Damon's intents than I do."

Fix had not denied what I'd named him, so let him digest both Damon and Pluvius. I needed to know where the Knight Defender's loyalties lay. With Damon? With the Marshal, who partnered with Damon but so pointedly distanced himself, as well? With the Archivist, who seemed fiercely loyal to the Marshal, yet friends with Inek? Or was the Knight Defender loyal only to the Order?

Arms folded, Fix peered at his agitated prisoner. "He insists he's come to bring warnings from a colleague who cares greatly about your welfare. He claims *he* does, as well. But he's refused to tell me more. I had to ferret out his identity for myself."

A shudder rippled through Pluvius like an earth tremor.

Coroner Bastien said Pluvius had made these same claims of concern for my welfare. He'd also said that Lucian de Remeni had never trusted Pluvius. But I greatly desired to know his secrets.

"His concern, at least, is a lie," I said. "From what I've seen, Curator Pluvius cares not a whit for anyone's welfare but his own. Damon might tell us why this man's here."

The prisoner shook his head vigorously, and his wordless grunting became angry, bawling insistence. Was he truly at odds with Damon or was he but Damon's partner, terrified for his coconspirator to learn he'd gotten caught?

"I knew from the first our impostor was a Registry man," said Fix. "Not so much as a polite good morning for the boatmaster. I'd hopes Inek might ferret out his intent. But Commander Inek fell victim to a vile enchantment before he could tell what the villain had to say." Fix squatted in front of Pluvius, who shrank backward as if to embed himself in the stone wall. "I've a special place I drop murdering sorcerers into the sea. They can usually keep themselves alive for an hour. Until the cold and dark get to them. And doubt creeps in as the chain on their ankles just won't break. Then fear begins to sap their magic."

Sweat beaded on Pluvius's brow. He was right to be afraid; every trainee spent his time at the bottom of the bay.

"Where has he been these few days?"

"He spent a great deal of the time crawling about the cellars. And foraging. Trying to catch you alone, I'd think, and find a way off-island. Your hours on the seaward wall—or wherever you've taken yourself during those hours—have likely frustrated him to his marrow. He thinks you don't sleep."

Pluvius latched his gaze to mine and growled, not pleading, but demanding. He was confident he had information I wanted. Though Damon had named Pluvius an idiot, he had also named him *Pluvius-the-not-so-much-a-fool-as-he-pretended*. My portrait had shown Pluvius guarding a gate marked with Xancheira's tree. He could have knowledge of *that* mystery, as well as Damon.

"You didn't question him yourself that night?"

"No," said Fix. "I let him think he'd played us. I hoped he'd help me discover the secrets gnawing at Evanide's foundations." The blue-masked face turned back to me. "*Your* secrets. Inek's secrets, such as silver bracelets left for you, one sigil containing only one of two names. Secrets in our highest ranks. Discipline must bend from time to time lest it grow brittle, but of late, lapses have become a dangerous habit at every level."

Even Pluvius quieted at Fix's menace. And both of them waited for me to break the silence.

Fix had told me he was not bound to the Marshal. That might mean he was Damon's man. But the more I saw, the less inclined I was to believe that.

"I would hear what this curator has to say," I said. "If you are what I named you—with all the implications of that office—and if you are your own man as you told me this morning, then I would be willing to question him in your presence. Once you've decided whether or not to drop him in the sea, I'll answer *your* questions."

One side of Fix's mouth curved upward beneath the dark mask. "You are a brassy whelp."

With a sharp pop, the scarf that silenced the curator split into scraps that drifted onto the ill-fitting mail shirt. My breath caught. Fix hadn't even twitched a finger.

"Spirits and demons!" Pluvius rubbed at his mouth with the back of his silkbound hand.

He had aged a bit in the two years since the scene in the Registry prison. Unless he was fooling me as Fix apparently had, he was surely well into his eighth decade.

"Must this blackguard stay with us, Lucian?" he said. Pompous, for a man yet bound and shackled. "My information is for you alone."

"He stays," I said. "For now, at least, I am his brother, and he out-ranks me."

Fix perched on a stool to one side like a cat ready to pounce. The lamp-light dimmed to a pool that encompassed Pluvius and me—and left him shadowed. But Fix hadn't touched the lamp . . . or any kind of bracelet or token . . . which hollowed my chest a bit. What kind of power did the Order's most formidable warrior bear?

"He has no respect for an old man," said Pluvius. "And my bones could use a softer seat and looser bonds. I couldn't outrun that decrepit boatmaster, so I could hardly best either one of you. Wherever would I run?"

"You're not a *simple* old man," I said. "An old villain, I think. A wily one. I wouldn't trust you bound by twice this weight of chains."

Though intensely aware of Fix at my shoulder, I settled on the floor in front of the curator and gave him my attention.

"You asked for Greenshank," I said, "and that's who sits before you. I no longer answer to that other name you speak or adhere to that man's loyalties. If you know enough to ask for me by my current name, and to dress as an Order knight in order to weasel into this fortress, then you know something of our practices. How is that possible without Damon's aid?"

"A colleague, a *noble* personage—unlike the perfidious Damon—sent me here. This colleague was once Damon's closest ally and so learned of this fortress." His gaze flicked nervously to Fix. "Damon confided his connection to a mysterious knightly brotherhood and assured his loyal partner that the Order's dedication to justice would ensure the success of their vision of reshaping pureblood power in Navronne."

Reshaping, not just purifying. What did that mean?

"His ally believed sincerely in that vision. And then you came on the scene and changed everything."

"I."

"Lucian de Remeni-Masson. Yes." His watery eyes squinted at me in a sly and probing way that made me happy for my mask. "You may not acknowledge that name, but it does not surprise you, and you recognize my own. If I'd not witnessed a bit of Damon's skill, I'd never believe they could erase a person's entire past. But you've regained yours, it seems. So you must surely recall all that happened in Montesard, your devotion to your grandsire and his to you, and how he brought you to me at the Registry, entrusting me with your first contract. You know that Vincente and I were close friends, long-time colleagues. . . ."

"My memory has *not* been restored," I said. "Curator Damon has chosen to share with me a memory of his own that revealed the Remeni name, my bent for portraiture, and how, with his assistance, my gift was perverted by his fellow curators—including you. That is the extent of my knowledge of Lucian de Remeni. If this grandsire contracted me to the Registry, then he must be my Head of Family, the same who consented to my presence here—a harsh and dangerous education to be mandated by one so *devoted*."

Fix's curiosity burned on my left. Let him hear. Let Pluvius prove his honesty against those things Bastien had told me.

"Listen to me, lad, your grandsire considered you the gods' greatest gift to him—beyond his own prodigious talents, beyond his own children, parents, brothers, and his other grandchildren, all of whom he adored. By the gods, Vincente de Remeni served as King Eodward's Royal Historian! But *you* were to be the work of his life—honorable, disciplined, talented beyond measure. . . ."

My kinsman, Eodward's Royal Historian? Despite mistrust, I was caught up, grasping at the image he sketched, willing it to feel familiar. And more than ever my own ignorance of the past gnawed at my certainties. Perhaps such a connection to Navronne's seat of power could explain Damon's choice of me for his scheme.

"Tell me, Lucian, are you aware that you were born with a second bent?"

This interview was very like running across the mudflats, dodging sinkholes. I sped through everything I knew—and Fix might know—to ensure I hadn't mentioned the dual bents myself.

"A second—"

Pluvius pounced, gleeful. "Damon didn't tell you that, did he?"

"No." Even in the relict-seeing, Damon never thought of my bent for history. "What difference would that make to anything? Second bents are excised in childhood."

"But yours were art and history," said Pluvius, relishing his little triumph. "An ideal combination, supremely powerful if you could learn to manage them together. Think of the insights—investigating a historical artifact or ruin, while using your art to interpret, to discover more. Vincente allowed you to pursue both *into your twenties*. He got waivers for your Declaration of Bent—and planned to get a permanent—"

"Whoa!" Fix was off his stool, a warning hand raised to his prisoner. "You have no leave to reveal Greenshank's past. It's not your decision to do so—nor his—nor even mine."

"No matter what kind of wharf thug you might be," said Pluvius, sneering, "you'd be a fool to silence me. Lucian de Remeni will destroy your Order and everything it stands for if you prevent my telling. These walls can hold back the sea, but they cannot withstand the corruption Damon brings. It is already here and growing; I learned that from Lucian's silver-haired commander. And be sure I laid no wicked enchantment on him, but only this same message I speak here. If Lucian could remember, he would tell you of my lackluster spellwork."

A leash of fire from out of nowhere circled Pluvius's neck. "Speak only what is necessary to the warning," said Fix, "else I'll lay a *wicked enchantment* on you both. And be sure, I am a most competent wharf thug."

Pluvius choked and growled as foam spewed from his mouth—a silencing spell beloved of children. It wasn't going to kill him.

I inclined my back to Fix. "I shall keep my questions strictly contained to the matters of concern to Commander Inek."

"Waste no time." Fix withdrew the leash, leaving a trail of gray smoke and a distinct odor of singed meat. Though I saw no evidence he'd actually burnt Pluvius, the old man's bundled hands blotted furiously at his brow and neck.

"Two mature bents lead inevitably to madness," I said. "Was that why my Head of Family sent me here?" Would he admit that wasn't possible?

Pluvius snorted. "Vincente didn't send you here. He indulged your talents, but that was not his mistake—his terrible, tragic mistake. At King Eodward's behest, he went looking for the lost city of Xancheira. And he told First Curator Gramphier he was going to do it."

"King Eodward and Xancheira . . ." An entirely new connection that made a kind of sense. Besides its magic and sophisticated arts, Xancheira was renowned for its just law and reasoned governance. Eodward, the noble soldier, had worked to bring such to Navronne.

Pluvius gave me no time to consider if or how that might redirect what I knew.

"After three years of investigation, ostensibly with no result, Vincente abruptly dragged you back to Palinur and excised your bent for history. He claimed it was because of— Well, I can't say." He cast a hate-filled glance in Fix's direction, as if the Defender might plant a fiery boot in his mouth at his first misstep. "But it seemed a mighty coincidence. Vincente contracted you to me at the Registry, so all could witness your reformation. But the excision didn't hold."

Another link in the chain snapped into place. Morgan said my disgrace was for my dalliance with her. But this hinted that *Registry secrets* were more likely the cause.

"If Damon showed you those most astonishing portraits of the six of us, then you saw the result of your two bents working in harmony. But the devil had taken an interest much earlier, when I, the fool, first showed him your drawings. Did you never wonder why you had to make copies of so many? Well, of course, you can't recall, but Damon required a copy of every drawing you did. Though truly, it was the curators' portraits made the danger insurmountable for those who keep Registry secrets—and thus for you and your family."

A folio of portraits to be used as blackmail, just as Fallon suggested, and a confirmation that the curators' portraits had caused my family's slaughter. Though it still didn't explain why so many had to die. Was it to disconnect me from the past so Damon's version would be my only truth?

Yet Pluvius's story was convincing—and its mesh with Bastien's account made it dreadfully plausible. So much so that I had to remind myself of what else Bastien had told me. I had not suspected the risk of my work as I did it. I had *not* invited murder by flaunting my power or being careless of the danger.

But the curator also hinted at a deeper mystery. Damon had told me he wanted my gift that could *depict the sins people want to hide*, but Fallon witnessed that I had already done that work. Damon also desired my *righteous anger* fed by the Registry's slaughter of my family. But his only mention of Xancheira was as an exemplar of Registry corruption. The lost city was the mystery . . . the key. What evidence had Bastien buried for me?

Pluvius was near quivering as he held his tongue, waiting for me to take in all this.

"You said it was my grandfather's investigation of Xancheira was the mistake. How is a lost city connected to my second bent or lack of it?"

Pluvius pounced, smug as a seedsman pocketing a twistmind's coin, knowing the customer must return again and again to feed his craving. "That is the question, isn't it? For two centuries the Registry has hidden all knowledge of Xancheira and the terrible crime that destroyed it. Only the First Curator and his successor—Attis de Lares-Damon—are privy to those secrets. I suppose you recall something of Navron history. . . ."

I dipped my head in agreement, letting it hide my surprise to hear of Damon's rank. I'd thought of him as playing for power from a lower position.

"Good," he said. "The curators have worked hard to make sure naught's left of Xancheira. And Vincente de Remeni worked hard to convince them that he learned nothing. But alongside his chastised grandson, Vincente brought secrets back from the north country, a chest filled with writings or magics that convinced him there was some great wound in the fabric of the world that only *you* could remedy."

"Because of my dual bents?"

"That chest changed the course of your life . . ."

Which did not answer my question.

". . . for my colleague, by a quirk of chance, encountered your grandsire as he was removing the chest from the Registry Archives to some new hiding place. He told her some of what he learned. She knew then that Damon had not told her everything."

"*She*. Your colleague is this woman curator, Pons?"

Of all the six curators, Pons was the mystery. I didn't know her sins, only that she'd not forced me to cover them.

"Elaia Pons-Laterus is a determined woman," said Pluvius, eager now, racing through his story. "She banished you to a necropolis, hoping to keep you from the curators' notice. Unfortunately you wouldn't stay hidden. So she made sure you came here—Damon's chosen refuge—because it was truly the only place you would be safe. But she vowed to wake you from this sleep before Damon's plans ripened."

All rang true. Damon had thought of Pons as *diabolically ruthless and morally conflicted*, a *formidable intellect*, and *perfect* for his plans.

"Damon used her," I said.

"Just as he plans to use you. Just as he uses everyone. Vincente begged her to protect you. Heed me, Lucian. Sila Diaglou and her lunatics grow bolder by the day; Palinur flounders in famine and lawlessness. This devilish war approaches its climax, and at that same time will Damon's scheming come to its fruition. Pons recruited me, her only trustworthy ally, to warn you."

"Warn me of what? What do you imagine is in this chest? What purpose does Damon have for me, and what *wound in the world* am I supposed to remedy?" Pluvius talked *around* everything that was important. Was he bringing information or seeking it? "How can one man possibly reshape pureblood power?"

"You are being driven to your destruction and that of Navronne," said Pluvius, eyeing the dark stillness that was Fix. "That's all I know, but I can help you find out more. I've a fortress of my own near Casitille. Together we can determine how to help Pons overturn Damon and search for Vincente's chest. Before you were spirited away, you and I set out to fetch it. Such a strange day. The two of us were attacked by . . . very odd strangers . . . who spoke of your magic destroying—"

"Ssss." Fix's movement was but a ripple compared to the waves crashing on the quay and his hiss but a droplet in the slop of the sea beneath the docks. But Pluvius's babbling fell silent and I popped to my feet. The lamplight flared a blinding silver as an invisible hand of iron shoved me into the deepest shadows in the back of the cottage, then dulled again as the door crashed open.

"Curator Damon!" said Fix, who now looked entirely himself—unmasked, gray hair, hunchbacked and older than Pluvius.

"I was just informed that you caught a most unusual fish from your docks a few nights ago," said Damon. The always cool little curator was disheveled, out of breath, and furious.

"Aye, we netted the sneaker again tonight," said Fix. "And you're just the one's needed. This fellow claims he's a Registry curator just like you. But he won't speak to none but Greenshank, as if we allowed sneakers to speak to just anyone they might name. That first night I locked up his boat and sent him off to Commander Inek, as was proper. And I've wondered since if Commander Inek's rebounded enchantment might truly be a curse from this'n. And then tonight, what do I find but him creeping about the boat-house, as if to snatch old Dorye to get away. The Knight Defender's spell-work caught him up. So I had a post guard drag him here, and notify the Marshal. Nary a word will he speak!"

Pluvius could not decide where to look—at Damon, at Boatmaster Fix so suddenly present, or at every corner of the room where the warrior who'd bound him might have vanished. None of them glanced at the back corner of the barren little room where a blanket of lead held me motionless. I had the distinct sensation that bellow how I might, they wouldn't hear me, either.

"You're not exactly *like* to me, are you, Pluvius?" Damon quickly settled into wintry composure. He strolled across the chamber to the old sorcerer and squatted in front of him.

Pluvius jerked his head back. "Don't touch me, devil! You, boatman, fetch that warrior who was here earlier. *This* is the curator who's cursed your Knight Commander."

Damon rested his palm on the old man's silkbound hands. "Clumsy and oafish, as always. Clever enough to see an advantage, but never quite think-ing it through. And, honestly, damaging a Knight Commander of the *Equites Cineré* and threatening a valuable paratus . . ."

"I didn't harm the soldier. And I'd never harm Lucian. I've never done aught but for his good."

"I've shown our young artist my worst faults. Did *you*? Or did you describe your idea of protection—the future you've planned for him *all these years*?" Damon glanced up at Fix hovering nearby. "Tell me, boatmaster, what did you find in the sneaker's boat? Something very much akin to these bonds, I'd wager. A spool of silk cord? Shackles?"

Fix's stillness deepened beneath the armor of his disguise. "Indeed. The bit of chain on his legs is his own. The silk, too, both of 'em tucked away in a bag in his boat. No need to use my own since I'd already stowed his in here. He's safely bound, so you'd best move away from him now, curator. He's the Order's prisoner."

Damon rose and drifted away. "I'd guess there was a mask, as well."

"Aye. This." Fix fetched something off a hook by the door. "Thought of using it on this'n, but I wanted him talking."

"Pluvius devised it to ensure a prisoner's silence. Lucian was forced to wear it for months, and of all his imprisonment, it came nearest driving him mad."

The mask was shaped of stiff leather, tangled with buckles and straps. The horrid-looking thing would encase half a man's head. Worse, one extra-wide strap could pass through the wearer's mouth like a horse's bit, depressing the tongue—muting him. For months on end . . . My bones shrank in revulsion.

"The bonds were for you, devil!" snarled Pluvius, spitting at Damon. "You're the one's going to send Lucian to his death!"

"What a ridiculous old man you are, Pluvius, a failure who lusts to own true power. You clawed and scrabbled and wheedled your way into position to influence Lucian, believing he could restore the fortune that was excised with your second bent. But honestly . . . a tool for common extortion? The gods would never permit such a waste. How often do they send us a man with a true passion for justice and the strength and talent to pursue it? Lucian de Remeni's proper destiny is to shape Navronne's future."

Appalled at their sordid bickering, I wanted to yell that I'd be a slave to neither of them. But Fix's damnable spellwork left me as helpless and mute as shackles and mask would have.

"Lucian will see through you," growled Pluvius. "Your insufferable arrogance will destroy this kingdom, purebloods and ordinaries alike. You haven't even told him why he is so impor—?"

"That's enough!" Enchantment erupted from Damon's hand in a bolt of yellow fire and a blizzard of residue that felt like dry leaves.

Even Fix leapt backward. "What have you done, curator?" he bellowed. "You've no right!"

Pluvius slumped against the wall, his staring eyes entirely white, as if replaced by orbs of alabaster. A thumb-sized pile of ash dusted his bundled hands. Damon pocketed a wooden token.

"He is still Evanide's prisoner, boatmaster," said Damon. "Haul him to the fortress dungeon, and I shall commend you to the Marshal for your efficiency in apprehending him."

Damon picked up the leather mask. He studied it as he ambled toward the door. "As for this"—he sucked his teeth in disgust—"show it to Green-shank next time he comes down to the docks. Let him see what his *friend* and former master was preparing for him—a lifetime mute and chained, his only free breath or glimpse of sky earned by doing Pluvius's nasty little tasks each day: a portrait of a young soldier to prove his betrayal; or of a young girl to reveal her maidenhead broken; a sketch of a treasury official to discover if his light fingers lifted the kingdom's gold. Whatever unhappy truth Pluvius imagined might fill his purse or enhance his stature."

Damon tossed the mask aside and pulled open the door. When the torch he'd left outside lit the entirety of the cottage room, his hawk-like gaze passed right over me. "Good Fix, Paratus Greenshank will surely join the rest of us in honoring Commander Inek for shielding him, and you for bringing the cur to justice. Perhaps even I shall earn his thanks for a mission of justice, cleansing the world of one perverse sorcerer. Though I doubt it. Greenshank knows I am neither his father nor his friend, only his master in the most noble work of our time."

CHAPTER 23

As the door slammed shut behind Damon, Fix knelt before Pluvius. Peering into the old man's ghastly eyes, he tapped the sagging cheeks and murmured words that charged the damp air with power. His own form had already reverted to his younger self . . . his true self, I thought . . . the Knight Defender.

"Get the iron off him," he snapped. "Key's in his bag. And cut the bindings."

By the time I realized I was free of his devilish prisoning, Fix had stripped off his jaque and shirt, baring powerful arms banded with silver, one fitted bracelet after another from wrists to shoulders.

I dropped the shackles outside the door. Once my dagger slashed ropes and silkbindings, Fix produced such an assault of magic as I'd never witnessed. Though his fingers never touched his myriad bracelets, he threw spell after spell at such speed that by the time I recognized one, he'd cast three more.

Half an hour in, Pluvius sat up, his eyes a solid milky blue. He shook his head. Stared at his hands. Then drummed his feet, frowned, laughed, spat, tilted his head, and wept. But these were no more reminiscent of a man's spirit than the cool, smooth surface of a mirror glass mimed human flesh. I captured his waving arms to stop his battering Fix, and eventually wrapped my arms around him so he couldn't distract the man wielding such magic.

When at last Fix sat back on his heels, Pluvius stilled. I released him, and the old curator curled up on the floor, instantly asleep. He'd spoken not a sensible word.

Fix stumbled to his feet and dragged himself to his small window. With arms that seemed weighted with iron instead of silver, he threw open a shutter to the cold night air, then leaned his head wearily on the thick oak. As the night wind riffled his dark hair and picked at his mask, his eyes closed. "Stupid, arrogant fool. Shouldn't have let their argument go so far. Should have seen that damnable token he stuffed in Pluvius's hand bindings."

It took me a moment to realize he railed at himself. Still, I kept silent.

"I could *not* reveal myself to Damon. I never imagined a failed paratus could inflict something I couldn't block or repair. The Archivist must see to Pluvius."

Unless the Archivist was involved as well. Fix didn't sound hopeful.

"I should get to the seaward wall," I said, returning the shackles' key to the damp leather bag. "Damon might go looking for me. He'll want to gloat and tell me more of Registry corruption. But if I could meet with you again, sir knight . . ."

"Damon's with the Marshal. When he leaves, I'll inform you. For now, you will stand here and tell me what in the seven halls of Magrog's unholy realm I just witnessed. Hold back nothing. And believe this, if you cross me, deceive me, or take me lightly in any fashion, you will not see another morning—at least not with a mind." He neither raised his voice, nor opened his eyes. "In this hour, everything you are or hope to become rests in my hand."

For a man who lived behind a veil, his words were unremittingly clear and his threat utterly, terrifyingly convincing. I told him everything—from the day I set out to fetch a supply of *cereus iniga* and met a Dané, to my frustrating visit to the archives that morning. He interrupted only to clarify some murky twist. Through every moment of that telling, I prayed . . . willed . . . that he would believe me. And with every passing moment, I observed a keen, unyielding honesty that glinted as cleanly as the edges of his silver bracelets. I came to trust him as I trusted neither the Marshal nor the Archivist.

". . . and so without knowing where else to look for another portal, I came down here to discover whether Fix—you—might have a portolan that could show me where to start a search for the ruins of the city or the five-fingered land itself, if they're not the same."

By this time Pluvius was gone, carried off in a canvas bundle by two fortress servitors who appeared and vanished as abruptly and soundlessly as Morgan. They'd seen only Fix the boatmaster, not the Knight Defender, and hadn't seemed to notice me at all.

We sat on the floor, each with a mug of ale in hand. A heavy shirt, cloak, and blanket now covered Fix's metal-banded arms and still he shivered. The extent and complexity of the spellwork contained in so many bands of silver was almost unimaginable; his expenditure of magic had been on a huge scale. Yet he refused to take my cloak or let me close the shutters.

"Deunor's holy, damnable, confusticated fire! Dual bents. Danae. And your relict *destroyed*." Fix drained his mug and refilled it from the flagon at his side. "And, oh yes, portals to another world that exists side by side with this we know. People who could be alive after two centuries. I can't decide which is worse. To believe you, or to think a man mad enough to create such a story could advance so far toward knighthood as you have—and without my realizing it."

"Two years I've lived in this unreal state every trainee endures," I said. "Never did I expect it to be the most normal part of my existence. But I am not mad, Fix, and no traitor to the Order. And I *must* see to both tasks— find out what Damon's up to and unravel this mystery of the Danae and Xancheira. If there's a possibility that Xancheirans have survived what was done to them, is their rescue not worthy of the Order's mission? We were founded to pay the debt of what our kind did to them."

"Deciding what work serves the Order's mission is the Marshal's responsibility. But"—he raised a hand to still my protest—"I concede your doubts. I've trusted the Marshal's practical strategies these two years since he took office—the gift of a pragmatic, worldly younger man after a decade of a philosopher Marshal. Why should he not consider Damon's objectives to cleanse the Registry and strengthen the position of sorcerers in regard to our new king, at least to the extent of allowing the curator access to Evanide and hearing him out? Yet hearing your story . . . I wouldn't reveal your secrets to the Marshal at this point, either. It distresses me to hear of his yielding authority to a man without conscience. And allowing Damon to solicit the submission of a paratus . . . to see such treacherous patterns coalescing around you and hear that they forward a plan so directly contravening our usual way . . . It makes me think I've been asleep. Never has the Order been mobilized as one entity. Never have we become a partisan in another's war. And yet, if the cause was right, and there was no other way to accomplish it . . ."

He blew a long exhale. "*My* responsibility is the integrity of this fortress and its inhabitants. Both are clearly compromised with Damon making free not just of our halls but of our brothers. And this matter of Inek . . . I detected the enchantment that harmed him, but I was not called on and cannot trespass the Archivist's demesne unless he asks. But the Archivist certainly should have brought a destroyed relict and the circumstances of Inek's injury to my attention and to the Marshal's, and I *will* find out why he didn't."

Fix did not pause and contemplate, but drew his thoughts together as he spoke.

"If I thought this Pluvius had perpetrated the attack on Inek, I would enlist my own successor tonight and drown myself in the bay as a fool and a failure. But I believe my initial judgment was correct. Whatever Pluvius told Inek likely reinforced what Inek was determined to do anyway—retrieve your relict and learn from it. And then he saw that spell waiting . . ."

Fix glanced up sharply. "Have you considered that he triggered it on purpose? Took the brunt of the spell's working. Such impactful memory work loses most of its virulence with a single use."

"I did. But why would he? He could have told me."

"If it makes you feel better, I'd say it was about saving his own life as well. Once he saw your relict destroyed, he knew that *someone* was determined to change the course of your life. To isolate you. To make you into something . . . other . . . and without interference. Which meant his own life wasn't worth a feather. They'd come after him next. This way, you'd know."

"Now he's in a prison of pain and madness . . . dying . . ."

"If anyone can rescue him, it's the Archivist. The Archivist is eminently trustworthy in his own demesne. If he believes your relict was destroyed and the trap set two years ago, I believe those things, too. His office is certainly compromised by the incident. Yet, though it sounds implausible, I don't doubt his intent to care for Inek with his best skills—which are more astonishing than you could possibly suspect."

Fix rubbed his eyes tiredly and scratched his head. "He wouldn't work so hard for just anyone, though. Mayhap that influenced Inek, too. Not that the Archivist bears malice toward the rest of us. He's just been the Archivist for too long. Tangled up every moment in other people's past and present, but never any time for his own. Picking and choosing through the detritus of personal histories, knowing that one minute slip could damage a soul forever. It's left him able to focus with incredible depth on any one task, but with a difficulty making connections on a large scale—like being able to look at a city on a map and knowing the names of all its streets and inhabitants, and the description and history of every house, but not comprehending the position of that city in the world or where the roads that lead out of it might lead. Not a job I'd want."

"Yours seems enormous. And incredibly complicated . . ."

His fingers idly rubbed his arms through his clothes, eliciting a wince now and then. There were only narrow strips of flesh between the bracelets.

". . . and uncomfortable. Do you ever take the bracelets off?"

"Mmm. Not a good idea. Threadings are permanent. Besides, I never know when I'll need them." With a rueful laugh, he clamped his hands beneath his upper arms. "They pose no difficulty on par with my brother Archivist's discomforts. Though, in truth, those you saw are not all I wear. I've others that might rank near his."

"Sky Lord's mercy." Every trainee heard rumors of threading—affixing a sliver of metal or chip of a gemstone to the body with threads of magic to hold a particular spell. But that was for one or two minute pieces, not a barrelful of hammered silver.

Fix rested his head on the cottage wall at his back. "You should go, Greenshank. The fortress will be waking soon. Come back on your next night watch and I'll dig out the north coast portolans. And you've permission to use old Dorye whenever you need. But if you think to bring an *ordinary* back to Evanide—or one of these Danae—give me a warning, if you please."

"Thank you, Knight Defender."

"And if I hear those words from your mouth again . . ." His finger wagged in warning.

Smiling, I sank to one knee and bowed my head, fist on my breast in all sincerity. "Boatmaster."

He snorted and scrambled off the floor as I rose. After dousing the remaining lamp, he walked into the night alongside me. We strolled up the quay, all quiet but the slop of waves and the muffled knocking of a boat loose at its mooring. The ponderous bulk of the fortress rising above us was just visible, but naught else, not even the man beside me, whichever form he wore.

When I started up the quayside stair, his words followed me. "I judge Pluvius *did* plan to enslave you. Damon wasn't lying about that."

The disembodied voice only reinforced a bone-deep horror at the thought.

I looked back, seeing nothing but night. "All right. But I'm also sure that Damon's plan is more than reforming the Registry. I've no idea what else, or how he thinks I can help him. And however outlandish it seems, Xancheira is a part of it, no matter Damon's never mentioned either Danae or Sanctuary."

"Don't assume anything. We know this: Damon plans a sea change. Your gift scares other purebloods into cooperating with him. Once accomplished, he will likely dispose of his sullied instrument—you—and install this Pons woman as head of his new Registry, while he attempts to maneuver her from behind. Being *diabolically ruthless*, she may or may not have her own plan. *Diabolically ruthless.* Perhaps that's a description I should aim for in my own work."

Fix's laughter was healthy, untainted with menace or irony. But unlike Cormorant, whose fair humor spread so easily to warm one's blood, Fix swallowed his almost as soon as it burst forth. "I'm sorry I can't help more just now."

"*Dalle cineré*, Fix."

"*Dalle cineré*, Greenshank. I'll be watching your back, but I'd say you'd best do that, too."

"I will. And I'll be back to see the maps as soon as I can."

I didn't get back to the docks to examine Fix's maps right away, nor to the infirmary to check on Inek. I had no opportunity to address any of the plaguing mysteries. On the morning after my adventure with Fix, the Marshal ordered all knights-in-residence, parati, and squires to the mainland for general exercises.

As the fortress erupted into frantic preparation, a tyro brought me a wax tablet:

> *Greenshank. Hone your skills and await your master's orders.*

The quaking fool couldn't tell me who sent it. But I knew. I couldn't fret; there was not a moment to consider Damon or anything but the present.

After a day's storm-wracked row up the coast to Val Cleve, we spent fourteen days of hard riding, hard marches, and hard fighting. We dueled and fought in the melee. We practiced attack formations in open country and skirmished with small determined cadres in dense forest. A series of increasingly difficult archery challenges for my little cadre while under attack put me in mind of Damon and his odd emphasis on my skill with the bow. But I'd no time or strength to question. Every tyro, squire, paratus, and knight was pushed to his limits.

This wasn't the first such general exercise since I'd been at Evanide, but it was by far the most brutal. By the seventh day, pain, blood, and exhaustion were the entirety of our existence. March. Fight. Ride. Fight. Crawl. Fight. Eating and sleeping were unimaginable, and yet magic failed without food or rest. One of Inek's former squires drowned when his boat capsized. Two men died of wounds in the melee. A knight was terribly burned when a panicked paratus's defensive spellwork rebounded. Not even pureblood heal-ing could remedy the virulent sepsis and sheer bodily damage from severe burns. The man would surely die in agony, and the paratus be dismissed. It was a dreadful loss.

My small cadre was fortunate. Dunlin broke his left arm, but fought on with determination and assurance. Heron escaped the melee uninjured, but ended with a harsh cough. He'd inhaled sea water while rescuing the drowned squire's two comrades. I'd been so intent on taking out a tricky target deep in a gloomy woodland with an arrow I could scarce aim, an attacker slashed my lower back. I never even saw who did it. I owed Dunlin's superior swordwork that the wound was not a fingertip deeper. The exhilaration of hitting the near-impossible target almost made up for the humiliation, and the pain merely blurred into the horrific landscape.

Reason peeped out from time to time warning of the implication: the Order was preparing for all-out war. Not immediately, but soon. The days until autumn and the Sitting were growing fewer. That was when all would come to a head. Damon's plot. Damon's war. I was sure of it.

T he fortress was subdued on the night of our return from Val Cleve. The Hall, often boisterous after a major tournament, was dead quiet at sup-per. Men fell asleep in their bowls, or were simply unable to eat from pain, exhaustion, or nerves yet aflame with battle fever.

Depletion had me shivering worse than wound or weariness, as I'd been tasked to navigate our fifty small boats through the tidal onrush to get us home. Such a heavy responsibility meant setting beacons, guide spells, and unbreakable signals to keep our force together as if we were pursued, yet far enough apart to prevent exhausted rowers from crashing into one another or falling victim to the naturally hazardous coastal passage.

"Nothing but sleep tonight," I said to Dunlin and Heron, as I stared at the rapidly cooling mess in front of me. For the moment, I couldn't recall what it was. "The tide charts say . . . I believe tomorrow is a running day. Eat beforehand if you feel up to it. Heron, if you're coughing up blood or your chest is still painful, see Adjutant Tomas before you come down to run. Dunlin, make sure he does that. If I'm late—"

"Greenshank, you're not going to—" Dunlin caught himself. "They had you stretched thin these days, Paratus Commander." He'd not slipped into familiarity for a tenday, so I paid no mind to the breach.

"I've already notified the Marshal that I'm not manning the wall tonight, *not* that it's any of your concern." Though I might as well. Mine were some of the nerves yet stuck at alert. I'd never sleep. "The Marshal has yet to schedule the cadre commander reports. That could delay me tomorrow."

"Are we to join the ordinaries' war?" asked Heron.

"I've not been told," I said, fearing he was right, "but we need to be prepared. You both did well. Your swordwork was exemplary, Dunlin, attacks and defenses both improved since the spring tourney. And your alertness saved me from a severe wound. Heron, I'm putting you in for a commendation. You saved two lives—and all the lives they may in turn save in their future as knights of the Order."

"Don't want a commendation," mumbled Heron. "We were all half crazed by that time. Near killing each other. Some of us were pushed too—" He clamped his mouth shut. "Guess we just need sleep. *All* of us."

I was glad he hadn't finished his grumbling. "Go. Sleep. Tomorrow we work on endurance, and keeping our wits when we're pushed to our limits."

They pressed fists to their breasts and left.

Alone at the long table, I drained the ale in my cup and waved it at the steward who promptly refilled it. Only because I needed to replenish my magic could I force down more of the pignut bread and fish stew, thick with turnips and bitter greens. Even the Order's granaries were bare after three years of famine. When my stomach threatened retaliation, I left the Hall. But instead of heading straight for my pallet to lie awake, I climbed to the infirmary.

Every bed and floor tile was occupied with wounded. More lay in the assembly chamber across the courtyard. Still insensible, Inek had been moved to a corner pallet, as the beds were needed for those who required more immediate care. Adjutant Tomas, on his way out with an armload of bandages, three well-laden servitors in his wake, rolled his eyes when I arrived. But he'd left the blanket covering the commander.

I told Inek of the exercise and Dunlin and Heron's excellent performance and my own successes and muddled failures. There were too many ears close by to speak of Fix or Pluvius or Damon, so I cut my visit short.

Descended from the heights, I trudged across the Hall again, and turned into the dimly lit passage of the barracks wing. A man in a squire's tunic was working on the lock at the weapons' store. As I walked past him, a thread of his unsubtle magic scored my back like another sword slash. A rusty sword. Or serrated.

My edgy nerves erupted. Grabbing his arm, I dragged him away from the locked gate and shoved him against the passage wall.

"Deunor's fiery balls, are you digging coal with a pickaxe?" Only respect for those sleeping kept my fury from raising the roof. "And unmask. Squires are never to be masked inside the fortress."

"A rough passage, eh, Greenshank? Three-and-fifty boats home safe. I believe the boatmaster was pleased. But it's not knightly to break a man's arm because you've had a difficult exercise. All is never as it seems."

A wind-roughened voice. A lean, powerful authority under the shapeless tea-colored tunic, and a metallic shell ringing the arm inside the loose sleeve.

I jerked my hand away.

"Sorry. I didn't know—" No excuses. And I knew better than to mention either of his names.

"Come, come, who do you think modifies all the locks? Though I don't usually do it with such . . . mmm . . . exaggerated awfulness. If you hadn't noticed, I'd have to put this little adventure off for another night until your head was back in place."

"Adventure?"

His only answer was to latch onto my arm and propel me along the passage, past my cell, and downward into Evanide's foundation—the labyrinthine old fort that had been the first human-built structure on the islet. Magelight shone from Fix's whole person, brushing the tiny, low-ceilinged chambers and narrow passages with a golden glow.

Half the rubble walls were collapsed, not worth the rebuilding for such meager space. The only use made of them was as an occasional depository for a cowardly tyro who needed some time to meditate amid dust, rats, the creaks of the weighty stone above his head, and the muted surging of the demonic sea as it tried to get through the rock and drown him.

"With everyone dead on their feet, I was thinking I might get the locks reset early for a change," said Fix. "Maybe snatch an hour of sleep. But my mind keeps parsing your nonsensical tale. I don't like discovering such astonishing doings going on under my nose. And so I drag out my maps and charts to see if I can find anything like you described on the north coast. Some of our portolans are quite ancient."

The ceiling got quite a bit lower when we had to crawl over a pile of rubble. I kept my eyes on the glowing body ahead of me and tried to ignore the weight of the fortress pressing ever closer.

Fix's chatting was a welcome distraction. "To get to the charts I wanted, I had to set aside my plan of the fortress—the Defender's Map—which shows every stone, brick, and timber of Evanide, maintained since the beginning by every holder of my office. And when I touched it, I remembered a curious mark on it, something like a white hand . . ."

Of a sudden the magelight ahead of me reoriented itself from a view of Fix's boots to the entirety of his person, standing in a chamber whose dimensions were lost in darkness.

". . . which designates our own small necropolis!" he said, spreading his arms and expanding his light into the chamber—a huge natural cavity in the rock.

Knights were buried in the sea, their resting place as anonymous as their lives. But others, who had occupied this place before the Order, had hacked niches from the native stone, hundreds of them, row upon row. Some folk had been laid here with swords or spindles, masks of metal or ivory combs. Some were laid face down—the mark of a coward; some were paired with another in the same niche. Here and there were the faded remains of painted god symbols or signs of the crescent moon with a slash across it—the most ancient representation of Samele, the Goddess Mother, who ruled over death and rebirth.

My breath caught. Neither dust nor skulls nor other reminders of mortality had struck me, but rather a small section of the far wall that had been rudely cleared of its burden, leaving heaps of rock and bone to either side of the flat. High on the wall was a chalked image of a white hand, and beneath it a bronze frame with a round arch.

The interior of the arch was no rippling light or notched rock slab. It was a bronze door. Its hammered center panel depicted a five-branched tree. And it also had hinges and a handle cast in the shape of a long, graceful hand. This door was meant to be opened.

"The Marshal told me that Evanide was once a hospice for Aurellians with magic-raddled minds," I said, excitement banishing weariness. "A sanctuary of a sort. Perhaps the Danae opened a way through their lands, shortening the traveling distance between Evanide and Xancheira."

"The door was masked with simple illusion." Fix folded his long body into a compact package and seated himself on the floor before the door as if waiting for it to speak to him. "I removed it. Likely I should replace it with something better. But the damnable door itself is locked. I am likely the finest locksmith in the world; what else is the Knight Defender of Evanide? But its key is nothing I can provide. I would call this a waiting-for-a-very-particular-kind-of-magic lock."

Neither mask nor feigned annoyance could hide his amusement.

"*My* kind of magic?"

"Try it. I would relish seeing you vanish."

The cool metal of the door handle reflected the racing blood pulse in my hand. No fire seared my arm. The Danae had not blocked this way to me.

A deep inhale to settle my ragged spirit. Then, closing my eyes, I laid both of my hands on the door—one on the handle, one on a hinge—and reached for Sanctuary.

Magic rose hot in my chest, between my eyes, and through the band of fire and power joining them. That was the gift I bore—two centers, two sources, two bents. Sounds and images rushed through me like the tide: *smoke and mouldering linen and old death, agonized wailing and hammering picks scattering rubble, the smells of paint and dust and burning herbs . . .*

Within moments, the flow sputtered and died. Spasms racked my limbs, and my stomach wrenched as if turning inside out. Depletion.

Strong hands gripped my shoulders. "Draw what you need. I've naught else of so much interest happening tonight."

Parents and devoted tutors offered reserves when teaching children, whose magical capacity was small. Naturally, I couldn't recall any such occasion. But we also practiced transfer at Evanide as a way to aid a comrade. It was a generous gift, fraught with risk. A dying or severely wounded man could drain everything the giver had and more, leaving that one sick and vulnerable, too. And to open oneself to take of another's power was the surest way in the world to have mind, soul, and magic enslaved. But even depleted, I wasn't helpless, and I trusted Fix. Thus—carefully—I accepted what he offered.

The Knight Defender's magic was very different, like pungent, fizzing cider compared to the smooth, robust wine of my own. The sheer volume of his provision was astonishing. Fix offered the sea, when every other person I'd drawn on yielded only pond or puddle.

And think . . . you need only the power of your bent for this purpose, not the visions or the artworks. He might have spoken this aloud, but it was not my ears that heard it. *The source is what's important.*

I'd never thought of them as separate.

I drew on Fix until the shakes were gone, my stomach had settled, and the fire in my breast raged with the heat of a smith's forge. I nodded, and he removed his hands.

Again, I sought sanctuary. Magic only. No visions, no history, no art. The magic flowing through my fingers had become mine, not Fix's. In mere moments, the door handle moved, the bronze door swung open, and I toppled off the edge of the world.

CHAPTER 24

Falling . . . falling . . . into endless night and boundless silence . . . into nothing . . . I screamed but no sound reached my ears. Without touch or hearing, sight or taste, my body was vanishing, shredding into flakes like flying ash.

But senses returned in a rush when the darkness of nothing was replaced with the darkness of the deeps—cold, black water. Limbs thrashed against its unrelenting weight. Eyes and wounded back stung. After the terrifying fall, I would have welcomed *any* sensation were my unprepared lungs not threatening to burst.

Still! Slow! Cast! Evanide's training lashed through mortal panic like the Disciplinarian's favored whip. My body hung limp in the water like sea wrack tethered to a rock, my arms its floating fronds. My heart slowed to an undetectable pace. The magic that had flowed into the bronze door now arrowed through the frigid water seeking air. Assuming, of course, that the end of the world was not entirely water.

No currents pulled at me. The sting was cold, not salt. This was neither Evanide's bay nor the estuary nor the northern sea.

A first layer of magic kept me near stasis, preventing me from gulping water instead of air. Though I did not breathe, the reserves of air stored inside me filtered through flesh or bone, however it did its work. There were always reserves, so Cormorant had assured me over and over when I would panic and swallow half the bay. There was always enough to give the deeper magic time to work . . . as long as I stayed disciplined. *Remain still, keep your heart slow, and do not ever, ever let yourself slide into sleep.*

My heavy boots settled. That would be down.

With the greatest possible strength and the least possible movement, I kicked in the opposite direction. Up. Once. Careful not to break stasis.

A second cast. Magic enveloped my flesh like a well-fitted mask so the heat would not escape me so quickly. Still adrift, but warmer. Eyes naught but slits—protected by the skin of magic.

Safia had warned me to do no magic here. But without magic I was already drowned. If I was trapped, so be it. Just let there be some end to this.

Not a glimmer of light. How deep was I? Two hours . . . three . . . I could maintain. But longer?

Still! Slow! Cast! Magic flowed through my fingers, shoving the water above my head to either side. A little more. Surely I was rising through the dark. But what waited above? Xancheira? Sanctuary? Was this Magrog's eighth hell? Morgan had seen the abyss. *A crack in the world,* she'd called it, *the unending dark whence come beasts to devour the Everlasting.* Please, Goddess, no beasts . . .

Another slight eddy allowed me to rise through the dark. And another.

When first I glimpsed a glint of gold, I squeezed my eyes shut and renewed the spells. Hurrying would kill me if I was too deep.

I held off looking until I couldn't bear it, then opened my eyes a slit. Gold specks darted like fish the size of sparks, leaving molten color in their wake.

The gold fish grew in size. Myriad silver ones joined them. Their swimming made glurps and garbles in the slowly swirling water. Words? *Dead . . . all accounted for . . . fool . . .*

Must not sleep. Must not allow seductive dreams. No senior paratus waited to pull me out.

". . . a corpse?" This voice was no dream.

"Not dead. Enchanted!" A woman's voice. ". . . could be the one!"

"Run, woman! Tell Signé we're breached!" The male speaker's ungentle hands dragged me from the water onto rocky ground. The gold fire of a torch vanished, leaving only the silver . . . stars. Uncountable stars. Not the stars of Evanide.

"Do not dare harm him," the woman called, distant.

"Hurry. They'll have felt his passage." But she couldn't have heard my rescuer's out-of-breath urgency.

A weight pressed on my chest, as my skin of magic began to dissipate in itching warmth.

"Aye, there 'tis. A living heart's in there somewhere. What vileness lurks inside it?"

My fingers twitched, but will stilled them . . . and forbade me open my eyes wider . . . and stifled the desperation to suck in air.

He lifted his head, but remained a warm bulk at my side as a chill wind blustered around us. "Ah, not-dead-sorcerer, thou'rt skilled indeed. By the Mother, I should end thee. But my lady would never forgive it. Aagh, these women."

My slitted vision picked out the crouching silhouette blocking the stars. No gards, either silver or blue, and his stink was nervous male human. Though his speech reflected their archaic lilt, he was not Danae.

Carefully I assessed leg and shoulder muscles. The man's hostility suggested caution until I could move everything. But before I was quite ready, the stasis magic winked out and my tortured lungs exploded. Harsh coughing threatened to rip my newly stitched wound as well as my chest. Unsure of my legs, I rolled to the side—toward my companion. In the matter of a few moments' grapple, I had the fellow on his face, hands pinned behind his back. Easier than I expected.

"I wish you no harm," I croaked, as soon as the spasms relented. "I do appreciate your not killing me."

"Tell me thy name, intruder," he growled. His breath smelled sharp, like bad wine.

"You first, I think." I emphasized the point with a bit more pressure on his strained arms.

"No name you know or are ever likely to."

Fair enough. "Then tell me where we are."

He crowed in bitter triumph. "Thou'rt the one who breached. Is it thy habit to blunder through the mysteries of the world without knowing what lies on the other side? Of course it is. Why would a Registry brute behave any different than his kind ever have? I tell thee nothing."

He was a big-boned fellow, but the starlight revealed his eyes sunk deep and his jaw and cheekbones much too visible through mottled skin. I could restrain both of his dry, fleshless wrists with one hand. The man was starving. Even so, I was not fool enough to let him go.

"I'm no Registry man, brutish or other," I said. "But I must know what this place is."

"The Fathomless Pool has belched thy carcass up in the farthest backwater of the Sky Lord's realm. May it be to thy sorrow of and that of all thy kin." He tried, without success, to buck me off.

"*Tell me*, poison tongue. Is this the land called Sanctuary?"

"Pssh! No." His scorn could have etched steel, but his feeble resistance relented.

"Go on."

He pressed his forehead into the ground, his breath coming in great wheezes. "So thou'rt he. The one she told of. The Remeni. The incomparable Deliverer. 'Tis unfortunate the deliverance comes a few decades too late."

"You know Safia!" I released his hands and scrambled off him. "Incomparable, no, but indeed I've come to help if I can. What do you mean, I'm too late?"

"Look round, Remeni-son. Excuse if I don't join thee." He remained prone as I stood up.

The pool, the starving man, and I were located on a broad, windy hilltop. The mostly level turf was lumpy and broken. Eight or ten stone benches had once ringed the pool. One was usable, three were cracked and fallen, the others rubble. And beyond . . . Goddess Mother!

I scrambled over and between the benches and a tilted slab to the edge of the steeps, where the hill fell away. A few scattered fires winked amid a sea of dark. Jagged shapes blocked the stars, hinting at what daylight would show. This was not Sanctuary, but the city portrayed in the Marshal's window . . . or its bony carcass. Atop the hill twin to this stood the citadel, bathed in pale luminescence, two of its three round towers fallen. Huge trees grew where fields and pastures and hay meadows should have spread like an apron before the hillside city, as if the countryside were besieging the human-built works.

All was silence and sadness. Ah Goddess Mother, only now that I paid attention did I feel it borne on the wind . . . a cold and weighty grief deeper than the waters of the Fathomless Pool. And beneath it all simmered a subtle fury that I recognized only because it mirrored the smoldering fire in my own belly. Bitterness. Betrayal. Of all things, I wished to call on my bent, to touch this ground and learn of its mysteries. But I dared not. I'd been warned.

The starving man was using a fallen slab to help him rise. It was one of four or five scattered about the hilltop. Others were overgrown like grave mounds or crumbled as if a giant's fist had crushed them.

I offered him my hand, but he refused it. "I'll keep moving on my own two feet for as long as I'm able. And for as long as I'm able—if thou'lt pardon me, Sorcerer Remeni—I'll not take the hand of thy kind."

"I was brought up in a Registry family, but I'm no longer one of them." He got himself up and sat on the tilted stone, panting.

"This was the place of the standing stones," I said.

"Aye. The holy place," he said, dry as chaff. "The gate to Sanctuary. The place where pride and hope and friendship came first to exaltation, then to grief."

I needed to know more of that, but seeing him . . . hearing his despair . . . fear hollowed my belly. "Where are they?" I said. "The group of Cicerons—Wanderers—who came through the portal two years ago. The Dané sentinel said they were safe."

"Safe, yes, for the nonce. Hidden in the citadel. They brought food with them. And they were accustomed to forgoing magic. Ironic, isn't it, that we'd been waiting for them to bring magic to save us? They told what's happened to them all these years—centuries, they said, though we've seen but eight-and-twenty. Centuries of running, extermination, forgetting. Hope died the night they came. Well, it did for those whose romantic notions had not been starved out already."

"But I thought—" Clearly much that I'd inferred from the portal in Osriel's cave had been wrong. "If you know who I am, then you know I sent the others, believing, as they did, that they would find Sanctuary—a place of safety and benevolent companionship with the Danae. But this is Xancheira—a human city—not Sanctuary, though you speak of mere decades, not centuries, which tells me that time spends differently here, and no one's laid an eye on your city all this time." Not even Morgan and her kind. "Where, in the name of all gods, are we?"

"'Tis not my place to tell stories. If you're to be trusted, our lady will tell thee."

"The Danae sentinel, you mean?"

He burst into acid-laced laughter. "Hardly. Safia is smitten with a dead man. Truly, she is the most sensible of all her kind, but I'd advise thee to rely on no more than two words of her every three. I speak of the Lady Signé, she who rules the living and dead of the vanished Duchy of Xancheiros. She who races up the path even as we speak."

He spoke with a despairing lightness, but as my waterlogged ears picked up the soft pelting of feet on grass, he slid from the bench he'd attained with such difficulty down to one knee, faced in my direction, and laid his fist on his heart. "Lady."

I spun around and had just enough time to glimpse a youth bearing a lantern pause at the verge of the hill before a second, smaller person came up behind him, screamed "ohhhhhhh," and barreled straight into me. All I could see of this one—a girl—was her dark head, which came only to my shoulder. The rest of her seemed to be all arms, thrown around me, touching, poking, patting. I tried not to flinch when she whacked the wound in my back.

"Oh, Luka! Merciful Goddess! Holy Deunor! All these months I told them you'd come. I never lost faith, but they are in such a terrible state, and Signé and Siever and all the rest so brave. You *must* help them. No one believes you can, but I told them that your magic is so powerful and so beautiful it made me weep every night in my bed. I know I never told you that, but if anyone can help, I know it will be you. Though they say we must use no magic here, just as we must keep hidden in the citadel and eat none of the food provided. But how in the Mother's heart will you get us out, if not with your magic?"

I was yet floundering, my hands sticking out like a scarecrow's limbs, unsure whether to touch her . . . to speak . . . to retreat . . . when the girl's babbling stopped. She peered upward, her head tilted to one side, puzzled. Dark-eyed, slight, and so very young. *"Ancieno?"*

Ancieno . . . elder brother. Indeed I felt ancient and foolish and wretched. Though I knew who she must be, she was a stranger.

"Luka?" She reached for my mask, and I flinched.

She snatched her hands away and stepped back, her eyes grown huge. "So like . . . but not."

Her gaze raked every quat of me before settling again on my mask. "Who in Magrog's fire are you? Where is my brother?"

"Step away, Juliana. I told you not to come." The woman's reprimand was commanding, though her low voice put me in mind of river currents, strong and steady beneath the raucous sea tides in the estuary.

There was no third person come. It was the one holding the lantern who spoke—no youth, but a woman, though her hair was hacked off to her ears and her garments were the shirt, jaque, and breeches of a man. She didn't hold the lantern high enough to reveal her face, but I saw enough to leave me wary. Bands of silver circled her wrists.

"Identify yourself, sorcerer, and state your purpose. Tell us why my friend now doubts you are the person she thought. And I'd advise you believe her warning that using magic here bears unhappy consequences."

No mistaking her authority. I inclined my back and touched my forehead. "Honored Lady . . ."

Then I laid my open palm on my breast as a family member would do.

". . . and *serena pauli.*" I used the formal address for *younger sister* because my tongue refused to speak the intimacy of the girl's name. "I am the man born Lucian de Remeni. But for reasons I've no time to explain just now, I am also . . . not he. Through strange effects of my magical bents, I've spoken several times to a Danae sentinel who calls herself Safia. She believes I can aid those trapped here—though I'm sorely confused about where *here* is."

Urgent for them to believe me, I removed my mask.

"I'm sorry it's taken me so long to find a way," I continued, feeling naked before their stares. "Even *that* was happy chance. But I feel the grief and sorrow bound in this land, and believe me, I've come to help make things right if I can. I've just no idea how."

"Goddess, Luka, what's—?" My sister's hand flew to her mouth. But even as her eyes welled with tears, her back straightened and her chin lifted, and she stepped back and to one side. "Pardon my intrusion, my lady."

"I am Signé de Tenielle," said the woman, passing the lantern to a scrawny, breathless woman who'd just come up the hill behind her. "My brother, Benedik de Tenielle, is the second Duc de Xancheiros."

Arms folded across her leather jaque, she strolled toward me. The woman with the lantern stayed close behind, as if she knew her mistress wished to get a better look at me without offering the same privilege. All I could glimpse of the woman Signé was thick, cropped hair the color of old honey and one light-sculpted cheek. That cheek was smooth . . . young. She was slim in her men's clothes, but no starveling waif.

"And your lineage?" I asked. Was this possible?

"Our father Gaiern ruled the lands of Xancheiros for one-and-thirty years," she said, stiff and resentful. "He was named the First Duc by Caedmon King and died at the hands of the Southern Registry, defending his lands and people until our magic and our friends of the long-lived could get the rest of us away to safety. Do not expect we'll trust anyone Registry-born."

Holy Deunor, it was all true. These were the actual survivors of Xancheira, not descendants hidden by magic for two hundred years.

"I expect nothing, lady. And I swear I mean you no harm. The sentinel Safia believes I can be of assistance . . . in whatever way you need assistance . . . and she spoke of urgent necessity. That you could be the very survivors of the horror at Xancheira, that the city itself exists, even ruined . . . is astonishment to me."

She leaned her back against a slab. "Our diviners warned us of the danger coming from the Southern Registry, and we prepared carefully for that day. Alas, circumstances—misjudgments, misunderstandings, but mostly the cruelties of passing time—have left us and our friends in a very difficult pass. I doubt a Registry-nurtured portrait artist can remedy it."

Her tongue was not tainted with bitterness, as the man's was. She was merely blunt and brittle, like grapevines cut back to await an end to our everlasting winter and then frozen dead.

She peered into the night behind me, where slow steps brought my rescuer to join us. "Siever, has he injured you?"

"Nay. But whoever this fellow is, he can easily outmatch a starveling. That's a starting place for a deliverance, I suppose, or whatever he's here for."

The dying man, tall and rail thin, halted beside my sister. She offered her hand to steady him, but he declined. He bent down close to her ear, but did not whisper, "Thy description was somewhat inaccurate when it comes to his skills in the area of physical conflict, young woman. If thou hast underrated his magic as much, perhaps he can do more than we expect."

The lantern light revealed an intelligent look and a grin of twisted humor. But his dull hair was sparse, and his skin patchy and peeling, almost transparent. Were he any more ill, his bones would poke right through it. Yet he retained more life in his despair and dying than did his mistress.

A distant horn call split the night, setting all four of them alert.

"Siever, escort Juliana and Celia back to the citadel. Tell the Wanderers their deliverance is at hand, though with Kyr hunting, we'll not dare move them tonight. I'll be along."

"Signé, do not stay out."

"No, my lady! We'll never leave the rest of you behind!"

The man Siever and my sister blurted their denials as one.

"I'll speak to Remeni before he leaves," said the woman, unrelenting. "The hunters won't bother me; Kyr knows I'll not leave without Benedik. And Juliana, you *cannot* be seen. Tell Hercule and the others of your brother's coming." She shifted her attention back to me. "You *will* take your sister and her companions back to where they belong, yes? If not tonight, then another time very soon?"

"If they want, certainly, and if I can, but—"

My sister stepped boldly between the lady and me. Confusion and whatever else was in my mind and on my tongue flitted away.

Somber, the girl touched my cheek and peered with such intensity my skin grew hot. "They did something to you, didn't they—those vile curators? It's as if you're encased in armor. But hearing you . . . Of course it's you."

She seized my hand and planted a ferocious kiss. Whirling about, she gently accepted Siever's proffered arm. With the lantern woman leading the way, they started down the hill. There was no illusion about who was escorting whom back to their citadel.

Speechless, I watched them go. I'd told myself I had to make my sister real. But Juliana needed no *making*. A spark of a girl, indeed, her light made even more extraordinary in this dark place.

As the torchlight vanished down the hill, the woman Signé unsheathed the blade of hostility and brandished it my way. "Is what she said true? From all I've heard, the two of you were as close as brother and sister can be, yet you look on her as a stranger. If you've been tainted . . . if you carry some geas to finish the work begun on that day my father and my city died . . . tell me now. For the rest of us death and ending is already accomplished, but I'll not have a Registry plot destroy these newcomers who yet have some hope of life."

Death *accomplished* . . . And Siever had said the Dané sentinel loved *a dead man*. My clammy flesh took on an even deeper chill.

"The Registry knows nothing of the doorway or those I sent here," I said. "Only one man and one woman in all the world—neither of them Registry—know of my theory that the survivors of the massacre at Xancheira were given refuge in a place of myth called Sanctuary. But your man Siever said we were *not* in Sanctuary, yet you clearly exist in a time and place that are not the world I know. And now you speak of me going 'back' and of yourself as if you're dead, though you seemingly breathe and talk and—" I had to hurry the asking before I felt too much the fool. "Lady, is this some byway of divine Idrium? Are you truly dead?"

"I am not a ghost, if that's what you're asking. You didn't *die* to get here, did you? Your sister certainly did not." Her mockery named me the idiot I felt. Which was a relief, to be sure.

"No. I'm yet living . . . I believe so." Unless a ghost could feel the bite of the wind when he was drenched. "But this is all so inordinately strange."

I scrubbed at my head and blew a long, slow exhale, unable to prevent a lapse into relieved prattle. "And if you truly aren't dead, then the only problem with taking *any* of you back the way I've come is that I've no idea how to do it. I'm not even sure if I can get back myself. Do I just jump in? Drag a few people with me? How in Deunor's light will I keep them all breathing?"

"You've found a path across a void in the foundation of the world." Dismayed fury swallowed her humor. "How can you not know how to go back? Are you a liar or a simpleton?"

"I but opened a door!"

"What *door*? All paths that could take us to the greater world were destroyed—cut off—by the Severing. We built twenty gates to bring the Wanderers back to save us. But your sister and her friends used the only one of them that survived, and those paths cannot be used a second time. Celia said they found you in the pool, but that was clearly meant to deceive us; not even the long-lived can enter Sanctuary anymore."

"*This* pool . . . this bottomless hole . . . leads to *Sanctuary*?" I retreated the few steps and pointed at the stone-rimmed pond. I needed to ensure we were talking about the same place.

"It doesn't lead there. It *is* Sanctuary."

"This is madness. I came from an island fortress, once a hospice where our ancestors could be cared for if coming to the lands of Navronne had made their magic unstable or too intense."

The woman had joined me beside the pool. "The House of Clarity. Aye. I know of it." Her every word was a challenge.

"In an old part of the fortress is a door set within a bronze frame, the same kind of frame as the portal my sister and the Cicerons—the Wanderers— passed through, although the hospice portal"—the artwork had not been half so refined, the bronze scratched and thicker—"yes, the hospice one is definitely older. My magic unlocked that door; I fell through a void and then came near drowning in this pool."

She held a thoughtful silence for so long, I wanted to shake her, duc's sister or no. But when she spoke again, her blade of a tongue had lost a bit of its edge. "The long-lived say our magic . . . what we did to hide the city . . . destroyed Sanctuary. They hadn't counted on that. I suppose"—she folded her arms around herself again, as if she were so full of things that needed saying, she could scarce keep to the subject at hand—"that somehow your magic bridges . . . Pssh. I don't know. If you've no way back, then you're a dead man as well as a fool."

I tried to match her cooler tone. "How can a bottomless pool be Sanc-tuary?"

"Were you never taught how the long-lived exist? Of course you weren't. Registry folk believe theirs the only power in the entire cursed world." At least her exasperation named me a child, now, rather than an enemy. "For one season out of every year, the long-lived must exist as a part of the land— truly a part of it, leaving behind their bodily forms. Each of them has a spe-cial place in his or her tending. A sianou it's called. It might be a stream or pool or grove, and their season of renewal is a blessing to them and to the place they inhabit. The refuge they call Sanctuary is such a place of renewal, but open to all of them, where they can recover from even the most dreadful injuries."

"But then humans could never go to Sanctuary!" Surely this was non-sense. Living bodies could not dissolve into ponds or groves. And I bore full witness that Danae bodies were just as solid as my own. Unless . . . was the Gouvron Estuary Morgan's sianou? Was that why I could find her with a touch of the water, and why she'd told me we could never be together?

"That was our dilemma when planning our deliverance," said Signé. "One of the long-lived can take a single human into his own sianou. It requires one of the long-lived with immense power and great patience . . ."

A tremor in her voice drew my fascination from the pool. But she held her emotion private and continued her story, steady and precise.

". . . but we numbered more than twenty thousand. And the long-lived of our lands—our friends since my ancestors first settled there—numbered scarce fifty. So with their help, we had to make our own sanctuary, a place where the Registry could not find us, where we could live as we wished until it was safe to rejoin the greater world. But we all miscalculated the cost."

"Twenty *thousand*." But of course, Xancheira had been a prosperous city on par with Palinur and, to them, only twenty-eight years had gone. "And you've all survived . . ."

I'd never considered so many. Even if I could set them free, where in the Goddess's mercy could I take them? Not to Evanide.

"Survival is a different matter altogether."

Another horn blast . . . closer.

Signé hissed and touched my wet sleeve. "Come, we mustn't be found here. A newcomer, especially."

"These hunters . . . who are they?"

"The long-lived. Our friends, our saviors. They helped us sever our home from the greater world, so we could all live safe until times were better there. But times never got better, it seems. And through the turning seasons, we real-ized the Severing had broken our friends as well as the land. Sadly, we cannot repair what we did, and they have no intention of allowing us to leave."

CHAPTER 25

Signé ran like a fox—fast, low, and silent, devouring distance with every bound, leaping obstacles without breaking stride. Before my longer legs could match her sure and steady rhythm on the downhill track, we'd cleared a grove of wind-stunted pines and come to paved streets. Once-paved streets, rather. Vines and thorny shrubs had bullied their way through cracked cobbles and left the place more wilderness than city lanes.

The crescent moon, risen huge and bright from behind the mount, revealed elegant houses with wide porticos . . . some intact, some half charred or collapsed . . . all dark and deserted. Courtyards, gardens, and orchards were overgrown, tangled and wild.

Down and down, alongside dry channels where the Marshal's window scene had shown flowing streams, arched bridges, and flowered lattices. The lower city was wild now, too, a woodland of great oaks and spruces, beeches, chestnuts, lime trees . . . many that startled me as they were out of place for the north of Navronne. It might have been purposefully planted with specimens from the farthest reaches of the kingdom, save these grew out from the broken cobbles of the boulevard, or straight through the ruin of homely houses that overlooked the market. As far as I could see down the hill and across the countryside, dark trees soared skyward.

"Why do the Danae hunt you?" I called softly to Signé's back, as another trumpet blast—closer—spurred our steps. "Surely not— Where *is* everyone?" All the way down, I'd seen not a movement save the wind in leaves and branches. No light but stars and moon.

"They don't *eat* us," she said with only a trace of scorn. "They hunt game for our sustenance."

"Then why are we running?"

She dodged a thicket of briars and sped through a colonnade where a third of the pillars had been toppled by a sturdy chestnut. "If they find humans out of the citadel at night, especially near the Sanctuary pool, they think we're plotting to leave—or that we've learned how to open the trees. If they find an outsider, we're all done for."

"Open—?"

"Hush." She paused at the end of another weed-choked lane. A bronze gate taller than I blocked our way.

Signé lifted the latch and drew the gate open without a sound. With a muffled curse, she reached back and pointed a finger at me. A flash from her silver bracelet and I fell back as if Dunlin's big fist had slammed me in the gut. She stepped out and let the gate swing free behind her. Sufficiently warned, I didn't follow, but flattened myself to the ground and crept forward, determined to see what had caused such an unmistakable deterrent.

As if lost in thought, Signé strolled across a courtyard centered by a single giant oak. Behind the tree, a narrow causeway snaked steeply upward to the luminescent citadel. The citadel's remaining tower was topped with a cupola sheathed in gold that glinted in the moonlight.

Signé didn't head for the causeway, but for the tree. She pressed her palms and forehead to the oak's great bole, and to my astonishment, began to sing.

The teeth of spring bite sea and stone.
Storm and mist shadow vale and cove.
Where is the fire? Where is the heart? Where is the gladness of the season?

All the sadness and anger I'd felt from this place were given voice in her singing, low and rich, like a posset flavored with mead and bitter plums. It put me in mind of the weeping goddess depicted in the Marshal's window.

Danger lurks mid trees yet barren.
And in the sea yet cold and dark.
Dance, my brother . . .

"Dost thou imagine singing will draw him, Tenielle-daughter?"

The man's question took advantage of her pause for breath. He was somewhere on her left; the gate blocked my view.

"Or dost thou imagine he can hear thee, as long as the song is a canticle of the long-lived? Lovely as is thy rendering, I regret that is not so."

His words were kindness itself. His regret sincere.

Though she no longer sang, Signé did not turn to the tall Dané who halted a few steps away. His body spoke power, bare flesh scribed in silver brilliance that dulled the scraps of moonlight, arms and thighs hugely muscled, as if he wrestled mountains. Over back and shoulders broader than Morgan's friend Naari's, he had slung a bow and quiver. One of the hunters, then.

He held back from Signé, respectfully it seemed, until she turned away from the tree and inclined her head. "*Envisia seru*, Kyr Archon."

Archon. Like Morgan's sire, he spoke for the Danae—the silver Danae.

"Singing brings my heart to life," said Signé, "and if anything can penetrate Benedik's prison, it will be a sister's song. Does that not seem reasonable, even to his gaoler?"

So Signé ruled the Xancheirans because her brother was in *prison*? A *Danae* prison. Morgan said Danae did not build, whether houses or prisons. But then . . .

The hairs on my neck rose. Tuari Archon had threatened to imprison his daughter in beast form. And Signé had said the long-lived feared the humans would learn how to *open the trees*. Goddess Mother, were these oversized trees *prisons*? Twenty thousand Xancheirans and I'd seen only four people and fewer lights.

"We saw fire upon the mount and felt a stirring of the pool," said the Dané. "We have asked thee to remain in thy fastness and leave the night for mysteries not meant for human trespass. Thou canst wander freely in the day. Is our agreement grown so burdensome?"

"We have spoken of this so often, Kyr. We *will not* leave without our friends and families. My spirit grieves tonight with Siever so close to death. So I walk under the stars and offer prayers on the mount and come down to sing to my brother."

"It is a grief to all that good Siever remains stubborn."

"He says he would rather be ash spread on our own small garden, than oak in—"

"—in ours. How sorely has our friendship lapsed since the Accord. Just now, a touch of human magic trembled the air. How shall we ever wake this land with human enchantment still disrupting it?"

"Clumsiness," she said dismissively. "I tripped. This bracelet yet retains traces of my brother's spellwork. I wear it that I might feel closer to him, just as you perform your rites, though they bear so little fruit."

Baiting him seemed foolish.

The Dané reached for the woman, sending my hand to my dagger and my body into a knot of readiness. But before I could launch an unrequested rescue, his hand stroked her short hair in unmistakable intimacy.

"What of thee, brave Signé? Tell me thou dost not share Siever's barren wish. I would spare thee his pain and all grief. I can show thee wonders, even in this broken land."

The night bloomed with his desire. Even from a distance, it bore the immensity of night and the insistence of the tidal onrush at Evanide.

I knew the body's lust, my own so recently and so kindly tended. But his was not the simple urgency to shed despair in breathless pleasure or tender intimacy. His hunger was as clear to me as if his intent were scribed upon the air. He wanted to possess her entire . . . to dissolve her human frailties and make her essence a part of himself. Could he do such a thing?

His hand, silver gards gleaming, slid down to her throat and traced its curve out to her shoulder. In the brightness of his silver was her face revealed at last, a fine-boned, pleasing oval. But an ugly, dark red blotch marred her brow and one cheek, sealing her left eye half closed.

"Ah, Kyr . . ." Her sigh wove another thread of love and sorrow into the night. It did not ring false. She laid her hand atop his, stilling its creeping movement. "Thou art all kindness, yet my duty remains to care for our people. We are so few. When the last day of Xancheiros comes and I am all that's left, then shall I hear thy offer and choose my way."

"So be it." His head bowed and he withdrew his hand. But flares of anger spiked his lust—fury scarce contained within his cold beauty. "Let me escort thee to thy rest."

"I beg thy indulgence, noble archon. I remain foolish and would companion my brother a while longer on this luminous night. The citadel is noisy and cramped, and it stinks. But an hour more and I'll make my way straight back as we've agreed. Good hunting, dear friend, and may thy rites bear fruit for us all."

With a curt dip of his head, the Dané strode out of sight. Signé rested her back on the oak's rugged bark. Only when she beckoned did I race across the broken cobbles to join her.

"You heard?" she said. Her breath came ragged as it had not when we ran.

"Lady Signé, this Dané is very dangerous. He wants to possess—"

"I know what he wants. Come, let's walk where we are not so exposed."

She led me deeper into the strange woodland, sure of her path through the dark. The track wound over broken bricks and cracked flagstones, heaved up by the trees' burgeoning roots and buried in generations of dead leaves.

"When I was a rebellious girl no older than your sister, I worshipped Kyr," she said, her fingers brushing the trunk of each tree we passed. "I refused to believe what our elders said was happening to him and to us. Our dalliance left a bond between us that makes it difficult to keep secrets. So mostly I tell him the truth, and when I speak of his kindness and grace, I must recall the way he was and how I felt when I was innocent of horror . . . and how my people's arrogance and failure caused this doom for all of us."

"They've gone mad," I said, half question, half declaration. Surely Morgan's fear—her father's fear—glared starkly. "The Danae who saved you."

"When we cut ourselves off from the greater world, the power . . . the grace . . . the great ordering of the Everlasting . . . whatever it is that binds them to the land and to the others of their kind with whom they are conjoined in their great mysteries was broken, too. Not only could they no longer enter Sanctuary or their own sianous, they could not make new ones. They suffer terribly, and without their nurturing, the plants and beasts the land produces cannot nourish us."

"So your people starve. . . ."

"Eventually, yes. Some sooner, some later. Yet by a terrible irony, the long-lived can transform our dying bodies into saplings, dissolving our physical form as if *we* were entering a sianou. Kyr and his brothers and sisters perform their mysteries in the night watches as they have always done. It gives them purpose, keeps them living. The trees thrive and grow to this monstrous size, while vines and waste plants breed uncontrolled."

Dissolving . . . so the prisoners were not *in* the trees; they *were* the trees.

"Some, like Siever, refuse this end, because we know the prisoners do not die. They are ever aware and can feel when we are near." She let her hand linger on a giant beech. "'Tis a terrible and lonely fate."

Some subtle sound or movement warned us both of an oncoming rush. As one, we dived into a pit of leaves beneath a half-fallen column. None too soon, for a great dark blur—a stag, I guessed by its size and smell—leapt over our shelter. Silver streaked the air as two bodies launched themselves after it. I cringed as I awaited the impact, for the slant and thickness of the sheltering column made it impossible for human-sized legs to clear.

Only they did. The two Danae raced after their quarry into the night.

When all was quiet, Signé scrambled out of the leaves. I followed, wincing at stabbing reminders of the wound in my back, agape at impossibility.

"That was entirely too close," she said, voice tight. "We must loop back

to the citadel. I doubt you came here to end as a tree. Kyr would not wait
for you to starve."

Sick in body and spirit, I followed her lead, stretching my every sense as
far as possible without magic.

"How do you know the prisoners yet live?" I whispered as we crept from
tree to rubble pile.

"Your friend Safia loves my brother, as I once loved hers, and from time
to time when she thinks it safe, she brings Benedik out to breathe the air of
the world. Sometimes she lets me speak with him. He says the prospect of that
brief respite keeps him sane, though returning to a tree of such size . . . it is an
agony. If Kyr ever learns of what she does—"

"He'll prison her in beast form."

Signé's head snapped around.

"I know a bit of Danae lore," I said. There was no time to explain about
Morgan. "Not nearly enough. Safia speaks in riddles. She says my magic
could save you all if I followed something called the Path of the White Hand.
But she didn't say what that was."

Signé darted from an elm as broad as a cart to a half wall, and then to a
beech, pausing to listen before speaking again. "I never heard of it."

Awash in history, I missed a step, tangling my boots. I reached for the
smooth, pale trunk of a birch, but yanked my hand away before touching it.

"Do it," said Signé. "Benedik says he experiences warmth from a human
touch. It helps him think, reminds him of what he truly is. Certain, he admits
the warmth might possibly be a bird." A trace of humor gleamed from her
sadness, like a single gold thread woven into a smothering blanket. "But he
prefers to think it's me, or Siever, who was his brother in all but blood, or one
of the others. We spend most of our days touching the trees. There are so few
of us now, I fear some of our people go days without comfort."

"How long has your brother—?"

"Seven years. Those who came here young—he was only twelve—
survived longer than the elders or those of middle years."

So I touched the trees as I followed her, hoping my presence was not so
alien as to frighten those inside. It was difficult to refrain from using my
bent. Surely magic could tell me if what she said was true. It seemed impossible, as if I had truly reached the halls of Idrium and found it a weasel's den.

"I'll do whatever I can to make this right," I said. "I'm just not sure how."

"Find your way back to the greater world," she said as the pale gleam of the citadel announced the edge of the trees. "When you've established that it's possible, take your sister and her friends back with you. Their provisions have run out. We've a good well and few gardens inside the citadel that yet thrive, ones planted and protected with the finest magics of Xancheiros to withstand siege. Mingling our grain and greens with what Kyr provides seems to help. But those gardens will soon fail as the rest of our enchantments have. The Wanderers must be out of here or they'll begin to fail, too."

"I'll find a way back," I said. "But all of you must leave with me that day. We can work together. Learn what must be done to free your brother and all these . . ." The sea of trees behind us seemed endless. Thousands. Goddess Mother.

"I was born on the day of the Severing," said Signé, "forever marked by its fire. I have just passed my twenty-eighth year. People began dying when I was eight. Starvation is ugly and painful, and most accept Kyr's offer, believing that in some fashion it pays our debt to those who tried to save us."

She brushed the bole of a monstrous elm. Naught of her was visible but the paleness of her fingers and her face—and the dark, palm-sized blight that intruded on it.

"While they yet had power to try, our finest mages worked to breach the trees. But what holds our people in them is not spellwork. Like all the rites of the long-lived, it is mystery. We've only seven-and-thirty of us left, all but one of us born here, and we'll not leave our family and friends, no matter if you show us a road paved with silver."

We'd returned to the overgrown courtyard and her brother's oak.

I understood her despair. Watching an entire people die out must smother hope and turn bone and spirit to iron. But Safia believed I could help, and my magic made the Danae of my own lands fear me, so I persisted. "What do you mean *while they yet had power*?"

"There is no point to all this yammering," she snapped. "Leave here and come back when you can take your friends. Stay and we all suffer."

But I could not let it go. "I came here in answer to your beacon. Why will using magic trap me here?"

"Because replenishing your power from this land will weaken it beyond use. Those who survived the Severing watched their magic wither even as their bodies starved. Recovering from depletion took longer and longer, and never did they attain the levels of power they'd known before. After a few years, none displayed talents greater than our ancestors had in the days before we moved to Navronne. Those of us born at or after the Severing have never even practiced greater magic—Aurellian magic as it was known in the Xancheira-that-was." Though she was no older than I, Signé's spirit was as dry and hard as old currants.

"More immediately, Kyr will not allow it. He is accustomed to the indwelling magic he senses inside the citadel, but any other use reaps punishment. He does not wait for transgressors to starve, nor does he take care in their disembodiment." Signé pointed up the hill toward the Sanctuary pool. "Leave while you can."

The overwhelming sorrow of the wood stilled any attempt to crack her resolution. And with the skewing of time, dawn would have long arrived at Evanide. Yet something in Bastien's report of the silver Dané nagged.

"Siever says not to trust Safia," I said.

She blew a note of exasperation. "Siever warned Benedik not to mate with Safia, as he saw early on what was happening to the long-lived. Safia never forgave him. His wife and three children are prisoned in the grove these ten years, and she'll not tell him which trees are theirs. They were not dying. She took no care in their dissolution. Now, that's enough questions."

She strode toward the bronze alley gate. I followed like an obedient pup, grieving for Signé and Siever—and Safia, too—and all those trapped here. But I could not let it distract me.

"Safia told me that my magic was the answer for my kind and *her own.* So she must think I can help the Danae, as well."

"The only way to help the long-lived is to rejoin Xancheira to the greater world. Even if you have the power required, the key to undo the Severing is two centuries lost. The Wanderers were to bring back the magic we need, but Hercule and his people know nothing of it. Now will you please go? I must not be caught out when you stir the Sanctuary pool again. Thank you for wanting to help, Lucian de Remeni. I hope you can find a way to take your sister back. If not, we shall cherish her for what time she has left."

Signé saw herself as dead already. Another tragedy amidst so many. The mere memory of her singing bound my spirit with every color of life.

"I *will* come back. I'll not leave my sister or you or anyone here to starve, do I need to breach the gates of Idrium itself to find the way."

With a shrug, she set out across the crumbling cobbles toward the causeway. My fingers traced the curves of the bronze gate. Bold words faded quickly in the deepening cold. I wasn't looking forward to drowning again . . . or falling back through the airless void. And how was I to . . . aim? The door at Evanide was meant to lead to this city when the proper magic was applied to it. But the pool—Sanctuary itself?—had no intrinsic destination as I understood it. It would help nothing if I ended up dead or halfway across the world from Evanide.

And then in a blurt of sense, my mind began functioning. Of course there was a door to take me back. Feeling an entire ass, I sprinted after the lady.

CHAPTER 26

Signé spun in surprise when I caught up with her. "Are you crazed entire? I told you—"

"Before the Severing, where did people leave the city to go to the hospice—the House of Clarity?"

"All I've ever known is this place," she snapped, "and no one's gone anywhere."

"Would one of your survivors know? Perhaps some of the Wanderers left here by way of the hospice gate."

"The Wanderers were sent out from the Silver Tower." She pointed to the taller of the broken stumps beside the citadel's sole remaining tower. "If we could reopen their paths and traverse the void, don't you think we would have done? If we could have *repaired* the Dark Divide, would we not have done that?"

"Of course, but—"

"We've not just thrown up our hands and yielded to fate. Our mages tried *everything*. Even diminished by the Severing, they were the most skilled and insightful practitioners of magic in the world. If Navronne is the Heart of the World, then the Duchy of Xancheiros was the Heart of Magic. We made our lives there for generations, developing our gifts and sharing them with all. That's why the Southern Registry hated us. I doubt you were taught the truth of those days."

This had naught to do with politics or history. "I look forward to learning whatever you will teach me, Lady Signé, but crossing the Dark Divide is the critical matter right now. The gate between the city and the hospice was much older than the Wanderers' gates, though it was surely the same kind of magic—a portal for humans to access a shorter way through the Danae's true lands."

"No human outside Xancheiros knows of the true lands or the short ways. How can you—?"

"Call me a coward, if you like. Call me a simpleton. I just don't want to drown or plummet into an abyss I can't crawl out of!" I said, striving for patience. "But if my magic can take me across the Dark Divide from the hospice side, surely I should be able to access the hospice from this side, if I can just find the door. And my magic—whatever it is about my magic that enabled me to detect your beacon and made Safia recognize me as one who could help—has already opened the way once today. I'm thinking my passage ended in the pool because I *expected* to find Sanctuary."

She was silent, staring at me for what seemed eternity with the moonlight bathing her scarred face. My jaw ached from staying silent.

"Siever might know. He was fourteen at the Severing. He's the only one left who was born in the greater world."

I couldn't help but smile. Somewhere deep inside her something . . . curiosity, at the least, or perhaps a hint of possibility . . . stirred. It was very like sensing the flutter of a pulse in a comrade's wrist when you'd dragged him out of the bay.

"Come on." She took out for the causeway at a spirited pace.

Vines and fat-leaved shrubs snarled the steep hillsides to either side of the causeway and had broken through the paving of the ramp itself. The mouldering greenery stank of sickness, not health, dank, decaying, acrid, unpalatable. When the great bronze gate swung open at Signé's whistle, a tide of fresher air rolled over us.

A bony youth who'd not seen fifteen summers cranked the great gate closed as soon as Signé was inside. "Lord Siever will be most relieved, my lady. He left strict orders . . ."

The boy's report faded when he saw me, and his dark eyes followed as wonder propelled me past Signé. Had any people ever created such high-soaring walls and graceful buttresses, such pleasing layers of terraces and bright-painted archways? Their sculptures were astonishingly refined in their likeness, not to the appearance but to the energies of life, whether bird or beast or human . . . and yes, Danae, too. All of these were lit with pale green magelight—the veil of luminescence visible from the twin height of the Sanctuary pool.

Rising behind all this in compact strength was a triangular bastion, that had once been defined by the three round towers. The edifice was wreathed in enchantments—defenses we of the Order considered our own and others of such making as I'd not yet learned, even if there was some master at Evanide to teach me.

At the height of its glory, the citadel of Xancheiros would have swelled my spirit with that sweet, hurtful fullness I knew only from perfection, like the moments when magic filled me or the knights raised their voices in the Order's anthem. Yet on this night, as if it were my own home, my heart ached for its broken carcass. Everywhere lay evidence of the ruined towers. Great slabs and cornices sat where they'd fallen, impossible to move without magic or the wooden scaffolds and pulleys ordinary builders used. Smaller rubble had been collected and used to reinforce the foundation of the broken towers.

"Where's Lord Siever?" called Signé to a pair of guards. Lances in hand, they stood at a wicket gate beside a sturdy portcullis. The wicket and portcullis were the only visible entry to the inner citadel that didn't require climbing three or four stories over the makeshift fortifications.

"Gone to the well, mistress," said a young woman, dressed in man's garb like Signé. "He prays you'll come to him there and wake him if he sleeps."

"Anything else to report? *Landieu*, attention!"

"All quiet," said the gawping youth, his eyes back to Signé. His voice yet displayed uncertain timbre. "But before I took post, I heard Mercier whisper to Ranold of vines in the barley. I didn't know . . . but I thought . . . you should hear of it."

"Mercier is a fool, and you can tell him so. Keeping it secret will not slow the vines' invasion. We knew the barley would go next. Now, let us in."

"They try to spare you ill news," I said, as we waited for an exchange of passwords and a third guard inside to unlock the wicket.

"Benedik swore them all to serve me to the last day of this world. I think that oath spikes my craw more than anything that's happened. Had he not paid for his every fault a thousand times over, I'd not forgive him for it."

The wicket swung inward and we crossed a deserted bailey into the oddest fortress imagining could conjure. The three-sided structure was strange enough, but the entirety of the interior was open to the sky. Its scents were not of unwashed soldiers or greasy smoke, but of dirt and healthy growing things, of grain and herbs and greens. Stairs led upward to innumerable levels of all shapes and sizes, staggered so that all could reap the benefit of sunlight and rain from the open roof and from vast sections of latticework wall that had appeared solid from the outside.

The level on which we entered was cluttered with long tables stacked with bins, bags, and implements for tending gardens. The underside of the level above was hung with net bags of turnips, onions, parsnips, and ropes of garlic. Some of the upper levels were entirely dark. Some were marked with pinpoint lights. And the only sound, as we passed between tables and stools, was that of water dribbling through myriad troughs.

"But where did you house your people?" I said, wonder yielding to curiosity. "The thousands."

"In the city, of course."

Signé hauled open a bronze door so eerily like that I'd found in Evanide's crypt, I almost jerked her back from the dangerous threshold. But it was only a stair that descended into cool dampness. A most ordinary smoking torch lit our way down.

"Once the Severing was accomplished, the city dwellers went home and took in those from the countryside. Others were housed in the towers. All of us stay in the Gold Tower now the city's dead. We've housed the Wanderers in what's left of the Silver and Bronze. Your sister stays with them, though I offered her to stay with me."

Even after so short an observation, Juliana's choice didn't surprise me. I'd so much to learn of her—and of this woman whose life was shaped by a broken world. But the mission took precedence. Though it was not imposed by the Order, heart and bones told me that this rescue was as important as anything the *Equites Cineré* had ever undertaken.

The stairs led us deep under the citadel into a network of passages. "Were the two fallen towers destroyed by the Registry?" I asked. "The story I heard spoke naught of war engines."

"There was no attack, no terms, no siege. As they set the fire to drive us out, we triggered the Severing. It was earthquakes over the next few years that destroyed the towers, the bridges, and so much else. And then the vines went wild. Kyr says the land grieves, trying to shake off the burden of human works and human magic before it, too, falls into despair."

Was that possible? Goddess Mother, I needed to speak to Morgan. Perhaps she'd know how to free the Xancheirans from the trees, or what to do about the silver-marked Danae, about the void, or about Sanctuary. But in the moment I told her any of it, my oath to her father would be in play, and I would have to bring him here. What did Danae do with mad ones of their kind?

Signé pulled open a waist-high gate. Even if the guard had not mentioned a well, I'd have known what kind of place this was. The misty dampness of a deep-buried spring, so like that at Evanide's heart, was unmistakable.

Another torch welcomed us to the cave, as did a familiar mechanism. A Semmonis pipe stretched at an angle from the pool into a tunnel in the rock, lifting the water to some other reservoir where another such pipe would take it farther yet to distribute among the troughs and gardens above us. The magic that turned the helical screw inside the pipe hummed just below hearing, a pleasing buzz on the skin. What incomparable magic to work without renewal for almost thirty years.

But we'd not come for mechanical or magical wonders. The gray-complected man, huddled in a blanket, sat leaning on the pipe beside the water. His sword lay at one hand, his walking stick at the other. His chest sank with a quiet wheeze, the only sign he wasn't dead.

Signé crouched a respectful distance from his weapon. "Siever!" she called softly, in a voice I'd thought reserved for her singing. "Our *Deliverer* needs your help."

"Not rid of him yet?" Either the man feigned sleep or he was clearer spoken in a doze than many I knew while awake. His eyes remained closed. "Has he a lust for trouble?"

"It would seem not, as his question has to do with his manner of leaving the city."

His eyelids dragged open as if they lifted the weight of the water. "Even rats know where their bolt-holes lie. Is the man a dolt?"

"Most likely," I said, which lured his gray-blue gaze away from Signé. Of course he did not sleep, not with such pain as I read in those sunken eyes. "I need to know where people left the city to go to the Aurellian hospice—the House of Clarity. I'm thinking it will be a more direct route home than jumping into a bottomless pool."

His torpid mask fell away and he sat up. "The *hospice*? Is *that* where you've come from? Am I afloat with the Last Ferryman or does that make a kind of sense?"

"If the Danae created a short path between Xancheira and the hospice through their true lands, the entries would be placed somewhere similar. The door that brought me is in the deepest part of our fortress. Not at the spring, though. I suppose . . . do you have a crypt?"

"No!" Signé's scorn would wither a rock. "Our dead are committed cleanly to the fire."

Siever's dry laugh set him coughing. "The answer 'tis not a crypt, but like. Come, let me up. I need to see this."

He labored to his feet. Signé did not offer him aid, though her body was urgent to do so. Instead of grabbing his arm, she grabbed the torch.

"Where?" she said. "Old chests and artworks couldn't possibly define a way of the long-lived."

"'Tis not the refuse room we need."

They took me back through the gate, and into a passage that sloped gently upward. Slow going for Siever.

"I appreciate this does not require climbing a stair," he said, breathless. "'Twould be wicked if rescuing the rescuer were to end me beforetime. Amid her incessant praises, the young Juliana *did* manage to name thy few faults. She says thou'rt always hard on those around thee, ever trying to make them better. She resented it terribly, as most of us do. So I must tell thee, exercise does little for me these days. Here!"

He turned a corner and waved his hand at a short passage.

"The cold store?" said Signé, distraught. "Siever, you mustn't tease! He needs to leave."

"'Tis true," he said. "All the way to the end."

A series of dark chambers opened off the passage between us and its blunt end. Odors cascaded from one to the other as we passed their doorways—of earth and roots, of smoke and fish, of brine and blood meats. But I had no mind to inspect the spare contents, for the chambers themselves oppressed my spirit so sorely, it was all I could do to walk past them. The walls, ceilings, and half-open doors were cast of solid iron, and the darkness inside the chambers seemed to eat the flaring light.

"Why *iron* larders?" I said.

"Necessary, back when the hospice gate was in use," said Siever. "Not for larders, certain, but for protecting our fellows from their own wild magics until they could cross to the hospice. After the Severing, 'twas no longer possible to go, and with the fading of our talents, no longer necessary. A small blessing amidst the harder things."

"You *confined* people in these rooms? I thought Xancheirans were enlightened!"

"How else were we to shield them from harm?" said Siever. "Their power was driving them mad. The iron walls not only kept them from overextending their senses but prevented them from harming others until they could be helped. They didn't remain here long—and they were gently tended. But 'tis sure the long-lived would consider this cavern the nearest thing to death."

"So where is the hospice gate?" said Signé, cutting off my retort that surely a thousand methods of protection would be more merciful than iron closets.

"There," said Siever, taking the torch and illuminating the end of the passage. "Behind yonder shelves."

The squarish alcove of native rock—quite similar to the rock of the crypt—had clearly been used at some time for storage. A sturdy oak frame held five shelves, littered now with dirt clots, shreds of straw, and empty baskets. Signé and I dragged the heavy cupboard aside, and there it was. A bronze portal framed a door almost the twin of that in Evanide's crypt, though instead of the tree, the door's center panel depicted a pair of open hands—the age-old symbol of healing.

"Why have you not told me of this, Siever?" said Signé, cold as the stone. "Why has no one tried it?"

"Certain, we tried it! Many times over, when the elder mages yet lived with grace. Benedik studied everything known about the gates and the Severing void, and when he reached his maturity, he tried everything to open a way. But it was already too late. None could summon power enough to budge it after the Severing. It was never supposed to be easy. The long-lived didn't want us making frivolous journeys through the true lands."

"Will Kyr detect the magic?" I said, as my gaze took in handle and hinges, so like the ones that had brought me here.

"He'll question me next time I go out," said Signé, drawing her fingers over the bronze. When the handle did not yield to her touch, she yanked her hand away. "He does not come inside, but he knows we have magical artifacts inside the citadel. I'll tell him something. If it's a massive enchantment and we do it often, he'll worry."

"I hope we'll use it again very soon," I said. Then I turned to Signé and bowed, touching my fingers to forehead. "It has been an honor to meet you, my lady. Whatever happens here, know that I'll not rest until—"

"Luka!" The faint call and running footsteps echoed through the caverns. "Where are you?"

Siever laughed from where he'd propped himself against the wall. "Benedik used to say that bold, clever younger sisters were the gods' greatest aid to a man's humility."

"You should go," said Signé, jerking her head at the portal. "To see you again will make the separation no easier. You can't even promise her you'll survive this."

Signé was likely right, yet I had left my sister behind in so many ways.

Without knowing my reasons for sending her here alone, I couldn't even say I'd had no choice. I waited.

"Oh!" She carried a lamp and halted abruptly at the first storage chamber, her face riven with horror. "This is just like what Coroner Bastien told me. What are you *doing* down here, Luka? Signé, you're not imprisoning him?"

"Certainly not," said the lady, more patient than I expected of her. "We've found a doorway your brother thinks will take him back where he came from."

"Well, I'm not going with you"—a frown twisted Juliana's fine features—"though it appears you weren't planning to take me."

"No."

"I'm not afraid."

An unlikely grin threatened to break out. I smothered it, not wishing to insult her. "I never imagined it, *serena*. But you were determined not to leave your friends here. *I* am determined to find a way to get everyone away who wishes to go, so I've no fear to leave you here a bit longer."

"So who *is* going with you?" she said. "Bek offered, when I told him. You likely don't remember him either—Bek the surgeon, less unsavory and more intelligent than he appears?"

"I can't take anyone with me," I said, shaking my head. "I've never done this, and I'm not sure . . . I may end up stuck here, too. Either way, here or there, there's a great deal I'd like to talk with you about."

Her frown only deepened.

"But if you don't take anyone with you, then next time you'll want to take only one person as a test, which means you'll have to come a *third* time to actually get anyone out, and if there's any delay . . ." Eyeing Signé and a bemused Siever, Juliana took on that kind of expression people use when they want to say more, but daren't say it aloud. "They are having a *terrible* time with the food supply, and I just had this idea that perhaps you would take *one*. It would have to be someone braver than me, because I'm not sure I *would* go with you even if you wanted me to."

"Dost thou imply, young woman, that *I* should venture this crossing, being wholly useless to my lady as I am?" Siever's dying eyes sparked like shooting stars on a clear midnight.

"Well, it certainly should be someone who can help Luka figure out what he needs to do. Perhaps it might get him back sooner than all these months just gone since we came here."

Siever and Signé glanced at each other—their silent exchange an entire conversation filled with logic and emotion and apology. My young sister had spoken what they could not. If I failed to get Siever across, he was no more dead than elsewise. No matter what vows he had made to his lord or his lord's sister, he could do naught more valuable than help me. But it was not my place to speak first.

And so Signé did. "There is merit in Juliana's suggestion. Every invocation of magic will draw Kyr's notice. Thus every invocation must move us nearer a solution. And Remeni will need more information if he's to formulate a plan for the Wanderers' recovery."

Now it was my turn. "I cannot promise safety, Lord Siever"—indeed I would have to depend on Fix's forbearance to conceal him—"but I'm willing to try, and I'd welcome your advice going forward. The women's argument is intelligent."

Siever sank to one knee and laid fist on his breast. "My Lady Signé, allow me to do this service for my lord Benedik and his people."

Signé laid a hand on Siever's scant hair. "Go with the blessings of all gods, dear friend. I shall count the hours till thy return, and all of Xancheiros shall sing thy courage and honor until the last day of the world."

"And if all goes well, my lady . . . what of the cache?"

"If you are well enough to go chasing myths, you are welcome to do so. But I'd rather you live and be at peace, whether there . . . or here." Signé glanced at me, burying emotion in severity. "*You*, Lucian de Remeni, have a care with my chancellor."

I inclined my back. "*You*, lady, have a care with my sister. I'll have your chancellor back before she can get notions of filling his office herself."

A hint of a smile illumined Signé's face. Even without her terrible scar, she'd be no transcendent beauty, nor did she shed warmth like Morgan's sun. I couldn't even call her friend. Yet even so slight a transformation filled me with unnamable pleasure.

For the very satisfied Juliana I could find no words, but pressed her hand to my brow, wishing memory could flow like magic through her fingers. Then, motioning for Siever to stand behind me and hold on to my waist, I faced the door. Truly, taking someone through *this* door should not be more difficult than taking myself. I hoped.

A deep inhale to settle my spirit. Then I laid a hand on the smooth, unyielding handle and one on a hinge and reached deep into my two wells of magic. Head and heart. Magic only; no visions, no history, no art. I reached for Evanide, my home. For a chance at life for the man behind me. For a chamber filled with the detritus of human striving . . .

As the magic welled from inside and became a tidal onrush worthy of Evanide, I heard Siever gasp . . . or sob. But I could pay him no mind. Will released the flood through my fingers, the handle yielded, the door swung open, and the two of us plummeted into the breathless void.

CHAPTER 27

Again the endless fall through night and boundless silence. As before, my senses served up nothing, yet when my armless panic reached for Siever . . . there was surely a difference. Though splintering and starved for air, I was not alone. I should have learned more of him, so as to hold him firmer. *What gift formed you before this long dying? Did you have a chance to experience greater magic? Did it shred your soul to lose it? Is it only duty that keeps you holding on? Or is it the Lady Signé? What is she . . . so hard . . . who thinks herself dead and the world's end within reach, yet gentles a tree with her singing? Are you her lover?*

We hit damp, close air that stank of blood and piss and boiling herbs. In the moment my body possessed arms again, I reached behind and pulled my bony, slumping companion into my embrace. As we slammed into slick stone and slid into a wall, I twisted round and absorbed what I could of the impact. A piercing pain in my back suggested a sword had been sticking out of the wall.

Even as the world spun, I knew this was not the crypt. For a moment, as I sucked in air and extracted my bruised head from the limp tangle of flesh-less limbs, I thought we were back in the atrium of Xancheira's citadel. Yellow light squeezed my seeing to a squint.

But the light was sun glare spilling through an embrasure. And between me and the embrasure, a man with spiky red hair and a bandage around half his head sat gawking down at Siever and me, whose feet were lost somewhere under the sling bed. "Sky Lord's balls," he croaked. "Thought I was done with visions."

The spiky-haired man collapsed backward, groaning. Snores and faint moans accompanied him on every side. A dreadful hacking cough was addressed by an abrasive voice, saying, "Drink this, tyro, or I'll pour it down your nose." Adjutant Tomas. We'd come to the infirmary.

I shook my limp companion's shoulder gently, and whispered, "Are you with me, lord? We've come to the right place, though likely at the wrong time."

The Xancheiran was dreadfully still. I rolled him over and ripped through his tattered shirt and felt his stuttering heart. "Come on, man, breathe. We've food can nourish you here. But it's going to look awkward if the fellow I'm hauling about is dead."

A spasm shivered his protruding ribs. "Lightwork," he rasped, eyes yet closed. "Yes. Yes. No. Yes. She is an exceptional spirit. In another life."

His whispered answers to my questions from the crossing brought a grin to my face. I slipped on the mask from my belt, then peeked over the bed to see Adjutant Tomas's back at his linen cupboard. No time for caution.

Like a spider I skittered across the room. All blankets were in use, so I snatched two cloaks from the hook by the outer door, raced back, and dived into the space between the sling bed and the wall.

As I bundled Siever in the damp wool, I whispered, "Imagine you're drunk . . ."

The infirmarian's heavy tread crossed from the linen cupboard to the row of beds.

". . . now."

Without a pause, I heaved Siever over my shoulder and marched briskly across the room, his long body shielding my head from everyone's view.

"Lazy lackwit of a tyro!" I growled. "Woolly head's not going to keep you from a dunking! You're into the deep every hour for the next ten. Swim or die. Might drown you apurpose . . ."

My blather was joined by a croaking bellow from inside the bundle. "Merry, merry, Cilla, show me thy toe. A glimpse of thy sweetness before I must go. Merry, merry, Cilla, show me thy leg. A taste of thy kneecap, else sure I must beg . . ."

By the time we had requested a sniff of Cilla's neck, I had poor Siever tucked amid the coal sheds and wood stores behind the kitchens. The hidden spot had been my refuge over the years when I could not bear the sight or sound of my guide, trainer, or comrades for one more moment. The niche was sheltered, though not exactly dry; few places at Evanide could make that claim. At least it wasn't raining. I'd rather have taken him straight to Fix, but mid-morning in the busy fortress was not a time to be hauling around a body you didn't want anyone to see, alive or dead. I'd had to dodge and hide ten times to get even so far as this.

"Much as I would love to hear more of Cilla's parts, we'd best stay quiet," I said, as I made sure I had him right side up and breathing. "Are you all right?"

His skin was gray, his cheeks fevered, his breaths harsh. "I'll tell thee in a while. Merciful—" He broke into a racking cough. I laid both borrowed cloaks over him.

"None will bother us out here," I said, when the spasm eased, "and I'll get you somewhere better soon. Warmer. Drier. But first something to drink, I think."

He bobbed his head.

"I'll be back as fast as I can. And, if you please, dead strangers are even more trouble than live ones. Besides . . . I need you to tell me what *light-work* is."

As I rose, his hand gripped my ankle. "Thy magic, Lucian de Remeni . . . 'tis a glory to banish grief."

"I pray it can," I said. "But we'd best get something in our bellies to feed our magics, yes? We've *both* got work to do."

The smell of bread near had me on my knees as I hurried through the deserted Hall toward the kitchen. No one was guarding the stocks, so I stuffed an entire still-warm loaf into my jaque, filled a mostly clean flask from the cider barrel, and dipped broth from the never empty pot on the hob into the biggest mug I could find. No cheese at hand, but I spooned a heap of beechnut paste onto a leaf and stuffed it into my jaque atop the bread. With a furtive glance to ensure no one had followed me in, I scurried back the way I'd come.

It seemed that naught but two or three hours had passed since I sat in this Hall staring into fish stew, so tired I couldn't remember what it was. But the sun through the clerestory spoke of late morning. If Morgan's seven-to-one estimates held for Xancheira, then it was only a half day gone since I'd left the crypt. Everyone would be at their proper business for a day following a grueling exercise—cleaning arms and armor, healing, mourning, training hard to repair the mistakes that were made. Some of the knights would be out on mission already; they'd surely give the rest of us time to heal and learn before sending us to war. But I had troubles enough for the nonce.

My charges, Dunlin and Heron, would think I was with the Marshal. I'd given no thought to Inek; I couldn't even say whether he yet lay in the corner of the overcrowded infirmary.

Fix would not be waiting for me in the crypt, but likely down at the docks this time of day, yelling at squires to get the boats swabbed and stored in proper order.

The Marshal would expect my report on the last sixteen days. The dunking in the Sanctuary pool had left me as damp as fourteen hours previous, as well as stinking, unshaven, dizzy from depletion, and weary to the bone. The Marshal would notice I'd not cleaned myself or rested.

But a man was sitting out in the rocks dying, and the means to aid him were in hand. Perhaps a small thing beside war and conspiracy to reshape pureblood life in Navronne. But it had to come first.

"Greenshank!" The call caught me as I was heading into the passage to the outside.

"Squire?"

I considered ignoring the squire, a man I didn't know, but squires were often detailed to carry the Marshal's messages.

"The Archivist would see you as soon as possible. And as I was searching for you, I spoke to your cadre second, who was also in search of you. He says you're to report to the Marshal at sixth hour as usual. And paratus"—I was already turned to go before I slopped the hot broth on my hand or had the loaf leap out of my clothes—"did you know your back is bleeding?"

"It's just seepage." Slamming into the infirmary wall must have torn the stitches. "Tell the Archivist I'll be in as soon as I complete my current task. And if you run into anyone else hunting me, tell them I'm seeing to an injured comrade."

Skeptical, he frowned and pointed to my back. "Uh . . . it's a deal of seepage. Mayhap you've lost enough blood it's gone numb. I could look. . . ."

"Be off, squire. I'm well." Or I would be if I *could* numb the damnable wound, which was hurting like the devil, and if I could get some food in Siever and me, then get the man to Fix . . . The list of tasks I had to do before I could sleep for even an hour was impossibly long. And I needed sleep before I could possibly address how to undo a severing in the foundation of the world, transform a forest back into human persons, and figure out what deviltry Damon thought to do with me.

Siever was curled up in the niche, shivering.

"Sorry it took me a bit," I said, trying to shelter him from the wind. "If you can sit up, this might be something other than frigid."

"Is this w-winter?" He snugged the cloaks tighter. "Or are we c-come to the lands of wolves, b-bears, and fur-beasts?"

I eased down beside him and tried to smile, despite a most unpleasant stretching of the wound on my back, accompanied by oozing warmth. "Kemen Sky Lord and Mother Samele seem to have had a falling-out over the last few years and forgotten to tend the seasons. *Every* season turns out winter. Drink this first."

I held on to the mug of broth until I was sure he had firm hold of it. He sipped slowly. Meanwhile I gripped the cider flask between my legs and pulled out the bread, somewhat damp and squashed, and the folded leaf— which had leaked out half its contents inside my shirt. My own hands were none too steady.

"I think I'm wearing my share of this stuff," I said, pulling off a hunk of bread and dipping it in the paste, "but I'm not generous enough to give you all of it. Besides, a starving man shouldn't put down too much at once, yes?"

"Depends on why he's starving." He took long swallow of the broth, then sighed as if he'd tasted the juice of Estigurean oranges. "We can eat as much as we want. It just tastes like clouds and satisfies the same. The citadel-grown plants prolong the inevitable, but sooner or later our bodies figure it out. So this delectable feast may not change anything. Which"—he scowled fiercely—"you will not bemoan like those soft-headed women." He took another sip and reverted to his former beatific expression. "But I'll say, this tastes like the Goddess Mother's own homely brew, and I *will* have a bit of that bread to soak in it. Maybe not that brown mess . . . whatever it is. I don't know that I could tolerate that in the best of times."

I passed him a small knob of bread; I still thought it unwise for him to overdo. His gut might not be able to handle what his mouth craved. I precluded such an unfortunate circumstance by cramming three-quarters of the loaf, all the nut paste, and half the cider into my own gut, which appreciated them very much. That took about five heartbeats. Then I scrambled to my feet.

"I've got to leave you again for a while. I'd hoped to get you to better shelter, but everyone's looking for me, and only one man here knows anything about my strange connection with your city. It *must* stay that way."

Already the truth of the adventure was fading. If Siever wasn't sharing my bread, I'd doubt my reason.

"Now we know you can get back and forth safely, you can fetch your sister and the Wanderers," he said.

Stupid with fatigue, it hadn't even occurred to me. "Yes, certainly, though to bring them here . . . It will be complicated. But yes. As soon as possible."

"So *here* . . . Where might that be?"

"The island hospice," I said, "only it isn't a hospice anymore. It's a military fortress, very secure and very secret. Which is why I'll need to make arrangements before bringing my sister and the Cicerons. And why, if anyone finds you, they're not going to like it. Tell them your fishing boat got swept out to sea from Ynnes—that's a fish town up the coast—and capsized. I'm guessing you can feign a state of half-drowned, half-starved confusion."

"Likely so." He grinned as he scooped the last soggy bread into his mouth, then wiped his hand on Tomas's cloak and extended it my way. It was still trembling. "My blessings, Lucian de Remeni-Masson."

"Lord Siever." Though it was neither pureblood nor Order custom, I touched his hand and bowed. "And for now, please call me Greenshank."

Happy that my own hand was no longer shaking, I picked up the empty mug and the telltale leaf and turned to go.

"Greenshank, is that blood on your back?"

Visiting the infirmary was not going to unravel my confusion of business, but bleeding to death wouldn't help, either. A quick stop at the barracks laver for a jar of water and a towel and I hurried to my sleeping cell. The lower left side of my jaque was, indeed, awash with blood. My nut-paste-infused shirt was no better. I did my best to blot the ripped-open wound with the towel, then wrapped a spare strip of bandage I kept for such necessities tightly around. It was not the most pleasant thing I'd done all day.

I'd no clean clothes. My kit, weapons, and mail lay where I'd dropped them the previous evening. Traces of rust already stained the steel like creeping poison. I rummaged in my kit and found a shirt less bloody than the one I'd taken off and threw my habergeon over it. It looked silly to wear heavy mail about the fortress when not on watch, but I'd naught better. Training made a good excuse for everything.

The bells announced the time. Eleventh hour of the morning watch. Abandoning the bloody towel beside the rest of the mess, I sped through the passages to Inek's office. The wax tablet sat as I'd left it the day before we'd gone to Val Cleve. I left a notation that I was speaking with the Archivist at eleven, and another assigning Dunlin and Heron to meet me at the docks at third hour of the afternoon watch for a navigation exercise. Meeting at the docks allowed me to see Fix.

I threw the stylus on the table and ran for the Archive Tower, slowing only when I felt a surge of seeping warmth under the bandage. I had no time for healers.

A tall writing desk sat just outside the Seeing Chamber, allowing the Archivist or his second to supervise the copying of pages from their rarest books. The Archivist sat on the high stool, with a sheaf of papers at one hand, and another page in front of him. He seemed to be transferring notations from different pages in his stack to the new page. He glanced up.

"Have you no manners, paratus? No respect?" He spoke through gritted teeth. "What tasks have you set higher than a tutorial appointment with the Knight Archivist of the *Equites Cineré*?"

He threw down his pen and scattered enough sand on his newly marked page to serve a copyist for a tenday, before setting the page carefully on his stack.

My jaw twitched. Too many matters of importance were clamoring for attention to care for anyone's pique. But Order discipline and my hopes to unravel mysteries forced me to care about the third most powerful knight at Evanide. And he held all hope for Inek.

Thus, with strict adherence to ritual, I sank to one knee, laid fist to breast, and lowered my eyes. "My apologies, Knight Archivist. I intended no disrespect."

"Come with me."

He snatched up his sheaf of pages, leaving his pens unwiped, ink unstoppered, and sand everywhere.

"Second!" he bellowed as we swept into the passage to behind the Hearth of Memory. "Clean up the mess on the copy desk!"

In moments he was unsealing the door to the relictory. He pulled a scroll from the clutter on his writing table and unrolled the portrait of Inek.

"What do these marks signify?" He pointed to the embossing I'd drawn on Inek's silver bracelet.

"Naught in themselves," I said, though he should know that. As on my own bracelets, the embossed or engraved symbols were easily recognizable locations to carry spellwork.

"The embossed shapes are not unique," he said. "Only the borders differ. I've tried every possible variant of repeated circles and addressed all likely semantics in my attempts to derive the trap spell's pattern, but to no avail. As Inek came here with *you* in mind, perhaps *you* can extract the meaning."

Repeated circles . . . great gods, how could I not have noticed? The raised circle did indeed have meaning for me. Inek wanted to tell me something.

"Was Inek wearing a silver bracelet when you found him, Knight Archivist?"

"I don't recall it." He looked at the heaped confusion of books, boxes, and implements as if confounded. "But I'd have stripped it off him with his belt and weapons. Steel, silver, enchantments . . . They interfere with my work."

He peered under the worktable and shook his head. Then, fingers to his masked temple, he turned slowly, surveying the relictory.

"Pssh." As he completed a full circle, he waved his hand at a stack of baskets and boxes heaped in the corner. "Second must have stowed them over there. Fool's a packrat."

We dismantled the mound of miscellany. Or rather the Archivist watched as I set aside a crate of glass piping, a rolled lap rug, a crock of ink, spools of bookbinder's string, another of dried honeycombs, and innumerable sealed packets. Under a box of parchment scraps, a familiar leather jaque and gray linen shirt lay neatly folded atop a flat, open crate. In the crate lay Inek's swordbelt, sword and dagger yet sheathed, along with his boots and spare dagger, his eating knife and spoon, the bronze medallion of a knight-retired, his kerchief, a ring bearing two keys and an iron stylus, and his waist pocket, sewn with a brass ring he could use to fix it to a saddle or a pack or his belt. No bracelet.

I sat back on my heels. I'd been so sure. Unless . . .

A search of the waist pocket yielded the worn leather-bound journal where Inek kept notes on his students' performance and a single band of embossed silver.

The bracelet was not at all the same as the one in the drawing, but one of its features was a small raised circle exactly like that on my own bracelets. At my touch—mine, not Inek's—the embossed circle hummed with faint magic. *Marshal.*

I almost dropped the bracelet, but wariness kept the strip of silver turning in my hands. Might he have given more? A raised circle with a spike in the middle tickled my finger. *Damon.*

No surprise.

I turned it again. A raised circle with an inner circle. *Archivist.*

Sky Lord's grace . . .

Each of the three spells vanished at its first expression. No other enchantment bound to Inek's bracelet was open to me—or anyone else, I'd guess.

So three names. No hierarchy between them.

On my bracelets Inek used the raised circle to tell me the initiator of my missions, so I knew to watch for hints of his purpose. Was he telling me that my mission as Damon's righteous warrior was not solely Damon's? I hated that thought. Damon was easy to despise. I wanted the Marshal to be worthy of his grace. I wanted to trust the Archivist with Inek's healing. . . .

"What does it mean?" said the Archivist, his patience exploded. "Something, clearly."

"The circle carried a name," I said.

Of all people in the Order, the Archivist was likely a judge of truth and lies. So why not tell him some truth?

"Inek used the circle on my bracelets to tell me the author of my missions or exercises. He linked this circle on his own bracelet to the name of Curator Damon. Perhaps he was telling me of the Marshal's plan to make the curator my new guide."

"Damon is *your* guide, too?"

Oddly, it was not the appointment of an outsider as an Order guide that struck the Archivist rigid. Nor even that the guide was Damon. But rather the realization that I was not the *only* person assigned to Damon's mentoring. So who else was? And if the Archivist was Damon's collaborator, why didn't he know?

"Indeed, I have given Curator Damon my submission, as the Marshal approves. Could Inek have been telling me the author of Inek's own mission? A reassurance that *Damon* had ordered him to retrieve my relict, not knowing that it was destroyed or enspelled. Yet they'd surely have come to you. . . ."

The Archivist had turned away, fidgeting with his pages.

I didn't need to ask the next logical question. He'd know it.

And indeed his answer came with his back to me, as if I *might* be able to judge his truth through the mask. "Inek came to me several times over the past two years to request your relict. He had serious concerns about you and your place here. He repeated his request a few days before the accident, highly anxious. He spoke of threats. But as before, I told him that the old Marshal had forbidden anyone to view your relict, and neither the old Marshal *nor our present one* had given me permission to release it. Access to relicts is a training matter, as are guides and outsiders; training matters are the Marshal's province, not mine."

The damning truth remained unspoken: The Archivist's province was preserving the relicts, and he had failed. Failed to secure it. Failed to report any mention of *threats* or my relict's destruction to the Knight Defender. The Archivist's name on the bracelet suggested those failures no accident.

"Would that I could change my decision," he said. "Rules are made for important reasons, and yet critical events . . . dire circumstances . . . do require them to bend from time to time. But how could I expect—? And for it to be Inek, of all people, honorable, disciplined . . ."

He whirled on me, fists raised, and magic rose in a stifling, invisible wind that whipped and billowed his rust-red robes. Worms wriggled in my head. Moth wings darkened my seeing.

"Why *you*?" he bellowed. "They told me you were *nothing*, a weakling paint dabbler who'd been seduced into murder."

Dizzy and nauseated from the pulsing magics, I dropped to one knee, and vomited words.

"Commander Inek should not have violated your ruling." My voice shook like every other part of me. "Likely my persistent weakness and insubordination made him curious about why Curator Damon chose such a stupid lout for his mission. The curator should have told him. It's this talent I have to create revealing portraits. Curator Damon has told me I'm to be his instrument . . . his broom to sweep the corrupted Registry clean."

Cold silence swallowed the gale of power and fury. The Archivist shoved a stool next to a worktable across the room and swept a litter of books and pages aside. "You arrogant twit," he spat as he sat down to work. "Get out of here."

The Archivist had seemed truly regretful that the spell trap caught Inek. Yet his angry slip gave credence to the truth the bracelet spoke. He had known the trap was there.

Why did it bother him so much that I was the focus of Damon's attention? Damon was one of the three the bracelet named. The Archivist clearly had not told Damon my bent had been returned or that I had seen the dust of my relict's destruction when Damon showed me my imprisonment. And no sooner had I given my oath to Damon than the Marshal revealed the curator's broken talents and his odd departure from the Order. The Archivist, the Marshal, and Damon might be the initiators of my mission for Damon, but they did not share everything. Was that what Inek wanted me to understand?

Still puzzled, I returned the bracelet to the crate, rose, and retrieved the portrait I'd set aside while delving. If only the man it portrayed might speak to me—tell me how the three men were linked or what the Archivist meant that I had been seduced into murder. They'd told me I was *not* a murderer, delivering the news by way of a memory prick—a fragment of memory recognizable as truth.

As I carried the portrait across the chamber, I examined it for more clues—

the shape of the blood droplets, the figures in the pool, his weapons, his bracelet again. . . .

My breath caught. It required all my discipline to keep moving and offer
the portrait to the Archivist. He didn't look up from his book.

"I plan to visit Commander Inek this afternoon to report on his cadre's
performance at Val Cleve," I said. "Adjutant Tomas thinks it foolish, but I
feel it's a matter of respect. Were there other questions about the portrait
that I might address before I go? Perhaps some of these other symbols on his
garb might be significant. . . ."

As if called to his senses, the Archivist snatched up the portrait from my
hand, rolling it so tightly the parchment must be near cracking.

"Clearly the spell pattern in the mail and neck chain were the significant
revelation," he said through clenched teeth. "The circle pattern of the bracelet was a clever insight on your part. Naught else remains a mystery. Be about
your duties, Greenshank, and arrive here promptly tomorrow with your
cadre or I'll drag you before the Disciplinarian, be you Damon's chosen
instrument or no."

"*Dalle cineré*, Knight Archivist."

He did not respond, so I bowed to his back and left.

Surely the Archivist knew what the bracelet suggested. Symbols and history were graven in my bones, and if in mine, then certainly in his. The
engraved border of the sketched bracelet's edges comprised two decorative
bands. The outer band showed a repeated pattern of the five implements of
the Order's blazon—sword, whip, pen, staff, and hammer. The inner showed
a flower and slashed crescent, linked within a circle. The flower was the royal
lily of Navronne; the slashed crescent was the Goddess Mother's signature of
death and rebirth. The linked symbols were repeated in an unbroken circle
that explained so much of Damon's strategy of the past months—my missions, his questioning. As if writ in fire, the bracelet told me what Inek had
learned, and why he understood his life was forfeit.

Damon's aide Fallon had told me that the Sitting of the Three Hundred
had all the signs of a move of power as we've not seen in Navronne since the
Writ. And truly, if I guessed right, that must be so. Damon, the Marshal, and
the Archivist had not initiated a mission solely to purge and reform the Pureblood Registry. They were planning the death and rebirth of Eodward's
kingdom as well.

CHAPTER 28

"And then I answered the Archivist's summons," I said, "and even a half day on, I'm not sure I believe what I learned."

It was near midnight and Fix sat at the small table in his cottage devouring the last of an enormous leek pie. Rough breathing whispered from the hastily assembled cot in the corner.

At the afternoon's navigation exercise with Dunlin and Heron, the boatmaster had bustled me aside long enough to order *Evanide's uninvited visitor* and me to his residence after nightfall. We'd spent two hours getting Siever warm and fed. Fix wrapped him in an enchantment that aided a warrior's ability to sustain himself on low rations, as well as one that relieved pain without dulling the mind. We hoped the two would help Siever hold to life until he could take nourishment from normal food. Now he slept, while I shared the tale of Xancheira's fate.

"So what did the portrait have to tell you?" asked Fix, scraping his dish with a spoon.

My theory was so outrageous, I couldn't just blurt it. So I presented my case as a man of the law might, in the way Bastien had given evidence to the Danae back in Palinur.

"I've assumed Damon was testing my Order training these last months—my loyalty, my diligence, my doubts and temper. The missions yielded interesting observations, but nothing any knight could not have done better. But look at the missions themselves. Damon sent me to observe Bayard at the moment he forever disgraced his father's name by allying himself with the Harrowers. Just days later, he showed me the horrific truth that the Registry had used the Harrowers for slaughter of purebloods, before telling me the victims were my own family. Then he sent me to observe Osriel, near a battlefield where the prince's diabolical practices were sure to be made clear. And Damon made sure I saw not just the Registry's cooperation in my own degradation, but in Perryn's plot to forge a dead king's will. He's asked me over and over, 'Which prince is worthy?' And how did I please him best? By saying, 'None of them.' Only then did he make me his servant. Then, today, I looked closer at Inek's portrait. . . ."

I laid out the story of Inek's silver bracelet and my outlandish conclusion. "Am I mad to believe Damon, the Marshal, and the Archivist are plotting to take the throne of Navronne itself?"

The Knight Defender's fingers flexed and curled about his spoon as if it were a dagger's hilt.

"Gah!" he spewed, after a shivering moment of immense control. "I'd call Damon a lunatic, but he is the farthest thing from it . . ."

Surely what angered him most was the same that plagued me: the fear that Damon's course was right. How could a kingdom so blighted with corruption prosper in these cursed times? Yet any cleansing forced by blackmail and murder was surely cursed as well.

". . . and *both* of my counterparts involved. Though I've only spoken to the Marshal once in the flesh, I'd have wagered my life on his honor. How is a man to believe in *anything*?"

His fury invited no simple answer.

"If they're partners, then why would your submission to Damon dismay the Archivist so sorely? Because you're a player, too, of course." The Defender's glare sprayed needles in my direction. "Your damning portraits terrorize the Three Hundred families into doing whatever Damon wants. Pureblood warriors would be a formidable force to reshape a kingdom, even if they're not Order trained. And certainly the slaughter of your family brings your righteous voice to speak of corruption. But Damon has all the portraits he needs from you . . ."

". . . and how persuasive is the righteous anger of a portrait artist *easily seduced to murder*?" I said.

Fix nodded slowly, eyes never leaving me. "Aye. There's that. So I just feel . . ."

". . . there must be more." We spoke the inevitable conclusion in unison.

If Damon didn't want something more from me, I would be a martyred memory, not nurtured in the bosom of the Order with my memories of the past dust.

"I've got to keep going, Fix," I said. "I've got to learn what is Damon's idea of Registry purity and the rebirth of Navronne. Does he plan to make a puppet of whichever prince wins the day? And if not one of Eodward's sons, then who does he intend to sit Caedmon's throne? Does the Marshal bring the Order to enforce their will? The second band on the bracelet suggests it."

Fix threw his bent spoon into the empty pie dish. "Boldest would be to sit his own king. Wait for one of the three to eliminate the other two and then trump the winner with his own man. But I've no idea who."

We had to leave the question there, as Fix had duties to attend. "I'll look in on your hungry friend from time to time through the night. Are you for the seaward wall? That could be a good time to consider magic that can knit the world back into one piece or set free a people trapped in trees. Gods' bones, I'll need to give those things some heartfelt contemplation myself!"

"Our seaward flank will go unguarded this night and several more," I said, dragging myself from the floor beside Fix's brazier. "Inek's pointed teaching tells me I am unfit to buckle my boot at present. And falling off the wall will do no one any good. But there is a matter of boats. . . ."

"*Boats,* as in more than one? I told you old Dorye—"

"I believe I can bring the Cicerons from Xancheira to anywhere in the fortress, if I focus my magic right. Two hundred people or so."

Fix closed the door he'd half opened and rested his back on it. "And when are you planning to perform this feat?"

"It needs to be soon. Tonight I sleep. Tomorrow night I'll take old Dorye to the estuary. By now Morgan should have Bastien waiting for me, assuming he was willing to come away, rather than waiting around to be murdered. I'm hoping the two of them will agree to get the Cicerons back to Palinur or wherever they want to go. As soon as we've a plan, I'll return to Xancheira through the crypt door and retrieve them. Hopefully I can bring more than one at a time."

"There's no place for your sister here. The Order doesn't believe you should even know she exists. Are you sure—?"

"I won't allow her to stay in Xancheira and starve. She's made friends with the Cicerons. . . ." I couldn't believe I was even considering sending my sister off with a troop of thieves and vagabonds, no matter their place in history. But where would a gently raised pureblood maiden of fifteen be safe? Evidently a place of legend I'd never seen, beyond a mystical boundary I myself couldn't cross, had seemed the best choice two years ago.

Fix folded his arms across his chest. "You won't need boats alone, but rowers; never heard of a Ciceron who knew an oar from a chicken leg. And you'll need a distraction, as we wouldn't want the Order, for the Mother's sake, to see *two hundred* people hauled out from their own confusticated docks!" As his voice rose, I'd swear the air rippled. "But certainly, paratus, Fix the boatmaster can provide whatever you need. Just give him a day's warning to create a bit of distracting spellwork and eight or ten rowers who can make a rough crossing twice in a night and whose minds can be safely mucked out at the end."

"I can do that. And this is your warning."

He jerked his body away from the door and reached for the latch again, then paused and looked over his shoulder, the moment's manic agitation profoundly stilled. "I felt what your magic wrought as you opened that door in the crypt, and again this morning when you returned. This Morgan and her kin, who seem devoted to preserving the natural order of things, are right to be concerned about you. Use such power wisely, Greenshank. I don't like thinking of a power-mad Damon having your kind of magic at his beck as he sets out to transform this kingdom. You *cannot* allow him to control it. I can't allow it, either. I won't."

His sobriety shot steel needles up my spine. "I understand, sir knight."

"And you'd best figure out what your friendly Danae do to mad ones of their own kind and to those humans who've befriended them. Two hundred ragtag Cicerons are one thing. But what happens when twenty thousand sorcerers, savaged by the Registry, are set free? Are these new wars in the making? Will your involvement bring them to my fortress? I won't allow that either."

His warnings jangled every nerve, but I refused to let fear take hold. "We can't turn our backs on them, Fix. We have to find a way to make it right."

A grin flashed through his mask. "Thought you'd say that. But *do* let me know what I must prepare for. If Damon thinks to use the Order to bring down the Registry and win Navronne's crown, and you think to bring in a legion of starvelings and mad Danae, I'm thinking I might have a very busy year."

His humor should have been reassuring . . . but Fix was a very serious man. I watched him stride down the quay, brushed by spotty lamplight . . . and felt the swift pulse of power that transformed the tall, brisk, sinewy knight into a round-shouldered, slow-moving elder. Had I not been waiting for it, the keen blade of enchantment would have been lost in the myriad threads that entangled Fortress Evanide.

"Dost thou count that extraordinary person as friend?"

The voice from the depths of the cottage spun me around so sharply I near broke my skull on the low lintel. "I thought you were sleeping, Lord Siever."

"Perhaps his potent spells cannot redeem this cadaverous frame any more than Kyr's new-bled meat does. Though, truly, I've not *felt* so well in months." Siever hefted his lank body to sitting. "This man Fix . . . danger drips from his tongue alongside jest as bee stings companion honey."

His wry observation raised a chuckle, but my answer came sober. "Fix is not my friend. His duties preclude friends, I think. He's let me know him, which implies a trust I believe extremely rare. *Never* would I presume on it. In return, I believe him eminently trustworthy. He'll not betray either of us."

"To this man Damon—who seems set to upend the world my people yearn to rejoin? Or to thy Danae friends?" Perhaps the fate of his people weighed especially heavy on Siever at that moment—or perhaps it was the cost of illness or Fix's spellwork—but his warmth had shifted into cool and weary resignation. "Thou didst not mention having friends among the long-lived."

"I didn't think—" Why hadn't I told them of Morgan and her kin? "I'd no intent to deceive. But it's a difficult situation, and I've no idea how to resolve it. Indeed, I could use some good counsel. . . ."

So I sat back down and told him of the blue Danae and their concerns about my magic and their silver-marked kin, of Morgan and the youthful liaison I could not remember, and of the terrible risk she'd taken to help me. ". . . so she agreed to bring this coroner back here. And I hope she can tell me what's necessary to set your people free of their prisoning."

Siever spoke carefully, as if paring away words he might otherwise have said. "I would accompany thee to meet this gentle lady. 'Tis inevitable that she have questions, and across a boiling sea is a very long way to shout an answer."

"I'd welcome you—and so would she."

The lamplight carved creases into his high forehead. "I doubt that. Truly 'twould be best not to speak truth of my origins, even to one who has so captured thy regard. Once the long-lived understand that the terms of thy oath are in play, thy choices will be limited."

His clarity shook me. I had sworn to take Tuari to the silver Danae as soon as I learned how. And Morgan's fate rested solely on my adherence to those terms. I was already in violation.

But Morgan had accepted my excuse that I had to understand what I learned before telling her father. "I trust Morgan, if not her kin. But I'll leave you to decide what she should know of you."

"But—" Again, he bit off words. "Well, we shall see."

Of course his dreadful experience would color his feelings about Danae. "Will you be strong enough to venture the sea tomorrow night?"

"A bit of sleep, another meal or two—this cider is extraordinary—and I shall likely be able to row."

I slept that night like the Sky Lord's hounds, who chase the Bull and Stag across the winter sky and sleep away the summer. After an early visit to the chart room and a hard run across the mudflats, Dunlin, Heron, and I sat our session with the Archivist. We had already studied the premises of memory magic—language, symbols, patterns, and the structure of human recollections—as well as the physical and ethical considerations underlying memory implantation and removal. To implant a new memory with a fullness of experience, understanding, and emotion was so complex and bore so many ethical burdens that it was taught only to vested knights who had substantial need for it. Memory preservation was quite delicate. Thus we began with the study of simple destruction.

We began by constructing the simplest kind of memory pattern—a word and its definition, a food and a preference, an action and result—and learning to wrap it in magic, so we could strip it from a person's mind.

The more one knew of the person, the more specific the memory you could construct—and the more complete the removal. The spells on our memory-wipe tokens used for strangers were extremely specific—this man's face, that particular location, this exact circumstance—else we risked intruding on memories we had no right to touch. Removing the memory of a knight's mission was dependent on the thoroughness and exactitude of his report.

Removing the past of a tyro was work that had been developed over decades, a sprawling net spell that touched those parts of every person's experience—family, teachers, lovers, residences. . . . It was brutal because of its extent, yet necessarily incomplete, so that the memories could be returned. Fragments always remained—perhaps like the greeting *Envisia seru* when one met a being of legend, and certainly those roots of familiarity, like the scent of ink, my hand's recognition of my signature, the understanding of my own artworks, the familiarity of Bastien's necropolis.

"Attend, Greenshank!" The Archivist's knuckle rapped on the table. And I bent to the work, exchanging memory patterns with Dunlin to examine and correct.

Creating memory patterns was art. Words, objects, faces, facts—these were lines, curves, dimensions: thick or narrow, sturdy or delicate, certainty or suggestion. Sensation and emotion were colors, blended and shaded, given depth or left vague. The memory itself was a composition, and if the artist was able to bring his bent to its creation, it would take on the aspect of truth. It was no delusion or excessive pride to believe I would be good at it, in the same way it was no false modesty to know I would never be a renowned swordsman. Delusion and false modesty did not last long at Evanide.

At midday, the Archivist dismissed us, grumbling that it would be the new year before we could dare try our workings on a person's mind. Disappointing. By the new year the world would be changed for good or ill. The fate of the Xancheirans would be determined. The Sitting of the Three Hundred would have done its work. Navronne's king would be one of Eodward's vile sons or perhaps, instead, a person of Attis de Lares-Damon's choice.

Was a man of such overarching confidence as Damon capable of stepping aside? And where was his belief in justice when he learned of my family's murder? I would bring him to account for that. But before I could know how to do it, I had to learn his plan.

Dunlin, Heron, and I spent a hard afternoon working with another cadre and the swordmaster on improving faults exposed at Val Cleve. When my back started leaking blood again, the swordmaster sent me to the infirmary for new stitches. An hour later I was fighting again, with knife and fists and magic, as if incinerating hay bales and slamming my brothers to the floor might drain the tumult inside.

The three of us were dull at supper. "What are we preparing for?" said Dunlin. "Magrog's coming?"

"*Whatever* comes," I snapped, my wounded back protesting the long row across the bay still to come before sleep. "We're not children."

The eighth-hour bells saved me from the urge to explain more. "We'll run again tomorrow. Heron, find the earliest hour we can slog through the ebb. Leave a message on Inek's tablet."

I ignored their eyerolls as I hurried to catch up with a knight just leaving the Hall. Exactly the person I needed to see.

"Knight Conall," I said, pressing my fist to my breast. "Might I have a word?"

"Greenshank! For certain!" The man I'd known as Cormorant inclined his head properly—and then grinned hugely. "That was a most excellent job of navigation on our return from Val Cleve. Inek could not have asked for better. Though he would have, eh?"

When I bent my head to acknowledge it, he nudged me as he'd have done a month ago. "We are yet brothers, Greenshank. I've a notion you'll join me vested sooner than you think. Tell me"—he drew me out one of the kitchen doors into the unlighted niche where emptied bins and crates awaited sorting—"what happened to Inek? I'd never believe him caught in a backlash, even if I didn't know about that odd business on my vigil night."

The Archivist had commanded me to secrecy, but I no longer trusted the Archivist. Someone needed to know the truth. Conall was Inek's man. "You cannot speak of this to anyone, not the Marshal, not the Archivist, not *anyone*."

I gave him a chance to stop me. But a jerk of his chin said continue.

"With Inek's knowledge and consent, I was—and still am—embroiled in a dangerous play for power that shadows the Order. I'm working to learn its objectives and its reach. Inek went to the archives that night to secure my relict, which was . . . guarded . . . by a virulent spell trap."

"Mother's heart! I knew it was something like, but you were the only one I dared ask. And he's—"

"In stasis for now, but at terrible risk. The Archivist seems to have high regard for him and says he's trying to work out a counter, but I don't know the whole story and don't trust him entirely. I try to visit when I can. The more who do so . . . perhaps, the safer he'll be."

"I'll get in there," he said. "It's been a rough month."

"Indeed, I wanted to ask how your tyros were shaping. I know a few, at least, are near squiring. Would you trust any of them with a double crossing to the estuary in a single night? I've talked to the boatmaster about an exercise I want to try for Dunlin, Heron, and me. The three of us would navigate. If you've one who could tail me, it would just be hard rowing for the rest. Rough conditions."

"Five of my eight would thrive on it, and one of those is going to make Marshal before I get my first mission out. I'd like to stretch him. A sixth is a possible. The other two would die for sure in the second return. Something different would be good for the five."

I hated drawing Conall into my scheming. I'd tell him the entire story if I had time. I believed he'd answer my need willing. But this could not get back to the Marshal or Damon, and until I had better evidence of their duplicity, I had to keep things simple.

"Good. I'm thinking tomorrow night or the next, but I'll let you know by midday so they can snatch some rest in the afternoon. And the boatmaster says it's an exercise works best with surprise—an evacuation drill—so if you'll keep it close . . ."

"I understand." His face livened with the generous humor that would make men die for him. "They won't realize it, but I'll hold back a bit the next couple of days. They're still a bit sagged. Inek would have been proud of them at Val Cleve, too."

"Tell him of it, Conall. I like to believe he hears what we say."

The night's venture had me inexplicably edgy. My snap at Dunlin shamed me. Whatever the reason, my agitation was helped not at all when I arrived at Fix's cottage to find Siever half in, half out of a thick cloak while doubled over with a violent cough.

"Thy not-friend has provided an elixir," he said, when he could croak a reply to my concern, "but it were a fool would drag me out to sea this night."

"And a worse fool who would allow himself to be dragged," I said, helping him back to the cot and throwing the cloak over him. "It may be only fever or the cough, but your color seems better."

"Some of all, I ween," he said. "My belly flourishes, for which I thank thee. And there's this . . ."

He held out his open palm and there rose from it a ball of rose-colored light and a sweet effusion of magic that brushed my spirit with joy. Though it vanished almost as soon as it was born, its glistening reflection lingered in the caverns of Siever's eyes.

"Lightwork," he whispered, hoarse.

"Ah, Siever. I am so glad."

"I could smell divine Idrium's mead and ysomar that night at the citadel's well and found the prospect of immortal feasting detestable; I'd sworn not to die before my lord and lady walked free. And now, perhaps, if the Mother wills it so, and thou art wise"—his words lingered on the air a very long time—"perhaps we can do something about that."

"Deunor's fire! Have you thought of—?"

But he waved me off as he hacked into his sleeve. And I had no time to press him.

"I've likely not reached the age of wisdom, but I do try," I said. "I'll have great care with what I say tonight."

"Work a bargain with your Danae lady," he croaked, with astonishing ferocity. "Agree to *nothing*, speak *nothing*, without her sworn word and, unlike thy first so-foolish oath, let the terms of that bargain be as strong and seamless as Syan silk. Friendship, honor, love, faith . . . the long-lived can express them all in such beauty the heart cannot hold it. But these are *human* qualities, not those of star or rock or grass. It is no simple madness that drives Kyr and his kin to do as they've done. Nor is it evil. 'Tis what they *are*, driven by nature to do as they do."

"She has defied her archon, her own father," I said, willing him to understand. "She's mortgaged her future to help me."

"Listen to her words. Not what they say, but what they mean. The long-lived do not lie, but the source of their truth is not the same as ours. Discover what she *wants* and what she *needs*. Trust her no further than that."

Throttling another spasm, he rolled over on the cot and shooed me away.

Of course he would mistrust. In Osriel's cave my bent had revealed love and reverence between Xancheirans and the Danae. Even the Danae themselves had not foreseen the outcome of such a unique and drastic solution to Xancheira's danger. Who could lay blame?

Yet as I guided old Dorye across the bay on the last of the onrushing tide, I could not shake Siever's warning—especially the eerie echo of Morgan's own. *'Tis not magic, but what we are. Though we share the same form, gentle Lucian, I am not human.*

CHAPTER 29

Moments after dragging my hand in the water of the Gouvron Estuary, threads of sapphire and indigo glimmered beyond the marsh. The memory of those threads entwining my flesh in exquisite heat obliterated every plan save one.

Leaning over old Dorye's gunwale, I dunked my head in the cold slosh of brine and muck. Only when my teeth ached from the cold and the rest of me declared the impossibility of such delights did I pull it out. And then I could see her entire and the sturdy man who hurried across the matted marshland alongside her. I kept my eyes on him and decided he was not entirely unlike an otter.

"Well met, sweet Lucian!" Morgan called cheerily. "Here's thy friend, an amiable traveling companion and most fascinating gentleman of the law. His questioning would have led our tutors in Montesard to speechless confusion."

I splashed through the mud, dragging the squinch farther into the marsh before tying it low on a well-rooted clump of reeds.

"Sorry it's taken me a few days to get here," I said, eyeing the dwindling crescent in the sky. Incredibly small it seemed, compared to the sliver that had lit Xancheira only two nights previous. "And I can't stay long. Are you well, Coroner Bastien?"

In fact he appeared quite well. The paleness of his teeth signaled a grin behind the snarls of his beard. "This is just the damnedest. Erdru's horns, I'd wholly forgot what it was like to have an adventure, and what man ever dreamed of such a one as this?"

The jerk of his head Morgan's way was unmistakable. She noted it as well and her own pleasure put the scrawny moon to shame.

"For certain the lady marches one hard," I said, "but then covers the ground at a rate that's kind to the feet, yes? I'd be ever grateful could she do the same for a boat!"

"However wouldst thou hone thy well-made shoulders in such a case?" Morgan's voice stroked my skin like silken ribbons. An hour's frigid dunking of my entire self might be needed to keep me thinking straight.

"So she explained why I was afraid for you to stay in Palinur?"

Bastien grew full sober. "I thank you for the warning, and your kind friend here for delivering it. I sent our few who were left—Constance and two diggers—off someplace safer. I'm no slouch to defend myself against the scum of Palinur, nor even against a prince's soldiers, but magic that makes *you* fearful enough to warn me . . ."

"I can't leave here just now . . . to protect you or your friends."

He examined me as he might one of his witnesses. "She says you're soldiering now; never thought I'd see that. No lack of courage—not in the least—but you were brought up soft. More drawing than wrestling or running. More books than weapons."

"Be sure that every weakness of my upbringing was made clear in my first days here," I said. "It was hard learning. . . ."

"No hiding that," he mumbled, "mask or no."

Such a reference to the past when I wasn't prepared set off the familiar throb inside my skull. I'd mostly avoided the headaches of memory probing of late. Even when meeting my sister, I'd been thinking more of present circumstance than our shared past. That frightened me in a way. I wasn't ready to relinquish what remained of my true self.

"So it's your *commanders* who want your friends dead? Or someone's paying them for it?"

"No. The Order is not a mercenary troop for hire. Our missions are not chosen for coin, but for merit, for right, for worthy needs that none else are prepared to meet. . . ."

Though chosen by a man compromised. Even now, I could not truly accept that the Marshal I believed in might harm a man whose only crime was to know me. Which showed how little of a military man I was. Sentimental, Inek had called me.

Knights gave up their personal memory of a completed mission, but they did not give up conscience or intelligence or judgment beforehand. Always we were taught to observe and ensure that our orders made sense. But how would that work if we were ordered to war?

"Damon has convinced some of our commanders that there is larger, more important work to be done with the kingdom in such chaos," I said. "He has plans to remake the Registry—clean out the corruption and put his own people at the head of it. I'm afraid he thinks to use our Order to enforce his will. And for some unknown reason he's fixed on me to play a part in this remaking since long before I worked for you."

"Since your grandsire brought this back from the north country?" Bastien pulled a small object from his belt pouch—a pale cylinder no thicker than my thumb with a dark knob protruding from each end.

"The Xancheiran spindle!" I'd almost forgotten.

I sank to a damp tussock, the canvas-wrapped wood in my hand. It was bound in enchantments that I'd once have imagined complex. One of them seared my hand with fire that left no mark.

Bastien crouched beside me to watch.

Morgan remained standing. "Hast thou more to tell before I go, Lucian? I've duties will not wait. The good Bastien knows the way to his cave."

Though her generous presence blunted Siever's warnings, I couldn't wholly ignore them. Neither could I get the Cicerons away without her help. I had to craft a story. . . .

"I found a portal in the crypt at the sea fortress," I said. "It was framed in bronze just like the one in the hirudo. The frame held neither a vision of light nor an abyss nor a blockage of stone, but a true door. My magic opened it. Beyond its threshold, I found the Palinur Cicerons."

Bastien goggled. "Shite!"

Morgan pressed her palms together and held them to her mouth. Slowly, she sank to her haunches, her whole body listening.

"The place was not Sanctuary," I said, "nor was it the five-fingered land. And the sentinel wasn't there. The land is wild, thick with vines and great trees, though surely a part of the true lands, for the Cicerons believed they had only been there a few months, not the years since I sent them. They'd brought their own provision and kept hidden, waiting for me to come for them. Cicerons don't work the land, Morgan, so they—"

Her quick hand pressed my lips. "Say no more, friend Lucian. I wouldst not have thee lie to me. What wouldst thou have me do?"

The flesh beneath my mask burned. "They'll starve if they stay there," I said. "And my sister's with them . . . my only family. So, I plan to return tomorrow night and fetch them. I've a scheme to get them across the bay, but two hundred men, women, and children can't stay here in the marshes. I need you and Bastien to take them to whatever place in Navronne they specify"—Siever's warnings dogged me—"by the shortest and safest route possible, leave them in peace to make their new home as they will, and bring the coroner back here if he chooses. Will you do those things for me?"

"I shall await thy coming on the morrow's eve and take thy friends where they will—exactly as you say. All shall be well." Morgan rose, brushed her glowing fingers across my masked cheek, and riffled my hair. "And when that work is done, we shall have time for other matters—some serious, some very much not. Bastien may have to dwell in his sea cave unsuccored as I have my way with thee."

Signé had spoken of a bond between her and Kyr, because of the intimacy they'd shared. I believed it. Morgan could tell when I was withholding truth. Likewise for me. Even as her desire infused and entangled me and became my own, so did a deep and mortal sadness.

I caught her hand and pulled her back down. "What do you need of *me*, sweet Morgan? What might I offer in return for your generosity? Always you give, but you never ask anything for yourself."

Her smile seemed to make her sapphire gards grow brighter. "What could I want that I do not have, save more days and nights with thee, my gentle warrior? Perhaps, someday, a new portrait to show us what beauty will come of our deeds."

Which was, of course, no answer at all.

My gaze lingered on the moonlit marshland long after all trace of sapphire and indigo had vanished. Beauty had gone with her, leaving frog croaks and bird calls, the slurp of backwaters and the stink of mold.

"Where will your sister go?" said Bastien, half startling me. "She can't stay with you, I'd guess."

"I'm hoping she'll have an idea. Or *you* might, since you've had more dealings with her than I can remember."

"I'll give it thought." The coroner eyed the darkness where Morgan had vanished. "Summat's changed with the lady Dané. From the moment you spoke of that door."

My fingers picked at the spindle, welcoming the stabbing fire of its binding magic. "Let's look at this. I've two mysteries on my hands, and my skull's going to cave if I don't get answers to one or the other."

"Curator Damon's plot and the Danae mystery. Same as two years ago. You're further along the path but still without a map to either one. Don't envy you." The coroner mimed a shudder. "So tell me, were you going to lie to her?"

"My commanders consider omission to be a lie," I said, fixing my gaze to the roll of canvas and wood. "If you see it that way, then yes, I was lying."

"So what else is beyond the door? The part you didn't tell her."

Bastien was easy to trust. He felt solid, not tenuous, not wavering. A man who was either on your side or not. As if his purposes sprang not from higher duty or demanding conspiracy, but entirely from who he was.

"Xancheira itself. Seven-and-thirty living survivors of the massacre. And some twenty thousand more of them who've been imprisoned in trees while yet alive by Danae whose gards shine silver. Morgan told me that silver gards imply madness. The survivors confirm it, though they say Safia, the one I spoke to, is the *most benevolent* of her kind. All of them—humans and Danae— will starve or die if I don't bring them back."

"Shite!"

"I'm afraid of what would happen—" I left off, drawing my cloak around me against the rising wind. Bastien didn't need me to explain my fears. He'd recognized the dangerous state between the blue Danae and the silver. A Danae war? A slaughter? Such a conflict was far beyond our understanding, but Morgan's father would surely summon overwhelming numbers to deal with mad ones of his kind, and if so, then what would be the fate of the Xancheirans? Siever had forced me to see the truth.

Morgan had spoken frankly of humans bringing danger, disorder, and violence wherever we traveled. She'd told me my magic was risky, because it thinned the boundaries that kept us out of the true lands, and that their Law of the Everlasting required them to eliminate such a threat as I was. The long-lived did not lie. Morgan was willing to help me when it did not conflict with her nature. If her people considered humans to be such a blight on the world, they wouldn't care what happened to twenty thousand Xancheirans as they dealt with a few of their own gone mad.

"I've got to learn how to release those prisoned in the trees and how we might rejoin the city and its surroundings to the world without Morgan's help. The abyss she saw in the hirudo portal does indeed lie between here and there. But if I keep the oath I swore her father and take him across it, I'm afraid the Xancheirans—prisoned or free—won't survive. I can't let that happen."

"And if you *don't* keep your oath, the lady will be a beast until the end of her days."

"If you can get me out of this one, Coroner Bastien, I'll conjure you a gift of your choosing from whatever's in my power to give."

"Seems to me a drawing or a bit of history delving might give answer."

"A drawing . . ." My bents could take me straight to Safia. "Gods, Bastien. I told you I wasn't thinking straight. She's *there*. The sentinel. I just didn't *see* her. Surely she can tell me how to get them out. Maybe even help."

"Add your thanks to the debt you owe me already. I paid good coin for four years of your service, but reaped only forty-six days."

Heaven's gates . . . assuming there was still an Order I wanted to be a part of at the end of all this, what would the Order make of an unfilled contract for my service? Did he mean it?

My sharp glance upward set Bastien laughing. "You're worrying about the rules, aren't you? Sky Lord's balls, no matter the formidable aspect, you *are* still Lucian de Remeni!"

Cheeks as hot as the spindle's magic, I laughed with him. "For now, I'm Paratus Greenshank who needs to get back to the fortress before anyone knows I'm missing. But you've come all this way to bring me this little mystery, and I'll be damned if I leave without seeing what it means."

I ripped away the spindle's annoying binding spell, several protective enchantments, and an outer covering of canvas, and spread a strip of fragile linen across my knees. Most of it, for it was a long piece that would be draped around someone's neck at a Temple rite, a funeral or wedding or other solemn event. A *stola*.

"Great gods of the universe . . ." *A bit of Xancheiran needlework*, so I'd told Bastien in that other life. Indeed it was, names and symbols formed by neat stitches—the crafted genealogy of two people on their wedding day. A simple witnessing that upended history and certainty in the single moment of comprehension, exposing the root of rivalry and slaughter, a truth that had spawned Xancheira's horror and the Registry's centuries of determination to bury its secrets.

A halfblood's children have no magic. That single incontrovertible truth was the foundation of the Registry's strict breeding rules. A pureblood who begat children with a mate not pureblood broke his or her bloodline, squandering the divine gift, because their every descendant would possess degenerate magic at best. Except it seemed that our incontrovertible truth was a lie.

The spindle had, indeed, changed the course of my life. The genealogy witnessed that I, or any other mature male or female of dual bent, could mate with a halfblood or even an ordinary and beget a child with pureblood talents—a feat which every pureblood believed as impossible as our backs sprouting wings. A pureblood woman could marry the man of her choice and her bent could reappear untarnished in her children or her grandchildren as long as one person in that lineage bore a matured dual bent. Every example was stitched onto that ancient genealogy. The magic we believed confined to descendants of the Three Hundred families—the uniqueness that had kept us wealthy and privileged, powerful and protected, and arrogant beyond telling—could be spread to any bloodline in this world. Even to ordinaries.

The *stola* testified that Xancheirans had allowed dual bents for at least six generations. And their magic had thrived and flourished, grown to power that could reshape the earth itself.

It was magic grown from dual bents that created my paintings that showed things I couldn't know, that allowed me to open the Xancheirans' portals and cross the crack they'd made in the world. Even Fix, with the all the power of Evanide's Knight Defender, could not do those things.

I, grown to maturity with dual bents, was an example of what the Registry had stolen from the world. And they could not allow anyone to know. How right Signé was that neither I nor any pureblood had been taught the truth of Xancheira's fall. Because the Registry had chosen to settle for a weaker gift so they could keep magic all to themselves.

"So am I destined to remain in ignorance?" said Bastien, his eagerness well cooled.

I'd done right by Bastien to keep this from him. Had the Registry a hint that he knew, he would have died in an eyeblink. Now danger stalked him anyway, because of me. And Siever—Goddess save him—a man who could confirm this conclusion in an eyeblink, was in peril with every breath.

Carefully I passed Bastien the *stola*, bathing it with magelight that he might read its tale. "On the day this secret comes to light, the world will change forever," I said.

He puzzled over it. Traced the marks of names and talents and lineage with a thick finger.

My portraits had borne witness that the Registry curators had passed the secret from one to the next, and were willing to protect that secret with blood. Cicerons, who claimed a magical gift, had to die. Historians who probed Xancheiran history had to die, along with anyone they might have told. And those like Pluvius and me, born with two bents, were mutilated in the name of the lie. Only in my case, it seemed, my grandsire had waited too late to rip my second bent away.

The stars wheeled and a delicate shift in the marshland told me the tide was on the ebb. I was on the verge of telling Bastien the answer when his head popped up, his ruddy cheeks gone ashen.

"Demons of night, Lucian! Of a sudden, I feel as if I've a signboard on my back that says *Kill me*. How is it you're yet living?"

"That's a very good question," I said, rolling the strip of linen carefully about the spindle. "One reason could be that you kept this buried and told no one I've come back from the dead. Damon has no idea that I'm aware of my dual bents, much less these implications. He's been very careful not to mention it and to ensure I can't discover it. As far as he knows, I've no personal connection with anyone in the world outside Evanide. Your old friend Pluvius turned up here babbling of my dual bents and how Curator Pons sent him to save me from Damon's clutches. Pluvius now lies in a dungeon with the mind of an infant."

"*Pons* sent Pluvius here!" said Bastien, as if he'd not had shocks enough. "Do you realize who she is? The plaguey Registry inquisitor that you believed responsible for everything that went wrong. And then damned if you didn't turn around and send your sister to her, when you got out of prison, so young Juli couldn't be named renegade. Pons seemed honorable in her stubborn way, and she was the only person you could think of to protect the girl. That was the hardest thing I ever saw a man do."

My turn to puzzle. "But on that last day, I sent her to Sanctuary with the Cicerons. . . ."

A thousand things could have happened in between those two events to set my sister free of the Registry: rescue, a bargain, an exchange of some kind. But if Pluvius had spoken true, this Curator Pons had already split with Damon. A relief to know that Damon likely didn't realize the girl lived. A young woman now . . .

"Juli. That's what I called her?"

"Are you sure you want me to tell you?"

However foolish, I needed to know this as much as anything in the world. "It's worth a headache."

"Aye, you did. And she called you—"

"Luka."

"That's right."

I ran my fingers through my damp hair. "There's a host of things I need to know. Pluvius made no mention of the spindle, but wanted me to help him find a buried chest that holds my grandsire's Xancheiran artifacts. He claimed Pons knew about the chest, but Damon didn't."

Bastien grunted. "I'd say that was likely. When Damon came to Caton, trying to chase you off to his 'house of healing,' he said naught of Xancheira or artifacts or historical investigations. He wouldn't have worried about asking, as he knew his people were going to scrape it all from your mind anyway, right? And since the chest wasn't buried, but still sat where your grandsire hid it five years previous, I'd say *no one* knew—"

"Wait"—I wasn't sure I'd heard him right—"you know where the chest is?"

"Aye." Bastien grinned. "Shall I tell you that?"

"No! Not that. Not now." I lived with people expert in memory manipulation. "Is it somewhere we can get to it?"

"Not easy. Not me alone, for certain. Likely we could do it together as we did before, if you've acquired better skills to go with all the rest of"—he waved his hand at me—"this."

"Oh, I've skills. But it's likely best I not know the chest's location until I learn what Damon plans to do about the secret. For whatever it's worth to you, Damon showed me I was right about those portraits of the curators; they even revealed who ordered my family's murder. Damon wanted the seeing . . . the *knowing* . . . to make me angry, and I let him do it and swore my allegiance to his cause. He says he wants to purge the Registry of corruption, but I'm sure there's more. Now more than ever."

So what was Damon's vision of Registry purity? Was it only eliminating his *corrupt* rivals, while keeping this secret buried and our privileges intact? Or would he risk overturning the world to cleanse our most fundamental sin—a cynical corruption of the divine gift that had led to centuries of murder? I needed to understand him better.

I restored the canvas sleeve and protective spells and entrusted the spindle to Bastien.

Spits of rain made the blustering wind sharp. "We've much to talk about," I said, "but weather's shaping, and I need to sleep. You, too. Tomorrow will be a rough night."

Bastien walked with me to the boat. The ebb was already stretching the slack out of the line.

"Will you need me to row? I did a stint on a coast runner one time down near Cymra."

"Might, if one of the tyros gets knackered. But mostly I'll need you to stay between Morgan and the Cicerons. These people will have heard terrible stories of Danae, and we can't have them spreading word of Evanide or

Danae or Xancheira or any link between them, just in case they're picked up before they find a haven. Morgan won't think that strange."

"Makes sense."

"And I'm going to tell them"—Goddess Mother, it felt vile to speak it aloud—"they mustn't mention anything about the Xancheirans or the prisoners in the trees in Morgan's hearing. I think they'll be cautious."

With a slow exhale, he nodded, then offered his hand.

"'Tis fine to partner with you again, pureblood," he said. "As I'm short of work right now—not that the Crown has paid any of its servants for a year or more—this is a sight better than soldiering for any of the princes. A man of the law enjoys an interesting case once in a while. And you do bring me the damnedest."

Which reminded me of something else. "You know the matter of the girl child you mentioned? Damon's military aide is a man named Fallon—"

"Fallon de Tremayne works for the *Registry*?"

"For Damon. Claims he supports some of Damon's work, maybe cleansing the Registry or maybe just Damon's other purpose"—he needed to know all, even if it was but supposition—"which I'm guessing is ensuring our new king is beholden to him."

"Great gods, Remeni! Are you involved in aught that won't get my neck stretched the length of my legs? You really mean that . . . treason . . . and murder . . . or a war such as this world has only begun to see, because there's no way that crown's hanging out there ready for a scrawny little sorcerer to snatch without drawing in every sorcerer in the Registry . . . or an order of magical warriors . . . and perhaps a young general, once Perryn's man, experienced in ordinary warfare . . . Ah, shite, shite, shite!"

"I'm not certain of it yet. But I've seen evidence."

We'd no time to analyze the ways Damon could install a challenger on Eodward's throne with use of the Order's magic or control one of the princes after their war was settled. The weather was closing in. But I needed to know one more thing.

"Fallon says he owes us a debt that will trump any other cause. Should I believe him? I don't know that we could convince him to betray Damon, but to have him willing to listen . . ."

"Aye. Believe him. The last thing in the world he'd want is Perryn on Eodward's throne." For a moment, a grin flashed through Bastien's dismay. "Told you we did good work together."

"It would seem so." I grinned back at him. "And I'm hoping we can do more after we get these people away. So put your mind to this. Who would a power-mad lunatic think to put on Eodward's throne instead of one of the three devil princes? It's likely to be someone Fallon believes in. Someone Fallon might convince Navron nobles to support. Would people listen to him? That seems the only way it would work."

"Aye, Fallon was well respected until his father's disgrace. A battle-tested field general. Nobs would give him a listen." He wagged his shaggy head. "Sky Lord's everlasting mercies."

Indeed. We'd need the cooperation of all gods to find a way out of this.

"Tomorrow," I said.

The rain drove harder. Bastien waded into the rushing water beside me, and together we gave the squinch a shove.

As I hopped in and grabbed the oars, he called after. "Enjoy your little row. I'll have a lovely night in my dry cave, eating the lady's smoked fish and figuring out where I'm going to hide while your friends, kin, and commanders tear this kingdom to shreds."

CHAPTER 30

My *little row* was not dry. Howling wind and sheeting rain churned the bay to frenzy, hiding or displacing beacons and driving me back toward the mainland. Sea and sky were a dizzying maelstrom of black water. When the flat-bottomed squinch tipped, it was the gods' own luck that the waves tumbled me onto a gravel shore. I'd scarce lifted my chin, desperate to crawl farther inland before the demon sea snatched me back, when the storm deposited old Dorye right atop my head.

Scalp bleeding into my eyes, I battled the sucking black water and wrestled the unwieldy squinch onto shore. Miraculously, one oar remained jammed in the grip of its lock, and blessed Fix's spare was yet lashed tight along the bottom boards. Less fortunate, the boat's water cask was lost. No magic could make salt water drinkable.

I sheltered beneath the upturned squinch, giving thanks for the divine gift as I set a pile of drift aflame with magic and huddled drenched and shivering in its tiny circle of warmth. Please gods we'd not see a repeat of such weather on the coming night. To take Conall's tyros out in such a storm would be murder.

Wind and cold made the night hellish. Sleep would have had a hard time coming anyway, what with carrying a secret that upended all that purebloods like me had ever believed. What in the name of all gods was I to do with the responsibility of such knowledge? Cleansing the Registry of corruption was one thing. Shattering the hard-won, complex balance of Crown, Temple, and magical discipline was entirely another.

Yet, the Xancheirans had accommodated the truth and thrived until the day the purebloods of the south had come to destroy them. Where was justice in all this? Certainly not in secret executions or purges or ripping away half a person's gift to serve a lie. Certainly not in a sorcerers' war where consequences could be unimaginable. Xancheira was proof of that.

. . .

The absence of drumming rain woke me from fitful sleep. Excited waves yet sloshed. The ashes of my little fire popped and smoked, the magic spent. All else was quiet. Wretchedly thirsty, the cut on my head bleeding, and the stitches on my back sore and fevered, I crept out to find the sky filled with fading stars. And I was still on the mainland. Time to row . . .

Three hours later, I staggered out of Evanide's boathouse, gulping stale water from a flask I'd grabbed from another boat. The boatmaster hurried down the quay to meet me. "No need to ask where you've been. Is Old—?"

"Old Dorye's fine," I rasped, draining the musty flask. "One oar lost. Water cask lost. A leak in the sternsheets. There's likely a dent in the keel where the devil boat attacked me." I blotted the stinging crack in my right temple that had started bleeding again. "I've things to tell you, Fix."

"There's others got first claim on you. Place is in an uproar. Marshal's been asking for you since dawn. Not even the *Knight Defender* could tell him where you'd gone. Most suppose you fell off the seaward wall, except they found your armor rusting in your cell."

No permission to leave the fortress. Absent overnight. I hadn't given that little problem any thought at all.

As we hurried toward the stair, I croaked quietly, "What of the hungry lord?"

Fix handed me a clean, filled water flask from somewhere about his person. "Still hidden," he mumbled. "Still alive. Eats like a tyro. He's a fiend for maps. The man's got tales . . . and ambitions. He's trying to convince me to set up some kind of expedition into the north. Some range of hills near *Montesard*. Says there might be a way to undo the Severing."

"What?" Stunned, I halted at the quayside steps. Siever had mentioned something about his lord and lady perhaps walking free. It had been right after he showed me his revived magic. "Hills near Montesard? That's where my grandsire—"

Deep inside, where the puzzle of Xancheira and the Danae churned like a milkmaid's cream, pieces began to clump together:

The northern city of Montesard, where Lucian de Remeni had lived with his testy grandsire, studied history, and met a Dané in disguise.

Siever's mention of a *cache* that Signé had called myth.

Cicerons who had promised to *bring back the magic* to undo the Severing—perhaps not referring to magic in their fingers.

My grandsire, the historian, who had brought back a chest of Xancheiran treasures *from the north*.

And now Siever wanted to go north to find an answer to the Severing.

"Move, fool!" Fix yanked the empty water flasks from my grasp. "This isn't the time. Get yourself to the Marshal with a plausible tale unless you yearn to spend a month in irons."

An avalanche was about to fall on my head from the Order, but it couldn't damp my excitement. "I don't think your guest will have to travel so far as Montesard," I said, backing up the stair. "As for tonight, we're planning an *escape drill*. Conall's loaning his tyros to row. Signs of another storm like last night's, though, and we'll have to wait one more day."

Fix jerked his head. I turned and ran.

"You've had the entire fortress in chaos, Greenshank. Training halted. Your brothers endangered, searching for you to seaward."

The Marshal circled his inner chamber for the third time as I knelt with my fist on my breast and eyes lowered, watching the nasty puddle I was leaving on his floor swell. Bleeding, filthy, and sodden, I'd seen no point in any attempt to portray myself other than I was. I just wanted to get this over with so I could speak with Siever and figure out how to retrieve my grandsire's Xancheiran chest. But the uproar over my absence was worse than I'd imagined and Order discipline could be brutal.

"I've reaped full sanction from the gods for prideful idiocy, Knight Marshal, and come near losing my paltry skills for the Order. No punishment you name will outweigh my fault."

"Be sure you'll spend an unhappy hour with the Disciplinarian. And in public, not private. Your brothers, those ranked above you and more especially those ranked below, will expect it when they hear that the morning's disruption was for naught but pride."

The Marshal's fingers had been twining his silver pendant, an unaccustomed disquiet. Yet the tenor of his words flowed as mild as ever, and worse, it was not anger, but disappointment shaped them. Shame choked me like a poison fog, even as reason named it ridiculous. I'd choose no differently even now. A good man's life had been in danger. And more lives awaited saving this night.

So I tried to reflect that shame onto the Marshal, who had fallen so short of my estimation, but I could not summon the accusations to support it. A lie, here. A concealment, there. The bulk of my suspicions were founded in his cooperation with the despicable Damon—the yielding of his authority to an outsider lacking moral boundaries. But even Inek's accusation by way of his bracelet remained shrouded in doubt.

The Marshal's bare feet halted an arm's length in front of me.

"This story rings false, Greenshank. I prize initiative in a senior paratus, but purposely challenging such a storm to prepare for an *exercise* is a sign of poor judgment wholly unlike you."

I'd never known him so agitated.

"Stand up." The order crackled like flame.

The Marshal and I were so similar in height and build, my lowered gaze rested on the white drape of his robe across his chest. His restlessness had left his silver pendant nestled in the fold, for that instant its back side fully exposed. Embedded in the silver was a coin-like gold disk with a woman's face. Recognition flashed with the brilliance of *cereus iniga*—

"Face me and speak truth, paratus!" His wrath demanded my attention. "Tell me why a man of strength, intelligence, and promise, one who has been singled out to help shape a better world, risks his life for *nothing*."

Stripes from the Disciplinarian, even in a public venue that would triple the humiliation, would be easy compared to standing before this man's righteous indignation and inventing more lies.

"Speak, Greenshank! Explain yourself."

Risky, the idea that came to me—warping my story so as to pry at the slight gap I'd noted between Damon and the Marshal. Were they partners or were they not?

"You're correct, Knight Marshal. It was no exercise. I didn't plan it. I simply . . . ran. I've given Curator Damon my oath of submission. How could I do elsewise after all that he—and you—have revealed to me? Centuries of corruption contaminating the divine gift. These unworthy princes ravaging the kingdom they want to rule. We must see these things remedied, yet your own warning gnaws at my commitment. How can one so compromised as the curator be the person to lead such an effort?"

"Curator Damon is a visionary," he said, anger reined in, the response unmarred by his body's disturbance. "Visionaries are rarely perfect. They're so intently focused on their cause, they oft disregard honor and common decency. We who cheer the vision must be mindful."

"But since that morning in the Seeing Chamber with Damon, my own decency and honor fail," I said. "Such rage consumes me, Knight Marshal. In our exercises at Val Cleve, we were ordered to halt at the death stroke. . . ."

Memory of those fourteen days came flooding back in sensations more vivid than in their immediate aftermath. Endless violence, blood, pain, exhaustion, and a continuous raging heat in my blood—fed by certainty that it was Damon's war we rehearsed.

". . . but my discipline broke. Several times, others had to stop me from dealing a killing blow."

My hands, clasped at my back, clenched and released and clenched again. I'd revealed more than I intended . . . more than I had even realized, for what I said of Val Cleve was true. Twice, Dunlin and Heron had struck my bow just as I released an arrow at another man. They knew how rarely I missed. A squire had prevented me finishing his partner. And only at this distance did I recognize the appalling nature of the incidents. No simple fatigue or battle confusion had brought me close to murder. It was this septic anger.

"You should have come to me with this, Greenshank. You were not the only one who discovered unpleasant things about himself at Val Cleve. That's the purpose of such violent exercises, to expose weakness that it may be remedied before the consequences are even worse. A man who goes into battle with magic is the most dangerous weapon the world can know."

"I know that. . . ." How broken was I not to have recognized such aberrance earlier? And how childish, that this Marshal's understanding helped ease guilt and horror.

I struggled to recapture purpose, which was neither atonement nor gaining sympathy, but understanding this man's place in conspiracy. Those of *us*, the Marshal had said of participants in Damon's plan. Yet he was not of a single mind with the devil, either. I needed more.

"A man who must run to his superior for reassurance that his sworn faith is not misplaced is no man at all. Once back from Val Cleve, I hoped to speak with Damon, to ask why, after so casual a restoration of my past, he'll not allow me to use what I know. If I could just pursue my bent *now* in the service of the Order. To seek justice for my family—"

"Damon restored your *past*? But that's imposs— Of course, you speak of the relict-seeing, the portraits you did in captivity." His shock, so quickly aborted, near cracked the great windows. And his swallowed denial suggested that he knew why *restoration* was impossible. "So it was Damon unmuted your bent. He should have told me."

So the Marshal, too, knew my bent was returned. It was surely the Archivist had told him. Damon certainly he hadn't known on the morning of the relict-seeing. Raising yet another question. *Bent*, the Marshal had said, not *bents*; did he even know I had two? Did he understand that my magic could restore a broken bloodline or bring witnesses to Registry villainy across the boundaries of nature?

"Yes, the seeing," I said. "To view myself through Damon's eyes, to witness my degradation at his hand and that of his colleagues . . . I watched myself alter the *truth* of my bent's creation, Knight Marshal, a perversion that corrupts the soul. I learned it was my own family savagely murdered with the knowledge of these same curators. Yet, monstrous as my rage is, I cannot help believing it is short of what I *ought* to feel, because I experienced these things through Damon's memory and not my own. Of all things, I desire to uphold the oaths I've sworn to the Order and to Damon's reform of pureblood corruption. But now I hear rumor of a stranger violating Evanide's boundaries, asking about me. If Damon knows where I am, the other curators must also. Doubts and fear gnaw my spirit and I've done *nothing* and I cannot mourn, cannot grieve, cannot hope. Last night, all I could think was that I needed to find my home, find my lost soul . . ."

I near squeezed my trembling hands to pulp. Somehow the playacting had taken on the sensation of truth.

". . . but it took a storm that shook the boundaries of the world to remind me that I have no home but Evanide."

The Marshal's curled fingers, gloved in their white silk, nudged my chin upward, so that we stood eye to eye. "I cannot give you what you desire, Greenshank . . . *Lucian* . . . as you well know."

His presence conveyed such stern and honest sympathy that in that moment I would have denied anyone who named him unworthy of his office. How could logic and certainty be so disjoint?

The Marshal blew a note of disgust and pivoted sharply to face the window.

"I have seen the dust of your past, as you have," he spat. "The evil that was done you is reprehensible, and the consequence for Commander Inek beyond vile. The Archivist sees Inek's healing as his life's redemption. I believe he'll manage it, and I've told him that *no one*, not Damon, not the Knight Defender, not the infirmarian, not a breathing soul save you or me is to know when that is accomplished. As for the stranger . . . A pureblood sorcerer indeed came here intending to take you captive. The Knight Defender ensured he was never truly a threat to your safety. Thanks to Damon's brutish questioning, he's no mind left to probe.

"But now what am I to do with *you*? Yesterday, I would have sent you straight to the Disciplinarian for a lashing and confined you in silence for thirty days while I considered further punishment. Your lack of control at Val Cleve could have merited anything from a reduction in rank to outright dismissal. This morning, however, everything is changed. . . ."

His eyes squeezed shut and the fist that gripped the silver pendant spasmed so violently, I thought he might crush it. To imagine what could so shake a man of the Marshal's demeanor did naught to soothe my own rioting blood.

"Last night I learned a few secrets regarding my own past—agreements made, secrets kept, mysteries deepened, including those shadowing you, thus I must stand in judgment while suffering a state very like your own. Ripped apart. Not knowing what to feel or whether feeling is even possible when I have but fragments."

To stay still poised on the verge of illumination required every scrap of control I could muster.

A blast of wind shook the broad windows. The day had clouded over and a draft raced through the chamber. Already, winter laid down its battle lines. Or perhaps it was only ghost memories and phantom answers caused the hairs on neck and arms to rise.

As if the wind had dispersed his uncertainty, the Marshal moved briskly to his great hearth, cold and dead this morning. Beckoning me to join him, he pressed his fingers to the wall beside the hearth. A panel swung open to reveal a modest sleeping cell.

The pallet, clothes chest, and washing table were little different from my own. But the Marshal's cell also contained a small brazier, a round window that overlooked the sea, and a neatly ordered worktable. At the foot of his pallet, he'd set an oil jar, a few rags, and an open armor chest containing the exact white and silver armor and regalia detailed in the centuries-old mosaic in his outer chamber—the equipage of the Knight Marshal of Evanide, should he ever ride out to war.

My back and arms were gooseflesh.

"Sit." The Marshal pointed to a rug on the floor beside the stone hearth. His touch to the brazier set the coals alight. As the fire pushed away the damp, he fetched a box from his table and joined me on the rug, placing a fist-sized, red lacquer casket between us.

"Until last night, the Order was the entirety of my existence," he said. "I cared naught for the man I had been. This was all I wanted—to live and die in these robes and mask, knowing that the world was more just than on the day I put them on. Knowing that the men who lived and the men who died by my word had found their proper destinies. But today . . ."

He extended his white-gloved hand between us as if it were newly attached to his arm.

"This hand destroyed my own memory relict on the day of my investiture as a knight," he said, flexing his silk fingers. "And I destroyed a second one on the day I first donned this cocoon of anonymity—erasing every personal memory of my training and my years as a knight. That act brought sensations so immensely strange, I think it must be very close to birth or death—to retain such immense and detailed knowledge of the world, the Order, history, the kingdom and its cities, yet be unable to say what gods I favored or if my own skin was dark or pale. Pale, as you see."

His bare toes poked out from his enveloping white, and a wry grin shone through his mask. For a moment, he might have been Dunlin, sharing an unseemly jest outside our commanders' hearing.

"As it happens, my hammer did not destroy all knowledge of what those relicts held. Though discovering that someone has retained a few of your memories might seem exactly what you desire, I can tell you that experiencing them is immensely unsettling. Have you learned how to deliver memory pricks, as yet?"

"Not yet." Another thing I relished learning. Speak a fact retrieved from a subject's missing memories, while delivering a jolt of tightly wrought enchantment—a memory prick—and the subject can recognize the memory as an inerrant part of himself. Truth. It was how the Marshal had told me I was eight-and-twenty, had once been wealthy but had fallen on hard times, and had been contracted to a necropolis. Memory pricks could be lasting, as those were, but they could also be crafted as ephemera, the knowledge vanishing at the moment the sorcerer unbound the spell.

"On the day I was invested as Knight Marshal," he continued, "not long after I destroyed that second relict, several old secrets were revealed to me by way of impermanent memory pricks. Such is not at all the usual practice. I was advised to write down my responses to those revelations before the memories vanished—not the information itself, as the memories themselves could snarl my official objectivity, but whatever I might need to carry forward to guide my decisions. I've carried those responses on my person every day of my tenure, almost two years now. Would you care to see what I wrote?"

"Very much so." More than anything, I wanted to understand this man. As ever, he had me dangerously inclined to believe in him.

He passed me a scrap of parchment pulled from his robe. It was worn to the pliability of cloth, and the ink was sorely faded, but quite readable.

Lares de Attis-Damon's vision of the future matches your own in almost every respect.

Do not deviate from his advice and guidance regarding the missions of the Order.

Beware of him at every step.

I handed back the scrap. Nothing startling. It was exactly what the Marshal had advised me on the day I submitted to Damon.

"You've no idea what prompted these responses?" That was the interesting part.

"Until last night I could answer *yes.*" He inhaled a great breath and expelled it slowly. "But now . . . It seems that you and I are both pawns in Damon's vision of the future."

As if his gaunt figure remained in the room with us, I knew the Archivist, the Order's keeper of memories and secrets, had paid the Marshal a visit last night. And I knew at least one of the things he'd revealed. "*You* were Damon's other paratus."

The Archivist had been furious that Damon had been named my guide. He'd come straight to the Marshal.

"Exactly so." Again the fleeting grin and a spiky satisfaction. "I'd long suspected I had some special relationship with Damon because of these, but I had no idea . . ." He waved his flimsy page, then peered at it as if it might tell him something new. "The matters revealed to me confirmed these conclusions in every respect. Understand, Lucian, I've only fragments, some of which are intensely personal. But it is clear that our fates, yours and mine, are bound one to the other for good or ill. Thus I'll share what I can that might illumine your own path. If you're willing, of course. Judgments based on fragments of information bear dangers. . . ."

"Yes. Please." The hungering rasp was scarce recognizable as my own voice.

"Understand first, I was given no explicit knowledge of the role Damon intends for you. The Archivist assumes one thing; I don't agree with him. But certainly this rage you feel—this divisive uncertainty and disconnection from the discipline and fraternity of the Order—is Damon's intent. But that's unhealthy for a man who has committed himself to the Order as you have; thus I've tried to enlarge that singular view. He demands that your training in weaponry and tactics take second place to your development in other kinds of magic and skills more appropriate to a commander than a warrior, as if you had some predilection to violence that made combat training risky. That's why one of the first memory fragments returned to you was that you were *not* guilty of a murder that had been ascribed to you. That struck true, did it not?"

"Yes." The fired memory yet remained as vivid as a single silver coin among a thousand brass ones, as it had on that morning when I ran the mudflats, retrieved a delivery of *cereus iniga*, and encountered Morgan again for the first time.

"In the same way, I made sure that when Damon showed you the relict of the Harrower assault, you also saw the Registry connection, and that you knew the Order was founded as *reparation* for such crimes, not as a conspirator."

"The two purebloods who laughed at the massacre," I said, stunned. "*You* showed them to me, not Damon. Do you know who they were?"

"No." There was no wavering in his answer, nor in the sincere sympathy that followed. "Until that very morning, I'd no idea the victims were your own family. Lucian de Remeni's exposure of Registry corruption in front of several hundred members of the Registry and Prince Perryn's entourage was legendary even here. The world believed Remeni captive or dead. Only Damon—and likely the Marshal of those days, my predecessor—knew better. Somehow Inek guessed, though. He referred to the possibility in one of his petitions to review your relict. To my lasting regret, I had no choice but to refuse him. My predecessor had declared that your relict would be unreviewable. At that time I didn't know it was nonexistent."

Belief and shifting understanding rearranged the world—Damon was not the sole manipulator in this business—even as reflex delivered the relevant question. "So did the old Marshal destroy the relict or did Damon?"

"Neither. I did it."

"You!" The world shifted yet again. "And the trap spell?"

"That, too." He opened his hands wide. "I ask no forgiveness or forbearance. The deeds were accomplished before I assumed this mantle, and I am not privy to the circumstances behind them. My predecessor must have approved both. Though I can scarce comprehend that I would consent to such deeds, the certainties that compelled me to write these instructions must have fed my choice. It can be no consolation to you, Lucian, but this tears at my own soul. I question my own decency. Justice required me to tell you."

His confession, abhorrent though it was, demanded belief. What purpose could be served by telling me? And if it was true, then what answer could I make? I had been no violent felon. Bastien's and Morgan's and my own sister's witness affirmed it. So why would the former Marshal agree to such a thing, unless he was Damon's partner in conspiracy? And yet . . .

"Was your predecessor the same who sent Damon away from the Order?"

"Yes. You see the conundrum. He must have believed in Damon's vision, too, though he viewed the man himself as seriously flawed. Unfortunately, his writings reveal nothing of his decisions with respect to you. Yet he didn't abandon you entirely to Damon's ministrations. He appointed Inek as your guide. Damon has always hated that."

Bitterness threaded my veins like poison. Had Damon somehow driven Inek into the trap spell? Considering all I'd revealed to my guide, it would not have been difficult.

"These other things you now know," I said, "this vision of Damon's . . . is it worth allowing a despicable man to continue to work his will?" Protocol, manners, and discretion had crumbled. "Is it righteous to achieve great ends no matter the cost? War? Murder? Purges?"

The Marshal's enveloping garb forbade any specific assessment of his demeanor, but as ever, the intensity of posture and voice communicated his conviction. "These Registry curators' cruel and perverse usage of a gifted colleague—you—*must* reap punishment. Such casual corruption, such hubris, cannot, must not, will not stand. And I do *not* exempt Damon from guilt. He gloated about your submission and claimed that your assurance of a future reckoning for his sins was but additional evidence of your suitability for his purpose. He knows and accepts and . . . relishes . . . that I agree with you. And yet . . ."

"Why do you tolerate him?" I growled. "You are the commander of the most powerful military force the world has ever known. Kill him. Pursue the right without the taint of his corruption."

"Listen to yourself, Lucian," he said softly.

The echo of my words sickened me. I had just demanded he use the Order to serve vengeance with murder.

"Justice and right are not simple in this case," he said. "Nor are strategy or logistics. Damon has been working on his plan for more than twenty years and has immense resources and complex strategies already in place. I've not been told how he plans to accomplish his goals. The Archivist maintains his own secrets, but he lives far removed from the realities of the world and knows nothing of how this will proceed, either."

"What of the Knight Defender?" I blurted.

"The Knight Defender is wise, and I cannot even comprehend half the magic he knows. But his single task is the defense of Evanide. He would be no more help in this matter than a villein from the river country called to design a fortress in the mountains of Evanore. It is you and I hold the opportunity for a better world in our hands, Lucian de Remeni, and we must decide how to move forward and when to unleash our righteous anger."

I could not argue the point without betraying Fix's trust and exposing too many other secrets. I certainly wasn't ready to trust the Marshal with everything I knew.

He pulled his box close. The lacquer gleamed like fresh blood in the firelight. The interior was divided into three compartments. One held a thumb-sized silk bag, tied with a thread. One held four smooth, round tokens of various sizes, like those that carried the spell that obliterated a memory. The third compartment held a litter of silver splinters, each the size of a nail paring. He pulled out two splinters.

"I know your trust in me wavers," he said. "Rightly so. Stay wary of everyone in Damon's sphere. But my faith in *you* does not waver—even after last night."

The Marshal held the two splinters up to catch the light. "I'm asking you to stay close to me, Lucian. There's still a great deal I don't know about myself, about your place in all this, about our future that is so entwined and how it is to be accomplished. But no matter your experience at Val Cleve, you are a man of honor and decency, and I trust you to keep watch both *on* me and *for* me. If you're willing to do so, I'll do the same for you."

He touched the two shards of silver together and a spark jumped between, confirming the link between them. As long as the two splinters were within a few quellae of each other—in the same house or the same town—a sorcerer could transfer power between them. It was a property unique to silver, as valuable as its property to hide evidence of enchantments. It enabled a sorcerer to work magic at a distance, as the Order did with the memory-wipe tokens.

"If you consent to carry one of these, an infusion of magic will leap between these splinters, not to destroy a memory, but to set a meeting place and time where we can exchange information."

I held out my hand. "I'd like to examine them."

He dropped the shining bits into my open palm. "I'd think less of you if you didn't."

"What if I don't consent?"

"We shall proceed as if this meeting never happened. If you wish to leave the Order, you may go with my blessing and my sincere regret, but you'll retain no memory of your time at Evanide, including what has transpired here today. If you choose to continue on your own path here, I'll not interfere with your actions, save as my duty to the Order and my convictions lead me, though I will continue to do everything I can to gain your trust. In any case, if you try to harm Damon or me or the Archivist, or interfere with our work, I *will* stop you."

"I appreciate your frankness," I said.

He rose and moved away, leaving me to my examination.

I picked apart every word and revelation, seeking flaws, inconsistencies, or contrivances. Though his refusal to be more specific about Damon's plan and the *personal matters* that had him so agitated could hide any manner of wickedness, I had no evidence to suggest what that wickedness might be. On the other hand, his feelings about the Order seemed genuine and heartfelt. I was not ready to exonerate him, but I was inclined to believe his story.

As to the examination, a splinter held but one spell, and the wooden tokens were magically sterile, so I quickly ensured he had not added any nefarious enchantments, subtle or otherwise to the simple declaration spell. It was precisely the same spell Inek had installed on my silver bracelets.

At my unspoken agreement, he returned to his place and charged one of the splinters with a spurt of magic. The one I'd kept spoke to me of the *seaward wall at eleventh hour*. The words vanished once released. No one else could perceive them. I charged the splinter in my hand, entwining the magic with a phrase of my own.

"The *boathouse at dawn*?" he said. "Old Fix would drop his aging teeth to see me walk in."

"Unless you stroll about the fortress from time to time, shed of your Marshal's garb."

No idea of jest had prompted me. But the Marshal shook his head and laughed softly. "Ah, Greenshank, that is ever a temptation. I shall take no position on whether I succumb to it."

It was that laughter . . . so entirely human, filled with regret and sparked with wit and good humor . . . that convinced me trust was worth risking.

Feeding magic to a tiny crescent on my left bracelet allowed my finger to embed the silver splinter easily into the smooth, hard wood of the token. Though I perceived no burst of magic, I assumed he'd done the same.

"We'll talk again soon," he said as his token vanished into his robe. "Damon has bound our fates together, so together we shall judge his actions. Together we shall determine whether his vision will create a new and better world or a new corruption. And together, we shall take what action is necessary to ensure the one and prevent the other."

"Take action . . . ?"

"Whatever is necessary to fulfill our oaths to the *Equites Cineré*—to ensure that justice triumphs. Those called upon to realize visions must take on the charge to ensure their humanity."

He led me back to his great chamber. As if a different man inhabited the white robes, he gestured me sharply to the floor. I knelt.

"Paratus Greenshank, your public discipline of forty lashes with the Order whip and a silent apology to your brothers will take place at first hour of this afternoon's watch in the usual place. Afterward, you will be confined to your sleeping cell. You will remain silent and solitary until dawn."

"As you say, Knight Marshal." My skin crawled. My only other adventure at the whipping post had been four lashes, easily dealt with. But forty—

"Your new orders arrived in a dispatch from Curator Damon this morning. You are forbidden to speak of them to anyone."

"Again, as you say." Every nerve stung, sharpened and ready.

"You are to join Curator Damon at Castle Cavillor twelve days hence, afoot, wearing no mark of the Order, and armed with only your bow. No dagger, no sword, no blade of any kind. You are to inform no one when you leave Evanide. Nor will you reveal to any person your destination, your route, your location at any time along that route, or anything we have discussed here this morning."

Cavillor. A town grown up around a castle of the same name, now the seat of the pureblood family Canis-Ferenc, and the site of the Sitting of the Three Hundred, scheduled for a month hence on the first day of autumn.

"As you command, Knight Marshal," I said with what breath remained in me after such orders. Did I hold to my word, everyone in the Order save the Marshal would believe me a deserter.

CHAPTER 31

As I left the Marshal's quarters, I gripped the token in my pocket, trying to reconcile the Marshal who had revealed himself behind his chamber door with the man I'd just left. He had created a trap designed to destroy a mind and crushed my past to dust, believing he had reason enough to commit crimes that should see him dead. He had just dispatched me into Damon's clutches as near naked as a paratus could be. Yet his call for justice thrilled in my blood. Terrible events demanded terrible risks.

What lay under that white robe? Rogue, villain, deceiver, or the man I wanted him to be? Were his limbs banded with silver like Fix's, the metal threaded into his flesh so that their spells and knowledge had become a part of his body? Or did that single silver pendant hold his favored spellwork? As I left his quarters he yet clutched it as if it held all the secrets he could not yet remember. Odd, that pendant and the gold coin embedded in its back. What had struck me about it?

I halted abruptly at the edge of the Marshal's courtyard. Doorward Horatio paused in his patrol. Inclining my head, I resumed my journey through the colonnade that led toward the infirmary. Once out of sight I closed my eyes and braced against the wall, dusting off bits of history and legend buried in corners of my mind little used since coming here. I laid those bits alongside what I had just seen and heard, and therein lay a possibility that near halted my breath.

The gold disk embedded in the Marshal's silver pendant had felt familiar because it was no common coin, but a historical rarity called a celebration medallion. Celebration medallions were easily recognizable. They bore a distinct raised rim of braided laurel and were slightly larger than a standard solé, the common gold coin struck with a king's image.

The medallion could fully explain the Marshal's agitation . . . the *intensely personal* secrets he'd not yet come to grips with . . . his compulsion to follow Damon's plan . . . and his conviction that, with the Order at his back, he could redirect any deviance from justice and right, because in all of Navronne's history, only six events had mandated the striking of a gold celebration medallion.

The kingdom's founding had been the first. The image of the strong-featured Caedmon on the medallion's obverse was so clear in my mind, I must have seen one at some time.

Two centuries later, the sixth and last medallion had celebrated Caedmon's distant grandson Eodward's final victory over the Aurellian Empire. Its face was the timeless symbology of peace.

But in between, in a stroke of vanity for a man born an illiterate petty noble, who had unified the most magnificent and generous of kingdoms, a medallion was struck for the birth of each of Caedmon's four children. And only one of those—one of all the six—would have shown a woman's face.

Our first king's two eldest sons had died in the war against Aurellia with no issue. His third son was but an infant when Caedmon abandoned the provinces of Morian and Ardra and retreated into the southern mountains. All trace of that third son was lost until his great-great grandson Eodward rode out of nowhere at the age of one-and-twenty to claim his ancestor's throne. But Caedmon had sired a daughter, as well.

In those days a king's daughter would have been discounted as a potential heir and married off, so that even her name was lost in the fogs of history. Why would the Marshal wear her birth medallion? Other than its weight of gold and its historical novelty, I could think of only one reason. It belonged to him.

Wishing to ensure the integrity of his heirs, Caedmon had hired sorcerers to enchant each celebration medallion, using a drop of the child's blood. Any example of those four birth medallions would glow with its own inner light when worn by an heir of Caedmon's blood—unless it was encased in pure silver to mask its enchantment. Caedmon had created undeniable proof of his lineage. And the Knight Marshal of Evanide wore that proof hidden in a silver pendant.

Was it possible Damon had discovered a fourth claimant to Eodward's throne? And one, assuredly by virtue of the Xancheiran secret, who possessed Aurellian blood? For unlike Caedmon, the Marshal was a sorcerer.

It would explain everything of Damon's secrecy, of the Marshal's story . . . the hints of conspiracy shown on Inek's portrait, a gravity that drew in the Archivist and even the previous Marshal. A king bearing magic could reshape not just the Registry, but all the Middle Kingdoms. Maybe soon, maybe well after the resolution of the prince's war. Damon had time. The Marshal was a young man.

What better place to hide and train a magical Pretender to the throne than Fortress Evanide? And what an unimaginable shock for a man with no personal memory, a man content with his anonymous life guiding the work of justice, to discover that he could be plunged into responsibility as great as any in the world. A sorcerer king.

If the Marshal was the obverse of this greater story, what was the reverse? What was my own role—a man of power trained in combat and steeped in rage? A threat to use and discard? A sword to enforce Damon's will on a puppet?

My feet had led me into the infirmary. Mother's grace, how I needed to speak with Inek. I was still missing something.

The scudding clouds allowed shards of sunlight through the arrow loops by each bed. A mere two days on and the crowding was greatly relieved. Pureblood healing sped recovery from most injuries. Despite my hard row of the morning, I'd near forgotten my stitched back.

"He's been transferred back to the Archive Tower," said Adjutant Tomas as he passed me by and poured some syrupy potion down an insensible man's throat. The infirmarian never stopped moving. "We weren't doing him any good here."

"Thank you, adjutant. Do you think he's made progress?"

"I've no experience with the mind's wounds. The body is complicated enough." His palm released an acrid bite of magic into the sick man's temple. Then he faced me, empty spoon in hand. "But if the Archivist's mumbling parallels my own, I'd say he's closing in on an answer, though not fast enough for his liking. Sorry."

Third-quarter bells rang.

"What's the hour?" I called after Tomas's retreating back. I'd lost all sense of time during the Marshal's interview.

"Eleventh hour almost gone."

There was naught to do about outlandish theories just now. The word would be out that I was under discipline. To avoid additional stripes, I had to be where I was expected—which was with the swordmaster for two hours of speedwork, and then the Inner Court for my appointment with the Disciplinarian. Forty lashes . . . gods save me.

Meanwhile, I was starving, parched, and desperately needed a trip to the chart room to assess the tides and the weather. No matter punishment, no matter the fate of kingdoms, magic, or a severed world, tonight I would bring my sister and two hundred others home to Navronne.

Agony without blood or bruise. Humiliation without words. Apology without excuse. Such was the nature of Evanide's punishment discipline. After forty blows with a lash that somehow marked the skin and seared the soul while leaving the receiver physically undamaged, an anonymous shepherd led me blindfolded from one observer to the next. At each I knelt and pressed my forehead to the paving and my hand to his foot.

My hand reported the infinite variety of shoes, sandals, and boots that populated Evanide, most of them damp. And surely someone had imported five thousand extra people to read the posted charges:

Greenshank, Paratus, recklessly endangered the lives of his brothers of the Order by abandoning his post and spending a night off-island without permission.

Focusing on such trivialities was the only way to keep from groaning every time I bent my back. Muscle and bone certainly believed they were damaged. By the time the low, brassy war horn crowed dismissal, I could not rise on my own.

Eventually, the departing shuffle of observers was replaced by the soft flutter of wings. Beaks pecked at the pavement. My shepherd remained my only human companion.

He must have felt the lash himself at some time, for rather than trying to support me under my agonized shoulders or around my savaged back, he guided my fingers to his arm and let me haul myself up. We crossed the courtyard and into the Great Hall, where the smells of supper, the clank of spoons, and a sudden hush greeted my passing.

That the fire in my cheeks did not melt my mask amazed me. And I near wept in gratitude when we at last moved into the barracks passage and through a leather curtain. My companion lowered me to my pallet.

"Before you lie down." He pressed a flask into my hand. "Drink it all and I'll bring another. The more you drink, the faster the pain will dissipate. And pull up the blanket. You fear it will hurt your back worse—and it will. But if you wait until you get cold—and you will—the muscles will seize. The cramps will be worse than the beating."

"Thank—" His finger hushed me.

The one being disciplined was not to know those who collaborated in his punishment or communicate with them. I raised the flask in acknowledgement, while cursing my idiot self who had not groveled to the Marshal and begged him to postpone the punishment. How in the name of all gods was I to carry out the night's work?

By the time the flask was empty, my companion had fetched another. I drained it, too. Hands helped me down to my side, then nudged my hip to roll me over. "Face down. This will hurt, but it's the only way you're going to be able to row tonight."

"Wha—?"

A splat of cold fat or mud or some such on my spine interrupted my surprised question and near shot me to the ceiling. The voice and . . . presence . . . were not those of my shepherd. But I was so entirely breathless with pain, I couldn't blurt the newcomer's name.

"Be still. Bite this."

My impotent hand wave was no deterrent to Sir Conall. He stuffed the leather strap—my belt? his?—in my mouth.

"I'm going to be fast and brutal," he whispered in my ear. "My laggard tyro guards the door, but you never know who'll peek in, and you're supposed to be suffering alone until dawn."

He unbuckled my blindfold and pulled it off.

"You never did tell me a time for your rowing exercise, so I consulted Fix. Astonishing what one can learn from a boatmaster, especially one who's been one's *mentor* for the last month."

Consideration of Conall's words was impossible as he kneaded his cold glop into my back with magic and unrelenting pressure. Pain devoured the world, along with thought, emotion, and self—a storm comparable to the lightless war of rain, sea, and wind the previous night. *Stay quiet. Stay quiet. Stay quiet.* And so passed an eternity of misery.

". . . be getting a bit better about now. Wriggle your finger if you're coming out of it."

I tried. Wasn't any more sure I'd done so than I'd feel a feather's touch while being stung by a swarm of bees. But my eyes opened to dusty sunlight.

"Excellent. I knew you weren't planning some ordinary navigation exercise. Not with all this business of Inek and that curator. Sweet Mother, have you ever seen Damon's eyes as he watches you? That's a lot more often than you could possibly know. Fix didn't tell me everything, but we revised your plan for tonight. *I'll* do principal navigation. My marshal-in-waiting will be my tailman. Dunlin and Heron can decide who leads, who tails for their boats. Fix has two other . . . mmm . . . henchmen who can lend an oar. My two laggards will remain behind, so tangled up in unresolvable spellwork that by tomorrow morning they'll not know where they were, what they did, or who was or was not with them. That way you can concentrate on getting your refugees here from . . . wherever they are . . . and get yourself across on the second pass."

"Good. Sorry," I said, in a rasping whisper. "So risky."

"The world is at risk. But my current knight-mentor is the Knight Defender of Evanide. You could have no stronger ally."

"Seems so." But my trust in my own judgment was well fractured.

"Wait and see." His cheerful whisper was punctuated by another pounding that left me speechless. But at the end of it and a great deal of blotting with a towel, I was able to sit up on my own. "Better?"

I raised both of my arms and twisted my torso—tasks I'd not thought to manage for a month or more. "Sir Conall, you are a *sorcerer!*"

He grinned hugely. "The Order lash is a brutal implement, but usually teaches what needs to be taught. The pain never lasts more than twelve hours, but molinara can provide a quicker recovery when needed. That's a knights' secret, you understand! You've collected several secrets beyond your rank of late." He rummaged around in my clothes chest. "Stars of night, Greenshank, do you never wash your clothes?"

He dropped a rank-smelling shirt over my head. "You'll have no visitors until sunrise tomorrow. If I didn't know a thousand smarter ways to work it, I'd say you planned all this to give yourself the night for this mysterious venture."

"I didn't know about the"—I kicked at a crockery jar slopped with gray paste—"whatever this mess is. And I'd not have been able to accomplish this greasy pummeling on my own. Conall, I can't thank—"

"You'll do the same for another one day. Now, it's half gone third hour. What time do you expect to have people at the boathouse?"

As I ignored residual twinges and shoved my arms into the shirt, I searched back through layers of pain and punishment, revelation, sea and storm to find the calculations I'd made. "Nine hours, maybe seven if I can get them moving quickly. I'm not sure how many I can bring at once, but if I don't have to row the first crossing, I should have a second lot back by the time the boats are back. Though truly I've no idea of the tides, and the boat crews will need a breather. Fix can explain why I'm so uncertain of it all."

"He'll explain as he will. I trust him. He sent you sustenance." From a leather sack he pulled a round packet the size of a plate and a small velvet bag.

The packet held an entire leek pie. I burst out laughing. "Pie feeds his power?"

"He said you'd need it after your meeting with the Disciplinarian. And that the other gift might help in case matters got difficult."

I blessed the Defender for the food, the surest remedy against depletion. Indeed a quarter of the heavy, greasy, astonishingly delicious pie was gone by the time I got the knots closing the little bag untangled. One more bite crammed into my mouth and I spread the crimped velvet open and dumped out a thin, flexible silver band set with four small rubies. Awe halted me in mid-swallow. "Deunor's holy fire . . ."

"Said he hadn't enough magic left this morning to light his oven, so it was a good thing he'd made the pie last night while he was filling the gems."

Almost any material could hold a worked spell. Metals like silver, bronze, and even steel could do so better than wood, cloth, or plants. Horn, ivory, or rare stones like jade or lapis were better—able to hold worked spells with enough magic bound into them to fuel a single working. But only gemstones could store pure magic itself—the power needed to feed a sorcerer's bent or spellwork of his choosing. If Fix couldn't stand at my shoulder to lend me his magic, as he'd done in the crypt, then he'd given me the next best thing—stored magic I could draw on at need.

I crimped the silver band midway up my right forearm, just above my own bracelet, and pulled my shirt sleeve over it. "How can I ever repay such a gift?"

"Honor his trust in you. The Order itself is the Defender's warrant—his life's work."

"Tell him Damon's play begins inside twelve days. And the Order will never be the same."

The Marshal might or might not be Eodward's heir, but if the Order was to put anyone on the throne or force the Three Hundred to do it, then our history and tradition were incomparably broken. Fix had to know.

"I'll tell him more once tonight's business is done."

Conall nodded, solemn, then peered around the leather curtain and let it fall back. "One of Sheldrake's tyros will relieve my man at the hour. You need to be gone by then. I'll confirm that you're not to be disturbed until dawn. *Dalle cineré*, Greenshank."

He slipped out before I, my mouth full of pie, could return the blessing.

I emptied my clothes chest onto my pallet, then rearranged and covered the pile with the wool blanket. After gulping most of the water Conall had left me, I used the rest to rinse out my mask and clean my face of dried sweat and leek pie. My body reeked, but given a choice of a bath or the rest of the pie, I'd have chosen the pie. Sadly, I'd no time for either.

Only my dagger went with me. I needed no encumbrances. Tonight would be tricky enough. The afternoon light from the small high window made my pile of clothes look like a . . . pile of clothes, so I closed the shutters. Better.

Conall's gray-clad tyro gripped his lance much too low and stood his watch several paces too far from my doorway. Cloaked and re-masked, boots in hand, I slipped out behind him and pelted silently along the barracks passage, down into the old fortress, and through labyrinthine ways to the crypt and the door to Xancheira.

*M*agic only . . . *no history, no art* . . . A shift of my shoulders did not entirely ease their lingering ache. The bronze latch and hinge were cool to my touch. *Beyond the door and the Severing void is a ruined citadel, unusual in its triangular shape. . . .*

Did the answer to the Severing lie in my grandsire's Xancheiran chest and a starving man born two centuries ago? Was the Marshal a legitimate heir of Caedmon? More important, was he worthy of Caedmon's throne?

Focus, Greenshank. . . . The passage must be precise. Consider the matching door to this one under your hands . . . the symbol of open hands shaped on its center . . . the smell of earth and root, smoky torches, and those terrible iron chambers. Juli recognized them as like to your Tower prison . . . your own soul recognized them. Lucian de Remeni's horror still lives in you. . . .

Was that possible? Extraction of personal memories left knowledge, understanding, the power to recognize ideas and facts. But so much of memory was linked with emotion—like the virulent *personal* sickness I had felt after viewing my family's slaughter, long before I knew who those victims were. Surely Lucian remained in me, alongside Greenshank.

I yanked my hands from the door. I'd thought this would be so easy. Consider the destination, invoke the power of my bents, and step through.

I sat for a moment, cross-legged, arms folded across my breast, fingers resting on my shoulders, and began to breathe. Once, when I was a tyro and woke on the cold hard floor of the Hall screaming with nightmares and excruciating headaches, someone had come in the dark and taught me this. I'd never known who. But the practice had kept me sane. With each breath, I erased a scrap of anxiety, curiosity, pain. . . .

Now, again, hands on hinge and latch. *The matching door . . . my spark of a sister's small hand . . . Signé's scarred face, transformed by traces of humor and glints of curiosity . . . dust and straw and the long sloping passage to the well . . . the hum of beautiful old magic that drew water from the well to water gardens . . .*

The latch yielded. I pushed open the heavy door and stepped through.

CHAPTER 32

The disembodied fall was more familiar than frightening. I instructed the body I could not feel to hold a breath, just in case I was wrong . . .

The smell hit first—old wood and straw—and then something heavy crashed on my head in the dark. Not old Dorye again!

But it was no wet squinch, and no storm waves doused my limbs. I hefted the wood frame and scrambled out from under through drifting dust and crumbling baskets. The abandoned storage shelves. Xancheira.

Breaking out in a grin, I ran, hands spread to guide me along the pitch-black passage. Where the passage ended at the turning to the well, I cast a weak magelight to illuminate the twisting ways. I should ask them to leave a lamp down here. Magelight used power and I needed to conserve every scrap.

A short time saw me to the citadel's great atrium.

An older girl stood on a ladder removing turnips from a hanging net and tossing them to a boy below. Before I could introduce myself, the girl yelled, "Eurus, get the mistress. Run!"

"I won't hurt you. I'm—"

"I know who you are," said the girl, perching her backside on the ladder step. "Your sister told everyone you'd come back. The mistress said that if any of us saw you, we should prevent you doing something stupid."

"No stupidity," I said, feeling inordinately good-humored. "I need my sister and the Wanderers to gather here right now. Time presses. Could you do that?"

"Where's Lord Siever?" She poked her narrow chin at me.

"Yesterday he worked a spell for me," I said, "a ball of blue light that hung above his hand and made me feel—"

"Delight!" she crowed. "I remember him doing that when I was small. He could juggle the balls and each one made you feel something different . . . but it's been so long. . . . You *saved* him."

"He's yet very ill. But I've hope. Now please . . ."

She scrambled down the ladder and bolted.

I waited, trying not to lose my good humor in the snarl of anxieties. Every hour I spent here was seven for Conall and the others. Dally too long and they'd not get back to Evanide before dawn. Would two trips be enough? A *hundred* each time. And what of the twenty thousand? I needed to see Safia.

"Remeni-son!" Signé hurried through the great doors.

"Lord Siever's alive," I said, knowing her first question. "He's safe. Eating. Not well, but stronger, so he says, and yesterday . . ." As I told of Siever's spellwork, tears welled in Signé's eyes, scarred and unscarred alike. She neither blotted them nor turned away. In no way did they diminish her.

"No news could be so welcome," she said. "Siever is beloved of all in Xancheira, everyone's brother, father, or son. So now you've come for your sister."

"I'll take all who'll go," I said. "Half to start. Then I'll come straight back for the rest. We need to be fast."

"Merro will bring them." Suspicion narrowed her unscarred eye. Her scrutiny did not waver. "Why the hurry? Is it safe where you'll take them?"

"The island hospice is now a military fortress. The men there are honorable, but very few know anything of Xancheira or my magic that brings me here. To see two hundred strangers arrive unexpectedly would cause no end of questions I'm not prepared to answer. But I've friends enlisted to get the Wanderers to the mainland and onward to a place of their choosing. Beyond that, I can guarantee nothing. The world is hard, more so even than when they left it."

She retrieved a few of the turnips the boy Euros had spilled when I arrived and tossed them into the righted basket. "Food. Roads to travel. Determining their own fate. Better than here."

"I've not given up on the rest of you. When I come back—in just a little while, I hope—I'd like to speak with you about that . . . and to Safia. She might tell me—"

"Luka!"

Sunlight burst through the doors to the outer courts. This time when my sister slammed into me, I knew better what to do. I pressed her head to my breast. "Juli. *Serena.*"

"I knew you'd come. Told them, but none believed you'd find a way. Celia scoffed you didn't know how. And you sound as if you . . . ?" She squinted up at me.

"I've just learned a bit more." I pulled back a little from her hope. "Naught else. So, will you go this time? Siever thanks you. He's likely eating leek pie just now and practicing his magic."

"Oh, such good news! And I'm ready any time . . . as long as they can come, too." Her head indicated a tide of gray, brown, red, and glinting brass flowing into the citadel from a distant corner.

"Come close, please, and quickly," I said, loud enough for all to hear. I shifted Juli to my side. "I'll take half to start. The passage will be different than when you came here, but no one has to die to open the way."

"'Tis surely the coroner's pureblood," said a rosy-cheeked young woman to those around as the crowd pooled about Juli and me. "Looked him in the eye once, when I poured him cider. Looked at the rest of him, too. He's . . . bigger, but I'd know those cheekbones anywhere."

Snickering broke out here and there.

I'd forgotten about the Cicerons knowing Bastien. One of these people worked for him. . . .

"Is the surgeon Bek here?" I said, scanning the crowd.

A slight man with deep-set eyes, gray-threaded hair, and ragged clothes stepped forward, a worn leather satchel in his hand. "So I'm allowed to speak to you now, pureblood?"

A good-humored quirk of his lips belied the snappish quip. He was likely forty or thereabouts, his speech educated, his eyes clear and intelligent. But the creviced landscape of his face and tremors in his hands bespoke years of decadence. Bastien had named Bek a twistmind, yet I doubted Xancheira had been able to provide much nivat to service his need. He was a strong man if he'd survived the lack.

"Speak as you wish," I said. "Coroner Bastien will be pleased to see you. He feared you dead or conscripted."

So many faces watching me, weathered, anxious, sullen. Hard-eyed women of every age, the younger kept protectively behind the elder. A few bold, suspicious youths. A few brawny, grizzled older men. Their fighters had died giving them time to get through the portal, Bastien had told me. Youngsters clung to the women's skirts. I'd not expected so many children. More than a third of them. "Which is your headman?"

One of the older men stepped out, bearded jaw jutting high. His wiry gray braids were bound with faded ribbons, and brass earrings dangled from drooping lobes. "I'm Hercule."

"Hercule." I inclined my back. Not so much as to make a mockery. "For now, I go by the name Greenshank. Though some use my birth name in various forms"—I nodded to Juli, who grinned hugely—"it's no longer familiar to me and . . . not safe to speak in the streets of Navronne."

A ripple of surprise. Curiosity.

"My sister may have mentioned that my memory of my days at Caton is broken. I live a different life now. More humble, I think. If I gave any of you offense in those days, I ask pardon. I showed your elder and your former head-man a way to open the portal in your commons house, believing, as they did, that this would be a refuge. You know more of the sad result than I."

"Where *is* Demetreo?" called several at once. A man in the back bellowed, "What of Jadia?"

"You'll see Coroner Bastien tonight. He'll know." He'd told me all left behind were dead. "I live on an island where you cannot stay, so you'll need to trust me. Trust my magic. Trust my friends who are waiting with Bastien to take you back to the world you know—difficult and dangerous as it is. Nothing has changed in that regard since you left it. Will you go with me? What say, Hercule?"

"Where will your friends take us?" he said.

"You can choose. Into the northlands or to Ardra. To Palinur, if you want to go back there. No one lives in the hirudo, but the war is two years' worse and the royal city ever vulnerable. The risks are likely worse than before. . . ."

Murmurs rose to babble about where might be better and who had relatives in what town. Some believed staying behind might be best after all.

I raised my hands, hoping to quiet them. "We've no time to argue. Coroner Bastien can give better advice. He's lived in the world these past few years, as I have not."

"How is it they have a choice of where to go?" Signé's question silenced them as my speech hadn't. "How will they travel to cities so distant?"

"I've a friend sworn to guide them safely to wherever they wish," I said.

"A *Registry* friend or someone even worse?" she asked, reeking of suspicion.

"I no longer bear allegiance to the Registry. The friends who will get them off the island are sorcerers of many bloodlines who risk much to do this service. They will be masked like me and will not speak to you. But underneath mask and silence, they are men like me and will do their best to keep you safe. Once off the island, you'll be in marshlands where it would be unhealthy to stay. Coroner Bastien and another very old friend of mine . . . a most *trustworthy* person who knows hidden roads and forgotten paths . . .

will take you onward." I didn't want to get into the matter of Morgan. Not here. "So will you go?"

Still they gabbled, even louder than before.

"I damned sure don't want to stay here and starve," said Bek the surgeon, loud enough to quell the talk. "Every one of us is weaker than a month ago, and we're eating the provender Lady Signé's people need to stay alive. I'd as soon go back to the starvation I know of as kill good folk who took us in."

"None of us got sick yet," shouted someone in the crowd. "Maybe we won't. We can work. Be of use."

"My granny told of the burning city," said a young woman, her skin already patchy and gray. "And how it was our duty to go back and save the ones lost. For my granny, I say we stay."

"But right now, the *saving* for Signé and her people is for us to leave," said Juli. "I'm going. My brother will do his best for you, the way Demetreo and Jadia and the others did. You need your families safe. And family has always meant everything to Luka—family and magic. He can bring you back later, if you want, when he comes to set the Xancheirans free. Because he wouldn't be able to sleep easy ever again if he didn't do that."

"Enough," I whispered. My hand found hers and squeezed it. "Hercule?"

The big man had listened carefully to every argument. "Them as want to stay, speak to the Lady Signé. If she says you'll be of more use than what you eat, you can stay. But the rest of us go. To Palinur to start. It's the place we know best. If it falls, we're the ones will know how to survive and get our-selves somewhere better."

"Good. Divide your people in two groups," I said, trying to decide how best to manage the passage. "We've boats only for a hundred. And make sure you've two adults for every child. Families together, but partnered with other adults if they've more than one child. Everyone must be holding on to each other."

Signé watched, stone cold, as the headman directed some of his people down the stair, some back toward the Bronze Tower. Four or five approached the lady about staying. Four she dismissed straightaway. One she spoke with longer, but eventually he rejoined the others, too. Through a melee of fare-wells and embraces, but no tears, Bek and Juli ushered the first group down the stair to where the portal waited.

Signé set herself between me and the stair. "You're putting them in the care of the long-lived."

"Yes. But my friend's gards are not silver. And she's sworn—"

"Does she know these people come from a land where her kind wear silver gards? Do *you* know that her kind fear that the silver madness breaks the world? Kyr says those with blue gards have their own form of madness, for they consider anyone—human, beast, or long-lived—who has been near the silver as aberrant."

Exactly what I was afraid of. "Siever warned me to be careful. And though Morgan has been naught but generous with me, I've heeded him. She and I have a bond like you and Kyr, forged years ago when I lived that other life, though unlike you, I can't feel— I can't remember what we shared or what I felt then that might be different now. But yes, she knows. I have to trust her. There's no other way to get these people somewhere they can survive before winter makes life on the road deadly. They cannot live in a swamp. Cicerons don't farm. They don't fish. They survive in cities where there are many people who have things they want and need."

"You're saying they're thieves," she accused, angrier than ever.

Goddess Mother, she really had no idea. But then, she had grown up in a ruin.

"They learned to live as they could manage." Which was strange coming from me who used *Ciceron* and *thief* interchangeably. "They dance and mime and do tricks for entertainment. They play games of chance. They perform services that people can't get elsewhere, services most people deem unsavory."

"And yet you're rescuing them."

"There are many reasons."

"I see. As your sister says, it's what you are."

"Don't presume too much from her chatter, my lady. I'm many things now that I was not before. Now, forgive me; I must go." The atrium had emptied. "I hope to be back within the hour. And when I come I need to ask you about the *cache* you and Siever spoke of. And I desperately need to speak with Safia about how we might free your people."

"The cache is two centuries lost. And Safia is mad."

"She guided me here believing I could help."

Signé acknowledged the point reluctantly. "I see her only when she brings provisions. That's usually when she plans to release Benedik for an hour or she brings me a message from him—to taunt me that he was out and I didn't know. But I'll try to find her."

"Is there a hilltop that looks out over the sea and five spits of land? White rocks like bones along fingers, grass, a few pines. She's been there every time I've spoken with her."

Her face opened up a little. "The place of the beacon, the boundary of our little fragment. We can walk forever along those spits, but never touch the sea. She and Benedik would often meet there."

She proffered her hand—not cold as I expected, but warm and grimy, hardened with work and smelling like herbs and clean earth. "For my people and the Wanderers, Lucian de Remeni, I thank you."

The echo of Signé's low voice followed me down the stair. It had made the syllables of that name sound very different from when others spoke it, as if it referred to yet a different version of me. What must it have been like to live all your days confined to a dead city—a necropolis of a sort? To see friends and a brother go mad or die or starve until desperate enough to become trees?

There was no time to go back and ask her all the things I'd like to know. Surely an hour had elapsed already. I'd not thought it would be so difficult to get the Cicerons to decide.

When I encountered the mass of people stopped in the cellar passage, they parted the way and let me through. Though they were subdued . . . anxious . . . a hundred seemed a great deal more when crowded into the narrow halls. Could I possibly hold so many through the void? Likely I should have tried it with a few before this. But I worried about Kyr sensing the magic—and the crossing took a great deal out of me. I hadn't slept since the fitful night under old Dorye. Even with Fix's rubies in reserve, I dared not overreach. What would happen if my magic failed halfway across the Severing void?

"Here's what we're going to do," I said, shaking off the nebulous terror these people already feared. "I need my hands to work the magic of the portal. So I'm going to have my sister hold on to me from behind. And someone must hold on to her, and another and another, as if we were dancing a galliard with the longest chain ever attempted. The chain must not break. Children must be held close between adults who hold each to the next adult, as well as to the child. I'll try to enfold each of you with magic, but I'm only a sorcerer, not the Goddess Mother who can embrace all her children at once. When you step through the door, you'll feel as if you're falling, but you're not. Hold on to each other with all your mind and strength. Think of each other, what he likes, how she looks in her new earrings, who makes the best bread, who's lucky at dice. This is your clan . . . your family . . . and for this moment, my family as well . . . and if we hold thought of each other, as well as the body in front of us, we'll stay together."

I peered over the crowd in search of the slight-bodied surgeon. He was off to one side, not wholly one of them. "Surgeon Bek, would you proceed down the line to make sure of our seamless joining? And, if you would . . . it would be helpful to have someone I know even a little at the end of the line. And no, that will not be you, *Doma* Remeni."

Juli shut her mouth quickly, as laughter rippled through those close enough to hear. The Cicerons started shifting themselves into line, hushing children, calling friends to join them. A few retreated into the passages. I'd best count on the second group being larger.

"I can do that," said Bek, easing through the anxious mob. "There's little use for barber surgeons in Xancheira. Most of the men are too young to need shaving. The dead are not available to be studied. And the living are too preoccupied with dying. *Doma* Remeni's conversation"—he bowed in Juli's direction—"has been the Sky Lord's own benefice. If ever you need someone to stand beside you in the gracious young lady's service, I am your man."

I should have taken my sister aside and offered a warning, but I was quickly absorbed in reinforcing my instructions. When we were as ready as we could possibly be, I moved to the portal, snugged my sister's arms around my waist, and sent a rope of magic down the column behind me, through nervous mothers and men who had never been afraid until facing magic and the void, all the way to the deep-eyed ruffian who enjoyed studying corpses and had once found sensual ecstasy in pain.

A stone harbor . . . mist, rain at the edge of the bay . . . the demesne of a lonely man who lives parallel lives . . . the scent of salt wind, bluster and tide rush muted by stone walls . . . brothers waiting . . . my family, both there and here behind me . . .

I let the power build well beyond what I'd done with Siever. Only when my skin felt thin as woven spidersilk, my every nerve aflame with lightning did I press the latch and push open the door. "Hold on!"

Oh, blessed Deunor . . . Luka!

I clung to that distant cry, even as I held our destination steady in my center and sent every scrap of my will up and down that line of magic: *hands tighter . . . who is behind you? . . . don't be afraid . . . trust me . . . who do you love? . . . who annoys you? . . . who sings best of home? of love? of sorrow?*

CHAPTER 33

"Oh, *ancieno,* you did it! Every person's crossed—a hundred and three of us. Bek, too."

Hearing trumped speech. Seeing, too. I flailed in the dark, glimpsing only streaks of light, but it was only the boathouse doors were closed. Torchlight seeped in through the seams. And the rhythmic thumps were not my heart splitting into fifty pieces, but an unsecured boat knocking gently on the pilings. Otherwise, it was deadly quiet.

I sat straight up. "Goddess Mother, where are they?"

"I just told them we needed to hush if we're not supposed to be here. See?"

A pearly light splayed from the warm, breathing solidity at my side, and I saw them lined up around the stone walls and stacked boats of Fix's boathouse. A hundred shabby bundles of human life, sitting, standing, tall, short, male, female, child, elder. Some were dripping. A few were sitting on the boats. But all two hundred dark eyes stared straight at me, and every one of those eyes dropped as soon as I met it.

"All right, then," I said, as the rest of my body came into focus. My feet dangled over the water, a dinghy banging gently against my boots. "Looks like I'm the last one to arrive."

I couldn't stop grinning. I'd aimed the crossing magic exactly here.

Hercule squeezed past the others, stopping not far away when he couldn't go farther without climbing in a boat. He bowed awkwardly and did not look up. Nor did he speak.

"Headman, is everyone all right?"

"Yes, *domé.* May I speak?"

Ah, yes. The rules. The law. Somehow in Xancheira things had been different, but now we were back in the world they knew. In Palinur he could have been whipped for speaking to me. For looking at me.

"For now, I am not *Domé* Remeni," I said. "I'm a soldier called Greenshank. You may speak to me any time you have something to say."

"What should we do?"

"Stay quiet, as my sister warned. Sit, if you wish. Rest. There might be water casks or packets of dry stores in these boats. You could send the children out to find them and share around—a game, but quietly, please, while I find out if we're ready for the next part of your journey. And tell them . . . everyone did well."

He wagged his head like a great dog. "We did *nothing*, *domé*. You carried us in your hand through the end of all things."

He whispered to those nearest him, and the word rippled through the others. A girl ventured into the boats first and squealed when she found a bag of currants. She clapped a hand over her mouth as a hundred people shushed her.

I scrambled to my feet, wobbling slightly. Juli grabbed one arm; Surgeon Bek the other.

"Might have overdone the magic a bit," I said. "There were just so many of them."

"Luka, do you have any idea—?" A whisper did not dim my sister's intensity in the slightest. "No, you couldn't, could you? Oh, Luka, if Capatronn could have felt what you just did. When you'd come home from Palinur, he'd often come and sit with me in the dark while you practiced your drawing in the studio. I would ask when I could make magic so beautiful as yours, for I was sure I would build a temple someday or a city to match the halls of divine Idrium. But he told me that I wouldn't match you ever. That none of us would. He and I would weep together, not so much for sorrow—though always a bit—but for the sheer beauty of it. And that was in no measure close to what you did this crossing."

"Some of it's sheer chance," I said. "And I've worked hard at magic these two years. But I think when we bring Signé and her people back here, we'll see such magic as we can only imagine. Siever's first raw attempt reminded me why we name the gift divine. But first . . . we go."

The boats should be waiting somewhere outside the boathouse. We hadn't wanted the rowers to see a hundred people appear out of nowhere. But I dared not open the doors, lest observers in the fortress notice. Which meant I needed to swim under the boathouse walls to meet Conall.

Leaving boots and jaque with Juli, I slipped into the water. A dive between the pilings, and I soon poked my head above the slopping wavelets. My spirits plummeted. The fog was thick as a tyro's head at dawn. I had to use the bulk of the massed enchantments shielding the fortress, the landward beacons, and the motion of the water to orient myself. It was nothing I'd not done a hundred times, but sweet Goddess, what were we to do about the crossing?

A few long strokes and I hauled myself onto the dock in the vicinity of Fix's cottage.

"Early." A good thing the hand gripped my wrist, else the invisible Conall's soft greeting might have toppled me right back into the water. "But we're ready."

"But this demon fog—"

". . . thins out amazingly just this side of the Spinner."

It took me several headshakings to comprehend. "Fix's distraction."

It was astounding. Magical fogs were as common as paralytic leashes in sorcerous combat. Their problem, of course, was that the wielder could see no better than anyone else. And they were always easily distinguishable. Magical fogs were dry, still, uniform in density, more like carded wool than natural fog. But this was wet and heavy, smelling of wet wood and saltmarsh. Drifting pockets and veils taunted the eye. The fog would ensure the Cicerons couldn't describe the fortress to anyone, and the enchantment was so delicately applied that the magic was indistinguishable from the common wards, locks, and training spells of the fortress. Masterful.

"We'll bring the boats to the water door one at a time," said Conall. "Are your people ready?"

"They've done well. But I doubt any can swim or have ever seen a boat. I told them the rowers won't speak to them."

"We'll have a care. Our oarsmen think they're a wandering band of Cicerons enlisted to serve our training needs and that we'll give them each a copper for their trouble. The tides are good. Weather's good. Should be three hours in with the hefty load, three back as usual. The second return will be the rough. You'll be here waiting with our second load, yes?"

"Close enough." He bared his teeth and vanished into the fog. I'd never thought of Conall's exceptional knightly skills as including conspiracy.

Back into the water and back to the boathouse. Restless murmurs were quickly hushed when I climbed out. Hercule was waiting with Juli and Bek.

"Pass this word to everyone," I said. "Crossing to the mainland should take three hours. I won't be with you, as I'll be fetching the rest of your people. Better for all if you puke outside the boat. Everyone does at first. The rowers believe you've been hired to give them a rough night. And please, please, Hercule, once you're landed, your people must not speak of Signé or her people or the ruined city or this place or me to anyone. I wish I knew how to erase these things from your minds, just to avoid laying this charge on you, but even a single mention—"

"Wanderers know how to keep secrets, Soldier Greenshank." Hercule pulled off one of his earrings and held it in his upraised palm. With a whisper of magic no stronger than a shift of the air from an opening door, the earring sparked and jingled. He passed his other hand over and the earring was vanished in a cloud of gray smoke. "'Tisn't quite what you do, but such tricks would see us dead in Navronne. Those of us here have managed not to be dead."

"Thank you for your trust," I said, near speechless. He was right about the danger of what he'd shown me. Though perhaps not in the future . . .

"Our *Naema* told us the coroner's pureblood was the one we'd been waiting for since we took up wandering," said the old man. "Whatever you asked of us, she said we were to do our best. And so we will."

Naema—not just *grandmother*, but a title bestowed upon the Goddess Mother or the human women who wore her mantle here on earth.

"She's the one who died opening the way to Sanctuary," I said, awed that I had met such a woman, wishing I could remember her. The title was never bestowed lightly, and even pimplebloods respected it. "I am so sorry."

"She wasn't. She'd waited her whole life for it. And from what the city folk told us, it should have been just what we sought. Maybe someday we'll make a fine song about the whole thing, and folk will puzzle over it." He raised his hand to belay any warning. "But no time soon."

"One more thing," I said. "Your guide on the mainland is my good friend and not at all like those of her kind in Signé's city. . . ."

He passed that startling news along to his people, too.

At Conall's signal, we doused Juli's magelight and drew open the water door just enough to accommodate one boat at a time. Bek and I handed the Cicerons into the boat; I nodded to Dunlin and Heron, but did not break the rule of silence Conall had laid on them. Conall's own boat was the last. I motioned Juli to take a seat just behind the knight.

She didn't move. "Bek and I thought we'd go back with you. Show the others that all's well."

"No," I said. "I'll take the surgeon. But not you." Too many things could go wrong. "Please, *serena*, I cannot— Would you consider sitting with Lord Siever? The man who looks after him is occupied in all this."

She tilted her head and squinted at me as if I were a half-wit. "They're frightened," she said. "Hercule won't be there. No one there really knows you. They might imagine that you don't mind losing a few of them as long as your kinswoman is safe."

I wanted to tell her that the thought of losing her was unbearable, and not simply for what she might share of our past. The tale of our grandsire had meant more to me in what it spoke about *her* than for grand sentiments from a dead man I would never remember. But she was right.

"Besides, I think Siever would rather me help you, *ancieno*. Because the sooner this is done, the sooner you can turn your mind to *his* friends. And I *choose* to go." Her mouth was set in a way that even a man without memory could interpret.

Bowing to the inevitable, I rapped on Conall's boat and gave it a shove. The loaded skiff melted into the fog.

"What do we do?" said Bek, looking about as if a doorway would appear out of nothing.

"First we've got to get the two of you to the crypt unnoticed. . . ."

I drew the water door shut and pointed to the slopping wavelets. "Jump in. Tonight you are going to be two sorry novice warriors."

They goggled for a moment, then did as I said. Fortunately there were plenty of bags around the boathouse that I could use to cover their heads—as was often done for tyros fool enough to lose their masks in a dunking. Juli already wore men's clothing, but I found a rag of canvas in one of the boats to wrap around her. We were entering a fortress that had seen no women for near two hundred years. Even the stones might notice.

Soggy and bedraggled, they trudged through the fog-shrouded halls, my hands on their shoulders to guide their steps. We encountered only a few people along the way; none who were interested. To my sorrow, an alert sentry was posted at my cell door in the barracks passage. I'd had dreams of snatching the remainder of my leek pie. Though likely congealed by now, it could have soothed the worrisome gnawing in my belly. I had to settle for two water flasks from the boathouse filled at the barracks laver.

When we arrived at the crypt, I gave Juli and Bek a drink and time to breathe without wet bags over their heads. Bek examined the dry bones, mumbling regrets that we had no recent corpses. It set Juli laughing, which bothered me. A surgeon's studies might be useful, but Bek was a man who sought pleasure in his own pain. Did he enjoy thinking of the pain of those he studied?

Juli started up with questions about the fortress and how I'd come to be here and what had caused me to lose my memory. When I said it wasn't the time, she offered to tell me of our hours together before I sent her with the Cicerons. I stopped her.

"Once we're back here we'll talk," I said. "I need to know everything you can tell me of that time. But to make the crossing, I need a clear head. Thinking about missing memories is like bashing my skull with a hammer."

"So do we dance our galliard as before?" said Bek. "I'll save my fascinating history for when we get back as well." I could see why Bastien valued him.

"Just as before."

After draining what was left of each water flask, I heaved a breath, then nodded to Juli. Her arms went around my waist.

Hands on handle and hinge. Thread a lifeline through my two companions. I drew up images of the ruined citadel and our purpose, of the bronze door in the bowels of the citadel and the symbol of healing. But when I focused on Signé's scarred face, instead I felt her capable hand stretched toward me . . . cold, not warm, and when she spoke the name that had once been mine, it was not appreciation, but urgency that flowed into my bones. *Lucian de Remeni . . . hurry . . .*

I poured magic into the door, pushed it open, and the three of us fell.

A basket of stunted parsnips and withered greens was the only casualty of our arrival in the citadel atrium. Evidently landing on one's feet was a matter of concentration as well as luck, and Juli stumbled after me. Bek had made some effort not to step on Juli and tumbled into the basket. Once the thumps of bouncing parsnips ended, no sound broke the damp and earthy silence but the trickle of water in the troughs above our heads. A lamp hung from a hook over the sorting tables.

Where was everyone? I'd thought they'd be waiting.

The urgency I'd felt at the portal hadn't left me. Without the press of people to intrude, simmering bitterness and an outsized rage too familiar of late seeped like autumn smoke through the citadel's every crack and crevice. Its source was outside the great entry doors . . . farther . . . perhaps beyond the outer wall.

"Bek, check downstairs and see if anyone's at the portal. Juli, how do I get outside the walls without stepping through those doors?" We dared not be seen.

"Out the Bronze Tower guardroom and through the herb garden," she said. "I'll show you."

"I'll follow when I've seen what's what," said Bek, darting for the cellar door.

Juli led me past garden beds and storage casks to a doorway punched through the rubble of the collapsed Bronze Tower. A passage had been rebuilt from the crumbled bits. Restraining her for a moment, I peered through. My senses reported no one ahead of us.

My sister's hand firmly in mine, we sped through the low arches to a dusty chamber lined with brackets and hooks—the Tower guardroom or what was left of it. Cloaks and canvas bags adorned the hooks. Wooden spears stood in the brackets. The residue of old spellwork lay everywhere.

A doorway had been cut through the original curved wall to the outside. A thick new door stood slightly open, its wooden barricades standing against the wall. Juli motioned me through.

Caution bade me leave my sister here while I found out what was so wrong. But even had I known the way, no force of will or reason would allow me to be separated from her. She already held her own dagger, as did I. We squeezed through the narrow opening into the night.

Surprising to find it night. I had assumed only a short time would have passed here in the hour or two we'd been away.

Morgan had told me that crossing the boundary from the human world into the true lands would always match in season and time of day, but that the slow meandering of life in the true lands caused the days to spend so differently and humans to age at a much slower rate than they expected. I wasn't sure I would ever understand that.

The citadel's eerie luminescence had faded, leaving the darkness of its precincts as profound as the wildlands bordering the Gouvron Estuary. Starlight revealed a great lump of stone had crushed half of the Bronze Tower portico—recognizable only from pale columns yet standing.

Anger and bitterness dripped from voices in the distance, like acid piercing holes in my gut.

Juli drew me faultlessly through a labyrinth of fallen cornices and vine-choked gardens. She hesitated for a moment at a wall's dark face, then crept rightward, halting at a simple garden gate, twisted at its hinges and smelling of rust.

The voices came clearer.

". . . 'tis a cruelty unworthy of thee, Kyr." Signé's desperate fury split the night. "What you felt is but a dying pulse of the old magic. We've no power like that anymore."

"Lies do not become thee, Signé. I am no senseless worm to judge every step and whisper as earthquake. Petra, choose the next, a male this time." Kyr Archon's rage could have crumbled Evanide itself.

"Mistress! Please! Don't let them . . ." The man's horror would have slashed the night even had he remained silent. But the darkness writhed as his pleading became panicked grunts . . . became moans . . . became a rising agony of screams.

I pressed Juli to the wall, willing her to wait. She acquiesced, and I slipped through the gate and alongside a fallen column until I could get a view.

Ten Danae, their flesh marked in fiery silver, stood in an arc between the top of the causeway and the citadel's gates. Twenty or thirty Xancheirans knelt on the paved terrace before the gates, Signé standing at the center front. At eight-and-twenty she was their eldest. Five slender trees, barren of leaves and lit eerily by the bright light of Danae gards, stood between Danae and humans. No tree had stood there on my first visit.

At first I thought yet another Dané stood in the very center of the saplings like a column of silver light, but he twisted around, the source of the dreadful cries. A young man I'd seen manning the gates on my first visit was being consumed by the argent fire. Feet and legs had vanished. Knees and thighs shattered like an exploding star. And as the light flared around groin and belly and chest, the lower part of the column turned dark and slender like scorched bone, transformed to wood and bark, rooted in the broken paving.

The Xancheirans did not wail or cover their ears, but clenched their fists and fixed their eyes on their friend as if to imprint his pain on their own souls. Nor did I betray the youth's agony by covering my own ears. This was retribution—not for the workings of old magic, but for mine.

A last cry, then chest and lungs were gone. Only his rictus of horror remained—and his spread arms, raised to keep them from the blazing light. When the light died, a sixth sapling stood with the others. Mother's mercy . . .

"Now again, Signé. Which one of thy people hast done this magic? And where is Siever?"

"You can feel my truth, Kyr. None of my people have done magic this day. And Lord Siever's long dying is ended."

The archon waved at one of his kinsmen. "Prepare another rooting, Petra. This time a female."

"Kyr, please no!" Signé cried.

Schemes to interrupt the dreadful standoff bloomed in me like deadly nightshade. A frontal attack? Or I could lure the Danae on a chase to the

Sanctuary pool. More than breathing, I needed to feel Kyr Archon's heart stop beating.

A touch on my back fired my reflexes. No time could have elapsed before I pinned the scrawny sneaker to the ground, knees on his arms and dagger at his throat.

"It's Bek," he croaked in a harsh whisper. "Bastien's friend."

His name alone would not have saved him, not in the dark where I couldn't see him, at a time when rage threatened reason. As it was, I jerked my hands away and shifted back so he could scramble away from me.

"They're waiting at the portal," he whispered.

The Cicerons. In the cellars, not the rooted ground beneath the paving. But how could I leave? A woman's shrill cries carved terror into my bones.

"Why do they allow this?" I spat.

"Those prisoned in the trees live," said Bek softly. "If they kill Kyr and his kin, who will *keep* them living? Who else will set them free?"

"Every one of my city's children kneels before thee, Kyr." Signé's words were built of the crumbled stone and ruined gardens, of strength and caring, of endurance and despair. "You can take us all, but it will not soothe thee. It is thine own broken power torments thee, not ours. When all of us have been devoured by this mockery of life and still the land does not yield to thee, how will you explain it? Let us work together to find an answer. . . ."

As if she knew I lurked close by, Signé had given me her answer. If all free Xancheirans were kneeling in the courtyard, my magic might prove they were not the sinners.

Bek and I slunk backward through the gate. I hated it. Sobs racked Juli, entirely silent. Gathering her close, I whispered in her ear, "We go. Now."

As a boy's yelling scoured the night, defiance dissolving into torment, Bek, Juli, and I pelted through ruined gardens.

The Bronze Tower stood against the brittle stars like a broken tooth. I held out a hand to slow my companions as we neared it. At the moment the tower doorway took shape from the night, a flare of silver blocked the way.

I shoved Juli and Bek behind me and readied a blast of fire from my bracelet.

"Hold, Remeni-son!" The quiet urgency stayed my hand, defining a dark shape behind the silver light. An eagle of wrought silver surrounded an eye colored deep as a spruce forest. Safia.

"Savages!" I snarled, low. "I should kill you all."

"No kind greeting for the one who guided you here," she said.

"With lies and childish mystery. You toyed with me when you could have told me the way. You could have told me about their desperate straits . . . and yours. You never mentioned this barbaric practice. Twenty thousand souls, and now these children . . ."

"Thou wert weak and unskilled," she said fiercely. "Through the passing season, I've felt the changes in thy power, though even yet thy human blundering leads Kyr to wreak his despair upon us all. Kill us and the prisoners die. Instead, use thy power to set them free!"

"Tell me how."

"Did I not say thy magic dissolves the boundaries? Must I etch the meaning on thy flesh?" Her green glare seared me.

"My power . . . you mean my magic can undo the Severing? But I've neither the knowledge nor the means." I'd only guessed about my grandsire's chest—and it lay in Palinur.

"No! To repair the Dark Divide is too much a risk." She ripped up a length of bloated, rotting vine and held it out to me. "Rejoin the lands while my kind yet walk this land and our blight will infest the true lands. The greater world will die as this one has. Take the prisoners from the trees, Remeni-son. Transport them across the Dark Divide, seal the crossings, and never look back."

"But how—? You're saying magic *alone* will release the Xancheirans from the trees."

"What is the shell of trees but another boundary? Lay thy magic upon each one and it shall release its prisoner, the most of them healthier than when we took them."

"But how in the shades of Idrium can I touch twenty thousand trees without one of you planting an arrow in my back or slaughtering any Xancheiran who yet lives?" Each of twenty thousand would take days.

"Thou'rt the sorcerer. Learn what's needed. But quickly." Her hand was an iron manacle on mine. "Give me thy promise, Lucian. Free Benedik first. Get him to safety before all others, and when the time comes, I'll keep my kin away."

More soul-searing cries dimmed the stars.

I wrenched my hand from her grip and locked hers in my own. "Stop Kyr from this horror or I'll stick a knife in him in the hour the Xancheirans walk free."

"Pah!" she said, wrenching her arms from my grasp with a strength entirely unlikely for her sylph-like form. "He'll not take all of them tonight. But do not delay. And though simple knives cannot end us, thou canst be well satisfied; once the trees are gone, we shall weaken and die."

"You, too?"

"Prove thy quality, Remeni-son." She vanished in a flare of silver.

As I started for the door, Juli stepped in front of me. "Luka, we can't leave Signé to this. . . ."

"We've no choice."

"But—"

"Our responsibility waits in the cellar."

Of course she was angry. So was I. As the three of us raced through the citadel, the earth trembled. Stones cascaded from the rubble walls of the Bronze Tower, rattling on the guardroom floor, and the makeshift arches of the passage creaked as we sped through on our way to the cellar.

The Cicerons were petrified by the rumbling earth. With my head full of Safia's warnings, Signé's desperation, human trees, and the magnitude of the tasks yet waiting, it was immensely difficult to concentrate on the crossing. Had it not been for Bek and Juli getting the people calm and in order, I could never have managed it. Even so, as I toppled into the void with Juli at my back and some hundred people strung out behind her, my binding thread slipped. Terror rippled through the darkness. Children.

Hold, hold, hold, I cried with every particle of my senses. Pouring magic into the tether, I stretched invisible arms from Juli all the way back to the surgeon. If only I'd planted splinters of silver in each person, linked with spells to hold us together, this would work better. . . .

CHAPTER 34

Head and shoulder crashed into a stone wall. The blow caused my belly to erupt, and I vomited so violently, it seemed I must be turned inside out.

The world bulged and retracted beneath me. I crawled toward a jouncing blur, grasped a gunwale, and heaved again. *Always puke over the side.*

As the shivering of depletion racked my bones, I clung to an imagining that I could do what was necessary. If I could just recall what that was. Or what had brought me to this disgusting state.

Concern was voiced in the language of squirrels. When frigid water splattered my face, the shock made me heave again. Only as stringy bile dribbled on my chin did I realize I was puking *into* a boat, not out of it. Fix would drown me. Or at least make me swab it out.

"Will something to drink help?" The low voice came from a short distance away.

"Yes. And he needs food."

I clamped my mouth shut and swallowed hard. Repeatedly.

"Truly?" The man seemed unperturbed. "Seems unlikely he could hold on to it. Mayhap, there's more food in the boats."

I squinted into a soft ivory light. Dark, lank hair framed deep-set eyes of charcoal. Haunted eyes. Bek. And with his name, the light took on its proper meaning. As did the slop of waves and muffled whimpers from the dark. The horror at Xancheira's gates shrilled in my ears and lurked behind my eyelids.

"How could you let them do it?" Juli stood over me, too, her fingers glowing, her small face a storm front. "What use is all this soldiering nonsense if you can't do something about a few naked, murdering creatures?"

"I'm just a man. D-danae are not." Teeth clattering like hailstones on a roof, I rolled up to sitting. "It profits nothing for us to end up trees. Signé knew that. D-did everyone make it across?"

"All safe—but scared," said Bek. "Almost lost three wee ones."

"Goddess Mother." I should have drawn on Fix's rubies. I should have figured out a way to transfer a holding spell through the line of people. I could have used—

"Splinters!" The solution exploded in my mind like a new sun. Not for the task just done, but for the one to come.

"What?" Juli and Bek chorused.

"Silver splinters! You can transfer magic through linked splinters, not just a particular spell, but raw power, too. Insert a splinter in the bark, a notch, a woodpecker hole. Anyone can do it . . . if there's anyone left." I scrambled, still shaking, to my feet. "Juli, I can open the trees."

"Woodpecker holes? Splinters? Luka, what have you done to yourself?" Juli patted my shoulder as if I were one of the children.

"I know how to set Signé's people free," I said. "Just have to eat. Sleep a bit. It will take everything I have." And everything Fix had loaned me. All temptation to draw on the rubies to cure my depletion vanished.

Fumbling at my sodden sleeve, I confirmed that the ruby bracelet was still in place. Baskets of silver splinters sat in the armory. Once the business of transporting a hundred Cicerons wasn't pressing, it wouldn't take long to link them. Then I'd need a plan to get the freed Xancheirans back to the greater world before they starved.

"Are the b-boats back? Have you heard bells? The time?"

"No bells," said Bek. "All's quiet outside. Still fogged in."

"I'll look," I said. "Keep your light shielded, *serena*. And pass the word to the people that we'll be leaving soon . . ."

". . . and to be silent, and they can have whatever food or drink they find on these boats. You mustn't get in the water again, Luka. You've no magic left. Someone else should go."

"I can swim without magic." I threw off my damp jaque and boots again. "None of you must be seen, and we mustn't open the doors." The danger was greater this time; someone could have been alerted.

Conall and I had agreed that we'd proceed only with contact, not signals on the second pass. Lights, enchantments, noises . . . anything we could do might be detected. Praying the knight and his rowers lay close in the fog, I dropped into the water and soon dragged my protesting body onto the quay.

The night bells did not ring the quarter hours as in the day, but myriad hours on the seaward wall assured me we were yet in the deeps of night.

Fix's fog yet drifted about the silent fortress. A light wind swirled the veils and pockets, making the Defender's task more difficult.

Senses alert, I scuttered along the quay in the direction that seemed right. No steps followed. Fix's door was exactly where it should be.

"Sssssshhh." A blade touched my neck and another pricked my back, nudging me forward. My hands flew up in surrender. Once the door closed behind us, the eye-searing magelight was not wholly unexpected.

"Greenshank!" Voices in front and behind spoke it together and with great relief.

The blades were withdrawn. The magelight dimmed. My muscles gratefully unclenched.

"He looks terrible," said Conall, the man in front of me.

"Seeing you here imp-proves matters."

Fire popped to life in Fix's brazier. Without invitation I dropped to my knees in front of it. The cold damp was making my back seize. Every shudder of depletion felt very like a new strike of the Order lash.

"It might be the only improvement," said the man beside the door, breathing hard. "Thou wert stealthy on thy approach?" The Xancheiran shoved a short sword into a sheath hung by the door.

"I was careful. It's g-good to see you up, Lord Siever."

"Prowlers patrol the docks," said Conall, throwing a blessedly dry cloak over my shoulders. "Dunlin was clever enough to swim in from outside the fog and bring back word. Don't know if someone spied the boats leaving or what. Fix's guest here"—he indicated Siever—"sent them on a merry chase. He does an astonishing imitation of the boatmaster."

"Nawt a man's ass is out in a fog like this'n," drawled Siever. The wind-rasp in his voice was perfect. And a twirl of his hand shifted the firelight so that I'd vow old Boatmaster Fix stood there instead of the tall, lordly Siever. It was not so much illusion as a reordering of light, like reflections in rippling water. Even better, it lacked the definitive sensations of illusion.

"More lightwork," I said, breathing in the glory of the magic.

Siever sagged onto one of Fix's stools. "Takes far too much out of me, though."

"And Fix?"

"Well hidden. But we can't bring in the boats while someone's watching," said Conall, crouching at my side. "And it's near midnight, which gives us no slack time. Fix has all he can manage with the fog."

"So we need another diversion." I blew a long exhale. "If you'll see to it, Conall, I'll take your place in the boat. I'm drained to the nubbins, but I'll need Fix's rubies later. And you'll do better covering if we're late back, as I can't modify the rowers' memories."

"Give me a quarter of an hour," said Conall, donning his cloak. "When you see fire on the mount, stutter the fog warning—three and one—and Heron will bring up the boats."

I appreciated that Conall didn't argue. And the sack of cheese and flask of ale they'd left me on the table was the gods' own benefice. The bells rang midnight. I cracked open the door and kept an eye on Idolon Mount while I ate and drank—likely far more than my share.

"Lord . . ." Siever had dozed off. Gods, I'd questions needed answering before I left.

Serena Fortuna provided. Wind swirled the flames in the brazier. Siever started, then wrapped his arms about himself and shook his head as if to clear it.

"I can open the trees," I blurted.

Siever's drooping head jerked up. "By the Goddess . . ."

"But Safia said we dared not repair the Severing while she and her fellows walked the land, lest they infect the true lands . . . and all this world . . . with Xancheira's sickness. She said we should take out your people, then seal off the portals and leave the Danae there to die."

"'Tis a dread ending for them." He shuddered. "Like to burning from the inside out. But certain, they no longer fulfill whatever purpose the Mother ordained. Never have humans lived in so close a friendship with the divine as we did in Xancheira. We presumed too much on that."

"I can't believe the only answer is to abandon them and leave the world broken. Is it true you might know how to undo the Severing?"

"In theory only." He poured himself a mug of ale and returned to the stool, rubbing his head tiredly. "My father created the Severing enchantments. He sickened early on. As he died, he repeated the undoing steps to me over and over. But I was very young, inexperienced, and angry, and I'd already lost my greater magic."

No wonder Siever refused to die.

"But you know how."

He glared in annoyance at his bony, tremulous fingers. "The tools to aid in the undoing were sent with the Wanderers to be hidden. Alas, none of these that dwelt with us have a notion what became of them. With the tools,

I might attempt it, though there's no assurance I'll regain the power necessary. Or live, to be perfectly frank. Thy knightly friend had to prop me up to guard the door."

"My grandsire was a historian," I said, grasping at hope. "He hunted Xancheiran artifacts for years, but only one remnant of your city did he ever find. Is it possible—?" I hated to risk the asking. "How would I recognize your father's tools?"

Siever lifted his head, his glance sharp. "He packed them in a small chest of painted wood alongside other objects that could tell Xancheira's story. Even if rescue never came, he'd not have us entirely forgotten."

My excitement could scarce be contained. "Objects like a wood spindle and an embroidered wedding *stola* that reveals how dual bents can reinvigorate a magical bloodline?"

"Merciful Goddess!" Siever sprang to his feet just as a burst of yellow flame on Idolon Mount cut through the fog.

For a moment I wasn't sure which had astounded him more.

"The *stola* and the spindle. By stone and sea, Remeni, the two together . . . *they* are the key!"

Conall's fire on the mount sufficed to draw off anyone who might have interfered with our loading the boats and setting out for the bay crossing. Whether it was Fix's cheese and ale or pure elation, I was able to take Conall's stern-seat oars *and* summon magic for navigating Fix's fog.

Despite the loaded boats, the row was not difficult, as the night was calm and the tide with us. Still, the normal swells had Juli and more than half the passengers sick. My sister curled up around her misery, her head on my foot.

Feeling more inclined to believe in divine interference than I had for years, I prayed fervently that Conall would come to no harm from his showy assistance and that Siever would thrive. We'd the means at hand to free the Xancheiran prisoners and reverse the breaking of the world.

Once I'd retrieved the *stola* from Bastien and got it to Siever, I'd acquire the silver splinters from the armory and take them to Signé. She needed time to get them distributed and for Siever to regain his strength. I couldn't assume I'd have power enough to help him work the magic.

Only one obstacle remained. We'd need to undo the Severing soon after opening the trees, for I could see no other way to feed so many or get them back to the greater world. Two hundred had near wrecked me. Twenty thousand would kill me a hundred times over. Which meant, if Safia spoke true, we'd have to find some way to ensure that Kyr and the silver Danae were not *walking the land* when Siever worked his magic. I hated the only solutions that came to mind.

But surely at sometime soon, we'd have a chance to set Xancheira free. The city would be a part of the living world again. Signé, her brother, and their people could take up their lives in the northland and, perhaps together with the Order, could take on the corrupt Registry—and Damon, if need be. For the first time, I dared imagine that such a healing might have some effect on Navronne's crippling winter.

Visions of grandeur, Greenshank! Damon likely started with such imaginings.

Yet the Danae were real; the void was real; and the decay of Xancheira and its people were real. Was it so mad to think such breakage as the Severing had caused some ill effect on the greater world, as well?

But, of course, all hope could end quickly. Damon and his gnarled plot awaited me at Cavillor.

As we entered the smoother water of the estuary, one of the Ciceron men who'd had some experience on the water agreed to take my oar. Grateful for the rest and the few moments peace, I scrunched down beside Juli, hauling her upright and tugging her damp cloak around her.

"Honestly, it helps to sit up and take deep, slow breaths," I said. "We're almost to the mainland and we've thinking to do. I understand you already know Coroner Bastien. He'll protect you as you head for Palinur. But you need to decide where you want to go after that."

"Will I ever see you again, Luka?" She leaned into my side, her spark considerably damped.

I would not lie to her. "Ah, *serena*, likely not. Beyond all this with Xancheira and the Danae, I'm involved in a game of power I don't entirely understand. It's all mixed up with the Registry and the princes' war and those awful things that happened in the months before I sent you away. If I lose, I'll be dead." Or worse.

"And if you win? Because I will never doubt you."

The flare of determination brought me a smile. Honesty did not require telling her how unlikely winning was when I didn't even know what winning meant. But, much as I wanted to console her, I had to speak what yet held my mind.

"My life cannot ever be what it was before, *serena*. I'm too much changed. I've found this place—good work to do that I'd like to think would make you and our family proud. But to do it well requires secrecy, anonymity, and leaving everything else—even family—behind."

"Sounds just like you." Her resentment was softened by her grip on my hand. "So what am I supposed to do?"

"Something extraordinary, I'll wager. It might require becoming someone else entirely. My name is too dangerous even to speak. For now, you must lie low. Which means—"

"I have to forswear you. Again. So that I can practice magic and keep our bloodlines alive. It didn't work before . . . well, the lying part didn't."

"Again? I don't—"

"That's exactly what you said when you sent me to Pons. You stood in that graveyard so broken, wearing that dreadful mask and chains, and you sent me away to your worst enemy. You were exactly right to do it. But I'm not so good a liar as you thought. It was just Serena Fortuna's blessing that Pons wanted to help us all along."

"She really did? You didn't *escape* her. . . ." So much of what Pluvius had said had been proven true—my grandsire's chest, his talk of a *wound in the world*, the significance of my dual bents—but I had never accepted his talk of the woman curator, Damon's protégé who had split with her devious mentor.

"She's not an easy woman. But she hid me, talked sense into me, sent me to the Mother's high priestess—the safest place in Palinur. She promised to see that you learned enough to survive. She said she'd fetch you back when the time was right, and clear your name and together you'd stand up to—" Juli stared up at me, her face pale in the starlight. "This game of power is about Curator *Damon*, isn't it?"

"Yes. And if Pons is secretly opposing him, she's in a very risky position. Curator Pluvius came here to fetch me away, claiming Pons sent him to warn me about Damon. I wasn't sure whether to believe him."

"Ugh. Pluvius tried to lure us into his *protection*. That's when you decided to send me off with the Cicerons. Prince Bayard's troops were laying the siege, and you were out of choices." Her face wrinkled into a frown. "Pons must be desperate to choose Pluvius for a messenger. Luka"—Juli sat up a little straighter—"I could go to her again, see what's what. If she's true, I could give her a message from you, tell her how she can find you . . . help you. She's a stone-hard witch, but she's truly powerful and believes you know things that could make purebloods . . . more honorable. That's her words. She refused to tell me more."

"She was right not to tell you. Holy gods, I never imagined—"

I wanted to reject Juli's offer. I preferred she hide and survive. But Pons might know more of Damon's plan and my place in it, and would surely have plotted her own strategy, lest I die or fail or lose myself along the way.

"Signal ho!" Dunlin's voice cried out from the lead boat.

Perhaps Fix was wrong about family.

"Truly, a few answers might make all the difference." None should have been able to hear anything we'd said, but I pressed my mouth to Juli's ear and drew a bit of enchantment around us. "Tell her this . . ."

In as few words as possible, I told of my strange mission as Damon's weapon to reshape the Registry, but sworn to justice, not the man; of my suspicions about the throne and the report I'd heard of coercion using my portraits. So short a time was not enough to tell all, but Juli knew a great deal on her own.

". . . and with what you can tell her of Xancheira and what we've done here, she should understand that Navronne's future rests in our hands. But please, *serena*, have a care. At the least sign of danger—"

Juli grabbed my hands and pressed them to her forehead. "To strike a blow for our beloved dead, to see you make right and honor grow from that horror, I will *not* fail. Hercule and the coroner will see me safe until Pons arrives in Cavillor. And I can tell Coroner Bastien whatever I find out. He'll be able to get it to you easier than I, especially once I'm in skirts and mask again."

"I'll arrange that with him."

All around us the rowers leapt into the water and dragged their boats into the muddy shallows of the middle estuary. Bastien watched from the upper bank as Hercule and others of the first party waded in enthusiastically to help their seasick friends go ashore, promising that fires and provisions waited just beyond the bank.

I jumped out and lifted Juli from the boat. As I carried her to solid ground, she flung her arms about my neck.

"Live," she said fiercely, "and swear to me that before the name Lucian de Remeni-Masson vanishes forever into myth and hero tales, you will tell me that you've done so."

"I can't promise—"

She gripped a handful of my hair. Came near yanking it out entire. "Swear it or I'll start screaming that a madman is posing as my brother!"

"All right," I said, my laughter laced with rue. Had the others in our family been so filled with spirit? "I swear it. And on that day you'll tell me what gods I offended to be birthed from the same parents as you!"

She wriggled and near leapt from my arms. It was surprisingly difficult to let her go. A part of me was no longer so empty as it had been. Perhaps our true lives were indeed graven in our bones, ready to recapture. I hoped.

"Hercule!" Juli called, catching the attention of the crowd. "Palinur's too far for all of us who've emptied our bellies in this wretched sea. I've heard favorable stories of a town called Cavillor. If I recall correctly from my lessons, it sits just inland from the port of Tavarre, which likely means it has a steady stream of sailors, merchants, and adventurers hungry for a taste of entertainments and games of chance. It could be a good way station on our journey home. . . ."

She chattered on to the Cicerons as I jogged back to the boats. The rowers awaited my orders.

"Well done," I said. "Check in with the boatmaster before you set foot in the fortress, else you'll have failed the exercise and will reap my Knight Commander's favored consequence—a month's tour on the seaward wall. If you've doubts as to your fitness for the crossing, speak now or the consequence will be doubled."

One of the tyros, a long-faced fellow with a bulging chin and heavy brow ridge, swallowed hard and raised his hand. "I'm flat, paratus." His speech quavered a little—a trait of ever-apprehensive tyros. "Had a bout of flux a few days since."

"No excuses. But better to speak now than after you're drowned. You"— I signaled my bow man, another of Conall's tyros—"will be a third in this honest man's boat. Trade off with him. Navigators and tails as before, save I won't be with you. I'll come after on my own, once I've seen our passengers off. Dunlin and Heron, lead out."

As soon as the small flotilla was under way, I joined Bastien at the top of the bank.

"You're sending the Cicerons to the place of the Sitting?" he snapped. "And your *sister*? Are you mad?"

"To the town, not the castle itself, and the Sitting's not for almost a month yet. Cicerons wander everywhere. And I don't *want* Juli there. But Pons will surely come for the Sitting, sooner or later. Juli knows her, respects her, and believes Pons can keep her safe and help us sort out this conspiracy. I'll be in Cavillor myself ten days from this. . . ."

I told him of my strange orders from the Marshal.

"I'm going to do exactly as he says—except for telling you and my ally back at the fortress. If Juli learns anything I need to know, she's trusting you to get it to me. Are you willing?"

"Told you I'd do what needs doing. There'll be a decent sop-house near the market. I'll stop in every night."

"Good. I'll share the rest of my news with you there. But first, I've someone needs to see the spindle. You have it?"

"Not leaving it in a sea cave, am I?" he grumped.

He rummaged in his sizeable rucksack—everything he owned, I supposed—and passed me a compact leather bundle tied with cord.

I tied it to my belt. "Thank you, coroner. To uproot yourself . . . to come so far to help in this business . . . It makes me wish I could remember more of our dealings."

"Some of them, you would as soon not," he said. "You were not a happy man. You didn't believe you and me could possibly get on, righteous prick that you were. But you . . . bent. Well, not the magical kind . . ."

"I understand. I've become a bit more flexible, I think. At least Cavillor will be a shorter journey for these people than Palinur." Which brought up the tender subject. "Where's Morgan?"

"Waiting just upriver where the bank joins a spur of rock. Keeping her distance so's not to spook them. She was hoping you'd come to her before you went back."

"Best I do that. Godspeed, Partner Bastien."

A grin split his thatch of a beard. "Watch your back, pureblood. I'm invested in you."

As he hurried back to the restless Cicerons, I picked a way through willow snags and slick alder roots along the muddy bank of the estuary. A few hundred paces upriver, Morgan sat atop a low rise, her gards like threads of indigo linking the stars one to the other. Across the splayed estuary, a reed forest whispered in the breeze. The beauty of the scene swelled my heart and slowed my steps halfway up the bank.

"Gentle Lucian," she said. "Are all who were so sadly marooned beyond the boundaries safely ashore? Thy sister, too?"

"Yes. The bay crossing was difficult for people unaccustomed to water travel, but they're ready to go onward. Bastien will tell you their destination."

As I resumed the short climb, she rose, her draping of spidersilk drifting on the air. The luminous gards and the background of stars made her very like a goddess in a temple painting. Until I saw her face.

Winter settled in flesh and bone. "Morgan, what's wrong?"

"I keep my bargain," she said, cool as frosted steel. "I trusted thee to do the same. To tell me of Sanctuary and of madness among our kind that must be remedied. I thought thee careful of the Everlasting. But it seems not."

With a glance behind me, she turned and walked into the starlight.

I whirled about and faced three blue-marked Danae, a glowering Tuari Archon in the center.

CHAPTER 35

"Thou'rt forsworn, sorcerer. Liar. Violator," said Tuari. "As every human before and after thee. Dost thou imagine us blind and deaf to the world? Over and over this very night hast thou violated our strictures, transporting humans across boundaries they were not meant to cross, corrupting the Everlasting in such fashion as breathes danger to all we know."

One of the archon's companions carried loops of vine rope. One held a bow with an arrow nocked. Tuari himself carried a thick branch.

"Morgan!" I bellowed over my shoulder, unwilling to take my eyes off the Danae.

"My daughter earns no grace amongst us any longer. Never fear, she will fulfill her noxious bargain before she pays the price of thy offenses. Does it please thee to think of her as vermin?"

"Of course it does not please me," I snapped. "I never meant for my ignorance to put her at risk. I've tried to learn of the world without jeopardizing her."

I dared not explain the Severing. Knowing what was done, Tuari might find a lingering thread that yet crossed it and destroy the silver Danae and imprisoned humans before we had them free. Surely Morgan would have told me if her father knew of the void. But then again, she had brought him here without warning me.

"Your treacherous daughter must have run out of patience with my human frailty."

"Dost thou deny her charges?" said Tuari, snarling. "Thou didst swear that the particular magic that damaged the boundaries was lost to thee. Thou didst swear to tell us of Sanctuary and our silver-marked kin as soon as they were found, and to lead us to this aberrant sentinel."

Tuari's companions moved to surround me. I edged backward, up the shallow spur of rock, keeping them in front. The terrain was slick with mosses and mud. Did I slip, our dance was done.

"I've regained my magic, as you've perceived," I said, "and spent it to recover those I sent across the boundary those seasons past when I had no understanding of my power. I thought they'd found the verdant beauty of the true lands. But instead they were trapped in a wasteland that could not nourish them. Mercy bade me retrieve them before they died there."

"This reeks of lies," spat Tuari, tossing his long braid. "What part of the true lands cannot nourish—even in these days of skewed seasons?"

He truly didn't know what had happened at Xancheira.

"Ask your daughter what she saw in the city portal. She did not deign to tell me what a *crack in the world* signified or who were the *beasts* who would come ravening. If the long-lived who understand these things will not tell me, then how am I to learn enough to satisfy you? Tell me what you'll do when you meet your kin who wear silver gards."

"No concern of any human are these matters. Hast thou spoken to the sentinel marked in silver since swearing thy oath?"

"Yes."

"Hast thou taken me to her?"

"No. But—"

"Then by thy own words art thou and my daughter condemned." Tuari spun his thick branch as if it were a twig. "Bind him to yon chestnut bole. Splay his hands. My stick shall break his fingers first . . . then wrists . . . then elbows. Only when he is ready to take us where we wish to go shall the breaking cease."

"That won't be so easy." I retreated another step, clasping my hands on my bracelets.

My power was naught but dregs. A firebolt . . . a leash . . . nothing worked. So, Fix's bracelet—

Blue-scribed arms clamped around me from behind, steel sinews pinning my arms and crushing the breath from me.

My head smashed backward, cracking fragile bone.

He bellowed, blood and phlegm gurgling. His grip loosened but did not drop.

I wrenched an arm free and slammed an elbow into his cheek. A quick follow with my forearm slammed a bull-thick neck.

My assailant staggered. Though blood poured from nose and mouth, he was still on his feet. But I didn't follow through with my fists. The three others charged like maddened bulls. I ran.

Drawing every scrap of strength from my legs, I sped across damp uneven ground, furrowed with rock spurs and clumps of vegetation. Surprise and quickness gave me the moment's advantage, but I'd no illusion that would last. Even using Fix's magic, I couldn't hide. Morgan had seen straight through my veil. And I would not kill them. To slay a guardian of nature's creation must surely wreak havoc—

An arrow whizzed past, scorching my cheek. I touched Fix's bracelet and my own and released a burst of fire and smoke behind me, then angled sharply seaward across the flats. Too much farther north and the low scarp separating me from the shore would become a cliff. Could Danae swim? Every natural being had a weakness. Morgan didn't tire; she ate rarely; she could vanish. There *were* places she wouldn't go. Indoors. And—

That was it! She'd admitted one tale of Danae weakness was true.

As the coast was so often foggy, the saltern had a blessed beacon that could guide me through the darkness. I dashed more directly seaward and circled wide. I needed to head back toward the lower estuary and the marshes to reach the Order's salt pans, but I couldn't let my pursuers know my destination too soon lest they cut across the flats to intercept me instead of following.

My feet tripped on a lump of broken ground. Stumbling forward, I used Fix's power to cast a faint magelight, colored deep so as not to ruin what night seeing I had. The beating, the rowing, and lack of sleep weighed on my legs like shackles. But I ran. Tuari would leave my bones dust.

By the time the beacon prickled my skin, the Danae's bare feet were pounding in my ears. I dared not look back, lest I see an arm reaching for me. Where to lead them? They likely wouldn't enter the boiling-hut. And with the recent storm, the brine in the pans might be too dilute. I needed crystals—a lot of them.

Past the hut stood a ruin of sandstone blocks, little more than two half walls and two leaning pillars sunk in the ground, evidence that this place had been used to harvest salt for centuries before the Order came. I jumped from a ragged line of sand blocks into the shallow well of the ruin and darted into the shelter of the fallen columns. Breathing hard, I let my magelight die.

The five Danae leapt over the wall as if they weighed no more than goose-down, landing softly in the pit.

"Hiding in a hole like a rabbit?" spat Tuari.

I backed into the deepest corner of the ruin. Those who worked the salt in ages past had used clay for their pans, vessels, hearths, and countless jars to transport the sea's gift. What remained was a heap of clay shards, clay dust, and plenteous salt. Crystals that could bind a Dané in place.

"Force me out!" I said, trying to slow my heaving lungs. "Bring your mighty sticks and arrows against a sorcerer."

With a gout of power borrowed from Fix's bracelet, I raised a fierce beam of magelight, focused exactly on their faces. Surely, even Danae could be blinded in the dark.

"Perhaps we could talk about this like reasonable souls," I said behind my light, watching the angry Danae enter the sheltered corner. My assailant's broken face yet dripped blood—as red as my own. "I'll not come out unless you drag me."

They came in a half circle: one, two, three . . .

"Archon, wait!" bellowed one, staring down at his bare feet. He shuffled, but could move only a few steps forward or back, like a hound on a short leash.

"I shall not—" The archon strode onto the spoil heap, arm raised to shade his eyes, until he, too, looked down. Appalled. "What have you done, sorcerer?"

"Prevented your crippling a man who only wishes to be of service," I said. "One who seeks answers for the world's disorder. One who cares a great deal about your daughter."

"So thou'lt leave us here to die."

"Crushing my joints with your stick is a surer death sentence for a human than this for you," I said. "If you agree to a new bargain, I'll tell Morgan where you are. Hear this: Before year's end, when *I decide* I have learned enough of consequences, I shall take you to the place where I saw the silver-marked sentinel. The sentinel's choice to speak with you is her own, and the matter of your dealings is between you and her, but at that time you will declare my oath upheld and we shall speak together as honorable beings about my magic. Until then, you will refrain from punishing your daughter or me or *any human* for my offenses."

"What value is a bargain made with one party held against his will?"

"The same value as a bargain tricked upon a party immersed in ignorance as I was in Palinur. As you knew very well."

He fought to step free of the spoil heap. When his sinews yielded the struggle, he cast a final furious lash. "Thou shalt ever be an enemy of our kind."

"I would regret that more than I can express," I said. "The beauty and grace of the long-lived bring your own divine magic to the world. But I will not be a party to a confrontation whose result I cannot see, especially when it is approached with such spite and grievance as yours."

"Thou'lt never speak with my daughter again."

"That is between you and Morgan. This night has shown me her true loyalty, so I doubt you have aught to fear."

"It is a bargain . . . your saying." Tuari Archon's disgust told me I'd chosen rightly.

"Will you wait until Morgan returns from her journey, or is there something I can do to set you free sooner?"

Tuari's face twisted into deeper hatred, if such was possible. To admit need of a human's help must certainly gall him.

"Water."

I bowed—without mockery—and clambered over the red mound of clay and salt well out of their reach. There was no water nearby save that in the tide-filled brine pans. I filled an empty jug with it. Several jugs of small beer sat in the boiling-hut, ready for those who worked to stoke the fires and collect the salt. If the water's purpose was to dissolve the salt around their feet, either should do. I sat for a moment to slake my thirst with a sizeable portion of the beer—and, ungenerously, to let Tuari stew a bit.

Then I hauled the two jugs into the ruin. "One is seawater; one is a mild brew of barley and herbs. Use as you see fit."

I set the jugs just out of their reach and climbed out of the ruin. Let them work at it a little. Tuari yet clutched his stick.

By the time I reached the boat, the marshes were deserted, the Ciceron fires ash, and my knees jellied with weariness. The air bore the certain freshness of dawn. I would be late back to the fortress again after rowing against the final onslaught of the surge—a dangerous crossing when I was unfit. And a second lashing or confinement would follow a public return. Either consequence could see me dead or near enough as to leave me useless. The only way to avoid those dangers was to wait out the daylight hours, replenish my magic, and sneak in after nightfall.

After a feast of fish and a full day of sleep, and no interference from searchers or troublesome Danae, I made good time across the bay. Night and cold rain veiled Evanide. I scuttled up the quay to Fix's cottage. As I lifted my hand to touch the latch, the door swung open.

"No blades this time?" I said, once the door closed behind me.

"Perhaps another taste of the lash suits better for a habitual miscreant," said Fix, as his brazier burst into flame and lamplight bloomed from over his table. The surge of power that effected these things was weak for the Knight Defender.

"Had I attempted a crossing this morning, I would have floated out to sea without a boat," I said. "Four times across the Severing void will take it out of a man."

He blew a scornful note. "Try holding a true fog for fifteen hours, then scraping a night's memory from eight half-minded tyros and two parati." Indeed his eyes were bleary and his shoulders tight. "Make your next rescue mission a shorter excursion, if you please. Better yet, do it somewhere else."

"That's entirely likely," I said. "Is Siever—?" I inclined my back as the Xancheiran emerged from the shadows, bearing a mug, fragrant and steaming. "Lord Siever, I've brought you a gift."

Setting the mug aside, he perched on a stool and carefully unwrapped the *stola* and its spindle. "Ah, Greenshank, thou dost intend to challenge me!"

"So this is the artifact," said Fix, peering over the Xancheiran's shoulder. "The bit of linen that could change the world, as well as repair it?"

"Though the genealogy is truth enough to upend the Registry, 'tis the spindle itself is the key to the Severing," said Siever, running his fingers over the spindle.

A whisper of elegant magic revealed raised sigils on the smooth, dark wood.

"A few of the names in the genealogy are contrived to guide the spellwork. I'll need pen and paper to work out the steps."

"I was hoping to take the *stola* to Cavillor," I said. "I might need the evidence."

"Better we keep it safe," said Fix. "Draw it from memory if you need. Even a fool of a curator will understand why it was too risky to carry."

Once Fix shoved a writing case and a few sheets of parchment in front of him, Siever retreated from the world. The Defender left him to it and joined me at the fire. He tossed a few strips of dried meat into my lap and wagged his head. "So much that we believed of ourselves. . . . How is this possible?"

"Two centuries of blood," I said, relishing the salt and savory of the leathery morsels. "And we're not done with it yet. . . ."

Over the next hour, I told him all I'd learned from Bastien and Safia. I described the horror of the silver Danae's torment of the Xancheirans, my broken pact with Morgan, and the new one I'd squeezed from Tuari. And lastly, I told him of my interview with the Marshal and my orders to desert the fortress and join the Marshal in Cavillor. So intense was Fix's listening and his questioning, he could likely have recited every scrap of my telling back to me.

It was the story of the Marshal shook him most. "You think the Knight Marshal could be a Pretender of Caedmon's own blood. . . . A man of honor who can make even a tyro believe he could be worth something in this world. Stone and sea, what a king he would make."

"But, Fix, *is* he a man of honor? Tell me why the Marshal everyone believes in—a knight of the Order we claim to value—destroyed my relict and set Magrog's own trap spell for anyone to trigger. He overlooked the fact that Damon allowed the slaughter of my family and allowed the corruption of my magic to go unchallenged. This is not just personal grievance . . . honestly. Thanks to the Marshal, I feel no personal grieving for my dead, only this monstrous outrage. I've no choice but to come to terms with that, but I need to know why the Marshal believes that Damon's purposes—cleansing the Registry? putting a sorcerer on Caedmon's throne? putting *him* on the throne?—are worth such abandonment of right. And are those purposes worth violating the Order's mission? The Order was founded to remedy injustice, not impose our will upon anyone."

Fix blew a long exhale. "They've certainly not confided in me."

"It's all conjecture, of course," I said. "I didn't see him invoke the medallion's magic or learn what evidence they might possess that would authenticate it."

"Could *you* affirm it?"

That gave me pause. I wasn't in the habit of considering myself a historian. "In theory, yes. But who would believe me? Registry records say my bent for history was excised by my own Head of Family. The Three Hundred believe me a murderer. And Damon has never admitted that I have any bent beyond portraiture. Makes me doubt he plans for me to use it. Publicly, at least."

Recalling the curators' coercion in the Registry cellars gnawed my gut.

"If I'm to play this out, I need to be on my way to Cavillor," I said. "It's two hundred quellae more or less. I'm to go afoot, and I certainly can't count on Morgan to speed my steps."

Every time I recalled Morgan's stony face and the contempt in her accusations, I tried to be angry with her. But, in truth, it was my own foolishness had led to our break. She had warned me that she answered to her archon as I answered to my commanders. I just hadn't wanted to consider what that meant.

"Before I go, I need to fetch the silver splinters from the armory, get them to Signé, and come up with a plan to contain the silver-marked Danae before Siever works his magic."

"Twenty thousand freed prisoners. I doubt you have to worry about a few Danae." No sooner had Fix said this than he rolled his eyes very much as my sister and Bastien did. "But that's too simple, isn't it?"

"Slaughtering Danae is out of the question. According to the coroner, Safia told me that my magic was the answer to a long waiting by my own kind *and* hers. At that time, at the least, she believed they could be saved . . . healed . . . whatever it takes. Perhaps she's fallen into despair the way Kyr has . . . and Signé has."

"That's so."

I whipped my head around. I'd almost forgotten Siever was there.

"When their gards began to fade, the long-lived visited the Sanctuary pool repeatedly. To our grief and theirs, it didn't help them. Many have vanished over the years. We assume they died, or were buried by their own. We rarely see them all together, but estimate there are but thirty or forty of them left."

"*Sanctuary,*" I said, feeling an idiot not to have thought of it. "Could they be healed there?"

"They'd drown as a human would," said Siever. "They cannot release their physical form and exist in the pool as is their true nature."

"But if you could reverse the Severing . . . Safia said her people could not be *walking the land* when the Severing was undone, else their sickness would pass to the greater world. But if they were *in* the pool when it became linked to the greater world—when it becomes Sanctuary again—then maybe they *could* do as they were made to do."

"Mayhap. 'Twould be a delicate dance. And whoever is convincing them to try would likely find himself a sapling after all. Thankfully, I can stay this side the void. This magic can be worked from either."

Fix shook his head. "Madmen. All of us. I've long concluded those who come to the Order are already lunatics. And Lord Siever, you most assuredly belong amongst us. As for you, Greenshank"—he jumped up and opened a clothes chest so weathered it might have been constructed when the Order was founded—"you've no need to visit the armory. Charge the entire length at once and then shatter it yourself."

He tossed me a silver disk that gleamed in the firelight—a thick, weighty coil of fine silver wire, the whole about the diameter of my hand. To infuse the wire with a receptor—a simple spell to accept a flow of magic—and shatter it into at least twenty-five thousand magically linked splinters was easy after my day's sleep. Brushing them into a fist-sized cloth bag took longer.

"I'll take them to Signé tonight. You know, lord"—I turned to Siever—"we have to make this work. Bringing two hundred souls across near drained me past recovering. It would take years to bring the rest. I can free them from the trees, but they must be able to walk into the greater world on their own."

Siever studied his pen. "If I fail, everyone I know—my children, my wife, the friend of my youth who is my good lord—will remain locked away forever or starve. I am sufficiently motivated. 'Tis the time—"

"If I could conjure us more time, I would," I said. "But whatever is to happen in Cavillor between now and the first day of autumn, I have to be there." And instead of the hospice door, my bent must take me across the void, as it had done from the Tower prison and from Bastien's necropolis. I'd best speak with Safia to ensure she would allow me past her boundary.

"Lord Siever will get what help he needs," said Fix.

"So, how am to I know when your spellwork's ready?" I said.

"Give me my bracelet," said Fix. "I'll signal you."

"Across *two hundred quellae*?" I could be all the way to Cavillor by that time. The links of the memory-wipe tokens would not work a spell beyond fifty or sixty *paces*. The declaration spell on the Marshal's location token required us to be closer than a quellé. Even the simplest beacon signals we used on the rocks in Evanide's bay could span a few quellae at most.

Fix glared at me in his most condescending manner. Of course he could do what he said. The rubies on his silver bracelet glittered as I pulled the band from my arm and passed it over.

"Understand that this will work for one exchange only," he said, squinting as he manipulated the band of silver in some way I couldn't see. "You don't want to know what it takes to generate a spell over such a distance. Wait for our signal. When you, in turn, are ready to make the passage to Xancheira, infuse the same point on the bracelet, so Lord Siever can judge when to begin his invocation. You can send only one signal. So be sure."

He returned the bracelet. A tiny embossed star pulsed green, then faded, waiting for magic. I raised my sleeve and crimped the band about my upper arm.

Fix glanced at me sidewise, then touched the star. Some sharp edge of the silver pricked my skin. Before I could interpret the spark in Fix's eye and the quirk of his mouth, the cottage disintegrated. . . .

Shards of color, fragments of light, stone, flesh, thought whirled into a great smear like spilled paint . . . spinning, condensing, the entirety of the world winding tighter and narrower until it pierced the flesh of my arm like a red-hot nail pounded into the very bone.

Abruptly, the structure of the world reasserted itself, and all was as it had been. The cottage. The fire in the brazier. Siever at the table. Fix's hand that gripped my other arm prevented dizziness toppling me. "Come, come, it's not *that* horrible," he said.

Siever stared at the two of us. "By the Mother, what was that?"

A good thing he asked. The words would have dribbled from my tongue with no more substance than foam.

"When one is dealing with a critical sequence of events to restore the world's health," said Fix, "one does not assume things such as 'Fix's bracelet will be with me when the time comes.' It was a simple threading. Only a tiny splinter of the bracelet, not the whole thing, which is a much more . . . mmm . . . violent experience. But if the bracelet itself is lost, the spell will remain."

Threading. A tentative finger shifted the bracelet. It moved. But where it had been a pinpoint of green pulsed. The color faded, but not the sensation of the sliver of metal embedded in my flesh or its threaded enchantment that extended from the skin of my arm all the way to the pit of my stomach. When I examined the spot in the firelight, I saw . . . imagined? . . . the glint of silver in my flesh.

Fix continued as if such things happened every day. "Signal us *before* you cross. Certainly this link won't reach across a crack in the world. So how long does Lord Siever wait after that signal to begin the undoing?"

Blinking, breathing as hard as if I'd just run the mudflats, I wrestled my thoughts into order. To estimate how much time I'd need to prepare for Siever's attempt to rejoin Xancheira to the greater world was akin to estimating how many invisible apples it would take to fill the maw of the wind. The crossing would depend on Safia. Once in Xancheira, I'd have to feed power to the linked splinters in the trees. Deal with the aftermath of freeing twenty thousand people. Persuade or force thirty or forty or sixty silver Danae into the Sanctuary pool. And then there was the skewed spending of time. "A day, more or less, by Evanide's reckoning?"

So I'd have three hours to make it work.

"Then I'd best get back to it," said Siever. "Go with the Goddess, Lucian."

But as he bent his head to the spindle and the *stola*, it was my turn to remind a man of his limits. "You need to sleep and eat as well, lord."

"Yes." He didn't look up.

Fix walked me to his door. "The Marshal does not give me orders," he said, "but I was advised that even though the entirety of the Order, including tyros, squires, parati, and combat-trained adjutants, is to muster elsewhere, the Knight Defender will not be needed. What does that say to you?"

"That despite the harsh tenor of our exercises at Val Cleve, they are not expecting much of a fight. They're to be a show of force. . . ."

"That is my estimate, as well. Skirmishes, perhaps. Demonstrations of our capabilities, perhaps. Controlled strength. If fortress rumors bear truth, which is usually the case unless I start them myself, the road to Palinur is supplied for a march."

"I heard that one as well," I said. "Perhaps an escort for a new king. The Order could put down any small resistance, but there is no plan for siege, no need for your kind of power. Or your judgment?"

"Be ever watchful, Greenshank. Find out what they're up to and get out again. We can decide how to respond once we know. Will you leave tonight?"

"Be sure of it. This visit to Xancheira should be quick. Then I'll need to fetch my bow, a few supplies, a map."

"The boatmaster cannot supply you a boat, since he has no idea of your orders," said Fix.

I ducked my head in acknowledgement. "I'd thought of caching my blades outside of Cavillor. I hate being without."

"Leave them here. If Damon commands you travel in this very anonymous and specific way, then he has something up his sleeve. He could join you at any time. He knows you can defend yourself, feed yourself."

"And using magic to stay alive will leave a trail for him to follow." Gods, what was the man planning? "I hope to arrive at Cavillor early enough to spy out the place, make sure Bastien is there and—"

"And your sister." Fix crossed his arms and breathed exasperation. "Do you see how that diverts your attention? We leave families, friends, and lovers behind for very specific reasons."

"I understand. But I can't pretend she's not a part of my life." I sank to one knee and pressed my fist to my breast. "*Dalle cineré*, Knight Defender."

"*Dalle cineré*, Paratus Greenshank." He laid his hand on my head and my every hair stood on end, as if he were no man, but rather embodied lightning. "Hold tight to your rage. Let it give you strength, but not control that strength. May Kemen Sky Lord, the Goddess Mother, and Deunor Lightbringer stand with you, as I do, in this hour of our need. May it be an hour of justice and right."

All was blackness beyond the Severing void. Yet my feet touched solid ground. I rocked the heel and toe of my boot to assure it and crouched to feel the dusty paving stones of the citadel atrium. The air bore the scents of soil, dry leaves, and herbs, but not a sound creased the silence. No trickling water. No breath. No glimmer of light revealed the layered gardens. Even when my initial panic subsided, dread replaced it.

Goddess Mother, was I too late? Were they all gone to trees?

The impossibilities of altering the rescue plan wreaked havoc in my gut, as I felt my way toward the outer doors.

"Remeni!" Even without the soft glow of a lantern, I would have recognized Signé's richly layered voice coming from behind me. A very angry Signé. "What are you doing here?"

"Told you I'd come back. But gods' breath, lady, are you the only one left? And your gardens . . ."

"Kyr stopped at ten new prisoners yesternight; he just wanted to make his point. After the burst of magic when you left, he took five more and said he'd take the rest did we not quench every remnant of magic in the citadel."

"The Simmonis pipe . . . your garden spellwork . . ." And there were only two-and twenty Xancheirans left free, doomed to starve the sooner without their scraps of magic.

"And now you've blundered in and what will I tell him when next he comes to the gates?"

"Tell him you were searching for other things that might offend him. You opened a chest, uncovered a crate of spelled jewels, whatever you can think of. Because very soon, we're going to open the trees and walk into the greater world. I can set your brother and the rest of them free, Signé. And once we have them out, Siever is going to undo the Severing. Xancheira will exist again."

She stood only a few steps away, but without the lamp dangling at her side, I wouldn't have known it, so still and silent she was.

"Lady?"

"We'll pay a terrible price for this foolery."

"Didn't you hear what I said? We can save them all. The same magic I use to cross the void can open the trees. And then . . . my grandsire found the cache Siever's father sent with the Wanderers. All these years I've had the key your people needed to undo the Severing and had no idea of it. Siever says his father taught—"

"Siever has practiced no magic in twenty years," she snapped. "And how do you know that you can open the trees? *Safia* told you, didn't she? She is mad, Lucian. She swears she will never bring Benedik out again because of your disrespect. Besides, Kyr can never permit this. Without the trees to consume their energies, unable to make new sianous or enter Sanctuary, his people will suffer horribly until they die. So they'll imprison you and the rest of us and let the trees start dying one by one until our punishment satisfies Kyr. They've done it before."

A slap to the face could be no colder. But I could not relent.

"Our first plan worked, lady. The Wanderers walk the lands of Navronne right now. My sister, too. I grieve for this dread price you've paid, but I believe Safia. She told me that I should follow the Path of the White Hand to prove my fitness—and I did, maturing in magic and strength along the way so that I'm able to do this. She told me I could save the people here by taking them across the boundaries of the world—and she was right. Yes, she is as sick as the others, but she has never guided me ill, and she desperately wants your brother to go free. She accepts that she and her kind will die here, telling me to transport you all, leave the void unrepaired, and seal the portals so they can't get out. But we can do better. Siever and I can set all of you free—Xancheirans and Danae, too. We just can't do it alone."

"What would you have us do?" Though she expressed no optimism, I took this as a step forward.

I pulled out the bag of enchanted splinters and explained about placing them in the trees. ". . . so I can stand here with one of these splinters, infuse it with magic, and open them all at once. And if Siever can do what he believes, then soon after, we shall rejoin Xancheira to the greater world."

"We dare not," she said, shaking her head in denial. "Even in madness, Kyr's nature is to tend the land. He says that if Xancheira is rejoined to the world, this sickness will poison the Everlasting. Your people and the rest of the long-lived will suffer with us. All will starve and beg to go to the trees."

"Only if the long-lived yet walk the land when the void closes . . ." And so I told her about our hope that if the Danae were in the Sanctuary pool, they would have a chance to heal as well.

"They'll never go. I wish it. Certain, I desire such a resolution. But they never will."

"Give them no choice. They're strong and elusive, but you'll outnumber them. You know them. Kyr and the others of the long-lived were your friends. *You* must convince your people to bring them safely to the Sanctuary pool. If your brother asks, Safia will help."

"You've no idea. . . . Benedik can scarce remember how to walk when he comes out of the tree."

"If the worst comes, you have weapons, and I've skills. . . . I know it's difficult to hope. Truly this plan is risky for all of us, and ill chance could yet see us fail. But this—all of this here—is wrong. You and your people are gifted in so many ways. You should be able to experience your magic's glory and share it freely with the rest of the world as you tried before. And the long-lived have their own gifts, awful and mysterious as they are, and this mad perversion is not of their own will. My bent allowed me to witness the pact they made with your people, and it was glorious and holy. We have a chance to make things right. We *must* try."

I pressed the bag of silver splinters into her hand. "A splinter for every tree. Save one for me. And maybe a few extra. They're easy to drop."

"Signé!" The bellowing came from outside the citadel.

"Kyr." Signé shoved the lantern at me and urged me toward the downward stair. "Go quickly."

"But I need to speak with Safia. . . ."

"Too dangerous. We can't lose any more of us if we're going to spread these."

Sweet Goddess! "Then, please, find her. Tell her that when Siever's spellwork is ready, I'll have to come here *the old way*. I need to travel away from the hospice, so she *must* let me through the boundary when my magic thins it."

Without a word, Signé slammed the bronze door behind me and her brisk steps vanished.

Leaving Fortress Evanide in the deeps of the night was far more painful than I had imagined. Rather than just another step on an impossibly long list that could be titled *Impossible Matters for Greenshank to Deal With*, it felt a lonely and fearful break. No matter my words to Juli, I wasn't sure I would ever have a place here again. Or if anyone would.

A group of squires huddled around a magelight lamp in the Hall, laughing and telling stories of their days as stupid tyros, while exhausted tyros slept or shivered, wakeful beneath the tables. A knight sat on a stool picking out a pensive melody on a cittern. On another night, I would have stopped to listen, or tell a stupid training story of my own, or comfort one of the terrified beginners as Cormorant had comforted me. But I wasn't one of them any longer. They must not see me, lest someone pinpoint the hour of my leaving.

I wished I could speak to Inek. But the Archivist worked at all hours, so I dared not venture the Archive Tower. Nor could I do my duty by Dunlin and Heron and pass off their training to someone else. Everyone would believe I'd run away after the beating. I hated that. Had Fix wiped Conall's mind of the night's events as well? Safer if he had.

I left my useless half relict behind, along with my dagger and sword bearing the Order blazon. Of Order garb, only my gray mask with the green threads came with me. The Marshal hadn't said one way or the other and I felt naked without it. Someone—maybe Conall—had left a clean shirt of thick gray wool on my pallet. It went on over my filthy layers, and my blood-stained leathers over that. A sketched map of possible routes to Cavillor lay on my clothes chest. Fix? Or the Marshal?

My bow went into its canvas case. My supply of a dozen arrows, in their own canvas wrap, would have to do. A flask of clean water and a few provisions stolen from the kitchen went into a small rucksack. The Marshal's token went into my waist pocket along with the few coppers I'd been allotted for the mission to Ynnes. Heavy cloak. Thick gloves. I hated being weighed down with them, but snow would fly any day now, especially in the upland vales where I was headed.

Fix's cottage was dark as I passed it by. I didn't stray from the deepest shadows of the quay to see if Siever was yet working, and I let the currents carry me away from the dock before setting to with the oars, so none could say they heard me go. It felt as if yet another piece of my soul was ripped away.

PART IV
THE GLORY TO BANISH GRIEF

CHAPTER 36

Demon winter arrived with the Hunter's Moon—the last full moon before autumn—descending with a fury the third morning of my trek to Cavillor. Scouring wind drove sleet so violently, it could cut flesh. By midday, I had to shelter in a mound of rocks lest I lose the road.

I'd already chosen to parallel the coast road up through Ynnes, the fish town where I'd glimpsed Bayard and Sila Diaglou, and on toward Tavarre. From there it was straight east to Cavillor. It was a slightly longer route than cross-country, but easier going for a man afoot and easier to keep my bearings in bad weather. With a day given to the Ciceron rescue and another to the storm, I could afford no more delays.

Only a lunatic would consider strict obedience to the Marshal's orders. How would he or Damon know if I slept in a sop-house in Tavarre or begged bread from a farmwife? But as with so much I'd done at Evanide, I believed the journey to be a test of some kind. The reason for it might be worthy, might not. But this was Damon's game and I was determined to play it. It was late to be reconsidering.

Two great strands of history had converged in me, warping my life beyond recognition. Against all belief, my peculiar combination of magics could dissolve the separation of the human world and the world of sacred myth, and I held a secret that could change the order of pureblood lives . . . all lives . . . in Navronne. Woven together, those strands spoke the possibility of the divine gift cleansed of corruption, and redemption for the terrible wounds my people had caused. If I were to break either of those strands now, if I refused to move forward or gave up the fight to save both Xancheirans and the Danae, I would spend the rest of my days wondering what might have been had I pushed a little further, a little harder. And for better or worse, arrogant, calculating Attis de Lares-Damon sat directly in my path, whether a gateway or an obstacle I still was not sure.

Snow and sleet reverted to cold, drenching rain, and I began to think the weather would defeat me sooner than Damon or the Danae. By the fifth morning my cheese and barley-flour biscuits had given out. Hunting hare or roe deer took far too much time, yet I dared not skimp on food or what sleep I could get. Nor did I dare use more magic than what kept me alive. Imagining the amount of power it might take to inflame twenty thousand silver splinters left me edgy. Fix and Siever could signal me at any moment.

My fitful sleeps were filled with dreams of Morgan. Lustful dreams, fearful dreams of crushed bones and hard green eyes, dreams that spilled into waking, for I imagined flickers of lapis and indigo among limestone scarps or deep in thickly treed gullies. But no one answered my challenges. Nor did I smell meadowsweet, or sense Morgan's presence or hear the eagle's yip that signaled her friends' approach. But I never closed my eyes without an arrow in hand.

One triumphant morning, I shot a wayward ryegoose. The wood I could find in the scattered copses was so wet, even magic could not keep it burning, so I ate the fatty bird half raw and was grateful for it.

Filthy, unshaven, and cold to the marrow, I felt increasingly raw, too, not just in every place wet wool and leather abraded tender flesh, but in spirit. I longed to gut Damon like a fish next time I saw him. That Damon would be unbothered by such hatred made it all worse.

Nine days on and no signal had come from Fix. Had Siever failed? Had Signé been able to distribute the splinters? What if she, too, was a tree by now? No alternatives came to mind. The anger I'd managed to keep buried behind schemes of rescue and salvation devoured me, driving me onward through the bitter night until my every bone ached.

Please gods, the next night I would be in Cavillor. Please gods, Bastien would tell me Juli was safe and had discovered what all this was about. Please gods, Damon's throat would be under my hands. Was anyone ever such a fool?

Sometime near midnight, after I had ensured, yet again, that no Danae lurked in the trees, a large insect whizzed past my head. And then another. A third stung my cheek. A beast started braying as exhaustion consumed me. . . .

Gods, my head! It hammered like the armorer's favorite mallet. Even my eyelids ached. Nasty grit caked lips and tongue. I spat and drew in my forearm to wipe my mouth, only to find it slathered with . . . muck?

"Doan ye move, cocksman!"

The girl wasn't on top of me, but was close enough to be a danger. And someone near my feet tugged on my cloak. The stink and a nearby wattle fence named the half-frozen ground under me farmyard.

"Not moving," I mumbled. "Just getting my face out of the mud."

Twisting my neck, I squinted into wan sunlight. A scrawny girl, her flimsy cotte and drooping hat stuffed with straw, tugged at a goat by a rope around its neck. The damnable beast was chewing my cloak.

I booted the beast in its muzzle.

The goat bawled as the girl hauled it backwards, leaving both of them well out of arm's reach. Rough-skinned and bony, the girl might have been twelve or twenty.

I made to rise. She wrapped the goat leash around one arm and yanked a mattock from her belt.

"Doan git up or I'll crown ye with my friend here," she said. Her mattock reminded me of how abruptly sleep had overtaken me.

"*Crowned* me already maybe," I snapped, feeling around for a bump on my head. "Prince of Dunces. What kind of witch are you?"

One who could sneak up on an Order paratus and clobber him? Gods, had I even set wards last night? Stupid, stupid to drive myself to carelessness.

"I'm no witch. And I didn't whack ye. Found ye just now when come to milk here goat. Figgered ye for a drunk." She jutted her sharp chin my way. "What's wrong with yer face?"

No use explaining that drunk wasn't possible. Or that a goat with the wrong parts wasn't going to give her much milk. Instead of scaring the girl into answers, I remained where I was, ready to spring should events warrant. She'd likely talk more if I let her keep the upper hand.

"Just cold, wet, and ugly," I said.

Her eyes slid away from the mask, diverted by its *obscuré*. My head felt like to split, and my left cheek was grossly swollen. Pressing it rattled boulders in my skull. There had been insects whizzing. . . .

"You see anyone with me?" I said.

"Naught. But ye best scat afore my da comes to trim ye like an irksome donkey. Da's a brute with any's lustin' after me."

"I don't tangle with fierce girls. I'm just a traveler got whacked by highwaymen."

Highwaymen with a poison dart of some kind and such practiced aim as to hit me by starlight. I assessed my possessions. The straps of the rucksack were in my hand, as if I'd been carrying it. My gloves, soaked with goose blood, were gone. My cloak was tangled under me in the mud. To my relief and puzzlement, my silver bracelets were intact, as were my boots, the Marshal's token, and my few coppers. Only one other object was missing.

"I want my bow back." I'd no time to waste hunting it. "Give you a copper for it."

"Did'n see a bow. Wudda took the copper were I a thievin' kind. I work; I get paid. Now git." She raised the mattock again. "Best you waked when you did. I were gonna trim yer balls myself. Or maybe just crush 'em. Done my uncle. Done my cousin." She slammed the mattock against a section of wattle fence, sending stakes and twigs flying.

I believed her. The bow was longer than she was tall, and no matter her strength with the mattock, she'd never be able to draw it. Best she forget about me.

So I crawled away, reprising Siever's song of merry, merry Cilla, as if pickled in mead. Once through a wide gap in the fence, I scrambled to my feet. The girl stood there alone, clutching the bleating goat. The slovenly cot behind her had half its roof caved in, and not a wisp of smoke rose from it. A crow settled atop the broken peak squawking, mocking us both.

"Are you lone?" I called back to her. "Do you need help?"

"Git!"

I didn't begrudge the girl my gloves did she have them. Maybe she'd burnt the bow to keep warm. But I'd wager someone had dragged me into the farmyard. Hoofprints—some that looked like horse prints, some like donkey prints—and fresh droppings marked a well-used tread through an ash copse. A fold of ripped canvas poking out from the muddy track proved to be my canvas bow case.

Why would a mounted thief, a practiced person with access to a poison dart, steal my bow and—I quickly counted—three arrows, while leaving me three silver bracelets, one set with rubies?

The trail led all the way to the road. And at the point just before the track and the road intersected in the trampled grass of a wagon camp, my bow dangled from a leafless beech, as if the thief had hung it in the tree after dropping me in the farmyard. As if to make sure I saw it.

There was certainly no use to it anymore. The springy yew was snapped a third of the way down its graceful curve. And there were marks . . . blood?

A closer examination revealed words scratched awkwardly in the smear of dry blood:

For the girl child.

Not the goat girl, who was an accident. No one would call Juli a child. We'd lost no Ciceron children that I knew. This deed spoke of deliberation, not vengeance. I'd been left alive and away from the road where little harm could befall. I rubbed my cheek, where only the prick yet stung. The swelling and the headache already seemed less. A girl child . . .

And then my sluggish mind recalled a scrap of parchment, a portrait of world-weary eyes, and a fierce young man's pledge of service. Fallon de Tremayne, Damon's military aide, had promised to repay me for identifying his young half-sister's murderer. Which suggested *who*, but not *why* or *why in such odd fashion.*

The unresolved mystery left me doubly wary that day. I kept entirely to the stands of trees alongside the road, and I stretched my senses farther—forward, behind, and to every side. A snapped stick, a rustle of leafless twigs, a plop of mud, a soft footstep . . . every sound fired my nerves.

Damon wanted me alone, raw, angry, and armed with a bow. He had accomplished all but the last. When my route joined that of the deep, fast-flowing river Oscur that twined around the town of Cavillor and the castle that overlooked it from a rocky height, I broke the useless weapon into smaller pieces and threw it in.

Cavillor was crowded between a thick forest of oak and beech and the river Oscur. Its massive walls and the hilltop castle embraced by a bend of the river left it in little danger from marauding Harrowers or common bandits. Even three years of war had left it unscarred. No doubt the fact that its lord was a pureblood sorcerer had a deal to do with that.

As the town bells rang the twilight warning, I joined the queue of travelers hoping to spend the night inside those thick walls. Following close behind a twitchy drover and his cartload of squealing piglets, I watched the gate. The guards seemed quite attentive to those passing. The Marshal had commanded I wear no symbol of the Order, and the guards served a pureblood lord, so caution bade me slip my mask off.

A scuffle broke out at the gate and a man was drawn aside, though I couldn't hear what caused it, as two blowsy women blocked the pig cart at the same moment, shouting that the pig man had stolen their weanlings. The drover thumped one of them in the breast with his staff, and yelled for an old man on a donkey to bear witness that he'd raised the pigs. The donkey rider agreed, and the two women retreated to a barrow stopped at the side of the road.

"The guards seem testy," I said to the nervous pig man, as he kept an eye on the women.

"Summat's gone on today," he said, tongue darting over his peeling lips. "They're looking for someone particular. Ought to pay attention to *thievin' hoors!*" He bellowed this last when the two women headed back his way dragging a brutish younger man.

I drifted away from the argument and stayed to the edge of the slow-moving crowd. Best not risk a veil or any other enchantment. Not in a pureblood's town.

My skin flamed as I drew closer to the gatehouse. A man in a wine-colored cloak and a half mask the green of unripe plums stood aloof, observing each person who passed. As protocol demanded, no one looked at him or even acknowledged his presence. I followed their lead. Guards queried travelers and poked inside wagons and carts. They gave no indication of what they were looking for.

My turn came. The pureblood's cool eyes turned to me. Though all the magic I carried was buried in unspeaking silver, my gut tried to crawl into my throat. I made sure my shirt covered my bracelets, but kept my hands clearly visible.

"State your business in Cavillor." The young guard's nose flared at my filthy turnout. Indeed, I reeked.

"Heard there was work here in the counting houses," I said. "I'm deft at numbers."

The young guard snorted. "You look better suited for deadhouses."

"Fell into a terrible storm a few days since. Lost my mule."

They didn't care. Guards and pureblood were already looking to the pig cart.

"Move on."

I quickly shouldered my rucksack and moved toward the verge of the gatehouse tunnel, where guards in crimson livery were subduing a shackled prisoner. Tall, dark-haired, built strong, the man fought them with a panicked frenzy until a blow to the head flattened him. His chains rattled on the cobbles as they dragged him into the dark tunnel. A ripped black cloak was left behind, and beside it a fine bow of yew and a scattering of arrows.

Skin creeping with dread, I bobbed my head at one of the remaining guards. "Stars and stones, what's that fellow done?"

"Planted a shaft straight through a pureblood's eye," said the guard, poking a sword into the pig cart before waving it onward. "The fool will die for it, less'n he can come up with a good story. An ugly death, certain. Our good lord'll see to that."

"Gods grant him mercy. . . ." Or a witness. Or powerful friends. Or a pureblood historian who could determine whether or not his weapon had slain the victim—one who might be believed as I would not.

Every step through the gatehouse torched my nerves. An arrow in a pureblood's eye! And they'd been watching for a dark-haired man with a particular kind of bow. It could be no coincidence. I'd no orders to kill anyone. And even angry and stretched as I was, no potential victim had crossed my path. Yet, I could not believe Damon had provided me two and a half years of training and done such purposeful twisting of my soul to make me the goat for a single murder. What of serving as his *righteous voice and strong right arm*? What of Registry cleansing?

One thing sure . . . by ruining my bow, Fallon de Tremayne had spared my life. For the moment at least.

I halted before leaving the gatehouse, just long enough to settle my demeanor. My hand strayed to the mask tucked into my belt, but jerked away again. The better disguise here was no mask at all.

A narrow, twisting, walled street led from the gatehouse into the city, a discouragement to any who broached the gates and thought to charge easily toward Canis-Ferenc's castle. Pent enchantments hung on those walls like the winter-dead vines, ready to blossom in the heat of battle. Watchmen, unseen above glaring torches, called clipped reports.

Smoke hung heavy in the evening damp. Women carrying baskets of dried fish, turnips, or reeds bumped shoulders in the crowded lanes. Men shoved and jostled to get to the few shopkeepers still open for business—a Syan oil seller, a chandler whose candles hung from horizontal rods in his stall like rows of teeth.

Many in the crowd wore livery—some crimson and silver like the pennants that flew from the castle, some in colors I didn't recognize. A disturbing number wore badges of black and scarlet, the colors of the Pureblood Registry. In twos or threes they stood at corners, or strolled purposefully through the crowds examining faces.

The Marshal had charged me to report to Damon by the twelfth day from his order. But in no way was I walking into Damon's arms, not until I knew more. I needed to find Bastien.

Brittle with nerves, I kept moving, not hunched or furtive or gawking like a newcomer. But as I slowed at a branching lane, the press of servants and householders surged sidewise like a river current flowing around a rock. A braying mule and its brawny master pressed me against a rough stone wall, one or the other of them trampling on my sore feet.

"Damnation, you clumsy oaf!" I shoved the beast aside and was ready to do the same to its master, when a party of twenty or more purebloods strode up the lane. They were not a family group, but elders, men and women each with distinct regalia. Bundled in fur-lined cloaks and elaborate half masks, surrounded by a ring of attendants and linkboys, they seemed oblivious to the crush their passing caused. Of course they were not. They expected it. Believed the gods had ordained it. But I knew they were wrong.

The bawling mule drew the notice of a black-and-scarlet-liveried attendant. The attendant—pureblood, too, from his mask—slowed and squinted in my direction. I quickly averted my eyes like everyone else.

Attend, Greenshank! The echoes of Inek's teaching reprimanded me. *No matter how tired you are, no matter how fraught your emotions, know it is the small things that will defeat you. The blister on your foot. A misplaced mark on a map.*

Failure to drop my eyes could have me arrested and whipped. And not with the ultimately merciful Order lash, but one that would force me to puke out my every secret.

When the pressure of the crowd relented, I fled into the darkening streets. By the time I reached the market, the stalls were shuttered, only a few people abroad in the expanse. How did one recognize a sop-house?

A thickset young man with a tidy beard strolled across the leaf-strewn pavement just in front of me, a meat pie in his hand. He'd a jaunty air and was dressed like a clerk, far cleaner than I.

I stepped into his path, dipped a knee, and touched my forehead in deference. "Pardon, goodman. I hear this market has places the likes of me might have a bath for the cheap. I be just come from my da's cot up the north coast to meet a girl he's matched me with. Oughta be clean."

"Alas for us vigorous men, the divine Arrosa's temple is closed down." He leaned in close and winked. "A fellow could have a holy wash and a divine tug in those precincts for naught but a prayer! Sop-houses will cost ye a copper for a tub and a tankard. Extra if you want a clean towel or soft hands to scrub you."

"Where would I find a place like that? Decent . . . I mean clean."

He grinned, displaying a mouthful of large brown teeth. "I could show you my favorites. Share a mug with you . . ."

According to my friendly informant—Jochen the Cob, he called himself, as he was "short, thick-legged, and hairy, but quite reliable"—the Gull had better ale than the Nag's Head and runners who could fetch almost any delicacy for a good price. The Nag's Head had prettier girls and the town's best piper. Unsure of which Bastien would choose, I decided to try the Gull first. The trick would be getting rid of Jochen.

A touch of my bracelet and a spit of magic before I grasped his wrist in thanks for his direction soon had his gut rumbling noisily. About the time we reached the tight, dark alley that hosted a litter of pigeon bones and the Gull, poor Jochen had to apologize and run for the deeper shadows. His forlorn retching bruised my conscience.

The Gull's door opened to a blast of heat, smoky lamplight, and two men wrestling to the ratting of a tabor. Perhaps twenty onlookers crowded around the wrestlers, exchanging cheers and jeers with equally good humor. I couldn't tell if Bastien was among them.

Pitchers and mugs stood on a plank laid across three casks. In the wall behind the plank, a half door whopped in and out as a thin man with long, pale, wet hair stepped out. He called for mead before dropping onto a stool. He looked more than a little nogged already.

"What's your pleasure? Bath? Ale? Both?" A flushed young woman with hair flying every which way paused in her mission to deliver two overflowing mugs. Her sooty eyes took my measure. "We've a mutton pottage in the kettle. And there'll be dancing when Thill and Pescar finish their nightly walloping."

"That last," I said. "The soup, I mean. And ale." The bath beckoned more than all, but it wouldn't feed magic. Nor did the idea of being naked behind that free-swinging door sit easy. By now Damon would know his net hadn't caught me. It was Bastien and information I needed most.

"Find a stool and I'll bring it," said the tap girl. "I'm Fycha."

I set up in a corner where the lamps wouldn't shine so bright on my naked face. The harried Fycha brought me a bowl of watery broth. Two chunks of carrot and a wedge of onion floated in it, and a sheep might once have walked close to the pot. No matter. My belly welcomed the warmth, along with the fresh, strong ale.

Though I hoped to hear gossip of the pureblood murder, the hooting crowd silenced all other conversation. I'd give Bastien an hour, then try the Nag's Head.

The wrestling match ended with both men insensible. Their audience dispersed, settling at two long tables or other upended barrels such as the one that held my bowl and mug. The pock-faced drummer dropped his tabor in favor of a pipe and began to play untunefully. Fycha asked me and three other customers to carry the wrestlers out and drop them in the alley. I obliged. We appeared to be the only ones sober.

No sooner had Fycha refilled my mug as payment for the drunk-hauling than a smallish man wreathed in steam pushed through the half door from the bathing room. Bek, the surgeon.

One might have thought he'd been in the wrestling match. His face was bruised and the back of one of his hands was bleeding. But he seemed well enough. At least his hands weren't trembling this night. One eyebrow ticked upward when he spotted me.

"I'd hoped for mead and conversation, fair Fycha," he said, lifting a cloak from a hook, "but I've lingered in your fine bath too late. A rotted tooth awaits my skills elsewhere."

Inexplicably annoyed, I swallowed the last of my ale, dropped a coin on the table, and strolled to the door. My nod to Fycha was ignored. The tap girl studied Bek as she'd not any other customer. "We'll see you again tomorrow eve, surgeon?"

"Like as not," he said. "I've taken a special fondness for the Gull."

It seemed an hour until the surgeon followed me out, carrying a small lantern. He'd wrapped a kerchief about his bleeding hand and seemed in no hurry.

"Well met, man of many names." He started down the alley, but I grabbed him.

"Why are *you* here?" I pressed him hard to the brick wall. "Where is the coroner?"

"Elsewhere. He thought better of being seen regularly in so public a house. Scratch a brick of this town and it bleeds spies. Didn't take us a day to figure that one out."

"Is my sister safe?"

"Aye," he said, his gaze cool. "She got a message to us yestermorn saying she's with that important person she mentioned, and you were to stay out of sight. That's all we know. Had a rough journey, did you?"

"And what of the others?"

"Most of Hercule's people chose to head for Tavarre, which is bigger and friendlier to their kind. Some have kin there. But Hercule and a handful stayed, as he wanted to be of service to you should you ever show up—which the coroner and I had doubts about when the glowing lady stayed mute as a marble pillar on the journey. Shouldn't we be getting on with our business?"

I let Bek go as abruptly as I'd taken him, elsewise I would have added more bruising to his hollowed cheeks. Which made no sense. The surgeon had been nothing but help.

Rage hovered just beneath my skin. Impatience, frustration, fear . . . all could trigger it. Drawing a deep breath, I summoned the discipline that had saved my life ever and again. I could not afford mistakes.

"Looks as if you had your own wrestling match," I said, indicating his face and hand.

"Aye," he said, "I did." And pointed the way we were to go.

We took a short circular route through the web of streets, stopping at every turn to ensure we weren't being followed. It wouldn't have surprised me had we ended back at the Gull. But this alley was even narrower and nastier than the first. A wooden shed nestled at its farthest end, its entrance closed only by a rag curtain.

I lagged behind, fingers on my bracelets, as Bek rapped three times on the wall, paused, and then twice more. Drawing the curtain aside, he motioned me in.

Three walls and a plank roof formed the shed. The back side was a tiny yard open to the sky, bounded by houses crammed so close together a man could scarce squeeze between. Bastien sat on a plank bench under the roof, sucking on a Ciceron smoking pipe, unsheathed sword close to hand. The smell of his pipe weed could not disguise that goats, donkey, geese, or per-haps all together had occupied the shed not so long past.

Bek hung the lantern beside the doorway and shuttered it. Bastien's pipe was a pulsing gleam.

A hostile silence hung about him like a shield.

"I'm glad to hear you're all safe," I said, curious.

"Did you do this pureblood murder?" Bastien blurted, before I could choose where to sit. "An *arrow* through his eye."

"Gods, no! Though I'm thinking someone wanted it to seem that way . . ." I told him of the poison dart and the goat girl, the broken bow and the man I'd seen shackled at Cavillor's gates.

"Aye, it was surely Fallon warned you," he said, cooler. "But why in such a roundabout way?"

"That's plagued me all day," I said. "Maybe someone else had to do it for him; he'd assume I'd never trust a stranger. Maybe he had some other mission. Damnation, maybe he paid the goat girl to do it once he shot the dart. It's no matter. It's what's next I need to be worrying about. And I think . . ." I didn't like the notion that had come to me.

"Surgeon Bek, will you leave us alone for the while?" I'd been far too free speaking of dangerous matters to Bastien, Juli, Siever. "It's for your safety."

"No tears. I'll watch." Bek's shuffling steps faded.

"Bek's a good man, Lucian. He's saved my life a number of times."

"Then you don't want him to hear these things."

I shoved Bastien's feet off his bench and sat beside him, so even someone standing in the open yard could not hear us.

"Back in the marshes, I told you I thought Damon was aiming for the throne as well as the Registry," I said. "I believe it even more firmly now. . . ." I told Bastien of the Marshal and how my perceptions of him had changed from my training to his partnership with Damon to our last interview. ". . . so am I mad to think the man who destroyed my memory of my past is trustworthy? He claims to believe in Damon's purposes. That could mean simply that he wants Damon to make him king. But if he's true, and now something's changed so that Damon is setting me up to be a murderer, shouldn't I warn him that Damon could be planning to betray him as well? All I have to do is infuse this token with a little magic and have him meet me."

"I think you're a blazing lunatic!" Bastien's clipped whisper scoured me. "You and the rest of these knights or whatever you are. Maybe every cursed pureblood. You've got my blood so cold, I don't know as I'll ever get warm again. You're talking about *treason*. Men have their bowels cut out of them and set afire for such a crime. And what the jolly shite does it have to do with your magic? The blackmail using your portraits I understand, but this *he's got a use for me* business? You should take your sister and run as fast and far away as you can. And I'll do the same, but in a different direction. You don't owe the Registry anything. You don't owe these princes . . . the kingdom . . . anything that's worth putting such magic as yours in the hands of villains who see themselves as gods. They've already killed your family. Stolen your life . . ."

He paused, unfinished. Even in the dark his gaze burned my face.

". . . but as you'll never in this cursed world do such an intelligent thing, here's what I propose. Set up your meeting with this Marshal. But I'll go instead of you, stay out of sight, see what he does. If all's well, he'll leave, imagining you're delayed, and you can set a new one."

"Tempting, but no. I'll meet him. You watch. If something happens to me . . . give it a few days. If you don't hear anything more from me or Juli, get back to the Gouvron Estuary. Persuade Hercule to go with you. I'll wager he can hang a bit of red fire in the air on and off three times every hour, until an old boatman shows up. His name will be Fix. Be sure, he'll sound fierce—and he is. But tell him everything I've told you. Everything you saw. He knows about you, about the plots, about everything."

"And what of the Xanch—?"

"Ssss." I laid a hand on Bastien's knee. What was it? A sound, a scent, a shifting of the air? Likely it was Bek. But it had seemed . . .

Magic infusing a large spell structure whispered cold, like falling snow.

"Get out," I breathed in Bastien's ear. "Silent. Fast."

I shoved him off the bench toward the beast yard and stepped through the leather curtain into the alley, just in time to touch my bracelet, raise a shield of magic, and absorb the firebolt that would have slammed shed and the two of us into the back wall of the yard.

I fell . . . forever it seemed before I slammed into the ground. At some great distance, as if I looked up from the bottom of a well, stood Damon and at least twenty men clad in black and scarlet, bristling weapons like great hedgehogs. As sight collapsed, words drifted down on me like falling leaves: "Lucian de Remeni-Masson, in the name of the Pureblood Registry, I arrest you for the crime of murder of the gods' chosen."

CHAPTER 37

"On your feet, Remeni." The terse command issued from the last voice I wished to hear.

"Curator Damon. Was on my way—"

"Yes, yes, I know. On your way to dally with an *ordinary* woman in a pigsty! It's not even a violation of orders, as who would think to command a pureblood warrior in-mission to contain his bodily urges? Or to avoid besotted babbling to a twistmind procurer?"

I squeezed eyes and lips tight. No more speaking. No more listening if I could help it, lest I discover I'd truly gone mad. Nothing made sense. I was alive, but lay prone on a very hard stone floor, and somehow the phrase *very ugly death* kept bobbing up in the dark behind my eyelids like a wayward boat on the demon tide.

But the more I fought to stay insensible, the more Damon's clipped annoyance cut through the fog like a honed blade.

"Your orders were quite simple and clear," he said. "Twelve days. Speak to no one. Wear no mark of the Order. Bring only your godforsaken bow. Yet you arrive without the bow and before deigning to report, you choose to spend an hour drinking and whoring. Did you think I wouldn't notice? How stupid do you think I am?"

Not stupid at all, save that he had the story all wrong. Dally with a woman? Twistmind procurer? Bek! The damnable, treacherous bastard. I should have seen it: the cut hand . . . the bruised face . . . the vanished tremors . . . A moment's ecstasy and an hour's pleasure wrought with self-inflicted pain and the enchanted nivat paste he'd likely bought with my life. And he knew of Xancheira and Juli. . . .

To my astonishment, I was not bound. I drew my knees up under me and sat back on my heels, assembling my shredded wits. The cold, hard floor was rose-threaded marble. The curved walls were not iron, but polished stone hung with vividly colored tapestries. Damon, robed in dark red, paced in a tight circle around me, arms folded, his over-bright, disturbingly hungry eyes never leaving me.

"I never imagined a crack in my cursed bow would gain me a reprieve from *execution*," I said, making my accusation as sharp as his. "Perhaps I needed a bit of human solace before I gave myself up for gutting by *Domé* Canis-Ferenc. You made me believe you cared about Registry corruption, and now we're back to secret executions?"

Damon halted, disdainful.

"Of course you're not going to die. You gave me your submission. You agreed to let me guide you to our shared purpose. Discipline is your joy and your strength; how could I imagine you would abandon it so near our goal? You can thank that twistmind's unholy need for getting our great ship back on course. In exchange, we've provided him a supply of extraordinarily potent paste. He'll not be able to form a cogent thought before summer."

It was difficult to muster sympathy for the traitorous Bek. But he'd provided a story, perhaps a caution for Bastien's sake.

"I was attempting to find out whom I was supposed to have murdered. Harlots know what gossip's worth hearing."

"You'll learn everything soon enough. Today is the day of our triumph, Lucian." Indeed Damon was cranked tighter than a crossbow.

"Today?" I shifted my joints, which were giving me notice that I had lain on that cold marble unmoving for too many hours. "You have me wholly mystified. You seem to take especial delight in that."

Twisting my neck to relieve the soreness revealed vertical slots spaced evenly around the ceiling vault—arrow loops. Arrows aimed in my direction protruded from at least three of them. Dared I imagine others might have firebolt spells trained this way as well? And I . . .

"You've taken my bracelets." And Fix's too. Regrettable, but not exactly surprising. I wriggled my toes. The Marshal's token remained in my boot.

"You presented yourself combatively, and I wished no accidents. They'll be returned to you in due time."

"So if I'm not to be executed and I'm clearly not to be your strong right arm until *due time*, then what?" I said, standing up slowly, hands visible to all who might be observing. "I am at your service, *domé*."

"If your petulance is properly satisfied, come. And quickly. The house will be stirring soon, and no one must see you. Put on your mask."

I did so. My spirit sighed with relief, which was wholly ludicrous. Damon had arrested me for *murder of the gods' chosen* in front of some twenty wit-

nesses. That was not anything that could be dismissed with apology or erad-
icated with explanation. Nor could I ignore the seven guards robed in black
and gray who appeared behind us. They wore hoods, so I could not see if
they wore full-face masks. But I'd wager so, and that their bows and blades
were marked with the Order blazon. If I was to get out of this, I'd need to
pick my time and place carefully.

"I'm not exactly garbed for a lord's house," I said as I matched Damon's
brisk pace. I couldn't get filthier than the ten days traveling had left me, but
being blasted into the beast yard had left my cloak missing, and breeches and
hose ripped. My hair was crusted with stinking mud, and twelve days growth
of beard itched under my mask.

"There will be a time for silks and velvets," said Damon. "Later."

We left the circular chamber by way of a vaulted passage. Jewel-colored
mosaics adorned the walls. Another time I would have stopped and looked
closer, but Damon's urgency drew me onward into a long gallery overlooking a hall of vast proportion.

A colonnade of slender, close-set pillars screened observers from below;
bronze grillwork screens had been built perpendicular to the colonnade to
shield observers from one another. Perhaps halfway down the gallery, I
dodged into one of these viewing alcoves to peer through the colonnade.

The hall below displayed appropriate grandeur for a Sitting of the Three
Hundred. Marble mantelpieces, carved in great elaborations of gods and
beasts, soared three stories high at either end of the chamber. The Hearth of
Memory at Evanide could have fit inside their cavernous maws. In between
sat a great table in the shape of a horseshoe. At the focus of its arc, between
its two long arms and clearly visible from every seat at the table—forty or
fifty of them—was a simple square dais, bordered by wood rails at waist
height.

But my eye was captured by an exquisite mural of Kemen Sky Lord and
Mother Samele that centered the high wall above the table. The brother and
sister divinities were each engaged with a Danae partner, the sapphire, lapis,
and indigo of their exquisite gards exactly as I knew them. Legend said those
couplings birthed Deunor, Lord of Fire and Magic, and Erdru, Lord of Vines.
The artistry of that painting . . . the muscular vigor of its subjects . . . the
lines and shading that revealed such passionate intimacy that my flesh and
blood heated . . . could make anyone believe such tales.

"Come along. Your aerie is a little farther."

As I followed Damon back to the open aisle of the gallery, my fingers glanced along the grillwork. His voice had sounded dead inside the alcove, and indeed subtle magics had been woven into the bronze screens. Those inside would not hear the comments from their neighbors, nor would their own be heard outside the space. A nice deterrent to spies.

"Here is where you will view the proceedings." Damon indicated an opening.

That the viewing alcove selected for me had a gate to close it off from the open walkway did not surprise me. Nor did the circumstance that these screens were wrought of iron, not bronze. The gate bore locks of spellwork so intricate even a paratus of Evanide would require a significant time to undo them. What kind of madman was I to walk in?

I halted. "Am I your prisoner, curator?"

"No." Yet seven hooded guards stood just beyond range of hearing. "You are my willing instrument. I need you to observe and learn—is that not what you desire? I also need you to remain silent, and refrain from any detectable trace of magic. Should any person down below have occasion to look up here I will have you bound and muted as befits a man accused of murder. Should we do that as a precaution?"

"No."

I could not leave. Not here, on the brink of enlightenment. Damon himself was so near bursting that I knew he spoke true—this was the day, whether of triumph or ending or simple understanding. Serena Fortuna . . . the Law of the Everlasting . . . whatever it was that determined the course of human fate . . . had driven me to this moment. I was not mad. The divine gift lived in me in a form that had shaped terrible events and it was my duty to serve its call, both here and in Xancheira. Even if it meant stepping into a cage.

Damon nodded, meeting my gaze, not with gloating, but with solemn understanding, as if he'd listened in on my argument. "I expect this session to last late into the night. Food and drink will be provided you. You will neither touch those who bring it nor speak nor expose your face to them. There is a slops jar for your use. This is not the Tower cellar. You are neither naked, nor stupefied by potions, nor subject to the other indignities of that prisoning. And no, I do not expect you to thank me for that. I accept responsibility for those conditions as I do for these. But your life will change today. One way or the other for the greater glory of Navronne . . ."

He turned to go.

But my patience was too much frayed. "Good gods, curator, just a hint.

What are these *proceedings?*" My muddled reckoning said the Sitting was not to begin for twelve days yet.

"Our trial. The Fifty are assembled to weigh judgment."

The gate slammed behind him and the lockspells settled into place.

The Fifty. The Fifty Judges, to be precise. Every year each of the three hundred original pureblood families designated one of their own to serve at the pleasure of the Registry to determine guilt or settle disputes in matters that involved more than one family. Most occasions required only one judge or three. But for the most serious adjudications, a random fifty would be chosen to hear arguments and witnesses.

Not long after Damon's departure, the judges arrived in solemn procession and took their places at the table. All wore robes the same blood-red as Damon's. Hoods hid their faces. No one knew which fifty families were represented at any hearing or which member of a family was designated its judge in any particular year. Yet I did not doubt that Damon knew exactly who sat on those fifty stools. He would have left nothing to chance—not with the folio of my portraits in hand.

It made sense that the Fifty would meet before a Sitting. The Three Hundred decided how pureblood society was to move forward in perilous times. But the Fifty had to lay the groundwork, determining what circumstances mandated change. Fallon had told me this Sitting was meant to address matters of corruption in the Pureblood Registry.

A very large man swept through the door trailing wine-hued velvet robes. A wool-cart's worth of black and gray hair was bound into ten fat braids. Kasen de Canis-Ferenc welcomed the noble judges to his demesne, and with a brief ceremony involving invocations, fragrant smokes, and a magical font of crimson and silver light, formally opened the Convocation of the Fifty. He paused for a moment, as if waiting for an invitation to stay. When all remained silent, he swept out, followed by quick-stepping attendants in crimson-and-silver livery.

One judge rose from his seat at the end of the curved table and walked around to stand beside the small dais. "Heed me, worthy Judges, as I present to you a case I have assembled over more than twenty years, tragic violations of law and custom that reach from the deeps of history to our present day, that touch on human wickedness, on greed and murder that have sullied our divine gift, and held us back from the fullness of destiny the gods intend for us. . . ."

Damon. He wandered as he spoke, sometimes drawing near the table, sometimes standing back and gesturing as he laid out a background of the perilous times. The everlasting winter. The ordinaries' war. The scouring madness of the Harrowers.

". . . and how have we—the Registry, the children of Aurellia who've come to this wondrous land where the gods infuse our magic with majesty and brilliance—responded to these perils? We look the other way. We hide inside fortresses of riches, citing the Law that keeps us separate from the world of ordinaries. Where is the advancement that should demonstrate the gods' favor? We preach of nurturing our gifts and sharing them impartially to better the world, but where is the magic? Where is the glory? Rather, behind our bastions of comfort and our prattling of duty, discipline, and distance, corruption festers. Centuries of corruption . . ."

His voice and his body bespoke passion, compelling every eye and ear in that chamber to heed him. He told the story of Xancheira, much as the Marshal had told it to me. He did not speak of the Order, nor mention the poisonous secret of dual bents. But he told of the city's death in a ring of fire, and the warriors who had never gone home from the shame of that day.

Perched on a stool that had been left in the viewing alcove, I took in every word as he moved on to other history I'd never heard—of the extermination of other magic wielders, of settlements razed, of caravans bringing new Aurellian settlers attacked and the travelers massacred.

". . . our lives and fortunes built not on divine magic, but on blood. And what have we done for the world but foster corruption that reflects our own? Consider our own day. Three princes vie in savagery to replace a great king. And among our own? All here know the name of Remeni. Vincente, whose bent for history was so powerful he became King Eodward's Royal Historian. Elaine de Remeni-Masson, whose glorious artworks grace these very halls . . ."

His hand pointed to the painting of Kemen and Samele—my grandmother's? My mother's? Gods!

". . . of countless others whose work stands amid the greatest of our kind. And the last of them, Lucian the portraitist, the quiet, impeccably disciplined young artist, whose deft hand and incomparable magic produced portraits of almost every pureblood man, woman, and child in Navronne over the span of five years. Ah, yes, I see some of you squirm. No matter what is spoken of the man now, no matter rumor or innuendo, Lucian de Remeni-Masson's portraits bore the glorious, undeniable aspect of divine truth in ways we have not seen in uncounted generations. And what did those portraits reveal?"

Indeed, every one of the red-robed judges, whose stillness to that point might have been attention or boredom, shifted uneasily.

"Corruption," said Damon. "Aberrance deep, foul, poisonous . . ."

And then Damon told the story of my great commission to paint the portraits of the six curators. Of the sudden and horrible savagery that destroyed my family not two days after the portraits' completion, of the growing anger among the curators at certain truths those paintings exposed. He told of the rumors of my madness that circulated through the city, and a second fire that had "killed Lucian de Remeni's young sister and six of their servants."

Juli. They'd set a fire to murder my sister and our servants—so they could blame it on me.

Revulsion and outrage pulsed in my veins. Cut me and I would bleed murder.

As he told of my imprisonment and how they forced me to alter the paintings, he displayed illusions that reflected the original and the altered works. They were true to every detail that I had witnessed in the relict-seeing.

"With the authority given me by the Fifty, I have summoned the architects of this current corruption. Let them speak to these crimes. Bring in First Curator Gramphier. . . ."

No matter my apprehension at my situation—locked in this cage, convinced of his duplicity—Damon's skill awed me. While no match for the Marshal and his ability to inspire, the little curator had laid out his case against the Registry with impeccable precision.

The First Curator of the Pureblood Registry was escorted into the hall and led to the railed dais by two men robed and hooded in gray. Gramphier's posture spoke arrogance and disdain.

"Three questions only, Curator. First, why did you wish the bloody dagger excised from your portrait?"

"This is nonsense, Damon," said Gramphier. "You know the answer very well. To protect the divine gift is a sacred duty that cannot be accomplished without bloodshed. But few wish to be confronted with ugly truth as they go about their lives. To display the harsh necessities of our calling in so public a way was not appropriate. Remeni was a madman, bound to—"

"Answer only what you're asked, First Curator, and heed your words. Perjury before the Fifty will see you dead before sunrise. And be sure, I can prove the truth or falsity of your answers. If the Fifty determine you innocent, no one beyond these walls will ever know what you've said. So, again. Why did you wish the bloody dagger removed?"

"I approved executions necessary to maintain our proper role in the world."

Damon nodded. "Second question: Did you approve the plan to exterminate the Remeni and Masson bloodlines by whatever means came to hand?"

Even so far above them as I was, I felt the heat of Gramphier's hatred. "Yes, but—"

"We are not interested in excuses or explanations. The last question: Was that decision precipitated by the revelations in Lucian de Remeni's portraits of the six curators?"

"What are you—?"

Silver flashed from a ring on Damon's hand. Gramphier choked on his words as if a knife had been planted in his throat.

"Answer the question. *Yes* or *no*."

Another glint from Damon's ring and Gramphier snarled. "Yes."

The livid Gramphier was dismissed, and a small, dapper man escorted to the dais, his gaze jerking between Damon and the judges. A twist in his spine left his head cocked to one side. This was Curator Scrutari-Consil, the man who had forged a will naming Prince Perryn as King Eodward's chosen heir.

Damon put a similar three questions to Scrutari. As with Gramphier, Scrutari affirmed his crimes.

Never did Damon mention dual bents, nor did he link the Registry's history of murder to the secret that halfbloods could pass on the gift of true sorcery by intermarriage with those so gifted. Every reference to the image of the white tree in the portraits was to the crime of burning Xancheira; none suggested that Xancheira had flourished, in part, through the richness of dual bents.

To my astonishment the next witness was Pluvius. Disheveled but clean, subdued and possessed of a mind, he shuffled onto the witness's dais, ducking his head before the formidable wall of faceless judges. When Damon stepped out from behind the table, Pluvius hissed.

The escorts stepped up smartly, but Pluvius raised his hands, fingers spread to stay them.

Three questions for Pluvius.

"Did you devise the plan for Lucian de Remeni-Masson to be tormented into modifying the portraits?" *Yes.*

"Did you devise private schemes to entice Lucian de Remeni into enslavement in your own house, intending to advance your fortune through blackmail?" *Yes.*

"When and where did you last see Lucian de Remeni?" This one surprised me.

"If this is the same year as when I traveled from Palinur, then I saw him not a month ago. He lives among a cadre of formidable warriors. I judged him damaged and violent."

"I did not ask for opinions." But neither did Damon interrupt those opinions as he had with Gramphier.

Spider feet prickled my spine. Where was this leading? Everything Damon had presented was truth that fired my own blood, but he had arrested me in front of witnesses. . . .

Pluvius, too, was escorted out. Damon faced the judges, hands pressed to his breast. "I am one of these infamous curators, as well," he said. "I did not coerce Lucian de Remeni into altering my unflattering portrait, but that yields me no virtue. I aided my colleagues in their despicable cruelty. Only one of our six refused to take part."

The doors opened and a woman strode across the marble floor without escort. She put me in mind of the standing stones that surrounded the Sanctuary pool in Xancheira: squared shoulders, hair more gray than black, gray eyes, gray complexion, worn down by the years. Yet, like those slabs of granite, she bore a fierce, unbending stature. Pons.

She stepped onto the dais, making it clear that it was no accident of light or the draping of her robes that gave her an asymmetrical appearance. She had only one arm.

"Three questions, Curator Pons-Laterus." Damon spoke over his shoulder as he strolled toward the table, cool and confident.

"No."

Damon spun in his tracks. "You were told—"

"Our single shared purpose is to root out corruption, Damon. You think to exalt me as virtuous, but I will not allow it. Because, of course, I had my portrait altered as well, just not by way of Lucian's torture. My portrait exposed evidence of my dalliance with an ordinary and the child we made together, a violation of Registry law. My son and his father are well hidden these twenty years, far from the reach of any consequence that may befall me. My second fault? I knew what went on in the Tower cellars, but did nothing to stop it. I left an innocent man in the netherworld at the mercy of monsters. And third"—her dagger gaze did not leave the furious Damon—"on the night Remeni exposed our perfidy to the world, I forced his fingers onto Gilles de Albin's chest and poured my own magic through those divinely gifted hands into a spell that burnt out the smirking villain's heart. I did the same to my own shoulder to its ruin, so that the blame for that wounding and Gilles's death would fall on Remeni's head. My reasons were my own, but I will not allow you to charge Lucian with those crimes. And perhaps the judges should know that Gilles's father, Guilian, did not—"

Damon raised a finger. Magic glinted from his silver ring, and Pons fell silent. She grasped the rail with her one hand.

"Quite clear, Curator Pons. Your sins are nobly confessed. Guilian de Albin, the sixth curator, was arrested that night and condemned for the slaughter of two bloodlines by Harrowers. His son Gilles had admitted to all of us—proudly—that he was complicit in his father's sins. Executing him was no crime, save in the method and the lack of official sanction. But it was through *your* diligence over the next months that it was discovered that Curator Albin escaped the execution that all assumed. Our colleagues on the Curators' Council refused to see Albin executed for a crime in which we had all conspired. Guilian de Albin has lived these two years in the bosom of his family. . . ."

Albin *alive*? The man who had locked more than two hundred people in a house and burnt them alive? Bestial rage rose from my belly, stung my throat, and threatened to breach the seal of silence I had sworn. At some time I had risen to my feet, hands splayed on the slender columns as if I could tear them down and leap to the floor below to right such an outrage with blood.

Four of the robed escorts strode through the hall below me, carrying a long table draped in blood-red silk. The escorts set down the table and whipped away the draperies. A muscular man with a bountiful beard and thick raven hair pulled straight back from his forehead was laid out on that table. A wealthy man, dressed in dark velvet and a black-and-silver half mask. Neither beard nor years had changed him so much that I could not identify the man who had tried to cut off my hand when I refused to hide evidence of his infamy. Guilian de Albin, an arrow stuck straight into one eye.

Gods, gods, gods . . . My bellowing protest died unreleased. As a clamor of voices rose from the hall, I slid to the floor, feeling sick and unendingly stupid. For I knew who Damon planned to put on trial next. A murderer. A violent, vengeful man, honed to raw edges by long, nervous days on the road in winter. The prosecutor would regret the lack of my bow, but the arrows missing from my pack were ones I had made myself. Like a stupid sheep, I'd let Damon lead me to the killing ground.

Visions of grandeur, Greenshank? You thought you were important.

As I flung my arms over my head and ground my teeth in self-loathing, a fiery sting stabbed my upper arm. Hotter and hotter. Unrelenting.

I tore at my sleeve, as the fire burnt through my flesh like a speck of *cereus iniga*, sending spikes of heat through my marrow. Damon must have left some magical spider in the alcove to ensure my compliance.

But I found only a fiery pinprick of silver gleaming on my arm.

Great Deunor's mercy! Fix's splinter. Siever was ready.

CHAPTER 38

Despairing laughter burst from my chest. It was time to free the Xanchei-rans, while I was, myself, imprisoned. Was Damon planning to parade me onto the railed dais and ask me three questions?

No, he'd never dare let me speak. Though indeed, what could I tell them about my guide? He freely admitted his own sins. And any argument that he had made me into something other than I was would be proof of his contention: Registry corruption perverted our gifts.

"Silence, good judges," cried Damon, arms spread wide. "We've enough business to carry us long into the night. I've brought you not only this dread tale of our guilt in the violent disintegration of a gifted young sorcerer, but also a way we might cleanse our past sins and ensure our future. What say you? Do we return to willful blindness or will you hear what I propose?"

"Hear, hear!" the Fifty yelled, caught up in the spider's web. Perhaps there were naysayers, but not enough to make themselves heard. My mad-ness would be proved by my murder of Guilian de Albin. Damon would convince them to purify the Registry and, in exchange, he would give them a king.

Meanwhile, Xancheira waited.

I had to get out of here. Three walls were bound in iron—a terrible risk when using magic. And surely someone—Damon down in the hall or his aides of the Order—would sense my magic and come to stop me, for I had no door to step through this time. No hospice entry to the void. I'd no notion how long it might take for Safia to allow me through the boundaries. And I could not allow Damon to silkbind my hands. Only one recourse. Risky.

I pulled the Marshal's token from my boot, fed magic into its splinter, along with the words *locked viewing gallery* and *now.* Surely he was in the castle already.

While the judges below took refreshment, I paced, imagining Siever and Fix doing the same. Every passing moment could weaken Siever's working, or make him doubt, which was the truer danger when working complex spells.

"I'm sent to bring refreshment." The man outside the cell spoke softly. "Is the gate locked?"

"Let me see what you've got there." Shuffling. Clinks. Thumps.

"Who is it inside?"

"A favored guest. You're not to speak to him."

"I was told to peel the oranges and pour the wine fresh."

"Then do so quickly."

The gate spells released with a sucking draft. Seven guards formed an arc before the open gate, blades blazing with enchantment. Order enchantments.

I turned my back to the door as the gate swung shut and the servitor set a tray on the second stool.

"Stay still, Lucian. Quick movements will be visible from below." The shuffling of dishes and the rip of orange peel masked the Marshal's quiet voice.

"He's set me up for murder," I said. "I am his trump, the culminating example of Registry corruption. They're going to execute me."

"Murder?" The sound of pouring liquid released the aroma of good wine.

"Please believe me. If I remain here, I'll be dead by morning."

"Sky Lord's balls . . . Here, cover your head." He thrust a cloth into my hand. "Guards!"

As the cell door opened, I draped the cloth over my head. A thread of magic scored the air, and the Marshal snapped, *"Cineré resurgé."*

Together, the words and the magic created a command imperative that only the Knight Marshal of Evanide could issue. Every knight was bound to obey.

"Relock the gate, and do not report my interference until Curator Damon himself comes here."

"As you say . . . Knight Marshal?" said a clearly bewildered guard.

"As you were, *equites.*"

The Marshal led me briskly along the gallery. Two turnings, a series of doorways, and we entered a small, enclosed chamber. He released me and snatched away the cloth.

We occupied a plain anteroom, furnished with cushioned benches, pegs for garments, a night jar, a washing bowl, and a bootscraper. A voluminous gray cloak hung from one peg, a white tunic and shirt from another, and white robes . . .

"None's followed." He drew a painted screen across the open arch with a grunt of satisfaction, then turned to me. "Now what is this about murder and execution? Damon has spent years grooming you."

The answer died on my tongue. The Marshal stood before me unmasked, a man in his prime, forty or thereabouts. And there was no doubt at all as to his lineage, not with the wiry red-gold curls of his Ardran heritage and the well-proportioned features so like those that graced every common coin in Navronne. King Eodward's features. My guess was right.

Only the eyes were unexpected. Dark Aurellian eyes, not the gold-flecked brown of Navronne's royal family. It wasn't simply that, however. No longer did those eyes reflect the serene, almost spiritual focus of the leader who counseled and inspired troubled parati. They displayed suspicions, impatience, anxiety, and hard, worldly, *personal* experience. Only one thing could alter an Order knight so dramatically in so short a time.

"You've been given your memories!"

"Most insightful. And you've no idea . . ." A rakish smile, far younger than his flesh, lit the dim chamber like magefire. The same smile he'd flashed in his chamber at Evanide. "But I believe we're in a hurry?"

I shook off amazement. "Damon intends for the Fifty to condemn me for the murder of Guilian de Albin. The devil, the man who slaughtered my family, was murdered with an arrow in the eye only yesterday. Damon charged me by name before twenty witnesses. It's why he had me bring the bow. Three of my arrows were stolen, and I'll wager my soul the shaft in Albin's eye is one of them. But on my honor as a brother of the Order we both value, I am innocent of it."

"Sky Lord everlasting . . ." Those unexpected eyes darkened, his wide brow creased, and he fingered his unshaven chin thoughtfully. "That makes no sense at all. The man's a devious prick, no doubt, but he's told me you were groomed to be"—he glanced at me sharply—"*my* right hand as we move forward. Counselor and bodyguard for tumultuous times."

A *king's* bodyguard. A counselor who could delve into history or depict hidden truths or dissolve nature's boundaries. I could not possibly unravel the myriad ways that made sense . . . or all the ways Damon could twist a man in such a position to his purposes. Then why kill me?

"Something's changed, then," I said to the Marshal's back as he circled the short dimensions of the chamber. "If I can hide until nightfall, I can get out of the castle and out of the city. I swear my aims are nothing contrary to the Order's interests. To serve the Knight Marshal of Evanide would be my privilege."

I would not pledge myself to *his* service. Not until I understood how his elevation was to be accomplished or more of his own intents. Inek had named the Marshal along with Damon and the Archivist as an *architect* of this plot.

"You should watch *your* back, sir," I said.

"Be sure of that." No, not serene at all. Anger simmered beneath his goodly exterior. "Yes, you should stay hidden until we sort this out. This is my dressing chamber. No one's going to disturb my clothes or my piss jar as I dine with Canis-Ferenc. I've already banished the servants."

"Whatever comes, Knight Marshal—for me or for you—I pray it will be for the honor of the Order and the glory of Navronne."

"As do I," he said. The simple words, spoken with such resonant conviction, demanded belief. Yet I would have given much for pen and paper, and freedom to use my bent to sketch him. He was changed.

He shucked his servant's livery, then buckled his knife belt and donned white robe, mantle, and mask. Before pulling up his hood, he drew a small gray silk bag from inside his mantle.

"I've kept this for a goodly while," he said, rolling the bag between his fingers. "A sort of luck charm. I know it seems odd; the Order is not at all about luck. Don't tell anyone that the Knight Marshal of Evanide tosses salt over his shoulder from time to time or buries his fingernail parings at the dark of the moon. Evidently I relied on such a great deal in my youth."

He poured the contents of the bag into his cupped palm. Before I could see what it was, he tossed it into the air.

I flinched. But it was merely dust that drifted over us. Magic made it sparkle in the lamplight. He laid his hand on my shoulder and laughed, his eyes glittering like black flame. "We both must find our forward path, and if we provide a little help for Serena Fortuna, all the better. *Dalle cineré*, Lucian de Remeni."

He pulled up his hood and departed, as brisk and rare as the east wind that bears hints of unfamiliar lands. The room was diminished without his presence. What a king he would make . . . if he was true.

Perhaps his dust was merely a luck charm. I felt nothing strange and no magic but that which sparked its fall. But I scraped up a little of the dust and dropped it into a pocket to investigate later. I didn't like anyone involving me in spellwork I didn't understand.

So I'd bought time to work and a hiding place. Though it was difficult to shift my focus to the duty that called, I rolled onto my knees and summoned magic. With will, not fingers, I infused power directly into the fading gleam of silver threaded into my arm. And indeed, with a ripping fire that astonished me with its immediacy, Fix's spell sent out the signal.

Pressing my hands to the floor, I summoned my bents and prayed that Safia would be waiting. As I let the magic flow, the boundaries of the world dissolved. I had three hours.

"Remeni-son!" The silver-marked sentinel sat on a rock overlooking the five-fingered land. As in Cavillor, it was mid-afternoon, a smeared disk of the sun just visible through the overcast. "Long have I awaited thy coming."

"*Envisia seru*, Safia," I said, shaking off the abrupt change from the Castle Cavillor dressing chamber to a bitterly cold and windy hilltop. "A great deal has happened since I saw you last."

"Indeed." She prowled around me like a cat making sure of its master. "Art thou abused? Suffering some sickness?"

"Just need a bath and new clothes and about fifty hours of sleep. But first I must go to Signé."

"We go to Benedik's tree. No need for the sour sister." Her fingers touched my hair and bristling chin and stroked my lips. "I shall sorely miss the body's pleasures. Humans do certain things very well."

"I intend to set all Xancheirans free," I said, gently removing her hand, "your kind as well. None of you should die for a deed of generous friendship."

"Signé told me of thy plan. A noble dream, but too risky."

"It's too late to change it, so please, take me to Signé and tell me how to convince your people to enter the Sanctuary pool."

"Kyr will root thee before following thy direction," she said spitefully, as she started down the hill toward the mainland. "Perhaps I should do it first and give thee a gentle dissolution." Pique sped her steps to a steady jog.

Every moment that flitted past was an agony. Three hours. Why the devil had I thought that would be enough?

"When the time is right, you can send me back as you've done before, yes?"

"Yes, else I'd never have been able to bring thee here. The sentinel and the boundary are one. Thy power creates a path to me, and it remains intact despite the Dark Divide."

"So I'll return to exactly the same place."

"Only thine own working can alter the path." She trotted even faster, so I couldn't query further.

Once we entered the coastal forest, I felt the subtle shifting that Morgan used. Soon the trees were no longer hardy birches and pines but the unnatural variety of the Xancheiran wood. Were the splinters in place? I should have kept one of my own before giving Signé the rest. *Should have . . .* So many things I should have done.

The first glimpses of the citadel dome above the trees had my blood racing faster than our pace. My thoughts churned with how to trigger the silver linkage in so many trees at once, when Safia halted abruptly, frowning at the dead leaves and bulging roots of the forest floor. She dropped to her knees, scrabbled through leaves and twigs, and laid her hands on the bare earth. After a moment, she glared up at me, green gaze filled with fury. "Liar! Violator! Death-bringer!"

"I don't underst—"

She lunged forward, elbow aimed at my knees. I twisted away, only to trip on a massive root and crash to earth. Safia leapt on top of me, scrabbling for advantage. She seemed to have four hands, six elbows, and eight feet, every one of them lethal. Her strength matched that of any Order sparring partner; her rage doubled it. Grunting, twisting, writhing, it took all I had to pin her without killing her—or her killing me. I straddled her back, her silver gards near blinding me in the dimness under the trees.

"What," I said, heaving and swallowing hard as I held her face down, "have I done now?"

"Brought our ruin!" Her bitter anguish was muffled by the ground.

It was other cries explained her distress. The shrill yip of a white-tailed eagle, followed by another and another echoing through the quiet from every direction at once—the hunting cries of Morgan and her kin.

"How is it possible they're here?" I said, horrified, shaking Safia's shoulders. "They couldn't have followed me. They weren't with me. I was within walls. The void is not yet repaired."

"In the true lands, there are no human walls," she said, sobbing. "And Signé says the blue one is thy lover, bound to thee across all lands. The blue one was likely watching thee, and when I allowed thy crossing, followed in thy wake. Now all will die. Benedik . . . beloved . . ."

I'd thought it was only *dreams* of Morgan had shadowed my journey to Cavillor.

"No one's going to die," I said, releasing my hold. "Get me to Signé."

Safia scrambled up and away from me. But she didn't run. Her lovely face was streaked with dirt, blood, and tears.

"I'm sorry," I said. "I am yet so ignorant. But I do know this: This is the hour of choosing. Live or die. For you. For Benedik. For the world. You've been my guide through so many seasons. Now show me how to find life when all seems ended. Is that not your place in the Everlasting? Your duty and your joy?"

"Thou'rt as mad as we are."

I took no offense, for she grabbed my hand and set out running through the wood. Three times on that journey, she slammed me against the bole of a tree. Each time terror insisted that bark consumed my legs and circled my throat. But always she drew me away when some danger I could not perceive passed. Or perhaps she merely wished to terrorize me.

We came to the verge of the wood. Streaks of blue fire were just visible through the branches of Benedik's great oak. Morgan and her kin blocked the outer gates.

"I need to get inside the citadel." I had to know if Signé had distributed the splinters.

"No. Set Benedik free. No more help until it's done."

"You can let him out yourself, once you've shown me a way inside."

"Never again can I free him." She stretched out her arms.

"Oh, Safia!" My finger traced the exquisite silver vines that encircled her arms, the leaves on the backs of her hand just on the verge of unfurling, the tendrils twining her long fingers. Someone had methodically drawn a blade across every vine and tendril and packed red clay into the wounds. Horrid scars formed as the cuts healed, destroying the sinuous continuity of the gards.

"I can no longer know his tree properly," she said. "For me to bring him out could kill him or leave him half tree, half man."

"Kyr did this," I spat through gritted teeth.

"Kyr is lost," she said with such grief as must wrench a stone's heart. "That he cannot enter this land or heal it, that he cannot show Signé the glories of the Everlasting, is hurtful beyond a human's dreaming."

"Come." I drew her with me, slipping across the yard to the great oak as soundlessly as bodies could move.

"Find a bit of silver left on the tree," I whispered. My fingers had to touch the linked splinter to carry my magic to Benedik and the rest of them. "It will be tucked into the bark or beside a root, as small as the gards on your fingers. It might be high, but I'm thinking not."

Please gods let it be here. We'd no time to spare. Dozens of blue-marked Danae stood between us and the citadel gates, some on the causeway, others scattering into the wood on either side of it. Where was Signé? And where was Morgan? She could locate me so easily . . .

"Here!" The silver splinter gleaming on Safia's fingertip might have been a sliver of her broken gards. She touched the oak gently then backed away. "Do as thou must. I'll keep them away."

I was already on my knees between the great roots of the oak, pressing the silver to the bark, ensuring my finger touched both splinter and tree. I had rehearsed this spellwork in my head a dozen times, but that was before the harrowing journey and Cavillor. The cries of hunting Danae split the air from every side; any one of them could be Morgan or Tuari.

Sorely regretting Fix's lost rubies, I closed my eyes and summoned magic. The power grew as I envisioned the chain of twenty thousand splinters, a spark of gleaming silver tucked in bark, in root, in branch or hole . . . each one marking a human spirit, itself like gleaming silver that hid such variety of enchantments. Children, women, men . . . duc and sorcerers and ordinaries . . . scholars and washwomen . . . farmers and artisans . . . fishermen and alewives . . . those who touched the divine with their magic . . . those who nursed infants . . .

When magic filled my every muscle, every bone, lungs and heart and veins, I poured it all through the splinter and the oak.

Never had I felt such an outrush of enchantment. Sheer power . . . heady and exhilarating . . . surely enough to dissolve the boundaries between heaven and earth, not just trees and humans . . . until the screams began. Men's cries, women's, the wails of children—all of them in pain. *Hold on,* I said. *I'm sorry it hurts. But you're free . . . you're going home . . . they're not going to hurt you any more . . . please . . .* The cries rattled my skull and clawed my entrails, and I was sure I was going mad and everything in the world was shaking. . . .

"Stop." The man's hand gripped mine. A big hand. Rough. Made of bark perhaps. Or scribed in brilliant light, silver or blue. But I'd no strength to spare to open my eyes.

"No," I growled. "This ends today!"

"Lucian de Remeni, get up. They're coming for you!" The woman's urgency pierced the roaring frenzy in my ears. Thunder in winter . . . or perhaps it was wind rocked the stones of Evanide . . . or an earthshaking . . . or the end of the world.

The hand held steady—not *my* hand, because every part of me was shaking, and still the magic flowed out of me. I dared not move until all were free.

"He's yet feeding the spell," said the man. "Only there's no magic in it. He has to stop."

"Lucian, open your eyes!" A body crouched in front of me, near enough I could feel her warmth like a brazier. She smelled of good earth and green things. "Stop feeding the spell or you'll die. It's your life flowing now, not magic."

"'Tis the silver in his hand," said a different woman, impatient. Cold fingers pried my own apart. The biting splinter fell away. "See? Humans think they know everything."

The outrush ceased. Chaos battered me. *Are they dying?* Screams, wails, moans, and thunder made it impossible to hear my own question.

"Open your eyes. You must get away." Hands—Signé's hands—cupped my head.

"Are they dying?" It sounded as if I'd been the one screaming. "I'm so sorry—"

Flames roared on every side of me—or was it *trees* burning?

I leapt upward, spun around, and would have fallen over if multiple hands hadn't caught me.

They'd brought me inside the citadel walls. Torches burned, not trees. But tremors racked the ground and night had fallen, which churned my belly more than it was already, though I couldn't say why. Depletion had my knees porridge, my head aching, and the rest of me shivering and sick.

"Not dying," said the man who stood between Signé and Safia. He was a big man, his thick hair the color of old honey, just like Signé's. Their kinship was clear. Though he did not bear his sister's terrible scars, Duc Benedik's own were visible—shadowed eyes and deep lines on gray skin. Will alone kept him upright.

"Emergence feels a bit like being sewn back together with broken glass and splinters. They've got to remember how to walk, see, and hear amidst a battle of the long-lived which makes the earth shake. My sister and I must go to them. But first we brought you inside for your safety. It seems the only thing the long-lived hate more than each other is you."

"We must get *you* to safety!" said Safia, tugging his arm.

"No," he said, and gently shed her grip. "Our duty is out there. My people and I are forever in your debt, generous one. And yours, too, Remeni. My sister says that Siever—"

"Mighty Deunor! Even now, Siever is working the magic to repair the void." Had it been three hours? "We must get Kyr and the others to Sanctuary."

The earth heaved and bucked as if a whale swam under its surface. Deep, hollow groans from below, scraping and sharp cracks from every side. New cries shrilled, nearer, as seams gaped in the outer wall. Mortar and rubble began to cascade from its heights . . . and from the citadel itself.

"Run!" All of them shouted together.

I could scarce stand, but Safia grabbed my hand and pulled me through dead gardens, broken gates, piled rubble, and down a perilously steep slope into a treed gully. More Xancheirans? How many were unchanged when I'd run out of magic? As trees swayed and earth buckled, ferocious shrills and shrieks resounded from every direction. Terror forced my legs to run.

I stumbled, but Safia didn't slow. Had I fallen, she would have dragged me.

Upward again, through trees and rocks and snarled vines until a stitch in my side had me short of breath. We rounded a fallen slab, only to be staggered by a blast of wind across the hilltop. Safia's hand slipped out of mine, but I could not move a step more or raise my head to see where she'd gone.

Bent over, hands on my knees, I fought for breath and sense. Lightning flickered. Thunder rumbled through the ground in company with the earth's own groaning.

"Safia," I panted when I could summon words. "Is the Severing undone? Are we too late?"

"Oh, gentle Lucian, she cannot answer just now. Or is it faithless Lucian? Lying Lucian?"

Morgan sat on a fallen slab. Safia sprawled unmoving on the grass in front of her.

"Goddess Mother, did you kill her?"

"We do not kill our own kind as brutish humans do." She smoothed Safia's hair even as the wind snarled it. "Especially those who've gone silver."

"Do you transform them into beasts?"

"Certainly not. They'll be returned, disembodied, to the land . . . to the Everlasting which will embrace and reshape them."

"So you destroy the bodies, the spirits, the beings that they were. It sounds very like murder, especially here where they cannot return to the land of their own will."

Morgan's skin blazed beneath her gards. "Our ways are merciful."

"Not to humans! The tales told of humans misled into storms and left to freeze or drown, tricked into bogs, or stolen from their beds, those are true, aren't they? No mercy for *my* kind. If you destroy Kyr and Safia and their people, will you stay to tend the humans trapped in trees or feed those who've been set free this day? Or must they die, too?"

"The life in this place is diseased, Lucian. It will poison the greater world for my kind and thine own."

"Not if Sanctuary can heal the silver madness. Love helped Safia hold on to herself all these seasons, as she guided me here. She believes that as the land is rejoined to the Everlasting, Sanctuary will be restored. Everything she's told me along the way has been true."

I knelt at Safia's side. Her breathing was easy; her blood pulse even. No blood or break was visible.

"*You* are not cruel, Morgan. Your father would condemn fifty of your brothers and sisters to die because of pique—because their deeds of kindness were done for *humans*. And if they die and the Severing is not repaired, twenty thousand humans will die. I can't get them all back to the greater world before they starve."

"Thou canst not comprehend our duties."

"If my friend cannot undo the Severing, none of this matters. But if it *is* undone, as I pray will happen this night, and if Safia and her kin are held in this pool, isn't it *possible* Sanctuary can return them to their true natures? Isn't that what the tale of Rhiain says?"

She snugged her arms about herself. "I should not have told thee Rhiain's tale."

"But you did. You *wanted* me to understand. And here is Rhiain's Sanctuary right in front of you. Healing cannot come from murder, however *gentle*. Nor will it solve the illness of our own world to leave Xancheira separate. You once told me that your nature is to heal and nurture the living world, and that you're free to choose the recipient of your gift. Morgan, what if this breaking has, at least in some part, caused our demon winter?"

She waited so long to answer, I feared we would be lost. I had to move. "So, how can we get Safia's people to Sanctuary to await the change? It could happen any moment."

When Morgan laid a hand on Safia's head, I moved to stop her. But her other hand held me back. "I do but wake her."

Safia stirred. When she saw Morgan, she scrambled backward, straight into me.

"Morgan won't hurt you." I hoped.

Morgan lifted her chin proudly. "If she will bring her people here, I'll bring mine after. I'll tell them I've found the proper place to seal our aberrant kin into the Everlasting, and I'll persuade Tuari to drive the silver ones into the water. If the change comes soon enough . . . and if they can be healed . . . so be it. But I make no promises if they harm one of our own."

"Is this one trustworthy?" asked Safia.

"Yes. We are bound together by love from our youth. And though we've drifted apart, she knows I speak truth, and I know she does as well."

"I'll tell Kyr thou'rt he whose magic intrudes on our peace," said Safia. "That thou dost threaten Sanctuary. He'll come."

"Whatever you think will draw them here. And, Safia, when I call your name twice over, send me."

She nodded. Then grabbing my head, she kissed me full on. She smiled wickedly at Morgan, and vanished in a streak of silver.

Morgan laughed, her sad humor giving texture to the night. "Clearly she does not know I betrayed thee. I'll tell my father that I spied thee here, without salt this time. I'll need no other tale to draw him. I am sorry, friend Lucian. I do love thee in my way. But I am the daughter of the archon and perhaps not so faithful as this Safia."

"You've saved my life ten times over. Helped me learn what I needed. Guided my friends safely. I'm grateful for that . . . friend Morgan."

Pleasure illumined her face more than did her gards. But I didn't feel it anymore.

It wasn't so long until I heard Kyr's bellowing. Silver streaked the wood down the hill. I stood beside the pool, close enough no one could squeeze between.

"Step away, meddler," said Kyr, his body sculpted by the gathered light of his kind, who quickly moved to encircle the pool and me. "So thou'rt the one who has ensured the doom of so many. Signé's people will suffer for thy deeds. They cannot survive until we heal the land."

"I cannot step away," I said. "And a healing will come. If not this night, then tomorrow or the next day. Lord Siever works, even now, to undo the Severing."

"Prideful fool," cried Kyr, anguished, "thou'lt destroy the Everlasting!"

I explained to him our plan for his people's healing in Sanctuary. But he sneered and hefted the spear in his hand. What madman ever recognizes his illness?

"Break Siever's magic, human, or I'll root thee myself. And when the humans begin to die again, thou'lt feel every whisper of their pain. . . ."

"Hold!" I said, as blue light glimmered in the wood behind him. "There's more to this."

I stepped up to the rim of the pool and extended my hand. Not to Kyr but to the one who waited at his right hand. "Safia, Safia."

And then did the world shatter. The ground shook. The stars exploded. Safia rushed forward and touched my brow, just as the blue Danae yipped like hunting kites from every side and Kyr let fly his spear. As I jumped backward into the Sanctuary pool, Safia toppled after me in a spray of blood.

"No!" I cried into blackness.

Entirely depleted, powerless to change my destination, I opened my eyes to the Marshal's dressing chamber, dead silence . . . and Damon.

CHAPTER 39

Damon sat leisurely thumbing through a large leather folio, his chair set squarely in the doorway of the dressing chamber. It would be hours before I could summon magic. I might be able to throttle him, but at least five people lurked on the other side of the dressing screen behind him. Likely they were Order knights, capable of killing me before I could break Damon's neck or fracture his fingers, both of which appealed to me just now.

Thus I remained sitting on the floor, leaning on the wall, and shivering uncontrollably.

The spider glanced up and produced that smile of paternal satisfaction that I loathed. I'd best wait for better odds before wiping it from his face with a fist. And then I would confront the Marshal, too, for how did Damon know I'd hidden here unless the Marshal had told him?

Damon closed the folio—my damning portraits?—and leaned forward like that pleased parent, watching his child learn to walk.

"My, my, Lucian," he said and blew a large sigh. "Someday you must teach me this astonishing veil magic. Had I not witnessed your occasional *disappearances* in those days you worked in the Registry Tower, I'd have had Ferenc's hounds scouring all of Cavillor at the first report of your vanishing. Instead I have spent this very long night in a closet, waiting for you to reappear. Would you like to hear how I knew you would?"

"Certainly."

"The spell produces a slight change in the quality of the air, as if you leave a hole in the world. Indeed it fills with oddments of scents and breezes as it waits for your return. But you don't leave, do you? It would be so much more useful if you could actually creep away while you hide—especially on a night when you believe you're going to die."

Laughter near choked me to think how close he was to understanding what I did . . . and yet so far. The laughter held no merriment, not while imagining thousands of people half emerged from trees when my magic failed, not while smelling Safia's warm blood on my jaque, not when I imagined the poisoned vines of Xancheira devouring Navronne or the dread alternative—thousands emerged from the trees starving all over again to the sound of Morgan's feral shrieks.

To die not knowing if any of the plan worked was bitter. To believe I'd left matters worse was insupportable.

"Do you think the Marshal would mind if I b-borrowed his gray cloak for my visit to the executioner? Holding the . . . vanishing spell . . . for so long has drained me dry. I'd not thought to have curators taking up residence in the Marshal's closet to prevent my escape."

He popped up from the chair and rapped on the dressing screen. "No cloak and no food. You will just have to shiver for a while. Thanks to your small rebellion, the Fifty have had all night to mull my proposals. It *was* unfortunate we could not produce you at your trial. After the grooming of your journey from Evanide, it would have saved a deal of persuasion. You look quite savage, and every one of these judges knows . . . knew . . . Lucian de Remeni as a quiet, well-disciplined young man of good family. Soft. Weak, save in magic."

The dressing screen was removed. As I feared, guards were ready with shackles and silk cord. Not Order guards, though. These wore Canis-Ferenc's crimson and silver. It cheered me to imagine Damon didn't trust Order knights to shackle one of their own at the word of an outsider. He couldn't know which knights might recognize me despite my savage appearance.

The first man who laid a hand on me crashed backward with a broken nose. The second would be feeling my boot in his balls until the moon fell. The third grabbed my hair and near twisted my head off. But the fourth laid a blow to my middle that near rammed my gut into my throat. I could tell I'd hurt them by the lack of consideration as they yanked off my boots, hobbled my ankles, and silkbound my hands. Damon likely approved the bloody split on my cheekbone.

"This is necessary, Lucian," he said, once the guards had left us alone. "But it is not the end you imagine. Trust me."

I bleated a laugh. Appropriate for a stupid sheep. Yet he was not smirking as he said it. Not gloating. Not sad or sorry. He was excited.

"Why in the name of every god should I trust you?"

"Because I have never lied to you. Not ever. Yes, I know the Order considers omissions a lie but today you will understand why I had to omit certain pieces of our plan. Lucian de Remini *will* die today or tomorrow"—though I'd known it, anticipated it, resigned myself to it, my gut hollowed—"but *Green-shank* . . . that one will have a choice to make."

"You're mad." No other explanation presented itself.

"Vainglorious, yes. Not mad."

He rubbed a thumb on his silver ring and my lips and tongue grew numb. "This is less grotesquely obvious than Pluvius's leather mask. Be sure I will give you voice again when the time of your choice comes. For now, observe and consider all you know and all you've learned—of yourself, of our kind, and of Navronne."

The eyes of the Fifty burnt holes in my skin as I stood chained to the railed dais in front of them. The pleasure of seeing Gramphier, Scrutari, and Pluvius led away similarly restrained and condemned to hang for their corruption did not alleviate my raging frustration at my enforced silence. But I resisted my body's demands to break the oaken rails of the dais or bellow in wordless rage. That would but confirm the verdict I knew was coming. Perhaps dignity and silence could make one of the judges question.

The judge at one end of the horseshoe table stood and read their finding. "It is with sincere regret that we, the Convocation of the Fifty, judge Lucian de Remeni-Masson, sole remaining descendant of two noble bloodlines, guilty of deliberate murder."

The faceless judge was a small woman who sounded sorry as she had not for the condemned curators. That made the words no easier to hear.

"That the victims were conspirators in his own family's murder . . . that the circumstances of that loss and the venal, repugnant actions of the Pure-blood Registry drove a virtuous man to such extremity . . . cannot relieve the combined danger of his moral decay and exceptional power for magic. We see no remedy for his evils but death. At the sun's zenith tomorrow, the time when power for magic is at its nadir, Lucian de Remeni's hands will be severed from his body and burnt, and he will find his merciful end at the headsman's block."

Merciful . . . So much work, so much loss, so much pain. Wasted. My sister left alone with a name she dared not use.

Numb and shivering, I watched the crimson-and-silver clad guards unlock my chains. I wished they would take me straight to the block and be done with it. No matter Damon's foolery, no matter what I'd believed since rediscovering my birth name, Lucian de Remeni and Paratus Greenshank were the same person. I relished the scents he loved and favored the food he liked. The places he'd walked felt familiar to me. When the axe severed Lucian's neck, Greenshank would die, too.

The hooded judges sat silent as the four guards led me out. My stumbling, shaking weakness gave them a good show.

The surprise came when my escorts deposited me in the viewing gallery again, albeit muted and chained to the iron grillwork. Damon must want me to witness his triumphal reshaping of the world. At first I refused to look, huddling in my corner and apologizing to the gods for the insufferable presumption that had got me into this fix. But then the spokesman judge began reading again, and the words drew me to kneel up to watch and listen. . . .

". . . we judge the Pureblood Registry guilty of deliberate, savage murder throughout two centuries, of conspiracy, persecution, false imprisonment, extortion, wanton cruelty, forgery, and uncountable other crimes listed herein. We therefore recommend to the Sitting of the Three Hundred that the Pureblood Registry be dissolved, that its administrative functions regarding authentication of birth and bloodline, approvals of applications for marriage or childbearing, and regulation of pureblood interaction with the population of ordinaries be controlled directly by the Three Hundred. As Curator Lares-Damon proposes, a single Administrator of Pureblood Affairs should be named to oversee these activities, that person reporting directly to the Three Hundred. The Administrator should be a pureblood sorcerer of strong intellect, independent mind, and familiarity with the tasks required. Curator Lares-Damon is hereby forbidden to serve in the capacity of Administrator."

Independent mind. I had to laugh. Damon had persuaded them to appoint Pons after all.

Once the judgment was signed and sealed, Damon rose again. Sincere. Glowing with solemn righteousness. Gods save all . . . anyone would believe him at peace with the gods, convinced that a plan approved by coerced judges would reform centuries of greed and self-interest.

"This is a painful day for all of us," he said. "But I feel the same relief as you, worthy judges. This age of infamy will soon be behind us. Now we must look to the future. Yestereve, I swore that purification of the Registry could change our position of authority in this dangerous world. What if I could bring you a leader who bears in his hand—and his blood—the means and the *right* to take us forward? A man who can break Caedmon's stranglehold on pureblood governance, and ensure that we shall never have to bow and scrape to ordinaries again. A man who can bring peace to Navronne with reason, might . . . and magic?"

The judges stirred.

"For many years have I searched for such a man. Not until seven years ago, when I heard rumor of some extraordinary portraits in the Registry Archives, did I find him." He tapped the leather-bound book in the crook of his arm. "A detail caught my eye in Lucian de Remeni's portrait of a man who lived in the eastern reaches of Morian. It was so small an ornament of his garments that neither Remeni nor anyone else noticed it. The man had grown up disadvantaged, lacking a great family to embrace or teach him of his bloodlines or his capabilities. I sought him out and found him immeasurably gifted. And he had in his possession an artifact of extraordinary rarity. Today, as we stand on the cusp of destiny, I've brought him to testify before you."

Damon opened his arms wide as the man I'd seen unmasked the previous night entered the hall. A majestic figure, not hooded this morning, not masked. He wore the white and silver armor I had seen in his quarters, though without blazon of any kind. Even the hilt of his sword was unmarked. Had I any notion that Damon could orchestrate the weather, I would have believed he arranged the beams of sunlight that shot through the clerestory at the moment to illuminate the Knight Marshal of Evanide and his red–gold hair. Was it only my imagining or did a gasp of recognition ripple through the Fifty?

"Step up, sir knight." Damon motioned to the railed dais. "Your name, if you will."

"Geraint de Serre."

"You are halfblood."

"Indeed so. My pureblood sire defied his family and took an ordinary to wife. Though to be sure, my mother's people, though fallen on hard times, never considered themselves *ordinary*, but claimed noble descent. On the day he took me to be registered, my father repented his crime and returned to his family. As required, my mother took me in for portraits, but warned me never to demonstrate the odd skills in my hands."

Spoken without apology. A quiet dignity testified of a man sure of his place in the world.

Damon again. "When I inquired about your mother's claim—for a noble bloodline was exactly what Lucian de Remeni's portrait revealed—what did you show me?"

The Marshal passed his silver pendant to Damon. . . .

All unfolded as I had imagined. Damon showed each judge the gold celebration medallion embedded in the plain silver. In fine dramatic fashion, he told the story of Caedmon's vanity and the birth medallions, so that when he removed the gold coin from the silver casing and handed it to the Marshal, every observer—myself included—held breath. The Marshal raised it high, and the medallion glowed of its own light. Beams of purple, azure, and green streamed into the aether, Caedmon's colors—the purple of Ardra, the azure of Morian, the loden green of Evanore, the three provinces Caedmon had united to build Navronne.

A tall judge burst from his seat. "How do we know this is not some trick? A halfblood born to an undisciplined servitor? A portrait done by a madman? This curator who has confessed to his own corruption happening upon the chimera—part royal, part sorcerer? Half of us here could create a coin that would shine such light when a hound licked it."

Even from my distance, I felt Damon's smile. He'd known the question would come.

The curator pulled two sheets from his folio and passed the first to the woman who had read the verdicts. "Here is the tale of our salvation, judges of the Fifty. The first is de Serre's portrait, drawn by Lucian de Remeni in his first year as a Registry portraitist. Its divine truth is clear. Note the lily of Navronne stitched into Geraint's tunic."

He gave them a while to pass the portrait one to the other. And then he passed along the gold medallion. "Examine this carefully. Commit its every detail to your memory. Those historians or examiners amongst you, use your skills to aid us."

Several of the judges called "affirmed" after examining it. Once he had retrieved the medallion, Damon gave the woman judge the second sheet. "This is the medallion's formal validation. An examination, description, and explanation written by the most gifted historian our kind has ever known. A man so revered for his intellect, insight, and magic that King Eodward made him his Royal Historian." My body tightened, knowing. "Vincente de Remeni."

My grandsire. Familiar only from story. It was but one more sorrow of this day that Vincente de Remeni's next-to-last heir, the one who had inherited at least a part of his extraordinary gift, was going to die a murdering madman, and that his last descendent, gifted in myriad ways, would never be able to use his name. *Ah, Juli, I am so sorry.*

As the last parchment passed down the line, one and then the other of the judges rose. By the time it had reached the end of the curved table they were leaving their seats in a flood, gone to touch a sorcerer of Caedmon's blood-line, clamoring to know more of him. How would any who had not heard de Serre's voice comprehend such instant willingness to believe?

The Marshal received each one with a nod and his hand, and I knew the flood of warmth they would feel, as if he looked into their souls and knew their strengths and weaknesses, his gaze promising to make them better men and women. Had any leader of men ever been gifted so generously with a quality so befitting a king? One and then the other bent a knee before him. As the uproar grew, Damon stood to the side, serene. Fool that I was, I still wanted to believe.

And then the Marshal raised his hands and spoke. "Know this about me, noble judges: I shall be no *ordinary* king."

Every one of them cheered at this, which struck me as unseemly. They were judges, vowed to be impartial in their considerations.

"I have served the past seven years in a strict military order," he continued, "learning of duty and justice and the power of magic to fight for them. I cannot change what I am. So you'll not see me dressing myself in silks and furs and dallying with rich men's daughters. Nor shall I mutilate the dead to bargain with Magrog or sail the coastal waters playing pirate captain to prove myself a worthy king."

They nodded, comparing him to Eodward's vile sons.

"From the day I am acknowledged by the Sitting of the Three Hundred, Geraint de Serre will be no more. Every hour of every day will I live masked to remind all that I have been and will ever be a bearer of a divine gift. When the day comes that I claim my birthright, I shall be known only as the Sorcerer King. Ordinaries, peasant and noble alike, will kneel to the power the gods have given those of our kind, and I and my heirs shall rule Navronne with righteous magic until the end of days."

So wild was the cheering, one would imagine him anointed already. My heart soared as well. As ever he spoke directly to my spirit, nourishing my deepest hopes. What a king he would make.

I'd said that before. Fix had said it. But did I believe it?

That glorious voice . . . that noble sympathy that woke my spirit . . . And yet where I saw a man of passion and vision, Dunlin believed the Marshal a man of ferocious rigor—which his own wild spirit craved. Fix believed the Marshal entirely pragmatic, yet could not shake faith in his honor after a single face-to-face meeting. The Archivist believed him devoted to the Order, even knowing he had violated the Order's most sacred trust by destroying my relict and setting a mind-destroying trap aimed at brother knights. Surely it was Geraint de Serre's bent to make others hear what they wanted to believe.

What had he actually said? A masked king. Apart. No face to present to the world. Separate. Elite. Pure. Would what worked so well for a small fraternity focused on works of justice be the right thing for a great kingdom?

Eodward had been a wise, generous, truly noble man who had brought Navronne out of war and into glory. His subjects saw his face, fought alongside him, and adored him. It was only his last years were blighted with the sad truth of his sons and the terrible turn in the weather, a mystery which no pureblood had been able to solve. If no one knew the identity of the Sorcerer King . . . then who would know his successor . . . or when his successor took over? Even more important, who in the world would hold him to account?

Misgivings festered in me like Xancheira's vines as the lauds faded and the hall emptied. What of Eodward's lost will? Navronne's succession was not based solely on primogeniture. Our king was empowered to choose his heir from any of his blood.

As darkness fell, the sickness of depletion had me dizzy, my thoughts blown to nonsensical. When they came for me, I was asleep.

I didn't fully wake when they moved me. And it was likely in my dreams I heard Damon.

"Did I not promise a day of triumph, Greenshank? Now we need to put you away for a while. Sleep well, knowing that the Remenis have determined the future of Navronne in glorious ways you cannot yet imagine."

When an iron door slammed, I embraced the dark.

CHAPTER 40

"Mother's blessing for this day."

I was astonished. "I'm not dead?"

"Nay, *still* not." Lantern light revealed a skinny old man as pale and dry as a withered turnip and just as expressive.

"What's the time?" I sat up on a hard bed, unhappy to find shackles and silkbindings still in place. I could have batted this man down with one elbow.

"Third hour of the morning watch. Sorry about the hobbles. The curator would not have you misbehave."

My execution was set for midday, not much time for misbehavior.

My fingers twitched in their bindings. Why did they bother with silkbinding? It had been late when they retrieved me from the viewing gallery, so I could have slept only a few hours. Far too short a time to replenish such depletion. And I couldn't recall the last time I'd eaten. My belly felt like to devour itself. Or perhaps that was just sickness at such abject failure at everything I'd tried to do.

The turnip and four guards soon led me out. Damon awaited us at the top of the dungeon stair.

"Will you not just get on with things?" I snapped. The hobble chain made going difficult. "Or feed me lest I puke bile on your executioner's boots."

"We'll get you cleaned up. But you'll likely appreciate not having anything in your stomach for the next few hours."

I didn't like the sound of that. Surely they didn't remove the hands while the condemned sorcerer yet lived.

A labyrinth of deserted, barren corridors brought us to a stone closet furnished with a drain, a tin tub, an incongruous lump of lavender-scented soap, and a servant who proceeded to strip, bathe, and shave me. Not just my chin, but head as well. It was unnerving for both of us, with four enchanted sword points touching my bare skin and Damon eyeing every move.

When I thanked the nervous youth for his care with the razor knife, he shook his head and pointed to his ears. Deaf. Goddess Mother . . .

Though the air on my hairless scalp was strange, it was glorious to be clean, and the underdrawers and sleeveless tunic given me were of decent linen. But false bravado died unspoken, for at Damon's gesture my hands were silkbound, separately this time, and the shackles replaced. He didn't speak. Nor did he smirk or patronize or provide additional garments, save one. When the black mantle enshrouded me bald head to bare toes, even covering my eyes, the sickness in my gut gnawed deeper. Indeed I was glad not to have eaten.

A short, brisk journey later, the mantle came off. We'd arrived at a chamber very like a smaller version of the Evanide armory, worktables littered with weapons, sharpening stones, engraver's tools, boxes of metal scraps, flasks of oil, and such. No headsman's block.

"Place him as I instructed you," said Damon. "Once he's fixed to the wall, remove the chains, but leave the silkbindings."

Fear brought back the dizziness, and my mind scrambled for some way to stay the devil spider's weaving before I lost my wits entire. Silkbound, I'd no way to work magic.

"It's too early," I croaked. "I've got till midday."

No one spoke. Guards bound me to a wall with leather straps, facing out. Even when they were done with all the buckles, I was not particularly uncomfortable. But I couldn't move anything the width of an eyelash, not even my head. Certainly not my hands.

"Deunor's fire, Damon, you value our magic and believe it should be protected. You know mine is unusual. How can you throw it away?"

"I do value you."

"Then what is all this?"

"Preparing you for your destiny. You're a stubborn man and I can't have you arguing or interfering. Once it's done, all will be clear."

"Give him wine at the least. I don't like my subjects twitching." The ever-present irritability, voiced in tones so like rusty gate hinges, came from my left, but of course, I couldn't turn my head to see if it was truly the Archivist, come all the way from Evanide.

And the Archivist's *subject*? No, no, no . . . "Merciful Goddess, Damon, what is this?"

"Better he should feel what's coming," said another man before my panicked question got an answer. "Sooner or later we must all pay for the power we bear."

The words' harsh meaning was wholly at odds with the mellow warmth of the speaker. But it was indeed the Knight Marshal who strolled into view alongside the Archivist. The three of them here together. Damon. The Archivist. The Marshal. Inek had warned me. *Fool, fool, fool.*

As the Archivist left the others and joined me, he dropped his rust-red hood and removed his mask. I'd never seen him in the flesh. Scant white hair and beard lay like frost upon a scarred, cragged landscape of experiences, not just his own, but those of uncountable knights, parati, squires, and tyros. His lips were thin and arid, and pond ice in the frozen realm of Hansk could be no colder than the blue eyes examining me so intimately.

"You will thank me," he whispered, entirely without mockery.

I would have laughed at such a solemn assertion, save for the knuckle-length splinter of silver he held in front of my eyes. With a blink of magic, he plunged it into my left wrist.

"What are you—? Gah!" A second splinter pierced the right wrist. Was this how they cut off a doomed sorcerer's hands?

Anger bloomed like balefire, blunting fear. "Magrog's unholy triumvirate. One servant, one puppet, one puppetmaster!"

Another splinter a finger length above the first, just above the strap that immobilized my wrist. A matching sting on the left.

"Knight Marshal, you can't believe Damon will allow you to rule."

The Marshal chuckled. Damon remained silent. And as the Archivist placed new splinters, the previous ones shot blazing spikes into the veins of my arm, into the bones, erasing sensible thought. I'd felt this before. . . .

The Archivist's deft hands moved quickly leaving a chain of fire up the inside of both arms. When he moved away to the worktable, I prayed he was done, for I would swear a dagger had opened my flesh from wrist to shoulder.

The Marshal stepped closer, tilting his head as if I were a curiosity. "I told you Damon had great plans for our future, Lucian. Yours just requires a bit more pain. Pain has always been the difference between us. While you dabbled in your art and learning, a soft youth of divine promise and nurturing family, I was arrested for practice of illicit magic. The Registry knew well how to teach halfbloods their proper place. Now I'll direct the course of their dissolution. Amusing, isn't it, how my *impure* blood will give me the life you assumed was yours alone?"

"I believed in you," I said, breathless from pain and the weight of my blindness. "I believed in the Order. You believed, too."

For an instant his eyes reflected the man he had been . . . yearning . . . focused on a righteous future just out of reach. But a blink left them hard again, and he flashed the rakish smile I'd glimpsed a lifetime ago in his dressing closet. "Ah, paratus, you shall certainly serve the Order's future."

Then he leaned close and spoke softly so that only I would hear. "All that was before I remembered how much I despise purebloods like you and Inek. Yon Archivist doesn't quite understand that Caedmon's heir is not so devoted to his arcane fraternity as he is. The Order will be useful these first few months. But then, just between the two of us, I think it will be time for those self-righteous pricks to drown. Perhaps I'll have you do it."

I couldn't respond. The Archivist had returned with a handful of splinters longer than the first ones. Where was he going to put these?

The inside of my left ankle. And then the right. My legs soon blazed from ankle to groin.

Another handful. Tiny ones. Merciful Goddess.

He planted the first just in front of my left ear, the next a knuckle length higher. The initial sting was bad enough, but it was the penetrating magic that cracked my skull as it shot all the way down to my gut. The Archivist had to step aside as I vomited.

"Get it all out now," he said, and then returned to his work. Another and another, across my forehead, down past the other ear, then another. I tried to stay sensible by counting or estimating what pattern he made, but I could not. None of this made sense.

The Archivist stepped away. Only the leather straps held me upright. Breath came ragged. Spittle and bile dribbled down my chin. Though legs and face yet blazed, the pain in my arms had settled into to a grinding ache, as if every bone was fractured.

Damon hurried over and I flinched when his hand reached for my face. But it was only a towel he offered to blot my chin. And then a sip of water from an earthen cup. Even if I could have spoken, I would not have thanked him. Whatever this was, it was his idea.

The Archivist returned and placed a basket at my feet. I could not move enough to see what it held. Instead I tried to slow my breathing and remember all that Inek had taught me about enduring pain. *Focus outside yourself . . . erase emotion . . . erase the body . . .*

It didn't help. Not when the Archivist knelt down and wrapped something about my left ankle atop the first splinter. It felt as if it ripped out a ring of flesh, and I could not hold back a cry. And then another ring, and another . . . My body shook and heaved. I vomited again.

A long interruption allowed my vision to clear. Damon and the Marshal stood together, drinking, well away from their puking, sweating prisoner. The aroma of wine near made me heave again.

The Archivist, his brow wrinkled, examined my shoulder, then ran a finger down the outside of my arm. He paused and snapped his gaze to mine. "Fix!"

Panting, trembling, I could not imagine what his quiet exclamation meant.

"Allow the pain to become a part of you," he said softly, "altering the body without obliterating the spirit. That will make this go easier. *Fix* would tell you so."

Fix. The Archivist had found the Knight Defender's splinter in my arm.

When he wrapped something . . . metal . . . around my right wrist, I panted through the burning and considered Fix and his splinter. *Threading?* Is that what this was about? But that would change everything . . .

I sought his eyes. "Archivist—"

Another band went on and ate its way into my arm.

This time, I let go of reason and followed the snaking fire into a well of pain.

"Time to move forward, Greenshank. Geraint and the Archivist are off to breakfast. We've an hour to alter the course of history."

It was an effort to open my eyes. The lids were stuck together and weighed of lead. "Don't want to move."

I hadn't lost consciousness. From some great distance, I had felt them take me down from the wall, sit me on a bench, and wrap me in the black mantle. Now Damon crouched in front of me, solemn and sympathetic. "Come, you survived it, did you not?"

"What have you done to me?" My ribs ached with every breath. To speak made the pounding in my head thunderous. However unlikely, arms, legs, and face no longer pained me. All I could feel was a certain tightness. But I was shaking so hard my teeth rattled.

"I told you the truth. We prepared you for your proper destiny." He leaned close. "Though not everyone who watched understands that destiny entirely."

Damon, ever the spider.

Spice-scented steam bathed my face. "Drink this. You need your strength and your magic."

"Can't." My gut was too unsettled as yet.

He held the cup to my lips. "Drink. Two hours hence you will stand before the Three Hundred."

He poured it down me slowly, giving it time to work. The flavorful posset was gloriously hot, the milk thick and soothing, the wine strong. For the first time in an aeon, the shivering stopped.

He refilled the cup and did it all again. Muscle and bone felt stronger already. Power swelled between my eyes and behind my breastbone. I slurped the third cupful like an infant at its mother's breast.

"What destiny?" I said, as the edges of the world became exceedingly sharp. The castle around us teemed with waking life . . . with householders . . . with strangers . . . hundreds of people.

Damon rose and picked through the items on the worktable. He returned with a bit of purple fabric dangling from his finger. Silk, it appeared, embroidered in gold. "This. Take it. It's yours. Well deserved and fairly earned."

But when my hand found its way out of the black mantle, my gut hollowed. My arm was banded in bracelets of hammered silver, finely engraved with a variety of sigils. No embossing. Trigger points weren't needed, because the bracelets were embedded in my flesh. Threaded. Like Fix's splinter, like Fix's own bracelets, their magic could be triggered with will alone, not touch.

I ripped off the mantle. My other limbs were banded the same. Six on each arm, eight on each leg. I fumbled about my face, and hairless scalp, relieved to find no trace of metal. Perhaps that part had been delirium.

"What *are* these?"

"Tools. You'll need the support they can provide for great magics." Damon sat on the bench beside me and held out the slip of purple again. "*This* is the answer you've been seeking, Greenshank. This is yours, do you but choose it so."

A full-face mask. Silk, yes, a deep purple. The mask told the tale of Damon's use for me, for the purple of Caedmon's Ardra was bordered with a chain of three-petaled lilies worked in gold. *Royal* lilies.

"You are entirely mad," I said, hoarse.

"Many would say that. Navronne needs a Sorcerer King. But it needs one with brilliant magic and the discipline to use it, one with a true passion for justice and the strength to pursue it, not an ill-educated marketplace charlatan with a golden voice. You heard him. Geraint will use the cleansing of the Registry to make himself a tyrant. His voice will gather men and women to his side, and they won't know what's happening until it's too late."

But the Marshal's flaws could not qualify me to be the king of Navronne. "This is ludicrous. I am not of Caedmon's blood, and the judges supported him because of that royal kinship. I'm condemned for murder. I've nothing: no past, no family, no follower, not even a name I can use."

"Caedmon's blood has been proved. No further validation is needed, not with the Fifty as witnesses. You'll likely never need to demonstrate the medallion's magic. But if you do . . . this might help."

He held up his hand and in a trick every pureblood child learned before age ten, twisted his fingers and produced a coin—a gold coin struck with a raised edge and a woman's face.

"You heard Geraint swear to go masked every hour of every day, for I told him that such appearance of humility would win him favor, as you saw it do. So this mask will be threaded to your face—the Archivist has prepared you for it—never to be removed. No one will ever know you are not the man who spoke to the Fifty."

The Marshal and I were the same height, the same build. And Damon had shaved off my black hair, so different from the Marshal's red-gold.

"*This* is what you've planned all these years—to put a true sorcerer descendant of Caedmon on the throne of Navronne, only to replace him with an *imposter*? With *me*?"

"Geraint de Serre is corrupt. Deceit and conjuring men's hearts are the pillars of his nature, just as discipline and a passion for justice are yours. Unlike any usurper in history, he is armed with magic . . . and the Order. The old Marshal, the good, wise man who read my own soul so clearly, threatened to revoke Geraint's knighthood for repeated recklessness. Then he died. Suddenly. Inexplicably. Using his divine gift, Geraint persuaded the Archivist to skew the count and name him Knight Marshal, for the Archivist is more devoted to the ideal of the Sorcerer King even than I. Geraint's first acts as Marshal were to destroy your relict and lay that abhorrent trap. In the same way, he will manipulate purebloods, crush those who defy him, and use the Order to work his will. Once he is untouchable, he will destroy the Order, too."

"He told me he would force me to destroy the Order." And Inek had told me how unexpected the old Marshal's death had been. He'd had suspicions . . .

"Listen to me, Greenshank. Beyond all these things, you've a qualification that no other sorcerer in Navronne has displayed for more than a century—two mature bents. It's the source of your extraordinary magic."

I was instantly wary. "You never mentioned two bents."

"Come, come, Pluvius admitted he told you. The greedy fool would have done anything to steal you away." Damon was near running over his own words in his eagerness, like the flood tide driving me closer and closer to dangerous shoals. "Your grandsire discovered a terrible secret in his investigation of Xancheira, a secret about bloodlines and those born with two bents."

"Yes. The Registry's great lie."

"How did you learn of—? No." A headshake erased his surprise. "It doesn't matter. But that's very good that you know, for I believe *you* can find a path to use that knowledge, to redeem our centuries of wickedness, to truly change the world without brewing a new and most terrible war amongst ourselves."

The world shook itself like a wet pup and trotted off in a new direction. Damon wanted the secret of the *stola told*, not buried . . . and he wanted *me* to do it. Me. The king of Navronne.

The audacity of such a plot—the blatant treason—was breathtaking. But such a trust . . . such opportunity . . . such responsibility . . . a responsibility I would welcome . . . justice on a grand scale . . .

"Why this way? You could have taken ten simpler courses. And what of the Marshal? *You* were the one who sought him out. Exposed him." Surely if I asked enough questions I would discern the course of right.

Damon blew a note of disgust. "My determination to find an alternative to Eodward's vile spawn outstripped my judgment. By the time I had proved Geraint was of Caedmon's blood, I had to ensure he didn't take off on his own and find himself an army. I prayed the Order would make him wise . . . nurture the discipline needed to accomplish great purpose . . . teach him of magic's glory and its responsibility. I saw glimpses of the man he could be—you saw them, too—but the true man ever bled through the masking. He persuaded the Archivist to feed him enough of the truth of himself to 'keep him focused.' Though his magic showed flashes of brilliance, his instincts remained those of the trickster and thief he was when I found him. His only true talent is to bind men's hearts. Fortunately I have none to bind."

"You could have stopped at any time. Wiped his memory of the Order, of his bloodline."

"What man who cares a sliver for the world could dismiss such opportunity as the gods had given me?" he said. "And in the very year I despaired at Geraint's indiscipline, I saw your portraits and watched you deal with adversities that would crush a lesser man, growing ever stronger, more determined. . . ."

"And you didn't think to tell me any of this."

"Couldn't. Geraint became Knight Marshal, who could have you drowned at his word. I was never sure what he knew of himself—or you. So I made sure you despised me; you certainly had reason enough. And I contrived a role for you that would fit with his expectations."

"*His* strong right arm."

Damon's hot gaze threaded itself into my flesh. "If Geraint de Serre becomes king of Navronne, I will bear the guilt of the worst mistake made since the Mother birthed the world."

I drew the black mantle around me, wishing it might hide temptation. I wanted it. Gods forgive me, every one of my aching bones wanted to take the mask from his hand that moment and strive to be a worthy successor to Eodward. I could not be worse than Bayard, who pandered to the Harrowers, or Perryn, the cheating coward, or Osriel, who stole the eyes of the dead. I wanted it, even if it meant giving up all other dreams. Even if it meant never feeling the sun on my face again. Even if it meant living as someone else . . . meaning Juli, Bastien, Conall, Fix could never know me, for there could be no chink in the armor of my identity. The scale of the work was so much larger than that of the Order. If by the grace of the gods, the Xancheirans lived, I could shape the peace between us, draw on their wisdom and experience. . . .

But thoughts of Xancheira brought me around to my own arguments. How could we repair centuries of lies and murder with more lies, more murder?

"So it's the headsman if I refuse."

"Lucian de Remeni was beheaded eleven days ago."

"What?" I leapt to my feet and backed away from him.

"Twelve nights you bided in that cell. Order magic allowed you to sleep most of the time and forget the rest. The Fifty saw incontrovertible evidence that their judgment was carried out at midday eleven days ago, three Registry curators hanged for corruption and one madman portrait artist named

Lucian de Remeni-Masson beheaded for murder. The news has been spread, likely to Palinur itself by now. The Sitting of the Three Hundred begins today."

He rose and wandered back to the worktable, leaning his back on it, his fingers working the purple mask. The magelight lamp above the bench revealed worry lines and weariness, but I refused to concede sympathy. My young sister believed I was beheaded. What could balance such cruelty?

I spat the next query. "Who did you choose to die in my stead?"

"Someone from Ferenc's dungeons. A poacher, a thief . . . I don't know. But it leaves your choices quite limited if you refuse my offer. You will either become Geraint's secretly disloyal lieutenant—a most dangerous road—or you must run for your life while he reshapes the world to his image. You've seen his true face, so he *will* find you. His magic is no match for yours, but he can convince men or armies to follow him anywhere. He will destroy the Order and destroy Navronne."

"This is no choice. You've manipulated lives, murdered innocents, cut off all routes for my future but the one you desire. The same way you drove me to the Order. The same way you used Geraint until you decided he wasn't quite what was wanted and decided to discard him. If I do what you want, you'll have to kill him. And what of Eodward's sons? They're not worthy, either. So what shall we do? Turn a few Order missions to assassination? Because how could we allow any of Caedmon's blood kin to live? They might claim it is not right for one man to impose his whim on tens of thousands of lives. Their rights have been approved by time and history. Whence comes yours?"

"The fact remains. You must choose."

"Do you not believe your own argument? A just kingdom cannot be built on murder."

He would not hear it. "The princes will do each other in. We wait until there is only one left and then make our move. As for the Marshal . . . You will never be safe if he lives, even if we seal him into an oubliette. I'll do it. It will be a small sin beside my others. I freely confess—"

The dark air behind him parted with a whisper, a muffled thump, and a quick expulsion of air. Damon lurched forward, until his spread hands gripped the worktable behind him. The purple mask dropped to the floor.

The Marshal emerged from the shadows on the far side of the table. "Perhaps, curator, you need to stop committing so many sins that you must constantly confess them."

Damon's knees buckled and I moved to catch him. But he had no need of me. Braced on the table, he pulled himself around to face the pupil who'd planted a dagger in his back. "I tried to make you worthy. You promised to give up the old Geraint. Remember your lessons, and perhaps you can still become what I hoped for."

"I've no interest in your hopes."

The Knight Marshal threw off the dark cloak that had kept him hidden and pawed at the litter of silver and cloth piled on the worktable. "No sooner did I reach my dressing chamber than I realized you'd run off with my medallion last night, after displaying it to Canis-Ferenc. So I came back to fetch it, and what have I heard but treason, my devoted mentor seducing my new bodyguard. I've not even trained Lucian to my service as yet. But I do thank you for him. And for my throne."

He lifted the silver pendant to the light, gold gleaming from its back. His eyes gleamed, too, his mouth twisted into a smile, and he spared not a glance for the dying curator. Damon's chin had dropped and his hands lost their grip on the table.

I caught Damon as he fell and lowered him to sitting. Though his expression was entirely contained, he would not stay still. He fought fiercely for breath, clawing his waist and the floor. When his hands stilled, his dulling eyes found mine and for one moment hardened with a burst of will. He stuffed a wad of silk in my hand. "Run."

I ran. Straight into five of Ferenc's guards who stood outside the chamber's only door. They were ordinaries and not particularly skilled. On another day I could have taken them. But the metal bands felt strange and awkward, slowing moves that should have been instinctive.

Only when I was on the floor with four of the brutes near disjointing my stretched limbs, and their comrade crushing my neck with his boot, did I notice that one of the bands on my right arm was inset with Fix's rubies.

I'd no time to guess whether it was Damon or solely the Archivist who had chosen to provide them. But they forced my mind to the power of threading. And in that same moment, with naught but willing it so, my own rebuilding magic produced a spray of paralyzing filaments—ropes of orange lightning erupting from my hands. Pinned to the floor, I couldn't direct them, but the four guards at my extremities fell still and the boot man collapsed backward, growling, when his braced foot failed him.

I wrenched free and scrambled away, halfway down the passage in an eyeblink.

"Halt, Lucian! No more combat spells for now. No more magic of any kind until I say."

My feet stopped. And though I brought every shred of will to bear they would not budge. I tried to raise another spell . . . any spell of paralysis, fire, or confusion that might be incorporated in my silver bracelets . . . but I could not conjure a wisp.

"Now turn around and come back. We've business to attend."

And to my horror, I turned around and went back.

CHAPTER 41

"Release my attendants," spat the Marshal. "Do no other magic."

"I cannot," I said, near choking as I frantically tried to command my own limbs, my own magic. "The spells must wear off on their own."

"Mmm. Simple paralytics. With your new accoutrements, you should have worked something more flexible." He swept into the passage.

The angry soldier with the immobilized leg was trying to rouse his comrades. He glanced up at the Marshal. "My apologies, *domé*, that we allowed him to escape. We didn't think—"

"The villain fooled me, too," said the Marshal. "That won't happen again." He touched each of the five with a sharp burst of power. The angry man, no longer angry and still unable to shift his leg, gaped at his paralyzed comrades in bewilderment.

"A vacant chamber sits at the end of the corridor, bodyguard. Drag these lumps down there—Damon, too. Leave them their weapons, seal the door, and then return. Indeed, you will always return to my presence when you've completed one of my commands, be it successful or no."

My throat constricted as I bent to do his will.

"When I give you orders, you will respond respectfully," he snapped. "For now you may address me as— Hmm. *Knight Marshal* is no longer appropriate, though I shall continue to serve in that capacity for a while. For now, call me *Master*. It will reinforce the training of a man who such a short time ago was offered the crown of Navronne and thought himself too good for it. So?"

"As you say, Master." I would have bitten my tongue off rather than say it or feel my body respond to his command. As I dragged the heavy guards one by one to the chamber at the end of the hall, anger and fear boiled beneath my skin.

Goddess Mother, how had he done this? Of all things, human will was the most difficult to bind with magic. I had given him no consent, an essential part of any working that touched the will. Yet I felt no magic when he spoke, only the unequivocal compulsion to obey. The damnable Archivist must have done something. He'd been the Marshal's partisan from the beginning.

The dull-eyed guards breathed, though displaying no intelligence. I assured them that their paralysis would wear off and that someone would find them. The act told me I could yet move and speak as I wished outside the necessity of the Marshal's commands. But clearly that freedom could end at his word, so I didn't attack him when I returned for Damon.

I dumped Damon's body beside the guards. For seven years, the dark little curator had directed a profound and terrible course for my life and the lives of all who knew me. Yet, in moments, he'd become no more than any other lifeless spider, its legs curled. The dagger in his back might be the pin to affix him to an arcanist's specimen board. What use to hate him anymore? He'd been right that he knew me better than I knew myself. Just not quite well enough.

A slip of purple, half hidden under one of the immobile guards, caught my eye. I must have dropped the royal mask during the fight and dragged it here under the bulky body.

I pulled it out and brushed off the dust—ephemeral, like that foolish moment I'd considered wearing it for the rest of my days. Something heavy was caught in the silk, or rather . . . purposely tied into it. When I undid the knot, a gold disk dropped into my hand. Raised edge. Struck with the head of Caedmon's daughter. Holy gods . . .

When the gloating Geraint had dangled his silver pendant in the light, a gold disk had certainly been nested in the back. But Damon had been fussing with a medallion before the Marshal's arrival. . . .

Burying all thought, lest Geraint's strange talents trespass belief and yield him my most disturbing notion, I bound mask and medallion under my tunic with the string of my underdrawers. Then I sealed the door and headed back to my master.

An argument rose from the chamber, slowing my obedient steps. ". . . was already dead," the Marshal was saying. "Lucian was wild when we took him from the wall. I had to use the dust."

The dust . . . the Marshal's spellwork in the dressing chamber?

"Why such haste?" said the Archivist. "The dust binding was only for specific rebellion against your interests. Damon deserved death. Greenshank meted out justice, exactly as he was trained. Why would he not consent to serve you? The Order's needs demand it; your cause is clear. The daughter was the eldest of Caedmon's children, senior to Eodward's progenitor. Eodward's own law says that daughters inherit equally, thus you are Caedmon's true heir—Navronne's rightful king. Did you not explain these things? I compromised my oaths to assure your ascension. To see such ill-considered actions . . . Pssh."

The Archivist dealt in reason, as if that were the antidote to his immersion in memories. But just like his relictory, his world was fragments, each logical in itself, but disconnected from any other. He could feel distress for Inek's condition, but could not connect that to Damon's death, or Geraint's trespass of the morality of magic, or the possibility that Geraint de Serre posed a threat worse than any of the three princes. The smooth-voiced Marshal would tear Navronne apart and implement his tyranny with the Order and an army of purebloods at his back—the ultimate perversion of the divine gift.

"Your world is your tower and your relictories, good Archivist." The Marshal's voice fell into his most persuasive cadence. "But a Knight Marshal sees the men of the Order as you cannot. Lucian de Remeni was ever vain and secretive, so that I often wondered if his memory was properly scraped. He never believed in our rules. Even Inek, who doted on him like a wet-nurse, had to send him to the seaward wall for lies and sneaking. Convincing him would be a waste of time. He will make a better servant now he cannot argue."

My feet insisted I join them in the chamber.

"Ah, here is my right arm. Nicely obedient, you see. I've forbidden him spellwork for the present. As he recognizes that our aims are the same, he will come to take pride in his submission. Then we can take measures to loosen the hold the dust has on him."

"I don't like it," grumbled the Archivist. "You are the rightful heir, the Sorcerer King. Your magic is sufficient. Seize the throne and purify the Registry. Why do you need Greenshank?"

"Damon taught me well. A great king's hand bestows stern guidance and benevolent warning. He must own a trusty arm to wield the sword and axe. Lucian's righteous anger will scour the Registry and his well-honed skills teach Navron nobles their place."

Geraint commanded me to step to the wall and put my hands and feet back in the binding straps.

As my body obeyed, fear and anger exploded. "What is it to be this time? Splinters in my eyes so I can't see Damon's blood on your hand? Or the blood of the old Marshal, or that of the man beheaded in my place, or whomever else you believe stands between you and power? Will it be splinters in my ears so I can't hear your plan to use the Order and then destroy it?"

The Marshal's hand crashed into my cheek, slamming my head against the wall.

Dizzy and sick, I pushed on. "Knight Archivist, you know that the worst of all crimes for those bearing the divine gift—worse even than using magic to take life—is enslaving the human will. *Never*, not to Damon, not to this man, did I consent to be Geraint de Serre's right arm, left hand, or slave."

"Stop babbling," said the Archivist, elbowing de Serre aside as he tightened the buckles. "You gave consent when you joined the Order. Your relict embodies your will, so the dust of it does as well. Why do you think we dispose of it so quickly?"

The dust of my relict. Horrified dismay jellied my knees. Geraint had woven me a noose from my own soul!

"No one disposed of mine," I said, choking on desperation. "Who failed in that duty? The guilt of the evils I'm forced to do will rest on that man. Just as the guilt of Inek's suffering falls on those who allowed him to find the trap, as well as the murderer who creat—"

"Enough!" snapped the Marshal. "Speak no word until I release your tongue. Consider how you would enjoy a lifetime mute, speaking only with your weapons and your magic."

I growled, wordless. That would not happen. I'd find a way out. Though he'd forbidden me to work magic for the moment, he'd not forbidden me to *construct* it. It was bitter that the sample of the relict dust I'd collected, the very element needed to construct a counter to his binding, remained in the pocket of my filthy clothes left in the bathing room. They were likely burnt by now. And even if I structured a counter, when would I get a chance to use it?

The Marshal held up a full-face silk mask the deep red of good wine, right side plain, the left embroidered in spirals of black. "This will be face of my new bodyguard. Properly fearsome and anonymous. Servantlike."

He tossed the mask to the Archivist. "My faithful brother of our beloved Order, I trust you will get my ferocious creature dressed in his new livery and delivered to me outside Ferenc's hall. As I see to my own preparation for this historic event, I'll consider what name to give him. Perhaps I'll call him *Sword*. Or simply *Arm*. You have an hour."

As the Marshal left the chamber, the Archivist set the mask aside and continued tightening straps.

Masking. This session was about threading the mask to seal my face from view. Though the silver bands felt strange, they would bring speed and depth to my magic. A threaded mask was far more frightening. Even at arm's length I could feel its incredibly strong *obscuré*. No one would ever look me in the eye. No gaze would linger long enough to recognize me.

Always under the Order mask lay flesh that I could touch and feel and know I was this person temporarily named Greenshank with all his knowledge and questions and hungers, and I was also a person whose true life was hidden in a chip of stone. But a threaded mask . . . after wearing it for months . . . years . . . would the flesh remain? Would the person remain? Or would I become something else altogether?

Heart thuttered with terror. Mind clawed at any escape—even at a risky notion that had flitted past as I bade farewell to Damon. Surely it was better to risk all than live as Geraint de Serre's slave.

I growled and wriggled my fingers. No need for silkbinding when my master had compelled me to forgo magic.

"Keep still." The Archivist yanked a thigh strap tight, pinching the flesh between the strap and a silver band. "This must be done, else . . ."

He did not—could not?—supply a reason. And he didn't meet my gaze.

Was it guilt? To support the ascension of a sorcerer king, he had violated his Order oaths. But he'd been appalled at Inek's injury. Finding Fix's splinter had told him . . . something . . . that caused him to help me. He had embedded the band of Fix's rubies discreetly on the inside of my arm. *You'll thank me,* he'd said.

I growled with greater urgency, using each of my fingers in turn to point to my waist.

"Be still. You don't want me to attach this to your eyeball!" But this time he glanced up. I redoubled my wordless pleading and pointing.

"So piss yourself, if you've no control. I'm not going to undo all this."

But as I kept up my noisy display, he puzzled and glanced at my waist. That part of my will that was yet my own, I aimed in his direction, commanding, pleading, begging him to understand.

Wrinkling his nose and pursing his thin lips into perfect disgruntlement, he raised the hem of the tunic. Another quick glance up.

When he had the medallion and the royal mask in hand, one might have thought I'd paralyzed him as well as the guards.

"You stole these," he accused.

No, I voiced soundlessly. His ice-blue eyes widened and he glanced at the worktable—and Damon's blood staining the floor. *Your friend Inek touched that trap spell for me, Archivist. Sacrificed his mind to warn me. You know it's true.*

The Archivist had recognized the trap spell. He knew who made it, and who destroyed my relict. And he had falsified the naming of the Knight Marshal of Evanide. Guilt dogged him.

He smoothed the mask. Rubbed the medallion in his bony fingers. Considered.

"Damon, you sly devil," he breathed at last. The curator's name carried every nuance of evolving understanding.

The Archivist's glance speared me. "He *did* intend it to be you, because he knew Geraint before the Order . . . this crass, hasty person who is not at all like the Marshal. But Geraint is the true heir of Caedmon. Even if he murdered Damon, he is surely better than Osriel the Devil or Bayard the Harrower Consort or Perryn the Forger, and yet you want me . . ."

I clenched my fists, pointed a finger at the mask, and then, signaling two, tried to tell him that Damon had planned to substitute me for Geraint. That wasn't going to happen. But what would the Three Hundred conclude if they saw two Pretenders at the same time—one enslaved to the other with illicit magic? It was all I could think of, and only the Archivist could help me prevail. My fists opened in pleading.

In grim, angry silence, the Archivist continued tightening straps. My wriggling and growling ceased. If he had not chosen to do as I wished, further annoyance wasn't going to make him. I couldn't see which mask he picked up and smoothed over my face. Lord of light, preserve . . .

The mask's own magic slipped it into position. But strangely, the first target of the Archivist's magic was my upper right arm. The world bucked and writhed as a red-hot nail penetrated my bones. Better to cut off the damnable arm so I could not do murder at Geraint's whim. Then the Archivist touched my temple and one of the tiny splinters reached out from inside my skull and looped over the mask's edge. Then another. The silk melted into my face and every thought crumbled to ash.

I plunged into the dark, hoping never to see light again. . . .

But of course I did. Eventually, the Archivist started loosening buckles, grumbling at the tedium. I still had both arms, for I clung to the straps to hold myself upright when he walked away.

"Well, get over here," he said from the direction of the bench. "I am the Knight Archivist of Evanide. Whatever you are, I am not going to dress you."

Blood pounding in my face and arm, I pulled on the black hose and leather braies he stuffed in my hands, then numbly reached for the plum-colored shirt.

"Are you not even going to look?"

I shook my head. There was no mirror glass and I was glad of it. I never wanted to see.

"Your right arm, fool! You have to know where it is. Pssh . . ." He yanked my arm out straight. Between two of the silver bands on my upper arm, where Fix's splinter had once gleamed, sat the gold medallion, embedded in my flesh.

"A pretty job, if I say so myself," he said, beaming a macabre satisfaction. "The medallion's original spellwork is primitive, and Damon jumbled it grotesquely, but it's repaired now. Threading should attune the thing to your blood, but that could take a great deal of time. I've anchored it through Fix's splinter, which might speed that, and I've moved his rubies to a band on your leg. How such a common, lackadaisical sort of man came to be so gifted is a mystery. . . ."

I scarce noticed his rambling. My hand flew to my face. The silk was smooth and did not shift or wrinkle as my fingers tested it, a sensation that set off gibbering panic. But it was the stitching I sought. No embroidered spirals, but an elaborate border stitched near the edges. Lilies. The Archivist had done as I asked.

Taking a shaking breath, I jerked my head in acknowledgment and drew the plum-colored shirt and black leather jaque over my sweat-soaked linen. An undecorated swordbelt of fine leather with empty sheaths for sword and dagger lay on the bench next to a pair of knee-high boots and leather gloves.

"Yes, put it on," he said, when I held it up. "The Marshal plans to present your weapons before the Sitting, and fortunately"—from the worktable he brought a cloak of thick wool, dyed in the claret hue prescribed for purebloods—"your cloak has a deep hood. Shadowing your face will give you more time to do . . . whatever you think to do . . . before he kills you for this."

Mind racing, I pulled on the boots and buckled the swordbelt. My idea seemed so flimsy. I pointed to my lips and wriggled my fingers to exhibit their uselessness. I needed to be able to speak. Work magic.

"I can't undo his compulsions, if that's what you're asking," he said. "He took all the dust. But gods' bones, you trained at Evanide. Your skills are not confined to magic. *Wits* might suffice."

Geraint could counter any assault with compulsion, but control of will with magic was a heinous crime, certainly no recommendation for a king. So I had to force him to expose his sin in front of the Sitting. But how? I ran through one scenario after another, finding only quicker ways to get myself killed or compelled to forgo thought completely. I needed help . . .

The Archivist was tapping his foot in impatience when I jumped up from the bench and made writing motions. He narrowed his eyes and pointed to a writing desk in the corner. With ink, pen, and scraps of parchment that had been used and scraped innumerable times, I set my plan in motion. First a request for the Archivist.

"Carry a message like a sweating tyro? Certainly not."

He didn't budge until I wrote a bit of what I had in mind. "Hmmph. That's not entirely stupid. There should certainly be a historian among the Three Hundred. I can think of several families. . . ."

While he rambled of names and bents, as if we weren't speaking of murder and magical enslavement and Navronne's future to be determined within hours, I wrote the message I needed delivered. And then I wrote another short request for him.

"You retrieved a bit of the dust! Well thought!" His face brightened, then fell just as quickly as he clucked disapproval. "But to rummage netherstocks in a bathing closet . . ."

The clangor of bells interrupted his grumbling. I pulled on gauntlets and the wine-hued cloak, and we hurried off to the hall and the Sitting of the Three Hundred. One way or another, Damon's misbegotten plot and the Marshal's leash on my will would end there.

CHAPTER 42

"'Tis done as you prescribed, Knight Marshal. None'll ever know his face, nor even think to look at it." In an eyeblink, the Archivist's rust-colored robes vanished into the crowd.

He had cleverly arranged to transfer me to the Marshal's custody just as trumpets signaled the imminent processional. With dignitaries swarming into the castle rotunda, the Marshal scarce had time enough to give my dress a cursory glance. Both masks were deep-colored. Only the removal of my hood would reveal that mine was not the one he had prescribed, but a match for that on his own face. Though the prospect of a lifetime with a silken face nauseated me, I relished the grim irony. The true Pretender's mask was not permanently affixed.

The Marshal dismissed his Order bodyguards and shoved a well-balanced sword and a similarly efficient dagger into my hands. "You're damnably late. You will not use these weapons save in my defense or at my command. . . ." He ordered me neither to speak nor to leave his side without his command; to keep watch for assassins and identify anyone displaying unease at his naming; to defend his life with mine. He reached as if to yank down my hood, but his hand paused. . . .

The lordly pureblood, Canis-Ferenc, joined us. As the ushers herded us forward, I ducked my head and breathed again.

Celebratory cascades of bells rang from castle and town, and trumpet fanfares greeted each of the three hundred Heads of Family, resplendent in their finest brocades and jewels. The dignitary's plainer-dressed secretary, footman, or bodyguard followed—one attendant allowed each delegate, three for *Domé* Canis-Ferenc, as the host of the greatest gathering of purebloods in half a century.

"We are allowing a small number of non-delegates—purebloods of importance—to attend the sessions," said Ferenc as he and the Marshal paused at the threshold of the Great Hall. "They shall sit behind the Three Hundred and are not allowed to speak. You, Lord de Serre, will sit at my right hand, and when we discuss the matter of supporting your claim, you will be invited to address the assembly. But just now, I must mention that it is customary at a Sitting for everyone's"—he glanced over his wide shoulder—"*attendant* to deposit his mundane weapons with the doorwards."

"My bodyguard shall carry all his weapons, mundane and elsewise," said the Marshal, with effortless command. "With due respect, good Ferenc, I've no confidence that the word of my identity has been contained to this house. My life shall be at peril from the three princes—and our own pure-blood dissenters—until I take my rightful seat."

The trumpets blared flourishes, and we moved into the Hall.

"Our own— Certainly. My apologies for my lack of consideration. May I summon my personal guard to stand with your man?"

"Be sure, my *man* needs no one to stand with him." The Marshal laughed in easy humor, hands at his back, then swiveled in my direction. *"Fetulé iniga!"*

The command pierced the air like a lance. Scarce a breath and I had dropped to one knee, sword and dagger drawn at the ready, a shoulder-high shield of fire surrounding me. Body and breathing were controlled as I pivoted slowly, my senses roaming the glittering crowd in search of threats, weapons, or smoldering magic. Only when convinced no danger threatened did I erase the fire, rise, and sheath my weapons. *"Infetulé*, Master."

Delegates and attendants goggled as the Marshal and Ferenc resumed their grand entrance. Had anyone been able to see my face, they'd have noted only horror.

For every member of the Order, the response to the *on guard* command became purest instinct, just like running when the tide horns sounded. But my reaction had been so swift as to defy my own belief—far, far faster than I had ever seen it done. Had I been standing in a city lane or a hayfield when the Marshal spoke that brief command, I could have ignited a holocaust.

The Order had drilled us in a dozen commands that could trigger similarly dangerous reactions, but always they were given by trusted commanders—and always with time to assess the threats and *choose*. But spellwork bound in the threaded bracelets was triggered in the very instant I reached for it, requiring no thoughtful construction, no summoning of power, no purposeful release. Geraint's compulsion bypassed any restraint of will, and the speed of my reactions eliminated the time to seek alternatives. This public display of the truest danger of my enslavement was terrifying—my master's purpose, no doubt.

Ferenc yielded Geraint his own grand chair at the head of the assembled dignitaries and took a lesser seat beside him. I stood at my master's right shoulder. Every eye in the hall was trained in our direction, the weight of awe heavier than Ferenc's vaults and pillars.

"Well executed, Axe," said the Marshal. "We'll do more of that. You are exactly as Damon promised, whether he intended this partnership be consummated or not." Was I the only one who smelled his greedy pleasure?

Ferenc, admirably undaunted, platooned his functionaries with the confidence of a powerful sorcerer lord, housed safely in his own keep. "The ceremonies and confirmation of our delegates shall be tiresome," he offered in brotherly fashion. "But be sure, my lord, that with matters of such monumental significance at hand, we shall dispatch miscellany and get on to our true deliberations by midday at the latest. Where is Curator Damon?"

With my hood pulled low to shadow the mask, my actual sight was somewhat limited, but I'd already begun to understand Fix's uncanny perceptions. My silver-threaded skin told me of a woman's cheeks flushed with excitement, an attendant's boredom amid so many whose powers he failed to comprehend, a man's uneasiness at the crowd, and everywhere a quivering anticipation as Ferenc introduced the Marshal to eager delegates and the ceremonies proceeded. Muted conversations flowed through the room like tangled streams of hope and doubt. *Caedmon's heir . . . sorcerer . . . Fine figure of a man. Noble bearing . . . Remeni's proof . . . a true medallion. Tragic about the grandson. Don't like these stricter rules . . . no idea about the Xancheira horror . . . Our own king at last.*

Whispers of war rose like vapors from a swamp . . . some stinking of lust . . . some ripe with trepidation . . . some with horror. To my disgust, Geraint's command ensured I noted each source of doubt or opposition, imprinting faces and blazons on my memory. Truly a sorcerer's war was my fear as well. Even if I discredited the Marshal and escaped this new prison . . . then what? Who would lead our kind out of corruption? Surely all Damon's mad hopes had not hinged entirely on me. And yet my own hope of deliverance rested solely on the fractured mind of a knight who lived with other men's memories . . . and a stranger who had vowed me a lifetime's service for a deed I could not remember. Had the Archivist delivered my message?

A disturbance at the door distracted me from my flimsy hopes. As a tautbodied soldier hurried toward Ferenc's three attendants, I wanted to crow in delight. A whispered conference and the grim-faced ordinary departed in the company of one of Ferenc's men, while another attendant whispered in Ferenc's ear. "Curator Lares-Damon is nowhere to be found, *domé*. We've given his military aide leave to search the castle." Damon's military aide, Fallon de Tremayne.

After hours of tedium and breaks for wine and pissing, the business of the Sitting was begun. My back and jaw ached from standing ready. I dared not relax, for the danger lurking inside me. My will could not control the initiation of my magic, but I might be able to control its focus and its speed. Physical and mental discipline could slow my reactions or complicate my methods, perhaps allowing time for someone to stop me. None of it mattered, however, if the seeds I'd planted with the Archivist didn't grow. Fallon had not yet returned.

Three of the judges gave a full accounting of Damon's arguments for purification. But one delegate after another rose to argue that dissolution of the Registry would encourage ordinaries and scoundrels to trespass on *the time-honored prerogatives that preserve the integrity of the divine gift*.

The Marshal gestured for recognition. "Delegates of the Three Hundred, I thank you for allowing me to address this noble assembly. I respect these arguments. Curator Damon told me that they might be raised. He advised that reading this book might illuminate particular concerns among you . . ."

He raised a leather-bound folio crammed with sheets of parchment. The portraits. Cold fear pelted my threaded skin like storm-driven sleet.

". . . but I care naught for transgressions of agreements with ordinaries. On my word, sworn by my noble ancestor, I hold to a vision of Navronne where divine magic shall *never* be sullied with corruption, nor will its practitioners be demeaned by the touch, gaze, or rule of ordinary hands. No sorcerer of true blood shall ever again be subject to the judgment of ordinaries or have his lands taxed by ordinary nobles. Every person of the blood may approach the Sorcerer King, assured that his or her concern will be heard. Our law will not be a matter of treaty or concession, enforced by the whim of ordinaries. *Our* law shall be the law of Navronne."

To persuade those few unconvinced by his melodious promises, the Pretender quite clearly passed the leather folio to me.

The Sitting quickly confirmed the dissolution of the Registry. Necessary tasks would be overseen by the Three Hundred until the day that Geraint de Serre, rightful heir of ancient Caedmon, sat the throne of Navronne, uniting the administration of pureblood society and that of ordinaries. Until that day, the Three Hundred would offer whatever aid the Pretender's strategy demanded.

The Marshal briefly thanked them for their trust, demonstrating his commitment to live behind his regal mask, abjuring personal glory to lead them forward. With mesmerizing serenity, he elaborated on his vision of a holy kingdom ruled by sorcerers. The Three Hundred and their guests came to their feet as one, their cheers filled with ferocious pride. It didn't matter that he'd subtly threatened them or described a tyranny alien to everything we believed of the divine gift. They adored him and believed.

Misgiving had not wholly vanished from beneath jeweled velvets and brocade. But who would dare speak it? Anxious eyes flicked to the one who stood at his shoulder, the one with the book, the hooded menace who might see to those dark necessities of power their new ruler abjured.

As deliberations moved to an actual muster of forces to support de Serre's claim, the doors of the Hall burst open. "Murder! *Domé* Canis-Ferenc, murder in your house!"

Members of the assembly shot to their feet. Before Ferenc's guards could prevent them, a knot of men carried in a draped litter and set it before the assembled purebloods. Fallon de Tremayne knelt before Ferenc, his eyes humbly averted and hands outspread. At Ferenc's word, he spoke.

"*Domé* Canis-Ferenc, it is my great sorrow to report that my master, the Curator Attis de Lares-Damon lies before you most cowardly murdered." Fallon's battle-trained voice boomed, so that even the delegates of lower-ranked families and the silent observers seated in the farthest reaches of the Hall must hear. "I beg the indulgence of the gods' chosen for my bold trespass on this assembly. But there is such urgency in this evil matter, I dared not hesitate to bring evidence before those who can address it, as an ordinary cannot. May I speak further, my good lord?"

"Proceed."

The Mother could not have felt more relief at birthing the world than I did when hearing Ferenc's decisive assent. Everything depended on it.

"Thank you, *domé*," said Fallon. "Curator Damon believed this day the culmination of his life's work. He deemed that a leader who shares the divine gift, as well as our greatest king's bloodline, would be the noblest legacy he could provide in service of Navronne. He commanded me that if anything threatened this legacy, I must warn the Sitting—"

"Pardon, noble Ferenc!" Geraint interrupted. "Attis-de Lares-Damon has been my guide and mentor. His loss leaves the world immeasurably diminished. Yet the Sitting of the Three Hundred is a sacred assembly, and if an ordinary is allowed to disrupt the proceeding, even for such a grievous event, does it not set unfortunate precedent?"

Though the Marshal expressed sincere concern and such grief as would twist the heart, the air between us trembled with his rage. I held tight to my magic. Compulsion mandated obedience, *not* speed.

"A wise observation, my Lord de Serre," said Ferenc, "especially in the face of your grief. Yet the victim is one of our own. And this ordinary is no common servant, but Curator Damon's military aide, Fallon de Tremayne. Once a famed general in Prince Perryn's legion, he has pledged his strength and wisdom to Damon's quest for cleansing. I advise we hear him out for the very reasons you wish your bodyguard to hold on to his weapons. I'd not have our rightful king harmed in my house."

So Ferenc was intelligent as well as bold.

The Marshal acknowledged the point without words.

"Proceed, Tremayne."

Fallon bowed to Ferenc and then to the Marshal. "Indeed, *domé*, I fear this villainy must be aimed at Lord de Serre as well. Since the convocation of the Fifty, Curator Damon has learned of a conspiracy to supplant Caedmon's true heir with an imposter. Where better to discover the perpetrator of this bloody murder than here among the gods' chosen, and immediately before time fades the evidence? Root out the devils and we can eliminate the direst threat to our kingdom's hope of peace and purity before more harm is done."

Damon had schooled Fallon well in the pridefulness of purebloods.

"Conspiracies . . . imposters . . . surely Damon would have told me," said the Marshal, baring his skepticism.

"We need a historian," Ferenc called out to the restless crowd, "or an examiner. Anyone who might discern the provenance of Curator Damon's death wound."

As several came forward from the three hundred delegates and one man from the guests at the back of the Hall, the Marshal stepped to my side, hands knotted at his back. He eyed the group gathering around Damon's corpse and spoke through clenched teeth. "You will reap Magrog's own wrath if you left that dagger in place. . . ."

I crossed my arms on my breast and inclined my back, shaking my head.

He spewed disgust at the apology, but he well knew he'd not told me to remove the weapon. He'd been too busy enjoying my submission.

"Join those at Damon's side and erase all trace of me from that dagger. And if one of these self-important peacocks even hints that he's learned anything from the dagger, you will do *whatever is necessary* to silence him. If it reaps you a lashing, so be it."

I brought my fingertips to my mouth and then opened my palm in question.

"No, you may not speak."

Good. I wanted my limitations on view. I dipped my head and stepped away.

As if he'd heard my thought, the Marshal held me back with a touch on my shoulder. "Have a care, Axe, or you will live out your days on such a leash that you will never piss without my command."

Blood cold, I acknowledged his warning and joined the small group at Damon's side. Fallon's men formed a circle around us.

Fallon should have brought me the means to end this. If I was lucky, it might be a ring or a pendant to drop over my head, maybe a wooden token set with a silver splinter—anything the Archivist might use to trigger a counterspell to set me free. If the Archivist had failed or decided he wanted to crown Geraint after all, Fallon's sword would end my servitude. The Marshal had not compelled me to protect myself.

A white-haired man swathed in froths of lace poured magic into the dagger, but concluded only that it was last touched by a sorcerer. "Without a suspect hand to match with the traces on the dagger, I cannot guess who might have done it. Bring me someone likely, and I could say more."

A statuesque woman, her half mask crusted with diamonds, entwined the dagger in powerful magic. She pronounced that the weapon had been wielded in cold malice, intended to kill. "Spellwork directed its flight and maximized the damage caused. The actual power used was of an unusual sort—"

My arm smashed into her mouth, knocking her into the embrace of the white-haired man. Whether or not she could actually implicate the Marshal was unimportant.

The group broke into complaints and indignation. "What have you done, *domé*?" snapped Fallon.

I crossed my arms in apology, and bowed to the fluttering woman, shaking my head in denial. That was my story's opening. Please gods, let them read it.

Geraint had left me no choice as to my task, but I would embellish the doing and try my best to fail. Compulsion did not permit failure, of course. I could slow completion, stumble, restart, but I could not stop myself entire.

Making a show of my dismay, I reached for the dagger and began constructing a spell of erasure to cleanse the blade of the Marshal's imprint. Erasure spells were quite complex and could not be cast until the precise details to be removed were known. Using my bent provided far more than I needed, but I incorporated all so as to delay. Inevitably, I completed the spellwork, but I forced my body to withhold the outpouring of magic, aborting my cast before it could destroy the evidence. As long as I possessed power enough to drive the spell to completion, I had not failed.

And so I began constructing it again. And again I strangled the rush of magic, as if I'd noticed something wrong. I had to avoid casting the spell until someone noticed my strange behavior.

The third time I denied the flow of magic, one of the silver bands on my left leg tightened, as if my deliberate rejection of its aid angered it. I'd no time to consider why. I had to stay in control.

A strong hand grabbed my arm from behind. "What is it you do here, bodyguard?"

This would be the man from the group of guests, whatever courageous fellow Fallon had recruited to help him. Eyes focused on the dagger, I wrenched my hand from his grasp, ignored the now-painful tightening of the leg banding, and started building the erasure spell once more. If I looked at anyone, lost concentration, I would wipe the Marshal's murderous imprint from the dagger.

"What is your purpose here, bodyguard?" said the man behind me. A stern voice. Familiar. "What magic is this? Are you an examiner?"

Groaning through my clenched jaw, I shook my head. I had to make them see I had no choice.

I began the spell construction yet again, ignoring the warm wetness seeping from the growing agony in my leg. Fix's rubies . . . gods. When I aborted the flow of power, the threaded gems tried to supply more as if I was depleted. I was fighting myself . . .

Fallon's hand yanked mine from the dagger. "Mayhap the dagger will tell us something about *this* man!"

My twisting lunge caught Fallon in his middle and slammed him to the floor. Tangled in his cloak I slammed a knee upward, only to have someone else pounce on my back. As Fallon scrambled away, the man at my back reached under my arms and around the back of my neck in a crushing lock hold.

An eye gouge, a head slam backward. Another twist and I planted an elbow in my captor's cheek. Leaving him lie, I crawled back toward Damon's body. The dagger was all I could see, all I could think of. I reached for it, all the while shaking my head. *Stop me!*

Shouts creased the rattling din in my head. Fallon's man must be careful.

Yet again I touched the dagger. *Do not let the magic flow. The rubies won't cut your leg off. People must see the evidence.*

A blade rested on my wrist. "Let go of it," said the stern-voiced man standing over me. The familiar voice again. He was hooded and masked in black. "Move away."

But, of course, I could not. The Marshal's compulsion threatened to crush my skull. I shook my head and began the erasure spell yet again.

Voices rose from every side. "What's wrong with him?"

"He's bleeding."

"You four, get his hands off the weapon." The snapped order was so familiar. . . . "I don't think he can stop what he's doing."

Hands grabbed me. Demonic rage and threaded magic lashed out with acid stings, paralysis, fire . . . *Hold tight,* Fix had said. *Let your rage give you strength, not control it.* Of all things, I didn't want to harm anyone, kill anyone. I tried. Held back. Threw counters. But at least two soldiers were laid out bleeding. Another crawled away with one of his feet turned entirely the wrong direction.

At last they dragged me away from Damon and crushed me to the floor. I writhed and twisted. My control was slipping. I doubted I could stop the flow of magic one more time. My left foot was numb; the band constricting my leg had me near howling. If my assailants let loose for an instant, I would go for the dagger again and kill anyone in my way.

"Tell us who you are!" demanded my captor.

"He's the Pretender's bodyguard," said Fallon. "We should—"

"Axe, are you bewitched?" Now the Marshal stood over me, too. My own dagger was in my hand. "You were to offer your magic to *aid* this investigation. Lord Canis-Ferenc, my apologies. This is entirely unlike my servant."

"Are you sure it *is* your servant?" And at last someone yanked off my hood. I growled and came near gutting him, before they wrestled me still. My knife slid away and I was dragged upright. . . .

"Lord of light, look at his face! A living mask . . . the design of it . . . the same royal mask!" Shock rippled through the bystanders. "The Pretender swore to wear a mask every hour of every day."

And the bold Ferenc: "Lord de Serre, what is the meaning of this?"

"You damnable, cursed— Who's done this to you, Axe?" The Marshal's fury was no pretense. "First my mentor, and now my most trustworthy servant."

Roaring, I shook my head, over and over, half crazed with the need to cleanse the dagger in Damon's back or kill any who touched it. I kicked out at those who knelt in front of me, trying to get a closer look. A cataclysm was building inside me.

Soldiers grabbed my feet. The man behind me was only one—strong, yes, and magic fed his grip like links of steel. But eventually I would take him down and kill him, too.

"Take the dead man out of the Hall," said Ferenc. "That's what's driving him mad."

"It seems strange that his mask is fixed as the Pretender promised," said Fallon, "while yours, Lord de Serre, is yet loose. Curator Damon warned of a plot . . . an imposter."

The Marshal raised his hand and Fallon's body jerked and flew across the floor, as if hit by a charging stallion.

"How dare you speak to me, ordinary?" spat the Marshal. "No matter who you were. Perhaps *you* know who's suborned my servant. Someone's using him to plant a false imprint on the dagger."

"But why this erratic behavior?" demanded Ferenc. "I'll bear witness that this is the very man who accompanied you into the Hall. The one who responded with such dread speed and skill to *your* command. You commended him for his performance. You *relished* it."

The man behind me loosened his hold on my right arm and ripped my shirt. I wrenched my arm free. Demon compulsion bade me gouge his eyes. The need to finish the task given me ate through my bowels like acid.

But my captor's fluid moves were well practiced, and he soon had me caged again. My body wanted to shred his flesh. My fading intellect begged him hold tighter.

Canis-Ferenc and the other purebloods moved closer to inspect a blaze from my arm.

"The medallion's a part of his flesh," one said. "It's certainly the one the judges verified."

". . . never seen the like of his face . . ."

". . . what honor . . . what humility for a king to mask himself . . ."

"What is this idiocy?" yelled the Marshal from somewhere I couldn't see. Beams of purple, azure, and loden green reflected on the polished floor. "I hold the true medallion. *I* am Caedmon's heir. This man is my *servant*. A traitor has mutilated him to discredit me."

"One of you is a murdering imposter," snarled Ferenc. "But which? Both wear a royal mask. Both wear a medallion. And by divine Deunor's grace . . . both medallions shine!"

The fire from my arm flamed purple, azure, and loden.

"Perhaps it is the gods' sign that it is not our place to decide." A square-shouldered woman, robed in Registry scarlet and black, swept into view like a tornadic wind. "Historian Geselle-Mando has just determined that the hand that wielded the dagger to murder Curator Damon is the same as the most recent person to occupy your chair, *Eqastré* Ferenc. Geraint de Serre."

"Do not dare touch me," said the Marshal, snarling as Registry guards surrounded him.

Lightning bloomed from his hand. The flame joined the clerestory sunlight and magefire, smearing into a blinding brilliance. "You're all mad. Who will sit Caedmon's throne? Some brawling ordinary? The madman of Evanore?"

"Not you," said Pons. "Attis de Lares-Damon, flawed as he was, forced us to see our own corruption, and you murdered him, using magic."

"Slay this witch and these fools who hold you, Axe," snarled the Marshal. "Rise up and slay any who threaten me. I am the rightful king of Navronne."

Magic rushed through me, wild, dreadful, bestial. Wordless, I roared with power, bucking and thrashing even as waning reason fought to hold it back. *Hold . . . hold . . .*

"Can no one see? This man"—the woman's finger pointed at me—"is the true Pretender, his will enslaved by de Serre's malice. Enslavement of will is the most ancient and most serious violation of Aurellian law. As the last Curator of the Pureblood Registry, charged by the Sitting of the Three Hundred to carry out its dissolution, I arrest you, Geraint de Serre, for murder and enslavement of the gods' chosen."

"Unleash your power, Axe!" yelled the Marshal. "Bring this house down on every cowering traitor! Show no mercy!"

The ground shook. Dust drifted from the vaults of the Hall. Magic boiled and flowed like molten rock from my bracelets, feeding on Fix's rubies and eating through my defenses until it became a monstrous flood of destruction. Bellowing, I yanked a hand free and raised it, shaking . . .

Screams rose from onlookers. A thunderous crack split my kinswoman's glorious mural. *Feel this loss, Lucian,* I begged, trying to direct the escaping power where it would do the least harm. *Find yourself. Greenshank, reach for your lost name. You cannot . . . cannot . . . do this, a crime for which there will be no redemption. If Pons is here, then surely your sister is here, too. The last of your family. The one who can help you reclaim your soul.*

For a moment, fervid longing muted my fury. But the battle raging inside me incinerated hope and desire, shame, horror, and reason. . . .

Cracks appeared in the grand pillars. The viewing gallery sagged, and the slender columns that masked it toppled one and then the other into the hall. The screaming crowd surged toward the doors.

Fallon stood before me, sword drawn, his skin scraped and bloodied, my last hope of salvation. Even as I snarled and summoned death, a deep-buried voice begged him, *Do it, do it . . .*

"Not yet," snapped the man behind me, strengthening his hold as he threw a magical shield between me and the sword.

I roared and tore at his flesh, but his stern voice ground through madness and into my ear. "The time of your choice has come, paratus. There is no counterspell. The dust you preserved was gone. But the Archivist reminds you that Geraint's chains were forged with the detritus of a man executed eleven days ago. But in truth, that man ceased to exist two years past."

"Axe!" screamed the Marshal. "Execute these traitors! First of all this cur who dares restrain my instrument."

But the one who held me would not yield. "You cling to sentiment instead of understanding, listen to echoes instead of voices; you yearn for what is ash, rather than shape what is silver. *Think.* The soul is not a name. Nor is it incidents of other times, or emotions, no matter how cherished. The soul endures. The divine gift endures. Who *are* you? Choose."

Fading reason searched for an answer . . . and found magic . . . my bents . . . my art. . . . I reached for line and color, shape and depth, and drew the portrait of a man of loving family who found life in a house of the dead, strength in a dark cellar, and purpose in works of justice. . . . And I wrapped this artwork in magic and linked it to the symbol of a knife.

I am not Axe. I invoked the spell in silence. *Nor am I Lucian de Remeni, the artist whose past was stolen and whose future is enslaved. Nor am I Greenshank, because that name was never anything but a placeholder for what Lucian was to become. The divine gift lives in me in generous measure. I am threaded with the power of the Knight Defender of Evanide, and I know truths that will help my people shake off the evils of the past. Even without a name, my soul lives. Unbound.*

I turned inward, and as the Archivist had taught us, I used the knife to cut away the image I'd drawn. Not even memory pricks would be able to return a seed of Lucian de Remeni's life, because I removed the soil where it could root and display its truth. Three times I invoked the spell, reaching deeper to excise the lingering fragments: a sister who sparked the universe . . . the yearning for home and kinship . . . the connection with a great house near Pontia . . . the intimacy with a being of myth . . . the craving for beliefs, memory, and experiences that waited just beyond my reach . . . the threads that took fire when I touched a signature or artworks done in other times . . . and all attachment to a name.

As my knife cut deeper, belief and certainty grew, and lust for murder faded.

. . . my soul lives. Unbound. When at last I raised my head, the spasms and the killing fever had gone, as if swept away by a god's hand. Though I yet trembled from weariness and the pain in my leg, my captor had released his hold.

"You think this is over, *servant?*" The Marshal backed away from the sword-wielding Fallon, from Pons and her Registry servitors, from Canis-Ferenc and his crimson-and-silver-liveried guards. Both of Geraint's hands were filled with flame, ready to spew into ropes and chains of spellwork. "My leash has bound your soul, Remeni, and though the traitorous Archivist has allowed you to slip it this time, I will have it back."

"No," I rasped. "You won't." But before I could raise a hand to defend myself, his magic flared. . . .

As if a shutter had blown open and admitted a gale wind, two dozen men in black and gray swooped in and surrounded the Marshal, erecting wards and shields so that his cannonade of fire and lightning shattered without damage— a maneuver we had practiced repeatedly in the bloody days at Val Cleve.

"*Cineré resurge!*" bellowed the Marshal. "Out of my way."

The knights did not move. A fog descended from the ceiling and blanketed the noisy melee. A very familiar kind of fog—textured, shifting, though we were indoors and nowhere near the sea. A commanding figure walked out of it.

"Alas, the Knight Marshal's imperative has no weight when spoken by one who is no longer the Knight Marshal." The lean, sinewy newcomer was armored and masked in the blue of storm seas and Order gray.

I grinned, though entirely confused. Even if Bastien had gone straight to Evanide after my capture in the alley, how could Fix have gotten here so quickly?

"Who in the name of all gods—?" Canis-Ferenc summoned a troop of his warriors, swords humming with power. Pons raced to his side, her single arm bearing a staff that spewed lightning.

"With all respect, *Domé* Canis-Ferenc, Curator Pons, and worthy purebloods of the Three Hundred, this arrest is not yours to make." The Knight Defender waved a hand.

Swords and shields clattered to the floor. Soldiers dropped to their knees. Pons and Canis-Ferenc halted, not of their own accord.

"We mean you no harm." Fix held out his hand to the curator and the lord. "Take one of these tokens and it will tell you, all who serve you, and all who are guesting under your protection, everything you need to know about who we are." Memory-wipe tokens, certainly, to ensure the Order's anonymity.

The Knight Defender opened his hand in Fallon's direction. I shook my head. Fallon deserved to understand what he'd done for me and Navronne.

After dispensing a few more tokens, the Knight Defender came to me. "I'll see *you* before you leave here. You've some things to learn about metallurgy. Silver tarnish is as annoying as a bastard cousin. And no matter what you decide about the future, you *will* do some work with me before embarking on it. You're something like a sword without guards or hilt—all points and sharp edges."

I dipped my head and laid a fist on my breast. He laughed, nodded to someone behind me, and plunged into the fog.

By the time the fog dissipated, Fix, the Marshal, and the Order knights had vanished with it. Arcs of magic had spit through the air of the Great Hall, leaving those remaining in that chamber, and likely hundreds of others, scratching their heads in confusion.

Though he'd released me when my resistance ceased, my captor of the stern and powerful voice had shielded my back until the Marshal was gone. I turned around and knelt up on one knee, fist on my breast. As with Fix, I most improperly raised my eyes and affirmed that he was indeed the only man who could have bested me in such a fight or reached me in the midst of raging frenzy. There was no measure for my gratitude . . . or my pleasure.

"Knight Commander Inek," I said hoarsely, "I report my mission complete."

In stern solemnity that helped soothe my lingering tremors, he shook his head. "I disagree with your assessment, paratus. You seem to have set forces in motion that will not be denied. You cannot abandon a mission in progress."

His strong hand pulled me to my feet. From a tumbled chair, he picked up my hooded mantle and threw it over me. "You'll want this. The weather's turning and there are three hundred purebloods in this castle ready either to kill you as an imposter, hang you as a traitor, or anoint you king of Navronne."

Inek strode toward the doors and I limped along beside him. I could scarce think beyond putting one foot in front of the other. Every part of me seemed stretched thin.

A clamor of voices rose from the rotunda. Now the ground had stopped shaking, a sea of bodies flowed through multiple doors from the outer courts and gardens. However unlikely, townspeople milled about the castle. Like the Gouvron Estuary where salt water and fresh mingled with the surge of the tides, so did streams of men and women in worn, patched garb surge through the flood of jeweled brocades and frothing lace. Yet from everywhere in that mingled tide, spears and nets of magic flew out to support pillars before they toppled, to strengthen walls and settle dust.

A disgusted Pons stood at the great doors, hands on her hips. She was dispatching Registry guards to search for Geraint de Serre, who had disappeared out from under her nose. I started toward her, anxious to learn of Juli.

Inek held me back. "Not yet," he said. "What you have to show the girl will not be easy for her to see, and what you have to tell her will not be easy for you to say or for her to hear."

"True," I said. Juli believed her brother dead. As he was. Only now they were gone did I understand the ghostly threads that had bound the girl and me. My spirit was a desert.

Inek and I moved unremarked through the throng. Only when I stumbled into a woman and she looked straight through me, puzzled, did I realize Inek had drawn a veil over the two of us.

"I recall distinctly. There were two of them, master and servant," said a young woman, swathed in black fur. "The servant had no face."

"His face was a mask," said another. "So he was the true Pretender. The Pretender promised the judges that he would wear a mask every hour of every day. . . ."

"It was the medallion in his flesh tells me the bodyguard was the true Pretender," said a man with a pointed white beard poking out from under his half mask. "That's how you would hide who you are, while making sure you and your evidence can't be separated. And the magic . . . Great Deunor did you feel his power?"

"Where did they go? I don't see either one of them. A king of our own kind . . . what a fine way to clean up the mess. Patronne has named the curators greedy gatzi for years."

"Over here, carpenter! We need you to hold these arches until we strengthen the supports, else the dome will fall in." Juli directed several of the townsmen into an area of fallen masonry. Pale dust smudged her half mask and mourning gown of black velvet. An elegance of power flowed from her hand as she helped clear a passage. So her art manifested with masonry and buttresses, not pens and ink. A smile teased at my lips. Such a small thing she was to build so large.

Inek tugged at my arm. "Your mission awaits."

"Where?" I said, swallowing regret. "Much farther and you'll have to drag me. Never would have thought you could best me just out of your sickbed. Though I suppose the Archivist—" He must have moved Inek from the infirmary when he found the proper counter to the trap spell. Even then he didn't trust the Marshal.

"He is retired to Evanide and will never leave. His successor is already in place."

"And what of the Marshal?"

"De Serre will die. A new Marshal is already named, but Fix will command for a time as we go through our own cleansing."

The gray evening was frigid as we emerged onto Castle Cavillor's deserted ramparts to a view that thrilled the eye. A lake of magelight lanterns pooled in the bailey just below us, rivers of them flowed through the town, and a sea lapped the town walls. "Is this Damon's legion?" I said. "The Marshal said he had long-laid strategies in place . . ."

"Not Damon's. Look there."

In the courtyard below, Canis-Ferenc and a troop of his soldiers were surrounded by ragged men and women bearing every manner of weapon, all bristling with dire magics. Horror snatched my gut. Harrowers, armed with magic?

But three horsemen headed the ragtag legion—a tall man with hair the color of old honey, a woman almost his twin but with a scar blighting half her face, and a cadaverous man whose black hair was threaded with gray. Benedik, Signé, and Siever. Above them flew a black ensign, its blazon a white tree.

"Deunor's light," I whispered, joy, relief, and wonder mingled in equal parts. "However can they be here?" Yes, I'd been kept asleep for ten days, but that was hardly enough time to bring them from Xancheira . . . and Siever from Evanide . . . and Fix and Inek, unless . . .

My gaze roamed the darkening world beyond the torchlit bailey and the streams of lanterns. Had I not known what I was looking for, I would have thought I glimpsed a phantasm or a trick of the light. Atop a round tower outside the light stood a naked man alone, his muscular body sculpted in cerulean light, his long hair bound into a braid that fell over his shoulder and almost to his waist. Kyr Archon. Pale blue gards . . . not silver.

Was it joy at his redemption or the certainty that Safia would have stood there instead if she yet lived that made my chest ache so fiercely? Or perhaps it was the release of despair held close since my abrupt leaving. They lived, the Xancheirans and the once-silver Danae. The Severing was undone.

Voices rose from the confrontation in the bailey.

". . . but I don't know who you mean," said Ferenc with stern dignity. "And I don't know who you are or how your people got inside my gates, but you will withdraw them immediately. If you are servants of the imposter de Serre, know that his plot has failed. If you are Curator Damon's allies, know that the curator is dead and his noble plan left in splinters. Give me the name of the one you want, and I'll see him brought down. Lay down your arms, and I'll hear your grievance and his."

"We call him the Deliverer," said Signé. "But he goes by many names, some of which he says are not safe to use."

"We'll not leave without him," said Benedik. "He has brought us back from beyond time, and we hear he is prisoner in this place. We *will* have him, and then will I, the Duc de Xancheiros, have speech with the Southern Registry about the ordering of magic in the world."

"Xancheiros! You're mad. . . . Leave this house and take your rabble with you, else the power of Navronne's sorcery will be brought to bear."

"Dismiss my lord and his *rabble* at thy peril," said Siever, spreading his arms wide. As he slowly raised his hands from shoulder height, a pillar of whirling white light rose between the Xancheirans and the outer wall of the castle. The display was not illusion, but a palpable construction. Eye and mind told me that my hand could wrap my arms about the pillar and feel an impossible solidity.

But when Siever's hands met above his head, the white light reversed to unlight—that's all I could think to call it. Not simple blackness. The portion of the castle wall his pillar crossed—wall, parapet, tower—was not masked, but empty.

"If I breathe the word, this void in thy demesne becomes permanent," said Siever, coolly sober. "Though if I'm mad, that's not likely, is it? Wilt thou see this city fall to ruin or wilt thou treat with my lord as a civilized man who happens to be graced with magic, as art thou?"

Inek nudged me. "Only you can settle this. I'll release your veil when you say."

Of all things, I wanted to be sitting in the Aerie at Evanide, feeling the sea wind on my face. Or asleep in my quiet cell as the storm tides raged outside those sturdy walls. But the moment must not be lost if we were to hold on to whatever good Damon had accomplished. Purebloods must take care of our own guilts. Then, perhaps, we could find a righteous course to heal the rest of the world.

I removed hood and mantle, shirt and tunic, so that my hairless head, fearsome mask, and threaded silver arms would distract from any familiarity. I nodded to Inek.

"Hold thy wrath, Xancheiran!" I called as the veil fell away. "My lords, in the name of those who have fallen to bring us to this day, I command you hear me!"

My bellowing drew every eye to the ramparts. Siever's enchantment vanished, but the veiled Inek provided light for all to see me. The bands on my arms reported the swelling whispers: *Caedmon's true heir . . . the Pretender . . . the Sorcerer King . . .*

Fending off guilt, I took advantage. "Summon the Three Hundred."

It took very little time for those in the rotunda to join the crowd in the bailey. Which was good, as the wind was freezing my bare flesh . . . and the non-flesh parts of me were colder yet.

"*Domé* Canis-Ferenc, I commend your forbearance. And I ask forgiveness for the damage I've wrought to your noble house. I was bound by an enslavement of will that is the exemplar of the corruption we have now abjured. Be assured that the one who perpetrated that most heinous of all crimes against the divine gift will never do so again.

"My lord of Xancheiros, Lady Signé, Lord Siever, the one you seek has himself been set free from a great evil. His deeds—and those of his friends and brothers—have released me from prisoning, as they did you. I cannot doubt that, wherever the gods have taken him, he rejoices to know of your deliverance and blesses you for your care, and that he would beg you treat with this worthy Canis-Ferenc and these ancient families who are assembled in the name of purification. Those who were once your enemies have heard the horror of your city's fall—and have vowed to ensure such things never happen again. But they don't yet understand the full truth of what happened to you. Nor were they ever told of the great discovery that lay at the root of the divergence between Xancheira and the Southern Registry. In the face of the world's upheaval, the time for that truth to be told must be chosen with wisdom and care. But it *must* be told. Make peace between you first, heal, and then it will come clear how to move forward.

"And lastly, to all of you, the time for a Sorcerer King is not yet. Unlike the man who preened as Caedmon's heir—our salvation from corruption— even as he paraded me in front of you as a living mockery of our most sacred law, I do *not* intend to claim the throne that time, history, and tradition have granted to good King Eodward and his heirs. Rather I will serve the divine gift in ways that forward the cause of justice. I ask all of you to do the same. But in the same way this mask proclaims that I serve Navronne and not my own interest, so will I take a new name to replace all other names. From this day I shall be known as the One-Who-Waits. I shall wait to see if we can purge ourselves of corruption. I shall wait to see if Serena Fortuna reveals King Eodward's intended heir or the gods impart some measure of redemption to his sons. But be sure, my gift will see these things done."

Raising my hands, I released the magic I'd fought to hold at bay—magic born of history and art, pain and outrage, of loss, betrayal, and grief, of joy at freedom and hope of healing, and of unbridled wonder at the glory that flowed through every part of me. For that moment, the ground trembled and boundaries faded. Dressed stone reverted to cliffs, paving to grassy hillsides. Lamps and torches vanished, leaving the world lit only by starlight. The sweet airs of the Everlasting mingled with Navronne's oncoming winter, and faint music twined with the scents of meadowsweet and sea wrack on the breeze, speaking of beauty and mystery just beyond what we could see.

When my hands began to shake, I released the thread of power and whispered, "Enough."

The crowd, as one, drew in a great breath when Inek's veil made me vanish. As they exhaled in a rising murmur of awe, I dropped to one knee, lowered my head, and laid a fist on my breast. "Knight Commander, I report my mission complete."

"Blessed return, Aros, the One-Who-Waits, Knight of the Ashes."

CHAPTER 43

Late autumn brought deep snow and bitter cold to central Ardra. The wood was quiet, every bare branch, every twig, every dormant bud coated with snow. My footsteps were muffled. Now and then a bird startled at my passing, fluttering wings causing small showers of fine snow. But the war had moved south to Evanore, and in such quiet, knowing the season's change was so close upon us, it seemed as if the world held its breath.

I was on a dual mission coming south. I needed to lay some ghosts. And I had a few people to speak to about the future, now it seemed I would have one. That had been doubtful for a while.

The first few days after the incidents at Cavillor, I spent encamped with Fix and Inek. Fix helped me deal with the practical problems of the threaded silver bracelets, everything from bathing to investing the bands with my own spellwork without singeing my skin or setting off rebounding enchantments. The two of them together helped me work on the discipline required to manage the bracelets' magic and the steadily increasing awareness of the world around me.

But the work was difficult and I couldn't concentrate. I fretted about Juli, about strife between the Xancheirans and the purebloods and the certain resistance to dissolving the Registry now there would be no Sorcerer King to ease the pain of it. I felt like a tattered blanket, all holes and loose threads, no pattern, no weaving.

The result was I couldn't sleep. Every attempt ended in nightmares of prisons or cages, of chains, of body parts removed and replaced with swords or brooms or animal feet. At least half my nightmares involved cutting away the mask to find some horror . . . or worse, nothing at all. I couldn't breathe.

"Come to Evanide," said Fix, at the end of the third day, when I could not set a twig alight without setting the whole tree afire. "We must do something about that mask. As long as you wear it, you're a walking dead man."

I huddled by our tame fire and stared stupidly at a rapidly cooling tisane meant to put me to sleep. "Can't go back," I said. "Greenshank is a deserter. And I've things to do."

"We'll keep you anonymous," said Inek. "Knights come and go."

"I don't— I'm not sure I can ever go back," I said. Though I still believed in the Order, and I very much craved the peace and purpose it represented, how could I ever offer the submission it required? I trusted Fix and Inek and many of my brothers, but I had trusted the Marshal, too. I was not ready to yield so much again.

The warm tisane sloshed over my hands. The tremors got worse whenever I thought of Geraint de Serre commanding me to slaughter everyone in Castle Cavillor. If not for these men and Fallon and Pons and the half-mad Archivist, I would have done it.

Fix added a few drops more of his soporific to my cup and forced me to drink. "On the ramparts of Cavillor, Inek named you a knight to honor your choice and to acknowledge your clear qualification. That was no idle gesture. The Order needs you—your magic, your discipline, your devotion to our cause. As ever, it is your own choice to accept that naming. But not on this day. The Knight Defender will never allow a knight, squire, paratus, or tyro to leave the Order while he is wounded."

And so we returned to Evanide. I near wept when I got inside fortress walls, sneaked in via private ways, given a cell in the commanders' barracks. But even the sea could not soothe me. No sooner had I dropped off to sleep that first night than I woke up screaming. Fits of the shakes attacked me with the regularity of the tides. I dubbed myself a weakling ninny.

Fix and Inek assured me that time and peace and work would mend what was only to be expected from such wounding as the Marshal's leash. The only serious matter they discussed with me was the royal mask. No matter what I chose to do, no matter where I went, it marked me as the man on the ramparts. I was of no use to myself, my friends, the Order, or the kingdom if I flaunted a symbol that could see me dead in an eyeblink. Despite the risks of undoing intricate magic never meant to be undone, I agreed to their recommendation to be rid of it.

Fix brought the old Archivist out of his forced retirement, and over the course of three days I would give much to forget, the old man and the new Archivist, once known as Second, unthreaded the mask, carefully undoing the magic that had bonded it to my skin, to my nerves, to my mind and magic. Somewhere in the blur of those days, the old Archivist leaned close and whispered in my ear so no one else could hear. "You said the day of the Sorcerer King is *not yet*, and you promised to wait and watch. Was that empty posturing? If I remove the threading splinters around your face, this mask can never be put back."

I had no intention of donning the mask again and no desire to do so. But neither would I retract the promise made at Cavillor. Perhaps it was delirium caused by unending pain, but I whispered hoarsely, "Leave them."

Two months it took me to recover from that ordeal and regain some semblance of my former skills, sleeping during the days, and working all night in the training rooms, alone or with Inek. Daylight hours when I was not sleeping, I spent in the bowels of the Archive Tower. The new Archivist taught me more of the memory magic I should have learned before my investiture. Intricate, glorious magic. Which made my growing certainties all the more difficult.

During that time of healing, Fix and Inek purposely kept me ignorant of the world outside, saying it was useless until I had the skills to deal with what I heard. They confirmed Geraint de Serre was dead, but didn't tell me how. I grieved for the Marshal I'd believed in, but not for the man whose seductive voice lurked in my dreams like leeches in a pond.

On the night Inek laid a hand on my shoulder and said I was to meet Fix at the boathouse an hour before sunrise, with my weapons and what kit I had assembled during my stay, I knew the time of my choice had come. "As you say, Knight Commander. I want to tell you how much—"

"You told me enough when I lay in the infirmary, unable to reply," he said. "*Dalle cineré,* Knight Aros, my friend and brother."

"*Dalle cineré*, Knight Commander." *From the ashes.* Never had the words meant so much.

"You sleep well; you can run the flats in the dark at a pace near your best," said the Defender, as we strolled down the quay toward the boathouse that morning. The wind frosted the scruff on my chin that was the only beard I could grow around the scars left by the unthreading. "Inek reports your swordwork has actually surpassed your last testing. . . ."

I laughed. "Every tyro would be at this level if he trained with Inek every night."

It was hard to know Fix was going to force me to a decision. I hated to disappoint those who put such faith in me.

"It's good to hear you laugh," said Fix. "Don't ever allow that skill to wane. I'm pleased your time has been profitable, but the Order will benefit now our new Knight Marshal can be invested instead of playing nursemaid every night. The mysterious Knight Defender is most inadequate to handle both offices and his boats, as well."

I glanced up sharply. "Inek is to be the Knight Marshal?"

"He was named two years ago—before the Archivist falsified the count. He will implement the reforms we've decided on and lead us into this new world you've made possible. As for you—"

"Knight Defender, I cannot stay." Only the need to get the painful words spoken could make me interrupt Fix. "I've matters to see to, some personal, which sounds strange for one who so recently relinquished all identity save the One-Who-Waits. But I meant what I said at Cavillor. And these days of work and solitude convinced me I cannot judge the world if I don't live there. I cannot allow others to filter my view. My heart is with the Order, especially now it is in such fine care, but Aros belongs elsewhere."

We stood at the end of the quay, gazing out on the restless sea.

He tilted his head my way and looked at me the way the boatmaster looked on a tyro who could not remember how to tie a knot. "This is not exactly a shock to me. Indeed, I've a proposition for you," he said. "But first I'll have to tell you a bit about what's come of your deeds. . . ."

T he dawn light tinted the sprawling town on the horizon a vibrant pink, as I emerged from the snowy wood and joined the eastern road. I'd walked for a month since that dawn on the quay at Evanide, and winter had set in with a vengeance though we were yet a few days from the solstice.

I'd spent my journey listening—to travelers, hostlers, and laborers at the side of the road, at sop-houses and taverns, in alleyways and gatehouses, and at the windows of pureblood enclaves and official chambers, most of the time veiled in Order magic. Ordinaries were accustomed to the uncertainty the tides of war left behind. Purebloods weren't. They were struggling to move forward from the Sitting.

A few powerful families like the Albins had declared their intent to re-create an administrative council with stricter rules—a new, purified, but harsher Registry. Duc Benedik had returned north to secure his people against winter and war. Canis-Ferenc had sent wagonloads of provisions, tools, and seed with him, and they had committed to further negotiation in the spring. Ferenc's partisans sewed white stripes on their wine-hued cloaks—many of them fashioned in the shape of Xancheira's tree. Rumors already spoke of intimidation by the traditionalists. I would have to see to that.

But first something even more important. Morning bells rang at a Karish monastery school that nestled in the valley upriver from the town. Half a quellé past the school, a side road led into gentle hills. I pulled my hood low to shadow my face. The two women were already waiting.

The larger, older of the two, wide-shouldered and severe in her claret-hued robe and mask, raised a hand. I raised mine and then laid it on the opposite shoulder in the signal Fix's message had arranged. The smaller rider in black mantle and mask—the variant garb permitted for purebloods in mourning—dipped her head gracefully and pulled her mount around to take the side road into the hills. Without a word, I followed, leaving the other woman behind to guard the way.

As I passed, Pons—the temporary Administrator of Sorcerer Registration—nodded. She knew only that I was a messenger from the Order. Neither she nor Juli knew that I lived.

Unkempt myrtle and bay had almost overgrown the road. Only rabbit tracks marred the pristine snow. We saw no sign of the horror that had happened here until we reached the top of a hill overlooking a broad valley. The black and broken stubble of a huge house and myriad outbuildings laid a blight upon the frosty morning.

"Here," I said, calling her to halt. "This is far enough."

I dismounted and offered her my hand, but she refused. "I don't understand why we're here," she said, as she dropped smoothly to her feet and stroked her mare's neck. "Administrator Pons says you are investigating matters of corruption brought before the Sitting of the Three Hundred last summer. I thought this particular matter was well understood."

"We've come for several reasons. I've the skill to learn a bit more about the night this happened." I gestured toward the ruin. "And I made you a promise."

Her hand stopped in mid-stroke, and she spun around, her eyes wide.

I lowered my hood and held out my hand. "I live."

One hand flew to her mouth, as the other reached for mine. Even through her glove it was cold as the ice glaze on the ponds below us.

"I'm so sorry I couldn't tell you sooner," I said. "By the time I knew what they'd told you . . . shown you . . . I'd no opportunity. And once I was free, I had to go away for a while. . . ."

"That was you in the mask," she said, tracing the dreadful scars its removal had caused. "On the ramparts. And all I could think was how like you he sounded—and how glorious was his magic, more so than even my dearest brother's—the one I'd just buried. Oh, Mother's heart, Luka, where have you been?"

I guided her to a bench I'd noted in that relict-seeing so long ago and held her until the racking sobs had eased. "I saw you working at Cavillor—after—shoring up the wreckage I'd caused. So your bent leads you to that . . . to—"

"Building," she said, blotting her eyes before fixing them on my own. "So you still don't remember."

"No. And I won't. Not ever. I can't regret it, as it was how I got free of a man who wanted to use my magic to murder his enemies. As long as I clung to the part of me that believed I was Lucian de Remeni—which was not so much, as you'd already seen—I was de Serre's slave. To break his magic I had to destroy every part of me that would enable me to reclaim the person I was—the experiences that shaped me, the kinship and love I held for my family, even the desire to know more. I am forever changed, Juli. The affection and admiration I feel for you, the responsibility I feel for you, is because of who you are now, not blood nor anything we shared before that night at the Sanctuary pool."

She didn't flinch. "But your bents, you still have them?"

"Yes. Indeed"—I fetched parchment and a stick of plummet from my pack—"I wanted to use them today. Two purebloods were here the night this happened, and I intend to discover who they were. To make sure justice is done. I thought perhaps I could draw something for you, too. If I search the history of this place—*your* home—and you told me something to look for, I could sketch it for you. A gift. A memory, since I've none to share with you."

"But it wouldn't put the memory back in your head where it belongs."

"No."

"Then there's no use to it. Everything I loved here is graven in my heart forever, including my eldest brother Lucian, who was supremely talented and brave, but a bit of a prig. So, go ahead, do your investigating."

My laughter made her smile. I'd not thought there would be any of either on this day.

Closing my eyes for a moment, I touched the ground and searched for what had happened here. As the terrible scenes raced through my head and my joined bents answered my call, I opened my eyes and began to draw.

If I needed any confirmation of what I'd done at Cavillor, it lay here. I grieved for those who died and felt horror at the manner of it, but even with my deepest magic, I could not say the victims' names or recognize their faces. The villains, though . . .

"Who were they?" asked Juli, when I was done.

I showed her that justice had been satisfied.

"Pluvius, the lying wretch!" she said. "And—"

"Attis de Lares-Damon."

What was I to think of Damon? He had countenanced savagery and brought a murderous tyrant a handsbreadth from Caedmon's throne. Yet, would the Fifty have dissolved the Registry and set purebloods on a new, albeit rocky, course without Damon's impassioned case? Would I have found my way to the Xancheirans without the strength Damon's horrors forced on me?

Mayhap. Yet I refused to believe that slaughter was necessary to evoke changes in the world. If I'd recognized the wily curator in the relict-seeing, I might have killed him, and the Marshal would almost certainly be on his triumphal journey to Palinur right now, the Order, the Three Hundred, and his murderous slave, Axe, at his beck.

As the sun moved inexorably upward, Juli told me of her plans. Pons had found a distant Massoni cousin who had married into another family several generations back. She wanted Juli to adopt their name and pursue her studies until she was ready to forge a contract on her own. ". . . so I'd get to keep one of my names at least. But I've decided to go back to Xancheira. Think of the skills I can learn there—even if I only have the one bent. Signé and I are great friends, both of us cursed with over-righteous brothers. She'll likely enjoy imagining that someday you'll come back to see me. But what of you, Luk— So what *is* your name?"

"Aros," I said, "though I may take on different names from time to time. Your eldest brother is dead and must stay that way. To raise him, even in memory, puts us both in danger."

"So what will you do? Vanish into the sea fortress and let them take away all memory of me? How can you spend your talents—your kindness—your loving, generous spirit—only to be a warrior, even an extraordinary warrior?"

"I'm not going back, for a while at least. Damon plowed a furrow amongst our kind thinking to grow a new world. Instead, it could divide us for generations, perhaps become a morass to drown our gifts. I'm going to dig a little, toss a few stones aside, plant some seeds, and, yes, fight a little, if necessary . . . to see if something worthy might grow in that soil."

"So you're going to wait and watch, like you said on the ramparts, and do the work of justice."

"Yes."

"That's all right, then." She took my scarred face in her small hands. "Goddess Mother protect thee, beloved. Deunor, Lord of Light, be thy guide. Kemen Sky Lord give thee strength. And know this: Even without a shared name, or blood, or hearth, shall I ever be thy sister."

I helped her mount, firmly removed her hand from my hair, kissed it, and gave it back to her. As she rode away, I fingered the wooden token in my pocket, the match for the one I'd just left in her fist. But in the end, I burnt the disk to ash, which would do the same to hers. My boot ground the neutered splinter that remained into the soil that had once been my inheritance.

Some things were too much to yield.

The wind howled across the white wilderness as I emerged from the slot gate in Palinur's outer wall. Across the plateau, mounded with graves of the unknowns, the gates of Necropolis Caton stood tall, the towers broken and lopsided. Flames shot high from stone cauldrons flanking the gatehouse, lighting the statues of Deunor and Magrog, yet grappling in their endless duel. The flames told me the coroner was at home.

Someone else lurked about Caton, as well. A tall woman, luminous with traces of sapphire and lapis, stood at the outer edge of the plateau. I did not go to her, nor did I call out. She soon vanished in a gust of winter wind and a swirl of snow. Perhaps she didn't recognize me anymore, now Lucian was gone.

Regret, but no sadness, followed me across a graveyard toward the necropolis. I paused once to pour out the dregs of my ale flask as libation to the Goddess Mother, thanking her for bringing me here safely. No familiarity, no echoes of chains or prisons or other times greeted me, even when I considered what had happened to Lucian here. And my head did not ache.

No one sat behind the gates when I rang the bell. But at my third ring, a shutter flew open above me and a shaggy head poked out. "What's your business so late of a night? The dead are not in so much hurry."

"I'm looking for work," I said.

"One man is useless. I need twenty washers and twenty diggers or no one at all. Go away."

"What of a sketcher? I've heard you employed one in the past, someone who can draw a dead face so it can be recognized. Folk pay well to know how their kinsmen die, who did the deed, and where they're laid. Folk pay to know their enemies are dead, or their neighbors' farm has no man to work it anymore. Nobles pay decent. Merchants pay better. If they learn the news before—"

"Sky Lord's everlasting balls! Lucian!"

"Name's Aros. Traveling artist . . ."

But he didn't wait to hear my pretty story. He trampled down the gate-house stairs like a herd of goats, wrenched away a barricade, and unlocked the gate. Lantern raised, he stared as I lowered my hood. "Stars and stone, did the headsman miss with his axe?"

I wore no mask to hide the scars.

"Lucian's death was a part of Damon's plan, and he must stay dead," I said. "Forever. I can make it easy for you to forget him, but I'd prefer not. I've work to do in Palinur, and thought I might apply for his former position."

"If *making it easy* means erasing memories, then, no. I'm moth-eaten enough. Don't need extra holes. And I wouldn't want a sorcerer unpracticed at the art to miss what he's aiming at."

My spirits lightened with every moment here.

"Actually, someone more proficient worked the token magic." I flipped his token into the air and frizzled it with a thought. The silver bracelets were sometimes annoying, but I'd grown to like them very much.

"All right." He looked askance at the drifting ash. "I saw the masked sorcerer on the ramparts of Cavillor. Rumor named him Caedmon's heir. But it was you, wasn't it? Should I be afraid of you? Are you still working out of the sea fortress?"

"I am not Caedmon's heir. As to the fear . . . yes and no, as I'm a great deal quicker with magic than I used to be, and I'm still getting used to it. And yes, my roots are still at Evanide. But I'm on a special mission, having to do with what was spoken at Cavillor. I thought a man of the law who liked a bit of adventure might be just the partner I need. Besides, you're owed three years and ten months service and a great deal more. Such debts must be paid."

"You'd do portraits for me . . . help investigate?"

"Yes."

He pretended to consider it. But his face was already sparked brighter than his gate fires. "When Bayard took the city, the Harrowers ran wild, but now the war's down to the south, it's quieter. We could likely take up where we left off. A few of the magistrates have come forward to keep order, hoping to find favor with the new king, whoever he might be. We could get Constance back to run things. She's sewing for a living now, but hates it. And what else would we be doing?"

I peered beyond him into the dark courtyard. "Maybe we could have a seat and a drink of something? I've just walked from Evanide without any Danae to shorten the distance. And first off, I need to bury a few things where no one's going to run across them."

"Good enough."

He locked the gates and led me through a strange courtyard filled with stone tables and columns and water troughs, through a bedraggled prometheum, and into a small burial ground. "Here," he said, and pointed to a small, snow-covered grave with a simple headstone marked *Ysabel*. From the back of the headstone, he removed a piece that revealed a deep cavity. "It's where I kept the spindle after I dug it up and before the Danae woman fetched me. The girl child kept it safe."

"The girl child," I said. "Fallon's sister."

"Aye."

Curious how the world ran in circles. If ever I needed a reminder of how small works of justice could change everything, I had but to come here.

I pulled a canvas packet from my rucksack and stuffed it in the hole. It held a slip of purple silk and a gold medallion. "If Serena Fortuna is kind, these will never see the light of day," I said, as he replaced the stones and I sealed it with magic. "As to our work . . . Damon, the Hand of Magrog, convinced the Sitting of the Three Hundred to dissolve the Pureblood Registry. He was well on his way to installing a sorcerer on Eodward's throne, when his Pretender—legitimate blood-kin of Caedmon and a halfblood mage—was proved worse than the three aspirants we've got. He tried to force someone he liked better into the role, but the stubborn prig he chose didn't like the idea . . ."

As we climbed the stair to the chamber beneath the dueling gods and between the blazing cauldrons, I told him of the strife among purebloods.

". . . and so your commanders sent you here to do what you could to dissolve the Registry."

"Works of justice," I said. "Some not exactly small. Those who want to go backward have made the Registry Tower their headquarters. At some time in this coming year, the One-Who-Waits is going to bring that Tower down. When it falls, a piece of this will come to light"—I pulled the *stola* from my jaque—"and as Benedik and Signé return Xancheira to glory, another piece, and then another. Someone once told me that perfection was ephemeral, but if the person who sits Eodward's throne thinks to take up wicked habits of whatever kind, his dreams might take such turns as he cannot imagine."

Bastien poured two mugs of new ale. We toasted our partnership and talked late. Neither of us could sleep. It was the night of the winter solstice and the world seemed restless. Yet even surrounded by the unquiet dead, I was at peace. I knew who I was—a man with such friends and such purpose as could fill a lifetime of magic. If I needed to don the mask again, I would, but for now I would watch and work and hope.

ABOUT THE AUTHOR

Carol Berg is a former software engineer with degrees in mathematics from Rice University and computer science from the University of Colorado. Since her 2000 debut, her epic fantasy novels have won multiple Colorado Book Awards, the Geffen Award, the Prism Award, and the Mythopoeic Fantasy Award for Adult Literature. Carol lives in the foothills of the Colorado Rockies with her Exceptional Spouse, and on the Web at carolberg.com.